WHAT IF?
CLASSIC

"What If Sgt. Fury and His Howling Commandos Had Fought World War II in Outer Space?"
Plotter: Gary Friedrich
Scripter: Don Glut
Penciler: Herb Trimpe
Inker: Pablo Marcos
Letters: Tom Orzechowski
Colors: D.R. Martin
Editor & Concept: Roy Thomas
Consulting Editor: Jim Shooter

"What If Someone Else Had Become Nova?"
Writer/Co-Editor: Marv Wolfman
Pencilers: John Buscema, Walter Simonson, Carmine Infantino, Ross Andru & George Pérez
Inkers: Joe Sinnott, Bob Wiacek, Frank Springer, Frank Giacoia & Tom Palmer
Letters: Michael Higgins & Irving Watanabe
Colors: Michele Wolfman, Nelson Yomtov & Roger Slifer
Co-Editor: Roy Thomas
Consulting Editor: Jim Shooter

"What If Ghost Rider, Spider-Woman and Captain Marvel Had Remained Villains?"
Writer: Steven Grant
Artist: Carmine Infantino
Inkers: Chic Stone, Frank Springer, Mike Esposito & Pablo Marcos
Letters: Tom Orzechowski
Colors: Roger Slifer, Carl Gafford & Bob Sharen
Editor: Mark Gruenwald

"What If Dr. Strange Had Been a Disciple of Dormammu?"
Writer: Peter Gillis
Penciler: Tom Sutton
Inker: Bruce Patterson
Letters: Tom Orzechowski
Colors: Glynis Wein
Editor: Mark Gruenwald

"What If Spider-Man Had Stopped the Burglar Who Killed His Uncle?"
Writer: Peter Gillis
Penciler: Pat Broderick
Inker: Mike Esposito
Letters: Tom Orzechowski
Colors: Roger Slifer
Editors: Dennis O'Neil & Mark Gruenwald

"What If the Avengers Had Fought the Kree-Skrull War Without Rick Jones?"
Writer: Tom DeFalco
Penciler: Alan Kupperberg
Inker: Bruce Patterson
Letters: Tom Orzechowski
Colors: Carl Gafford
Editors: Dennis O'Neil & Mark Gruenwald

Cover Art: Gene Colan & Jack Abel
Cover Colors: Tom Chu
Color Reconstruction: Jerron Quality Color

Senior Editor, Special Projects: Jeff Youngquist
Associate Editors: Jennifer Grünwald & Mark D. Beazley
Assistant Editor: Michael Short
Vice President of Sales: David Gabriel
Production: Jerron Quality Color
Book Designer: Carrie Beadle
Vice President of Creative: Tom Marvelli

Editor in Chief: Joe Quesada
Publisher: Dan Buckley

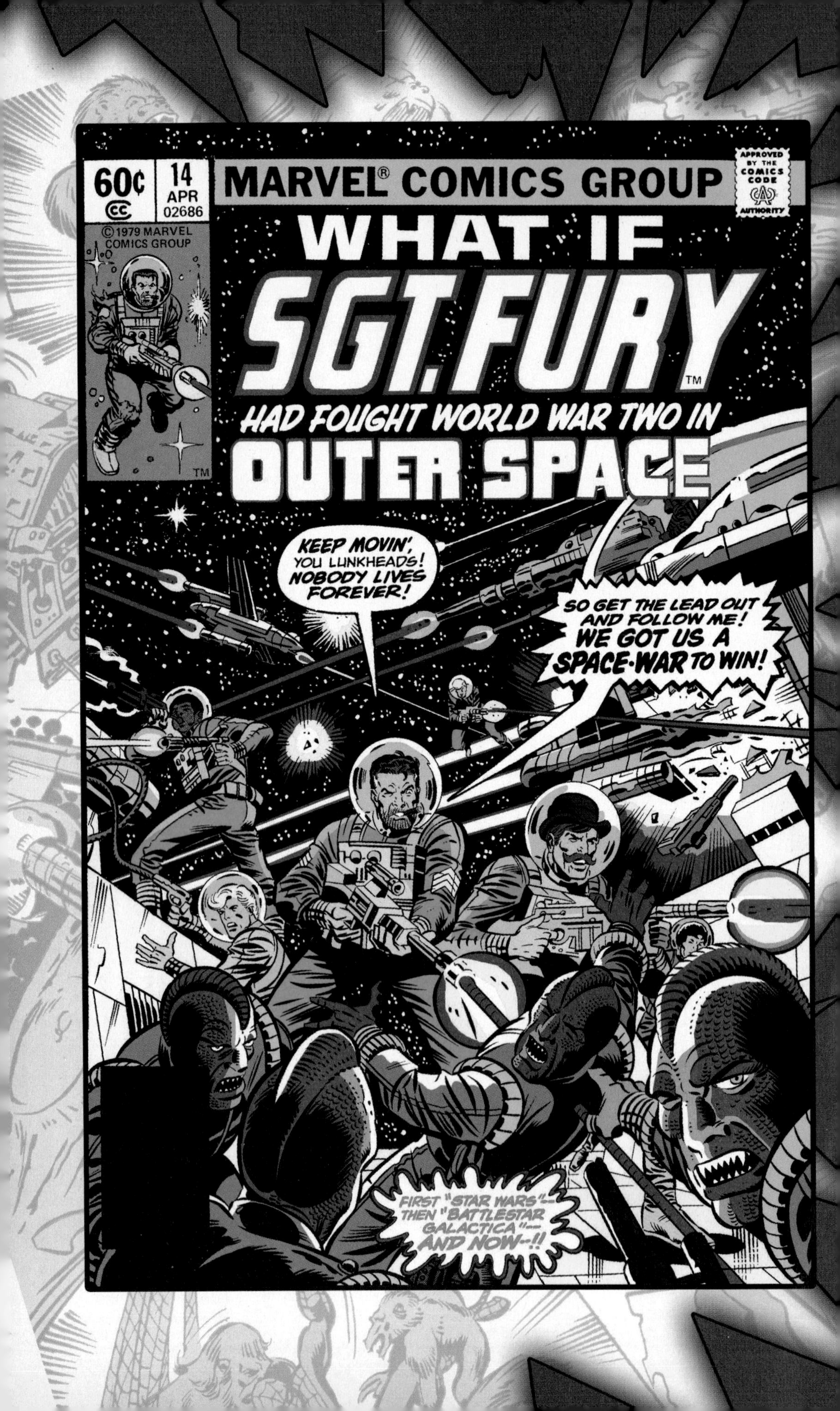
60¢
14
APR
02686
MARVEL® COMICS GROUP
APPROVED BY THE COMICS CODE AUTHORITY
©1979 MARVEL COMICS GROUP
WHAT IF
SGT. FURY
HAD FOUGHT WORLD WAR TWO IN
OUTER SPACE
KEEP MOVIN', YOU LUNKHEADS! NOBODY LIVES FOREVER!
SO GET THE LEAD OUT AND FOLLOW ME! WE GOT US A SPACE-WAR TO WIN!
FIRST "STAR WARS"-- THEN "BATTLESTAR GALACTICA"-- AND NOW--!!

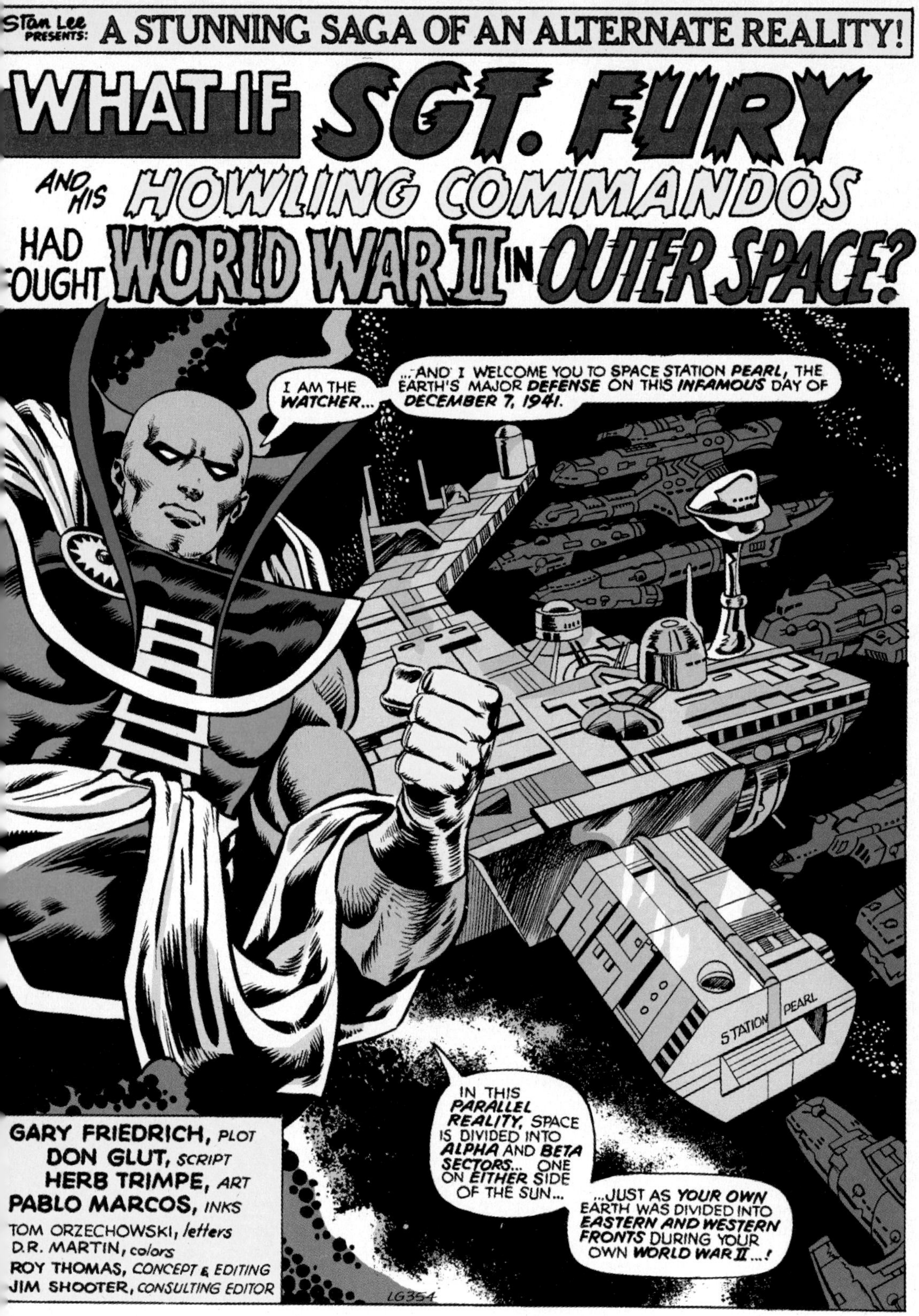
Stan Lee PRESENTS: A STUNNING SAGA OF AN ALTERNATE REALITY!
WHAT IF SGT. FURY AND HIS HOWLING COMMANDOS HAD FOUGHT WORLD WAR II IN OUTER SPACE?
I AM THE WATCHER...
...AND I WELCOME YOU TO SPACE STATION PEARL, THE EARTH'S MAJOR DEFENSE ON THIS INFAMOUS DAY OF DECEMBER 7, 1941.
STATION PEARL
IN THIS PARALLEL REALITY, SPACE IS DIVIDED INTO ALPHA AND BETA SECTORS... ONE ON EITHER SIDE OF THE SUN...
...JUST AS YOUR OWN EARTH WAS DIVIDED INTO EASTERN AND WESTERN FRONTS DURING YOUR OWN WORLD WAR II...!
GARY FRIEDRICH, PLOT
DON GLUT, SCRIPT
HERB TRIMPE, ART
PABLO MARCOS, INKS
TOM ORZECHOWSKI, letters
D.R. MARTIN, colors
ROY THOMAS, CONCEPT & EDITING
JIM SHOOTER, CONSULTING EDITOR
LG354

"STATION PEARL FLOATS WITHIN THE ALPHA REGION OF SPACE. AND, AT THIS INSTANT, INSIDE THE GREAT DEFENSE BASE...

HEY, FURY! YOU DAYDREAMIN' AGAIN ABOUT WHEN WE USETA FLY THOSE STUNT ROCKETS?

I SAID I'M CALLIN' YOU.

HUH? WHAZZAT, HARGROVE?

AWWW! HOW IN BLAZES AM I SUPPOSED TO KEEP MY MIND ON THESE BLAMED PASTEBOARDS--

--WHEN I'M ITCHIN' FER SOME ACTION MUCH AS YOU!

HECK! EVERYBODY KNOWS THAT EARTH CAN'T STAY OUTTA THIS STINKIN' INTERPLANETARY WAR FER LONG!

SHIP TIME 07:45

MAYBE THE TWO OF US SHOULDA STAYED OUTTA THIS MAN'S ARMY, RED...

YOU KNOW SOMETHIN', NICK? SOMETIMES I WISH THOSE BETA GOONS'D JUST GET IT OVER WITH...

...JUST DO SOMETHIN' TO GET EARTH INTO THIS WAR AND--

AT THAT MOMENT, RED HARGROVE GETS HIS WISH...

STATION PEARL

"..FOR, JUST AS ON YOUR WORLD, WHEN THE JAPANESE MADE THEIR UNEXPECTED ATTACK ON THE AMERICAN NAVAL BASE AT PEARL HARBOR, SO NOW DOES STATION PEARL FALL PREY TO A SNEAK BOMBARDMENT!

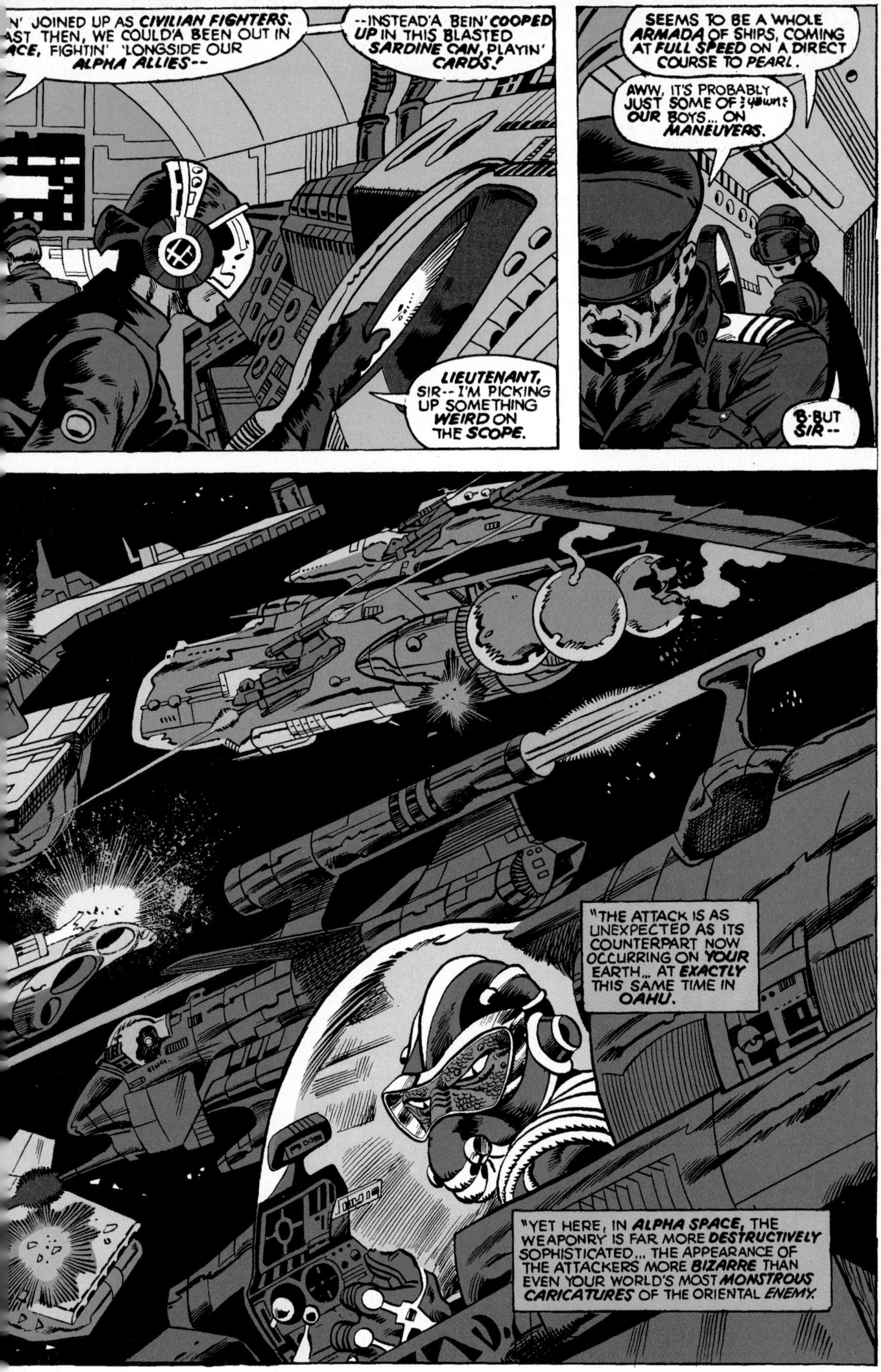
N' JOINED UP AS CIVILIAN FIGHTERS. AST THEN, WE COULD'A BEEN OUT IN ACE, FIGHTIN' 'LONGSIDE OUR ALPHA ALLIES--
--INSTEAD'A BEIN' COOPED UP IN THIS BLASTED SARDINE CAN, PLAYIN' CARDS!
LIEUTENANT, SIR-- I'M PICKING UP SOMETHING WEIRD ON THE SCOPE.
SEEMS TO BE A WHOLE ARMADA OF SHIPS, COMING AT FULL SPEED ON A DIRECT COURSE TO PEARL.
AWW, IT'S PROBABLY JUST SOME OF yawn OUR BOYS... ON MANEUVERS.
B-BUT SIR--
"THE ATTACK IS AS UNEXPECTED AS ITS COUNTERPART NOW OCCURRING ON YOUR EARTH... AT EXACTLY THIS SAME TIME IN OAHU.
"YET HERE, IN ALPHA SPACE, THE WEAPONRY IS FAR MORE DESTRUCTIVELY SOPHISTICATED... THE APPEARANCE OF THE ATTACKERS MORE BIZARRE THAN EVEN YOUR WORLD'S MOST MONSTROUS CARICATURES OF THE ORIENTAL ENEMY.

WEEEE

YOU HEAR THAT *ATTACK SIGNAL* AND FEEL THAT DANGED *ROCKIN'?*

HARGROVE, YER FAIRY GODMOTHER MUST'A BEEN *LISTENIN'* TO YA...

...'CAUSE YA *GOT* YER BLASTED *WISH.*

QUIT *JAWIN'* AND *SUIT UP,* FURY--

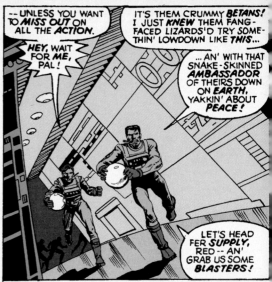

--UNLESS YOU WANT TO *MISS OUT* ON ALL THE *ACTION.*

HEY, WAIT FOR *ME,* PAL!

IT'S THEM CRUMMY *BETANS!* I JUST *KNEW* THEM FANG-FACED LIZARDS'D TRY SOME-THIN' LOWDOWN LIKE *THIS...*

...AN' WITH THAT SNAKE-SKINNED *AMBASSADOR* OF THEIRS DOWN ON *EARTH,* YAKKIN' ABOUT *PEACE!*

LET'S HEAD FER *SUPPLY,* RED -- AN' GRAB US SOME *BLASTERS!*

"IT IS A STRANGELY *SILENT* BATTLE IN WHICH NICK FURY AND RED HARGROVE PROMPTLY FIND THEM-SELVES--

"--OUT ON THE *EXTERIOR HULL* OF *SPACE STATION PEARL.*

"YET, THOUGH THEY HEAR *NONE* OF THE *EXPLOSIVE* SOUNDS OF EARLIER, MORE *MUNDANE* WARS, THE *CARNAGE* IS NEVERTHE-LESS THE *SAME.*

YOU *HOLDIN' OUT* OKAY, FURY?

AIN'T DEAD *YET,* OL' BUDDY! BUT SURE AS *SHOOTIN'* WE WON'T LAST MUCH *LONGER* WITH NOTHIN' BUT *HAND-GUNS* AGAINST THEM *SHIPS!*

WHAT *WE* NEED IS TO GET OURSELVES SOME *HEAVY ARTILLERY!*

YOU *CALLED* IT, SPACE-FIGHTER!

JUST DON'T START *BLASTIN' AWAY* TILL *I* GET UP THERE!

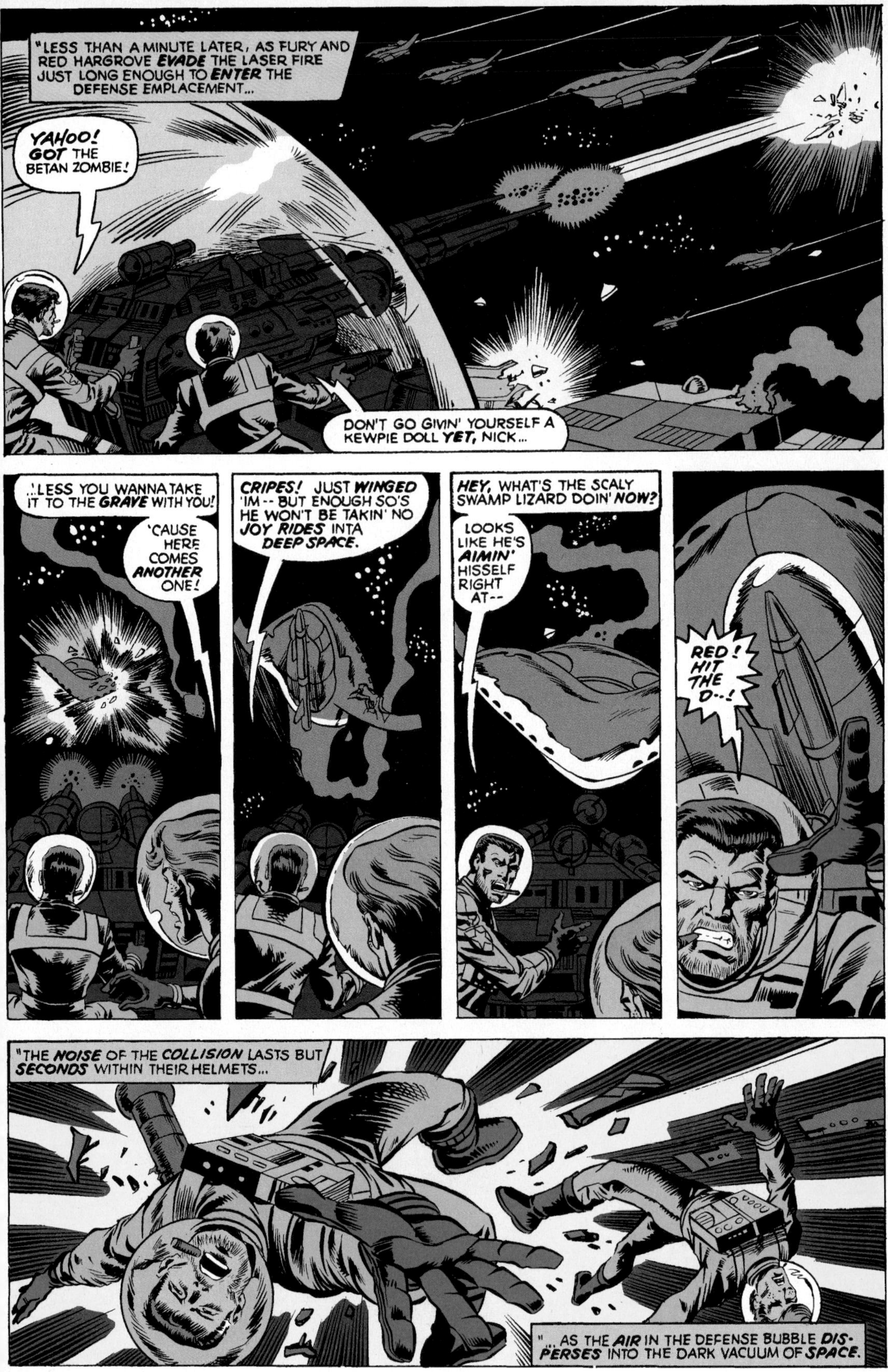
"LESS THAN A MINUTE LATER, AS FURY AND RED HARGROVE EVADE THE LASER FIRE JUST LONG ENOUGH TO ENTER THE DEFENSE EMPLACEMENT...
YAHOO! GOT THE BETAN ZOMBIE!
DON'T GO GIVIN' YOURSELF A KEWPIE DOLL YET, NICK...
..LESS YOU WANNA TAKE IT TO THE GRAVE WITH YOU!
'CAUSE HERE COMES ANOTHER ONE!
CRIPES! JUST WINGED 'IM -- BUT ENOUGH SO'S HE WON'T BE TAKIN' NO JOY RIDES INTA DEEP SPACE.
HEY, WHAT'S THE SCALY SWAMP LIZARD DOIN' NOW?
LOOKS LIKE HE'S AIMIN' HISSELF RIGHT AT--
RED! HIT THE D--!
"THE NOISE OF THE COLLISION LASTS BUT SECONDS WITHIN THEIR HELMETS...
"...AS THE AIR IN THE DEFENSE BUBBLE DISPERSES INTO THE DARK VACUUM OF SPACE.

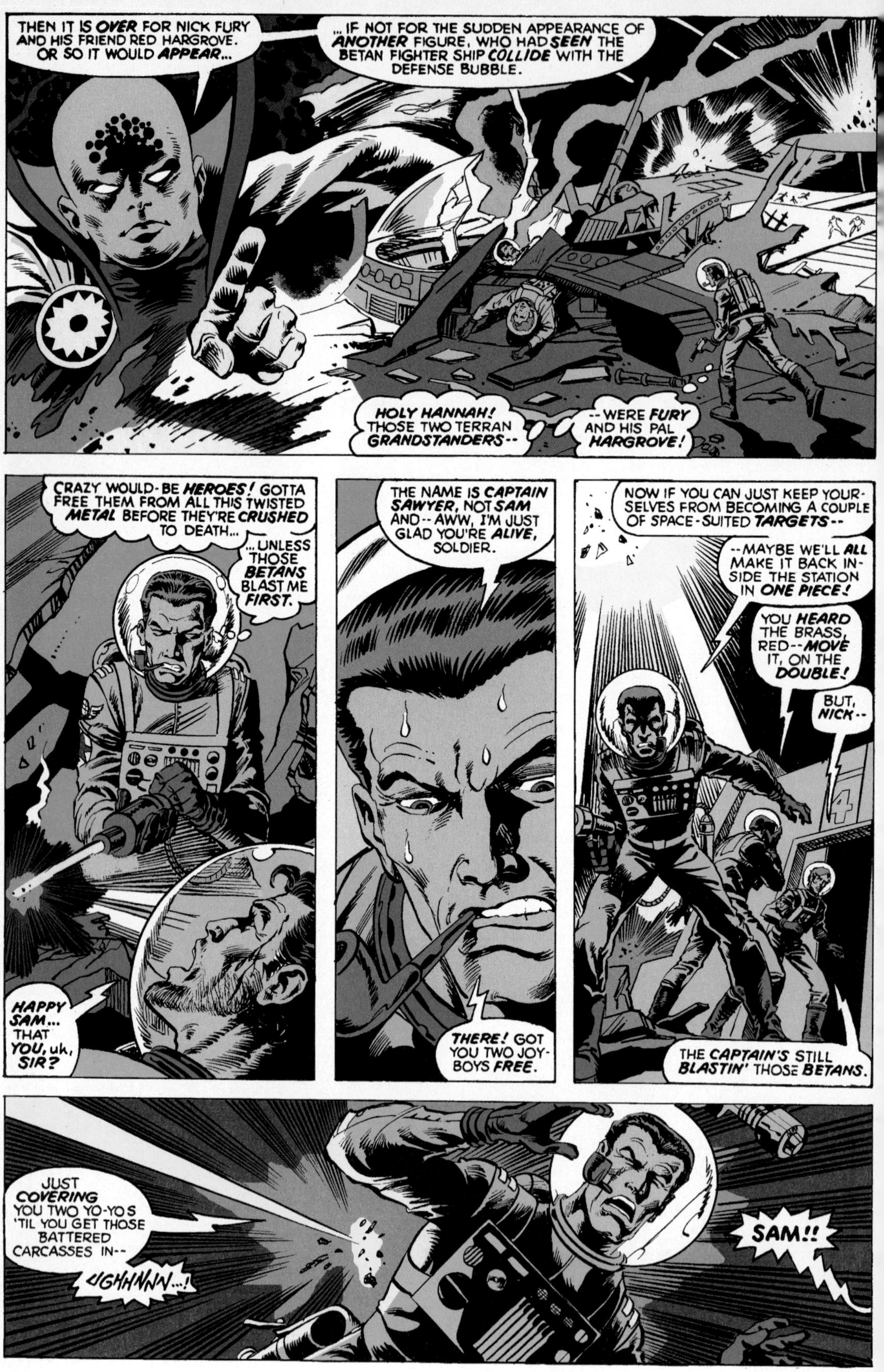
THEN IT IS OVER FOR NICK FURY AND HIS FRIEND RED HARGROVE. OR SO IT WOULD APPEAR...
...IF NOT FOR THE SUDDEN APPEARANCE OF ANOTHER FIGURE, WHO HAD SEEN THE BETAN FIGHTER SHIP COLLIDE WITH THE DEFENSE BUBBLE.
HOLY HANNAH! THOSE TWO TERRAN GRANDSTANDERS--
--WERE FURY AND HIS PAL HARGROVE!
CRAZY WOULD-BE HEROES! GOTTA FREE THEM FROM ALL THIS TWISTED METAL BEFORE THEY'RE CRUSHED TO DEATH...
...UNLESS THOSE BETANS BLAST ME FIRST.
HAPPY SAM... THAT YOU, uh, SIR?
THE NAME IS CAPTAIN SAWYER, NOT SAM AND--AWW, I'M JUST GLAD YOU'RE ALIVE, SOLDIER.
THERE! GOT YOU TWO JOY-BOYS FREE.
NOW IF YOU CAN JUST KEEP YOURSELVES FROM BECOMING A COUPLE OF SPACE-SUITED TARGETS--
--MAYBE WE'LL ALL MAKE IT BACK INSIDE THE STATION IN ONE PIECE!
YOU HEARD THE BRASS, RED--MOVE IT, ON THE DOUBLE!
BUT, NICK--
THE CAPTAIN'S STILL BLASTIN' THOSE BETANS.
JUST COVERING YOU TWO YO-YO'S 'TIL YOU GET THOSE BATTERED CARCASSES IN--
UGHHNNN...!
SAM!!

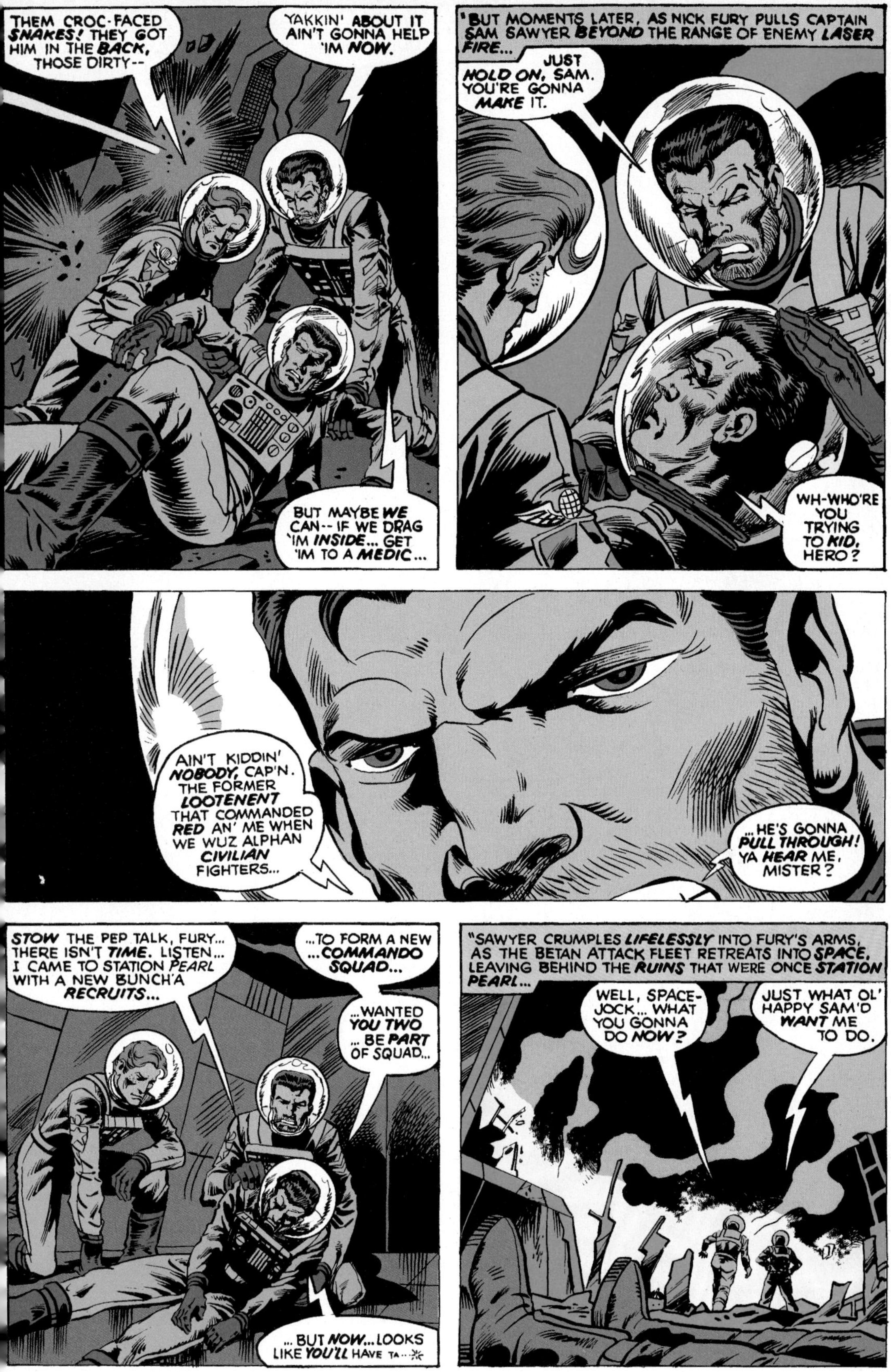
THEM CROC-FACED SNAKES! THEY GOT HIM IN THE BACK, THOSE DIRTY--
YAKKIN' ABOUT IT AIN'T GONNA HELP 'IM NOW.
BUT MAYBE WE CAN-- IF WE DRAG 'IM INSIDE... GET 'IM TO A MEDIC...
"BUT MOMENTS LATER, AS NICK FURY PULLS CAPTAIN SAM SAWYER BEYOND THE RANGE OF ENEMY LASER FIRE...
JUST HOLD ON, SAM. YOU'RE GONNA MAKE IT.
WH-WHO'RE YOU TRYING TO KID, HERO?
AIN'T KIDDIN' NOBODY, CAP'N. THE FORMER LOOTENENT THAT COMMANDED RED AN' ME WHEN WE WUZ ALPHAN CIVILIAN FIGHTERS...
...HE'S GONNA PULL THROUGH! YA HEAR ME, MISTER?
STOW THE PEP TALK, FURY... THERE ISN'T TIME. LISTEN... I CAME TO STATION PEARL WITH A NEW BUNCH'A RECRUITS...
...TO FORM A NEW ...COMMANDO SQUAD...
...WANTED YOU TWO ... BE PART OF SQUAD...
... BUT NOW... LOOKS LIKE YOU'LL HAVE TA--
"SAWYER CRUMPLES LIFELESSLY INTO FURY'S ARMS, AS THE BETAN ATTACK FLEET RETREATS INTO SPACE, LEAVING BEHIND THE RUINS THAT WERE ONCE STATION PEARL...
WELL, SPACE-JOCK... WHAT YOU GONNA DO NOW?
JUST WHAT OL' HAPPY SAM'D WANT ME TO DO.

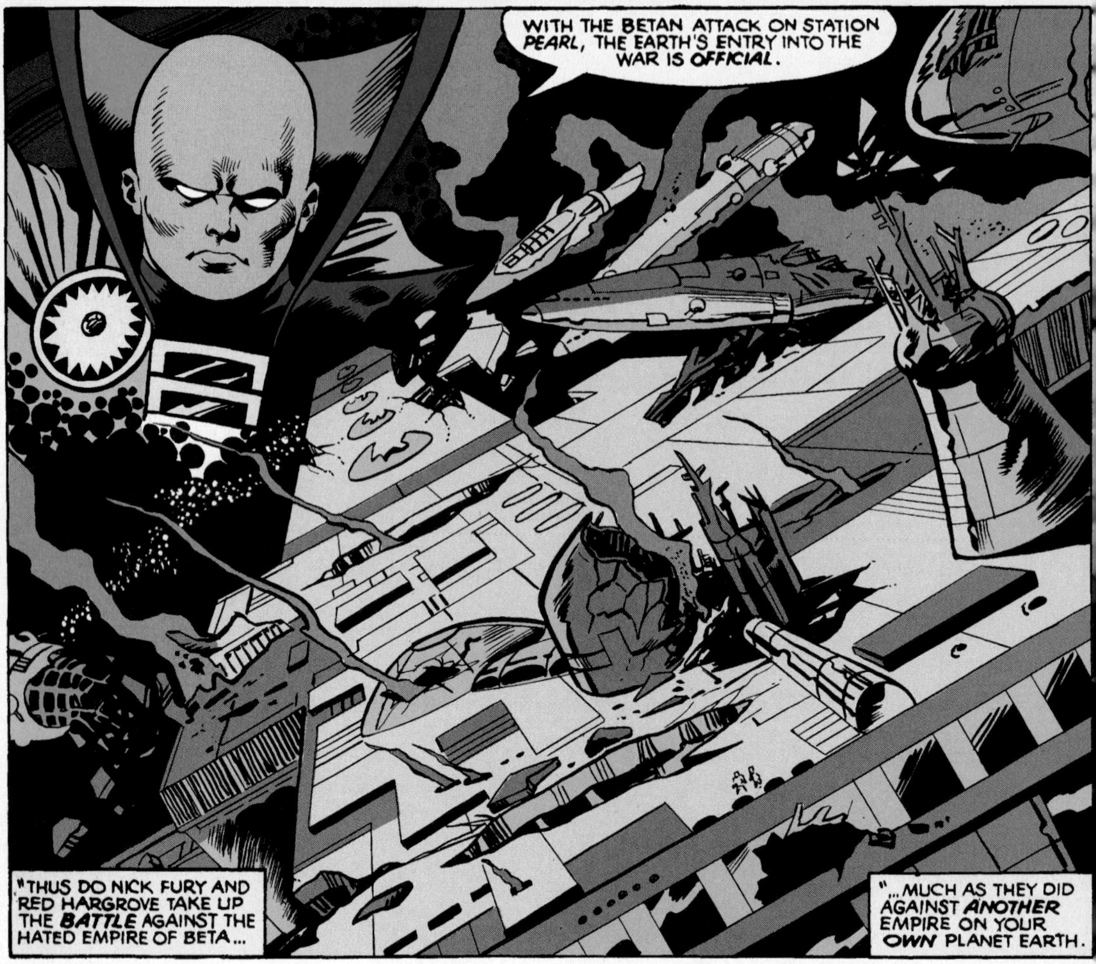
WITH THE BETAN ATTACK ON STATION PEARL, THE EARTH'S ENTRY INTO THE WAR IS OFFICIAL.
"THUS DO NICK FURY AND RED HARGROVE TAKE UP THE BATTLE AGAINST THE HATED EMPIRE OF BETA...
"...MUCH AS THEY DID AGAINST ANOTHER EMPIRE ON YOUR OWN PLANET EARTH.

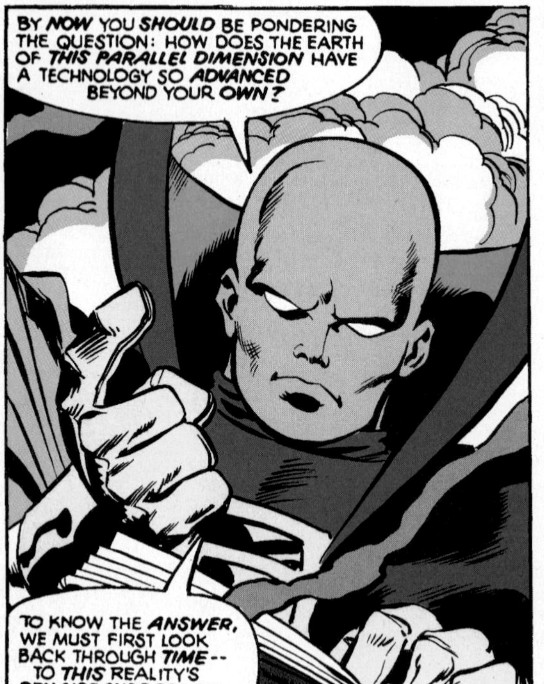
BY NOW YOU SHOULD BE PONDERING THE QUESTION: HOW DOES THE EARTH OF THIS PARALLEL DIMENSION HAVE A TECHNOLOGY SO ADVANCED BEYOND YOUR OWN?
TO KNOW THE ANSWER, WE MUST FIRST LOOK BACK THROUGH TIME-- TO THIS REALITY'S RENAISSANCE PERIOD--

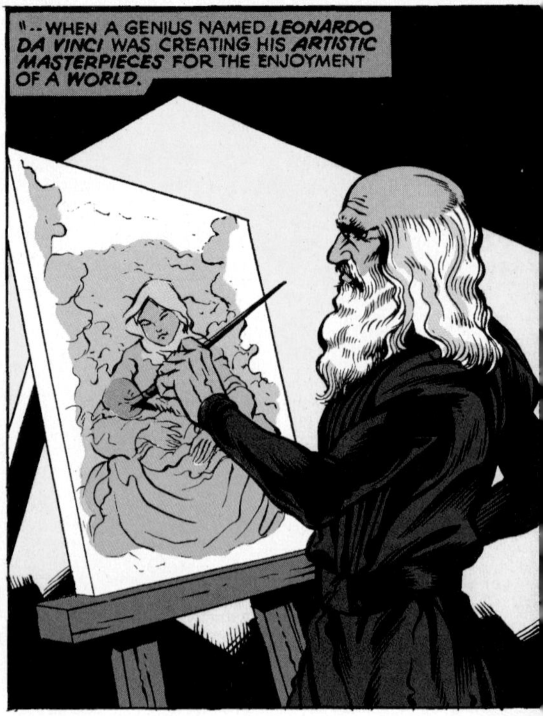
"--WHEN A GENIUS NAMED LEONARDO DA VINCI WAS CREATING HIS ARTISTIC MASTERPIECES FOR THE ENJOYMENT OF A WORLD.

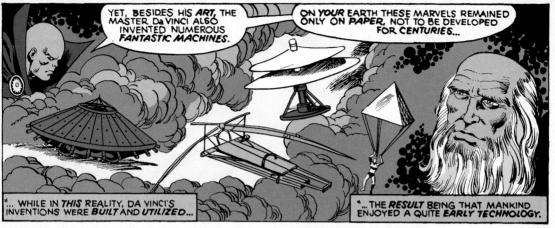

"... WHILE IN *THIS* REALITY, DA VINCI'S INVENTIONS WERE *BUILT* AND *UTILIZED*...

YET, BESIDES HIS *ART*, THE MASTER DaVINCI ALSO INVENTED NUMEROUS *FANTASTIC MACHINES*.

ON *YOUR* EARTH THESE MARVELS REMAINED ONLY ON *PAPER*, NOT TO BE DEVELOPED FOR *CENTURIES*...

"... THE *RESULT* BEING THAT MANKIND ENJOYED A QUITE *EARLY TECHNOLOGY*.

"LOOK *BACK* WITH ME THROUGH CORRESPONDING TIMES OF *TWO PARALLEL EARTHS*. ON ONE, A *NEW WORLD* WAS EXPLORED DURING THE *1500'S*...

"... WHILE ON THE *OTHERS*, MEN EXPLORED THE *SKIES* IN *FLYING MACHINES*...

"... THE *DESCENDANTS* OF DaVINCI'S TECHNOLOGICAL *VISIONS*.

"ON *YOUR* EARTH, DURING THE *1800'S*, NAPOLEON WATCHED THE *SUN* RISE OVER *AUSTERLITZ*...

"... WHILE IN *THIS* REALITY, MEN OBSERVED THE *EARTH* RISING OVER THE *MOON*.

"MAN, AT LAST, TOOK TO *YOUR* EARTH'S SKIES WHEN, ON DECEMBER 17, 1903, A HEAVIER-THAN-AIR CRAFT SOARED OVER *KITTY HAWK*, NORTH CAROLINA...

"... WHILE, PRECISELY ON THAT SAME DAY-- THOUGH IN THE REALITY OF *ANOTHER* DIMENSIONAL PLANE --

"--MANKIND WAS REACHING OUT TO TOUCH OTHER *GALAXIES*."

END OF PART ONE

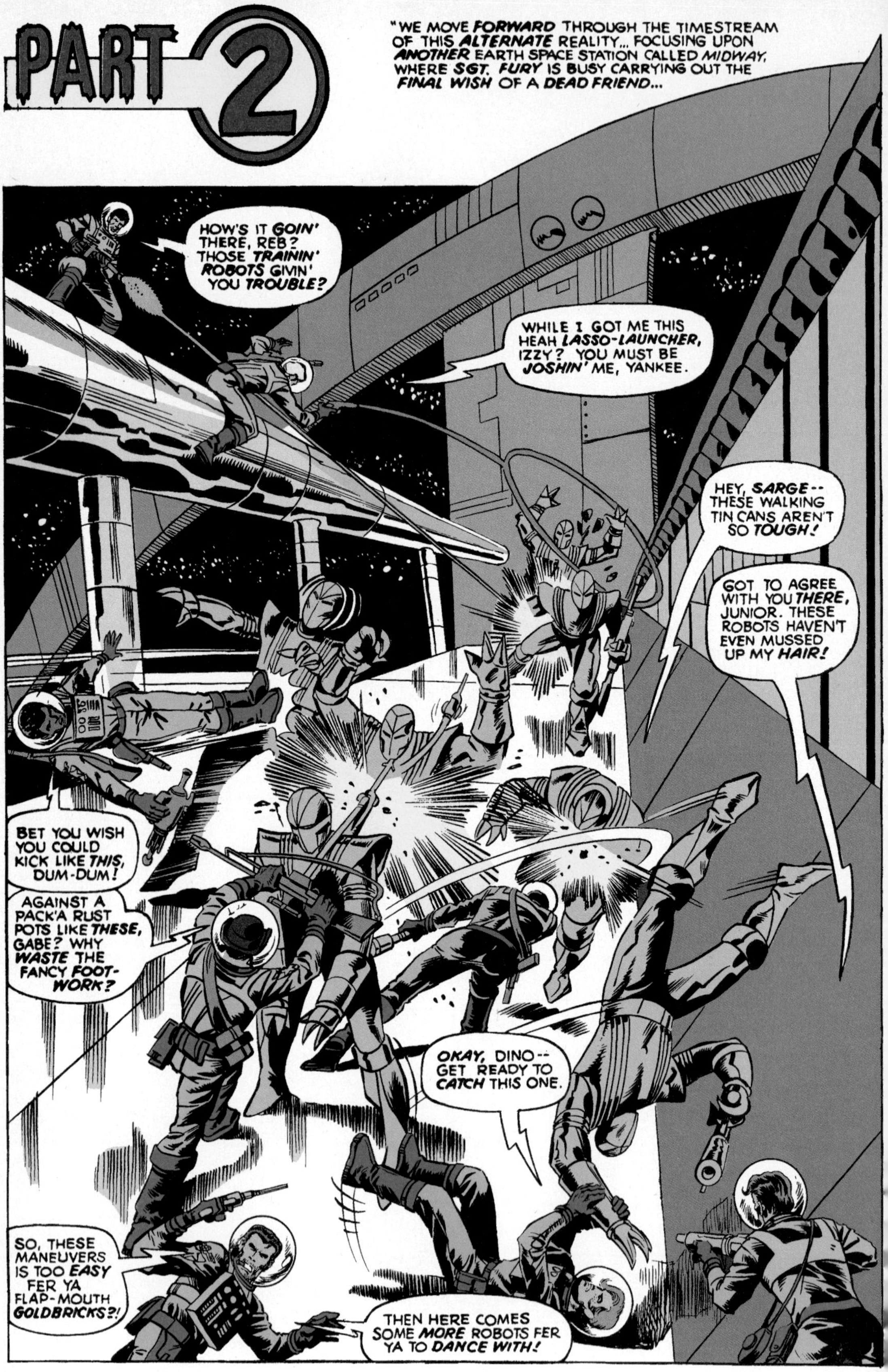
PART 2
"WE MOVE FORWARD THROUGH THE TIMESTREAM OF THIS ALTERNATE REALITY... FOCUSING UPON ANOTHER EARTH SPACE STATION CALLED MIDWAY, WHERE SGT. FURY IS BUSY CARRYING OUT THE FINAL WISH OF A DEAD FRIEND...
HOW'S IT GOIN' THERE, REB? THOSE TRAININ' ROBOTS GIVIN' YOU TROUBLE?
WHILE I GOT ME THIS HEAH LASSO-LAUNCHER, IZZY? YOU MUST BE JOSHIN' ME, YANKEE.
HEY, SARGE-- THESE WALKING TIN CANS AREN'T SO TOUGH!
GOT TO AGREE WITH YOU THERE, JUNIOR. THESE ROBOTS HAVEN'T EVEN MUSSED UP MY HAIR!
BET YOU WISH YOU COULD KICK LIKE THIS, DUM-DUM!
AGAINST A PACK'A RUST POTS LIKE THESE, GABE? WHY WASTE THE FANCY FOOT-WORK?
OKAY, DINO-- GET READY TO CATCH THIS ONE.
SO, THESE MANEUVERS IS TOO EASY FER YA FLAP-MOUTH GOLDBRICKS?!
THEN HERE COMES SOME MORE ROBOTS FER YA TO DANCE WITH!

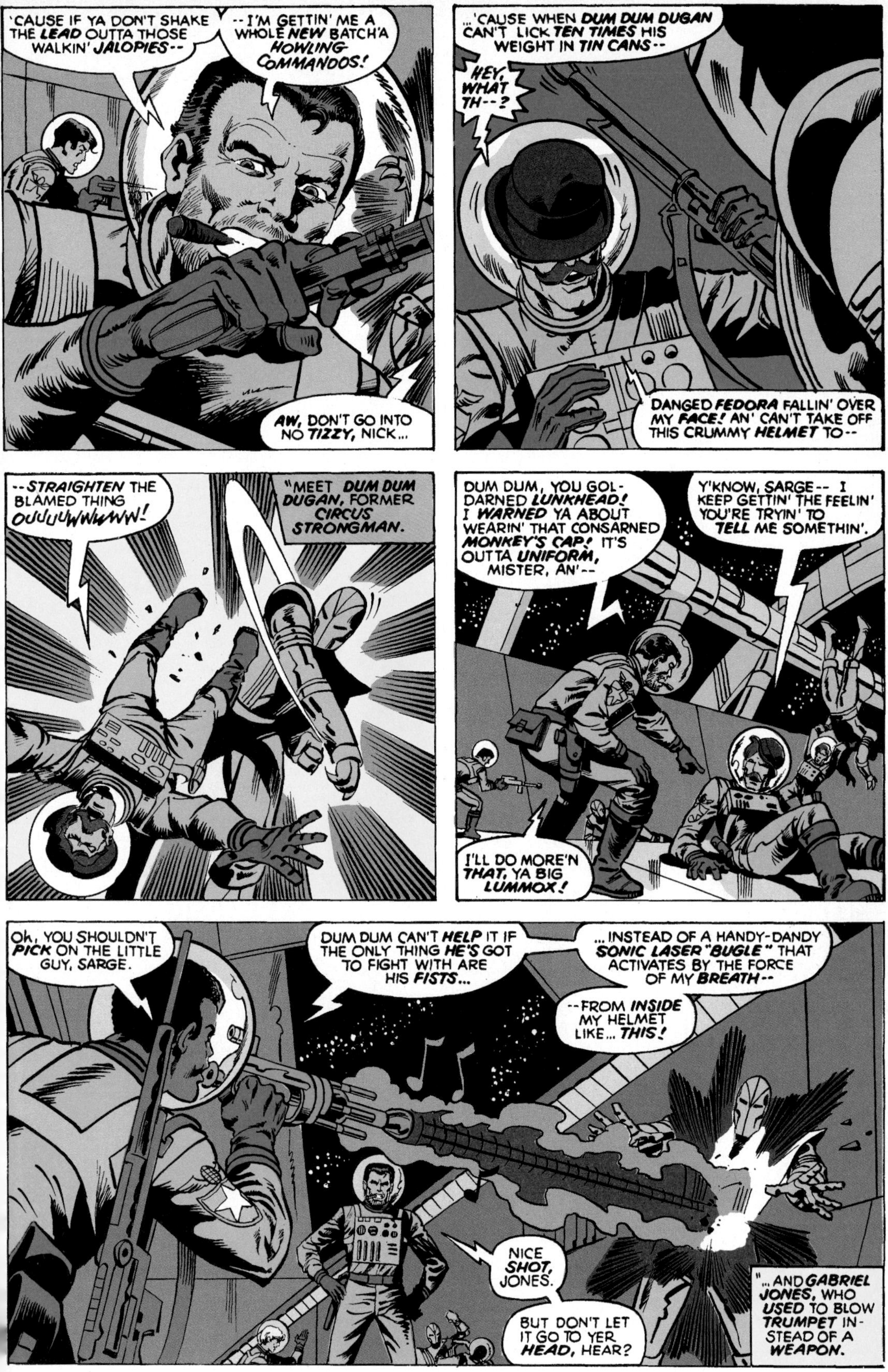
'CAUSE IF YA DON'T SHAKE THE LEAD OUTTA THOSE WALKIN' JALOPIES--
--I'M GETTIN' ME A WHOLE NEW BATCH'A HOWLING COMMANDOS!
AW, DON'T GO INTO NO TIZZY, NICK...
...'CAUSE WHEN DUM DUM DUGAN CAN'T LICK TEN TIMES HIS WEIGHT IN TIN CANS--
HEY, WHAT TH--?
DANGED FEDORA FALLIN' OVER MY FACE! AN' CAN'T TAKE OFF THIS CRUMMY HELMET TO--
--STRAIGHTEN THE BLAMED THING OUUUUWWWWW!
"MEET DUM DUM DUGAN, FORMER CIRCUS STRONGMAN.
DUM DUM, YOU GOL-DARNED LUNKHEAD! I WARNED YA ABOUT WEARIN' THAT CONSARNED MONKEY'S CAP! IT'S OUTTA UNIFORM, MISTER, AN'--
Y'KNOW, SARGE-- I KEEP GETTIN' THE FEELIN' YOU'RE TRYIN' TO TELL ME SOMETHIN'.
I'LL DO MORE'N THAT, YA BIG LUMMOX!
Oh, YOU SHOULDN'T PICK ON THE LITTLE GUY, SARGE.
DUM DUM CAN'T HELP IT IF THE ONLY THING HE'S GOT TO FIGHT WITH ARE HIS FISTS...
...INSTEAD OF A HANDY-DANDY SONIC LASER "BUGLE" THAT ACTIVATES BY THE FORCE OF MY BREATH--
--FROM INSIDE MY HELMET LIKE... THIS!
NICE SHOT, JONES.
BUT DON'T LET IT GO TO YER HEAD, HEAR?
"...AND GABRIEL JONES, WHO USED TO BLOW TRUMPET IN-STEAD OF A WEAPON.

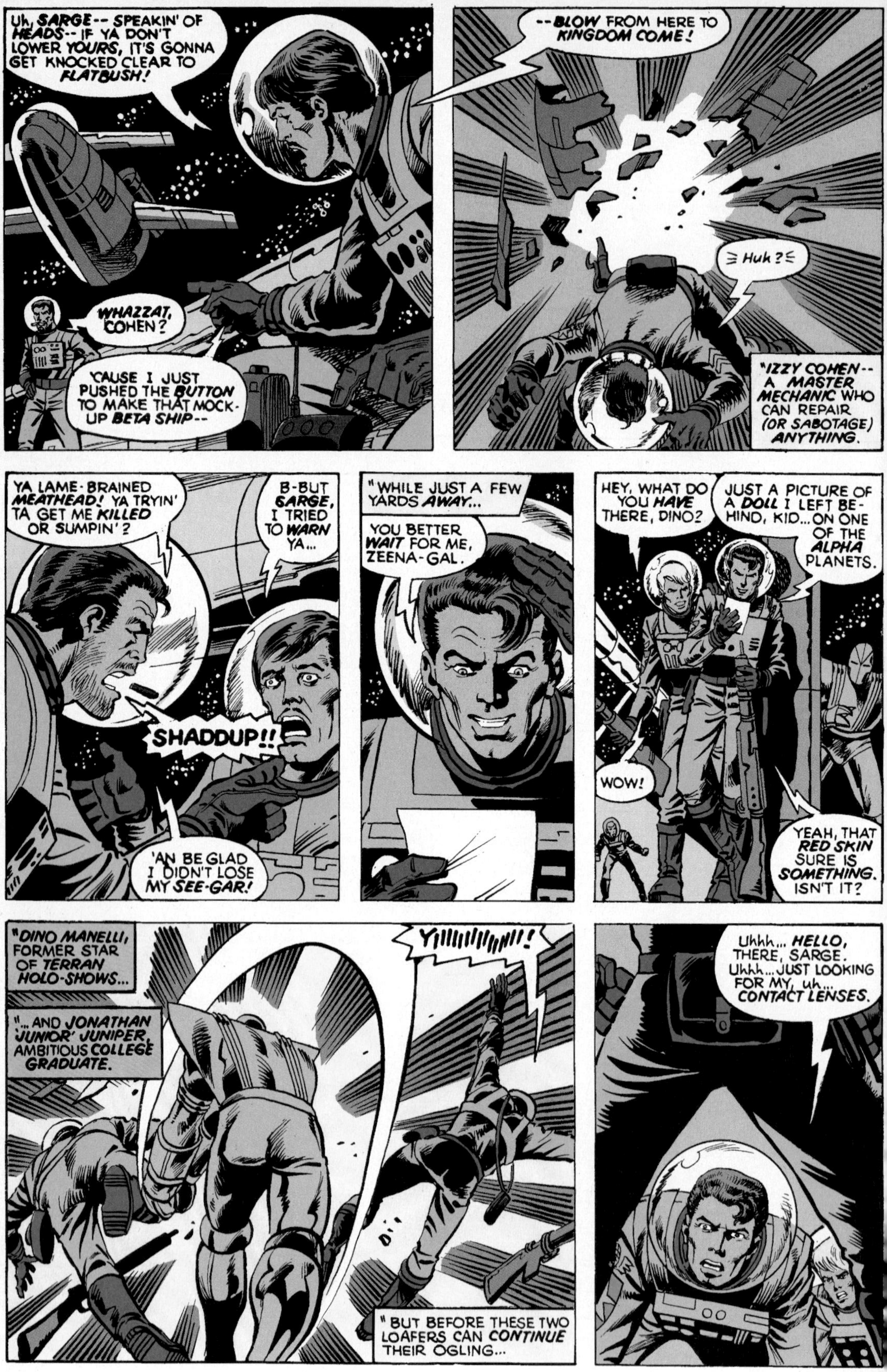
Uh, SARGE -- SPEAKIN' OF HEADS -- IF YA DON'T LOWER YOURS, IT'S GONNA GET KNOCKED CLEAR TO FLATBUSH!
WHAZZAT, COHEN?
'CAUSE I JUST PUSHED THE BUTTON TO MAKE THAT MOCK-UP BETA SHIP --
-- BLOW FROM HERE TO KINGDOM COME!
Huk?
"IZZY COHEN -- A MASTER MECHANIC WHO CAN REPAIR (OR SABOTAGE) ANYTHING.
YA LAME-BRAINED MEATHEAD! YA TRYIN' TA GET ME KILLED OR SUMPIN'?
B-BUT SARGE, I TRIED TO WARN YA...
SHADDUP!!
'AN BE GLAD I DIDN'T LOSE MY SEE-GAR!
"WHILE JUST A FEW YARDS AWAY...
YOU BETTER WAIT FOR ME, ZEENA-GAL.
HEY, WHAT DO YOU HAVE THERE, DINO?
JUST A PICTURE OF A DOLL I LEFT BEHIND, KID... ON ONE OF THE ALPHA PLANETS.
WOW!
YEAH, THAT RED SKIN SURE IS SOMETHING, ISN'T IT?
"DINO MANELLI, FORMER STAR OF TERRAN HOLO-SHOWS...
"... AND JONATHAN 'JUNIOR' JUNIPER, AMBITIOUS COLLEGE GRADUATE.
YIIIIIIIIIII!
"BUT BEFORE THESE TWO LOAFERS CAN CONTINUE THEIR OGLING...
Uhhh... HELLO, THERE, SARGE. Uhhh... JUST LOOKING FOR MY, uh... CONTACT LENSES.

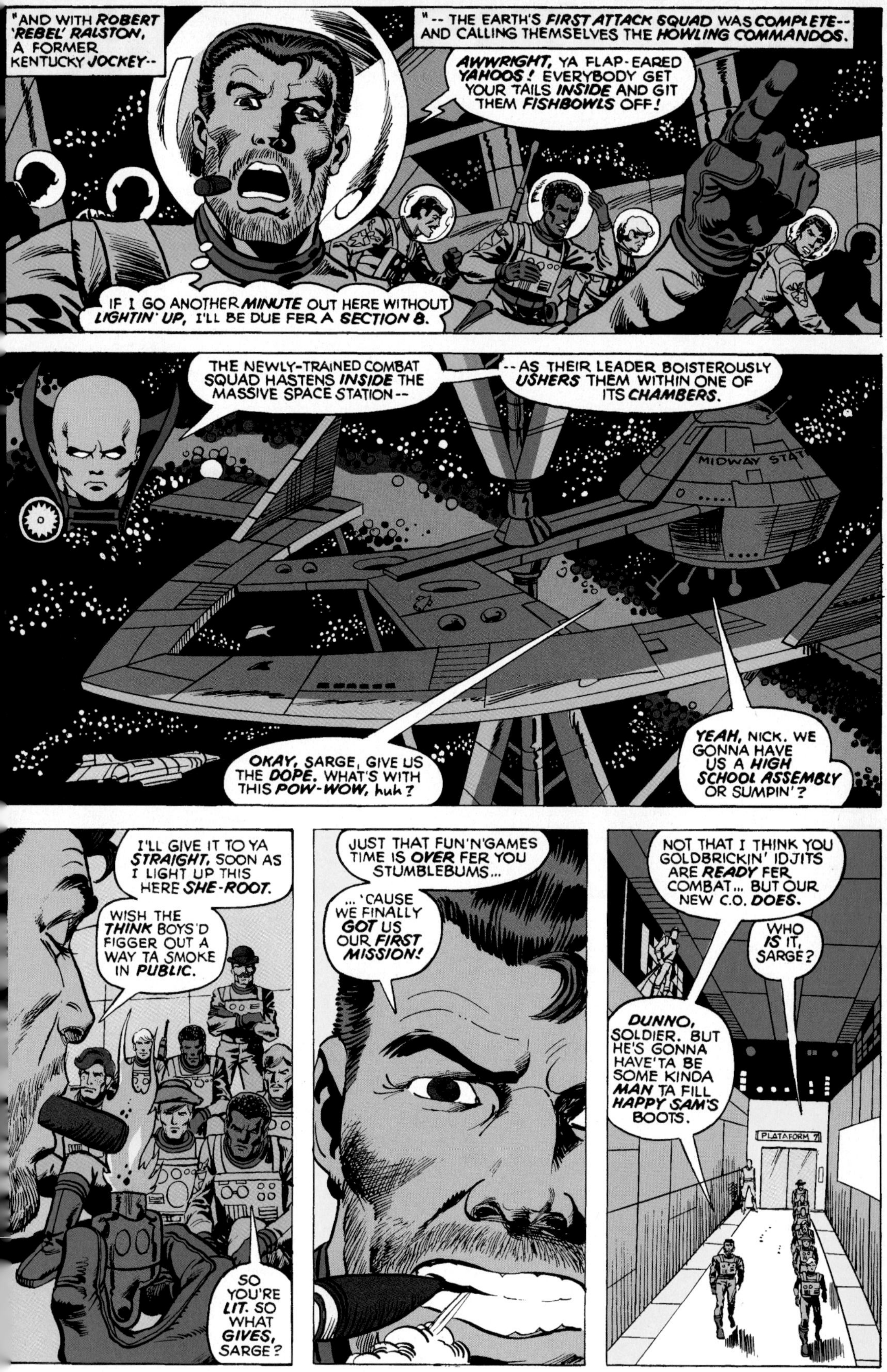
"AND WITH ROBERT 'REBEL' RALSTON, A FORMER KENTUCKY JOCKEY--
"-- THE EARTH'S FIRST ATTACK SQUAD WAS COMPLETE-- AND CALLING THEMSELVES THE HOWLING COMMANDOS.
AWWRIGHT, YA FLAP-EARED YAHOOS! EVERYBODY GET YOUR TAILS INSIDE AND GIT THEM FISHBOWLS OFF!
IF I GO ANOTHER MINUTE OUT HERE WITHOUT LIGHTIN' UP, I'LL BE DUE FER A SECTION 8.
THE NEWLY-TRAINED COMBAT SQUAD HASTENS INSIDE THE MASSIVE SPACE STATION--
--AS THEIR LEADER BOISTEROUSLY USHERS THEM WITHIN ONE OF ITS CHAMBERS.
MIDWAY STAT
OKAY, SARGE, GIVE US THE DOPE. WHAT'S WITH THIS POW-WOW, huh?
YEAH, NICK. WE GONNA HAVE US A HIGH SCHOOL ASSEMBLY OR SUMPIN'?
I'LL GIVE IT TO YA STRAIGHT, SOON AS I LIGHT UP THIS HERE SHE-ROOT.
WISH THE THINK BOYS'D FIGGER OUT A WAY TA SMOKE IN PUBLIC.
SO YOU'RE LIT. SO WHAT GIVES, SARGE?
JUST THAT FUN'N'GAMES TIME IS OVER FER YOU STUMBLEBUMS...
...'CAUSE WE FINALLY GOT US OUR FIRST MISSION!
NOT THAT I THINK YOU GOLDBRICKIN' IDJITS ARE READY FER COMBAT... BUT OUR NEW C.O. DOES.
WHO IS IT, SARGE?
DUNNO, SOLDIER. BUT HE'S GONNA HAVE'TA BE SOME KINDA MAN TA FILL HAPPY SAM'S BOOTS.
PLATAFORM 7

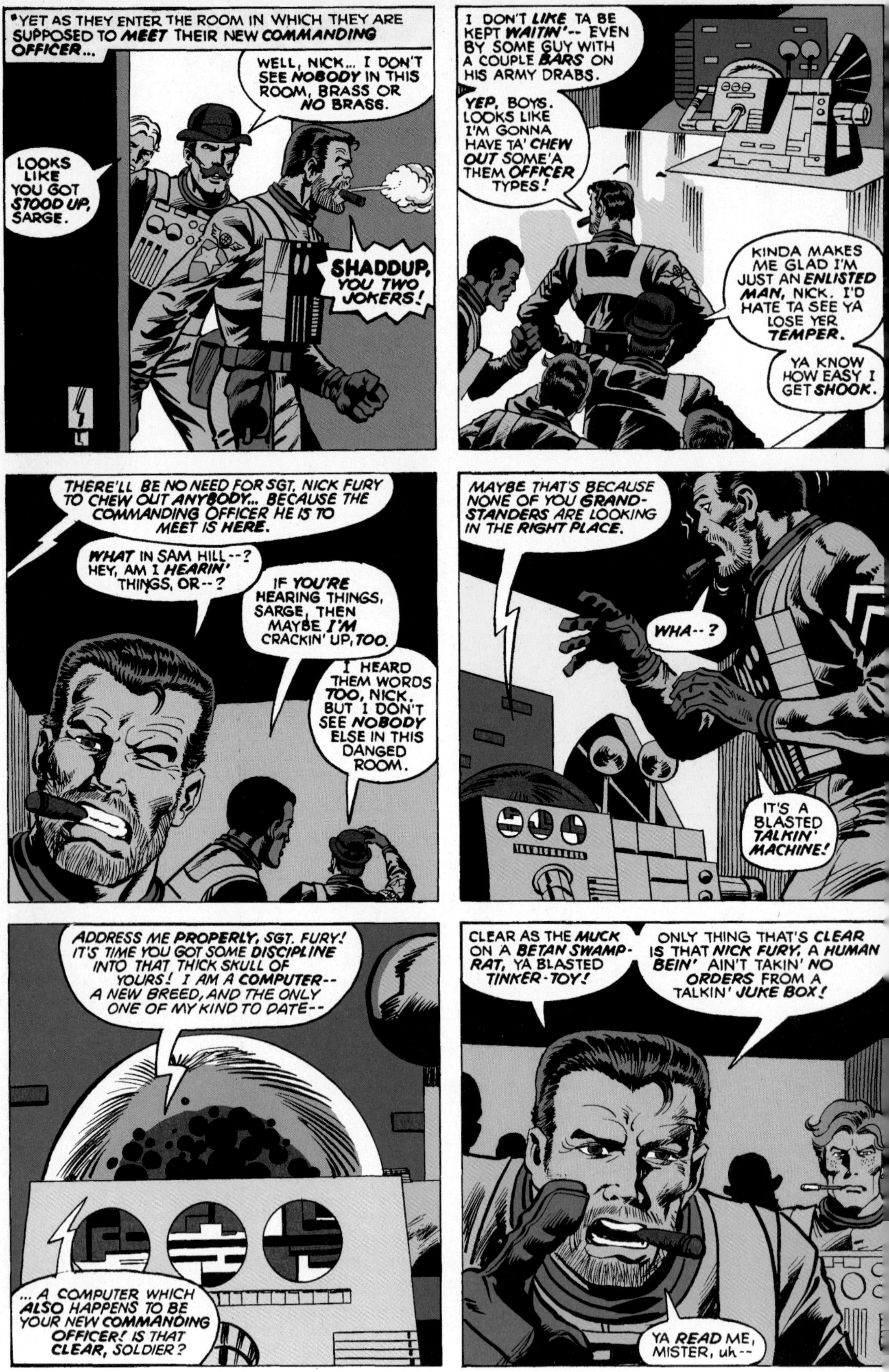
*YET AS THEY ENTER THE ROOM IN WHICH THEY ARE SUPPOSED TO MEET THEIR NEW COMMANDING OFFICER...
WELL, NICK... I DON'T SEE NOBODY IN THIS ROOM, BRASS OR NO BRASS.
LOOKS LIKE YOU GOT STOOD UP, SARGE.
SHADDUP, YOU TWO JOKERS!
I DON'T LIKE TA BE KEPT WAITIN'-- EVEN BY SOME GUY WITH A COUPLE BARS ON HIS ARMY DRABS.
YEP, BOYS. LOOKS LIKE I'M GONNA HAVE TA' CHEW OUT SOME'A THEM OFFICER TYPES!
KINDA MAKES ME GLAD I'M JUST AN ENLISTED MAN, NICK. I'D HATE TA SEE YA LOSE YER TEMPER.
YA KNOW HOW EASY I GET SHOOK.
THERE'LL BE NO NEED FOR SGT. NICK FURY TO CHEW OUT ANYBODY... BECAUSE THE COMMANDING OFFICER HE IS TO MEET IS HERE.
WHAT IN SAM HILL--? HEY, AM I HEARIN' THINGS, OR--?
IF YOU'RE HEARING THINGS, SARGE, THEN MAYBE I'M CRACKIN' UP, TOO.
I HEARD THEM WORDS TOO, NICK. BUT I DON'T SEE NOBODY ELSE IN THIS DANGED ROOM.
MAYBE THAT'S BECAUSE NONE OF YOU GRAND-STANDERS ARE LOOKING IN THE RIGHT PLACE.
WHA--?
IT'S A BLASTED TALKIN' MACHINE!
ADDRESS ME PROPERLY, SGT. FURY! IT'S TIME YOU GOT SOME DISCIPLINE INTO THAT THICK SKULL OF YOURS! I AM A COMPUTER-- A NEW BREED, AND THE ONLY ONE OF MY KIND TO DATE--
...A COMPUTER WHICH ALSO HAPPENS TO BE YOUR NEW COMMANDING OFFICER! IS THAT CLEAR, SOLDIER?
CLEAR AS THE MUCK ON A BETAN SWAMP-RAT, YA BLASTED TINKER-TOY!
ONLY THING THAT'S CLEAR IS THAT NICK FURY, A HUMAN BEIN' AIN'T TAKIN' NO ORDERS FROM A TALKIN' JUKE BOX!
YA READ ME, MISTER, uh--

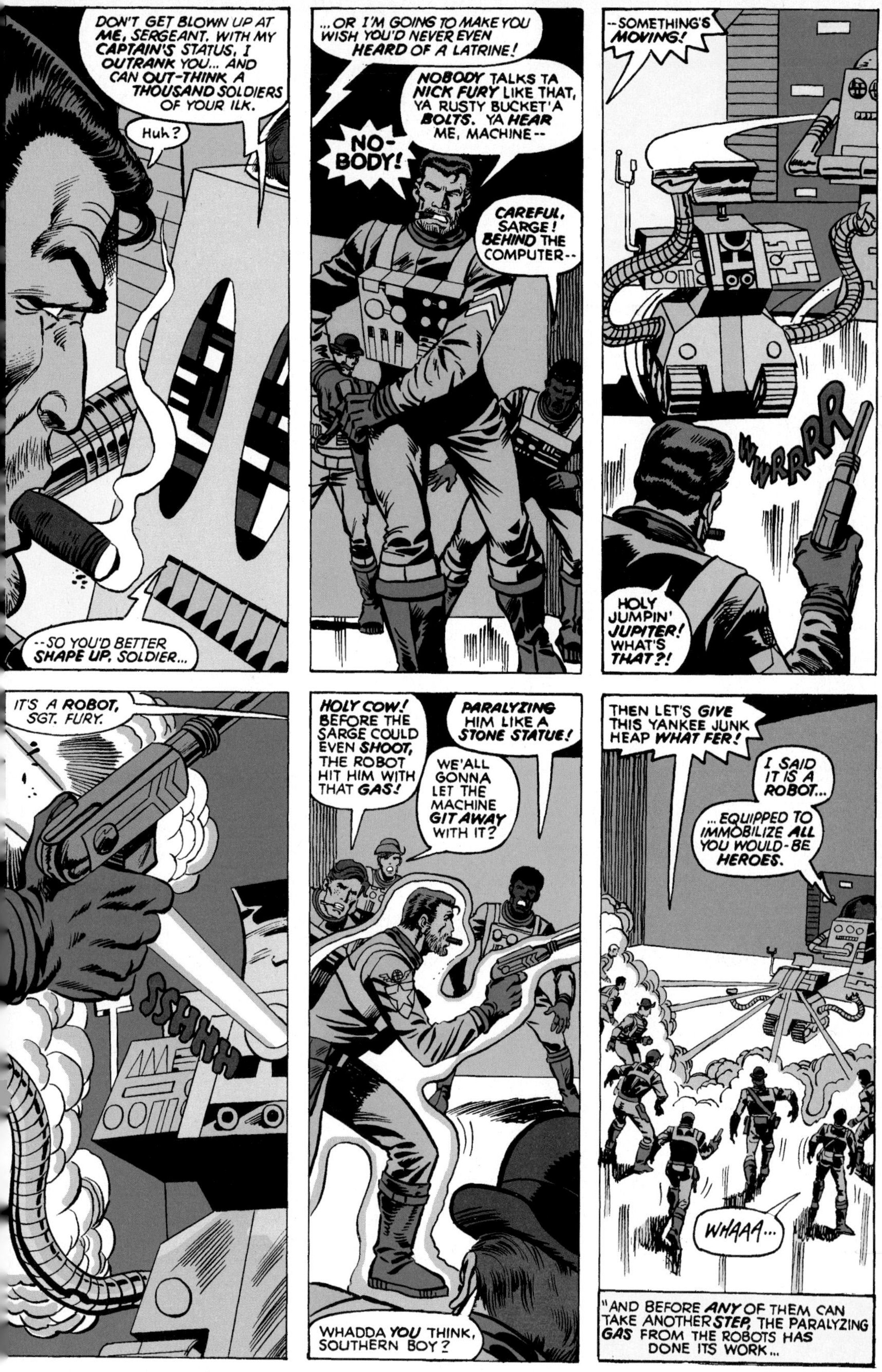
DON'T GET BLOWN UP AT ME, SERGEANT. WITH MY CAPTAIN'S STATUS, I OUTRANK YOU... AND CAN OUT-THINK A THOUSAND SOLDIERS OF YOUR ILK.
Huh?
--SO YOU'D BETTER SHAPE UP, SOLDIER...
...OR I'M GOING TO MAKE YOU WISH YOU'D NEVER EVEN HEARD OF A LATRINE!
NOBODY TALKS TA NICK FURY LIKE THAT, YA RUSTY BUCKET'A BOLTS. YA HEAR ME, MACHINE--
NO-BODY!
CAREFUL, SARGE! BEHIND THE COMPUTER--
--SOMETHING'S MOVING!
WWRRRRR
HOLY JUMPIN' JUPITER! WHAT'S THAT?!
IT'S A ROBOT, SGT. FURY.
SSHHHH
HOLY COW! BEFORE THE SARGE COULD EVEN SHOOT, THE ROBOT HIT HIM WITH THAT GAS!
PARALYZING HIM LIKE A STONE STATUE!
WE'ALL GONNA LET THE MACHINE GIT AWAY WITH IT?
WHADDA YOU THINK, SOUTHERN BOY?
THEN LET'S GIVE THIS YANKEE JUNK HEAP WHAT FER!
I SAID IT IS A ROBOT...
...EQUIPPED TO IMMOBILIZE ALL YOU WOULD-BE HEROES.
WHAAA...
"AND BEFORE ANY OF THEM CAN TAKE ANOTHER STEP, THE PARALYZING GAS FROM THE ROBOTS HAS DONE ITS WORK...

"... ALLOWING THEM ONLY THEIR ABILITIES TO *HEAR* AND *UNDERSTAND* THE COMPUTER'S REVERBERATING WORDS.

NOW *GET THIS,* SPACE-SOLDIERS, AND GET IT *STRAIGHT!*

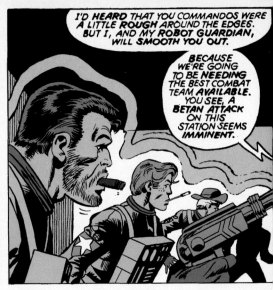

I'D *HEARD* THAT YOU COMMANDOS WERE A LITTLE *ROUGH* AROUND THE EDGES. BUT I, AND MY ROBOT GUARDIAN, WILL SMOOTH YOU OUT.

BECAUSE WE'RE GOING TO BE *NEEDING* THE BEST COMBAT TEAM *AVAILABLE.* YOU SEE, A *BETAN ATTACK* ON THIS STATION SEEMS *IMMINENT.*

YOUR ORDERS: YOU WILL REMAIN ON *24*-HOUR *CALL* UNTIL THE ATTACK *HAPPENS*... OR THE DANGER *PASSES*... ALL EXCEPT *HARGROVE.*

AS A PILOT, HE WILL BE ASSIGNED TO *CARRIER DUTY* ABOARD THE *ROCKET CARRIER YORKTOWN.*

YOU *HAVE* YOUR ORDERS, ROBOT--

--*MOBILIZE* THEM!

HUH? WHAT'S *HAPPENIN'* NOW?

WHADDA YA *THINK,* YA-RED-HEADED OL' *WALRUS?* THE ROBOTS HITTIN' US WITH A *RAY* SO'S WE CAN *MOVE* AGAIN.

ALL OF YOU, EXCEPT *HARGROVE*... ARE DIS-*MISSED!*

AWWRIGHT, YOU HOWLERS *HEARD* THE MAN--*er,* MACHINE. SO GIT THEM BUTTS *MOVIN'*... ...ON THE *DOUBLE,* HEAR?

≥ groan ≤

"THE MEN ARE *GRUMBLING* UNDER THEIR BREATHS AS THEY MARCH DOWN THE CORRIDOR.

THEY DON'T LIKE THIS SET-UP NO BETTER'N I DO... TAKIN' *ORDERS* FROM SOME BLASTED *WURLITZER.*

BUT I AIN'T FINISHED *YET.*

WRRRR

NO SIREE! SOON AS I FIGGER OUT SOME WAY TA PUT THAT COMPUTER OUTTA COMMISSION, I'M GONNA--

EEYOW!

WHY, YA DIRTY, BACK-ZAPPIN', HUNK'A--

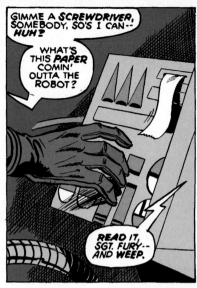

GIMME A SCREWDRIVER, SOMEBODY, SO'S I CAN-- HUH?

WHAT'S THIS PAPER COMIN' OUTTA THE ROBOT?

READ IT, SGT. FURY-- AND WEEP.

WHY, OF ALL THE--

I WILL ...WITH YOU AT ALL TIMES TO ENSURE YOUR COMPLIANCE WITH ORDERS

"AND, AS FURY STORMS DOWN THE CORRIDOR, SNARLING EXPLETIVES BEST LEFT UNHEARD BY EARS IN YOUR DIMENSION...

"...LET US RETURN TO THE COMPUTER ROOM AND RED HARGROVE."

I WILL BRIEF YOU. WE BELIEVE THAT THE BETANS ASSUME WE HAVE NO OPERATIONAL CARRIERS IN THE MIDWAY AREA.

SO WE WILL SURPRISE THEM WHEN THEY ATTACK. YOU WILL FLY AN ATTACK CRUISER FROM THE YORKTOWN, LAUNCHING A CARRIER ATTACK ON THE ENEMY.

GOTCHA, SIR.

YOU WILL FLY OUT WITH THE INITIAL ASSAULT WAVE, HARGROVE... IN WHAT MAY BE THE MOST CRUCIAL BATTLE IN THE ENTIRE WAR.

FOR IF EARTH STATION MIDWAY IS LOST, THE BETANS WILL CONTROL VITAL BASES--

-- FROM WHICH TO LAUNCH AN ASSAULT UPON THE EARTH ITSELF!

"WHILE AT THAT MOMENT, IN DEEP SPACE, SOME VERY NON-STELLAR LIGHTS STEADILY APPROACH STATION MIDWAY."

END of PART TWO.

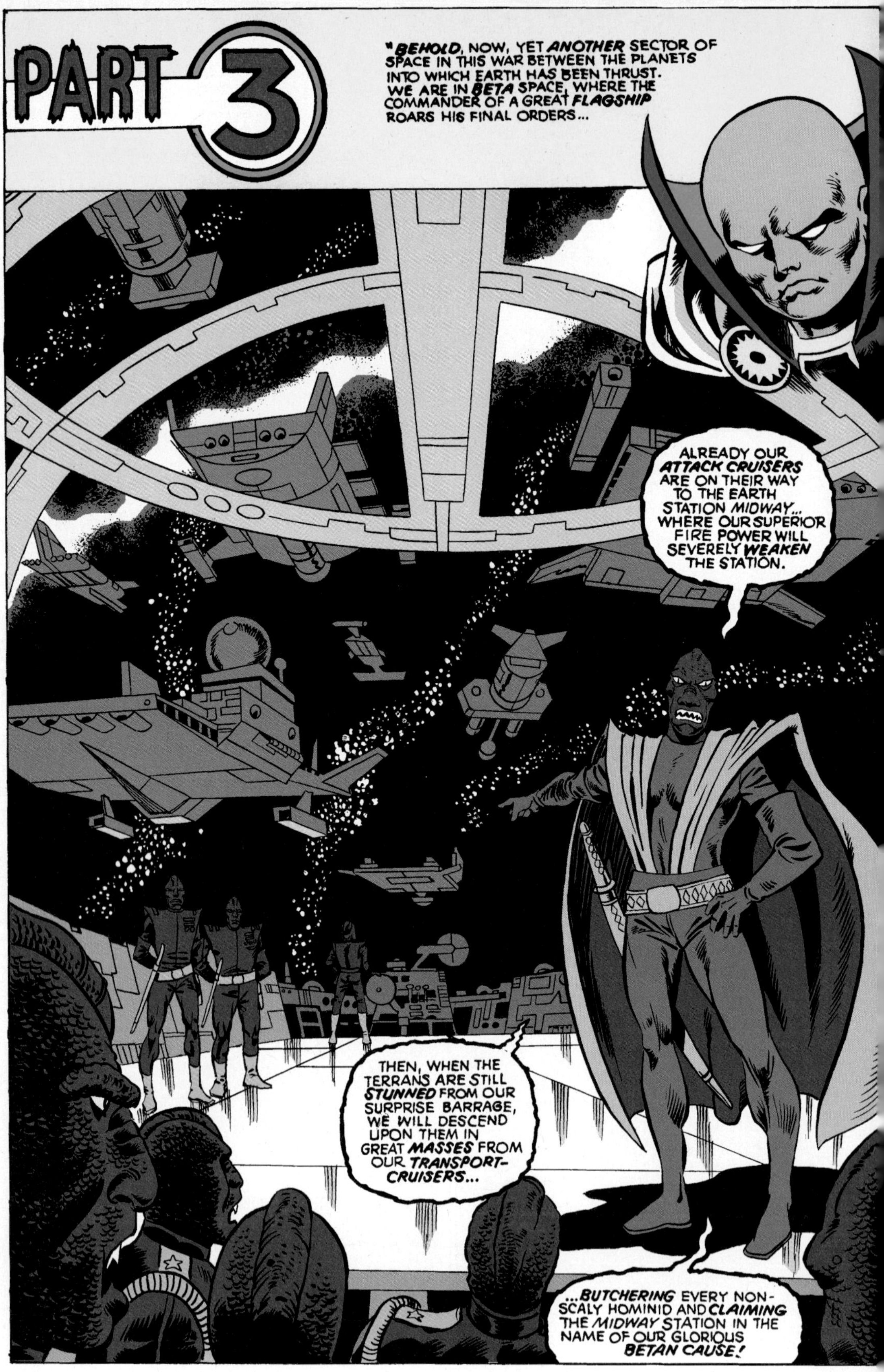
PART 3
"BEHOLD, NOW, YET ANOTHER SECTOR OF SPACE IN THIS WAR BETWEEN THE PLANETS INTO WHICH EARTH HAS BEEN THRUST. WE ARE IN BETA SPACE, WHERE THE COMMANDER OF A GREAT FLAGSHIP ROARS HIS FINAL ORDERS...
ALREADY OUR ATTACK CRUISERS ARE ON THEIR WAY TO THE EARTH STATION MIDWAY... WHERE OUR SUPERIOR FIRE POWER WILL SEVERELY WEAKEN THE STATION.
THEN, WHEN THE TERRANS ARE STILL STUNNED FROM OUR SURPRISE BARRAGE, WE WILL DESCEND UPON THEM IN GREAT MASSES FROM OUR TRANSPORT-CRUISERS...
...BUTCHERING EVERY NON-SCALY HOMINID AND CLAIMING THE MIDWAY STATION IN THE NAME OF OUR GLORIOUS BETAN CAUSE!

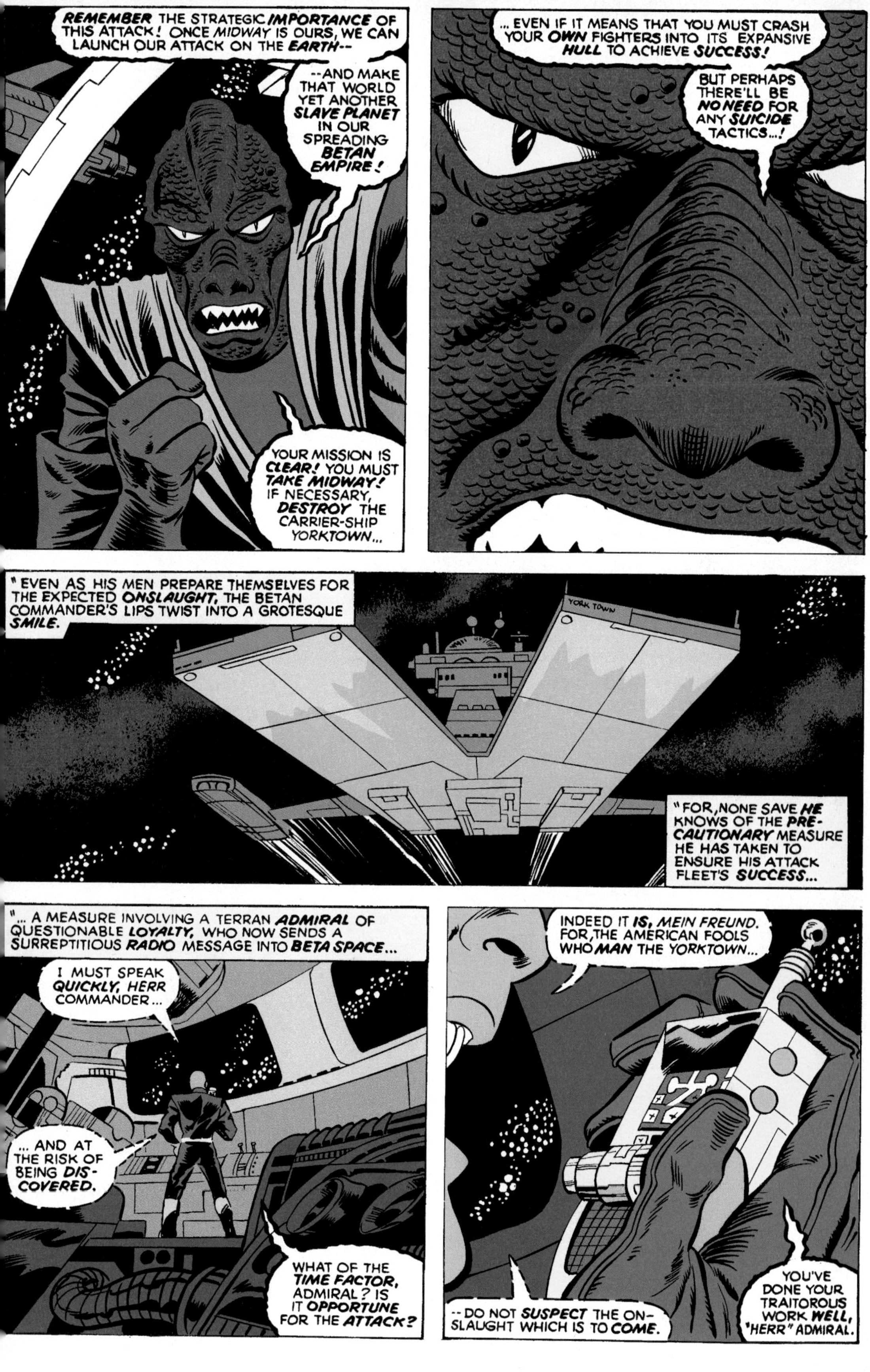
REMEMBER THE STRATEGIC IMPORTANCE OF THIS ATTACK! ONCE MIDWAY IS OURS, WE CAN LAUNCH OUR ATTACK ON THE EARTH--
--AND MAKE THAT WORLD YET ANOTHER SLAVE PLANET IN OUR SPREADING BETAN EMPIRE!
YOUR MISSION IS CLEAR! YOU MUST TAKE MIDWAY! IF NECESSARY, DESTROY THE CARRIER-SHIP YORKTOWN...
... EVEN IF IT MEANS THAT YOU MUST CRASH YOUR OWN FIGHTERS INTO ITS EXPANSIVE HULL TO ACHIEVE SUCCESS!
BUT PERHAPS THERE'LL BE NO NEED FOR ANY SUICIDE TACTICS...!
" EVEN AS HIS MEN PREPARE THEMSELVES FOR THE EXPECTED ONSLAUGHT, THE BETAN COMMANDER'S LIPS TWIST INTO A GROTESQUE SMILE.
YORK TOWN
"FOR, NONE SAVE HE KNOWS OF THE PRE-CAUTIONARY MEASURE HE HAS TAKEN TO ENSURE HIS ATTACK FLEET'S SUCCESS...
"... A MEASURE INVOLVING A TERRAN ADMIRAL OF QUESTIONABLE LOYALTY, WHO NOW SENDS A SURREPTITIOUS RADIO MESSAGE INTO BETA SPACE...
I MUST SPEAK QUICKLY, HERR COMMANDER...
... AND AT THE RISK OF BEING DIS-COVERED.
WHAT OF THE TIME FACTOR, ADMIRAL? IS IT OPPORTUNE FOR THE ATTACK?
INDEED IT IS, MEIN FREUND. FOR, THE AMERICAN FOOLS WHO MAN THE YORKTOWN...
-- DO NOT SUSPECT THE ON-SLAUGHT WHICH IS TO COME.
YOU'VE DONE YOUR TRAITOROUS WORK WELL, "HERR" ADMIRAL.

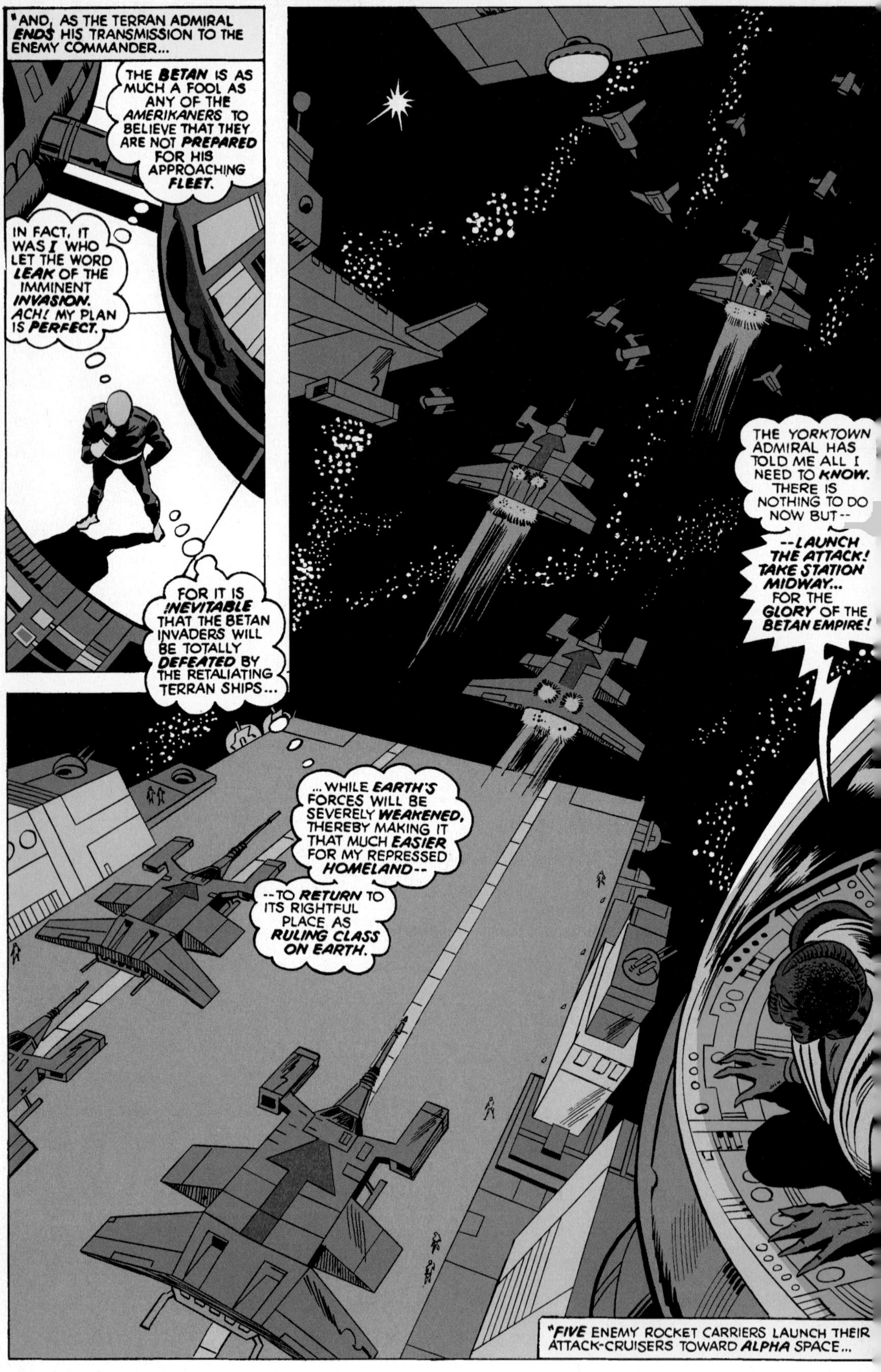
"AND, AS THE TERRAN ADMIRAL ENDS HIS TRANSMISSION TO THE ENEMY COMMANDER...
THE BETAN IS AS MUCH A FOOL AS ANY OF THE AMERIKANERS TO BELIEVE THAT THEY ARE NOT PREPARED FOR HIS APPROACHING FLEET.
IN FACT, IT WAS I WHO LET THE WORD LEAK OF THE IMMINENT INVASION. ACH! MY PLAN IS PERFECT.
FOR IT IS INEVITABLE THAT THE BETAN INVADERS WILL BE TOTALLY DEFEATED BY THE RETALIATING TERRAN SHIPS...
...WHILE EARTH'S FORCES WILL BE SEVERELY WEAKENED, THEREBY MAKING IT THAT MUCH EASIER FOR MY REPRESSED HOMELAND--
--TO RETURN TO ITS RIGHTFUL PLACE AS RULING CLASS ON EARTH.
THE YORKTOWN ADMIRAL HAS TOLD ME ALL I NEED TO KNOW. THERE IS NOTHING TO DO NOW BUT--
--LAUNCH THE ATTACK! TAKE STATION MIDWAY... FOR THE GLORY OF THE BETAN EMPIRE!
"FIVE ENEMY ROCKET CARRIERS LAUNCH THEIR ATTACK-CRUISERS TOWARD ALPHA SPACE...

"... WHILE, A GOOD DISTANCE *AHEAD* OF THE BETAN SHIPS, WITHIN THE ROCKET CRUISER *YORKTOWN*...

THERE'S NO DOUBT *ABOUT* IT, SIR...

IT'S A FLEET OF *UNIDENTIFIED SHIPS*... HEADIN' *THIS WAY.*

ALL RIGHT, SPACE HEROES...

... THIS IS WHAT WE'VE BEEN *WAITING* FOR! HIT THOSE *ATTACK CRUISERS* AND GET YOUR TAILS *INTO SPACE!*

YOU *HEARD* THE MAN, SPACE-JOCKIES! SO WHAT SAY WE *SHOW* THOSE SNAKE-FACED UGLIES WHAT IT MEANS TO TRADE *BLASTS*--

--WITH THE BOYS OF THE *MISSILE 8 ATTACK SQUAD!*

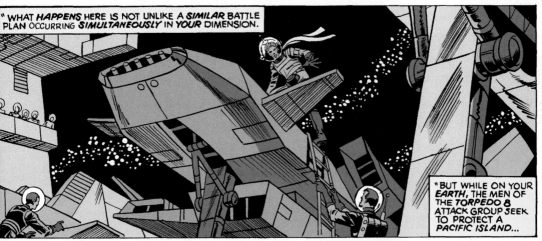

"WHAT *HAPPENS* HERE IS NOT UNLIKE A *SIMILAR* BATTLE PLAN OCCURRING *SIMULTANEOUSLY* IN *YOUR* DIMENSION.

"BUT WHILE ON YOUR *EARTH*, THE MEN OF THE *TORPEDO 8* ATTACK GROUP SEEK TO PROTECT A *PACIFIC ISLAND*...

... *RED HARGROVE* AND THE COURAGEOUS ROCKET PILOTS OF *THIS* REALITY WILL BE FIGHTING TO DEFEND MUCH *MORE*...

"... THE *OUTCOME* OF THEIR ENDEAVORS DETERMINING THE FATE OF *A WORLD.*

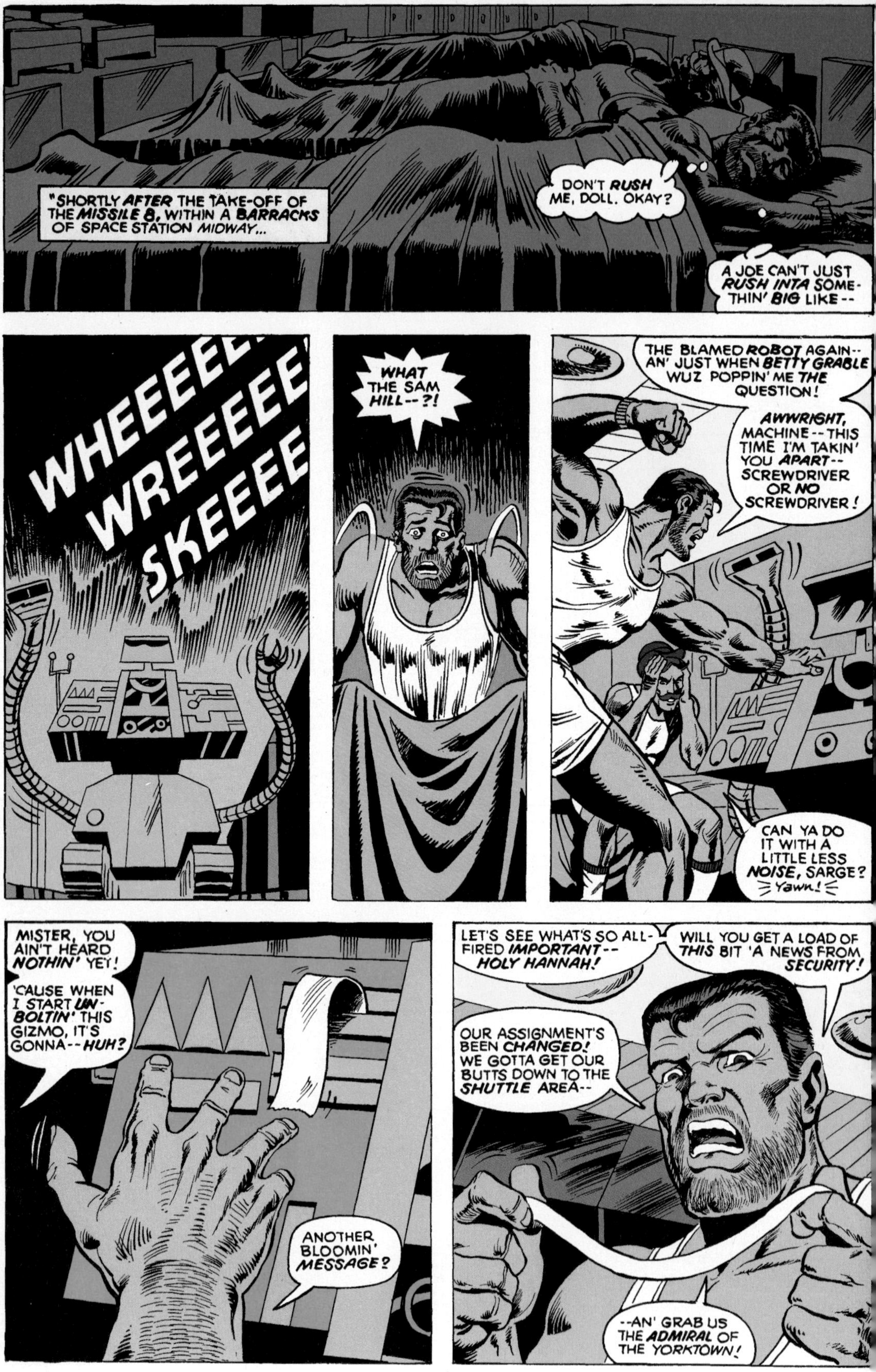
"SHORTLY AFTER THE TAKE-OFF OF THE MISSILE 8, WITHIN A BARRACKS OF SPACE STATION MIDWAY...
DON'T RUSH ME, DOLL. OKAY?
A JOE CAN'T JUST RUSH INTA SOMETHIN' BIG LIKE--
WHEEEEE
WREEEEE
SKEEEE
WHAT THE SAM HILL--?!
THE BLAMED ROBOT AGAIN-- AN' JUST WHEN BETTY GRABLE WUZ POPPIN' ME THE QUESTION!
AWWRIGHT, MACHINE--THIS TIME I'M TAKIN' YOU APART-- SCREWDRIVER OR NO SCREWDRIVER!
CAN YA DO IT WITH A LITTLE LESS NOISE, SARGE? Yawn!
MISTER, YOU AIN'T HEARD NOTHIN' YET!
'CAUSE WHEN I START UN-BOLTIN' THIS GIZMO, IT'S GONNA--HUH?
ANOTHER BLOOMIN' MESSAGE?
LET'S SEE WHAT'S SO ALL-FIRED IMPORTANT-- HOLY HANNAH!
WILL YOU GET A LOAD OF THIS BIT 'A NEWS FROM SECURITY!
OUR ASSIGNMENT'S BEEN CHANGED! WE GOTTA GET OUR BUTTS DOWN TO THE SHUTTLE AREA--
--AN' GRAB US THE ADMIRAL OF THE YORKTOWN!

WHAT'S THE FUSS, NICK? NEED YOURSELF A DANCIN' PARTNER?

KNOCK IT OFF, YOU OVERSTUFFED OX!

TURNS OUT THE ADMIRAL'S SOME STINKIN' YELLA-LIVERED TRAITOR! AN' WE GOTTA GET THE RAT BEFORE HE--

BLA-DOOM

WE BEEN HIT!

HANG ON-- AN' GET THEM HELMETS OVER YER UGLY KISSERS!

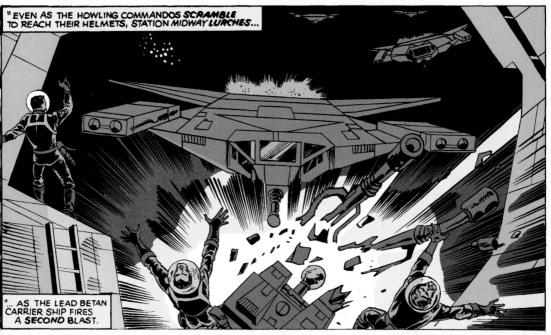

"EVEN AS THE HOWLING COMMANDOS SCRAMBLE TO REACH THEIR HELMETS, STATION MIDWAY LURCHES...

"... AS THE LEAD BETAN CARRIER SHIP FIRES A SECOND BLAST.

THUS, THE FULL-SCALE ATTACK IS NOW UNDERWAY...

... WHILE ON YOUR WORLD, A SIMILAR ATTACK IS MADE BY AN AIR FLEET FROM IMPERIAL JAPAN.

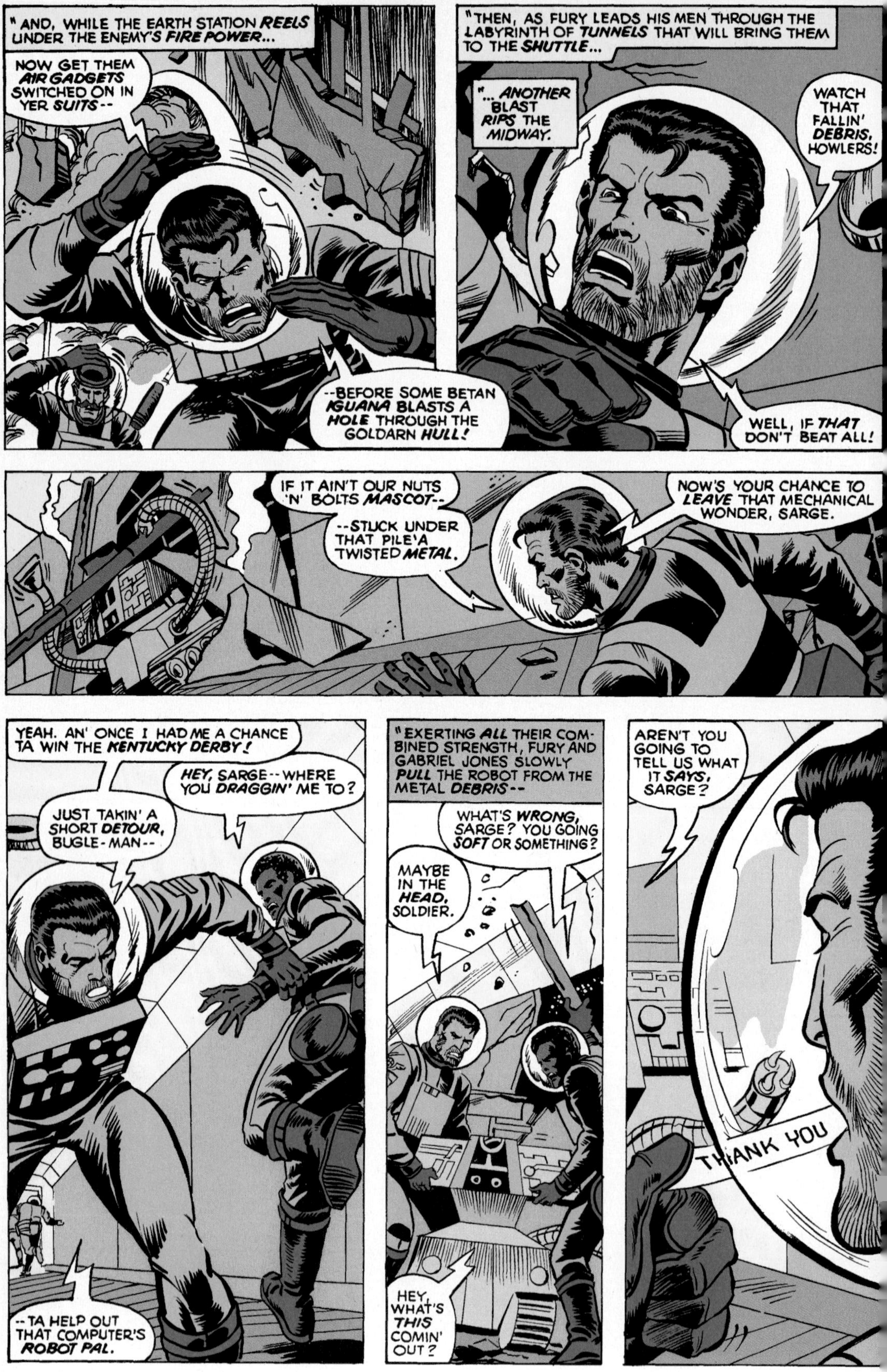
"AND, WHILE THE EARTH STATION REELS UNDER THE ENEMY'S FIRE POWER...
NOW GET THEM AIR GADGETS SWITCHED ON IN YER SUITS--
--BEFORE SOME BETAN IGUANA BLASTS A HOLE THROUGH THE GOLDARN HULL!
"THEN, AS FURY LEADS HIS MEN THROUGH THE LABYRINTH OF TUNNELS THAT WILL BRING THEM TO THE SHUTTLE...
"... ANOTHER BLAST RIPS THE MIDWAY.
WATCH THAT FALLIN' DEBRIS, HOWLERS!
WELL, IF THAT DON'T BEAT ALL!
IF IT AIN'T OUR NUTS 'N' BOLTS MASCOT--
--STUCK UNDER THAT PILE'A TWISTED METAL.
NOW'S YOUR CHANCE TO LEAVE THAT MECHANICAL WONDER, SARGE.
YEAH. AN' ONCE I HAD ME A CHANCE TA WIN THE KENTUCKY DERBY!
HEY, SARGE--WHERE YOU DRAGGIN' ME TO?
JUST TAKIN' A SHORT DETOUR, BUGLE-MAN--
--TA HELP OUT THAT COMPUTER'S ROBOT PAL.
"EXERTING ALL THEIR COMBINED STRENGTH, FURY AND GABRIEL JONES SLOWLY PULL THE ROBOT FROM THE METAL DEBRIS--
WHAT'S WRONG, SARGE? YOU GOING SOFT OR SOMETHING?
MAYBE IN THE HEAD, SOLDIER.
HEY, WHAT'S THIS COMIN' OUT?
AREN'T YOU GOING TO TELL US WHAT IT SAYS, SARGE?
THANK YOU

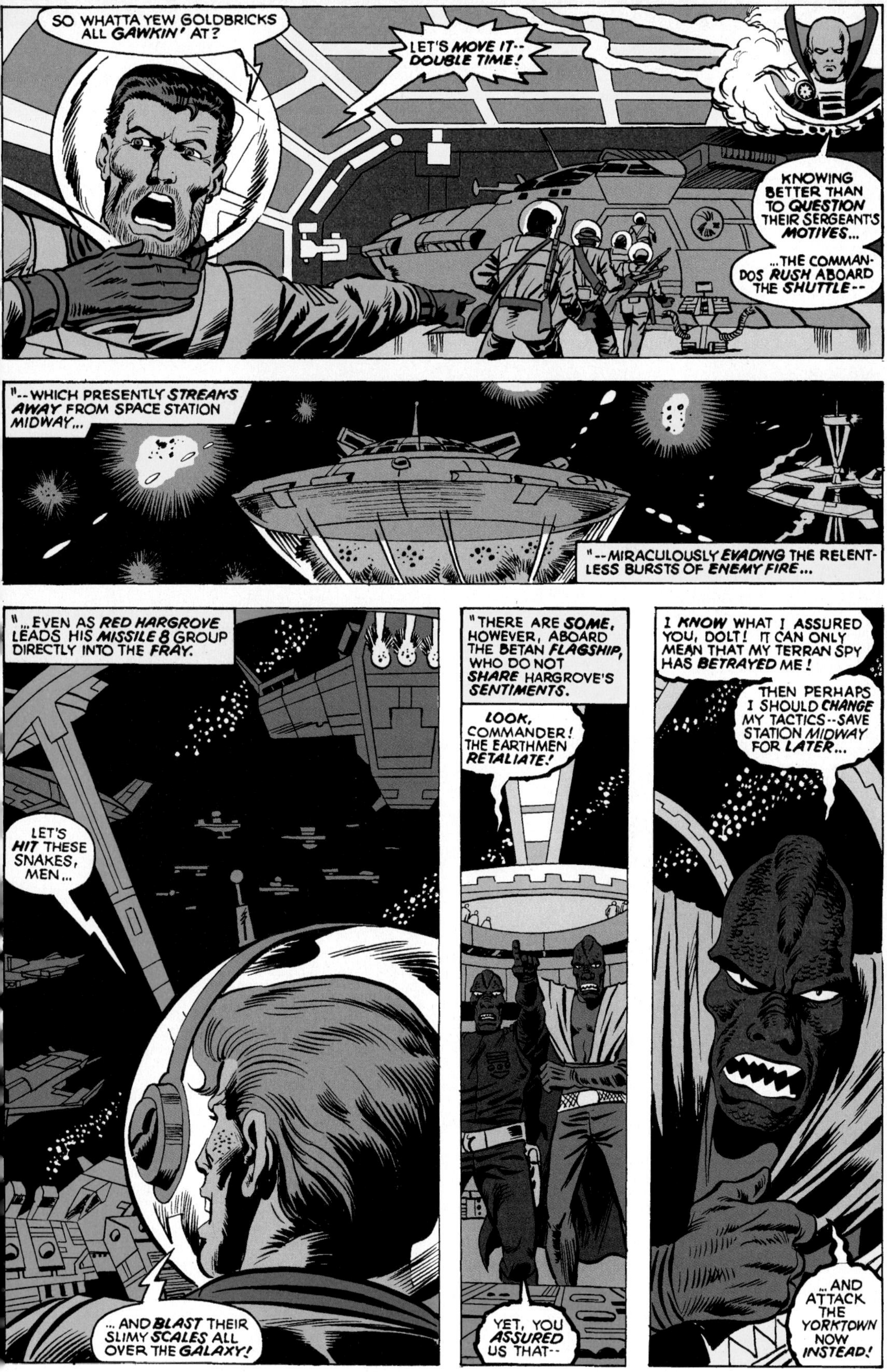
SO WHATTA YEW GOLDBRICKS ALL GAWKIN' AT?
LET'S MOVE IT-- DOUBLE TIME!
KNOWING BETTER THAN TO QUESTION THEIR SERGEANT'S MOTIVES...
...THE COMMANDOS RUSH ABOARD THE SHUTTLE--
"--WHICH PRESENTLY STREAKS AWAY FROM SPACE STATION MIDWAY...
"--MIRACULOUSLY EVADING THE RELENTLESS BURSTS OF ENEMY FIRE...
"...EVEN AS RED HARGROVE LEADS HIS MISSILE 8 GROUP DIRECTLY INTO THE FRAY.
LET'S HIT THESE SNAKES, MEN...
...AND BLAST THEIR SLIMY SCALES ALL OVER THE GALAXY!
"THERE ARE SOME, HOWEVER, ABOARD THE BETAN FLAGSHIP, WHO DO NOT SHARE HARGROVE'S SENTIMENTS.
LOOK, COMMANDER! THE EARTHMEN RETALIATE!
YET, YOU ASSURED US THAT--
I KNOW WHAT I ASSURED YOU, DOLT! IT CAN ONLY MEAN THAT MY TERRAN SPY HAS BETRAYED ME!
THEN PERHAPS I SHOULD CHANGE MY TACTICS--SAVE STATION MIDWAY FOR LATER...
...AND ATTACK THE YORKTOWN NOW INSTEAD!

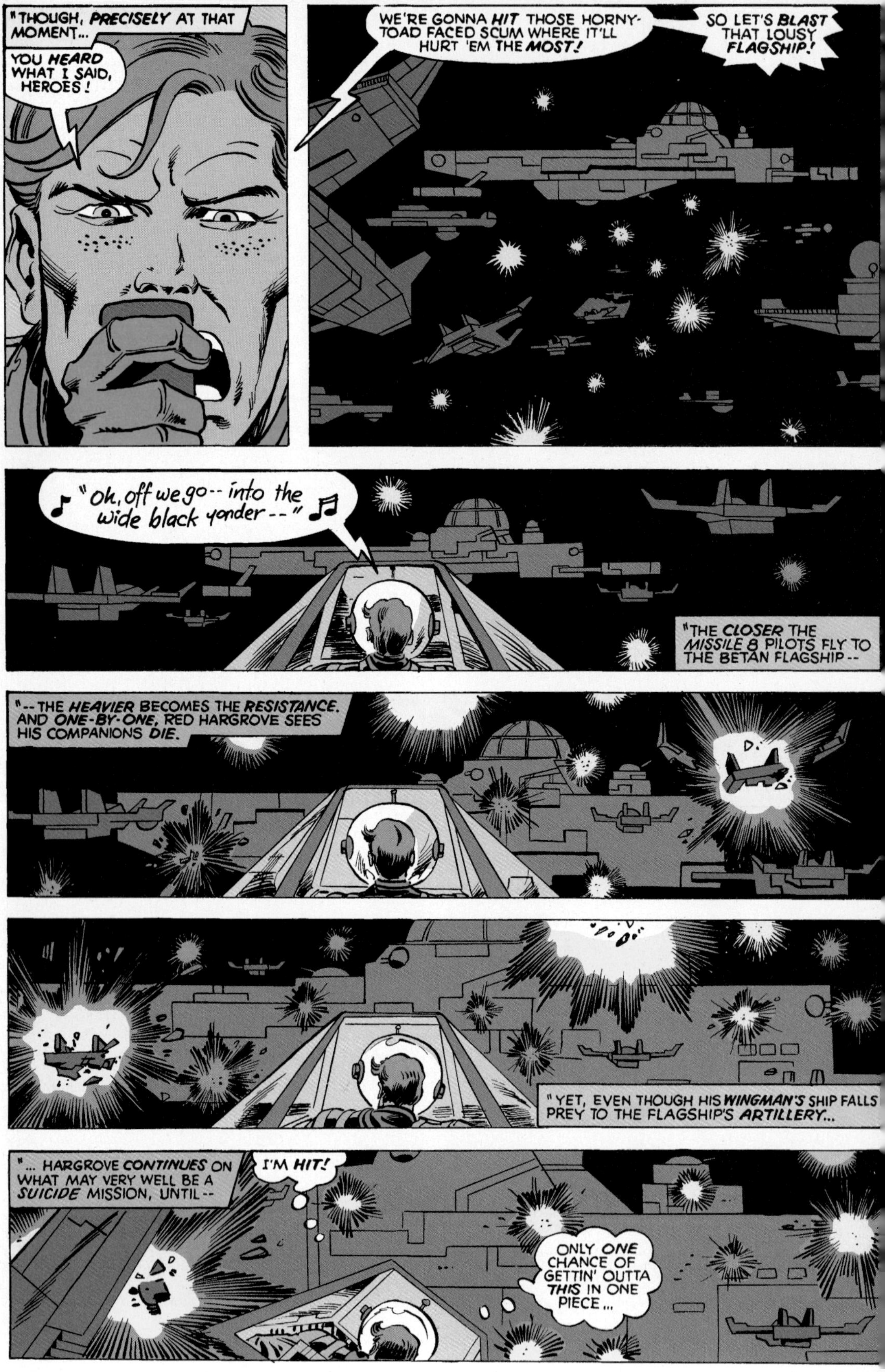
"THOUGH, PRECISELY AT THAT MOMENT...
YOU HEARD WHAT I SAID, HEROES!
WE'RE GONNA HIT THOSE HORNY-TOAD FACED SCUM WHERE IT'LL HURT 'EM THE MOST!
SO LET'S BLAST THAT LOUSY FLAGSHIP!
"Oh, off we go-- into the wide black yonder--"
"THE CLOSER THE MISSILE 8 PILOTS FLY TO THE BETAN FLAGSHIP--
"--THE HEAVIER BECOMES THE RESISTANCE. AND ONE-BY-ONE, RED HARGROVE SEES HIS COMPANIONS DIE.
"YET, EVEN THOUGH HIS WINGMAN'S SHIP FALLS PREY TO THE FLAGSHIP'S ARTILLERY...
"... HARGROVE CONTINUES ON WHAT MAY VERY WELL BE A SUICIDE MISSION, UNTIL--
I'M HIT!
ONLY ONE CHANCE OF GETTIN' OUTTA THIS IN ONE PIECE...

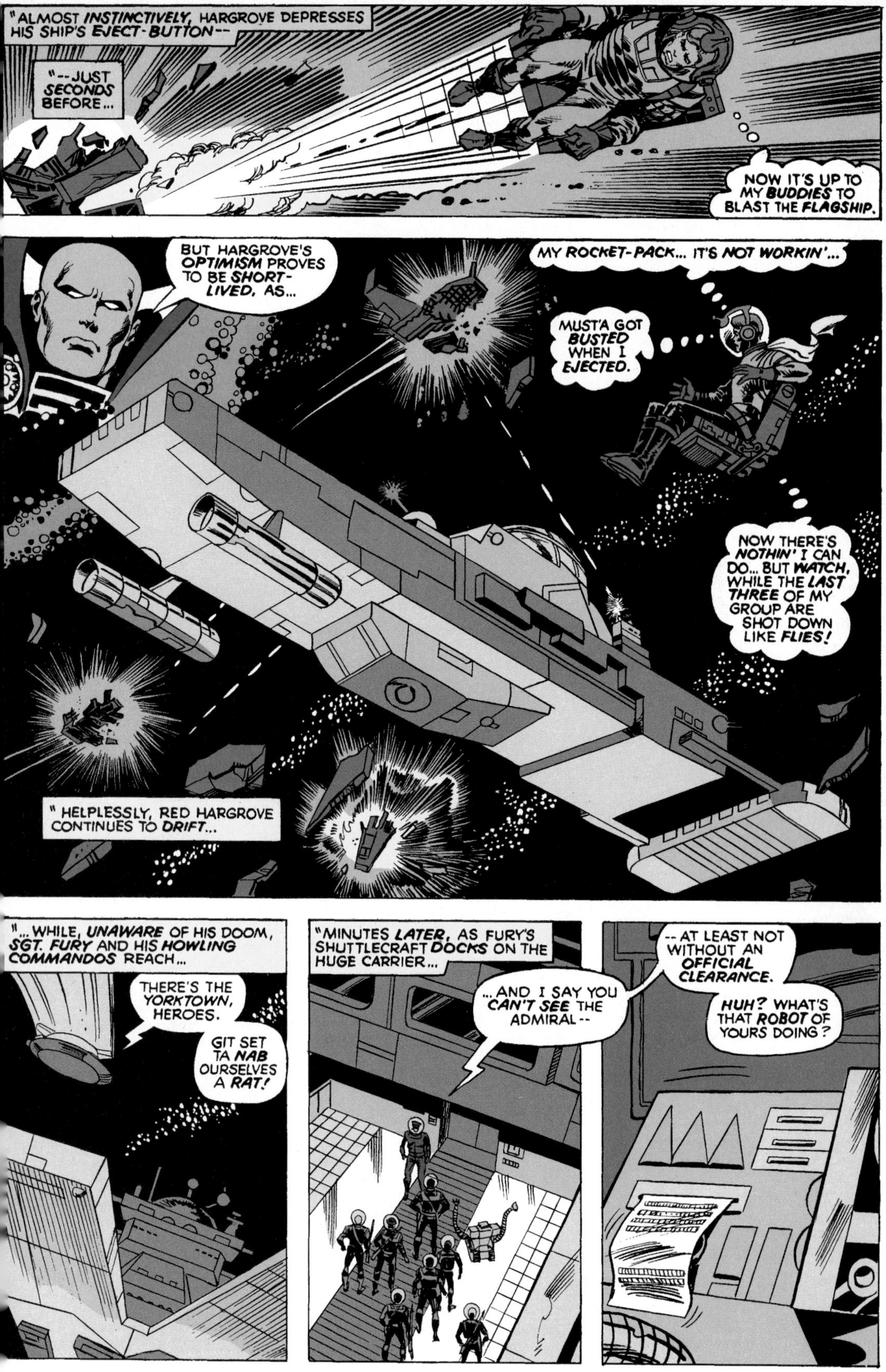
"ALMOST INSTINCTIVELY, HARGROVE DEPRESSES HIS SHIP'S EJECT-BUTTON--
"--JUST SECONDS BEFORE...
NOW IT'S UP TO MY BUDDIES TO BLAST THE FLAGSHIP.
BUT HARGROVE'S OPTIMISM PROVES TO BE SHORT-LIVED, AS...
MY ROCKET-PACK... IT'S NOT WORKIN'...
MUST'A GOT BUSTED WHEN I EJECTED.
NOW THERE'S NOTHIN' I CAN DO... BUT WATCH, WHILE THE LAST THREE OF MY GROUP ARE SHOT DOWN LIKE FLIES!
" HELPLESSLY, RED HARGROVE CONTINUES TO DRIFT...
"...WHILE, UNAWARE OF HIS DOOM, SGT. FURY AND HIS HOWLING COMMANDOS REACH...
THERE'S THE YORKTOWN, HEROES.
GIT SET TA NAB OURSELVES A RAT!
"MINUTES LATER, AS FURY'S SHUTTLECRAFT DOCKS ON THE HUGE CARRIER...
...AND I SAY YOU CAN'T SEE THE ADMIRAL --
-- AT LEAST NOT WITHOUT AN OFFICIAL CLEARANCE.
HUH? WHAT'S THAT ROBOT OF YOURS DOING?

JUST PRINTIN' UP A LITTLE *LOVE-NOTE* ON THAT BUILT-IN *TYPEWRITER* HE'S GOT INSIDE.

WELL, OFFICER? OFFICIAL *ENUFF*?

IT'S FROM A *COMMAND COMPUTER.* ALL RIGHT, SERGEANT...

...FOLLOW *ME.*

" ANXIOUSLY, FURY AND HIS COMMANDOS FOLLOW THE OFFICER *INSIDE* THE *YORKTOWN,* AND...

Y'KNOW SOMETHIN'-- MAYBE THIS ROBOT AIN'T SUCH A *BAD* JOE *AFTERALL* ...

...'SPECIALLY WHEN THEY *BUILD* THESE DOOHICKIES SO'S THEY *CAN'T LIE.*

MIND *TELLING* ME, SERGEANT--

--WHY YOU'RE IN SUCH A *HURRY* TO SEE THE *ADMIRAL?*

" INSTANTANEOUSLY, THE ROBOT *RESPONDS* TO THE OFFICER'S QUESTION.

GOOD LORD! THEN--THERE'S NO TIME TO *WASTE!*

ADMIRAL IS TRAITOR

THE ADMIRAL'S *QUARTERS* ARE JUST DOWN THIS *CORRIDOR.*

THERE HE *IS,* SERGEANT-- OUR *"TRUSTED"* ADMIRAL.

YEAH, *THANKS,* MISTER.

GREETINGS, SERGEANT FURY. AND FROM NOW ON YOU MAY ADDRESS ME BY MY *REAL* NAME...

...*BARON STRUCKER!*

IF YOU HAVE COME TO *PROTECT* ME FROM THE *BETAN* ATTACK--

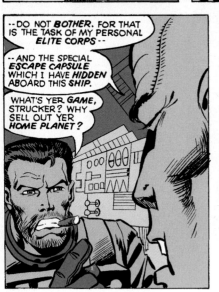

--DO NOT *BOTHER.* FOR THAT IS THE TASK OF MY PERSONAL *ELITE CORPS*--

--AND THE SPECIAL *ESCAPE CAPSULE* WHICH I HAVE *HIDDEN* ABOARD THIS *SHIP.*

WHAT'S YER *GAME,* STRUCKER? WHY SELL OUT YER *HOME PLANET?*

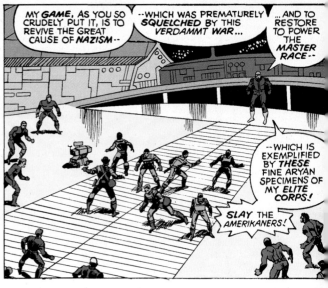

MY *GAME,* AS YOU SO CRUDELY PUT IT, IS TO REVIVE THE GREAT CAUSE OF *NAZISM*--

--WHICH WAS PREMATURELY *SQUELCHED* BY THIS *VERDAMMT* WAR...

...AND TO *RESTORE* TO *POWER* THE *MASTER RACE*--

--WHICH IS EXEMPLIFIED BY *THESE* FINE ARYAN SPECIMENS OF MY *ELITE CORPS!*

SLAY THE *AMERIKANERS!*

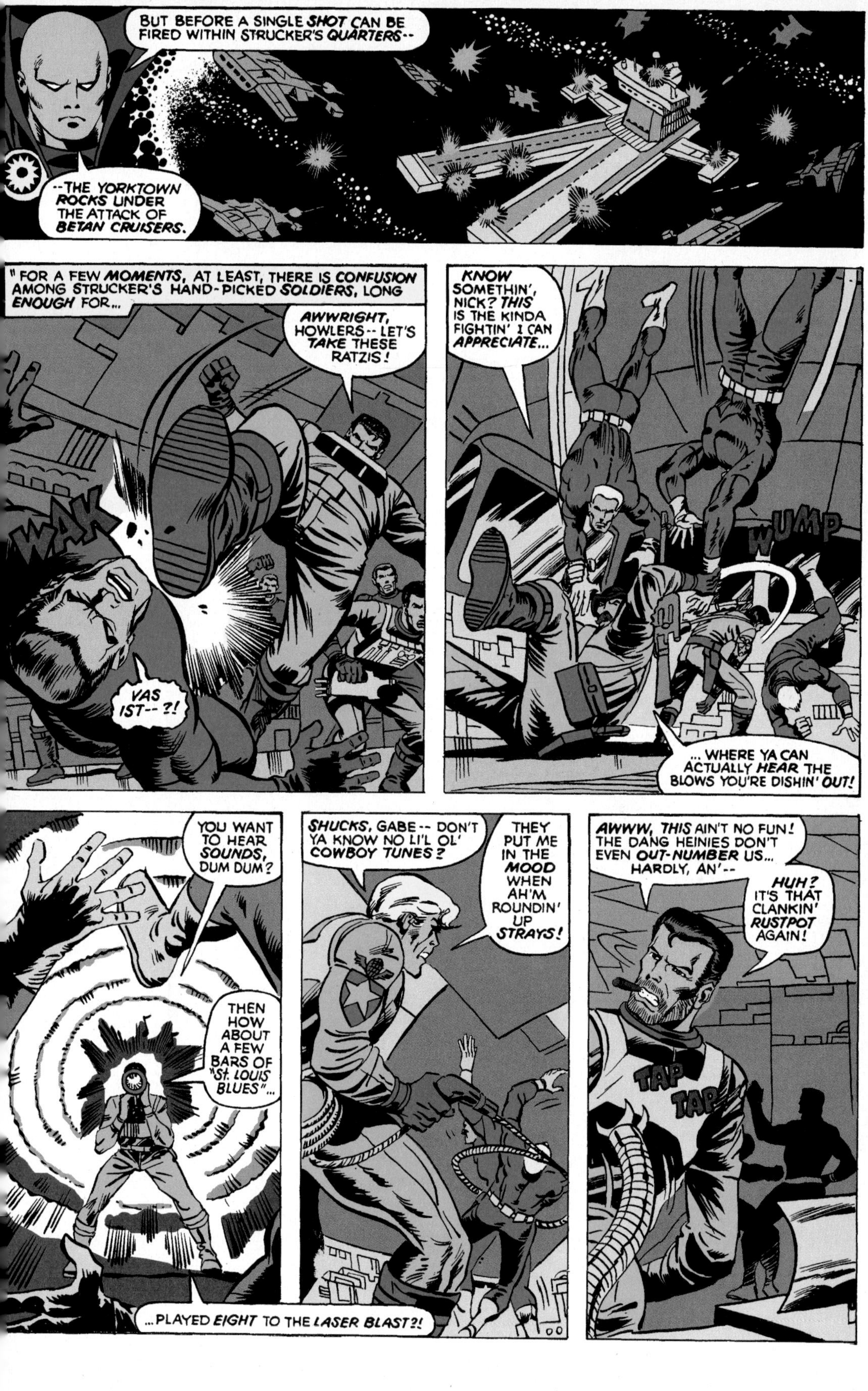

BUT BEFORE A SINGLE SHOT CAN BE FIRED WITHIN STRUCKER'S QUARTERS--
--THE YORKTOWN ROCKS UNDER THE ATTACK OF BETAN CRUISERS.
"FOR A FEW MOMENTS, AT LEAST, THERE IS CONFUSION AMONG STRUCKER'S HAND-PICKED SOLDIERS, LONG ENOUGH FOR...
AWWRIGHT, HOWLERS-- LET'S TAKE THESE RATZIS!
WAK
VAS IST-- ?!
KNOW SOMETHIN', NICK? THIS IS THE KINDA FIGHTIN' I CAN APPRECIATE...
WUMP
... WHERE YA CAN ACTUALLY HEAR THE BLOWS YOU'RE DISHIN' OUT!
YOU WANT TO HEAR SOUNDS, DUM DUM?
THEN HOW ABOUT A FEW BARS OF "St. LOUIS BLUES"...
...PLAYED EIGHT TO THE LASER BLAST?!
SHUCKS, GABE -- DON'T YA KNOW NO LI'L OL' COWBOY TUNES?
THEY PUT ME IN THE MOOD WHEN AH'M ROUNDIN' UP STRAYS!
AWWW, THIS AIN'T NO FUN! THE DANG HEINIES DON'T EVEN OUT-NUMBER US... HARDLY, AN'--
HUH? IT'S THAT CLANKIN' RUSTPOT AGAIN!
TAP
TAP

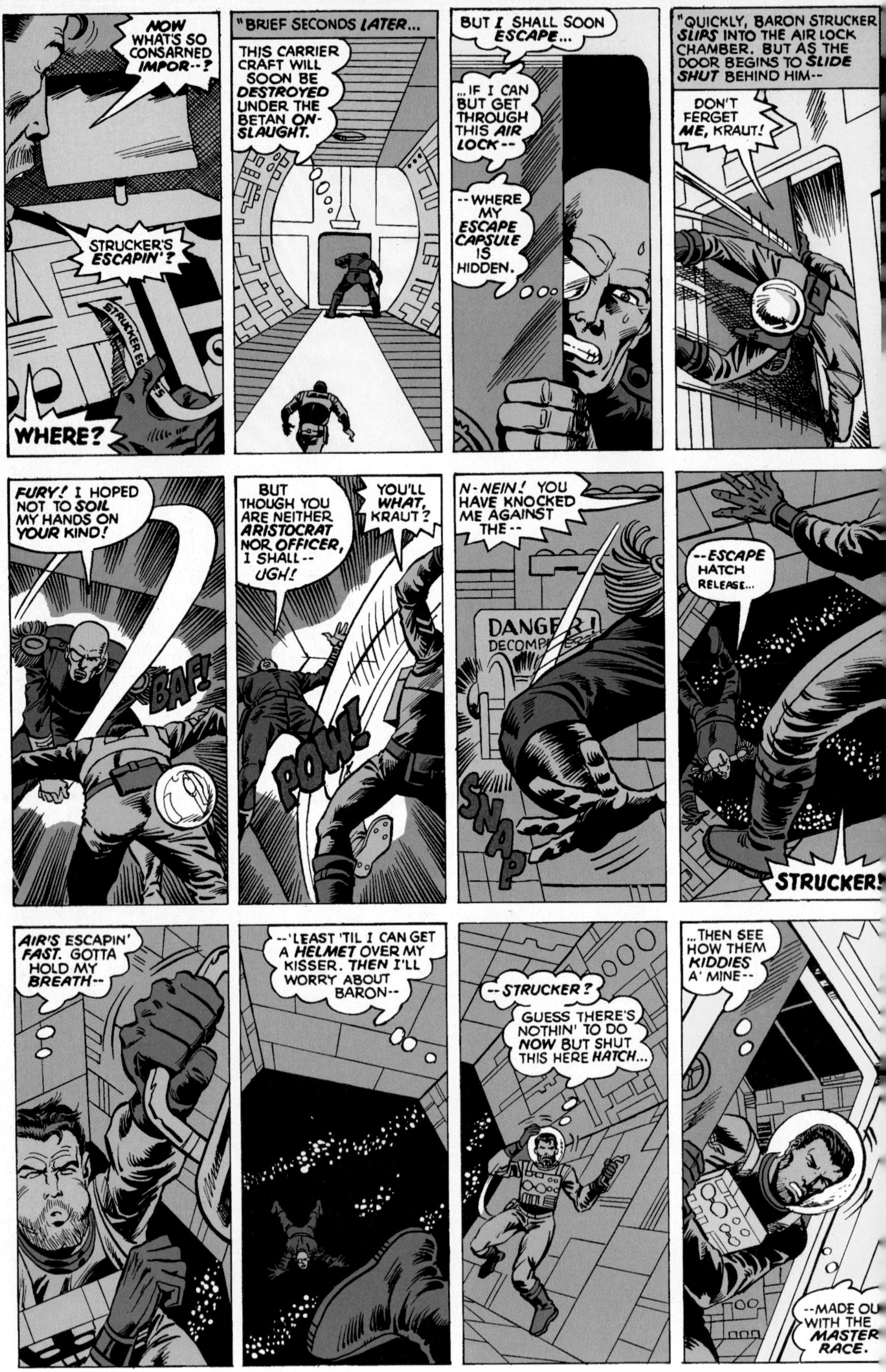
NOW WHAT'S SO CONSARNED IMPOR--?
STRUCKER'S ESCAPIN'?
WHERE?
"BRIEF SECONDS LATER...
THIS CARRIER CRAFT WILL SOON BE DESTROYED UNDER THE BETAN ON-SLAUGHT.
BUT I SHALL SOON ESCAPE...
...IF I CAN BUT GET THROUGH THIS AIR LOCK--
--WHERE MY ESCAPE CAPSULE IS HIDDEN.
"QUICKLY, BARON STRUCKER SLIPS INTO THE AIR LOCK CHAMBER. BUT AS THE DOOR BEGINS TO SLIDE SHUT BEHIND HIM--
DON'T FERGET ME, KRAUT!
FURY! I HOPED NOT TO SOIL MY HANDS ON YOUR KIND!
BAF!
BUT THOUGH YOU ARE NEITHER ARISTOCRAT NOR OFFICER, I SHALL-- UGH!
YOU'LL WHAT, KRAUT?
POW!
N-NEIN! YOU HAVE KNOCKED ME AGAINST THE--
SNAP
--ESCAPE HATCH RELEASE...
STRUCKER!
AIR'S ESCAPIN' FAST. GOTTA HOLD MY BREATH--
--'LEAST 'TIL I CAN GET A HELMET OVER MY KISSER. THEN I'LL WORRY ABOUT BARON--
--STRUCKER?
GUESS THERE'S NOTHIN' TO DO NOW BUT SHUT THIS HERE HATCH...
...THEN SEE HOW THEM KIDDIES A' MINE--
--MADE OU
WITH THE MASTER RACE.

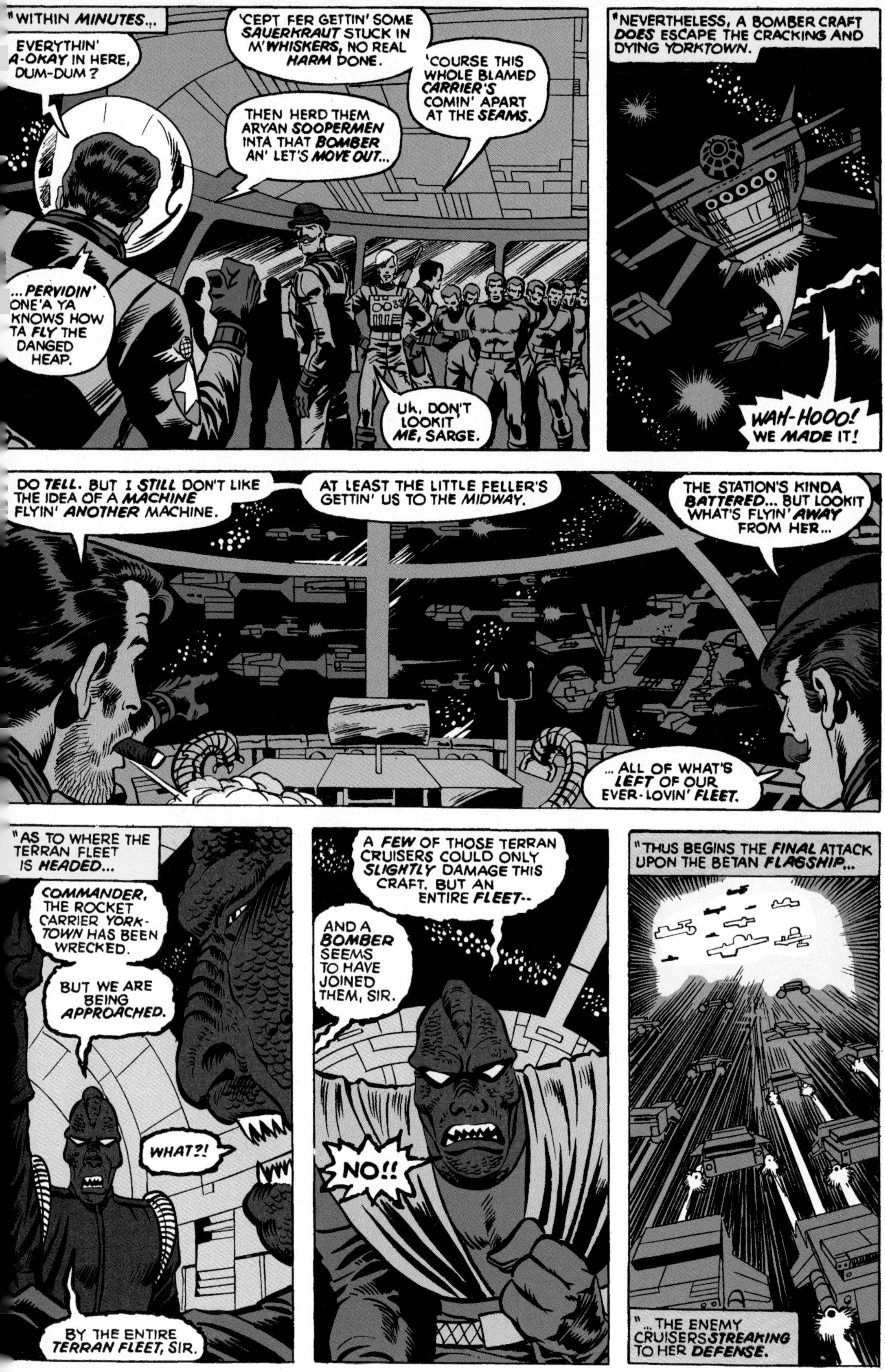
"WITHIN MINUTES...
EVERYTHIN' A-OKAY IN HERE, DUM-DUM?
'CEPT FER GETTIN' SOME SAUERKRAUT STUCK IN M'WHISKERS, NO REAL HARM DONE.
'COURSE THIS WHOLE BLAMED CARRIER'S COMIN' APART AT THE SEAMS.
THEN HERD THEM ARYAN SOOPERMEN INTA THAT BOMBER AN' LET'S MOVE OUT...
...PERVIDIN' ONE'A YA KNOWS HOW TA FLY THE DANGED HEAP.
Uh, DON'T LOOKIT ME, SARGE.
"NEVERTHELESS, A BOMBER CRAFT DOES ESCAPE THE CRACKING AND DYING YORKTOWN.
WAH-HOOO! WE MADE IT!
DO TELL. BUT I STILL DON'T LIKE THE IDEA OF A MACHINE FLYIN' ANOTHER MACHINE.
AT LEAST THE LITTLE FELLER'S GETTIN' US TO THE MIDWAY.
THE STATION'S KINDA BATTERED... BUT LOOKIT WHAT'S FLYIN' AWAY FROM HER...
...ALL OF WHAT'S LEFT OF OUR EVER-LOVIN' FLEET.
"AS TO WHERE THE TERRAN FLEET IS HEADED...
COMMANDER, THE ROCKET CARRIER YORK-TOWN HAS BEEN WRECKED.
BUT WE ARE BEING APPROACHED.
WHAT?!
BY THE ENTIRE TERRAN FLEET, SIR.
A FEW OF THOSE TERRAN CRUISERS COULD ONLY SLIGHTLY DAMAGE THIS CRAFT. BUT AN ENTIRE FLEET--
AND A BOMBER SEEMS TO HAVE JOINED THEM, SIR.
NO!!
"THUS BEGINS THE FINAL ATTACK UPON THE BETAN FLAGSHIP...
"...THE ENEMY CRUISERS STREAKING TO HER DEFENSE.

"BUT, THOUGH THE DAMAGE IS SEVERE FOR *BOTH* SIDES, A *BOMBER-CRAFT* SUDDENLY APPEARS IN THE *MIDST* OF THE CONFLICT...

KEEP *MANEUVERING* LIKE THAT, TIN-MAN. YER DOIN' *FINE*...

...WHILE *WE* KEEP BLASTIN' AT THAT LOUSY *FLAGSHIP* WITH EVERY GUN WE *GOT*!

"AT LAST, THE RELENTLESS *BARRAGE* ON THE BETAN FLAGSHIP TAKES ITS *TOLL*...

"...AND A *DYING COMMANDER* COMES TO REALIZE THAT THE BATTLE IS ALREADY *LOST*.

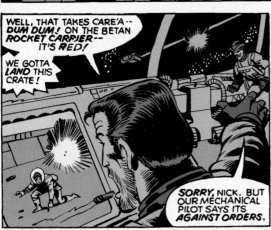

WELL, THAT TAKES CARE'A -- *DUM DUM*! ON THE BETAN ROCKET CARRIER -- IT'S *RED*!

WE GOTTA *LAND* THIS CRATE!

SORRY, NICK. BUT OUR MECHANICAL PILOT SAYS ITS *AGAINST ORDERS*.

NOW AIN'T THAT *TOO BAD*!

NOW *LISSEN*, ROBOT! EITHER YA PICK UP MY *BUDDY* DOWN THERE --

-- OR I *OPEN YA UP* LIKE A BLASTED CAN'A *RHUBARB*!

"AND... LOOKS LIKE HE HURT HIS *LEG*. SWING 'ER ON *DOWN*, ROBOT.

THE RATS ARE GONNA *STRAFE* ME!

NO! THAT'S ONE'A *OUR* BABIES!

NICK: I GUESS I SPRAINED MY *ANKLE* WHEN I BANGED AGAINST THE *CARRIER*.

SO TELL ME ABOUT IT *LATER*, OKAY? WE GOTTA HUSTLE OUR BUSTLES ABOARD THAT *BOMBER*!

SEE WHAT YA *MEAN*, FURY. LOOKS LIKE THE BATTLE AIN'T OVER YET!

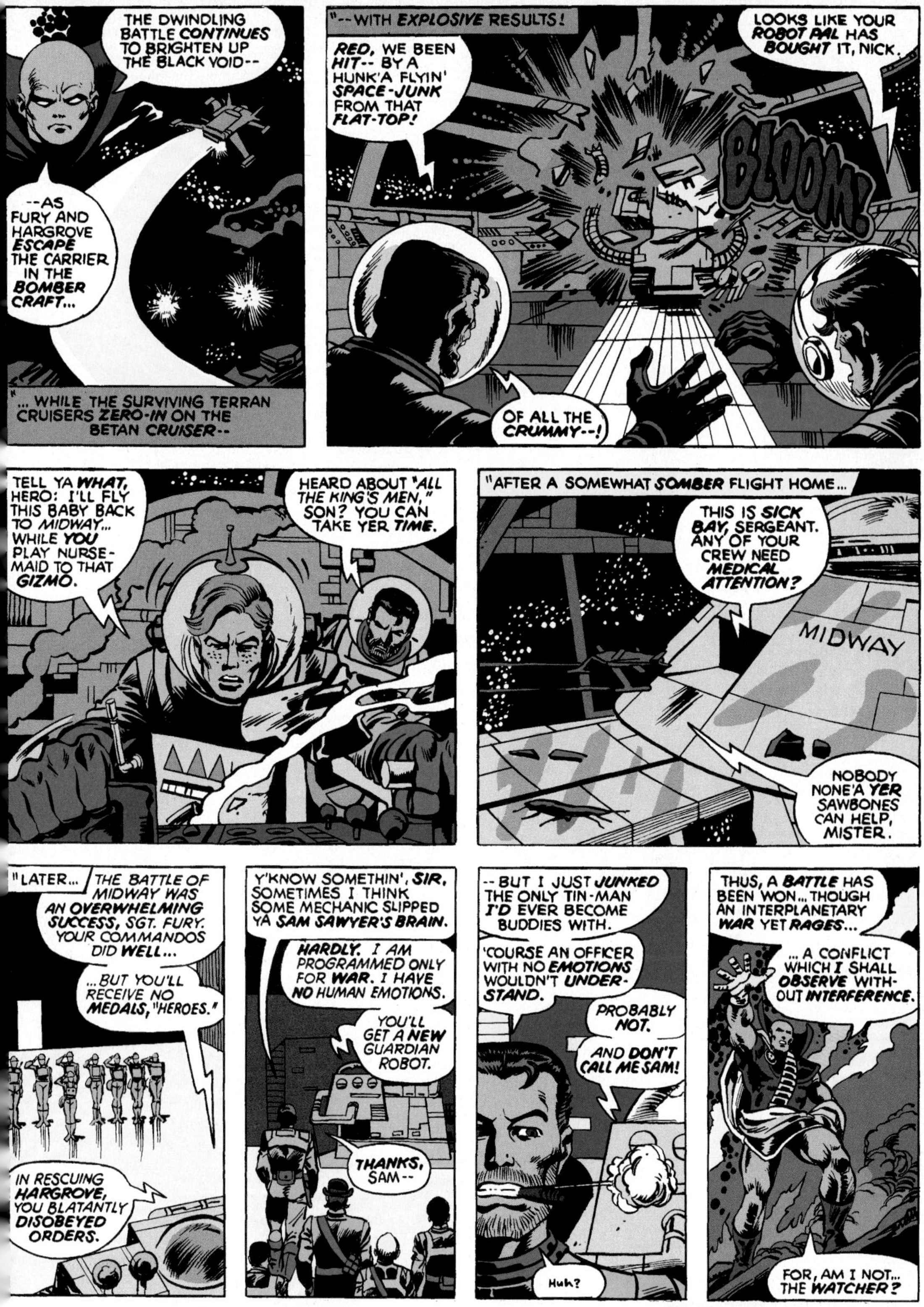
THE DWINDLING BATTLE CONTINUES TO BRIGHTEN UP THE BLACK VOID--
--AS FURY AND HARGROVE ESCAPE THE CARRIER IN THE BOMBER CRAFT...
... WHILE THE SURVIVING TERRAN CRUISERS ZERO-IN ON THE BETAN CRUISER--
"--WITH EXPLOSIVE RESULTS!
RED, WE BEEN HIT-- BY A HUNK'A FLYIN' SPACE-JUNK FROM THAT FLAT-TOP!
LOOKS LIKE YOUR ROBOT PAL HAS BOUGHT IT, NICK.
BLOOM!
OF ALL THE CRUMMY--!
TELL YA WHAT, HERO: I'LL FLY THIS BABY BACK TO MIDWAY... WHILE YOU PLAY NURSE-MAID TO THAT GIZMO.
HEARD ABOUT "ALL THE KING'S MEN," SON? YOU CAN TAKE YER TIME.
"AFTER A SOMEWHAT SOMBER FLIGHT HOME...
THIS IS SICK BAY, SERGEANT. ANY OF YOUR CREW NEED MEDICAL ATTENTION?
MIDWAY
NOBODY NONE'A YER SAWBONES CAN HELP, MISTER.
"LATER...
THE BATTLE OF MIDWAY WAS AN OVERWHELMING SUCCESS, SGT. FURY. YOUR COMMANDOS DID WELL...
...BUT YOU'LL RECEIVE NO MEDALS, "HEROES."
IN RESCUING HARGROVE, YOU BLATANTLY DISOBEYED ORDERS.
Y'KNOW SOMETHIN', SIR, SOMETIMES I THINK SOME MECHANIC SLIPPED YA SAM SAWYER'S BRAIN.
HARDLY. I AM PROGRAMMED ONLY FOR WAR. I HAVE NO HUMAN EMOTIONS.
YOU'LL GET A NEW GUARDIAN ROBOT.
THANKS, SAM--
-- BUT I JUST JUNKED THE ONLY TIN-MAN I'D EVER BECOME BUDDIES WITH.
'COURSE AN OFFICER WITH NO EMOTIONS WOULDN'T UNDER-STAND.
PROBABLY NOT.
AND DON'T CALL ME SAM!
Huh?
THUS, A BATTLE HAS BEEN WON... THOUGH AN INTERPLANETARY WAR YET RAGES...
... A CONFLICT WHICH I SHALL OBSERVE WITH-OUT INTERFERENCE.
FOR, AM I NOT... THE WATCHER?

NEXT: WHAT IF FOUR DIFFERENT PEOPLE BECAME NOVA?

WHY NOT?

c/o MARVEL COMICS GROUP
575 Madison Avenue
New York, New York 10022

ROY THOMAS
EDITOR
MARK GRUENWALD
ASSISTANT EDITOR

BETTER LATE THAN EVER Dept.: Many moons ago, we asked you rhapsodic readers to send in explanations as to how, 'way back in WHAT IF #5, Captain America and Bucky's surviving World War Two could have led to the death of Nick Fury— an event for which no adequate explanation was given in that issue itself.

Actually, the explanation we choose to believe is that submitted by Dinosaur Don Glut himself— the writer of that particular tale. He says:"Apparently I assumed that most readers would have been familiar enough with time-paradox stories so that an explanation wouldn't be required. But subtleties do not, alas, always work in comics. Simply put: In 'our' existence, Nick and his Howlers fought through the final days of the war *without* the help of Cap and Bucky— intimating that, in that parallel world, Nick's teaming up with our two heroes threw the succeeding events of his life 'off schedule,' either slightly or drastically. Some of the off-schedule events would have to have occurred during the Korean conflict. Fury would *not* have been in the exact same locations at the exact same moment during this war on *both* earths. In the parallel world, his schedule had been altered just enough so that he happened to be near that grenade, when it exploded. Thankfully, in *our* reality, Nick happened to be somewhere else."

Which, now that we think of it, is *still* pretty vague.

Several other readers sent much more *exact* explanations, which we wish we had room to print. It'll have to suffice to say that these were the best of those received: Phil Jones of Sewanee, Tennessee; Andy Kocher of Bath, Ohio; Anil Pisharoty of Passaic, N.J.; and someone who signed himself "The Red Skull." Hmmm. . . Well, anyway, it seemed to us we ought to print *something* by the time Nick and the Howlers fought a WHAT IF war in outer space, just to show we're not as forgetful as folks say we are. Which folks? Uh. . . we forget!

NOT MUCH BETTER THAN THE LAST ANSWER Dept.: We also presented a sort of "Hitler paradox" back in WHAT IF #6, in answer to events detailed in issue #4, which featured Uncle Adolf's death at the hands of the original Human Torch (retold from an early-1950's comicbook). The best response by far we had to *that* paradox, asking whether the Hitler who died in YOUNG MEN #24 and WHAT IF #4 was the real one, or whether the true Fuhrer was the character reincarnated in a CAPTAIN AMERICA issue by Jack Kirby, was the following:

Roy:

Re: Your Hitler problem presented in WHAT IF #6.

(1) There is an already expressed concept that Adolf Hitler had several doubles who could, if the Third Reich fell, be killed and presented as the dead body of the deranged paperhanger. This concept seems to be popular at Marvel, since 'way back in FANTASTIC FOUR #21 the Hatemonger was unmasked to reveal the face of Hitler, and Reed made a speech expressing the "double" concept.

(2) In the very recent past, Jack Kirby has shown absolutely no consideration for any Marvel writer or artist concerning the Marvel Universe, making large mistakes with well-established characters aimlessly. Of the two "truths," Jack's is the easiest to ignore, since Arnim Zola's master plan was just so plain silly.

So the logical consideration would be that Arnim found himself a double. Consider the source.

(3) Kurt Vonnegut Jr. has expressed the idea that Adolf Hitler is more a concept of pure evil and hatred than a human being. And almost every writer, graphic-story or otherwise, who has dealt with or on this person treats him as a mad god of evil, instead of a deranged paper-hanger. He is thus a concept as much as your Captain America, and thus can never die.

My choice is #3, since Adolf Hitler has been as much an object of perverse fascination as Jack the Ripper. The death of the *man* Adolf Hitler has been a subject of mystery at least as long, and with your own mythical creations you have given us answers. In that case, I choose, of course, #1.

I hope this settles the matter, and I hope *you* are more careful next time when you link your "present" stories with your "past." I won't bring up the point that at the climax of the Kree/Skrull War, when Rick Jones recreated images from old comics, you positively stated that such noteables as the Fin and the Blazing Skull were not real, when later stories and letters page commentary "proved" they really did exist.

My WHAT IF story idea (since most of your letter-writers throw one in): How about explaining that story in CAPTAIN AMERICA'S WEIRD TALES which appeared in 1949, in which Cap went to hell to fight the Red Skull, by having Mephisto pull both characters' souls from their sleeping bodies to continue their eternal battle? This was one concept Jack Kirby had which was really fascinating— that Cap and the Red Skull were joined in time, which is why neither can defeat the other. Anyways, thanks for some most interesting reading!

Steven Alan Bennett
842 Hunt St.
Akron, OH 44306

And your *letter* was just as intriguing to *us*, Steve. Our thanks for summing up the pros and cons of the Great Hitler Debate— and we think we will indeed consider the Hitler in CAPTAIN AMERICA a couple of years back to have been a double. But as to whether the original Torch really killed the true Hitler, or only thought he did, we'll have to leave to the future to decide. Roy knows he'd opt for the former, but the final decision rests in other hands than his.

Much as we appreciate your suggestion of a new Captain America tale in WHAT IF continuing that strange "final" battle between Cap and the Skull, though, we think we'll just let it stand as a 1949 curiosity— though we concur fully in believing that Jack Kirby's idea of Cap and the Skull being "joined in time" is a fabulous concept.

One final note, from Roy, as the author of the much-remembered Kree/Skrull War (or was it Skrull/Kree War— we guess it depends on which side you were on):

"Steve's definitely correct in pointing out that we erred when we referred to the Fin, Blazing Skull, etc., as being fictitious characters back in that climactic story. However, remember— it was *Rick Jones* talking, as a youngster who truly *believed* the characters to be fictitious— mainly because he hadn't delved more carefully into the matter. Some old comics heroes were doubtless fictitious, pure and simple; others, as I've explained in the pages of THE INVADERS from time to time, existed more or less (emphasis often on "less") as seen in the old Timely Comics, at least— I can't speak for the various competitors' mags of the day. Rick, when he conjured up the Torch, Namor, Fin, Skull, etc., was conjuring up the *comicbook images* he recalled from finding stacks of old magazines, so it makes little difference whether the characters were real or *not*. The ones *he* remembered, and thus brought to life, were the fictional comicbook heroes, as they appeared in the 40's! Clear enough, I hope so— 'cause I haven't got energy enough to go thru it again! The defense rests— passes out, in fact."

And so, truth to tell, does this letters page.

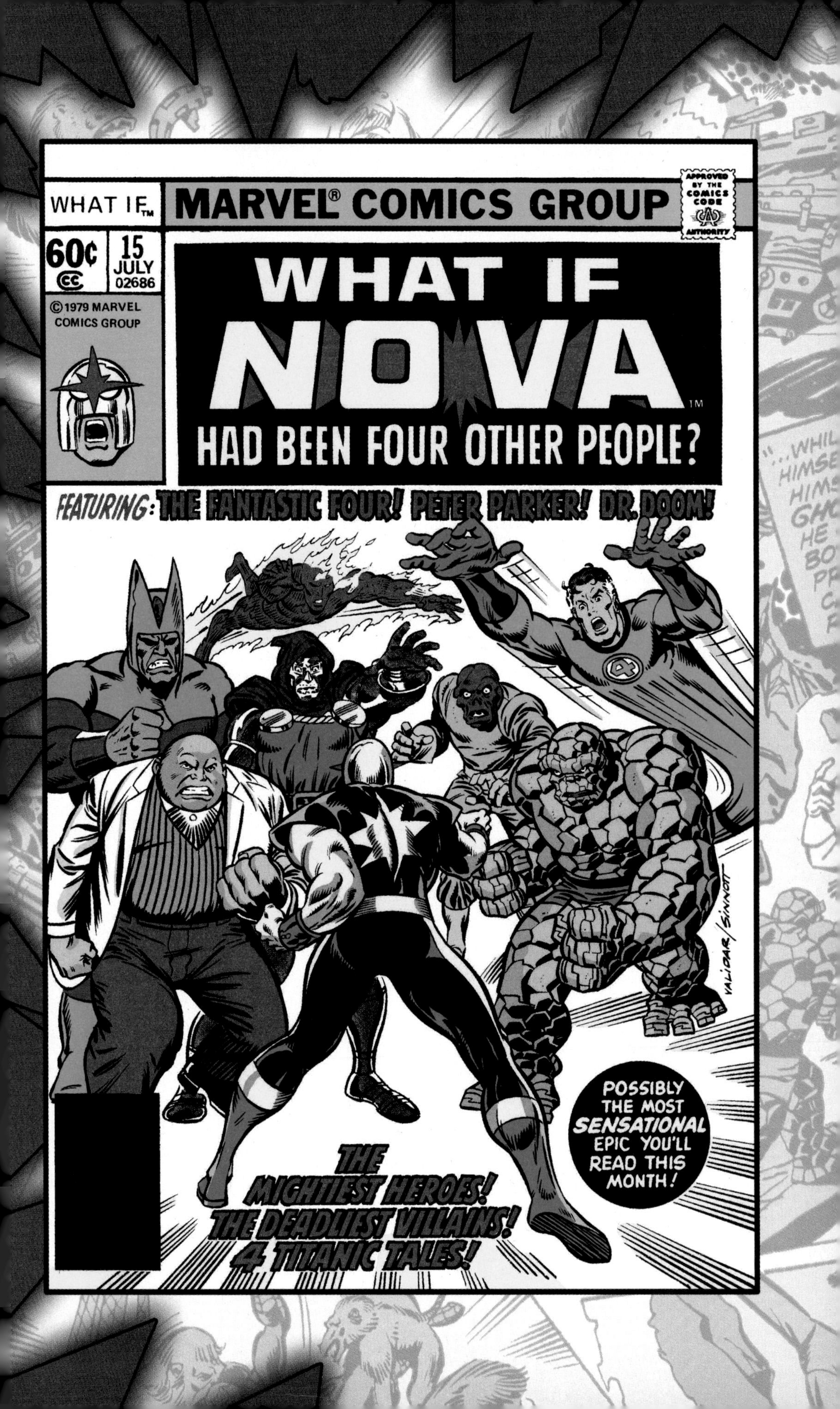
WHAT IF™
MARVEL® COMICS GROUP
APPROVED BY THE COMICS CODE AUTHORITY
60¢
CC
15
JULY
02686
© 1979 MARVEL COMICS GROUP
WHAT IF
NOVA™
HAD BEEN FOUR OTHER PEOPLE?
FEATURING: THE FANTASTIC FOUR! PETER PARKER! DR. DOOM!
VALIDAR/SINNOTT
POSSIBLY THE MOST SENSATIONAL EPIC YOU'LL READ THIS MONTH!
THE MIGHTIEST HEROES! THE DEADLIEST VILLAINS! 4 TITANIC TALES!

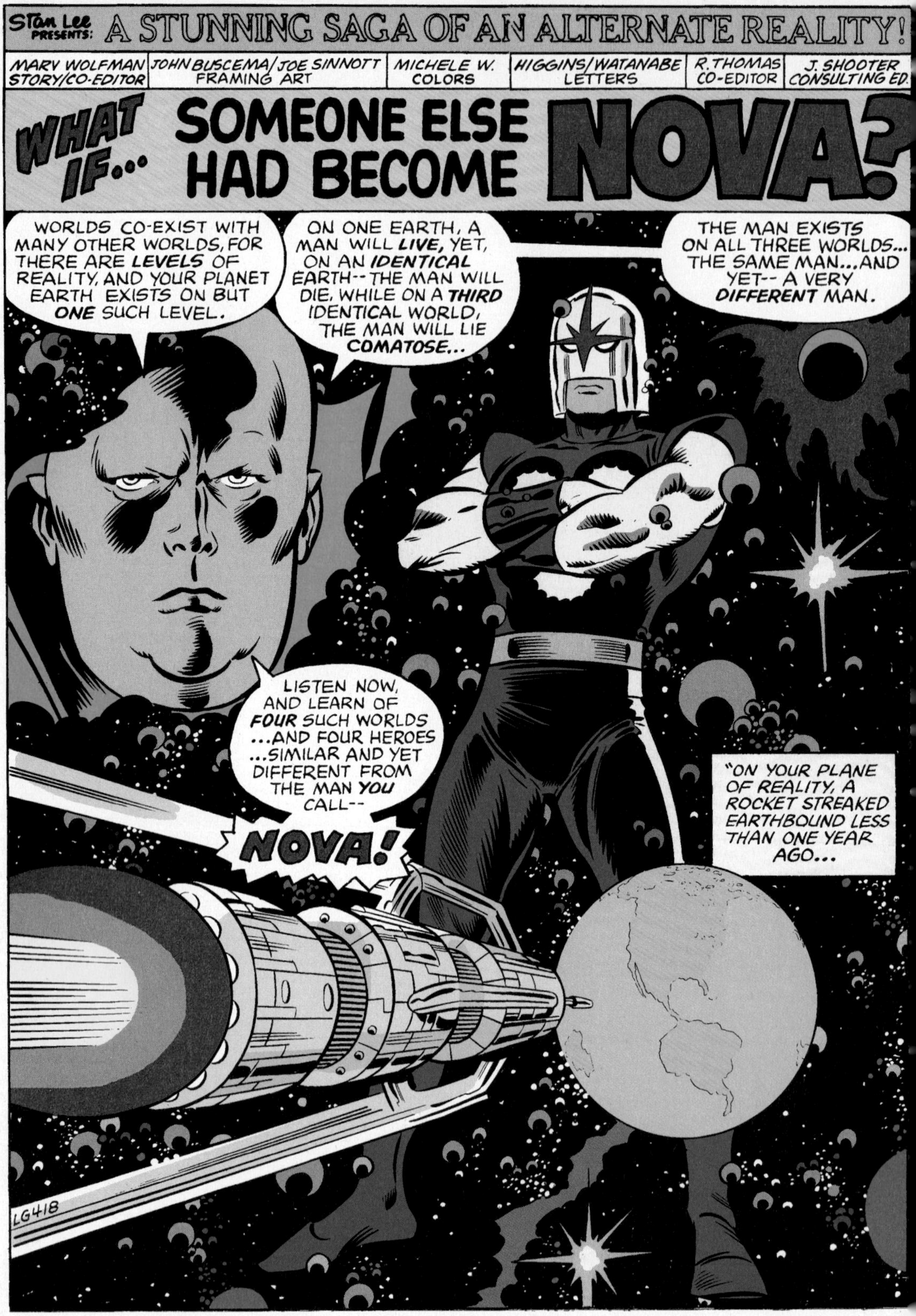
STAN LEE PRESENTS: A STUNNING SAGA OF AN ALTERNATE REALITY!
MARV WOLFMAN STORY/CO-EDITOR
JOHN BUSCEMA/JOE SINNOTT FRAMING ART
MICHELE W. COLORS
HIGGINS/WATANABE LETTERS
R. THOMAS CO-EDITOR
J. SHOOTER CONSULTING ED.
WHAT IF... SOMEONE ELSE HAD BECOME NOVA?
WORLDS CO-EXIST WITH MANY OTHER WORLDS, FOR THERE ARE LEVELS OF REALITY, AND YOUR PLANET EARTH EXISTS ON BUT ONE SUCH LEVEL.
ON ONE EARTH, A MAN WILL LIVE, YET, ON AN IDENTICAL EARTH-- THE MAN WILL DIE, WHILE ON A THIRD IDENTICAL WORLD, THE MAN WILL LIE COMATOSE...
THE MAN EXISTS ON ALL THREE WORLDS... THE SAME MAN...AND YET-- A VERY DIFFERENT MAN.
LISTEN NOW, AND LEARN OF FOUR SUCH WORLDS ...AND FOUR HEROES ...SIMILAR AND YET DIFFERENT FROM THE MAN YOU CALL--
NOVA!
"ON YOUR PLANE OF REALITY, A ROCKET STREAKED EARTHBOUND LESS THAN ONE YEAR AGO...
LG418

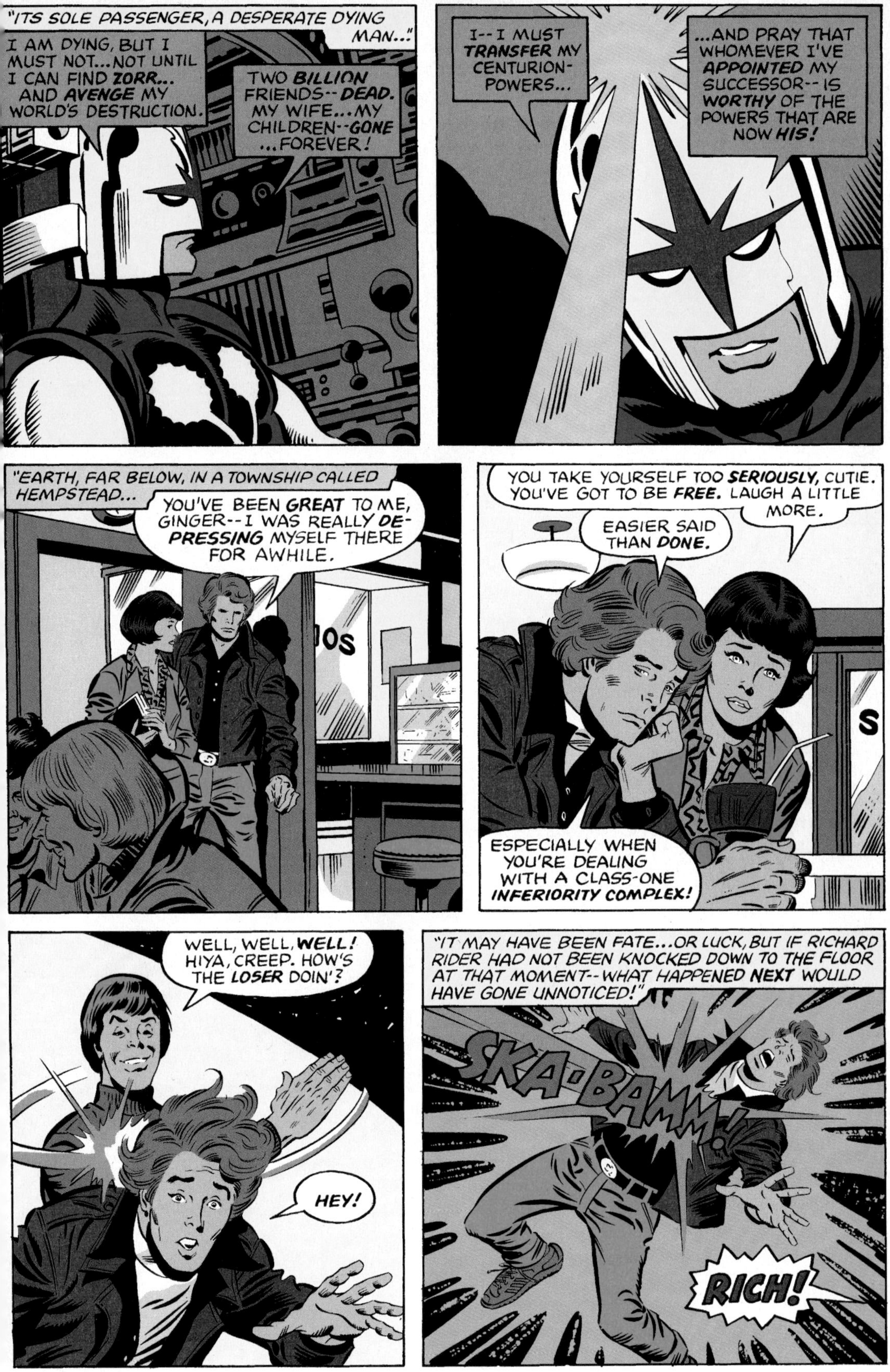
"ITS SOLE PASSENGER, A DESPERATE DYING MAN..."
I AM DYING, BUT I MUST NOT...NOT UNTIL I CAN FIND ZORR... AND AVENGE MY WORLD'S DESTRUCTION.
TWO BILLION FRIENDS--DEAD. MY WIFE...MY CHILDREN--GONE ...FOREVER!
I--I MUST TRANSFER MY CENTURION-POWERS...
...AND PRAY THAT WHOMEVER I'VE APPOINTED MY SUCCESSOR--IS WORTHY OF THE POWERS THAT ARE NOW HIS!
"EARTH, FAR BELOW, IN A TOWNSHIP CALLED HEMPSTEAD...
YOU'VE BEEN GREAT TO ME, GINGER--I WAS REALLY DE-PRESSING MYSELF THERE FOR AWHILE.
YOU TAKE YOURSELF TOO SERIOUSLY, CUTIE. YOU'VE GOT TO BE FREE. LAUGH A LITTLE MORE.
EASIER SAID THAN DONE.
ESPECIALLY WHEN YOU'RE DEALING WITH A CLASS-ONE INFERIORITY COMPLEX!
WELL, WELL, WELL! HIYA, CREEP. HOW'S THE LOSER DOIN'?
HEY!
"IT MAY HAVE BEEN FATE...OR LUCK, BUT IF RICHARD RIDER HAD NOT BEEN KNOCKED DOWN TO THE FLOOR AT THAT MOMENT--WHAT HAPPENED NEXT WOULD HAVE GONE UNNOTICED!"
SKA-BAMM!
RICH!

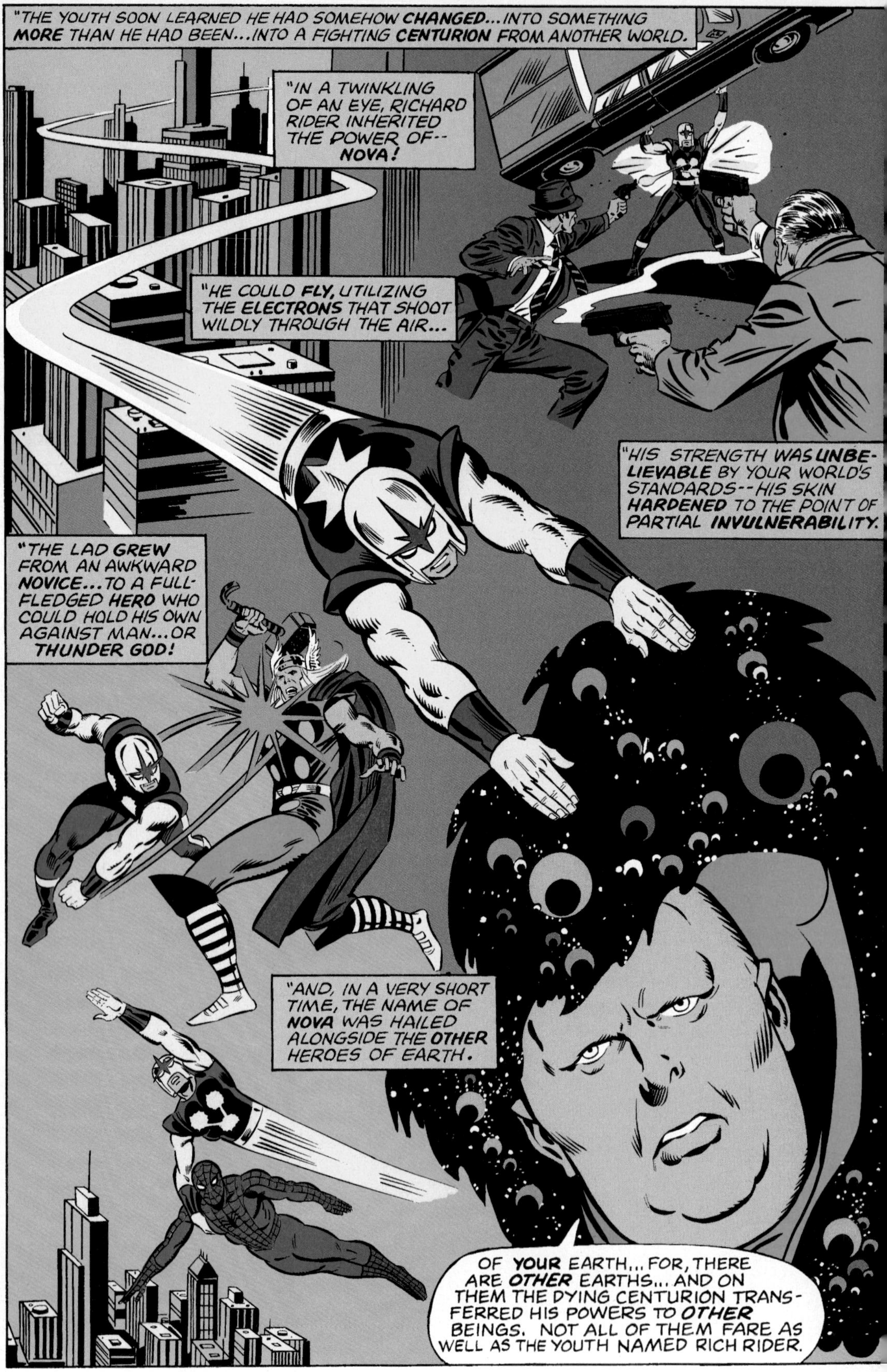
"THE YOUTH SOON LEARNED HE HAD SOMEHOW CHANGED... INTO SOMETHING MORE THAN HE HAD BEEN... INTO A FIGHTING CENTURION FROM ANOTHER WORLD.
"IN A TWINKLING OF AN EYE, RICHARD RIDER INHERITED THE POWER OF-- NOVA!
"HE COULD FLY, UTILIZING THE ELECTRONS THAT SHOOT WILDLY THROUGH THE AIR...
"HIS STRENGTH WAS UNBELIEVABLE BY YOUR WORLD'S STANDARDS--HIS SKIN HARDENED TO THE POINT OF PARTIAL INVULNERABILITY.
"THE LAD GREW FROM AN AWKWARD NOVICE... TO A FULL-FLEDGED HERO WHO COULD HOLD HIS OWN AGAINST MAN... OR THUNDER GOD!
"AND, IN A VERY SHORT TIME, THE NAME OF NOVA WAS HAILED ALONGSIDE THE OTHER HEROES OF EARTH.
OF YOUR EARTH... FOR, THERE ARE OTHER EARTHS... AND ON THEM THE DYING CENTURION TRANSFERRED HIS POWERS TO OTHER BEINGS. NOT ALL OF THEM FARE AS WELL AS THE YOUTH NAMED RICH RIDER.

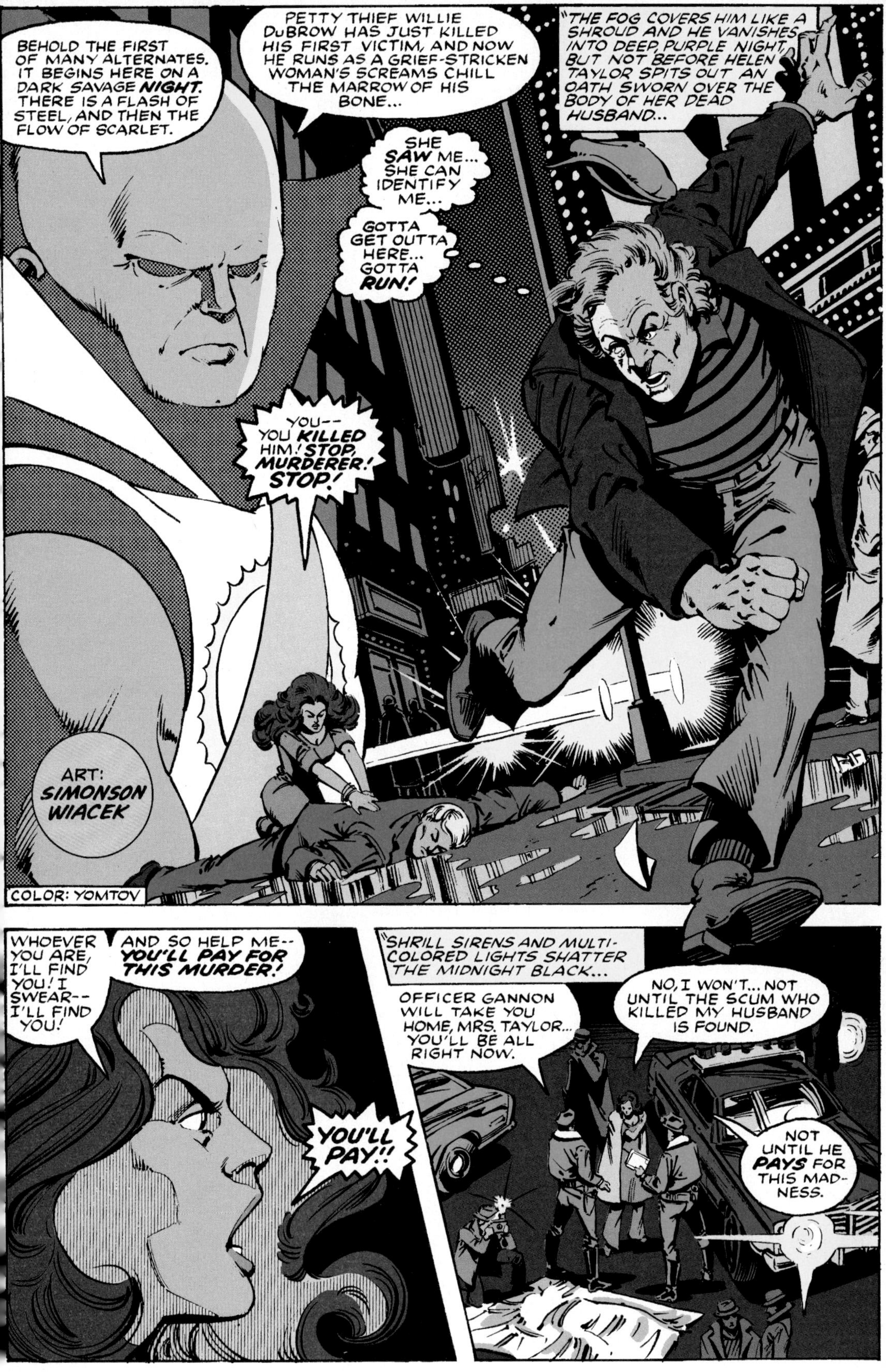
BEHOLD THE FIRST OF MANY ALTERNATES. IT BEGINS HERE ON A DARK SAVAGE NIGHT. THERE IS A FLASH OF STEEL, AND THEN THE FLOW OF SCARLET.
PETTY THIEF WILLIE DuBROW HAS JUST KILLED HIS FIRST VICTIM, AND NOW HE RUNS AS A GRIEF-STRICKEN WOMAN'S SCREAMS CHILL THE MARROW OF HIS BONE...
"THE FOG COVERS HIM LIKE A SHROUD AND HE VANISHES INTO DEEP, PURPLE NIGHT, BUT NOT BEFORE HELEN TAYLOR SPITS OUT AN OATH SWORN OVER THE BODY OF HER DEAD HUSBAND...
SHE SAW ME... SHE CAN IDENTIFY ME...
GOTTA GET OUTTA HERE... GOTTA RUN!
YOU-- YOU KILLED HIM! STOP, MURDERER! STOP!
ART: SIMONSON WIACEK
COLOR: YOMTOV
WHOEVER YOU ARE, I'LL FIND YOU! I SWEAR-- I'LL FIND YOU!
AND SO HELP ME-- YOU'LL PAY FOR THIS MURDER!
YOU'LL PAY!!
"SHRILL SIRENS AND MULTI-COLORED LIGHTS SHATTER THE MIDNIGHT BLACK...
OFFICER GANNON WILL TAKE YOU HOME, MRS. TAYLOR... YOU'LL BE ALL RIGHT NOW.
NO, I WON'T... NOT UNTIL THE SCUM WHO KILLED MY HUSBAND IS FOUND.
NOT UNTIL HE PAYS FOR THIS MADNESS.

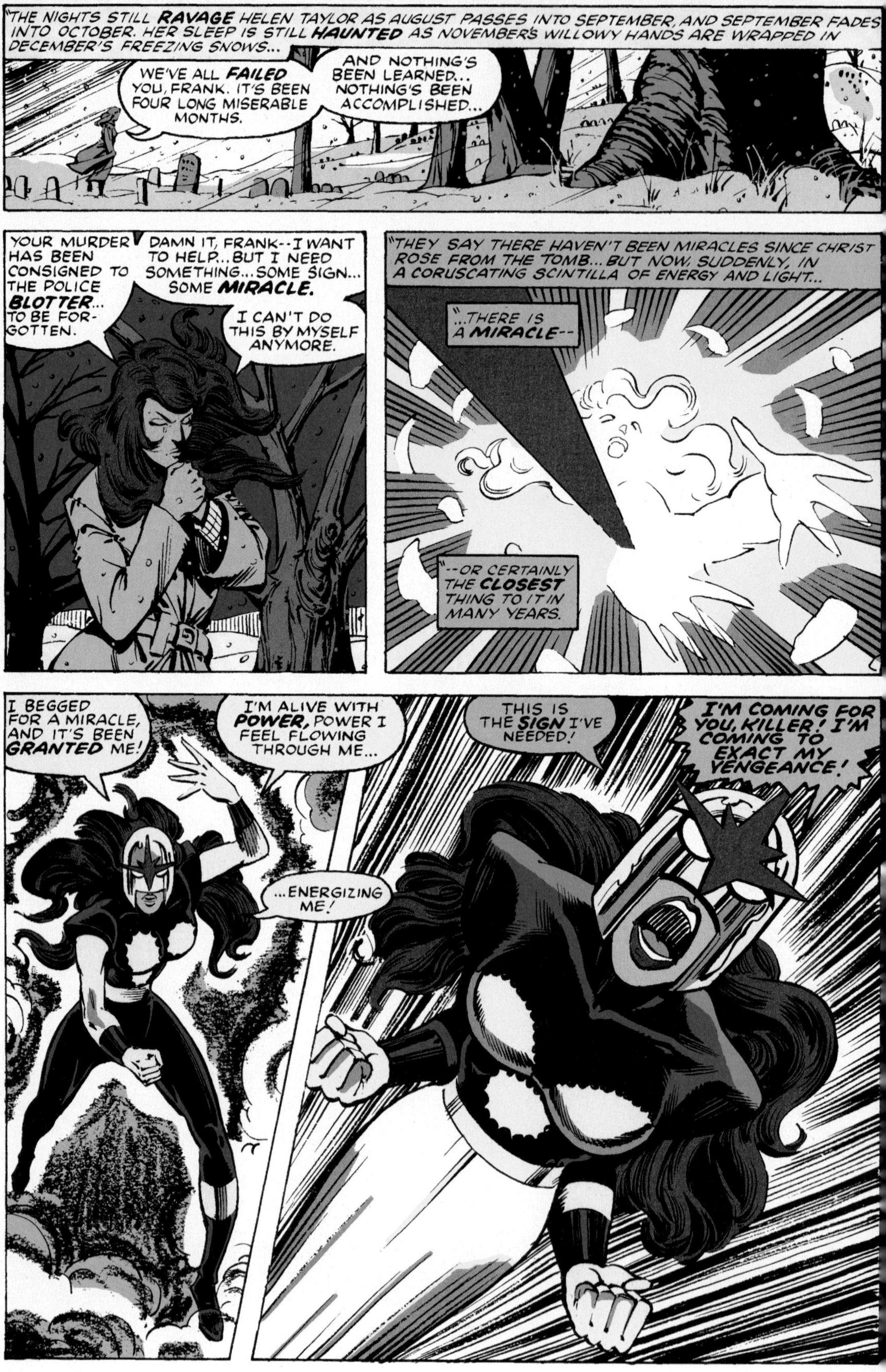
"THE NIGHTS STILL RAVAGE HELEN TAYLOR AS AUGUST PASSES INTO SEPTEMBER, AND SEPTEMBER FADES INTO OCTOBER. HER SLEEP IS STILL HAUNTED AS NOVEMBER'S WILLOWY HANDS ARE WRAPPED IN DECEMBER'S FREEZING SNOWS...
WE'VE ALL FAILED YOU, FRANK. IT'S BEEN FOUR LONG MISERABLE MONTHS.
AND NOTHING'S BEEN LEARNED... NOTHING'S BEEN ACCOMPLISHED...
YOUR MURDER HAS BEEN CONSIGNED TO THE POLICE BLOTTER... TO BE FORGOTTEN.
DAMN IT, FRANK--I WANT TO HELP... BUT I NEED SOMETHING... SOME SIGN... SOME MIRACLE.
I CAN'T DO THIS BY MYSELF ANYMORE.
"THEY SAY THERE HAVEN'T BEEN MIRACLES SINCE CHRIST ROSE FROM THE TOMB... BUT NOW, SUDDENLY, IN A CORUSCATING SCINTILLA OF ENERGY AND LIGHT...
"...THERE IS A MIRACLE--
"--OR CERTAINLY THE CLOSEST THING TO IT IN MANY YEARS.
I BEGGED FOR A MIRACLE, AND IT'S BEEN GRANTED ME!
I'M ALIVE WITH POWER, POWER I FEEL FLOWING THROUGH ME...
...ENERGIZING ME!
THIS IS THE SIGN I'VE NEEDED!
I'M COMING FOR YOU, KILLER! I'M COMING TO EXACT MY VENGEANCE!

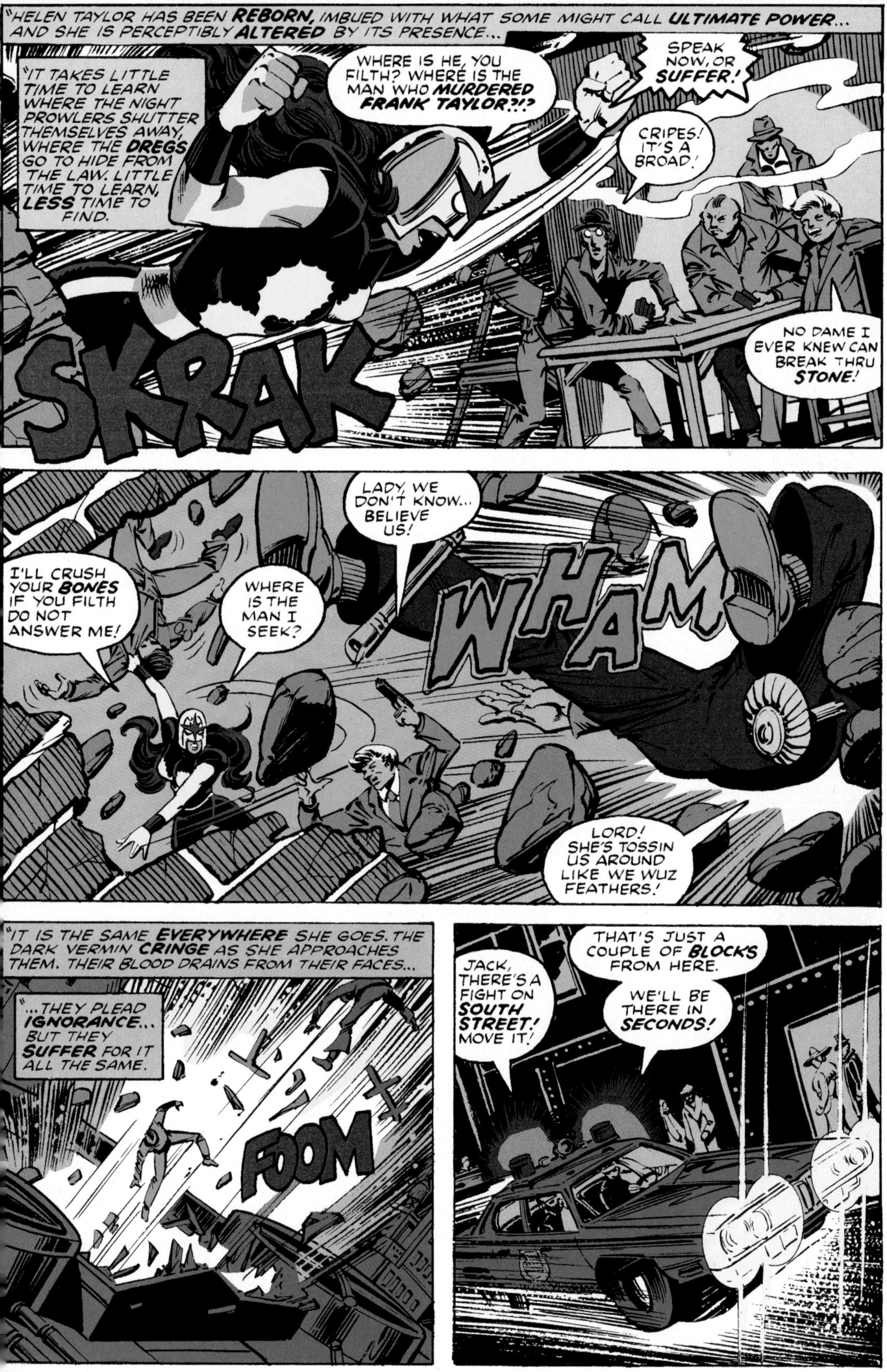
"HELEN TAYLOR HAS BEEN **REBORN**, IMBUED WITH WHAT SOME MIGHT CALL **ULTIMATE POWER**... AND SHE IS PERCEPTIBLY **ALTERED** BY ITS PRESENCE...
"IT TAKES LITTLE TIME TO LEARN WHERE THE NIGHT PROWLERS SHUTTER THEMSELVES AWAY, WHERE THE **DREGS** GO TO HIDE FROM THE LAW. LITTLE TIME TO LEARN, **LESS** TIME TO FIND.
WHERE IS HE, YOU FILTH? WHERE IS THE MAN WHO **MURDERED FRANK TAYLOR**?!?
SPEAK NOW, OR **SUFFER**!
CRIPES! IT'S A BROAD!
NO DAME I EVER KNEW CAN BREAK THRU **STONE**!
SKRAK
I'LL CRUSH YOUR **BONES** IF YOU FILTH DO NOT ANSWER ME!
WHERE IS THE MAN I SEEK?
LADY, WE DON'T KNOW... BELIEVE US!
WHAM
LORD! SHE'S TOSSIN US AROUND LIKE WE WUZ FEATHERS!
"IT IS THE SAME **EVERYWHERE** SHE GOES. THE DARK VERMIN **CRINGE** AS SHE APPROACHES THEM. THEIR BLOOD DRAINS FROM THEIR FACES...
"...THEY PLEAD **IGNORANCE**... BUT THEY **SUFFER** FOR IT ALL THE SAME.
FOOM
JACK, THERE'S A FIGHT ON **SOUTH STREET**! MOVE IT!
THAT'S JUST A COUPLE OF **BLOCKS** FROM HERE.
WE'LL BE THERE IN **SECONDS**!

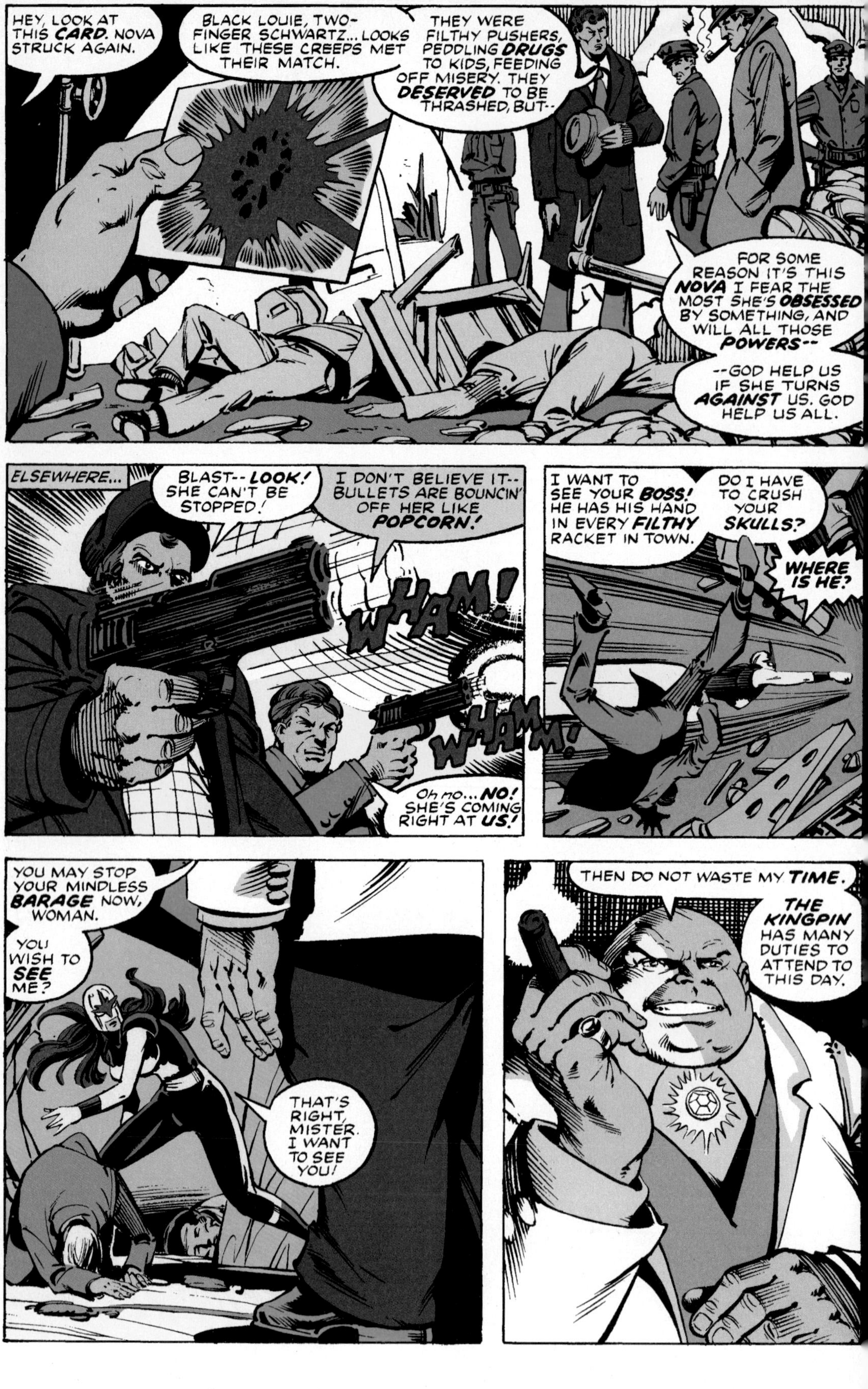

HEY, LOOK AT THIS CARD. NOVA STRUCK AGAIN.
BLACK LOUIE, TWO-FINGER SCHWARTZ... LOOKS LIKE THESE CREEPS MET THEIR MATCH.
THEY WERE FILTHY PUSHERS, PEDDLING DRUGS TO KIDS, FEEDING OFF MISERY. THEY DESERVED TO BE THRASHED, BUT--
FOR SOME REASON IT'S THIS NOVA I FEAR THE MOST SHE'S OBSESSED BY SOMETHING, AND WILL ALL THOSE POWERS--
--GOD HELP US IF SHE TURNS AGAINST US. GOD HELP US ALL.
ELSEWHERE...
BLAST-- LOOK! SHE CAN'T BE STOPPED!
I DON'T BELIEVE IT-- BULLETS ARE BOUNCIN' OFF HER LIKE POPCORN!
WHAM!
WHAMM!
Oh no... NO! SHE'S COMING RIGHT AT US!
I WANT TO SEE YOUR BOSS! HE HAS HIS HAND IN EVERY FILTHY RACKET IN TOWN.
DO I HAVE TO CRUSH YOUR SKULLS?
WHERE IS HE?
YOU MAY STOP YOUR MINDLESS BARAGE NOW, WOMAN.
YOU WISH TO SEE ME?
THAT'S RIGHT, MISTER. I WANT TO SEE YOU!
THEN DO NOT WASTE MY TIME.
THE KINGPIN HAS MANY DUTIES TO ATTEND TO THIS DAY.

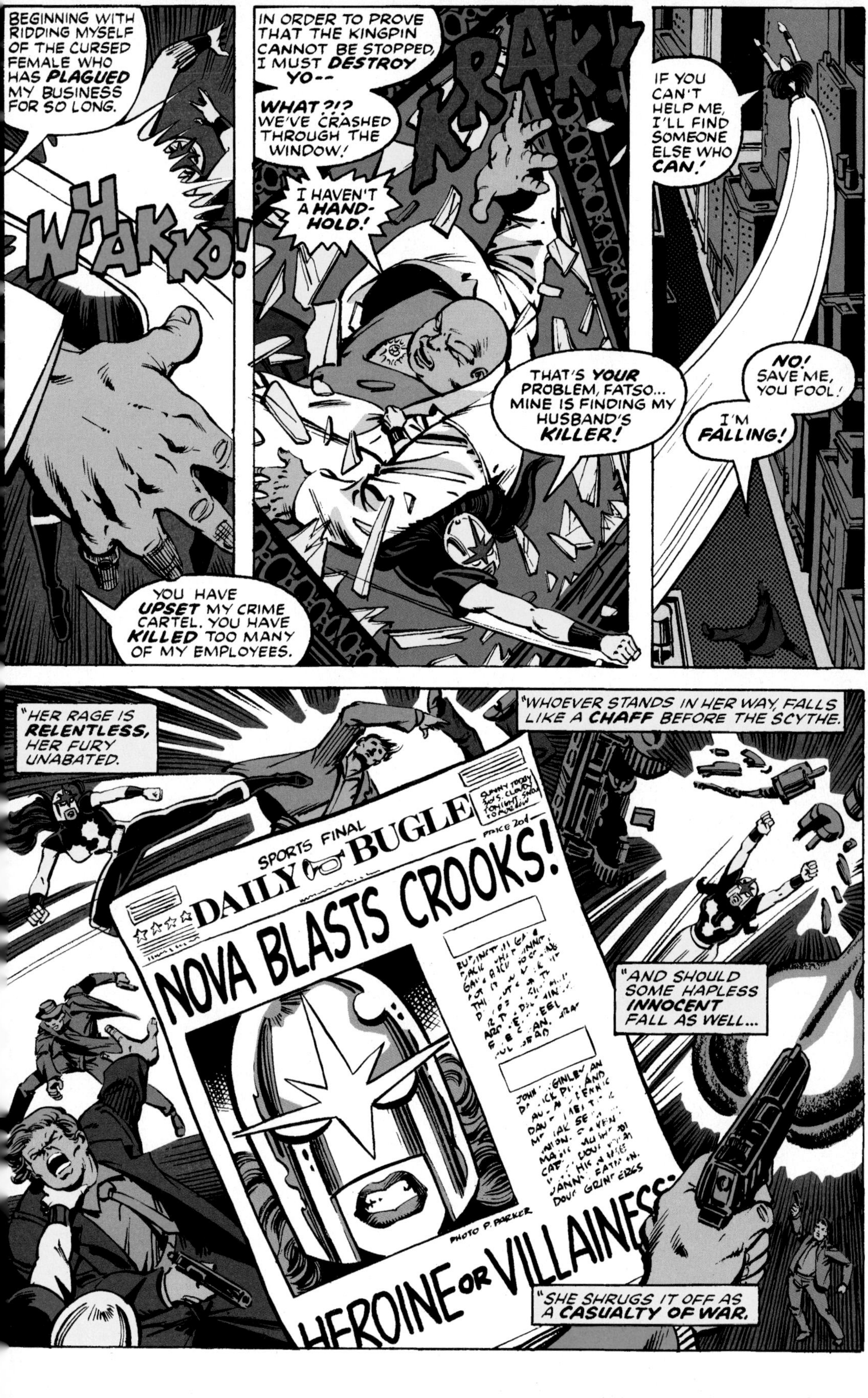
BEGINNING WITH RIDDING MYSELF OF THE CURSED FEMALE WHO HAS PLAGUED MY BUSINESS FOR SO LONG.
WHAKKO!
YOU HAVE UPSET MY CRIME CARTEL. YOU HAVE KILLED TOO MANY OF MY EMPLOYEES.
IN ORDER TO PROVE THAT THE KINGPIN CANNOT BE STOPPED, I MUST DESTROY YO--
WHAT?!? WE'VE CRASHED THROUGH THE WINDOW!
KRAK!
I HAVEN'T A HAND-HOLD!
THAT'S YOUR PROBLEM, FATSO... MINE IS FINDING MY HUSBAND'S KILLER!
IF YOU CAN'T HELP ME, I'LL FIND SOMEONE ELSE WHO CAN!
NO! SAVE ME, YOU FOOL!
I'M FALLING!
"HER RAGE IS RELENTLESS, HER FURY UNABATED.
"WHOEVER STANDS IN HER WAY, FALLS LIKE A CHAFF BEFORE THE SCYTHE.
SPORTS FINAL
DAILY BUGLE
NOVA BLASTS CROOKS!
PHOTO P. PARKER
HEROINE OR VILLAINESS?
"AND SHOULD SOME HAPLESS INNOCENT FALL AS WELL...
"SHE SHRUGS IT OFF AS A CASUALTY OF WAR.

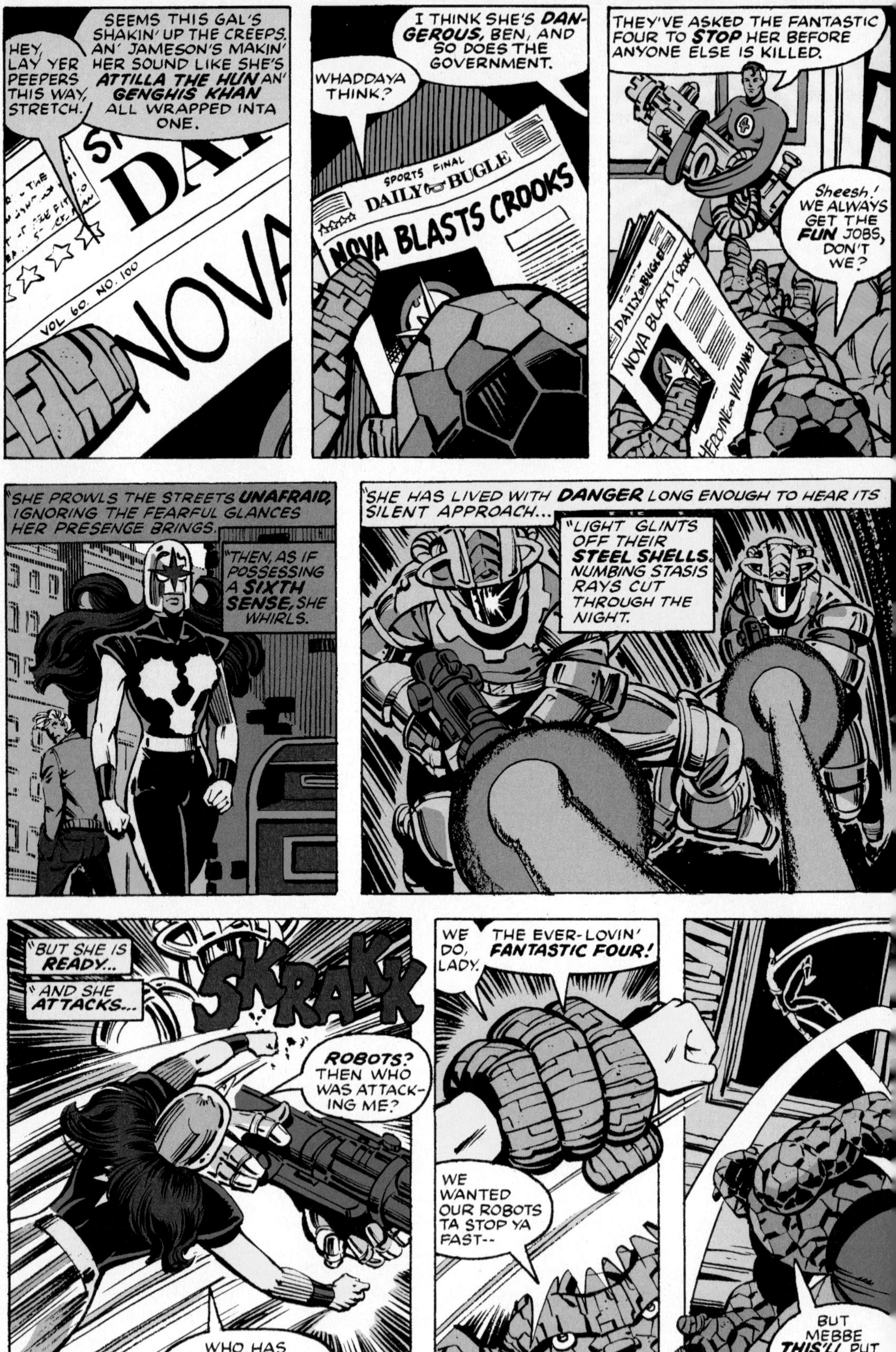
HEY, LAY YER PEEPERS THIS WAY, STRETCH.
SEEMS THIS GAL'S SHAKIN' UP THE CREEPS. AN' JAMESON'S MAKIN' HER SOUND LIKE SHE'S ATTILLA THE HUN AN' GENGHIS KHAN ALL WRAPPED INTA ONE.
DAI
NOVA
VOL 60. NO. 100
WHADDAYA THINK?
I THINK SHE'S DANGEROUS, BEN, AND SO DOES THE GOVERNMENT.
SPORTS FINAL
DAILY BUGLE
NOVA BLASTS CROOKS
THEY'VE ASKED THE FANTASTIC FOUR TO STOP HER BEFORE ANYONE ELSE IS KILLED.
Sheesh! WE ALWAYS GET THE FUN JOBS, DON'T WE?
DAILY BUGLE
NOVA BLASTS CROOKS
HEROINE or VILLAINESS
"SHE PROWLS THE STREETS UNAFRAID, IGNORING THE FEARFUL GLANCES HER PRESENCE BRINGS.
"THEN, AS IF POSSESSING A SIXTH SENSE, SHE WHIRLS.
"SHE HAS LIVED WITH DANGER LONG ENOUGH TO HEAR ITS SILENT APPROACH...
"LIGHT GLINTS OFF THEIR STEEL SHELLS. NUMBING STASIS RAYS CUT THROUGH THE NIGHT.
"BUT SHE IS READY...
"AND SHE ATTACKS...
SKRAKK
ROBOTS? THEN WHO WAS ATTACKING ME?
WHO HAS ENOUGH ABILITY TO CONSTRUCT--?
WE DO, LADY.
THE EVER-LOVIN' FANTASTIC FOUR!
WE WANTED OUR ROBOTS TA STOP YA FAST--
BUT MEBBE THIS'LL PUT YA DOWN FER NOW!

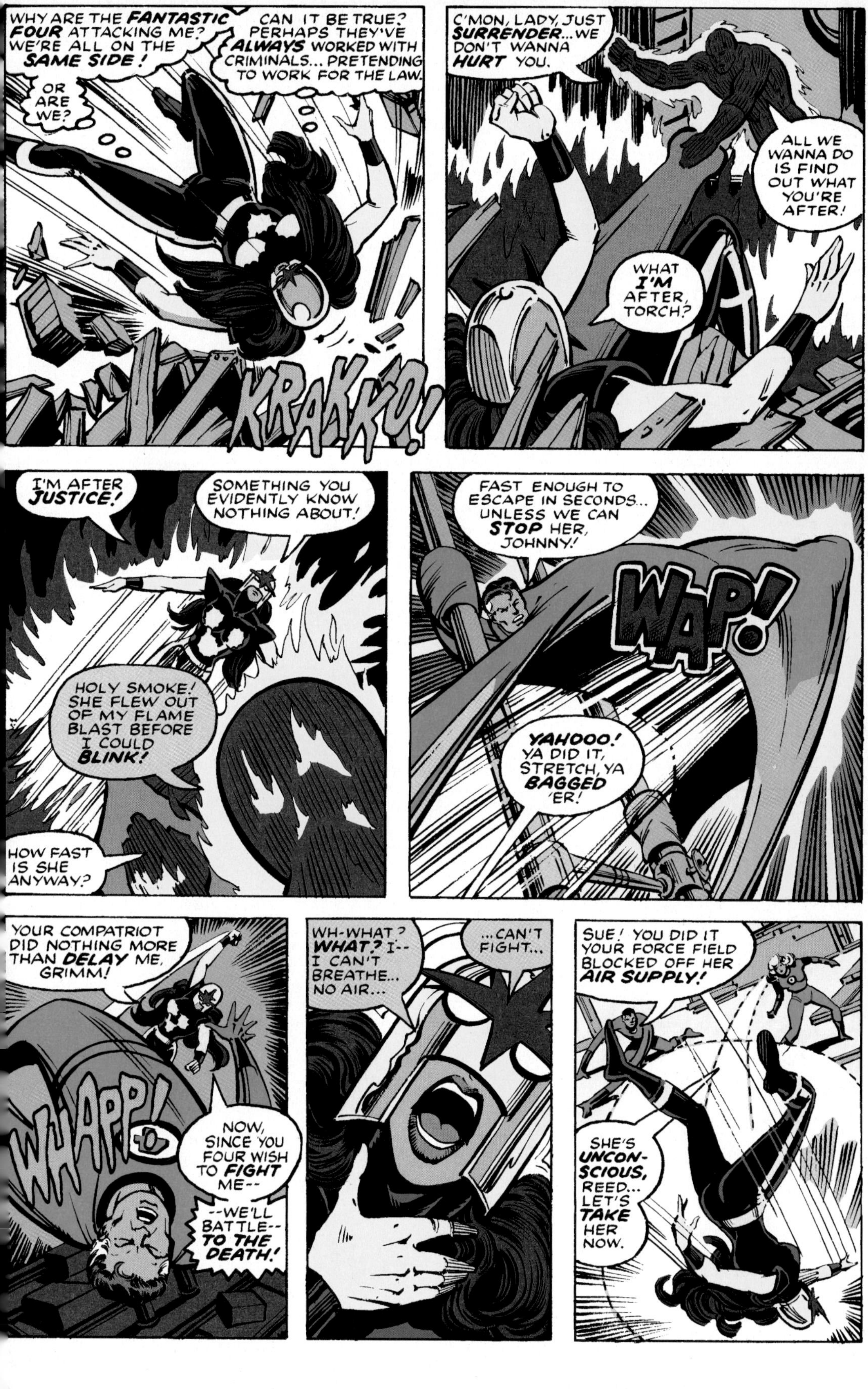
WHY ARE THE FANTASTIC FOUR ATTACKING ME? WE'RE ALL ON THE SAME SIDE!
OR ARE WE?
CAN IT BE TRUE? PERHAPS THEY'VE ALWAYS WORKED WITH CRIMINALS... PRETENDING TO WORK FOR THE LAW.
KRAKKO!
C'MON, LADY, JUST SURRENDER...WE DON'T WANNA HURT YOU.
ALL WE WANNA DO IS FIND OUT WHAT YOU'RE AFTER!
WHAT I'M AFTER, TORCH?
I'M AFTER JUSTICE!
SOMETHING YOU EVIDENTLY KNOW NOTHING ABOUT!
HOLY SMOKE! SHE FLEW OUT OF MY FLAME BLAST BEFORE I COULD BLINK!
HOW FAST IS SHE ANYWAY?
FAST ENOUGH TO ESCAPE IN SECONDS... UNLESS WE CAN STOP HER, JOHNNY!
WAP!
YAHOOO! YA DID IT, STRETCH, YA BAGGED 'ER!
YOUR COMPATRIOT DID NOTHING MORE THAN DELAY ME, GRIMM!
WHAPP!
NOW, SINCE YOU FOUR WISH TO FIGHT ME--
--WE'LL BATTLE-- TO THE DEATH!
WH-WHAT? WHAT? I-- I CAN'T BREATHE... NO AIR...
...CAN'T FIGHT...
SUE! YOU DID IT YOUR FORCE FIELD BLOCKED OFF HER AIR SUPPLY!
SHE'S UNCONSCIOUS, REED... LET'S TAKE HER NOW.

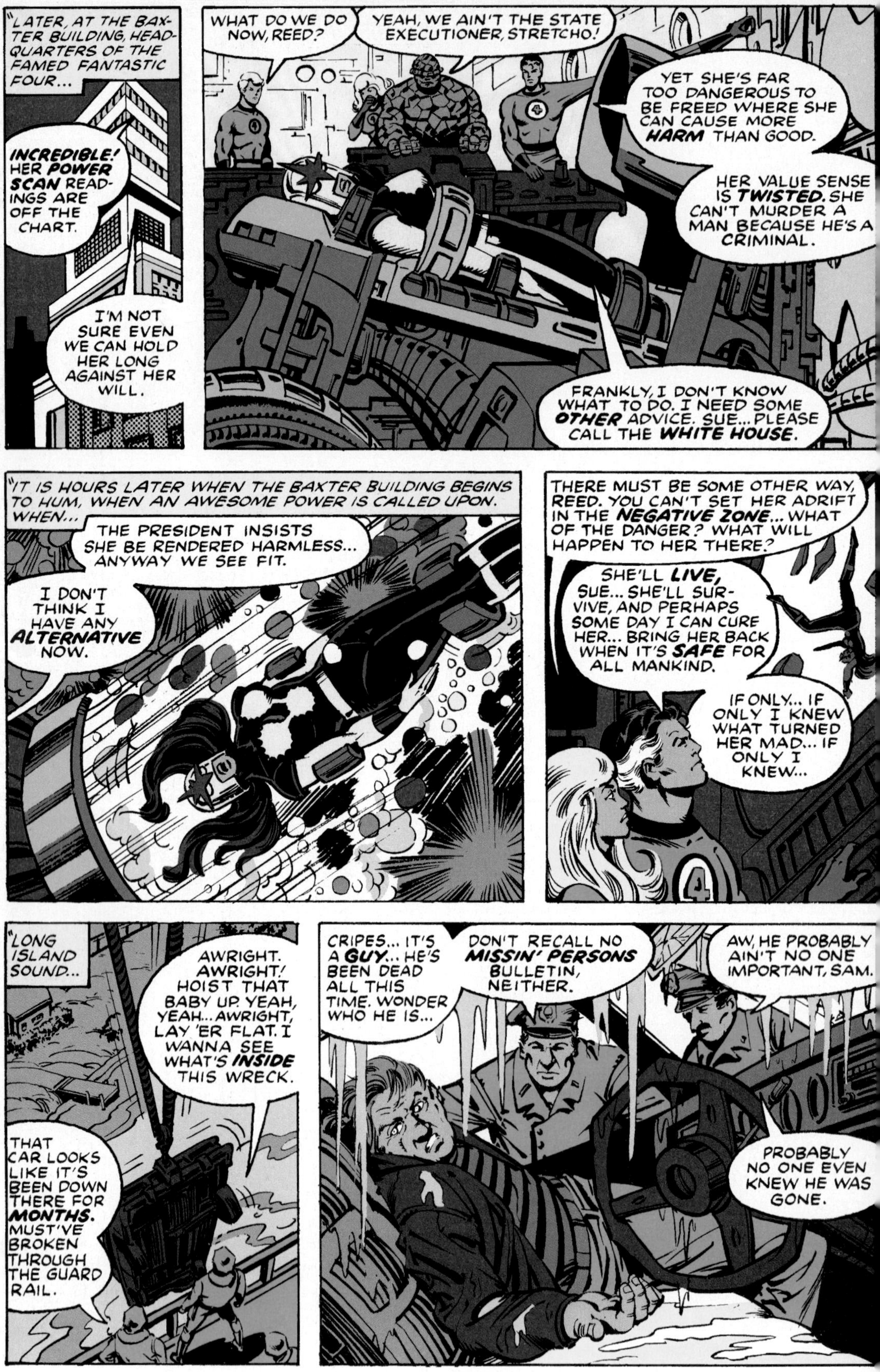
"LATER, AT THE BAXTER BUILDING, HEADQUARTERS OF THE FAMED FANTASTIC FOUR...
INCREDIBLE! HER POWER SCAN READINGS ARE OFF THE CHART.
I'M NOT SURE EVEN WE CAN HOLD HER LONG AGAINST HER WILL.
WHAT DO WE DO NOW, REED?
YEAH, WE AIN'T THE STATE EXECUTIONER, STRETCHO!
YET SHE'S FAR TOO DANGEROUS TO BE FREED WHERE SHE CAN CAUSE MORE HARM THAN GOOD.
HER VALUE SENSE IS TWISTED. SHE CAN'T MURDER A MAN BECAUSE HE'S A CRIMINAL.
FRANKLY, I DON'T KNOW WHAT TO DO. I NEED SOME OTHER ADVICE. SUE... PLEASE CALL THE WHITE HOUSE.
"IT IS HOURS LATER WHEN THE BAXTER BUILDING BEGINS TO HUM, WHEN AN AWESOME POWER IS CALLED UPON. WHEN...
THE PRESIDENT INSISTS SHE BE RENDERED HARMLESS... ANYWAY WE SEE FIT.
I DON'T THINK I HAVE ANY ALTERNATIVE NOW.
THERE MUST BE SOME OTHER WAY, REED. YOU CAN'T SET HER ADRIFT IN THE NEGATIVE ZONE... WHAT OF THE DANGER? WHAT WILL HAPPEN TO HER THERE?
SHE'LL LIVE, SUE... SHE'LL SURVIVE, AND PERHAPS SOME DAY I CAN CURE HER... BRING HER BACK WHEN IT'S SAFE FOR ALL MANKIND.
IF ONLY... IF ONLY I KNEW WHAT TURNED HER MAD... IF ONLY I KNEW...
"LONG ISLAND SOUND...
AWRIGHT. AWRIGHT! HOIST THAT BABY UP. YEAH, YEAH... AWRIGHT, LAY 'ER FLAT. I WANNA SEE WHAT'S INSIDE THIS WRECK.
THAT CAR LOOKS LIKE IT'S BEEN DOWN THERE FOR MONTHS. MUST'VE BROKEN THROUGH THE GUARD RAIL.
CRIPES... IT'S A GUY... HE'S BEEN DEAD ALL THIS TIME. WONDER WHO HE IS...
DON'T RECALL NO MISSIN' PERSONS BULLETIN, NEITHER.
AW, HE PROBABLY AIN'T NO ONE IMPORTANT, SAM.
PROBABLY NO ONE EVEN KNEW HE WAS GONE.

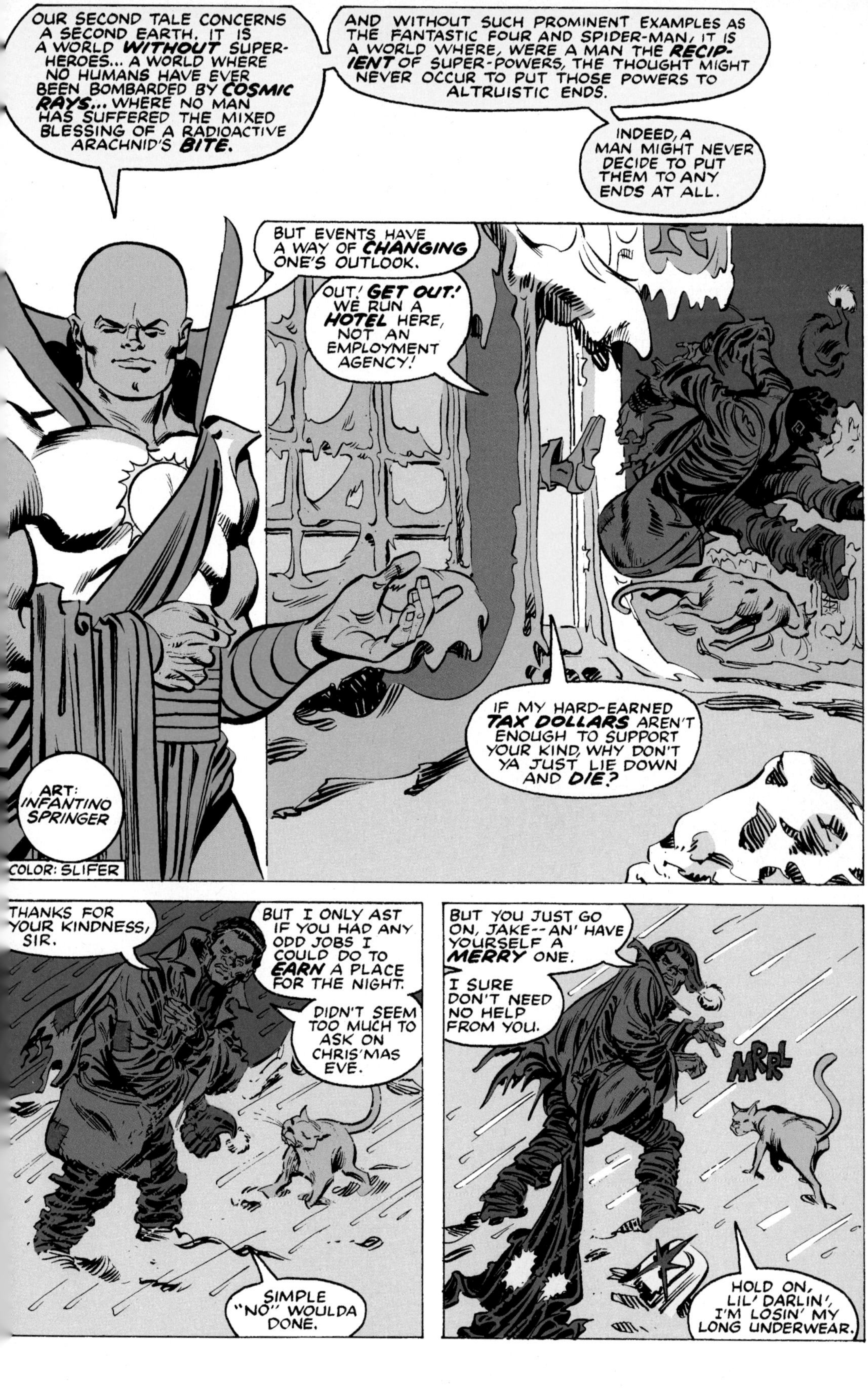
OUR SECOND TALE CONCERNS A SECOND EARTH. IT IS A WORLD WITHOUT SUPER-HEROES... A WORLD WHERE NO HUMANS HAVE EVER BEEN BOMBARDED BY COSMIC RAYS... WHERE NO MAN HAS SUFFERED THE MIXED BLESSING OF A RADIOACTIVE ARACHNID'S BITE.
AND WITHOUT SUCH PROMINENT EXAMPLES AS THE FANTASTIC FOUR AND SPIDER-MAN, IT IS A WORLD WHERE, WERE A MAN THE RECIP-IENT OF SUPER-POWERS, THE THOUGHT MIGHT NEVER OCCUR TO PUT THOSE POWERS TO ALTRUISTIC ENDS.
INDEED, A MAN MIGHT NEVER DECIDE TO PUT THEM TO ANY ENDS AT ALL.
BUT EVENTS HAVE A WAY OF CHANGING ONE'S OUTLOOK.
OUT! GET OUT! WE RUN A HOTEL HERE, NOT AN EMPLOYMENT AGENCY!
IF MY HARD-EARNED TAX DOLLARS AREN'T ENOUGH TO SUPPORT YOUR KIND, WHY DON'T YA JUST LIE DOWN AND DIE?
ART: INFANTINO SPRINGER
COLOR: SLIFER
THANKS FOR YOUR KINDNESS, SIR.
BUT I ONLY AST IF YOU HAD ANY ODD JOBS I COULD DO TO EARN A PLACE FOR THE NIGHT.
DIDN'T SEEM TOO MUCH TO ASK ON CHRIS'MAS EVE.
SIMPLE "NO" WOULDA DONE.
BUT YOU JUST GO ON, JAKE--AN' HAVE YOURSELF A MERRY ONE.
I SURE DON'T NEED NO HELP FROM YOU.
MRRL
HOLD ON, LIL' DARLIN', I'M LOSIN' MY LONG UNDERWEAR.

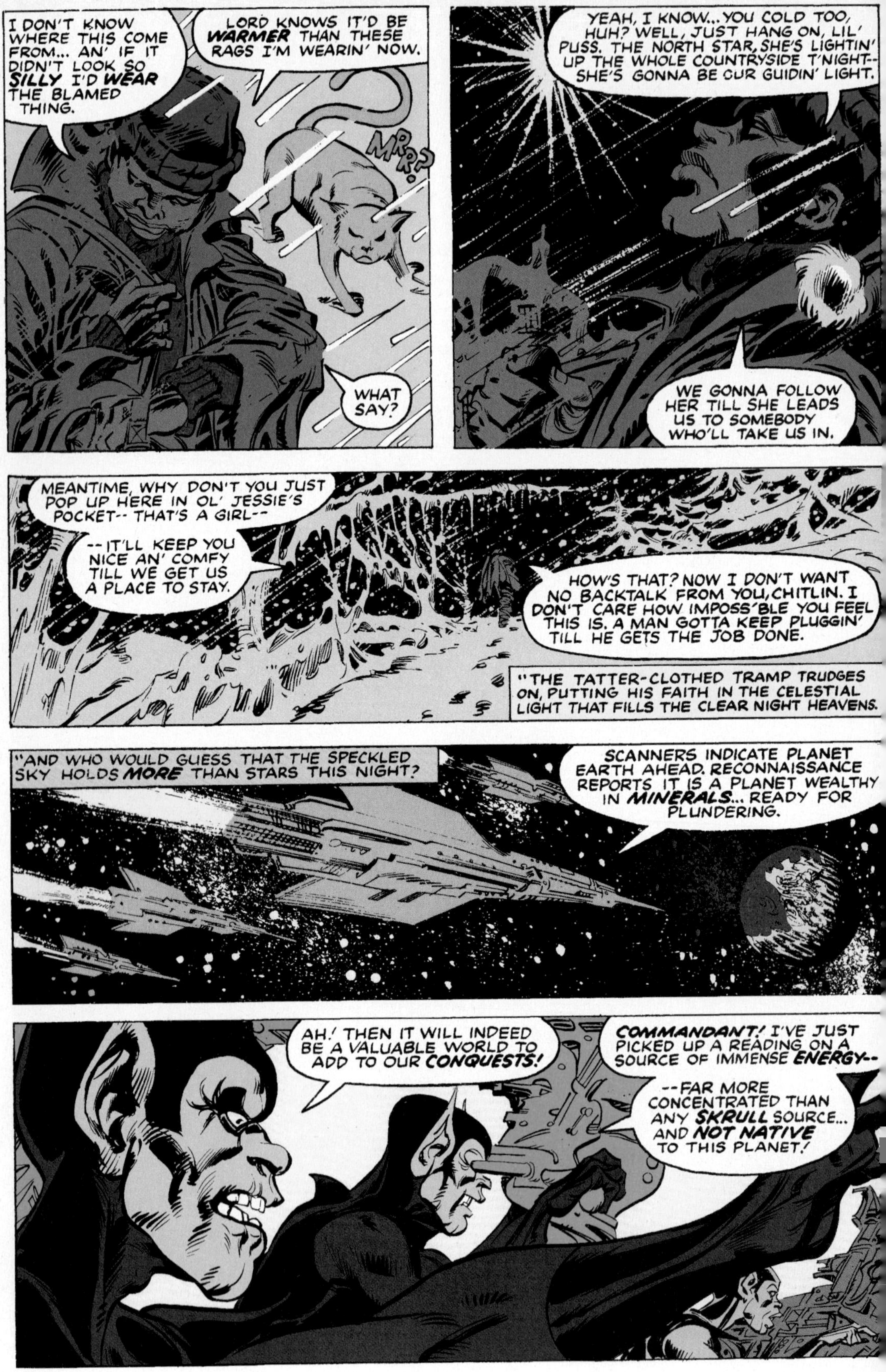
I DON'T KNOW WHERE THIS COME FROM... AN' IF IT DIDN'T LOOK SO SILLY I'D WEAR THE BLAMED THING.
LORD KNOWS IT'D BE WARMER THAN THESE RAGS I'M WEARIN' NOW.
MRRR?
WHAT SAY?
YEAH, I KNOW... YOU COLD TOO, HUH? WELL, JUST HANG ON, LIL' PUSS. THE NORTH STAR, SHE'S LIGHTIN' UP THE WHOLE COUNTRYSIDE T'NIGHT-- SHE'S GONNA BE OUR GUIDIN' LIGHT.
WE GONNA FOLLOW HER TILL SHE LEADS US TO SOMEBODY WHO'LL TAKE US IN.
MEANTIME, WHY DON'T YOU JUST POP UP HERE IN OL' JESSIE'S POCKET-- THAT'S A GIRL--
--IT'LL KEEP YOU NICE AN' COMFY TILL WE GET US A PLACE TO STAY.
HOW'S THAT? NOW I DON'T WANT NO BACKTALK FROM YOU, CHITLIN. I DON'T CARE HOW IMPOSS'BLE YOU FEEL THIS IS. A MAN GOTTA KEEP PLUGGIN' TILL HE GETS THE JOB DONE.
"THE TATTER-CLOTHED TRAMP TRUDGES ON, PUTTING HIS FAITH IN THE CELESTIAL LIGHT THAT FILLS THE CLEAR NIGHT HEAVENS.
"AND WHO WOULD GUESS THAT THE SPECKLED SKY HOLDS MORE THAN STARS THIS NIGHT?
SCANNERS INDICATE PLANET EARTH AHEAD. RECONNAISSANCE REPORTS IT IS A PLANET WEALTHY IN MINERALS... READY FOR PLUNDERING.
AH! THEN IT WILL INDEED BE A VALUABLE WORLD TO ADD TO OUR CONQUESTS!
COMMANDANT! I'VE JUST PICKED UP A READING ON A SOURCE OF IMMENSE ENERGY--
--FAR MORE CONCENTRATED THAN ANY SKRULL SOURCE... AND NOT NATIVE TO THIS PLANET!

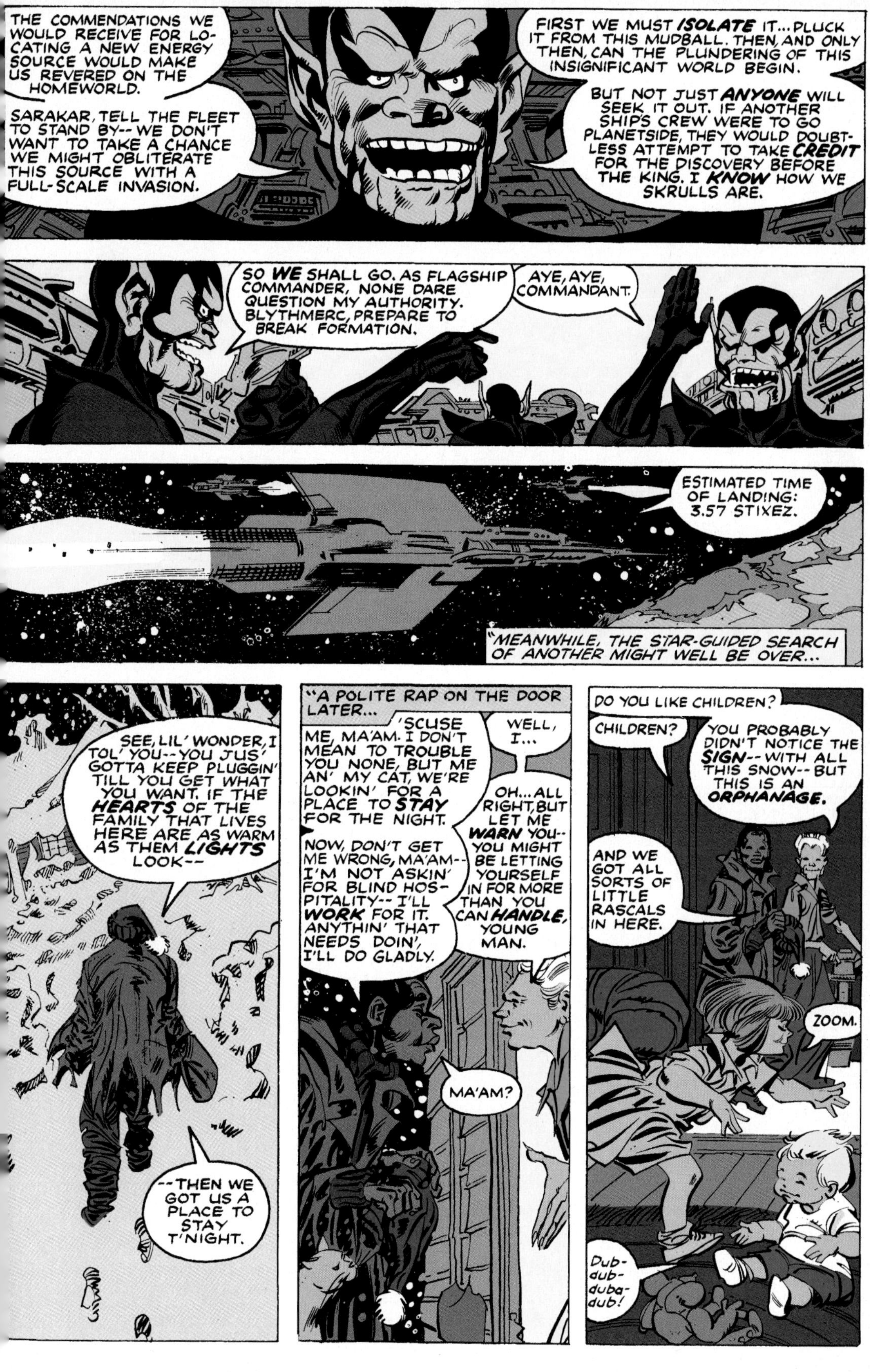
THE COMMENDATIONS WE WOULD RECEIVE FOR LOCATING A NEW ENERGY SOURCE WOULD MAKE US REVERED ON THE HOMEWORLD.
SARAKAR, TELL THE FLEET TO STAND BY-- WE DON'T WANT TO TAKE A CHANCE WE MIGHT OBLITERATE THIS SOURCE WITH A FULL-SCALE INVASION.
FIRST WE MUST ISOLATE IT... PLUCK IT FROM THIS MUDBALL. THEN, AND ONLY THEN, CAN THE PLUNDERING OF THIS INSIGNIFICANT WORLD BEGIN.
BUT NOT JUST ANYONE WILL SEEK IT OUT. IF ANOTHER SHIP'S CREW WERE TO GO PLANETSIDE, THEY WOULD DOUBTLESS ATTEMPT TO TAKE CREDIT FOR THE DISCOVERY BEFORE THE KING. I KNOW HOW WE SKRULLS ARE.
SO WE SHALL GO. AS FLAGSHIP COMMANDER, NONE DARE QUESTION MY AUTHORITY. BLYTHMERC, PREPARE TO BREAK FORMATION.
AYE, AYE, COMMANDANT.
ESTIMATED TIME OF LANDING: 3.57 STIXEZ.
"MEANWHILE, THE STAR-GUIDED SEARCH OF ANOTHER MIGHT WELL BE OVER...
SEE, LIL' WONDER, I TOL' YOU--YOU JUS' GOTTA KEEP PLUGGIN' TILL YOU GET WHAT YOU WANT. IF THE HEARTS OF THE FAMILY THAT LIVES HERE ARE AS WARM AS THEM LIGHTS LOOK--
--THEN WE GOT US A PLACE TO STAY T'NIGHT.
"A POLITE RAP ON THE DOOR LATER...
'SCUSE ME, MA'AM. I DON'T MEAN TO TROUBLE YOU NONE, BUT ME AN' MY CAT, WE'RE LOOKIN' FOR A PLACE TO STAY FOR THE NIGHT.
WELL, I...
NOW, DON'T GET ME WRONG, MA'AM-- I'M NOT ASKIN' FOR BLIND HOSPITALITY-- I'LL WORK FOR IT. ANYTHIN' THAT NEEDS DOIN', I'LL DO GLADLY.
OH... ALL RIGHT, BUT LET ME WARN YOU-- YOU MIGHT BE LETTING YOURSELF IN FOR MORE THAN YOU CAN HANDLE, YOUNG MAN.
MA'AM?
DO YOU LIKE CHILDREN?
CHILDREN?
YOU PROBABLY DIDN'T NOTICE THE SIGN-- WITH ALL THIS SNOW-- BUT THIS IS AN ORPHANAGE.
AND WE GOT ALL SORTS OF LITTLE RASCALS IN HERE.
ZOOM.
Dub-dub-duba-dub!

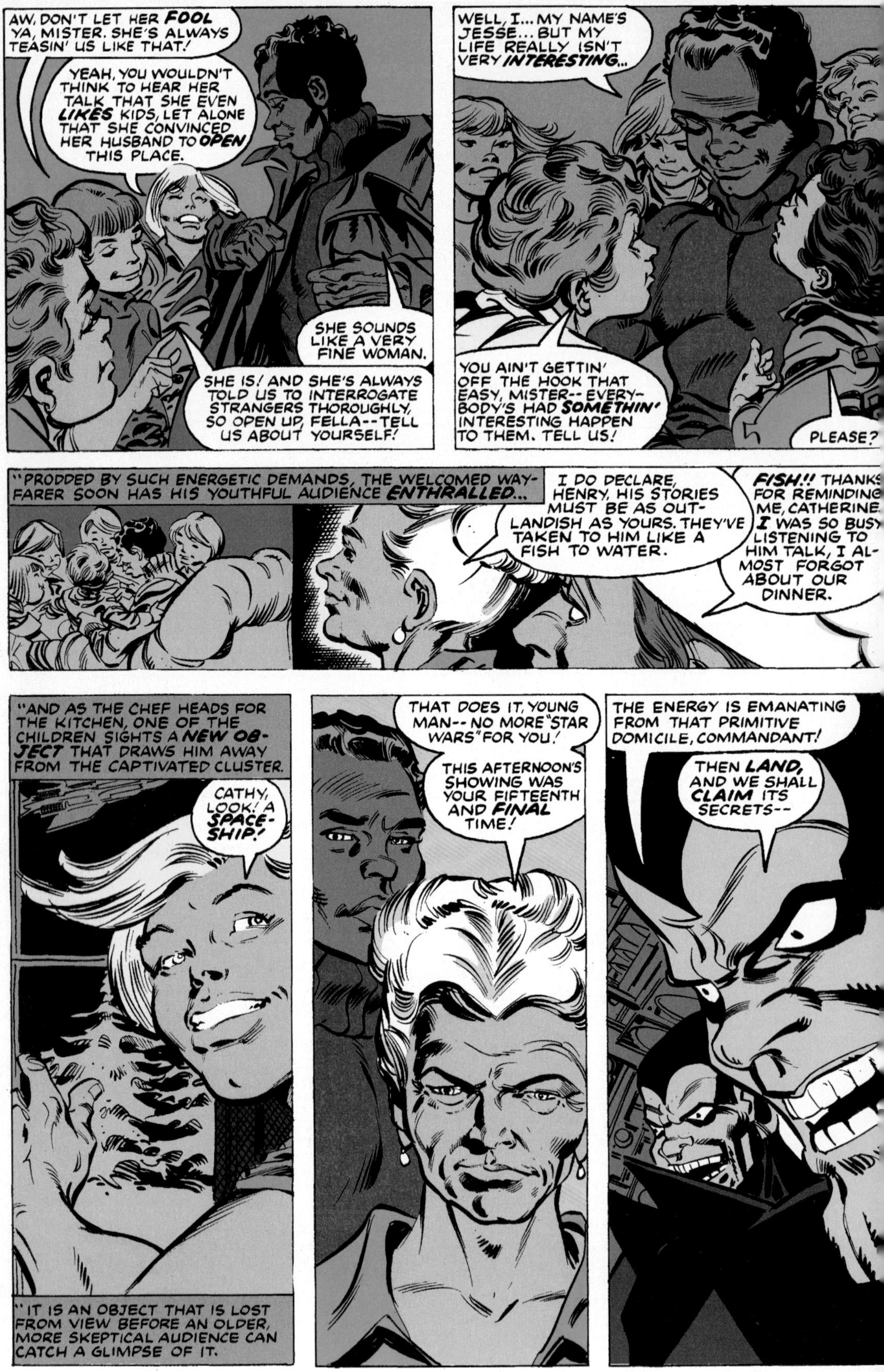
AW, DON'T LET HER FOOL YA, MISTER. SHE'S ALWAYS TEASIN' US LIKE THAT!
YEAH, YOU WOULDN'T THINK TO HEAR HER TALK THAT SHE EVEN LIKES KIDS, LET ALONE THAT SHE CONVINCED HER HUSBAND TO OPEN THIS PLACE.
SHE SOUNDS LIKE A VERY FINE WOMAN.
SHE IS! AND SHE'S ALWAYS TOLD US TO INTERROGATE STRANGERS THOROUGHLY, SO OPEN UP, FELLA--TELL US ABOUT YOURSELF!
WELL, I... MY NAME'S JESSE... BUT MY LIFE REALLY ISN'T VERY INTERESTING...
YOU AIN'T GETTIN' OFF THE HOOK THAT EASY, MISTER-- EVERYBODY'S HAD SOMETHIN' INTERESTING HAPPEN TO THEM. TELL US!
PLEASE?
"PRODDED BY SUCH ENERGETIC DEMANDS, THE WELCOMED WAYFARER SOON HAS HIS YOUTHFUL AUDIENCE ENTHRALLED...
I DO DECLARE, HENRY, HIS STORIES MUST BE AS OUTLANDISH AS YOURS. THEY'VE TAKEN TO HIM LIKE A FISH TO WATER.
FISH!! THANKS FOR REMINDING ME, CATHERINE. I WAS SO BUSY LISTENING TO HIM TALK, I ALMOST FORGOT ABOUT OUR DINNER.
"AND AS THE CHEF HEADS FOR THE KITCHEN, ONE OF THE CHILDREN SIGHTS A NEW OBJECT THAT DRAWS HIM AWAY FROM THE CAPTIVATED CLUSTER.
CATHY, LOOK! A SPACE-SHIP!
"IT IS AN OBJECT THAT IS LOST FROM VIEW BEFORE AN OLDER, MORE SKEPTICAL AUDIENCE CAN CATCH A GLIMPSE OF IT.
THAT DOES IT, YOUNG MAN-- NO MORE "STAR WARS" FOR YOU!
THIS AFTERNOON'S SHOWING WAS YOUR FIFTEENTH AND FINAL TIME!
THE ENERGY IS EMANATING FROM THAT PRIMITIVE DOMICILE, COMMANDANT!
THEN LAND, AND WE SHALL CLAIM ITS SECRETS--

"—BY FORCE!'"

SHRAM!

DUNG-DOG! WHERE IS THE ENERGY SOURCE YOU HAVE HERE? TAKE US TO IT IMMEDIATELY, OR BY THE SKRULL SUPREME, WE WILL ELIMINATE YOU!

HEY, LISTEN, I DON'T KNOW WHAT YOU GUYS WANT—IT'S KINDA LATE FOR HALLOWEEN—BUT IF YOU LEAVE RIGHT NOW, WE'LL FORGET ALL ABOUT THIS.

PROVIDED YOU PAY FOR THE DOOR, OF COURSE.

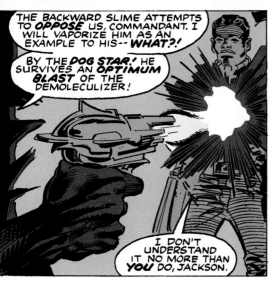

THE BACKWARD SLIME ATTEMPTS TO OPPOSE US, COMMANDANT. I WILL VAPORIZE HIM AS AN EXAMPLE TO HIS—WHAT?!

BY THE DOG STAR! HE SURVIVES AN OPTIMUM BLAST OF THE DEMOLECULIZER!

I DON'T UNDERSTAND IT NO MORE THAN YOU DO, JACKSON.

ALL I KNOW'S THAT THE SAME DAY I FOUND THIS SILLY COSTUME, I ALSO FOUND OUT NOTHIN' COULD HURT ME NO MORE!

NOW, I DON'T KNOW WHY YOU BUSTED IN HERE OR WHAT YOU WANT—

—BUT YOU AIN'T GONNA ATTACK THESE FINE FOLKS—

WITHOUT ANSWERIN' TO ME!

GET BACK, CHILDREN—GET INTO THE OTHER ROOM.

OKAY, CATHY—BUT ONLY IF YOU COME, TOO!

YOU COULD GET HURT AS EASILY AS US!

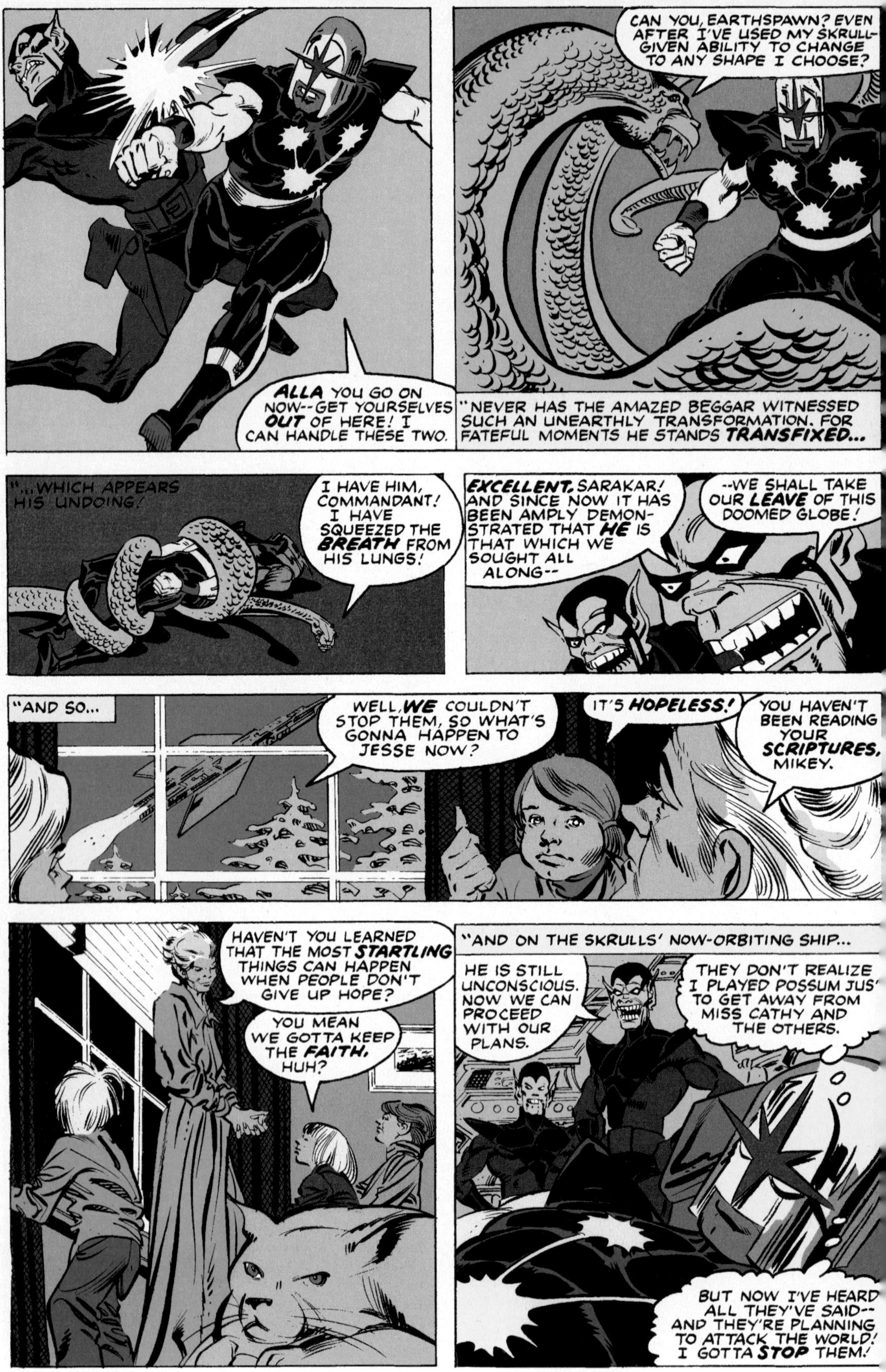
ALLA YOU GO ON NOW--GET YOURSELVES OUT OF HERE! I CAN HANDLE THESE TWO.
CAN YOU, EARTHSPAWN? EVEN AFTER I'VE USED MY SKRULL-GIVEN ABILITY TO CHANGE TO ANY SHAPE I CHOOSE?
"NEVER HAS THE AMAZED BEGGAR WITNESSED SUCH AN UNEARTHLY TRANSFORMATION. FOR FATEFUL MOMENTS HE STANDS TRANSFIXED...
"...WHICH APPEARS HIS UNDOING!
I HAVE HIM, COMMANDANT! I HAVE SQUEEZED THE BREATH FROM HIS LUNGS!
EXCELLENT, SARAKAR! AND SINCE NOW IT HAS BEEN AMPLY DEMONSTRATED THAT HE IS THAT WHICH WE SOUGHT ALL ALONG--
--WE SHALL TAKE OUR LEAVE OF THIS DOOMED GLOBE!
"AND SO...
WELL, WE COULDN'T STOP THEM, SO WHAT'S GONNA HAPPEN TO JESSE NOW?
IT'S HOPELESS!
YOU HAVEN'T BEEN READING YOUR SCRIPTURES, MIKEY.
HAVEN'T YOU LEARNED THAT THE MOST STARTLING THINGS CAN HAPPEN WHEN PEOPLE DON'T GIVE UP HOPE?
YOU MEAN WE GOTTA KEEP THE FAITH, HUH?
"AND ON THE SKRULLS' NOW-ORBITING SHIP...
HE IS STILL UNCONSCIOUS. NOW WE CAN PROCEED WITH OUR PLANS.
THEY DON'T REALIZE I PLAYED POSSUM JUS' TO GET AWAY FROM MISS CATHY AND THE OTHERS.
BUT NOW I'VE HEARD ALL THEY'VE SAID--AND THEY'RE PLANNING TO ATTACK THE WORLD! I GOTTA STOP THEM!

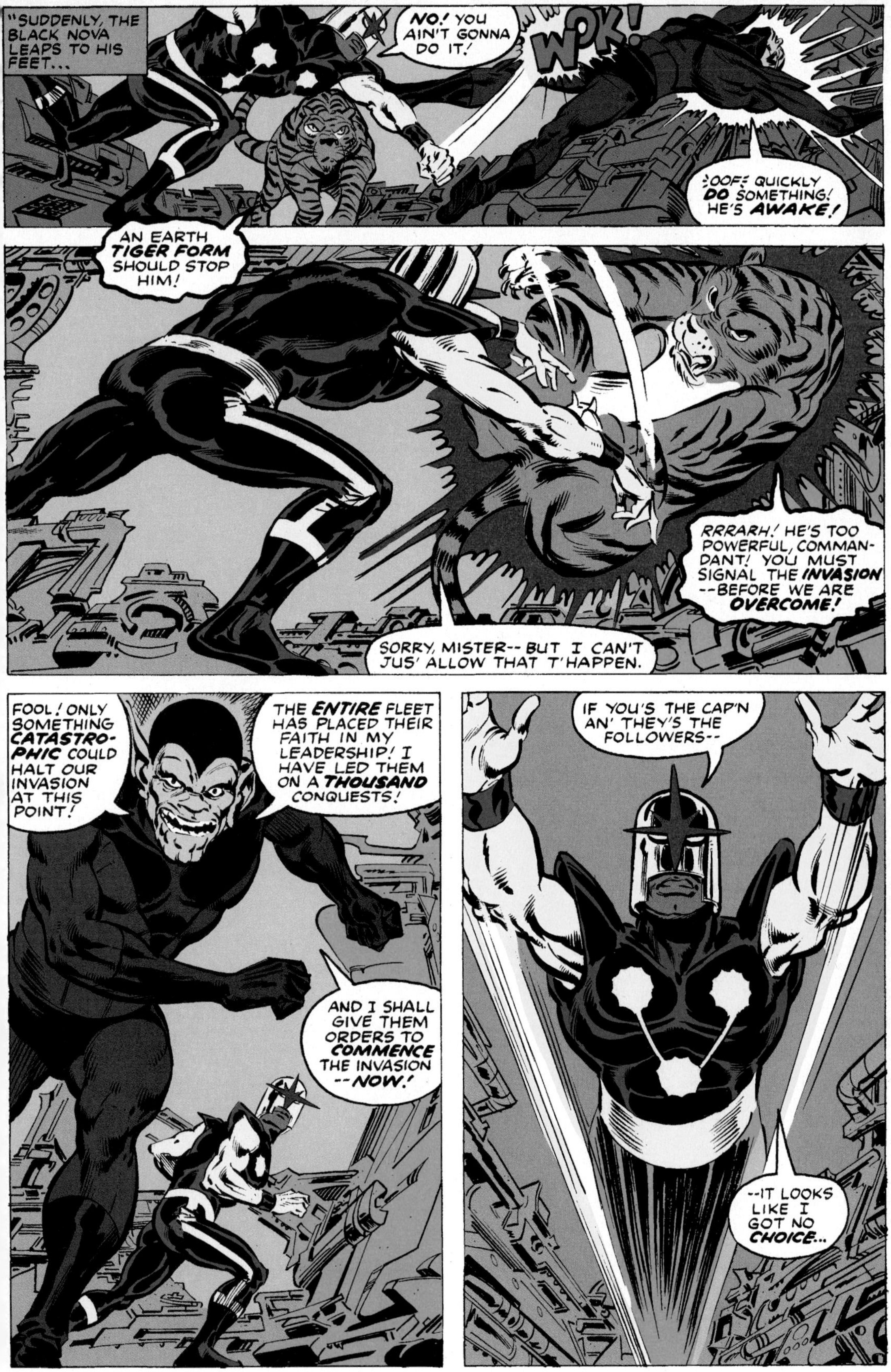
"SUDDENLY, THE BLACK NOVA LEAPS TO HIS FEET...
NO! YOU AIN'T GONNA DO IT!
WOK!
OOF! QUICKLY DO SOMETHING! HE'S AWAKE!
AN EARTH TIGER FORM SHOULD STOP HIM!
RRRARH! HE'S TOO POWERFUL, COMMANDANT! YOU MUST SIGNAL THE INVASION --BEFORE WE ARE OVERCOME!
SORRY, MISTER-- BUT I CAN'T JUS' ALLOW THAT T'HAPPEN.
FOOL! ONLY SOMETHING CATASTROPHIC COULD HALT OUR INVASION AT THIS POINT!
THE ENTIRE FLEET HAS PLACED THEIR FAITH IN MY LEADERSHIP! I HAVE LED THEM ON A THOUSAND CONQUESTS!
AND I SHALL GIVE THEM ORDERS TO COMMENCE THE INVASION --NOW!
IF YOU'S THE CAP'N AN' THEY'S THE FOLLOWERS--
--IT LOOKS LIKE I GOT NO CHOICE...

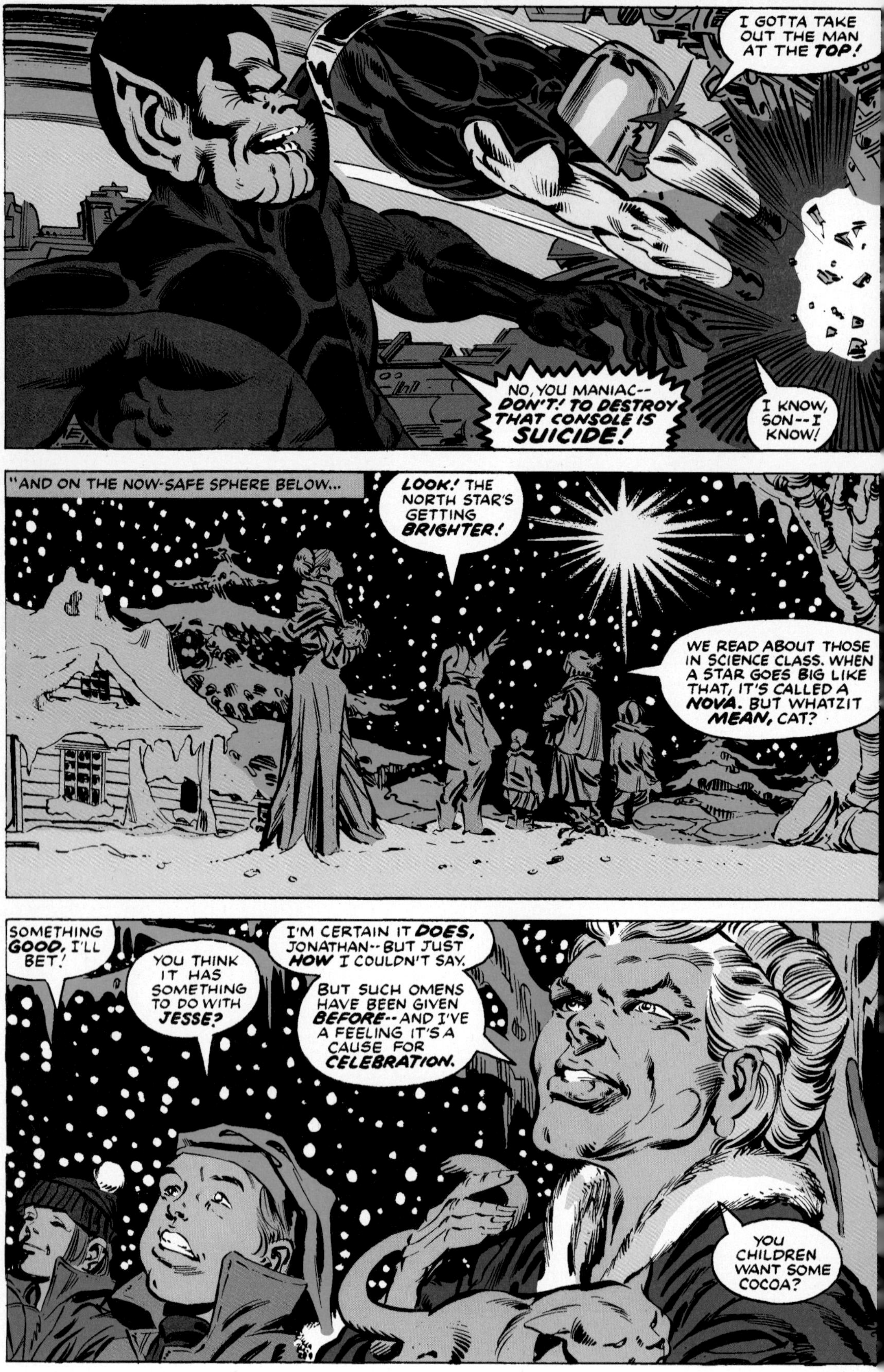
I GOTTA TAKE OUT THE MAN AT THE TOP!
NO, YOU MANIAC-- DON'T! TO DESTROY THAT CONSOLE IS SUICIDE!
I KNOW, SON--I KNOW!
"AND ON THE NOW-SAFE SPHERE BELOW...
LOOK! THE NORTH STAR'S GETTING BRIGHTER!
WE READ ABOUT THOSE IN SCIENCE CLASS. WHEN A STAR GOES BIG LIKE THAT, IT'S CALLED A NOVA. BUT WHATZIT MEAN, CAT?
SOMETHING GOOD, I'LL BET!
YOU THINK IT HAS SOMETHING TO DO WITH JESSE?
I'M CERTAIN IT DOES, JONATHAN--BUT JUST HOW I COULDN'T SAY.
BUT SUCH OMENS HAVE BEEN GIVEN BEFORE--AND I'VE A FEELING IT'S A CAUSE FOR CELEBRATION.
YOU CHILDREN WANT SOME COCOA?

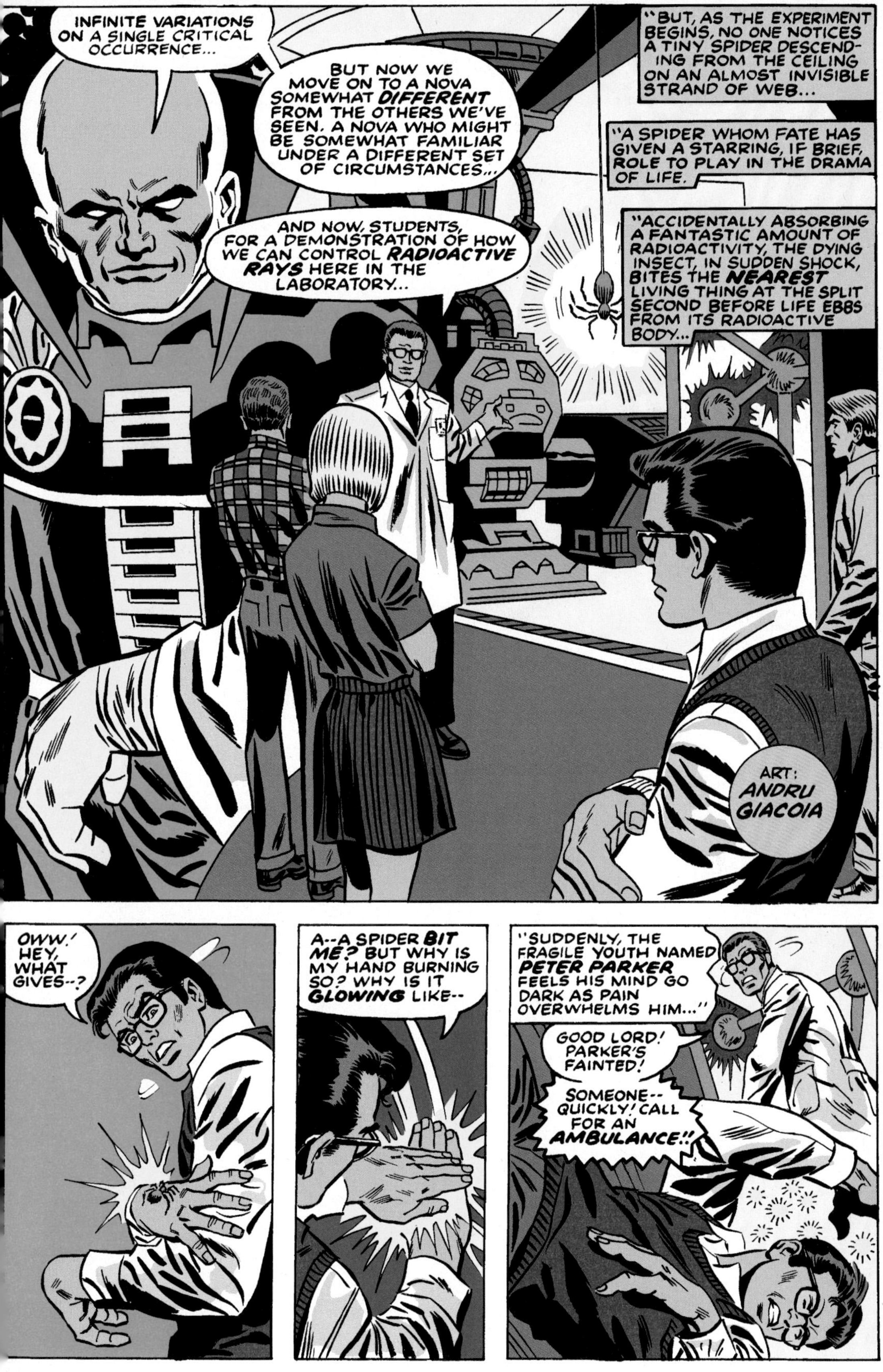
INFINITE VARIATIONS ON A SINGLE CRITICAL OCCURRENCE...
BUT NOW WE MOVE ON TO A NOVA SOMEWHAT DIFFERENT FROM THE OTHERS WE'VE SEEN. A NOVA WHO MIGHT BE SOMEWHAT FAMILIAR UNDER A DIFFERENT SET OF CIRCUMSTANCES...
AND NOW, STUDENTS, FOR A DEMONSTRATION OF HOW WE CAN CONTROL RADIOACTIVE RAYS HERE IN THE LABORATORY...
"BUT, AS THE EXPERIMENT BEGINS, NO ONE NOTICES A TINY SPIDER DESCENDING FROM THE CEILING ON AN ALMOST INVISIBLE STRAND OF WEB...
"A SPIDER WHOM FATE HAS GIVEN A STARRING, IF BRIEF, ROLE TO PLAY IN THE DRAMA OF LIFE.
"ACCIDENTALLY ABSORBING A FANTASTIC AMOUNT OF RADIOACTIVITY, THE DYING INSECT, IN SUDDEN SHOCK, BITES THE NEAREST LIVING THING AT THE SPLIT SECOND BEFORE LIFE EBBS FROM ITS RADIOACTIVE BODY...
ART: ANDRU GIACOIA
OWW! HEY, WHAT GIVES--?
A--A SPIDER BIT ME? BUT WHY IS MY HAND BURNING SO? WHY IS IT GLOWING LIKE--
"SUDDENLY, THE FRAGILE YOUTH NAMED PETER PARKER FEELS HIS MIND GO DARK AS PAIN OVERWHELMS HIM..."
GOOD LORD! PARKER'S FAINTED!
SOMEONE--QUICKLY! CALL FOR AN AMBULANCE!!

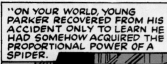

"ON YOUR WORLD, YOUNG PARKER RECOVERED FROM HIS ACCIDENT ONLY TO LEARN HE HAD SOMEHOW ACQUIRED THE PROPORTIONAL POWER OF A SPIDER.

"ON *THIS* WORLD, HOWEVER, PETER PARKER IS NOT QUITE SO LUCKY...

"...AS THE SPIDER THAT BIT HIM HAD ABSORBED A GREATER DOSE OF RADIATION THAN PARKER COULD METABOLIZE.

LOOK AT HIM, HARRY! HE'S WHITE AS A *SHEET*.

I'M AFRAID THIS KID BOUGHT IT.

THERE'S STILL A *CHANCE*, JACK-- REMEMBER THAT RADIOACTIVE CONTROL UNIT STARK INDUSTRIES LOANED US FOR EXPERIMENTATION?

IT JUST MIGHT TURN THE TRICK!

"PARKER'S WRITHING BODY IS WHEELED INTO THE HOSPITAL'S SPECIAL RADIOACTIVE WARD, WHILE..."

DOCTOR, I'M *BEN PARKER!* PETER'S UNCLE... HOW'S MY BOY DOING?

HE'S GOT TO BE ALL RIGHT, DOCTOR. TELL US HE'LL LIVE.

MRS. PARKER, I CAN'T PROMISE ANYTHING. HE'S SUFFERED A MASSIVE DOSE OF RADIATION POISONING.

WE'VE NEVER WORKED ON A CASE LIKE HIS BEFORE. WE JUST DON'T KNOW IF--?

MRS. PARKER!

MAY!

NO! PETER MUSTN'T DIE! HE-- Uhhh... MY *HEART!*

" THE FRAGILE OLD WOMAN FAINTS AT THE NEWS OF HER NEPHEW'S CRITICAL ILLNESS. BUT..."

MY SWEET HEAVEN-- *DOCTOR!* SHE HAS A WEAK HEART. PLEASE... DO SOMETHING!

WE'LL DO OUR BEST, MR. PARKER!

NURSE! WE'VE GOT A *RED BLANKET CASE!* MOVE IT!

"MAY PARKER'S UNCONSCIOUS BODY IS WHEELED INTO THE EMERGENCY WARD. IMMEDIATELY, THE FINEST DOCTORS ON CALL ARE AT THE LOVING WOMAN'S SIDE.

"BEN PARKER SLUMPS INTO HIS CHAIR...WEAK, TIRED, AND ALL-TOO WORN OUT, THE GENTLE OLD MAN *PRAYS*..."

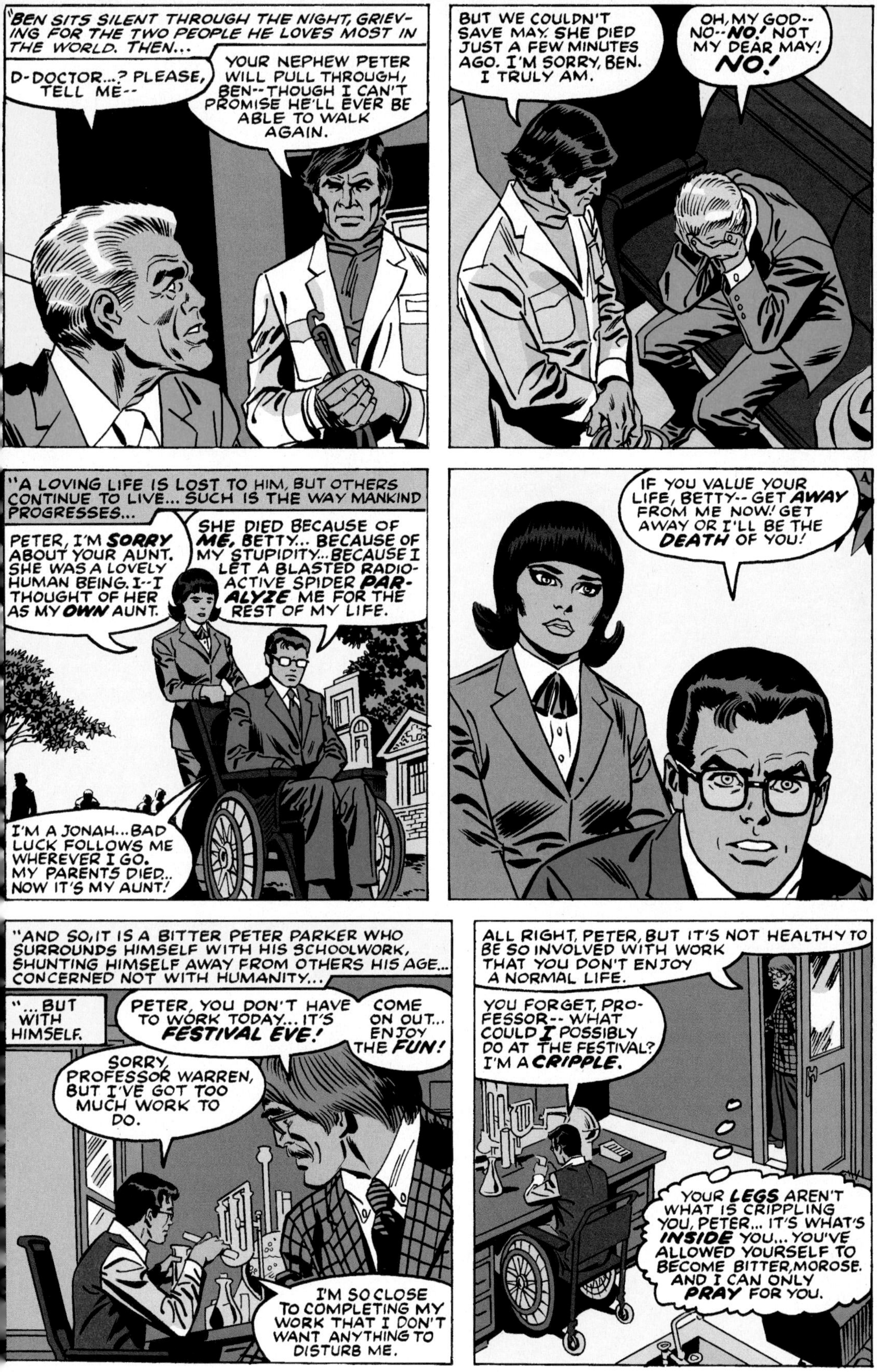
"BEN SITS SILENT THROUGH THE NIGHT, GRIEVING FOR THE TWO PEOPLE HE LOVES MOST IN THE WORLD. THEN...
D-DOCTOR...? PLEASE, TELL ME--
YOUR NEPHEW PETER WILL PULL THROUGH, BEN--THOUGH I CAN'T PROMISE HE'LL EVER BE ABLE TO WALK AGAIN.
BUT WE COULDN'T SAVE MAY. SHE DIED JUST A FEW MINUTES AGO. I'M SORRY, BEN. I TRULY AM.
OH, MY GOD-- NO--NO! NOT MY DEAR MAY! NO!
"A LOVING LIFE IS LOST TO HIM, BUT OTHERS CONTINUE TO LIVE... SUCH IS THE WAY MANKIND PROGRESSES...
PETER, I'M SORRY ABOUT YOUR AUNT. SHE WAS A LOVELY HUMAN BEING. I--I THOUGHT OF HER AS MY OWN AUNT.
SHE DIED BECAUSE OF ME, BETTY... BECAUSE OF MY STUPIDITY...BECAUSE I LET A BLASTED RADIO-ACTIVE SPIDER PARALYZE ME FOR THE REST OF MY LIFE.
I'M A JONAH...BAD LUCK FOLLOWS ME WHEREVER I GO. MY PARENTS DIED... NOW IT'S MY AUNT!
IF YOU VALUE YOUR LIFE, BETTY-- GET AWAY FROM ME NOW! GET AWAY OR I'LL BE THE DEATH OF YOU!
"AND SO, IT IS A BITTER PETER PARKER WHO SURROUNDS HIMSELF WITH HIS SCHOOLWORK, SHUNTING HIMSELF AWAY FROM OTHERS HIS AGE... CONCERNED NOT WITH HUMANITY...
"...BUT WITH HIMSELF.
PETER, YOU DON'T HAVE TO WORK TODAY... IT'S FESTIVAL EVE!
COME ON OUT... ENJOY THE FUN!
SORRY, PROFESSOR WARREN, BUT I'VE GOT TOO MUCH WORK TO DO.
I'M SO CLOSE TO COMPLETING MY WORK THAT I DON'T WANT ANYTHING TO DISTURB ME.
ALL RIGHT, PETER, BUT IT'S NOT HEALTHY TO BE SO INVOLVED WITH WORK THAT YOU DON'T ENJOY A NORMAL LIFE.
YOU FORGET, PROFESSOR-- WHAT COULD I POSSIBLY DO AT THE FESTIVAL? I'M A CRIPPLE.
YOUR LEGS AREN'T WHAT IS CRIPPLING YOU, PETER... IT'S WHAT'S INSIDE YOU... YOU'VE ALLOWED YOURSELF TO BECOME BITTER, MOROSE. AND I CAN ONLY PRAY FOR YOU.

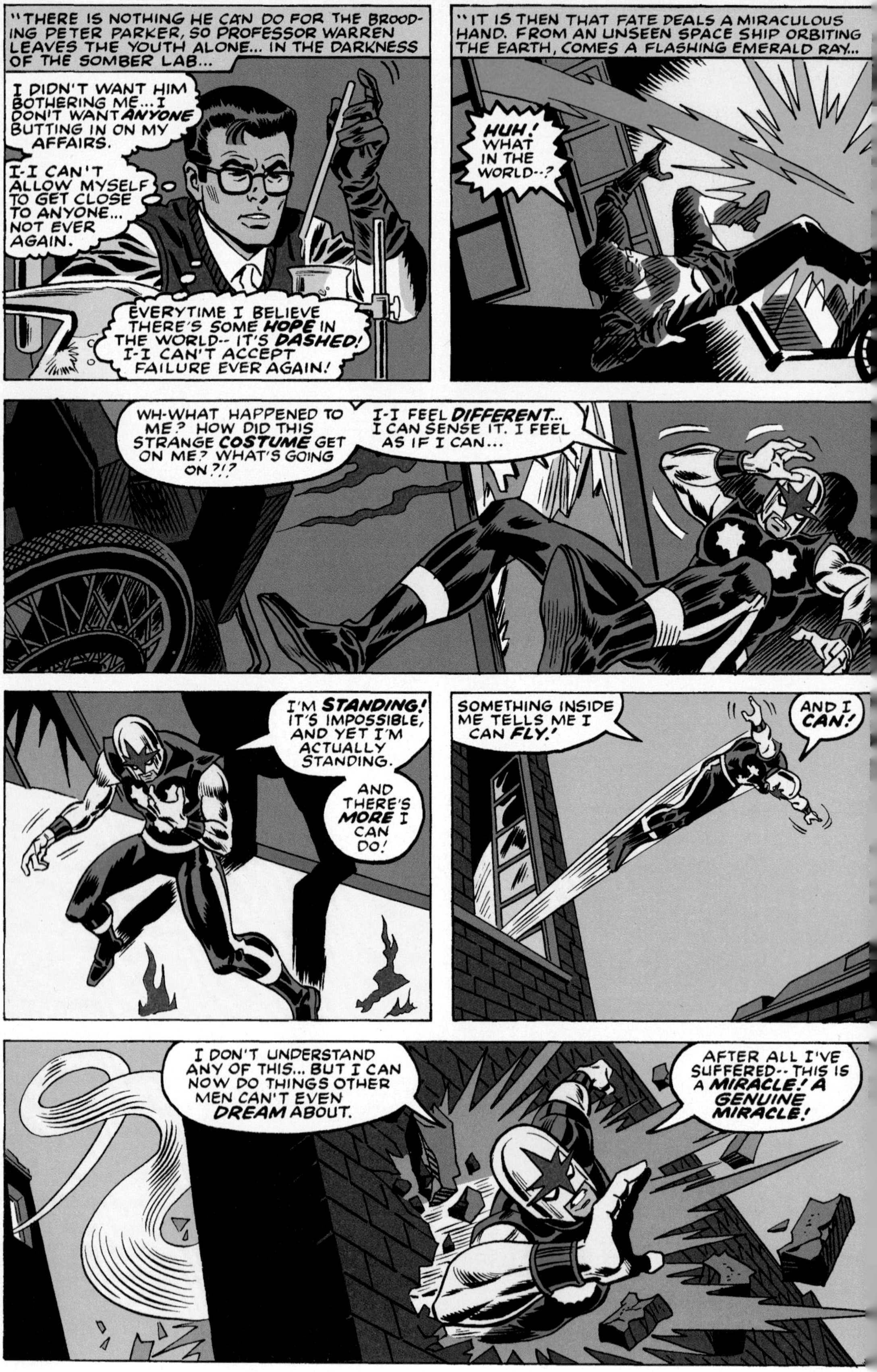
"THERE IS NOTHING HE CAN DO FOR THE BROODING PETER PARKER, SO PROFESSOR WARREN LEAVES THE YOUTH ALONE... IN THE DARKNESS OF THE SOMBER LAB...
I DIDN'T WANT HIM BOTHERING ME... I DON'T WANT ANYONE BUTTING IN ON MY AFFAIRS.
I-I CAN'T ALLOW MYSELF TO GET CLOSE TO ANYONE... NOT EVER AGAIN.
EVERYTIME I BELIEVE THERE'S SOME HOPE IN THE WORLD-- IT'S DASHED! I-I CAN'T ACCEPT FAILURE EVER AGAIN!
"IT IS THEN THAT FATE DEALS A MIRACULOUS HAND. FROM AN UNSEEN SPACE SHIP ORBITING THE EARTH, COMES A FLASHING EMERALD RAY...
HUH! WHAT IN THE WORLD--?
WH-WHAT HAPPENED TO ME? HOW DID THIS STRANGE COSTUME GET ON ME? WHAT'S GOING ON?!?
I-I FEEL DIFFERENT... I CAN SENSE IT. I FEEL AS IF I CAN...
I'M STANDING! IT'S IMPOSSIBLE, AND YET I'M ACTUALLY STANDING.
AND THERE'S MORE I CAN DO!
SOMETHING INSIDE ME TELLS ME I CAN FLY.
AND I CAN!
I DON'T UNDERSTAND ANY OF THIS... BUT I CAN NOW DO THINGS OTHER MEN CAN'T EVEN DREAM ABOUT.
AFTER ALL I'VE SUFFERED-- THIS IS A MIRACLE! A GENUINE MIRACLE!

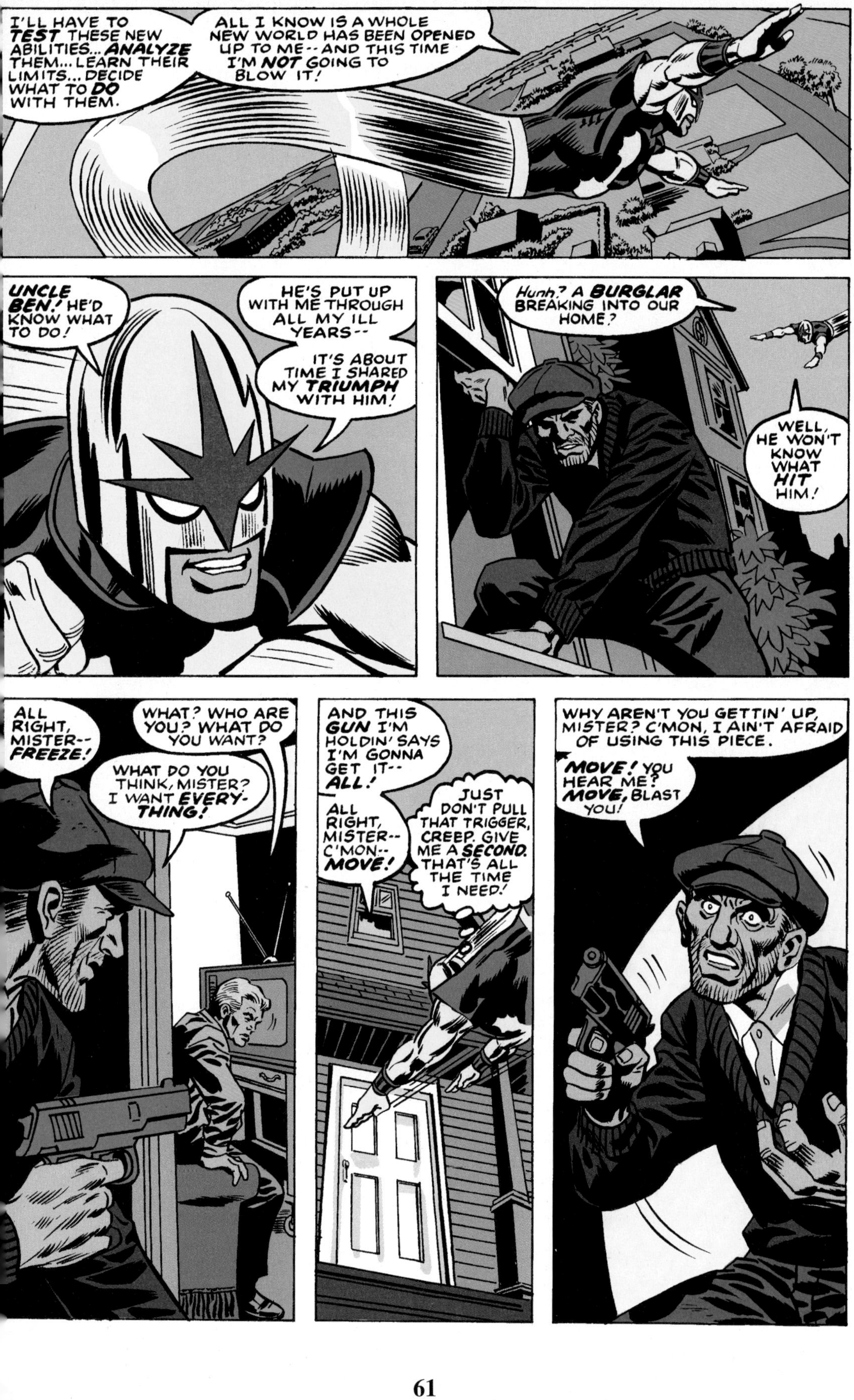
I'LL HAVE TO TEST THESE NEW ABILITIES... ANALYZE THEM... LEARN THEIR LIMITS... DECIDE WHAT TO DO WITH THEM.
ALL I KNOW IS A WHOLE NEW WORLD HAS BEEN OPENED UP TO ME--AND THIS TIME I'M NOT GOING TO BLOW IT!
UNCLE BEN! HE'D KNOW WHAT TO DO!
HE'S PUT UP WITH ME THROUGH ALL MY ILL YEARS--
IT'S ABOUT TIME I SHARED MY TRIUMPH WITH HIM!
Hunh? A BURGLAR BREAKING INTO OUR HOME?
WELL, HE WON'T KNOW WHAT HIT HIM!
ALL RIGHT, MISTER-- FREEZE!
WHAT? WHO ARE YOU? WHAT DO YOU WANT?
WHAT DO YOU THINK, MISTER? I WANT EVERY-THING!
AND THIS GUN I'M HOLDIN' SAYS I'M GONNA GET IT-- ALL!
ALL RIGHT, MISTER-- C'MON-- MOVE!
JUST DON'T PULL THAT TRIGGER, CREEP. GIVE ME A SECOND. THAT'S ALL THE TIME I NEED!
WHY AREN'T YOU GETTIN' UP, MISTER? C'MON, I AIN'T AFRAID OF USING THIS PIECE.
MOVE! YOU HEAR ME? MOVE, BLAST YOU!

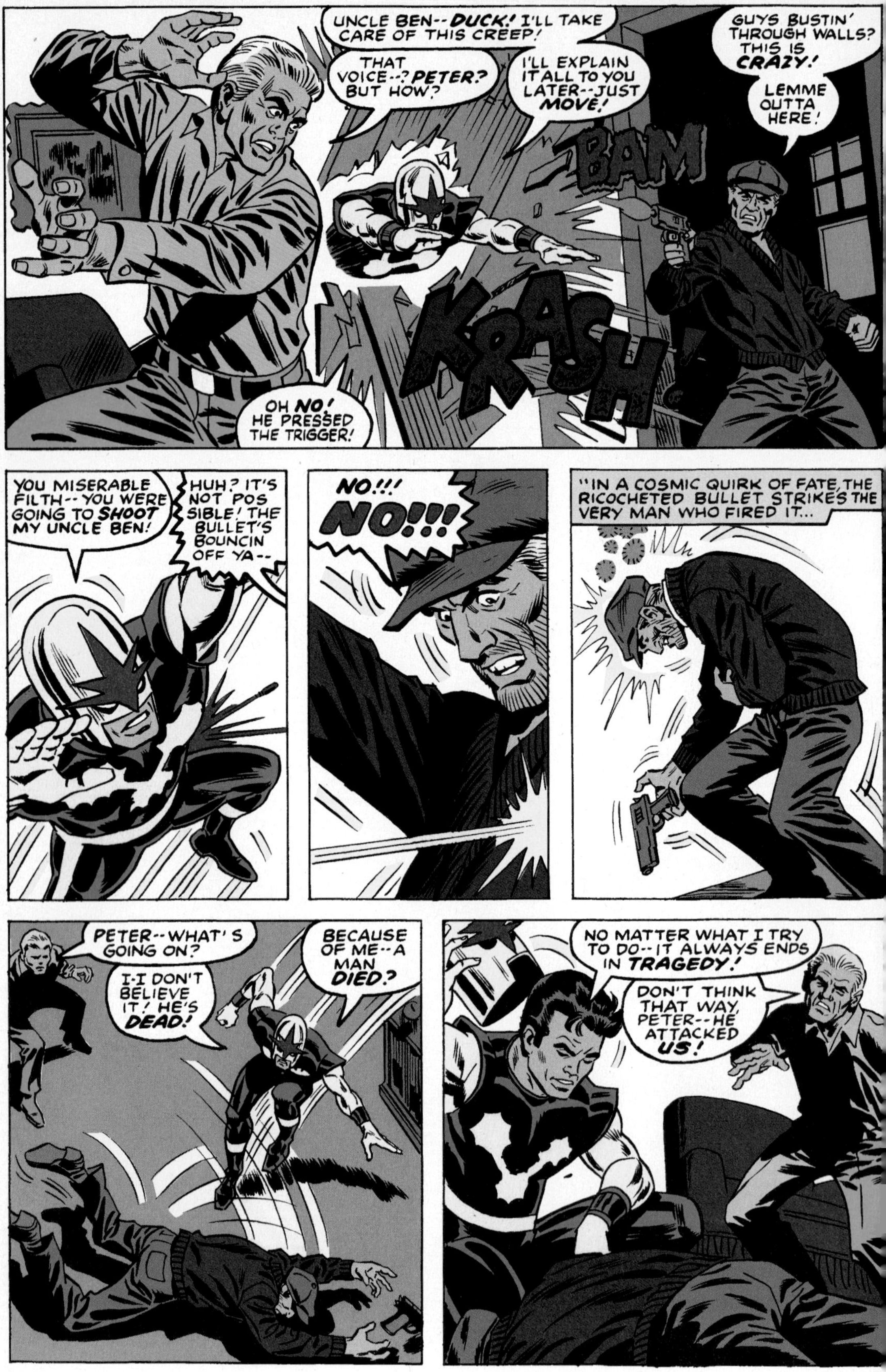
UNCLE BEN--DUCK! I'LL TAKE CARE OF THIS CREEP!
THAT VOICE--? PETER? BUT HOW?
I'LL EXPLAIN IT ALL TO YOU LATER--JUST MOVE!
GUYS BUSTIN' THROUGH WALLS? THIS IS CRAZY!
LEMME OUTTA HERE!
BAM
KRASH!
OH NO! HE PRESSED THE TRIGGER!
YOU MISERABLE FILTH--YOU WERE GOING TO SHOOT MY UNCLE BEN!
HUH? IT'S NOT POS SIBLE! THE BULLET'S BOUNCIN OFF YA--
NO!!! NO!!!
"IN A COSMIC QUIRK OF FATE, THE RICOCHETED BULLET STRIKES THE VERY MAN WHO FIRED IT...
PETER--WHAT'S GOING ON?
I-I DON'T BELIEVE IT! HE'S DEAD!
BECAUSE OF ME--A MAN DIED?
NO MATTER WHAT I TRY TO DO--IT ALWAYS ENDS IN TRAGEDY!
DON'T THINK THAT WAY, PETER--HE ATTACKED US!

YOU DON'T UNDERSTAND, UNCLE BEN... IT'S BEEN THIS WAY ALL MY *LIFE!*

AUNT MAY DIED BECAUSE OF ME... NOW THIS MAN.

IT'S ME... CAN'T YOU SEE IT? IT'S *ME!* I'M A *JINX!*

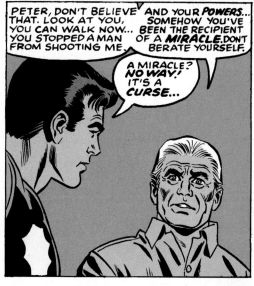

PETER, DON'T BELIEVE THAT. LOOK AT YOU, YOU CAN WALK NOW... YOU STOPPED A MAN FROM SHOOTING ME.

AND YOUR *POWERS*... SOMEHOW YOU'VE BEEN THE RECIPIENT OF A *MIRACLE.* DON'T BERATE YOURSELF.

A MIRACLE? *NO WAY!* IT'S A *CURSE...*

AND IT'S A CURSE I CAN'T *LIVE* WITH ANY LONGER.

HELLO... POLICE? THERE'S BEEN A *MURDER!*

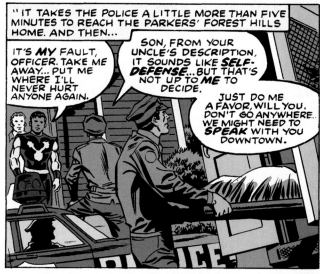

"IT TAKES THE POLICE A LITTLE MORE THAN FIVE MINUTES TO REACH THE PARKERS' FOREST HILLS HOME. AND THEN...

IT'S *MY* FAULT, OFFICER. TAKE ME AWAY... PUT ME WHERE I'LL NEVER HURT ANYONE AGAIN.

SON, FROM YOUR UNCLE'S DESCRIPTION, IT SOUNDS LIKE *SELF-DEFENSE*... BUT THAT'S NOT UP TO *ME* TO DECIDE.

JUST DO ME A FAVOR, WILL YOU... DON'T GO ANYWHERE... WE MIGHT NEED TO *SPEAK* WITH YOU DOWNTOWN.

"THE YOUTH IS ANGRY, EMBITTERED, AND HE ALLOWS HIS SELF-HATRED TO BLIND HIM TO THE TRUTH...

SO I GOT SUPER POWERS... AND WHAT DO I DO WITH THEM? I *KILL* SOME ONE!

WHAT IS IT ABOUT ME? WHATEVER I TOUCH *WITHERS AWAY*... DIES LIKE A FLOWER IN WINTER.

WELL, AS THEY SAY ABOUT HORSES AND WATER-- MAYBE I GOT SUPER-POWERS...

... BUT I DAMN WELL *DON'T* EVER HAVE TO USE THEM...

... DON'T HAVE TO USE THEM... EVER AGAIN...

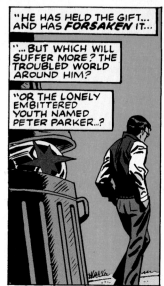

"HE HAS HELD THE GIFT... AND HAS *FORSAKEN* IT...

"... BUT WHICH WILL SUFFER MORE? THE TROUBLED WORLD AROUND HIM?

"OR THE LONELY EMBITTERED YOUTH NAMED PETER PARKER...?

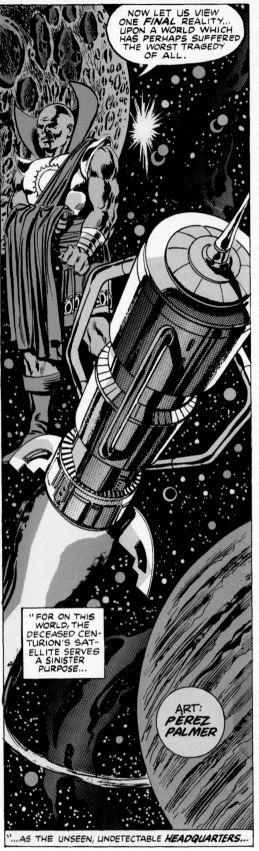

NOW LET US VIEW ONE *FINAL* REALITY... UPON A WORLD WHICH HAS PERHAPS SUFFERED THE WORST TRAGEDY OF ALL.

"FOR ON THIS WORLD, THE DECEASED CENTURION'S SATELLITE SERVES A SINISTER PURPOSE...

ART: PÉREZ PALMER

"...AS THE UNSEEN, UNDETECTABLE *HEADQUARTERS*...

"...OF THE WORLD'S MOST INFAMOUS *VILLAINS*...

IT IS *DONE.* THE FANTASTIC FOUR LIE *DEFEATED,* THEIR LIVES EXPUNGED BY THE PEERLESS POWER OF VICTOR VON DOOM!

AT LAST THE GAME IS *OVER!*

CAN'T YOU SIMPLY SAY THEY ARE *DEAD?* MUST YOU ALWAYS SPEAK AS THOUGH CONQUEST IS BUT A *RECREATION.*

ACTS OF TYRANNY AND MURDER SHOULD BE BASKED IN *FULLY,* DOOM, NOT HIDDEN AWAY WITH *WORDS!*

BAH! YOU SIMPLY FAIL TO UNDERSTAND THE *SUBTLETIES* OF CONQUEST!

LOOK, JUST THIS ONCE *CAN* THE PHILOSOPHICAL DEBATES!

I MEAN, WE SHOULD BE CELEBRATIN'! WE'VE DONE WHAT NO OTHER VILLAINS COULD EVER *DREAM!* BUT INSTEAD OF WHOOPING IT UP, YOU TWO KEEP *BICKERING--*

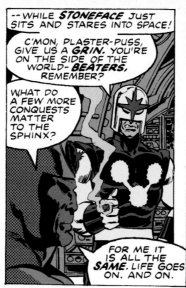

--WHILE *STONEFACE* JUST SITS AND STARES INTO SPACE!

C'MON, PLASTER-PUSS, GIVE US A *GRIN.* YOU'RE ON THE SIDE OF THE WORLD-*BEATERS,* REMEMBER?

WHAT DO A FEW MORE CONQUESTS MATTER TO THE SPHINX?

FOR ME IT IS ALL THE *SAME.* LIFE GOES ON. AND ON.

"...A FEW MORE CONQUESTS..."?! *THAT'S* HOW YOU SEE THIS-- AS JUST A FEW MORE CON-QUESTS?!/ MAYBE I'D BETTER REFRESH YOUR MEMORY A BIT, SPHINX! TAKE A GANDER AT THE *VIEWSCREEN.*

USIN' THE COMPUTER PRIME, WE'VE *OFFED* EVERY SUPERHERO ON EARTH! WE STRUCK WHEN WE WERE STRONGEST AND THEY WERE AT THEIR WEAKEST.

THE MACHINE IS RATHER A *SIMPLE* DEVICE, ACTUALLY-- AS I DISCOVERED ONCE I HAD THE OPPORTUNITY TO EXAMINE IT.

I SHOULD HAVE INVENTED A *SIMILAR* APARATUS LONG AGO.

BUT YOU *DIDN'T,* DOOM.

I *INHERITED* THAT MACHINE ALONG WITH MY *POWERS.* AND IT WAS *ALSO* ME WHO TRANSPORTED THE THREE OF US HERE.

I'M THE ORGANIZER OF THIS GROUP, AND DON'T ANY OF YOU *FORGET* IT!

BAH! IS THE PEASANT THAT *BUYS* THE HEN THE LAYER OF THE EGGS?

I *APPRECIATE* THE WAY YOU STATE YOUR POSITION, NOVA. IT IS SO REFRESHINGLY *DIRECT* NEXT TO DOOM'S CIRCUMLOCU-TIONS AND THE SPHINX' IRRITA-TING *SILENCES!*

THEN... A *TOAST* TO *NOVA,* MASTER OF THE MASTER VILLAINS!

"NOVA'S EXUBERANT TOAST IS MET WITH AN AWKWARD *SILENCE...*

"...FOR THE ASSEMBLAGE WHICH ORBITS THE NOW-DEFENSELESS EARTH IS AN *UNEASY ALLIANCE* AT BEST.

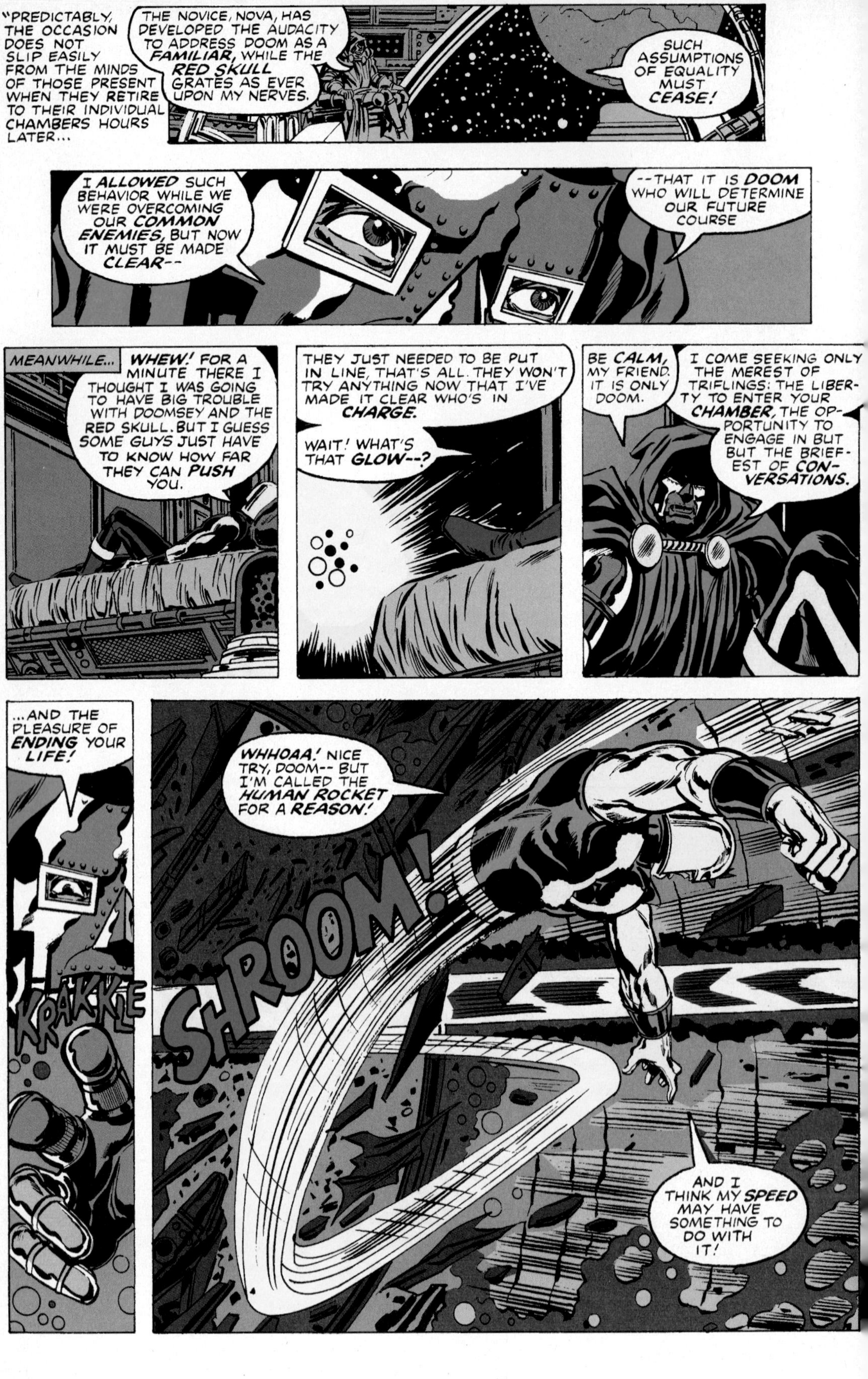
"PREDICTABLY, THE OCCASION DOES NOT SLIP EASILY FROM THE MINDS OF THOSE PRESENT WHEN THEY RETIRE TO THEIR INDIVIDUAL CHAMBERS HOURS LATER...
THE NOVICE, NOVA, HAS DEVELOPED THE AUDACITY TO ADDRESS DOOM AS A FAMILIAR, WHILE THE RED SKULL GRATES AS EVER UPON MY NERVES.
SUCH ASSUMPTIONS OF EQUALITY MUST CEASE!
I ALLOWED SUCH BEHAVIOR WHILE WE WERE OVERCOMING OUR COMMON ENEMIES, BUT NOW IT MUST BE MADE CLEAR--
--THAT IT IS DOOM WHO WILL DETERMINE OUR FUTURE COURSE
MEANWHILE...
WHEW! FOR A MINUTE THERE I THOUGHT I WAS GOING TO HAVE BIG TROUBLE WITH DOOMSEY AND THE RED SKULL. BUT I GUESS SOME GUYS JUST HAVE TO KNOW HOW FAR THEY CAN PUSH YOU.
THEY JUST NEEDED TO BE PUT IN LINE, THAT'S ALL. THEY WON'T TRY ANYTHING NOW THAT I'VE MADE IT CLEAR WHO'S IN CHARGE.
WAIT! WHAT'S THAT GLOW--?
BE CALM, MY FRIEND. IT IS ONLY DOOM.
I COME SEEKING ONLY THE MEREST OF TRIFLINGS: THE LIBERTY TO ENTER YOUR CHAMBER, THE OPPORTUNITY TO ENGAGE IN BUT BUT THE BRIEFEST OF CONVERSATIONS.
...AND THE PLEASURE OF ENDING YOUR LIFE!
KRAKKLE
WHHOAA! NICE TRY, DOOM-- BUT I'M CALLED THE HUMAN ROCKET FOR A REASON!
SHROOM!
AND I THINK MY SPEED MAY HAVE SOMETHING TO DO WITH IT!

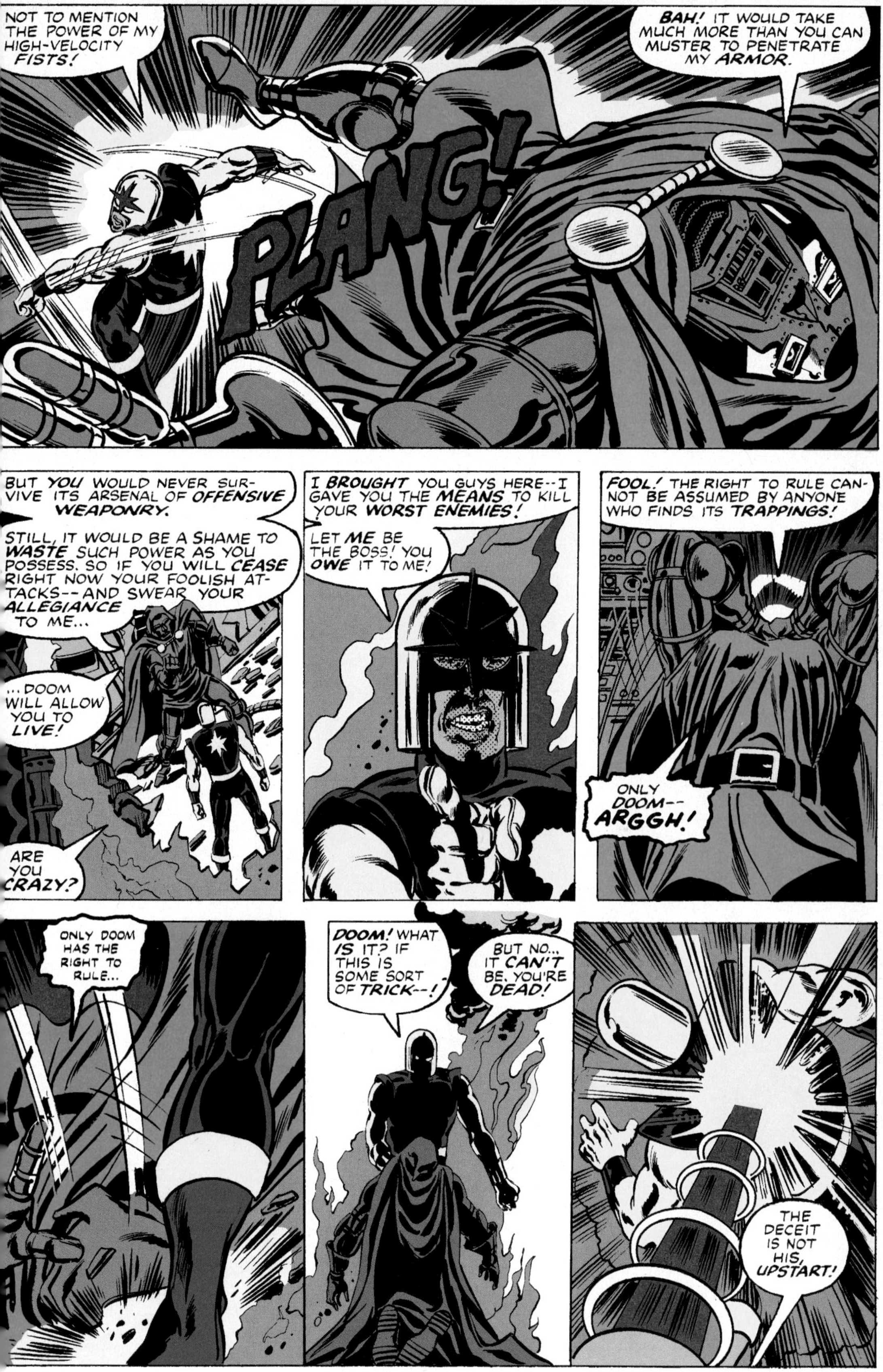
NOT TO MENTION THE POWER OF MY HIGH-VELOCITY FISTS!
BAH! IT WOULD TAKE MUCH MORE THAN YOU CAN MUSTER TO PENETRATE MY ARMOR.
PLANG!
BUT YOU WOULD NEVER SURVIVE ITS ARSENAL OF OFFENSIVE WEAPONRY.
STILL, IT WOULD BE A SHAME TO WASTE SUCH POWER AS YOU POSSESS. SO IF YOU WILL CEASE RIGHT NOW YOUR FOOLISH ATTACKS--AND SWEAR YOUR ALLEGIANCE TO ME...
...DOOM WILL ALLOW YOU TO LIVE!
ARE YOU CRAZY?
I BROUGHT YOU GUYS HERE--I GAVE YOU THE MEANS TO KILL YOUR WORST ENEMIES!
LET ME BE THE BOSS! YOU OWE IT TO ME!
FOOL! THE RIGHT TO RULE CANNOT BE ASSUMED BY ANYONE WHO FINDS ITS TRAPPINGS!
ONLY DOOM-- ARGGH!
ONLY DOOM HAS THE RIGHT TO RULE...
DOOM! WHAT IS IT? IF THIS IS SOME SORT OF TRICK--!
BUT NO... IT CAN'T BE. YOU'RE DEAD!
THE DECEIT IS NOT HIS, UPSTART!

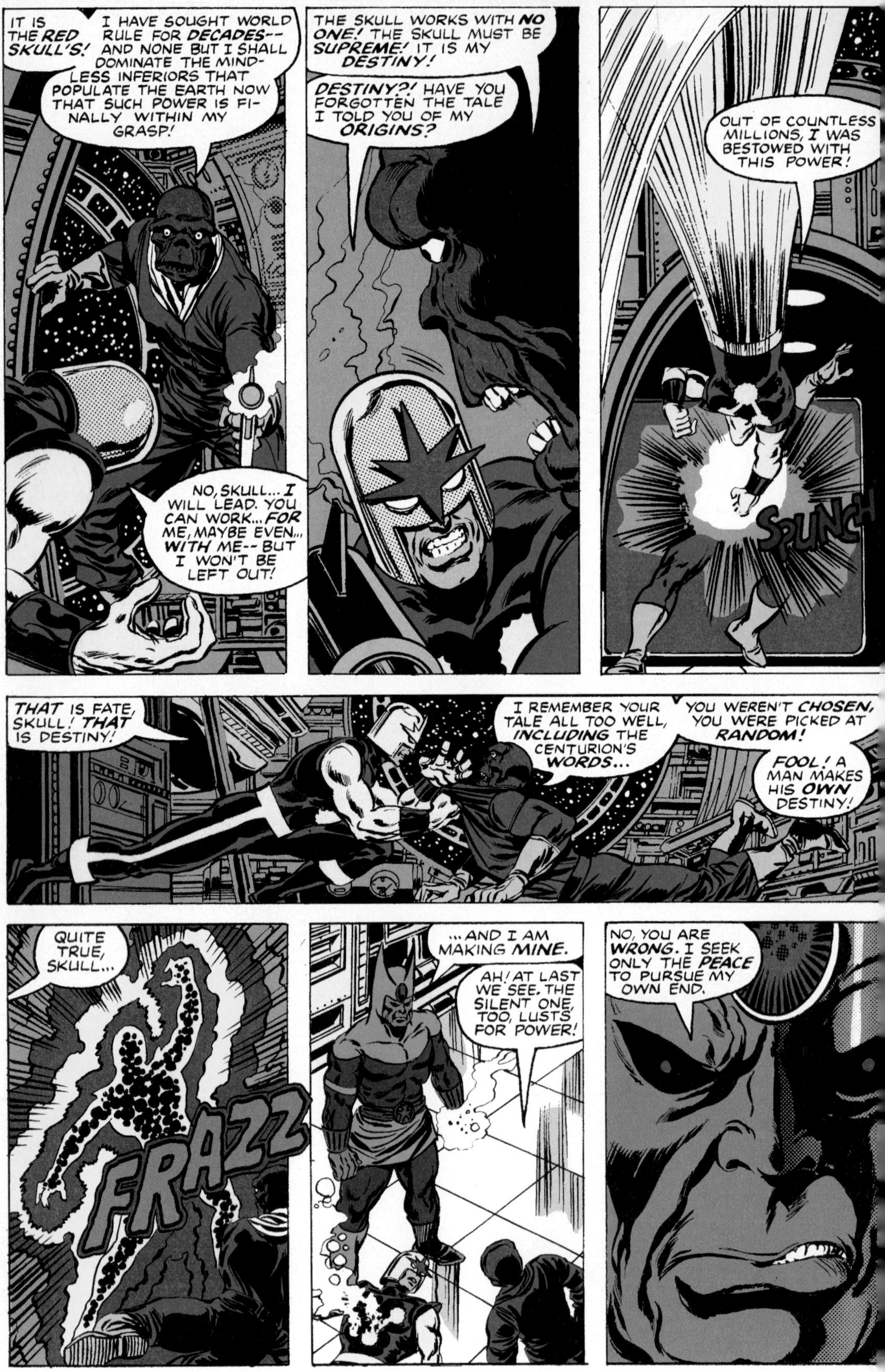
IT IS THE RED SKULL'S!
I HAVE SOUGHT WORLD RULE FOR DECADES-- AND NONE BUT I SHALL DOMINATE THE MINDLESS INFERIORS THAT POPULATE THE EARTH NOW THAT SUCH POWER IS FINALLY WITHIN MY GRASP!
NO, SKULL... I WILL LEAD. YOU CAN WORK... FOR ME, MAYBE EVEN... WITH ME-- BUT I WON'T BE LEFT OUT!
THE SKULL WORKS WITH NO ONE! THE SKULL MUST BE SUPREME! IT IS MY DESTINY!
DESTINY?! HAVE YOU FORGOTTEN THE TALE I TOLD YOU OF MY ORIGINS?
OUT OF COUNTLESS MILLIONS, I WAS BESTOWED WITH THIS POWER!
SPUNCH
THAT IS FATE, SKULL! THAT IS DESTINY!
I REMEMBER YOUR TALE ALL TOO WELL, INCLUDING THE CENTURION'S WORDS...
YOU WEREN'T CHOSEN, YOU WERE PICKED AT RANDOM!
FOOL! A MAN MAKES HIS OWN DESTINY!
QUITE TRUE, SKULL...
FRAZZ
...AND I AM MAKING MINE.
AH! AT LAST WE SEE. THE SILENT ONE, TOO, LUSTS FOR POWER!
NO, YOU ARE WRONG. I SEEK ONLY THE PEACE TO PURSUE MY OWN END.

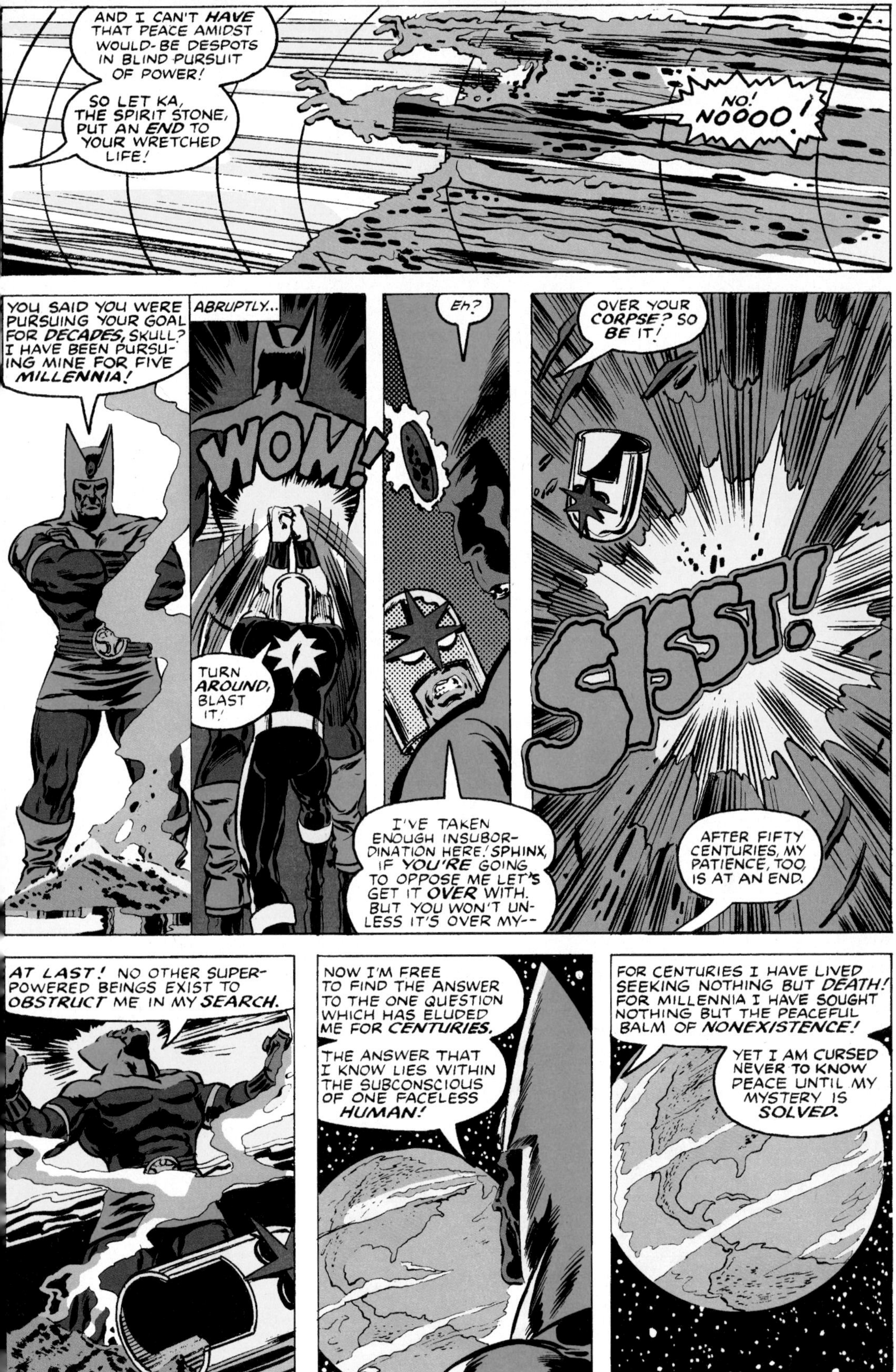
AND I CAN'T HAVE THAT PEACE AMIDST WOULD-BE DESPOTS IN BLIND PURSUIT OF POWER!
SO LET KA, THE SPIRIT STONE, PUT AN END TO YOUR WRETCHED LIFE!
NO! NOOOO!
YOU SAID YOU WERE PURSUING YOUR GOAL FOR DECADES, SKULL? I HAVE BEEN PURSUING MINE FOR FIVE MILLENNIA!
ABRUPTLY...
WOM!
TURN AROUND, BLAST IT!
Eh?
I'VE TAKEN ENOUGH INSUBORDINATION HERE! SPHINX, IF YOU'RE GOING TO OPPOSE ME LET'S GET IT OVER WITH. BUT YOU WON'T UNLESS IT'S OVER MY--
OVER YOUR CORPSE? SO BE IT!
SISST!
AFTER FIFTY CENTURIES, MY PATIENCE, TOO, IS AT AN END.
AT LAST! NO OTHER SUPER-POWERED BEINGS EXIST TO OBSTRUCT ME IN MY SEARCH.
NOW I'M FREE TO FIND THE ANSWER TO THE ONE QUESTION WHICH HAS ELUDED ME FOR CENTURIES.
THE ANSWER THAT I KNOW LIES WITHIN THE SUBCONSCIOUS OF ONE FACELESS HUMAN!
FOR CENTURIES I HAVE LIVED SEEKING NOTHING BUT DEATH! FOR MILLENNIA I HAVE SOUGHT NOTHING BUT THE PEACEFUL BALM OF NONEXISTENCE!
YET I AM CURSED NEVER TO KNOW PEACE UNTIL MY MYSTERY IS SOLVED.

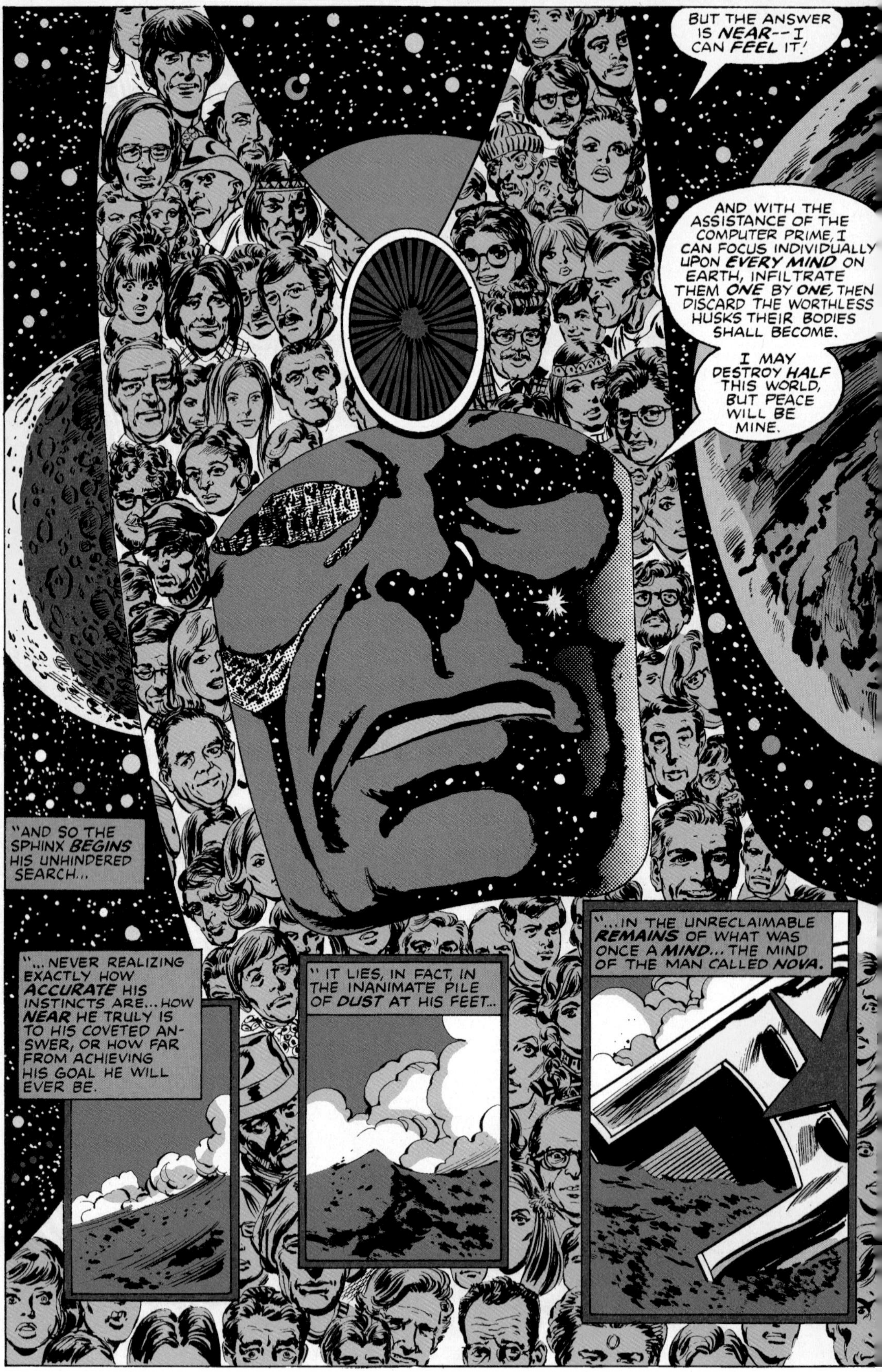
BUT THE ANSWER IS NEAR--I CAN FEEL IT!
AND WITH THE ASSISTANCE OF THE COMPUTER PRIME, I CAN FOCUS INDIVIDUALLY UPON EVERY MIND ON EARTH, INFILTRATE THEM ONE BY ONE, THEN DISCARD THE WORTHLESS HUSKS THEIR BODIES SHALL BECOME.
I MAY DESTROY HALF THIS WORLD, BUT PEACE WILL BE MINE.
"AND SO THE SPHINX BEGINS HIS UNHINDERED SEARCH...
"...NEVER REALIZING EXACTLY HOW ACCURATE HIS INSTINCTS ARE... HOW NEAR HE TRULY IS TO HIS COVETED ANSWER, OR HOW FAR FROM ACHIEVING HIS GOAL HE WILL EVER BE.
" IT LIES, IN FACT, IN THE INANIMATE PILE OF DUST AT HIS FEET...
"...IN THE UNRECLAIMABLE REMAINS OF WHAT WAS ONCE A MIND... THE MIND OF THE MAN CALLED NOVA.

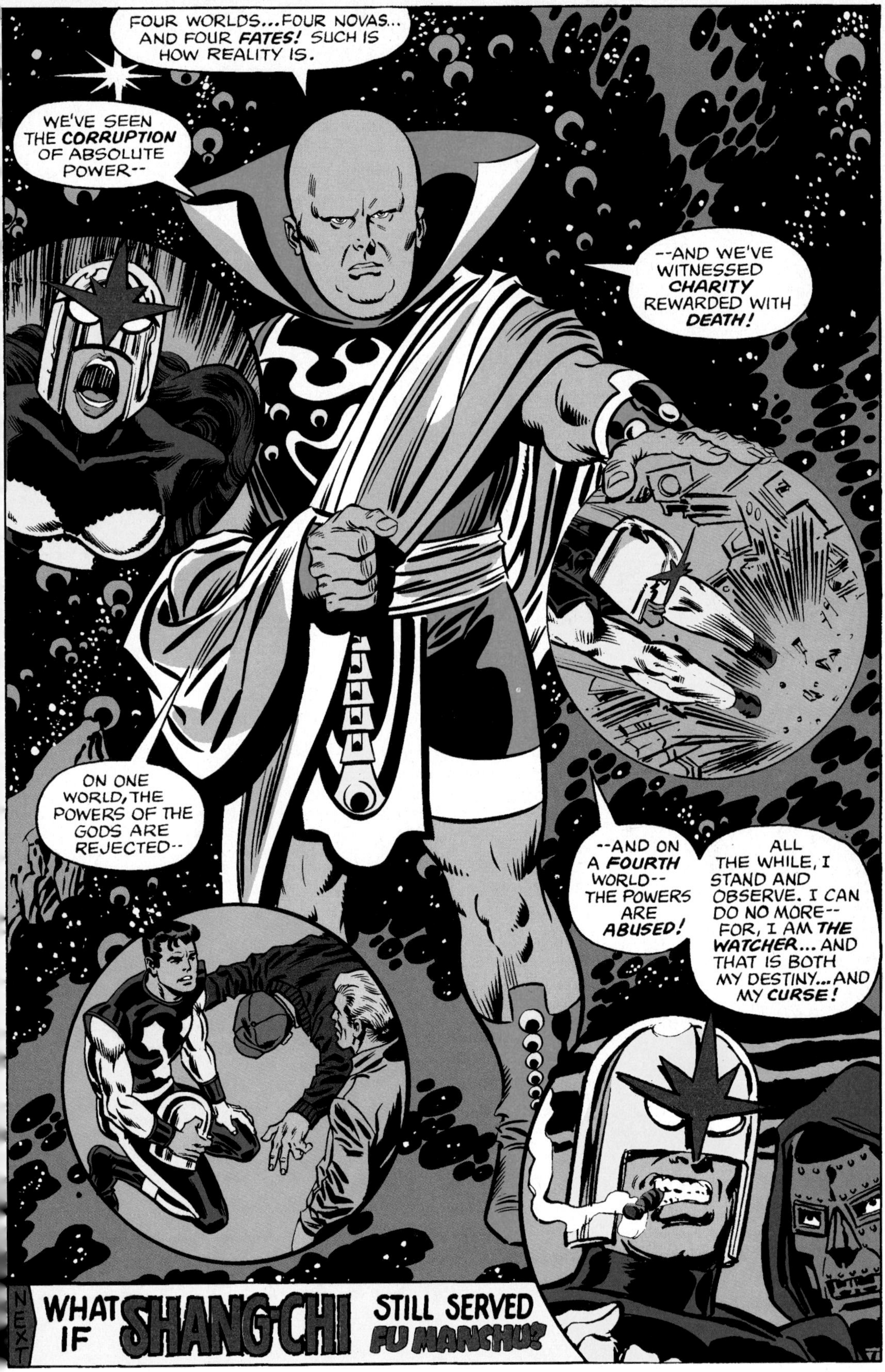
FOUR WORLDS...FOUR NOVAS... AND FOUR FATES! SUCH IS HOW REALITY IS.
WE'VE SEEN THE CORRUPTION OF ABSOLUTE POWER--
--AND WE'VE WITNESSED CHARITY REWARDED WITH DEATH!
ON ONE WORLD, THE POWERS OF THE GODS ARE REJECTED--
--AND ON A FOURTH WORLD-- THE POWERS ARE ABUSED!
ALL THE WHILE, I STAND AND OBSERVE. I CAN DO NO MORE-- FOR, I AM THE WATCHER... AND THAT IS BOTH MY DESTINY...AND MY CURSE!
NEXT
WHAT IF SHANG-CHI STILL SERVED FU MANCHU?

WHY NOT?

c/o MARVEL COMICS GROUP
575 Madison Avenue
New York, New York 10022

ROY THOMAS
EDITOR
MARK GRUENWALD
ASSISTANT EDITOR

Dear Roy,

It's strange. This was the comic that I dreaded. I thought that a brilliant character would be ruined because of the publication of this comic. In fact, I very nearly didn't buy it because I was sure I would hate it. However, curiosity prevailed. I bought it. I loved it more than any other comic I've ever read. The reason I loved this comic so much was that the supporting character was the most beautiful person I've ever seen.

Oh yes. The comic was "What If Conan Walked the Earth Today?" The character was Danette.

Before I talk about Danette in particular, let me talk about the comic as a whole. Roy, I can't believe it. I visualized the comic as a rip-off item. I couldn't conceive such a story being the sensitive work of art that you made it. It seems you took everything into consideration.

First of all, there was the language barrier, and this was very sensitively handled. More importantly, your handling of Conan as a character in 1977 was brilliant. The task, I thought, was impossible, and hence I thought Conan's character would be degraded as a result of his time travel. The Conan we know and love— the thief, the reaver, the slayer— could not possibly be a sympathetic character in 1977. How could we sympathize with a character who would lop off the head of one of New York's finest at the slightest threat? To have Conan behave otherwise would mean compromising his character.

Thus, I reasoned logically, there was no conceivable way to satisfy both the purists and the casual reader. I was wrong. You did it. You keyed on Conan's tendency towards impulse and actually stated that, on another occasion, he might choose to do something that would not be acceptable to our moral sensibilities. Good reasons are given for all his out-of-character actions. He didn't kill the thieves in front of Danette's place because she didn't want him to. He didn't *join* the thieves because he was protecting Danette. He didn't try to kill the "city guards" because Danette kept him away from them. Finally, with Danette unconscious and his protective instinct at its peak, he does what the purist fully expects: he brutally kills five thieves.

Still, our modern moral dignity is not aroused because the victims are all unsavory and murderous characters. Still, Roy, you never suggest once that Conan wouldn't be equally brutal to the "good guys" if he felt threatened. We are left with the feeling that it is just chance that none of the "good guys" were killed, thereby satisfying the purists.

For the above reasons I consider the story an unqualified success. Obviously, a lot of thought went into this tale. I imagine you yourself were somewhat hesitant about attempting it. In any event, had the above been all you did, I would consider the story a superior CONAN story. The extra touch made it a classic.

Danette is the most moving character I have ever encountered in a comic, perhaps anywhere. She is totally unselfish and yet totally alone. Her loneliness accentuates her unselfishness. First of all, she immediately tries to protect Conan even though he attacked her cab, perhaps because she can understand his sense of alienation because he can't speak her language. Next, she takes him to her apartment, where we learn of her loneliness. This loneliness is apparent from your script, Roy, but it's John's pencils that really emphasize it. Danette's face on page 24, panel 3, exudes loneliness. It was the best picture I've ever seen of what I would imagine is the hardest emotion to portray. In any event, we know she's "alone in this mad, monstrous world," but now she's got Conan.

However, she realizes that Conan wants to return to where he came from, so she immediately tries to help him. She doesn't even ask herself, "Should I help him or should I just keep him

with me?" She just helps him, even though she knows it will mean losing him if she succeeds. Then, in the museum, when she is grabbed by the "Professor" as a hostage, she risks her life and kicks him rather than let him shoot Conan. When she's free, she tells Conan to run, rather than screaming for him to save her, and is shot for her pains. Next, when all the fighting is done, with Conan victorious, she wakes up and *she* asks *Conan* if *he* is okay— and is worried because she sees that he has been hurt. Now those wounds were scratches to Conan, whereas her wound was enough to knock her out, and yet she worries about him.

Danette is a beautiful person and should not be left in comic limbo. I would like to meet her. Maybe some day I will. Maybe I already have. My girlfriend is a lot like her, but without the empty loneliness. In any case, I think you should introduce Danette into the real Marvel world. Perhaps THE HULK would be a good magazine for her to appear in. She worked so well with Conan, and I can't think of any Marvel character that more closely approximates Conan in the 70's.

"The Great Aims"
Queens University
Kingston, Ont., Canada

We (that means Roy) chose your letter not only because it was one of the first to arrive, but because it seemed to sum up so much of what a horde of Conan-lovers adored about WHAT IF #13. We'd be liars (which we ain't) if we said there were no detractors at all among the responders— but the overwhelming majority of fans, both of Conan and of WHAT IF itself, were wildly extravagant in their praise for the story, even if rarely so eloquent as yourself. Thus, rather than print random paragraphs from many letters, we decided to let your letter speak for all.

A few hasty notes, however, just to set things straight:

(1) While Big John Buscema did indeed outdo himself penciling the issue, it was Earnest Ernie Chan who was primarily responsible for one of the major artistic qualities for which you laud the issue. Most importantly, it was he who, working over John's rough pencils, turned the lady cabbie Danette from a standard comicbook heroine into a very particular lass, which we feel gave the feeling of individuality you loved in the artwork. Y'see, while attending Phil Seuling's lavish comic-art convention in Philadelphia and New York in the summer of '78, Roy was accompanied by his own lovely strawberry-blonde lady...whose name just happens to be Danette. Roy had indeed been wrestling for some months with certain aspects of the long-delayed "Conan in the 70's" epic, and it was his decision to use Danette as the heroine (at least in physical aspects and certain character traits) that fired him with enthusiasm for the project when various problems raised their hydra-like heads. The photographs, taken by professional photographer/journalist Nick Arroyo were not available when John penciled the story, so Ernie volunteered to render a likeness of the real Danette in close-ups.

(2) It is unlikely that Danette will ever again appear in any Marvel comic. She and Roy would like that character to stand alone in that single special issue, as one of the women Conan encounters in his wild road to kingdom— the *only* one in the Twentieth Century, of course. Nor, we fervently hope, will there ever be a *sequel* to WHAT IF #13, no matter what the sales (we suspect they will be very good indeed) of the issue. If Conan ever again visits the 1970's or 1980's, it will certainly be over Roy's loudest, sincerest protests— and frankly we just don't think it will happen. We're commercial; we are not necessarily as crass as our harshest critics prefer to believe.

So, if you liked WHAT IF #13, treasure it, friend. You'll not see its like again. But thanks. . . for understanding.

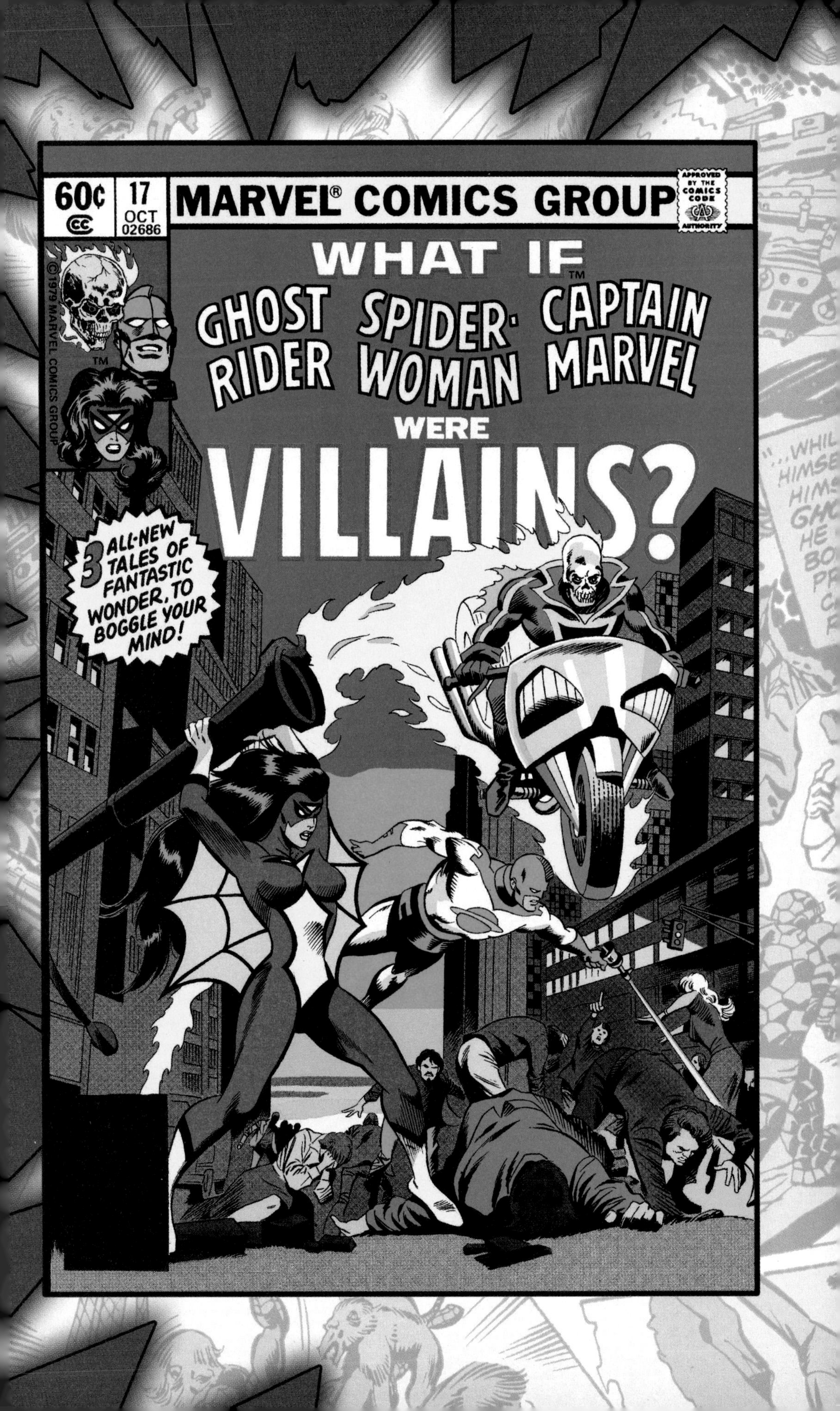
60¢
CC
17
OCT
02686
MARVEL® COMICS GROUP
APPROVED BY THE COMICS CODE AUTHORITY
©1979 MARVEL COMICS GROUP
TM
WHAT IF™
GHOST RIDER SPIDER-WOMAN CAPTAIN MARVEL
WERE
VILLAINS?
3 ALL-NEW TALES OF FANTASTIC WONDER, TO BOGGLE YOUR MIND!

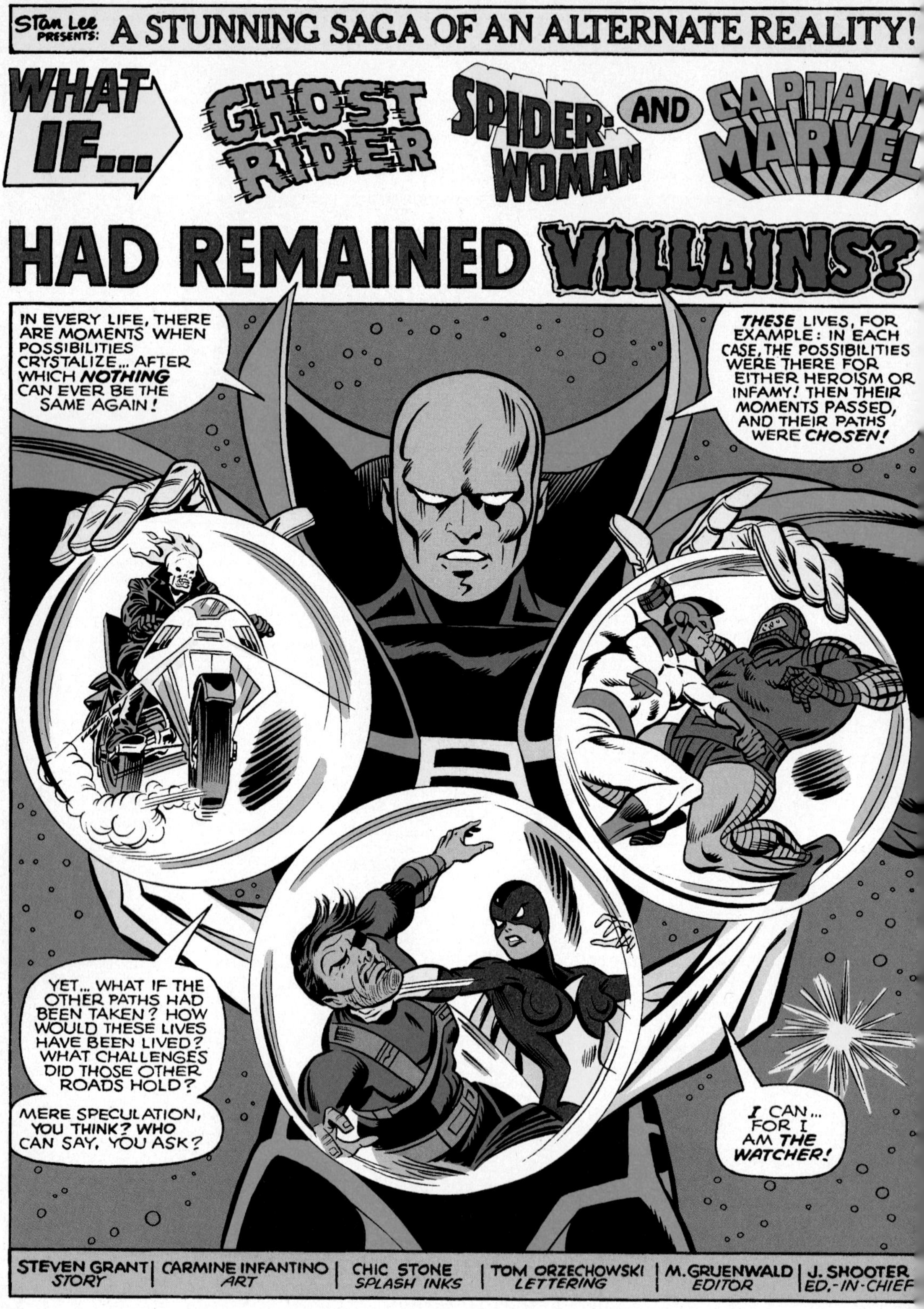
Stan Lee PRESENTS: A STUNNING SAGA OF AN ALTERNATE REALITY!
WHAT IF... GHOST RIDER SPIDER-WOMAN AND CAPTAIN MARVEL
HAD REMAINED VILLAINS?
IN EVERY LIFE, THERE ARE MOMENTS WHEN POSSIBILITIES CRYSTALIZE... AFTER WHICH NOTHING CAN EVER BE THE SAME AGAIN!
THESE LIVES, FOR EXAMPLE: IN EACH CASE, THE POSSIBILITIES WERE THERE FOR EITHER HEROISM OR INFAMY! THEN THEIR MOMENTS PASSED, AND THEIR PATHS WERE CHOSEN!
YET... WHAT IF THE OTHER PATHS HAD BEEN TAKEN? HOW WOULD THESE LIVES HAVE BEEN LIVED? WHAT CHALLENGES DID THOSE OTHER ROADS HOLD?
MERE SPECULATION, YOU THINK? WHO CAN SAY, YOU ASK?
I CAN... FOR I AM THE WATCHER!
STEVEN GRANT STORY | CARMINE INFANTINO ART | CHIC STONE SPLASH INKS | TOM ORZECHOWSKI LETTERING | M. GRUENWALD EDITOR | J. SHOOTER ED.-IN-CHIEF

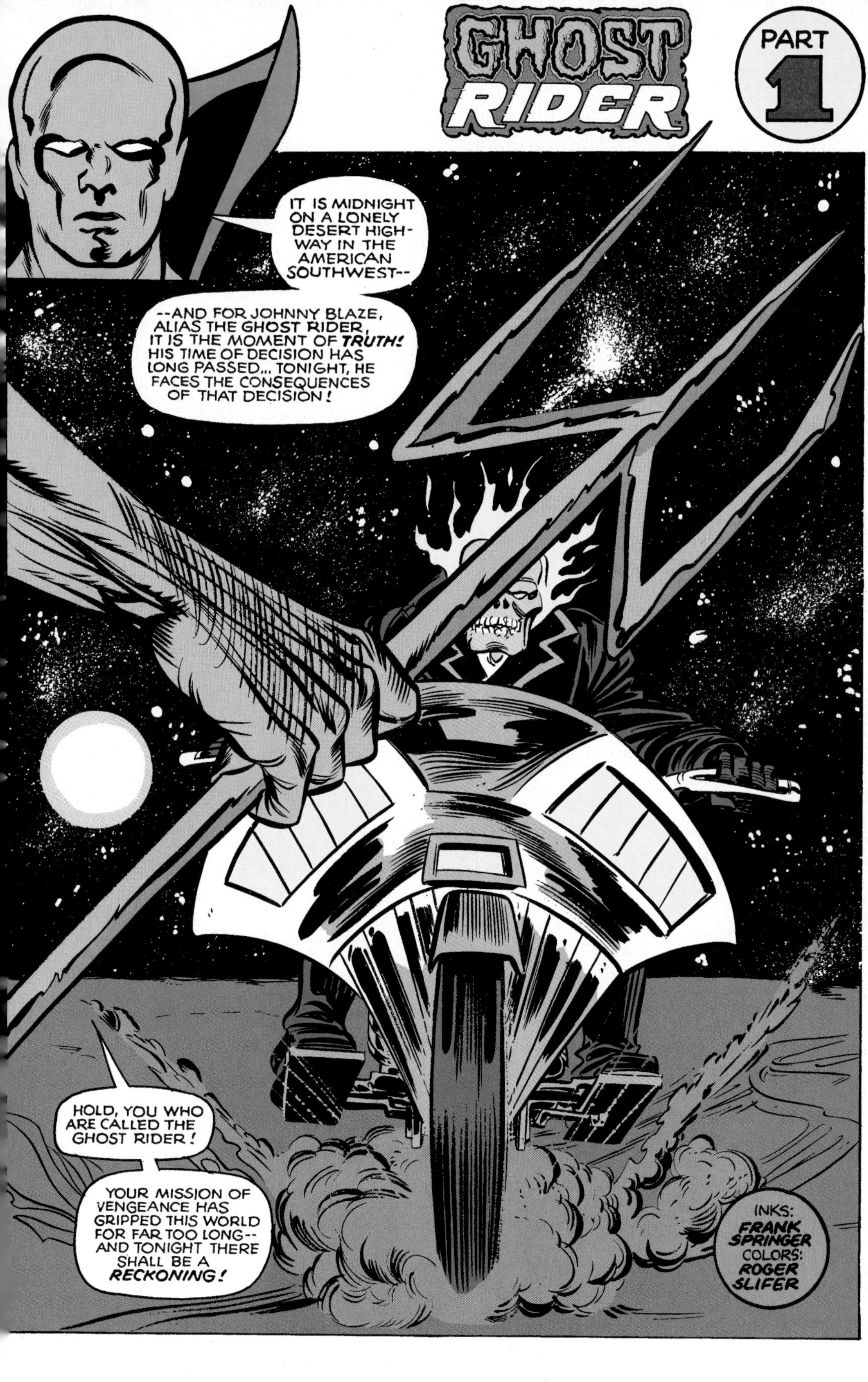
GHOST RIDER
PART 1
IT IS MIDNIGHT ON A LONELY DESERT HIGHWAY IN THE AMERICAN SOUTHWEST--
--AND FOR JOHNNY BLAZE, ALIAS THE GHOST RIDER, IT IS THE MOMENT OF TRUTH! HIS TIME OF DECISION HAS LONG PASSED... TONIGHT, HE FACES THE CONSEQUENCES OF THAT DECISION!
HOLD, YOU WHO ARE CALLED THE GHOST RIDER!
YOUR MISSION OF VENGEANCE HAS GRIPPED THIS WORLD FOR FAR TOO LONG-- AND TONIGHT THERE SHALL BE A RECKONING!
INKS: FRANK SPRINGER COLORS: ROGER SLIFER

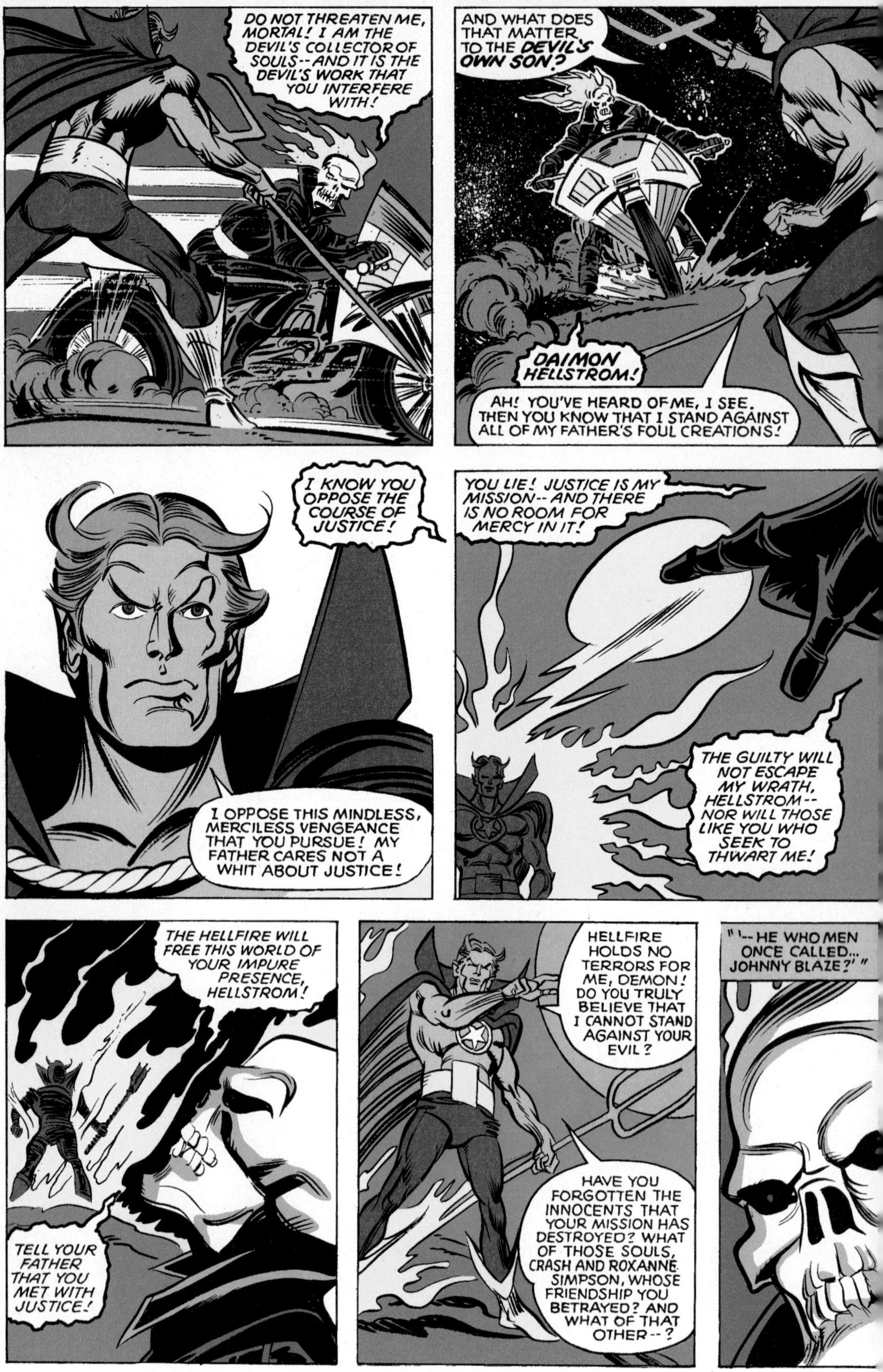

DO NOT THREATEN ME, MORTAL! I AM THE DEVIL'S COLLECTOR OF SOULS--AND IT IS THE DEVIL'S WORK THAT YOU INTERFERE WITH!
AND WHAT DOES THAT MATTER TO THE DEVIL'S OWN SON?
DAIMON HELLSTROM!
AH! YOU'VE HEARD OF ME, I SEE. THEN YOU KNOW THAT I STAND AGAINST ALL OF MY FATHER'S FOUL CREATIONS!
I KNOW YOU OPPOSE THE COURSE OF JUSTICE!
I OPPOSE THIS MINDLESS, MERCILESS VENGEANCE THAT YOU PURSUE! MY FATHER CARES NOT A WHIT ABOUT JUSTICE!
YOU LIE! JUSTICE IS MY MISSION--AND THERE IS NO ROOM FOR MERCY IN IT!
THE GUILTY WILL NOT ESCAPE MY WRATH, HELLSTROM--NOR WILL THOSE LIKE YOU WHO SEEK TO THWART ME!
THE HELLFIRE WILL FREE THIS WORLD OF YOUR IMPURE PRESENCE, HELLSTROM!
TELL YOUR FATHER THAT YOU MET WITH JUSTICE!
HELLFIRE HOLDS NO TERRORS FOR ME, DEMON! DO YOU TRULY BELIEVE THAT I CANNOT STAND AGAINST YOUR EVIL?
HAVE YOU FORGOTTEN THE INNOCENTS THAT YOUR MISSION HAS DESTROYED? WHAT OF THOSE SOULS, CRASH AND ROXANNE SIMPSON, WHOSE FRIENDSHIP YOU BETRAYED? AND WHAT OF THAT OTHER--?
"'--HE WHO MEN ONCE CALLED... JOHNNY BLAZE?'"

"INVOLUNTARILY, THE SKULL-FACED WRAITH REMEMBERS THE EVENTS THAT LED TO HIS DAMNATION..."

HELLO? ALFIE? WHAT'S -- *WHAT?* YOU GOT IT?

DAD! WE'VE DONE IT! THE CYCLE SHOW'S BEEN BOOKED INTO *MADISON SQUARE GARDEN!*

THAT'S GREAT, ROCKY HONEY! THAT'S REAL GREAT!

I DON'T GET IT, CRASH! YOU'VE BEEN WAITING FOR THIS ALL YOUR LIFE -- AND NOW YOU ACT LIKE IT'S *NOTHING!*

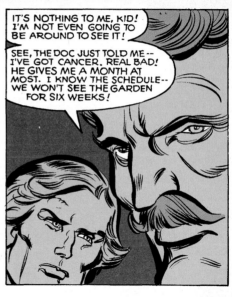

IT'S NOTHING TO ME, KID! I'M NOT EVEN GOING TO BE AROUND TO SEE IT!

SEE, THE DOC JUST TOLD ME -- I'VE GOT CANCER. REAL BAD! HE GIVES ME A MONTH AT MOST. I KNOW THE SCHEDULE -- WE WON'T SEE THE GARDEN FOR SIX WEEKS!

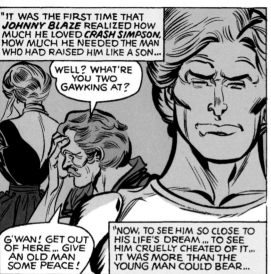

"IT WAS THE FIRST TIME THAT *JOHNNY BLAZE* REALIZED HOW MUCH HE LOVED *CRASH SIMPSON*, HOW MUCH HE NEEDED THE MAN WHO HAD RAISED HIM LIKE A SON..."

WELL? WHAT'RE YOU TWO GAWKING AT?

G'WAN! GET OUT OF HERE... GIVE AN OLD MAN SOME PEACE!

"NOW, TO SEE HIM SO CLOSE TO HIS LIFE'S DREAM ... TO SEE HIM CRUELLY CHEATED OF IT... IT WAS MORE THAN THE YOUNG MAN COULD BEAR..."

"...SO JOHNNY BLAZE TURNED TO SUPERNATURAL AID..."

HEAR ME, SATAN! APPEAR, O PRINCE OF DARKNESS! YOUR HUMBLE SERVANT BECKONS!

THROUGH TIME ETERNAL, THROUGH ENDLESS SPACE, I BEG THEE JOURNEY TO THIS PLACE!

"THE ROOM IS STILL AND SILENT, AND FOR A MOMENT -- ONLY A MOMENT -- JOHNNY BLAZE THINKS THAT HE HAS FAILED..."

"...AND THEN ALL HELL BREAKS LOOSE!"

SATAN HAS ANSWERED! FROM THE DEPTHS OF HELL, I COME TO AID HIM WHO WILL SERVE ME!

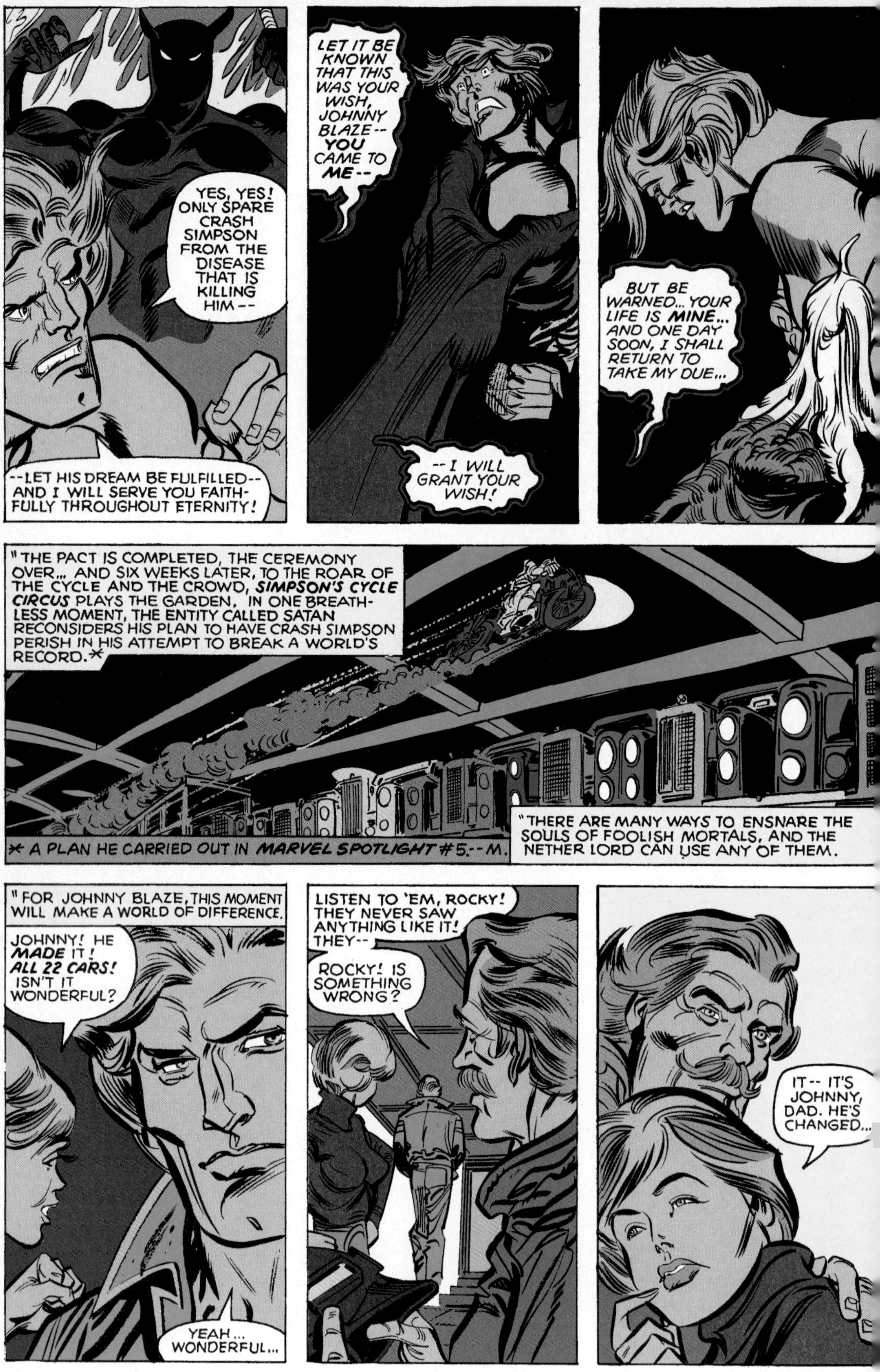
YES, YES! ONLY SPARE CRASH SIMPSON FROM THE DISEASE THAT IS KILLING HIM--
--LET HIS DREAM BE FULFILLED-- AND I WILL SERVE YOU FAITHFULLY THROUGHOUT ETERNITY!
LET IT BE KNOWN THAT THIS WAS YOUR WISH, JOHNNY BLAZE-- YOU CAME TO ME--
--I WILL GRANT YOUR WISH!
BUT BE WARNED... YOUR LIFE IS MINE... AND ONE DAY SOON, I SHALL RETURN TO TAKE MY DUE...
"THE PACT IS COMPLETED, THE CEREMONY OVER... AND SIX WEEKS LATER, TO THE ROAR OF THE CYCLE AND THE CROWD, SIMPSON'S CYCLE CIRCUS PLAYS THE GARDEN. IN ONE BREATHLESS MOMENT, THE ENTITY CALLED SATAN RECONSIDERS HIS PLAN TO HAVE CRASH SIMPSON PERISH IN HIS ATTEMPT TO BREAK A WORLD'S RECORD.*
* A PLAN HE CARRIED OUT IN MARVEL SPOTLIGHT #5.--M.
"THERE ARE MANY WAYS TO ENSNARE THE SOULS OF FOOLISH MORTALS, AND THE NETHER LORD CAN USE ANY OF THEM.
"FOR JOHNNY BLAZE, THIS MOMENT WILL MAKE A WORLD OF DIFFERENCE.
JOHNNY! HE MADE IT! ALL 22 CARS! ISN'T IT WONDERFUL?
YEAH... WONDERFUL...
LISTEN TO 'EM, ROCKY! THEY NEVER SAW ANYTHING LIKE IT! THEY--
ROCKY! IS SOMETHING WRONG?
IT-- IT'S JOHNNY, DAD. HE'S CHANGED...

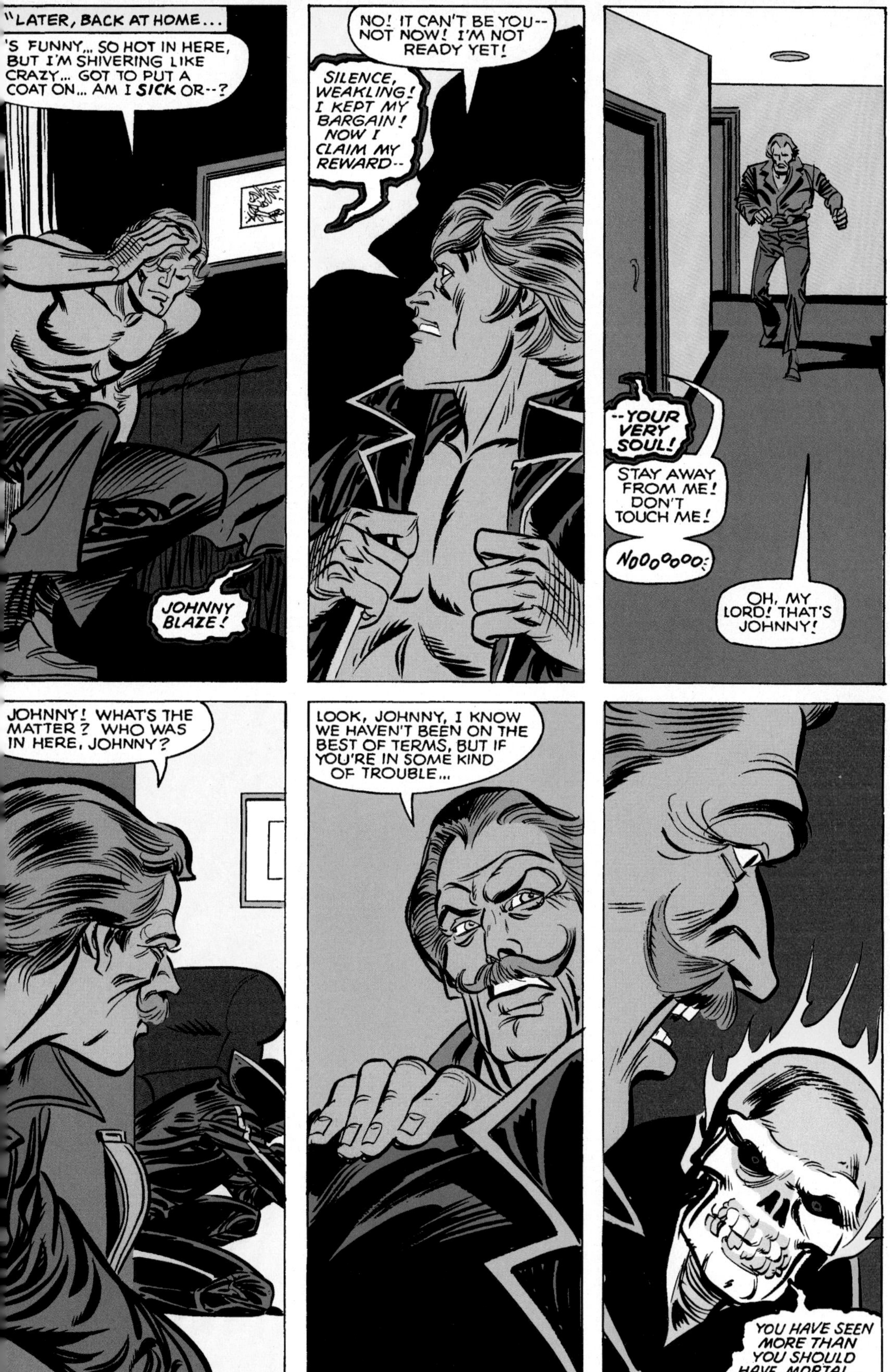
LATER, BACK AT HOME...
'S FUNNY... SO HOT IN HERE, BUT I'M SHIVERING LIKE CRAZY... GOT TO PUT A COAT ON... AM I SICK OR--?
JOHNNY BLAZE!
NO! IT CAN'T BE YOU-- NOT NOW! I'M NOT READY YET!
SILENCE, WEAKLING! I KEPT MY BARGAIN! NOW I CLAIM MY REWARD--
--YOUR VERY SOUL!
STAY AWAY FROM ME! DON'T TOUCH ME!
NOOOOOOO!
OH, MY LORD! THAT'S JOHNNY!
JOHNNY! WHAT'S THE MATTER? WHO WAS IN HERE, JOHNNY?
LOOK, JOHNNY, I KNOW WE HAVEN'T BEEN ON THE BEST OF TERMS, BUT IF YOU'RE IN SOME KIND OF TROUBLE...
YOU HAVE SEEN MORE THAN YOU SHOULD HAVE, MORTAL...

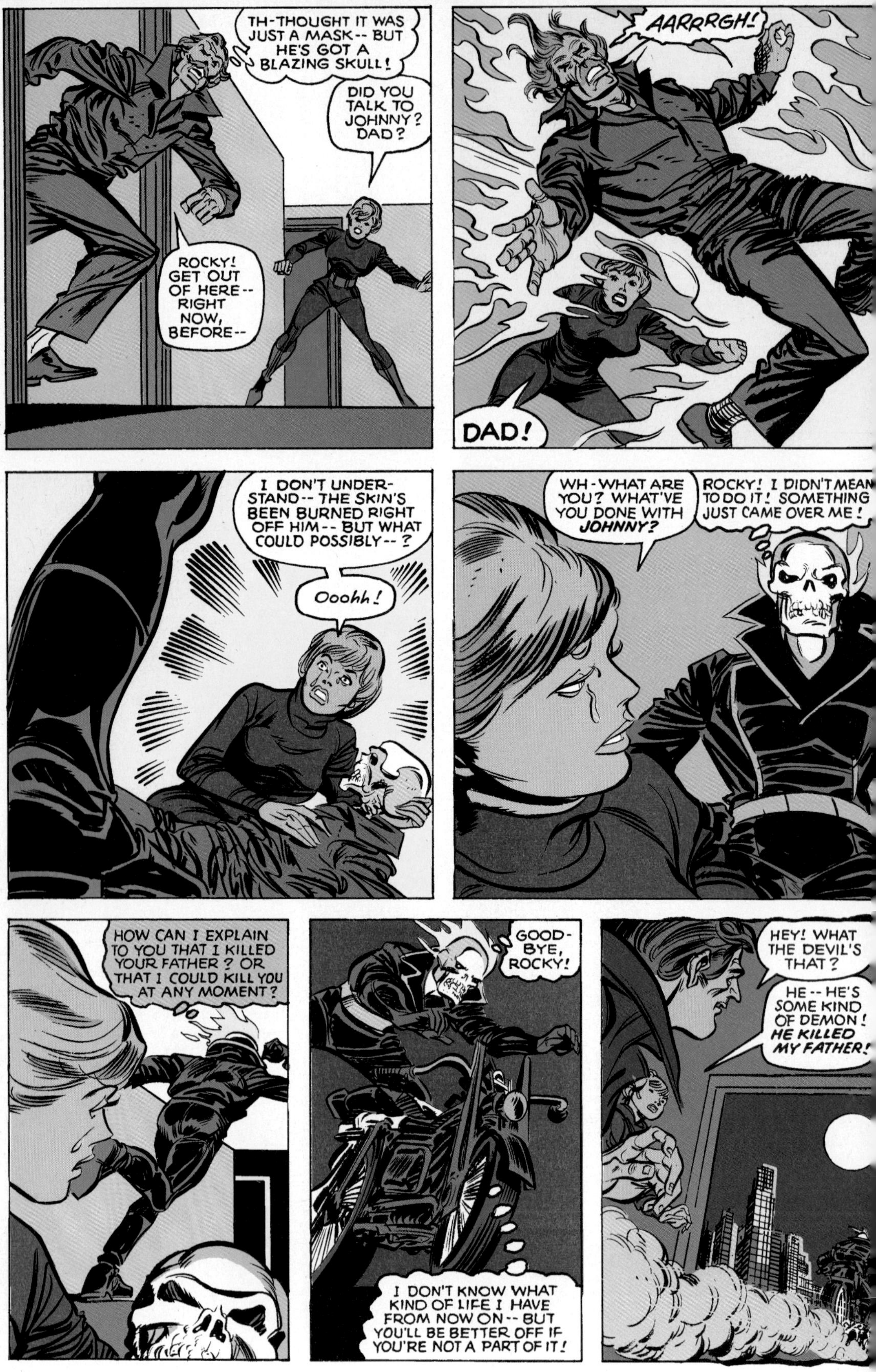

TH-THOUGHT IT WAS JUST A MASK-- BUT HE'S GOT A BLAZING SKULL!
DID YOU TALK TO JOHNNY? DAD?
ROCKY! GET OUT OF HERE-- RIGHT NOW, BEFORE--
AARRRGH!
DAD!
I DON'T UNDER-STAND-- THE SKIN'S BEEN BURNED RIGHT OFF HIM-- BUT WHAT COULD POSSIBLY--?
Ooohh!
WH-WHAT ARE YOU? WHAT'VE YOU DONE WITH JOHNNY?
ROCKY! I DIDN'T MEAN TO DO IT! SOMETHING JUST CAME OVER ME!
HOW CAN I EXPLAIN TO YOU THAT I KILLED YOUR FATHER? OR THAT I COULD KILL YOU AT ANY MOMENT?
GOOD-BYE, ROCKY!
I DON'T KNOW WHAT KIND OF LIFE I HAVE FROM NOW ON-- BUT YOU'LL BE BETTER OFF IF YOU'RE NOT A PART OF IT!
HEY! WHAT THE DEVIL'S THAT?
HE-- HE'S SOME KIND OF DEMON! HE KILLED MY FATHER!

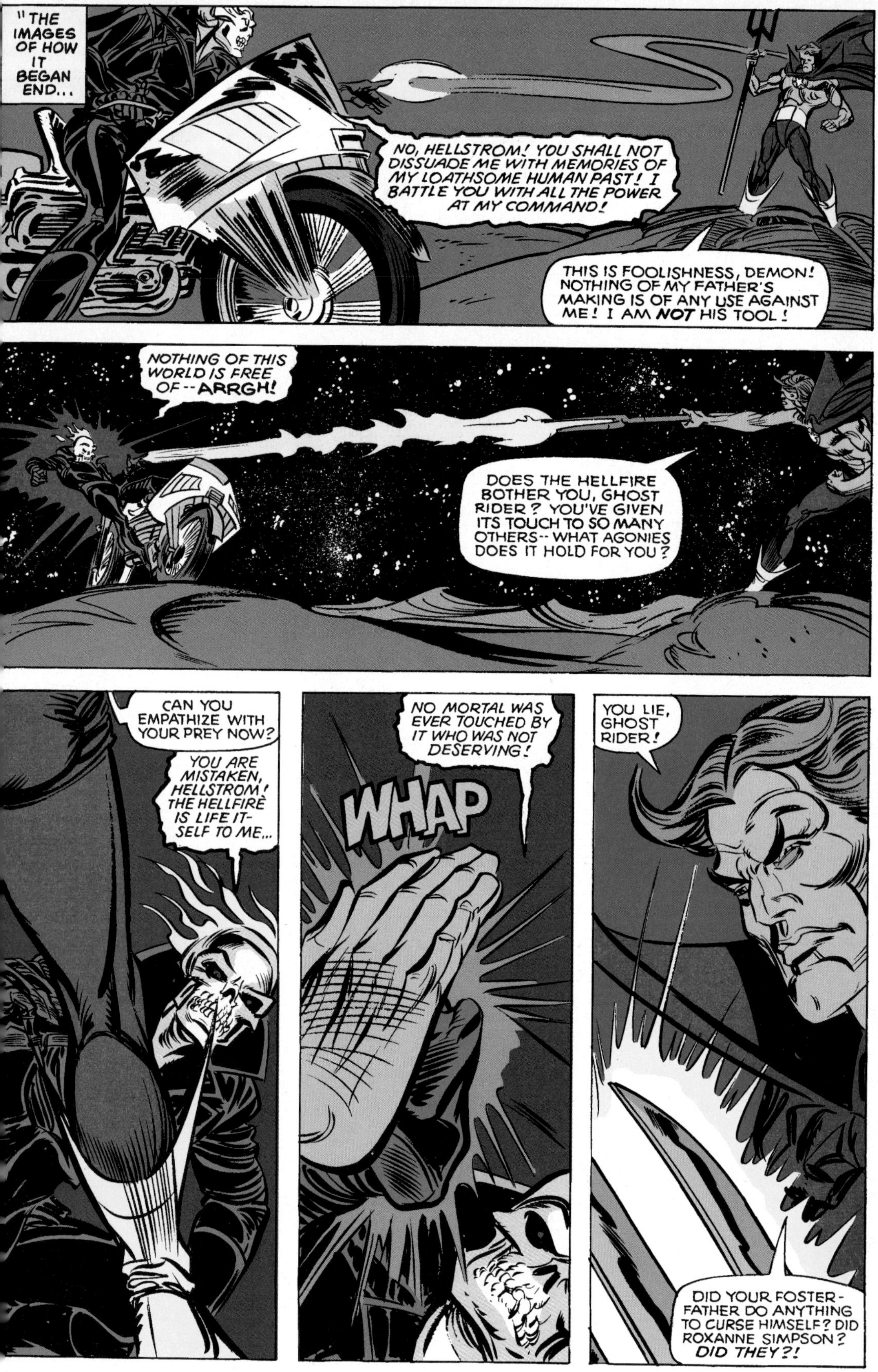
"THE IMAGES OF HOW IT BEGAN END...
NO, HELLSTROM! YOU SHALL NOT DISSUADE ME WITH MEMORIES OF MY LOATHSOME HUMAN PAST! I BATTLE YOU WITH ALL THE POWER AT MY COMMAND!
THIS IS FOOLISHNESS, DEMON! NOTHING OF MY FATHER'S MAKING IS OF ANY USE AGAINST ME! I AM NOT HIS TOOL!
NOTHING OF THIS WORLD IS FREE OF--ARRGH!
DOES THE HELLFIRE BOTHER YOU, GHOST RIDER? YOU'VE GIVEN ITS TOUCH TO SO MANY OTHERS--WHAT AGONIES DOES IT HOLD FOR YOU?
CAN YOU EMPATHIZE WITH YOUR PREY NOW?
YOU ARE MISTAKEN, HELLSTROM! THE HELLFIRE IS LIFE IT-SELF TO ME...
NO MORTAL WAS EVER TOUCHED BY IT WHO WAS NOT DESERVING!
WHAP
YOU LIE, GHOST RIDER!
DID YOUR FOSTER-FATHER DO ANYTHING TO CURSE HIMSELF? DID ROXANNE SIMPSON? DID THEY?!

"HELLSTROM'S COLD ACCUSING VOICE CUTS INTO THE GHOST RIDER...

MYSTERIOUS CYCLIST: 2 DIE

DAILY BUGLE

MOTORCYCLE PHANTOM SEEN IN ARIZONA

IS SPIDER-MAN INVOLVED?

...GHOST RIDER NOW IN CALIFORNIA...

...REIGN OF TERROR!

"...AND HIS MIND TWISTS BACK TO EVENTS PAST, AND THE HORROR OF THE LAST FEW MONTHS..."

SOOO... YOU'VE GOTTEN ALL THE WAY TO NEW MEXICO, JOHNNY...

IT WASN'T HARD TO FIGURE OUT THAT IT WAS YOU -- ONCE I'D STOPPED CRYING AND STARTED THINKING... IT WAS YOUR ROOM AND YOUR JACKET...

NOW YOU'RE HEADING TOWARD THE STATE PENITENTIARY... AND IF I COULD FIGURE THAT OUT, YOU CAN BET THE POLICE KNOW, TOO...

MAYBE YOU'LL EVEN GET PAST THEM, JOHNNY... BUT THEN I'LL BE THERE ...

I'LL BE THERE TO PUT AN END TO YOU...

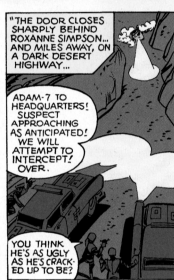

"THE DOOR CLOSES SHARPLY BEHIND ROXANNE SIMPSON... AND MILES AWAY, ON A DARK DESERT HIGHWAY...

ADAM-7 TO HEADQUARTERS! SUSPECT APPROACHING AS ANTICIPATED! WE WILL ATTEMPT TO INTERCEPT! OVER.

YOU THINK HE'S AS UGLY AS HE'S CRACKED UP TO BE?

GEEZ! LOOK AT 'IM -- HE'S EVEN UGLIER!

THIS IS THE POLICE, GHOST RIDER! PULL OVER -- OR WE'LL SHOOT!

HA HA HA! FOOLISH MORTALS!

PING

PING

YOU CANNOT STOP THE GHOST RIDER!

HOLY COW! YOU HIT 'IM DEAD CENTER, FRANK -- AND HE DIDN'T EVEN FLINCH!

THERE IS NO LAW ON EARTH THAT IS ABOVE THE LAW I SERVE -- AND NO ONE WHO LIES OUTSIDE MY JUDGMENT!

AARRGH!

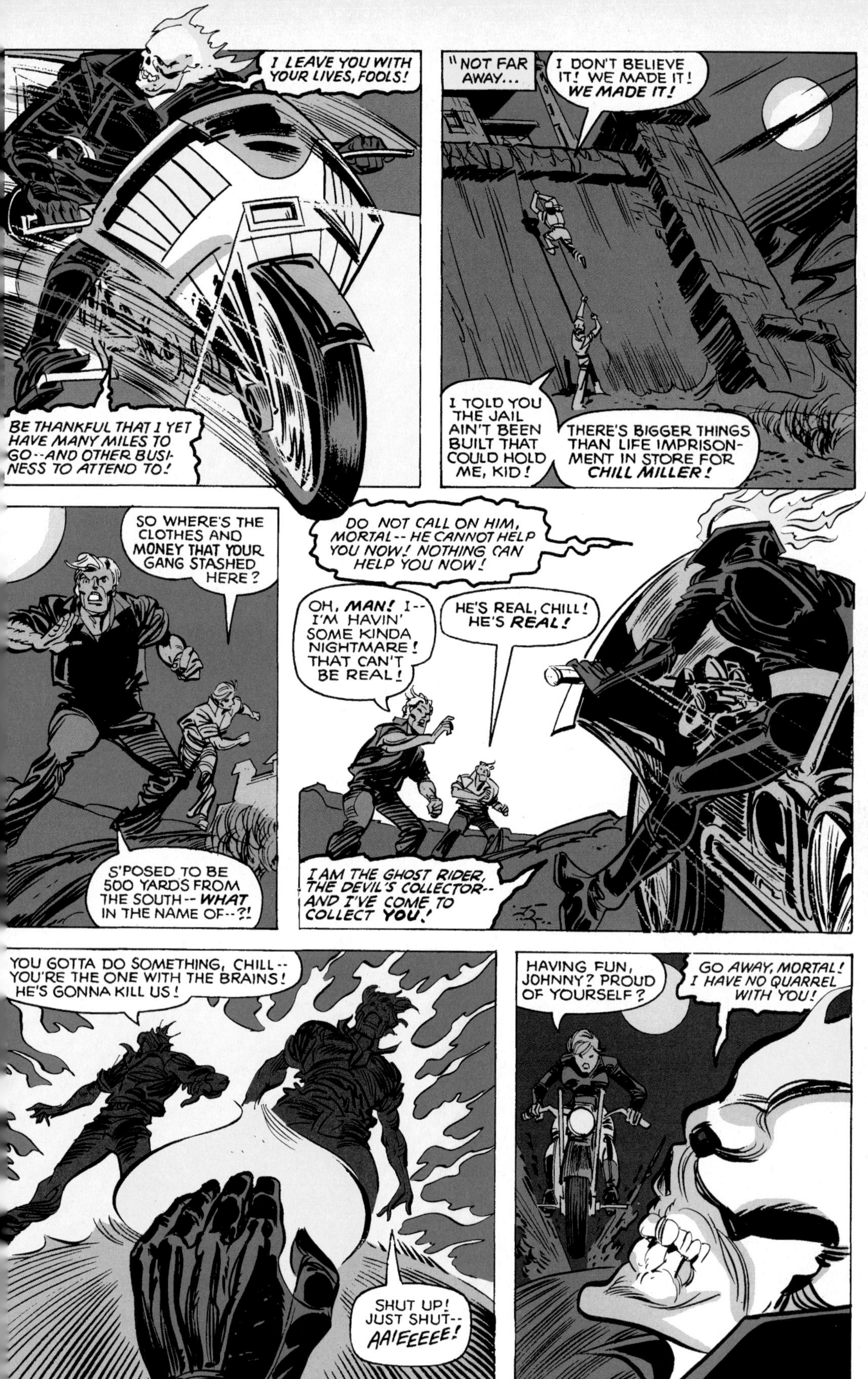
I LEAVE YOU WITH YOUR LIVES, FOOLS!
BE THANKFUL THAT I YET HAVE MANY MILES TO GO--AND OTHER BUSINESS TO ATTEND TO!
"NOT FAR AWAY...
I DON'T BELIEVE IT! WE MADE IT! WE MADE IT!
I TOLD YOU THE JAIL AIN'T BEEN BUILT THAT COULD HOLD ME, KID!
THERE'S BIGGER THINGS THAN LIFE IMPRISONMENT IN STORE FOR CHILL MILLER!
SO WHERE'S THE CLOTHES AND MONEY THAT YOUR GANG STASHED HERE?
S'POSED TO BE 500 YARDS FROM THE SOUTH--WHAT IN THE NAME OF--?!
DO NOT CALL ON HIM, MORTAL--HE CANNOT HELP YOU NOW! NOTHING CAN HELP YOU NOW!
OH, MAN! I--I'M HAVIN' SOME KINDA NIGHTMARE! THAT CAN'T BE REAL!
HE'S REAL, CHILL! HE'S REAL!
I AM THE GHOST RIDER, THE DEVIL'S COLLECTOR--AND I'VE COME TO COLLECT YOU!
YOU GOTTA DO SOMETHING, CHILL--YOU'RE THE ONE WITH THE BRAINS! HE'S GONNA KILL US!
SHUT UP! JUST SHUT--AAIEEEEE!
HAVING FUN, JOHNNY? PROUD OF YOURSELF?
GO AWAY, MORTAL! I HAVE NO QUARREL WITH YOU!

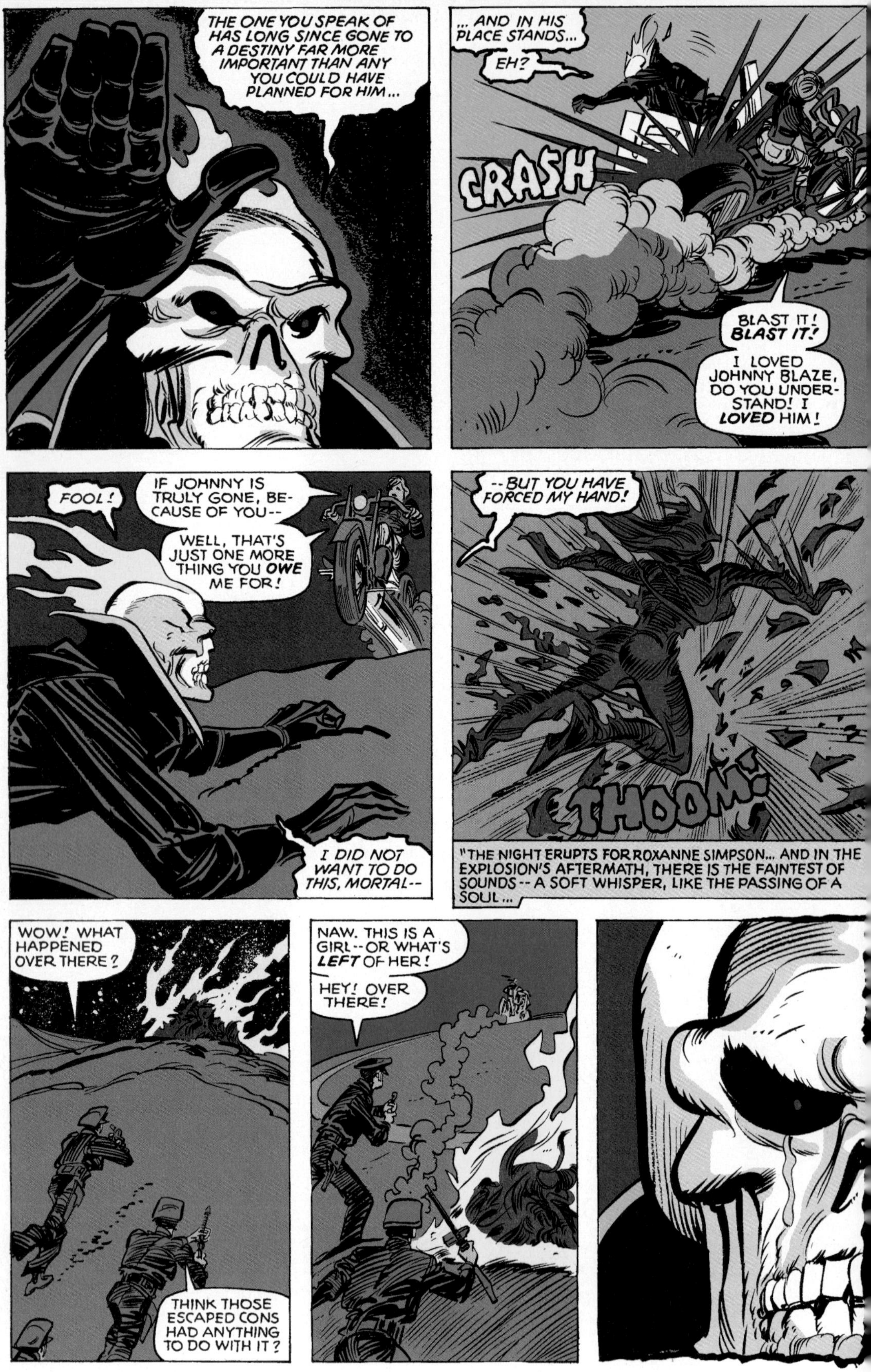
THE ONE YOU SPEAK OF HAS LONG SINCE GONE TO A DESTINY FAR MORE IMPORTANT THAN ANY YOU COULD HAVE PLANNED FOR HIM...
... AND IN HIS PLACE STANDS...
EH?
CRASH
BLAST IT! BLAST IT!
I LOVED JOHNNY BLAZE, DO YOU UNDERSTAND! I LOVED HIM!
FOOL!
IF JOHNNY IS TRULY GONE, BECAUSE OF YOU--
WELL, THAT'S JUST ONE MORE THING YOU OWE ME FOR!
I DID NOT WANT TO DO THIS, MORTAL--
--BUT YOU HAVE FORCED MY HAND!
THOOM!
"THE NIGHT ERUPTS FOR ROXANNE SIMPSON... AND IN THE EXPLOSION'S AFTERMATH, THERE IS THE FAINTEST OF SOUNDS -- A SOFT WHISPER, LIKE THE PASSING OF A SOUL...
WOW! WHAT HAPPENED OVER THERE?
THINK THOSE ESCAPED CONS HAD ANYTHING TO DO WITH IT?
NAW. THIS IS A GIRL--OR WHAT'S LEFT OF HER!
HEY! OVER THERE!

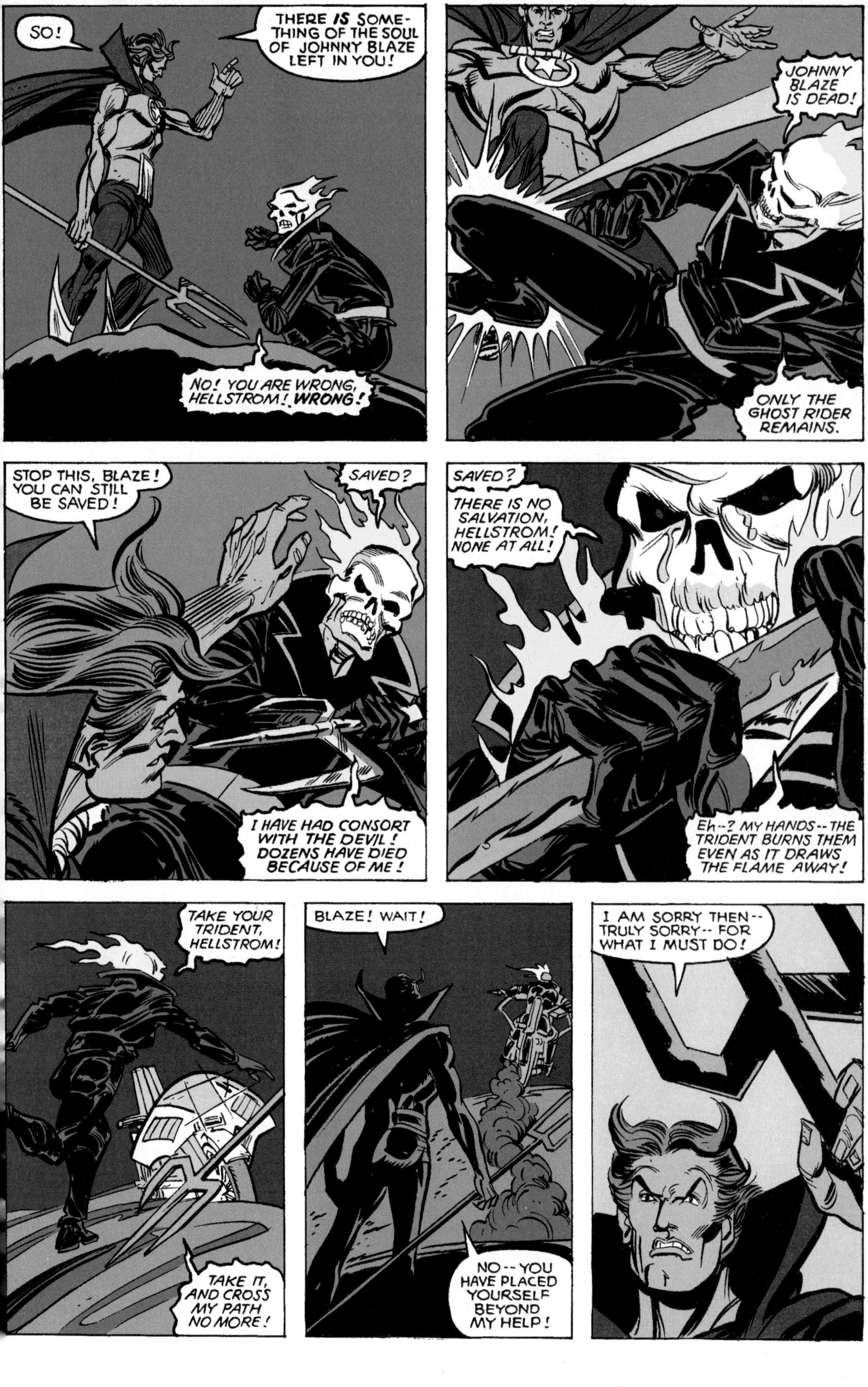
SO!
THERE IS SOMETHING OF THE SOUL OF JOHNNY BLAZE LEFT IN YOU!
NO! YOU ARE WRONG, HELLSTROM! WRONG!
JOHNNY BLAZE IS DEAD!
ONLY THE GHOST RIDER REMAINS.
STOP THIS, BLAZE! YOU CAN STILL BE SAVED!
SAVED?
I HAVE HAD CONSORT WITH THE DEVIL! DOZENS HAVE DIED BECAUSE OF ME!
SAVED?
THERE IS NO SALVATION, HELLSTROM! NONE AT ALL!
Eh--? MY HANDS--THE TRIDENT BURNS THEM EVEN AS IT DRAWS THE FLAME AWAY!
TAKE YOUR TRIDENT, HELLSTROM!
TAKE IT, AND CROSS MY PATH NO MORE!
BLAZE! WAIT!
NO--YOU HAVE PLACED YOURSELF BEYOND MY HELP!
I AM SORRY THEN--TRULY SORRY--FOR WHAT I MUST DO!

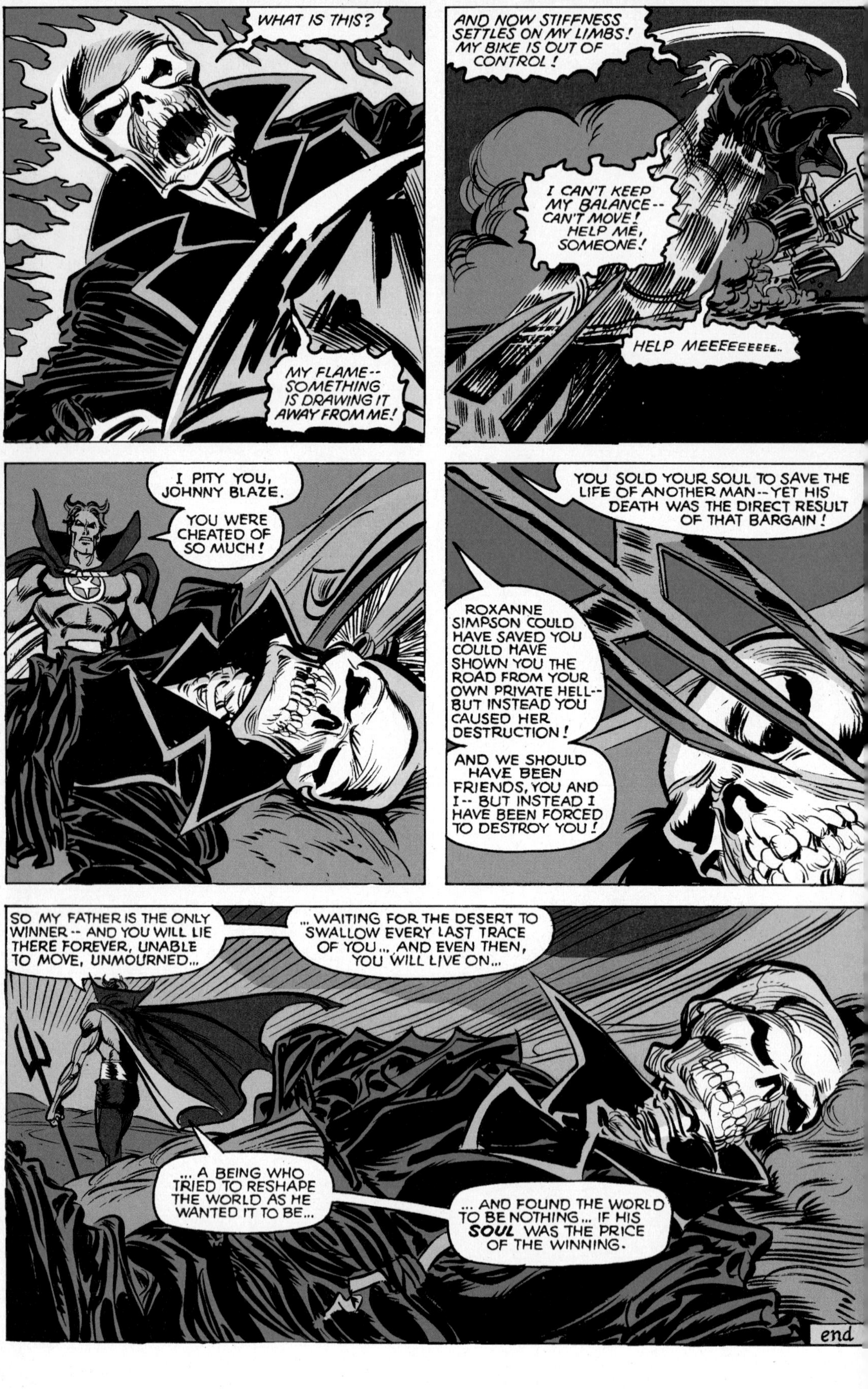
WHAT IS THIS?
MY FLAME-- SOMETHING IS DRAWING IT AWAY FROM ME!
AND NOW STIFFNESS SETTLES ON MY LIMBS! MY BIKE IS OUT OF CONTROL!
I CAN'T KEEP MY BALANCE-- CAN'T MOVE! HELP ME, SOMEONE!
HELP MEEEEEEEEE..
I PITY YOU, JOHNNY BLAZE.
YOU WERE CHEATED OF SO MUCH!
YOU SOLD YOUR SOUL TO SAVE THE LIFE OF ANOTHER MAN--YET HIS DEATH WAS THE DIRECT RESULT OF THAT BARGAIN!
ROXANNE SIMPSON COULD HAVE SAVED YOU COULD HAVE SHOWN YOU THE ROAD FROM YOUR OWN PRIVATE HELL-- BUT INSTEAD YOU CAUSED HER DESTRUCTION!
AND WE SHOULD HAVE BEEN FRIENDS, YOU AND I-- BUT INSTEAD I HAVE BEEN FORCED TO DESTROY YOU!
SO MY FATHER IS THE ONLY WINNER-- AND YOU WILL LIE THERE FOREVER, UNABLE TO MOVE, UNMOURNED...
... WAITING FOR THE DESERT TO SWALLOW EVERY LAST TRACE OF YOU... AND EVEN THEN, YOU WILL LIVE ON...
... A BEING WHO TRIED TO RESHAPE THE WORLD AS HE WANTED IT TO BE...
... AND FOUND THE WORLD TO BE NOTHING... IF HIS SOUL WAS THE PRICE OF THE WINNING.
end

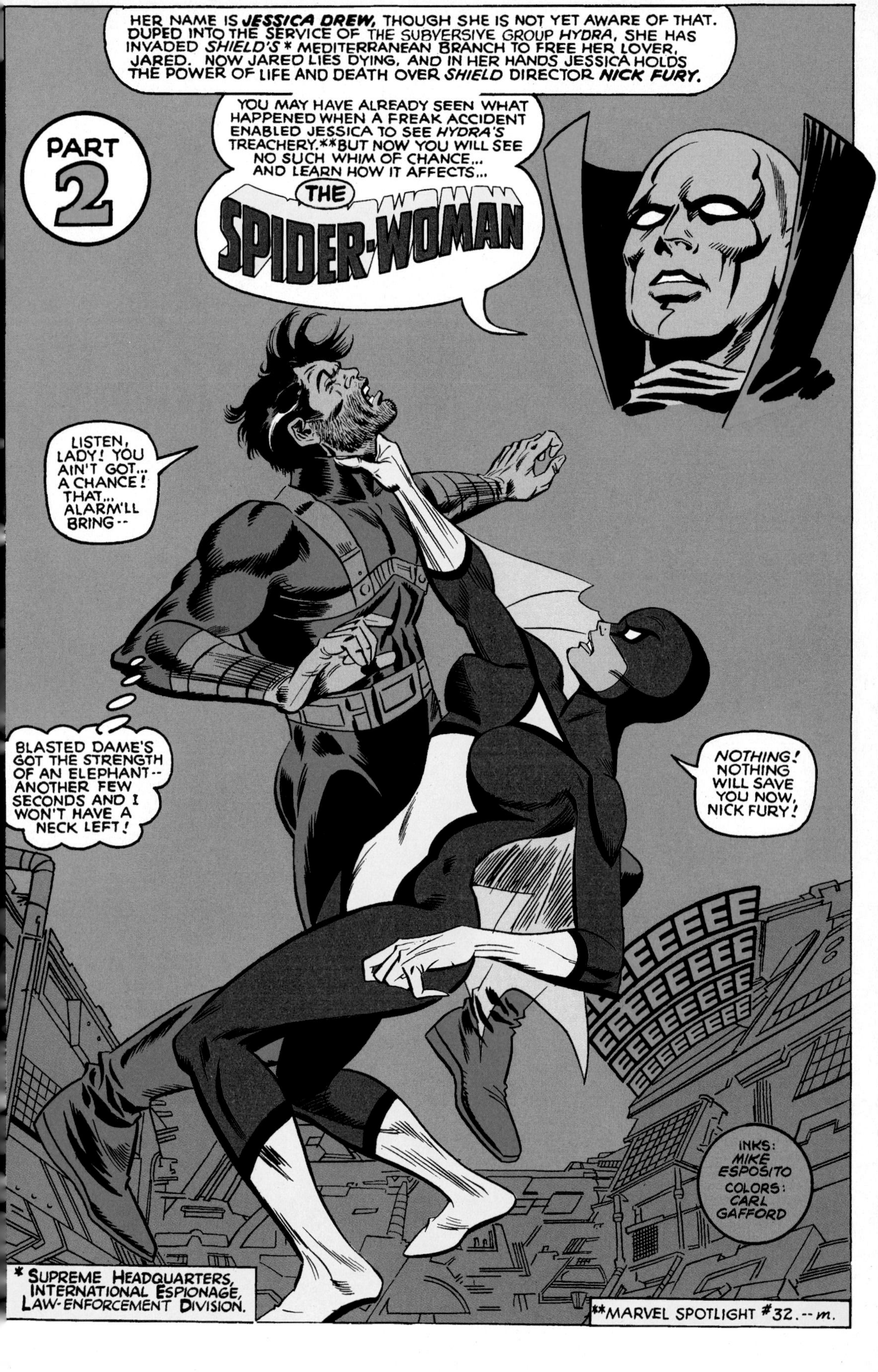
HER NAME IS JESSICA DREW, THOUGH SHE IS NOT YET AWARE OF THAT. DUPED INTO THE SERVICE OF THE SUBVERSIVE GROUP HYDRA, SHE HAS INVADED SHIELD'S* MEDITERRANEAN BRANCH TO FREE HER LOVER, JARED. NOW JARED LIES DYING, AND IN HER HANDS JESSICA HOLDS THE POWER OF LIFE AND DEATH OVER SHIELD DIRECTOR NICK FURY.
PART 2
YOU MAY HAVE ALREADY SEEN WHAT HAPPENED WHEN A FREAK ACCIDENT ENABLED JESSICA TO SEE HYDRA'S TREACHERY.** BUT NOW YOU WILL SEE NO SUCH WHIM OF CHANCE... AND LEARN HOW IT AFFECTS... THE SPIDER-WOMAN
LISTEN, LADY! YOU AIN'T GOT... A CHANCE! THAT... ALARM'LL BRING--
BLASTED DAME'S GOT THE STRENGTH OF AN ELEPHANT-- ANOTHER FEW SECONDS AND I WON'T HAVE A NECK LEFT!
NOTHING! NOTHING WILL SAVE YOU NOW, NICK FURY!
EEEEEEE
INKS: MIKE ESPOSITO COLORS: CARL GAFFORD
* SUPREME HEADQUARTERS, INTERNATIONAL ESPIONAGE, LAW-ENFORCEMENT DIVISION.
**MARVEL SPOTLIGHT #32.--m.

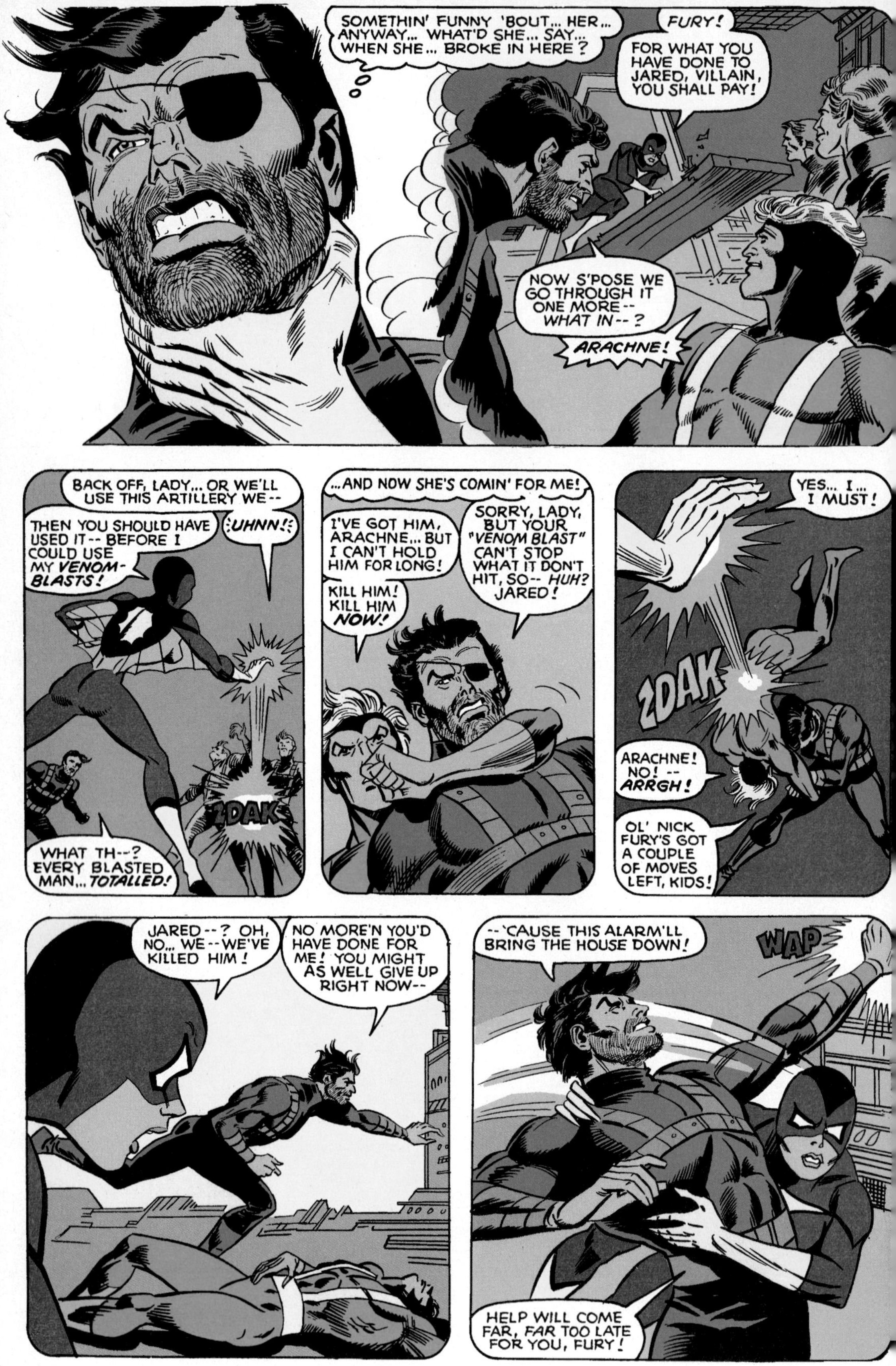
SOMETHIN' FUNNY 'BOUT... HER... ANYWAY... WHAT'D SHE... SAY... WHEN SHE... BROKE IN HERE?
FURY!
FOR WHAT YOU HAVE DONE TO JARED, VILLAIN, YOU SHALL PAY!
NOW S'POSE WE GO THROUGH IT ONE MORE-- WHAT IN--?
ARACHNE!
BACK OFF, LADY... OR WE'LL USE THIS ARTILLERY WE--
THEN YOU SHOULD HAVE USED IT-- BEFORE I COULD USE MY VENOM-BLASTS!
UHNN!
ZDAK
WHAT TH--? EVERY BLASTED MAN... TOTALLED!
...AND NOW SHE'S COMIN' FOR ME!
I'VE GOT HIM, ARACHNE... BUT I CAN'T HOLD HIM FOR LONG!
KILL HIM! KILL HIM NOW!
SORRY, LADY, BUT YOUR "VENOM BLAST" CAN'T STOP WHAT IT DON'T HIT, SO-- HUH? JARED!
YES... I... I MUST!
ZDAK
ARACHNE! NO! -- ARRGH!
OL' NICK FURY'S GOT A COUPLE OF MOVES LEFT, KIDS!
JARED--? OH, NO... WE--WE'VE KILLED HIM!
NO MORE'N YOU'D HAVE DONE FOR ME! YOU MIGHT AS WELL GIVE UP RIGHT NOW--
--'CAUSE THIS ALARM'LL BRING THE HOUSE DOWN!
WAP
HELP WILL COME FAR, FAR TOO LATE FOR YOU, FURY!

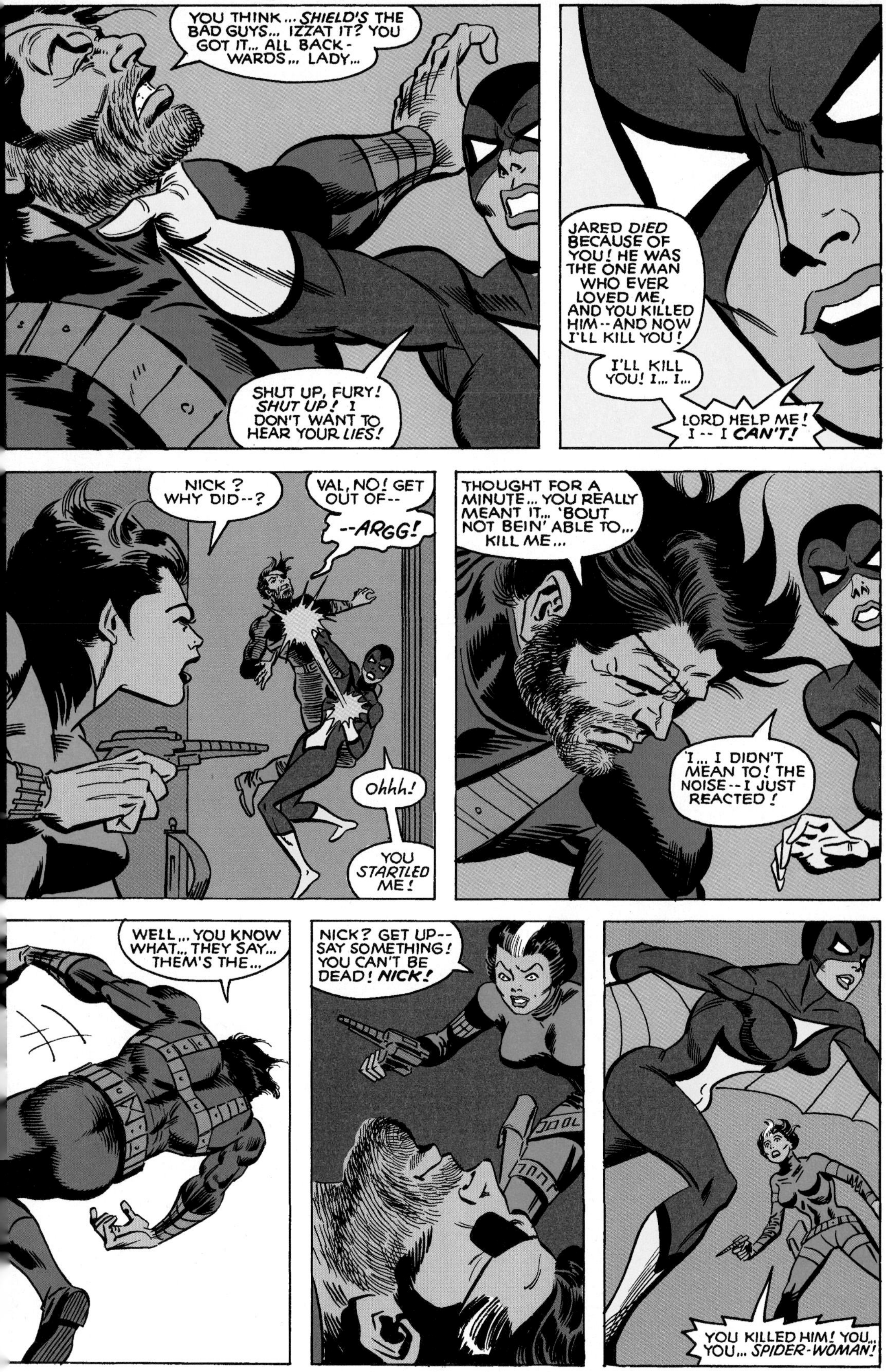
YOU THINK... SHIELD'S THE BAD GUYS... IZZAT IT? YOU GOT IT... ALL BACK-WARDS... LADY...
SHUT UP, FURY! SHUT UP! I DON'T WANT TO HEAR YOUR LIES!
JARED DIED BECAUSE OF YOU! HE WAS THE ONE MAN WHO EVER LOVED ME, AND YOU KILLED HIM--AND NOW I'LL KILL YOU!
I'LL KILL YOU! I... I...
LORD HELP ME! I -- I CAN'T!
NICK? WHY DID--?
VAL, NO! GET OUT OF--
--ARGG!
Ohhh!
YOU STARTLED ME!
THOUGHT FOR A MINUTE... YOU REALLY MEANT IT... 'BOUT NOT BEIN' ABLE TO... KILL ME...
I... I DIDN'T MEAN TO! THE NOISE--I JUST REACTED!
WELL... YOU KNOW WHAT... THEY SAY... THEM'S THE...
NICK? GET UP--SAY SOMETHING! YOU CAN'T BE DEAD! NICK!
YOU KILLED HIM! YOU... YOU... SPIDER-WOMAN!

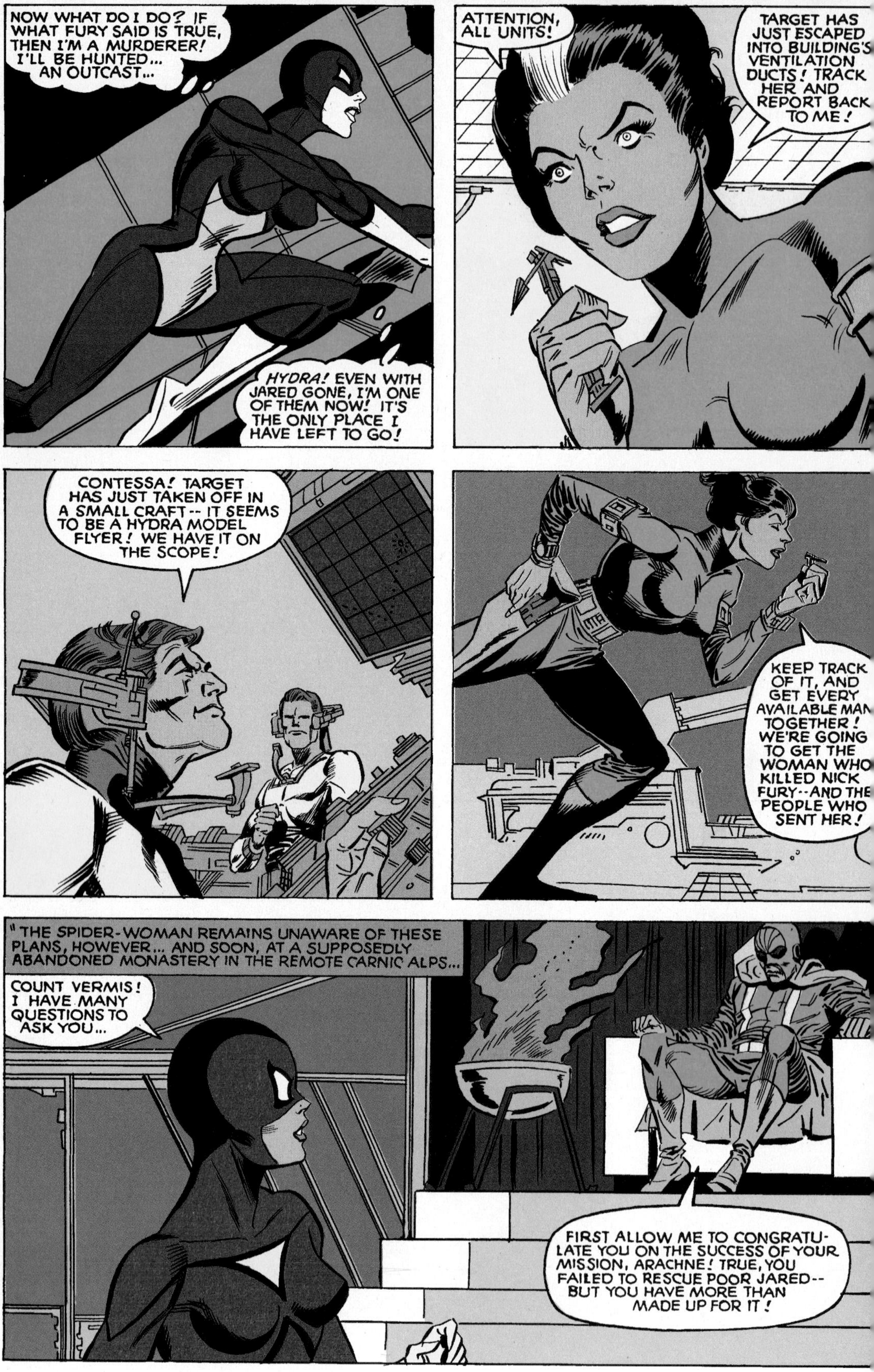
NOW WHAT DO I DO? IF WHAT FURY SAID IS TRUE, THEN I'M A MURDERER! I'LL BE HUNTED... AN OUTCAST...
HYDRA! EVEN WITH JARED GONE, I'M ONE OF THEM NOW! IT'S THE ONLY PLACE I HAVE LEFT TO GO!
ATTENTION, ALL UNITS!
TARGET HAS JUST ESCAPED INTO BUILDING'S VENTILATION DUCTS! TRACK HER AND REPORT BACK TO ME!
CONTESSA! TARGET HAS JUST TAKEN OFF IN A SMALL CRAFT -- IT SEEMS TO BE A HYDRA MODEL FLYER! WE HAVE IT ON THE SCOPE!
KEEP TRACK OF IT, AND GET EVERY AVAILABLE MAN TOGETHER! WE'RE GOING TO GET THE WOMAN WHO KILLED NICK FURY--AND THE PEOPLE WHO SENT HER!
"THE SPIDER-WOMAN REMAINS UNAWARE OF THESE PLANS, HOWEVER... AND SOON, AT A SUPPOSEDLY ABANDONED MONASTERY IN THE REMOTE CARNIC ALPS...
COUNT VERMIS! I HAVE MANY QUESTIONS TO ASK YOU...
FIRST ALLOW ME TO CONGRATU-LATE YOU ON THE SUCCESS OF YOUR MISSION, ARACHNE! TRUE, YOU FAILED TO RESCUE POOR JARED-- BUT YOU HAVE MORE THAN MADE UP FOR IT!

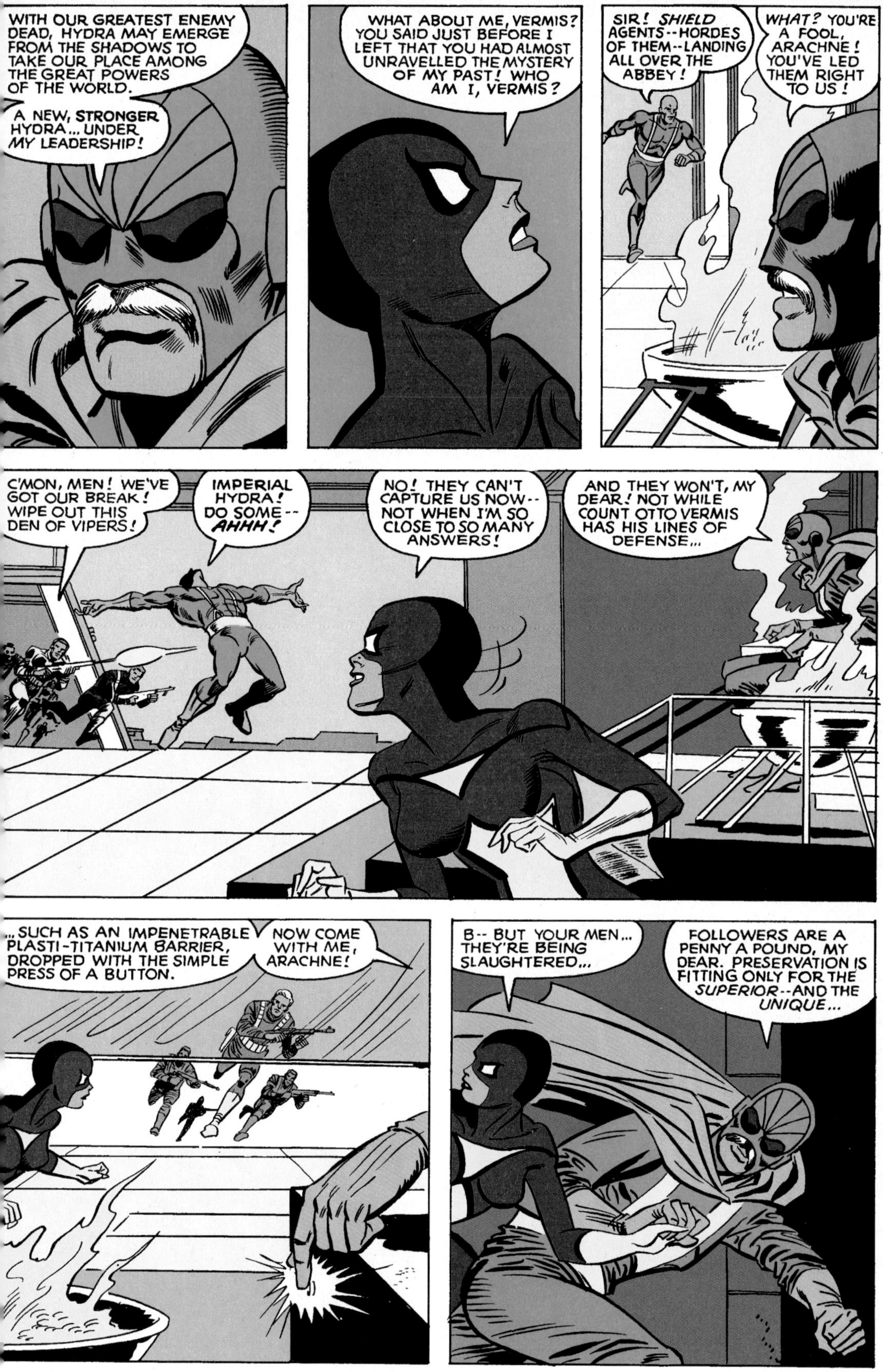
WITH OUR GREATEST ENEMY DEAD, HYDRA MAY EMERGE FROM THE SHADOWS TO TAKE OUR PLACE AMONG THE GREAT POWERS OF THE WORLD.
A NEW, STRONGER HYDRA... UNDER MY LEADERSHIP!
WHAT ABOUT ME, VERMIS? YOU SAID JUST BEFORE I LEFT THAT YOU HAD ALMOST UNRAVELLED THE MYSTERY OF MY PAST! WHO AM I, VERMIS?
SIR! SHIELD AGENTS--HORDES OF THEM--LANDING ALL OVER THE ABBEY!
WHAT? YOU'RE A FOOL, ARACHNE! YOU'VE LED THEM RIGHT TO US!
C'MON, MEN! WE'VE GOT OUR BREAK! WIPE OUT THIS DEN OF VIPERS!
IMPERIAL HYDRA! DO SOME-- AHHH!
NO! THEY CAN'T CAPTURE US NOW-- NOT WHEN I'M SO CLOSE TO SO MANY ANSWERS!
AND THEY WON'T, MY DEAR! NOT WHILE COUNT OTTO VERMIS HAS HIS LINES OF DEFENSE...
...SUCH AS AN IMPENETRABLE PLASTI-TITANIUM BARRIER, DROPPED WITH THE SIMPLE PRESS OF A BUTTON.
NOW COME WITH ME, ARACHNE!
B-- BUT YOUR MEN... THEY'RE BEING SLAUGHTERED...
FOLLOWERS ARE A PENNY A POUND, MY DEAR. PRESERVATION IS FITTING ONLY FOR THE SUPERIOR--AND THE UNIQUE...

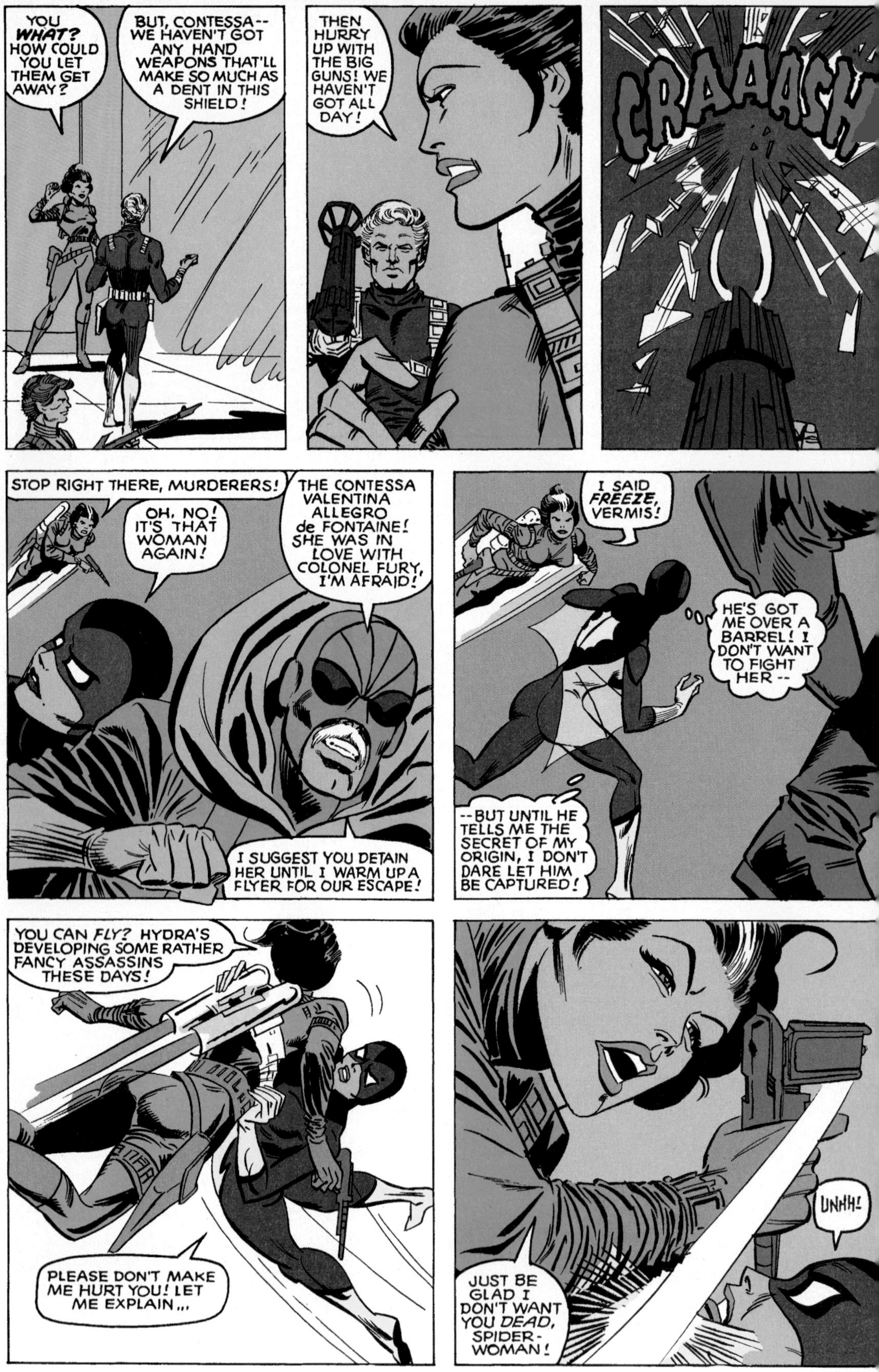
YOU WHAT? HOW COULD YOU LET THEM GET AWAY?
BUT, CONTESSA-- WE HAVEN'T GOT ANY HAND WEAPONS THAT'LL MAKE SO MUCH AS A DENT IN THIS SHIELD!
THEN HURRY UP WITH THE BIG GUNS! WE HAVEN'T GOT ALL DAY!
CRAAASH
STOP RIGHT THERE, MURDERERS!
OH, NO! IT'S THAT WOMAN AGAIN!
THE CONTESSA VALENTINA ALLEGRO de FONTAINE! SHE WAS IN LOVE WITH COLONEL FURY, I'M AFRAID!
I SUGGEST YOU DETAIN HER UNTIL I WARM UP A FLYER FOR OUR ESCAPE!
I SAID FREEZE, VERMIS!
HE'S GOT ME OVER A BARREL! I DON'T WANT TO FIGHT HER --
--BUT UNTIL HE TELLS ME THE SECRET OF MY ORIGIN, I DON'T DARE LET HIM BE CAPTURED!
YOU CAN FLY? HYDRA'S DEVELOPING SOME RATHER FANCY ASSASSINS THESE DAYS!
PLEASE DON'T MAKE ME HURT YOU! LET ME EXPLAIN...
UNHH!
JUST BE GLAD I DON'T WANT YOU DEAD, SPIDER-WOMAN!

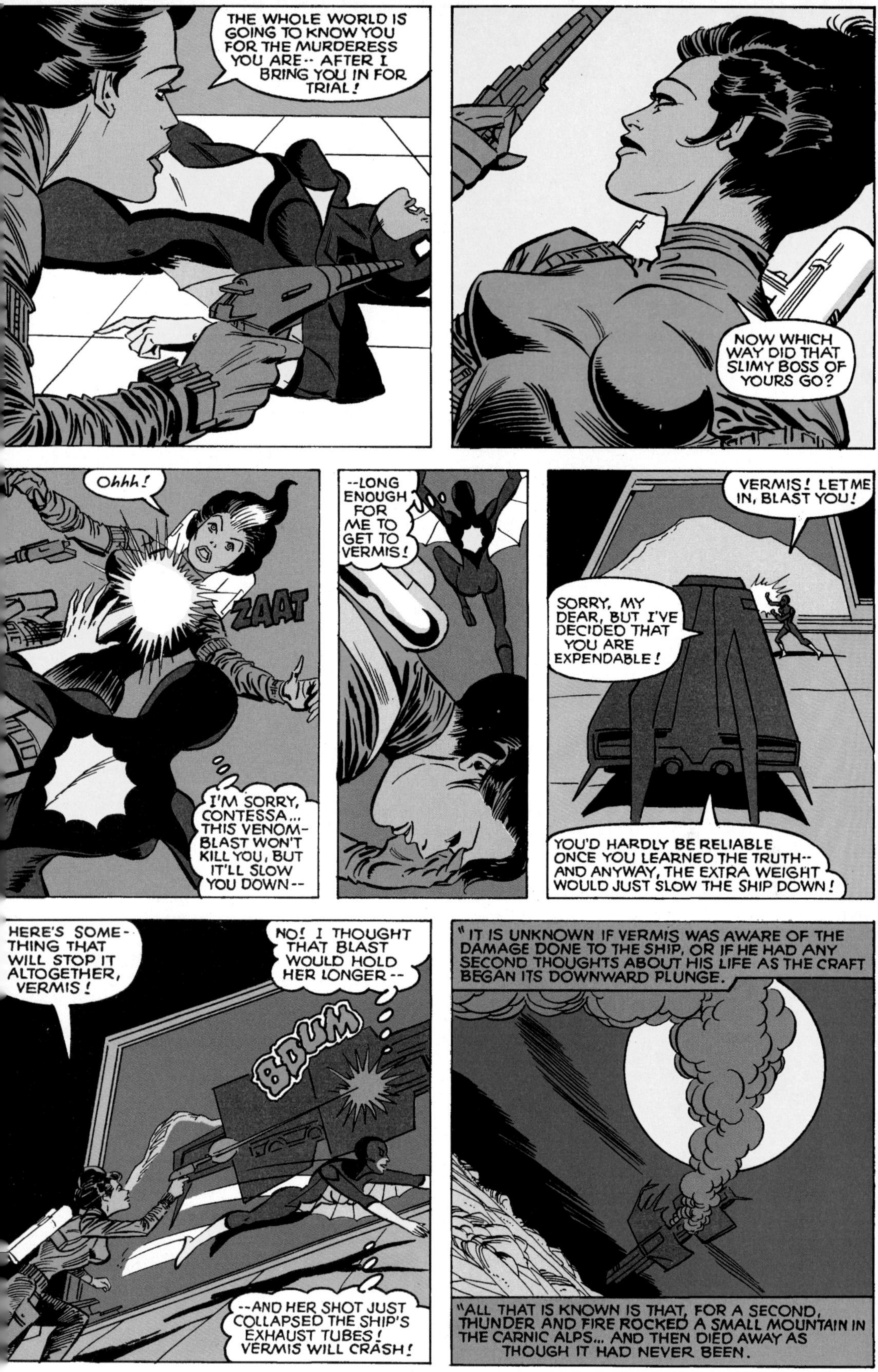
THE WHOLE WORLD IS GOING TO KNOW YOU FOR THE MURDERESS YOU ARE-- AFTER I BRING YOU IN FOR TRIAL!
NOW WHICH WAY DID THAT SLIMY BOSS OF YOURS GO?
Ohhh!
ZAAT
I'M SORRY, CONTESSA... THIS VENOM-BLAST WON'T KILL YOU, BUT IT'LL SLOW YOU DOWN--
--LONG ENOUGH FOR ME TO GET TO VERMIS!
VERMIS! LET ME IN, BLAST YOU!
SORRY, MY DEAR, BUT I'VE DECIDED THAT YOU ARE EXPENDABLE!
YOU'D HARDLY BE RELIABLE ONCE YOU LEARNED THE TRUTH-- AND ANYWAY, THE EXTRA WEIGHT WOULD JUST SLOW THE SHIP DOWN!
HERE'S SOMETHING THAT WILL STOP IT ALTOGETHER, VERMIS!
NO! I THOUGHT THAT BLAST WOULD HOLD HER LONGER--
BDUM
--AND HER SHOT JUST COLLAPSED THE SHIP'S EXHAUST TUBES! VERMIS WILL CRASH!
"IT IS UNKNOWN IF VERMIS WAS AWARE OF THE DAMAGE DONE TO THE SHIP, OR IF HE HAD ANY SECOND THOUGHTS ABOUT HIS LIFE AS THE CRAFT BEGAN ITS DOWNWARD PLUNGE.
"ALL THAT IS KNOWN IS THAT, FOR A SECOND, THUNDER AND FIRE ROCKED A SMALL MOUNTAIN IN THE CARNIC ALPS... AND THEN DIED AWAY AS THOUGH IT HAD NEVER BEEN.

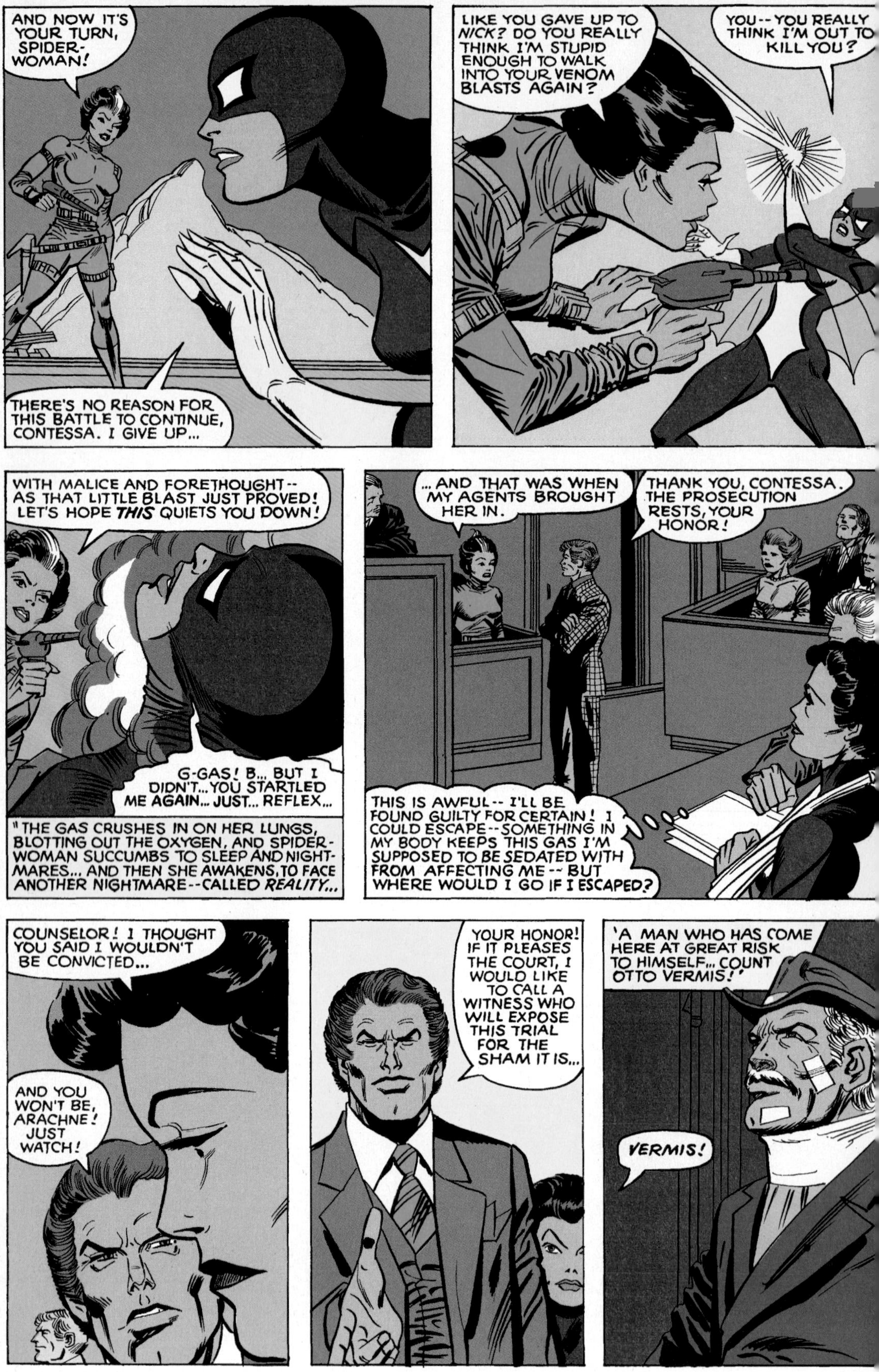
AND NOW IT'S YOUR TURN, SPIDER-WOMAN!
THERE'S NO REASON FOR THIS BATTLE TO CONTINUE, CONTESSA. I GIVE UP...
LIKE YOU GAVE UP TO NICK? DO YOU REALLY THINK I'M STUPID ENOUGH TO WALK INTO YOUR VENOM BLASTS AGAIN?
YOU--YOU REALLY THINK I'M OUT TO KILL YOU?
WITH MALICE AND FORETHOUGHT--AS THAT LITTLE BLAST JUST PROVED! LET'S HOPE THIS QUIETS YOU DOWN!
G-GAS! B... BUT I DIDN'T... YOU STARTLED ME AGAIN... JUST... REFLEX...
"THE GAS CRUSHES IN ON HER LUNGS, BLOTTING OUT THE OXYGEN, AND SPIDER-WOMAN SUCCUMBS TO SLEEP AND NIGHT-MARES... AND THEN SHE AWAKENS, TO FACE ANOTHER NIGHTMARE--CALLED REALITY...
...AND THAT WAS WHEN MY AGENTS BROUGHT HER IN.
THANK YOU, CONTESSA. THE PROSECUTION RESTS, YOUR HONOR!
THIS IS AWFUL--I'LL BE FOUND GUILTY FOR CERTAIN! I COULD ESCAPE--SOMETHING IN MY BODY KEEPS THIS GAS I'M SUPPOSED TO BE SEDATED WITH FROM AFFECTING ME--BUT WHERE WOULD I GO IF I ESCAPED?
COUNSELOR! I THOUGHT YOU SAID I WOULDN'T BE CONVICTED...
AND YOU WON'T BE, ARACHNE! JUST WATCH!
YOUR HONOR! IF IT PLEASES THE COURT, I WOULD LIKE TO CALL A WITNESS WHO WILL EXPOSE THIS TRIAL FOR THE SHAM IT IS...
'A MAN WHO HAS COME HERE AT GREAT RISK TO HIMSELF... COUNT OTTO VERMIS!'
VERMIS!

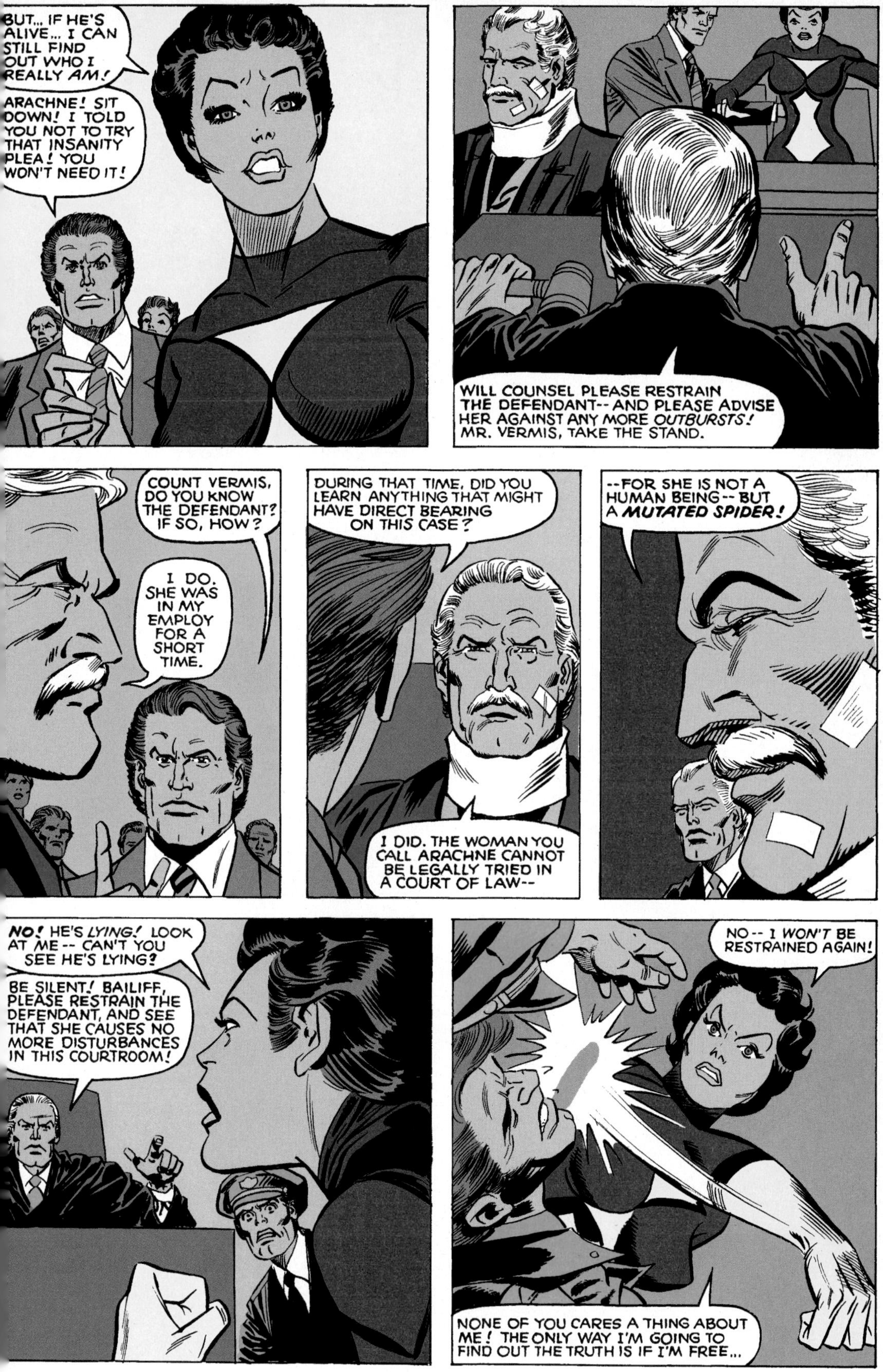
BUT... IF HE'S ALIVE... I CAN STILL FIND OUT WHO I REALLY AM!
ARACHNE! SIT DOWN! I TOLD YOU NOT TO TRY THAT INSANITY PLEA! YOU WON'T NEED IT!
WILL COUNSEL PLEASE RESTRAIN THE DEFENDANT-- AND PLEASE ADVISE HER AGAINST ANY MORE OUTBURSTS! MR. VERMIS, TAKE THE STAND.
COUNT VERMIS, DO YOU KNOW THE DEFENDANT? IF SO, HOW?
I DO. SHE WAS IN MY EMPLOY FOR A SHORT TIME.
DURING THAT TIME, DID YOU LEARN ANYTHING THAT MIGHT HAVE DIRECT BEARING ON THIS CASE?
I DID. THE WOMAN YOU CALL ARACHNE CANNOT BE LEGALLY TRIED IN A COURT OF LAW--
--FOR SHE IS NOT A HUMAN BEING-- BUT A MUTATED SPIDER!
NO! HE'S LYING! LOOK AT ME -- CAN'T YOU SEE HE'S LYING?
BE SILENT! BAILIFF, PLEASE RESTRAIN THE DEFENDANT, AND SEE THAT SHE CAUSES NO MORE DISTURBANCES IN THIS COURTROOM!
NO -- I WON'T BE RESTRAINED AGAIN!
NONE OF YOU CARES A THING ABOUT ME! THE ONLY WAY I'M GOING TO FIND OUT THE TRUTH IS IF I'M FREE...

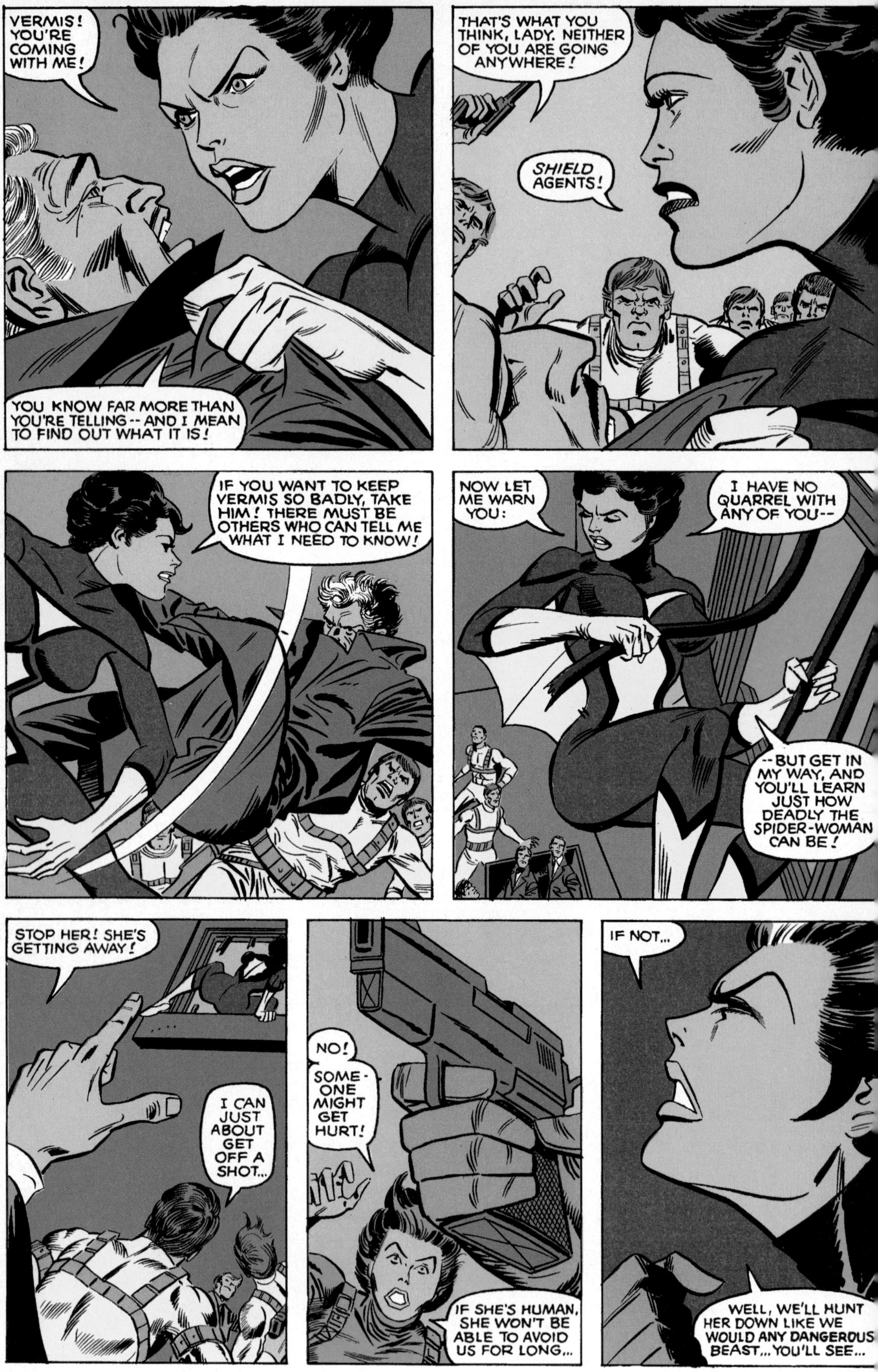
VERMIS! YOU'RE COMING WITH ME!
YOU KNOW FAR MORE THAN YOU'RE TELLING -- AND I MEAN TO FIND OUT WHAT IT IS!
THAT'S WHAT YOU THINK, LADY. NEITHER OF YOU ARE GOING ANYWHERE!
SHIELD AGENTS!
IF YOU WANT TO KEEP VERMIS SO BADLY, TAKE HIM! THERE MUST BE OTHERS WHO CAN TELL ME WHAT I NEED TO KNOW!
NOW LET ME WARN YOU:
I HAVE NO QUARREL WITH ANY OF YOU--
--BUT GET IN MY WAY, AND YOU'LL LEARN JUST HOW DEADLY THE SPIDER-WOMAN CAN BE!
STOP HER! SHE'S GETTING AWAY!
I CAN JUST ABOUT GET OFF A SHOT...
NO!
SOME-ONE MIGHT GET HURT!
IF SHE'S HUMAN, SHE WON'T BE ABLE TO AVOID US FOR LONG...
IF NOT...
WELL, WE'LL HUNT HER DOWN LIKE WE WOULD ANY DANGEROUS BEAST... YOU'LL SEE...

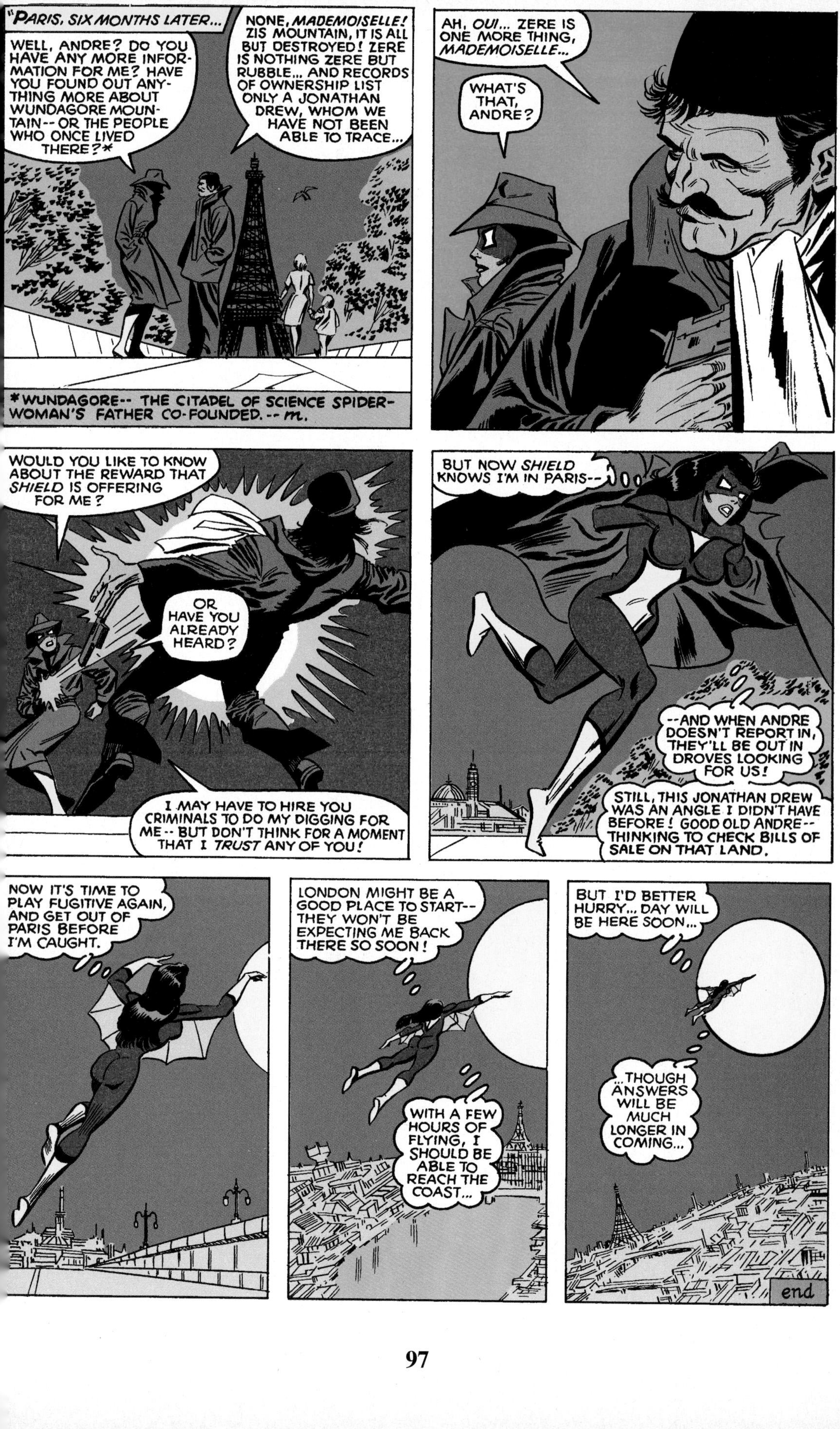
"PARIS, SIX MONTHS LATER...
WELL, ANDRE? DO YOU HAVE ANY MORE INFORMATION FOR ME? HAVE YOU FOUND OUT ANYTHING MORE ABOUT WUNDAGORE MOUNTAIN -- OR THE PEOPLE WHO ONCE LIVED THERE?*
NONE, MADEMOISELLE! ZIS MOUNTAIN, IT IS ALL BUT DESTROYED! ZERE IS NOTHING ZERE BUT RUBBLE... AND RECORDS OF OWNERSHIP LIST ONLY A JONATHAN DREW, WHOM WE HAVE NOT BEEN ABLE TO TRACE...
*WUNDAGORE-- THE CITADEL OF SCIENCE SPIDER-WOMAN'S FATHER CO-FOUNDED. -- m.
AH, OUI... ZERE IS ONE MORE THING, MADEMOISELLE...
WHAT'S THAT, ANDRE?
WOULD YOU LIKE TO KNOW ABOUT THE REWARD THAT SHIELD IS OFFERING FOR ME?
OR HAVE YOU ALREADY HEARD?
I MAY HAVE TO HIRE YOU CRIMINALS TO DO MY DIGGING FOR ME -- BUT DON'T THINK FOR A MOMENT THAT I TRUST ANY OF YOU!
BUT NOW SHIELD KNOWS I'M IN PARIS--
--AND WHEN ANDRE DOESN'T REPORT IN, THEY'LL BE OUT IN DROVES LOOKING FOR US!
STILL, THIS JONATHAN DREW WAS AN ANGLE I DIDN'T HAVE BEFORE! GOOD OLD ANDRE-- THINKING TO CHECK BILLS OF SALE ON THAT LAND.
NOW IT'S TIME TO PLAY FUGITIVE AGAIN, AND GET OUT OF PARIS BEFORE I'M CAUGHT.
LONDON MIGHT BE A GOOD PLACE TO START-- THEY WON'T BE EXPECTING ME BACK THERE SO SOON!
WITH A FEW HOURS OF FLYING, I SHOULD BE ABLE TO REACH THE COAST...
BUT I'D BETTER HURRY... DAY WILL BE HERE SOON...
...THOUGH ANSWERS WILL BE MUCH LONGER IN COMING...
end

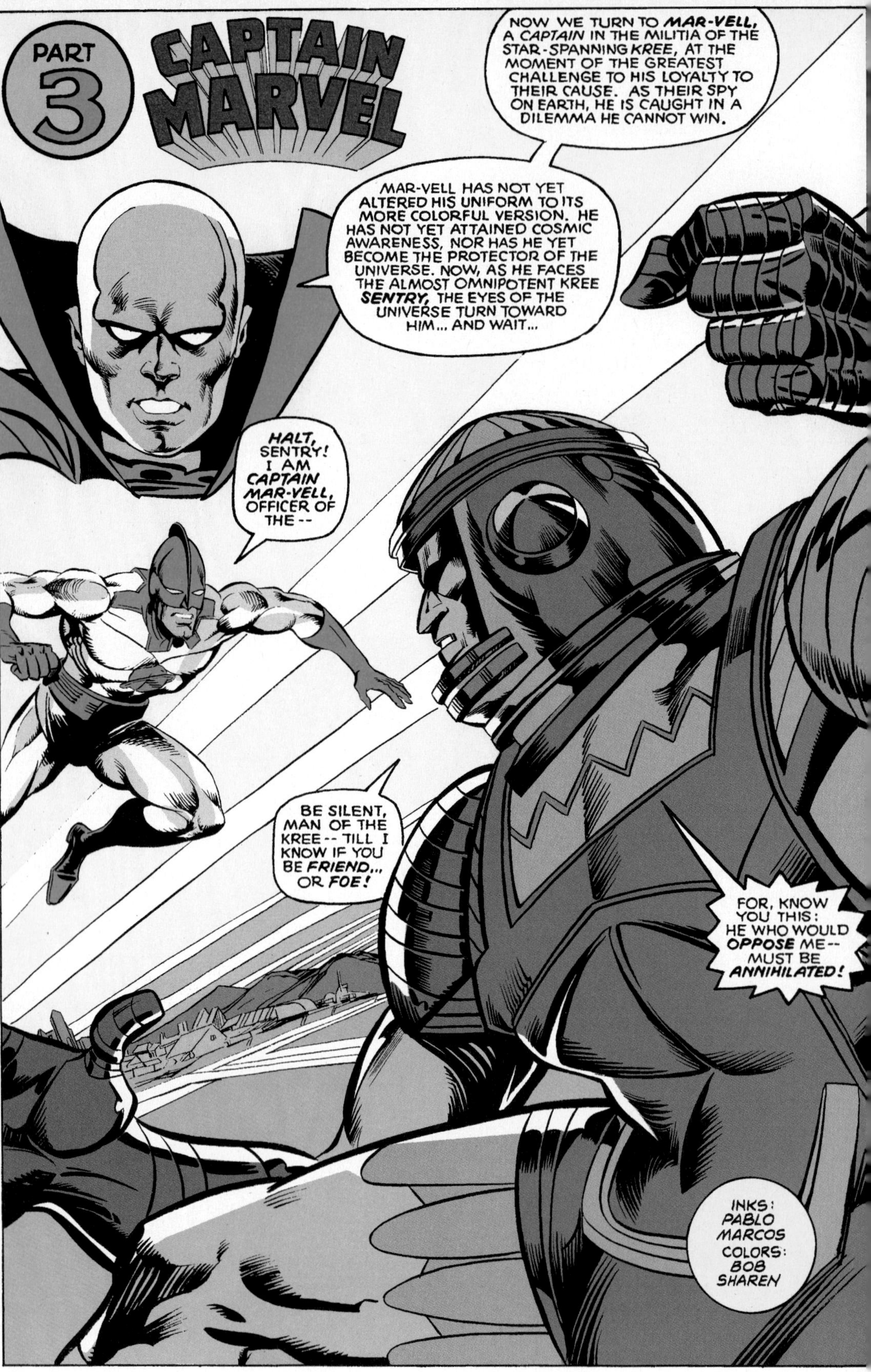
PART 3
CAPTAIN MARVEL
NOW WE TURN TO MAR-VELL, A CAPTAIN IN THE MILITIA OF THE STAR-SPANNING KREE, AT THE MOMENT OF THE GREATEST CHALLENGE TO HIS LOYALTY TO THEIR CAUSE. AS THEIR SPY ON EARTH, HE IS CAUGHT IN A DILEMMA HE CANNOT WIN.
MAR-VELL HAS NOT YET ALTERED HIS UNIFORM TO ITS MORE COLORFUL VERSION. HE HAS NOT YET ATTAINED COSMIC AWARENESS, NOR HAS HE YET BECOME THE PROTECTOR OF THE UNIVERSE. NOW, AS HE FACES THE ALMOST OMNIPOTENT KREE SENTRY, THE EYES OF THE UNIVERSE TURN TOWARD HIM... AND WAIT...
HALT, SENTRY! I AM CAPTAIN MAR-VELL, OFFICER OF THE --
BE SILENT, MAN OF THE KREE -- TILL I KNOW IF YOU BE FRIEND... OR FOE!
FOR, KNOW YOU THIS: HE WHO WOULD OPPOSE ME -- MUST BE ANNIHILATED!
INKS: PABLO MARCOS
COLORS: BOB SHAREN

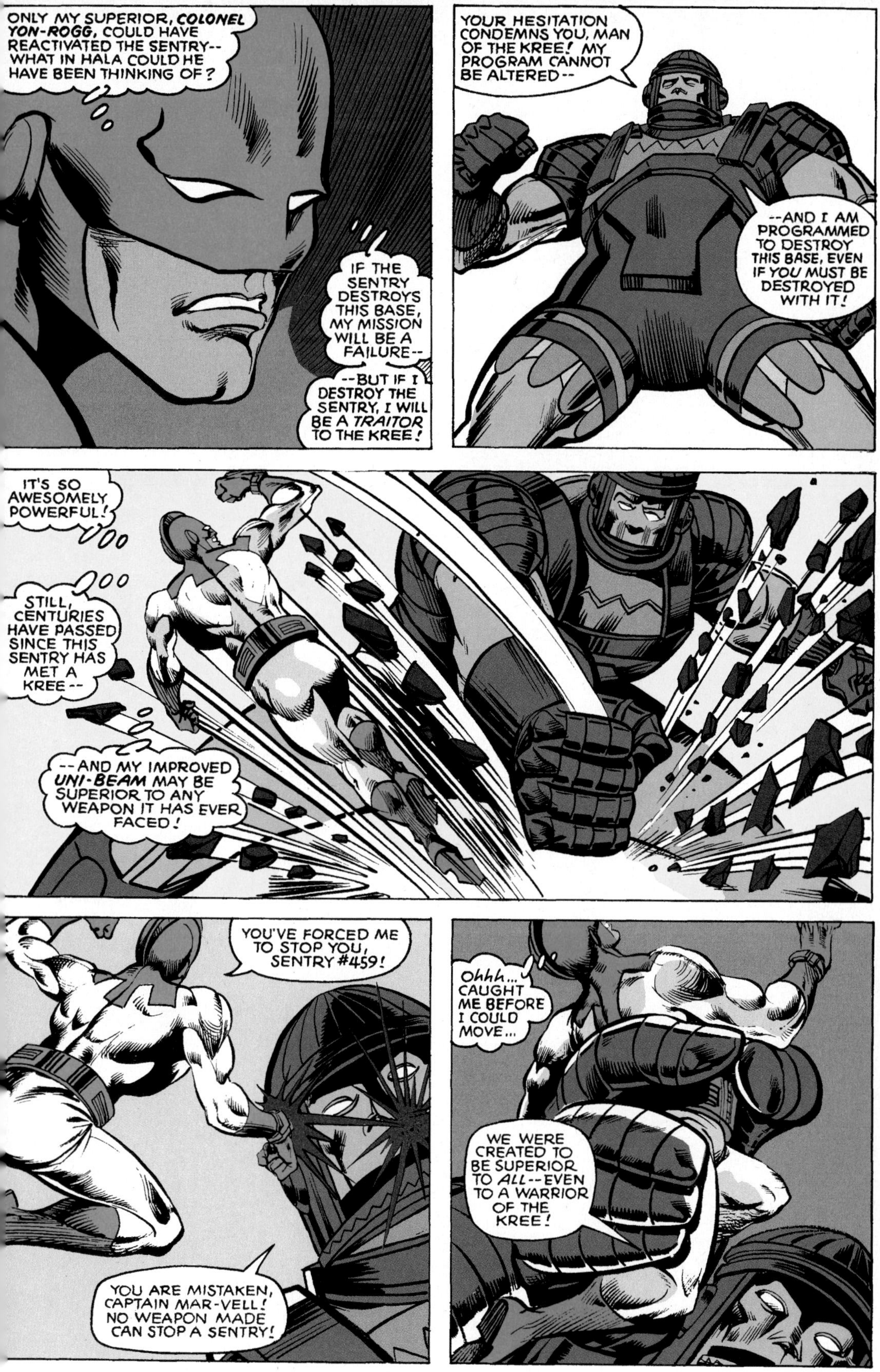
ONLY MY SUPERIOR, COLONEL YON-ROGG, COULD HAVE REACTIVATED THE SENTRY-- WHAT IN HALA COULD HE HAVE BEEN THINKING OF?
IF THE SENTRY DESTROYS THIS BASE, MY MISSION WILL BE A FAILURE--
--BUT IF I DESTROY THE SENTRY, I WILL BE A TRAITOR TO THE KREE!
YOUR HESITATION CONDEMNS YOU, MAN OF THE KREE! MY PROGRAM CANNOT BE ALTERED--
--AND I AM PROGRAMMED TO DESTROY THIS BASE, EVEN IF YOU MUST BE DESTROYED WITH IT!
IT'S SO AWESOMELY POWERFUL!
STILL, CENTURIES HAVE PASSED SINCE THIS SENTRY HAS MET A KREE--
--AND MY IMPROVED UNI-BEAM MAY BE SUPERIOR TO ANY WEAPON IT HAS EVER FACED!
YOU'VE FORCED ME TO STOP YOU, SENTRY #459!
YOU ARE MISTAKEN, CAPTAIN MAR-VELL! NO WEAPON MADE CAN STOP A SENTRY!
Ohhh... CAUGHT ME BEFORE I COULD MOVE...
WE WERE CREATED TO BE SUPERIOR TO ALL--EVEN TO A WARRIOR OF THE KREE!

"AS THE BATTLE RAGES BELOW, ANOTHER CONFLICT TAKES PLACE...ON THE *KREE SPACESHIP* ORBITING HIGH ABOVE THE EARTH. YOU MAY HAVE ALREADY SEEN WHAT HAPPENED WHEN YON-ROGG'S TRANSGRESSIONS WERE OVERLOOKED BY HIS SUPERIORS.* NOW WITNESS A WORLD OF DIFFERENCE...

DISGRACEFUL, YON-ROGG -- UTTERLY *DISGRACEFUL*...

*MARVEL SUPERHEROES #12-13.

IN YOUR PURSUIT OF A PERSONAL *VENDETTA,* YOU HAVE JEOPARDIZED A MISSION OF UTMOST IMPORTANCE TO THE EMPIRE! IN SENDING MAR-VELL TO THE EARTH ALONE, YOU HAVE BROKEN REGULATIONS...

RONAN... IF I MAY SPEAK...

I ACTED WITH THE INTENTION OF PROVING MAR-VELL TO BE A TRAITOR TO THE EMPIRE! HE IS WEAK...

SILENCE! YOUR LIES AND SUSPICIONS DO NOT ENTER-TAIN US!

IN THE NAME OF *ZAREK,* THE IMPERIAL MINISTER, YOU ARE RELIEVED OF YOUR COMMAND, YON-ROGG... AND YOU SHALL BE PLACED IN CUSTODY UNTIL SUCH A TIME AS I CAN STUDY YOUR CASE!

VERY WELL, ACCUSER! I ACCEPT YOUR DECISION!

AMAZING! YON-ROGG HAS NEVER BEEN SO DOCILE! AND NOW WHAT OF MY POOR MAR-VELL?

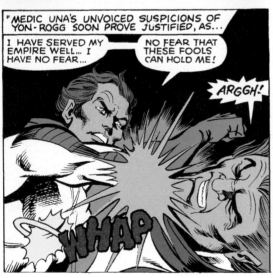

"MEDIC UNA'S UNVOICED SUSPICIONS OF YON-ROGG SOON PROVE JUSTIFIED, AS...

I HAVE SERVED MY EMPIRE WELL... I HAVE NO FEAR...

NO FEAR THAT THESE FOOLS CAN HOLD ME!

ARGGH!

WHAP

IF ANY OF YOU THINK THAT YOU WOULD LIKE TO INTERFERE WITH MY DEPARTURE --

-- REST ASSURED THAT THIS WOMAN'S LIFE DEPENDS ON YOUR DECISION NOT TO.

YON-ROGG! THIS IS MADNESS!

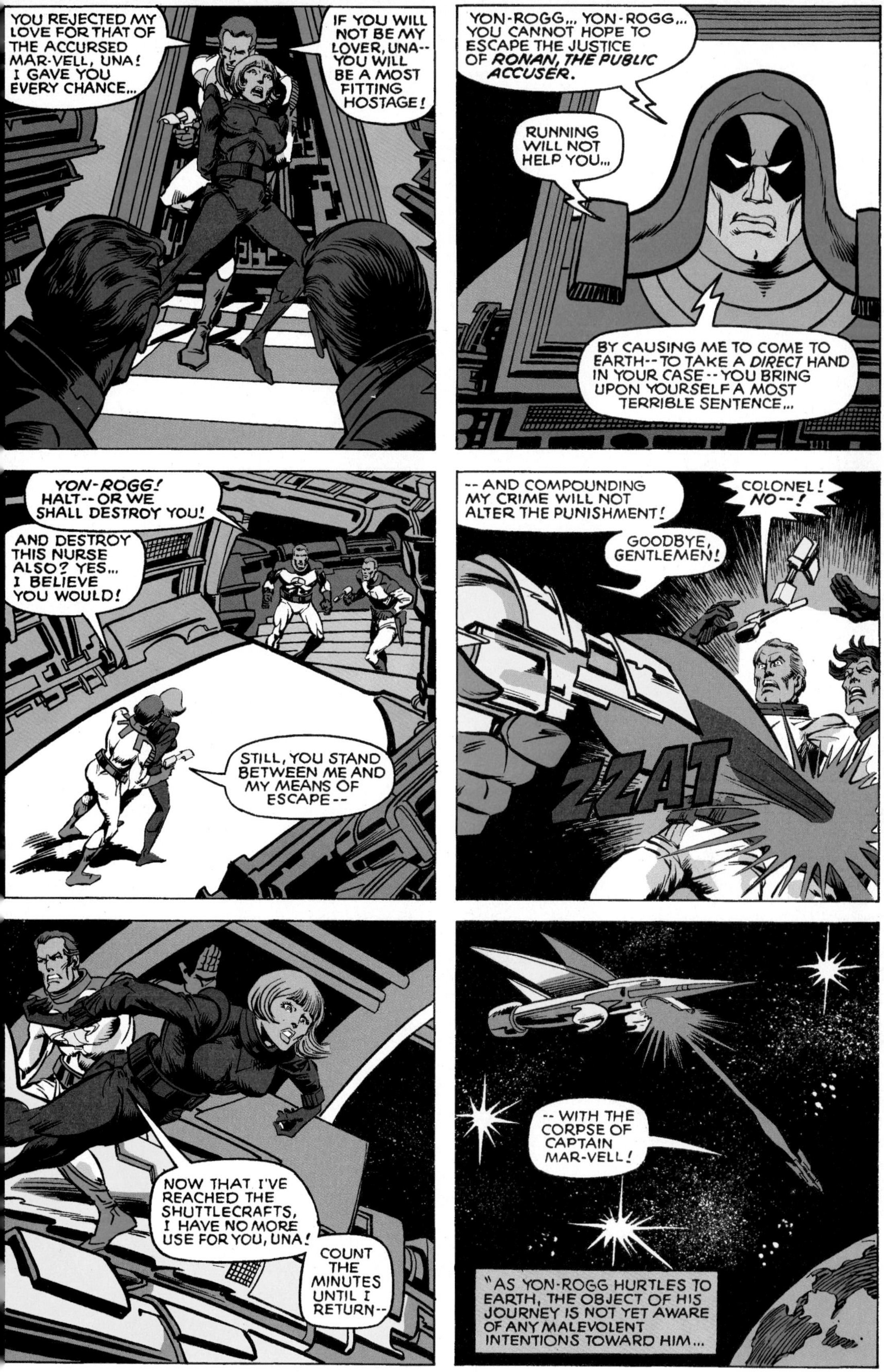

YOU REJECTED MY LOVE FOR THAT OF THE ACCURSED MAR-VELL, UNA! I GAVE YOU EVERY CHANCE...
IF YOU WILL NOT BE MY LOVER, UNA-- YOU WILL BE A MOST FITTING HOSTAGE!
YON-ROGG... YON-ROGG... YOU CANNOT HOPE TO ESCAPE THE JUSTICE OF RONAN, THE PUBLIC ACCUSER.
RUNNING WILL NOT HELP YOU...
BY CAUSING ME TO COME TO EARTH--TO TAKE A DIRECT HAND IN YOUR CASE--YOU BRING UPON YOURSELF A MOST TERRIBLE SENTENCE...
YON-ROGG! HALT--OR WE SHALL DESTROY YOU!
AND DESTROY THIS NURSE ALSO? YES... I BELIEVE YOU WOULD!
STILL, YOU STAND BETWEEN ME AND MY MEANS OF ESCAPE--
--AND COMPOUNDING MY CRIME WILL NOT ALTER THE PUNISHMENT!
COLONEL! NO--!
GOODBYE, GENTLEMEN!
ZZAT
NOW THAT I'VE REACHED THE SHUTTLECRAFTS, I HAVE NO MORE USE FOR YOU, UNA!
COUNT THE MINUTES UNTIL I RETURN--
--WITH THE CORPSE OF CAPTAIN MAR-VELL!
"AS YON-ROGG HURTLES TO EARTH, THE OBJECT OF HIS JOURNEY IS NOT YET AWARE OF ANY MALEVOLENT INTENTIONS TOWARD HIM...

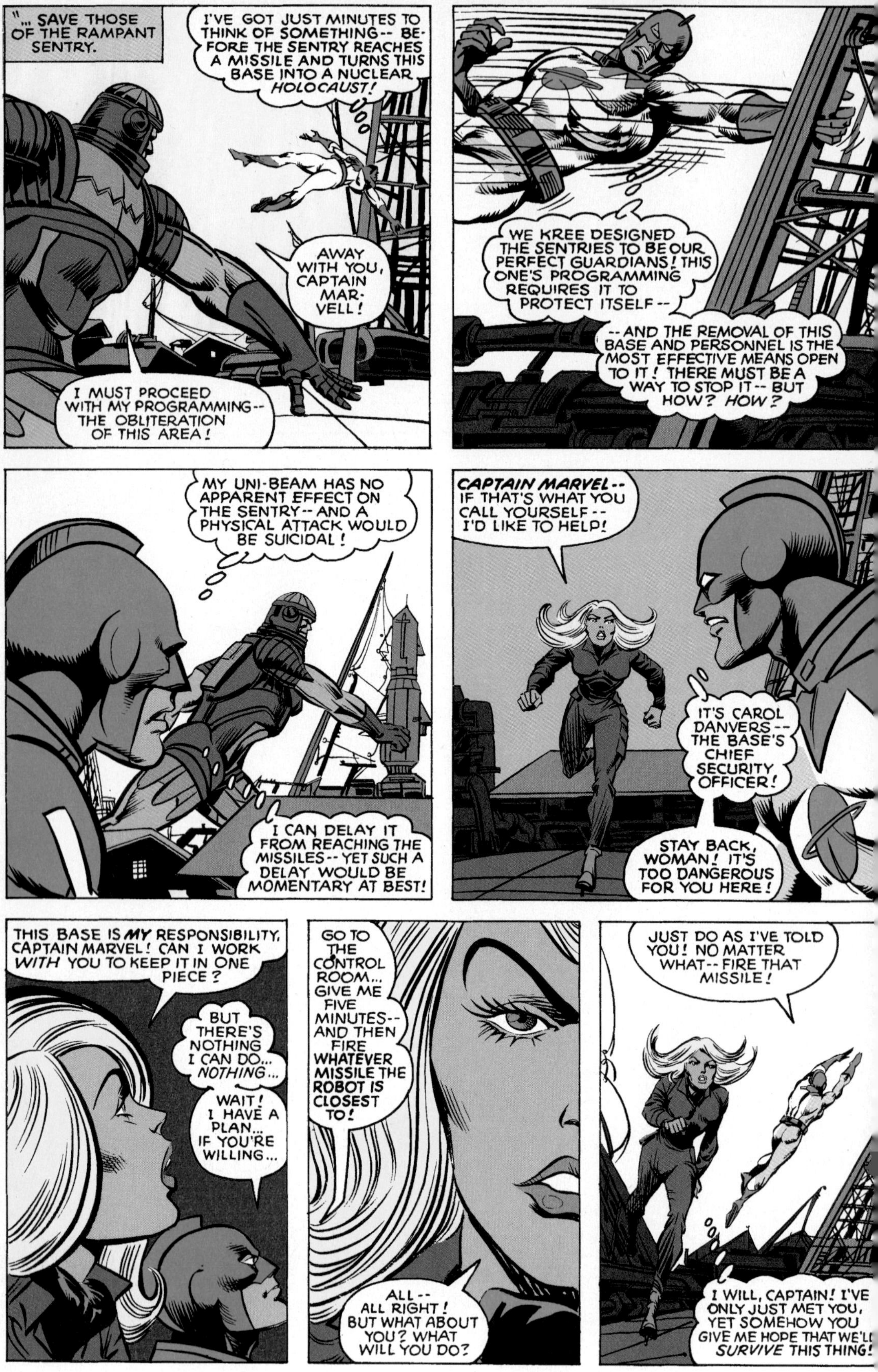
"... SAVE THOSE OF THE RAMPANT SENTRY.
I'VE GOT JUST MINUTES TO THINK OF SOMETHING-- BEFORE THE SENTRY REACHES A MISSILE AND TURNS THIS BASE INTO A NUCLEAR *HOLOCAUST!*
AWAY WITH YOU, CAPTAIN MAR-VELL!
I MUST PROCEED WITH MY PROGRAMMING-- THE OBLITERATION OF THIS AREA!
WE KREE DESIGNED THE SENTRIES TO BE OUR PERFECT GUARDIANS! THIS ONE'S PROGRAMMING REQUIRES IT TO PROTECT ITSELF --
-- AND THE REMOVAL OF THIS BASE AND PERSONNEL IS THE MOST EFFECTIVE MEANS OPEN TO IT! THERE MUST BE A WAY TO STOP IT -- BUT HOW? *HOW?*
MY UNI-BEAM HAS NO APPARENT EFFECT ON THE SENTRY-- AND A PHYSICAL ATTACK WOULD BE SUICIDAL!
I CAN DELAY IT FROM REACHING THE MISSILES-- YET SUCH A DELAY WOULD BE MOMENTARY AT BEST!
CAPTAIN MARVEL-- IF THAT'S WHAT YOU CALL YOURSELF -- I'D LIKE TO HELP!
IT'S CAROL DANVERS -- THE BASE'S CHIEF SECURITY OFFICER!
STAY BACK, WOMAN! IT'S TOO DANGEROUS FOR YOU HERE!
THIS BASE IS *MY* RESPONSIBILITY, CAPTAIN MARVEL! CAN I WORK *WITH* YOU TO KEEP IT IN ONE PIECE?
BUT THERE'S NOTHING I CAN DO... *NOTHING*...
WAIT! I HAVE A PLAN... IF YOU'RE WILLING...
GO TO THE CONTROL ROOM... GIVE ME FIVE MINUTES-- AND THEN FIRE **WHATEVER MISSILE** THE **ROBOT IS CLOSEST** TO!
ALL -- ALL RIGHT! BUT WHAT ABOUT YOU? WHAT WILL YOU DO?
JUST DO AS I'VE TOLD YOU! NO MATTER WHAT-- FIRE THAT MISSILE!
I WILL, CAPTAIN! I'VE ONLY JUST MET YOU, YET SOMEHOW YOU GIVE ME HOPE THAT WE'LL *SURVIVE* THIS THING!

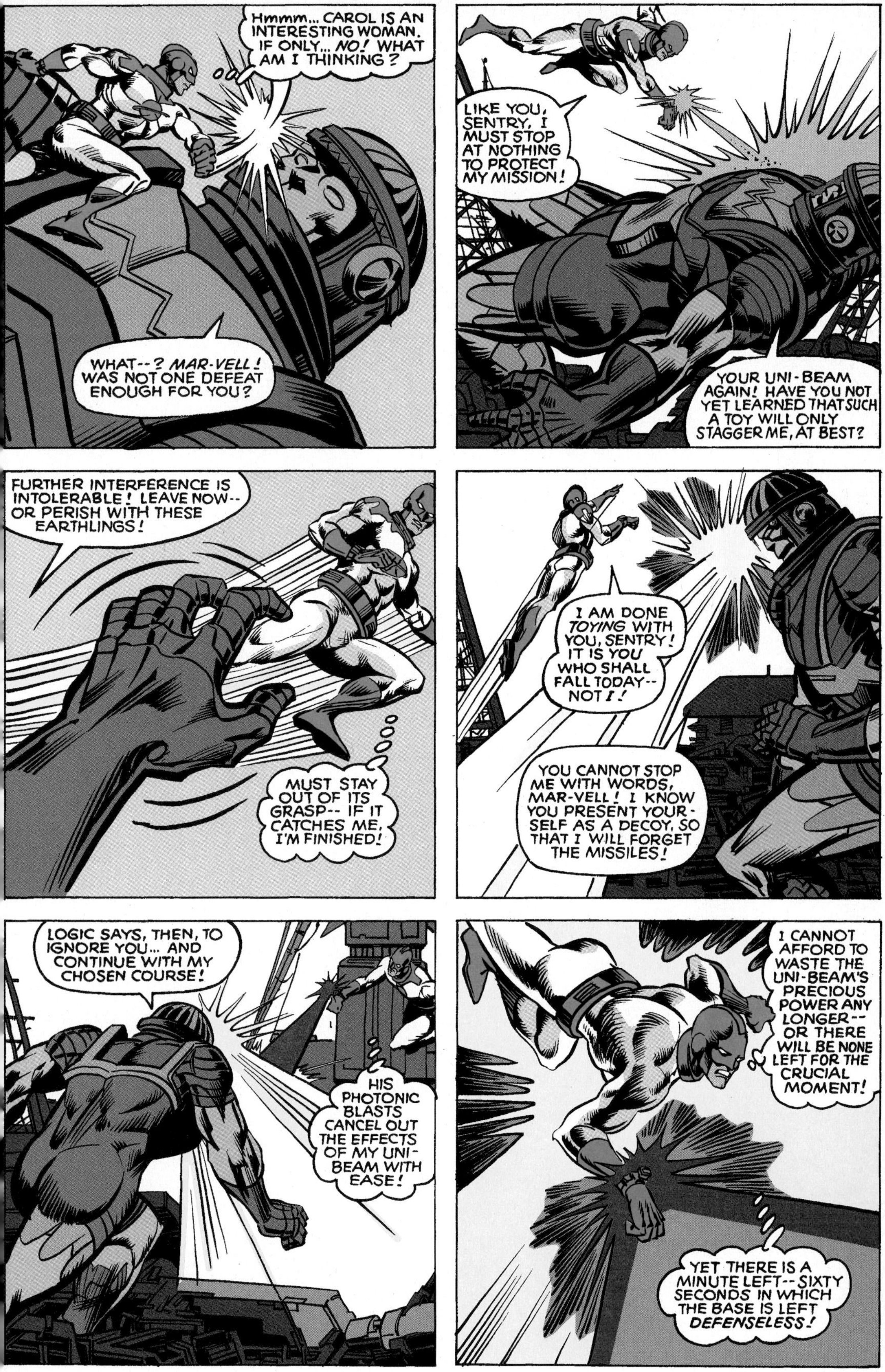
Hmmm... CAROL IS AN INTERESTING WOMAN. IF ONLY... NO! WHAT AM I THINKING?
WHAT--? MAR-VELL! WAS NOT ONE DEFEAT ENOUGH FOR YOU?
LIKE YOU, SENTRY, I MUST STOP AT NOTHING TO PROTECT MY MISSION!
YOUR UNI-BEAM AGAIN! HAVE YOU NOT YET LEARNED THAT SUCH A TOY WILL ONLY STAGGER ME, AT BEST?
FURTHER INTERFERENCE IS INTOLERABLE! LEAVE NOW--OR PERISH WITH THESE EARTHLINGS!
MUST STAY OUT OF ITS GRASP-- IF IT CATCHES ME, I'M FINISHED!
I AM DONE TOYING WITH YOU, SENTRY! IT IS YOU WHO SHALL FALL TODAY--NOT I!
YOU CANNOT STOP ME WITH WORDS, MAR-VELL! I KNOW YOU PRESENT YOURSELF AS A DECOY, SO THAT I WILL FORGET THE MISSILES!
LOGIC SAYS, THEN, TO IGNORE YOU... AND CONTINUE WITH MY CHOSEN COURSE!
HIS PHOTONIC BLASTS CANCEL OUT THE EFFECTS OF MY UNI-BEAM WITH EASE!
I CANNOT AFFORD TO WASTE THE UNI-BEAM'S PRECIOUS POWER ANY LONGER--OR THERE WILL BE NONE LEFT FOR THE CRUCIAL MOMENT!
YET THERE IS A MINUTE LEFT--SIXTY SECONDS IN WHICH THE BASE IS LEFT DEFENSELESS!

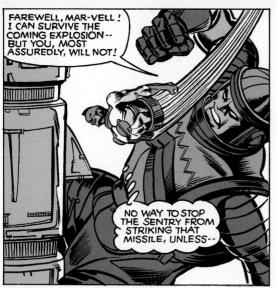

FAREWELL, MAR-VELL! I CAN SURVIVE THE COMING EXPLOSION-- BUT YOU, MOST ASSUREDLY, WILL NOT!

NO WAY TO STOP THE SENTRY FROM STRIKING THAT MISSILE, UNLESS--

--I USE MYSELF!

CRUNCH

N-NO... CAN'T PASS OUT... IT'S ALMOST TIME...

CAPTAIN MARVEL! THE MISSILE IS PRIMED! WHATEVER YOU'RE PLANNING--

--DO IT NOW!

"SUDDENLY, THE UNI-BEAM STABS OUT AGAIN, BATHING THE SENTRY IN ITS GLOW...

"...AND THE SENTRY LAUGHS!

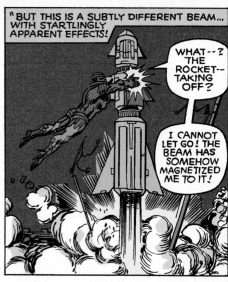

"BUT THIS IS A SUBTLY DIFFERENT BEAM... WITH STARTLINGLY APPARENT EFFECTS!

WHAT--? THE ROCKET-- TAKING OFF?

I CANNOT LET GO! THE BEAM HAS SOMEHOW MAGNETIZED ME TO IT!

IT WORKED! THE MISSILE-- AND THAT MONSTER-- ARE HEADING INTO SPACE!

THE UNI-BEAM'S MAGNETIC CHARGE WAS AN ADAPTATION MADE AFTER THE SENTRY WAS PLACED ON EARTH...

"... AND THAT CHARGE WILL TAKE THE SENTRY FAR FROM THE EARTH'S SURFACE...'

KAR·ROOM

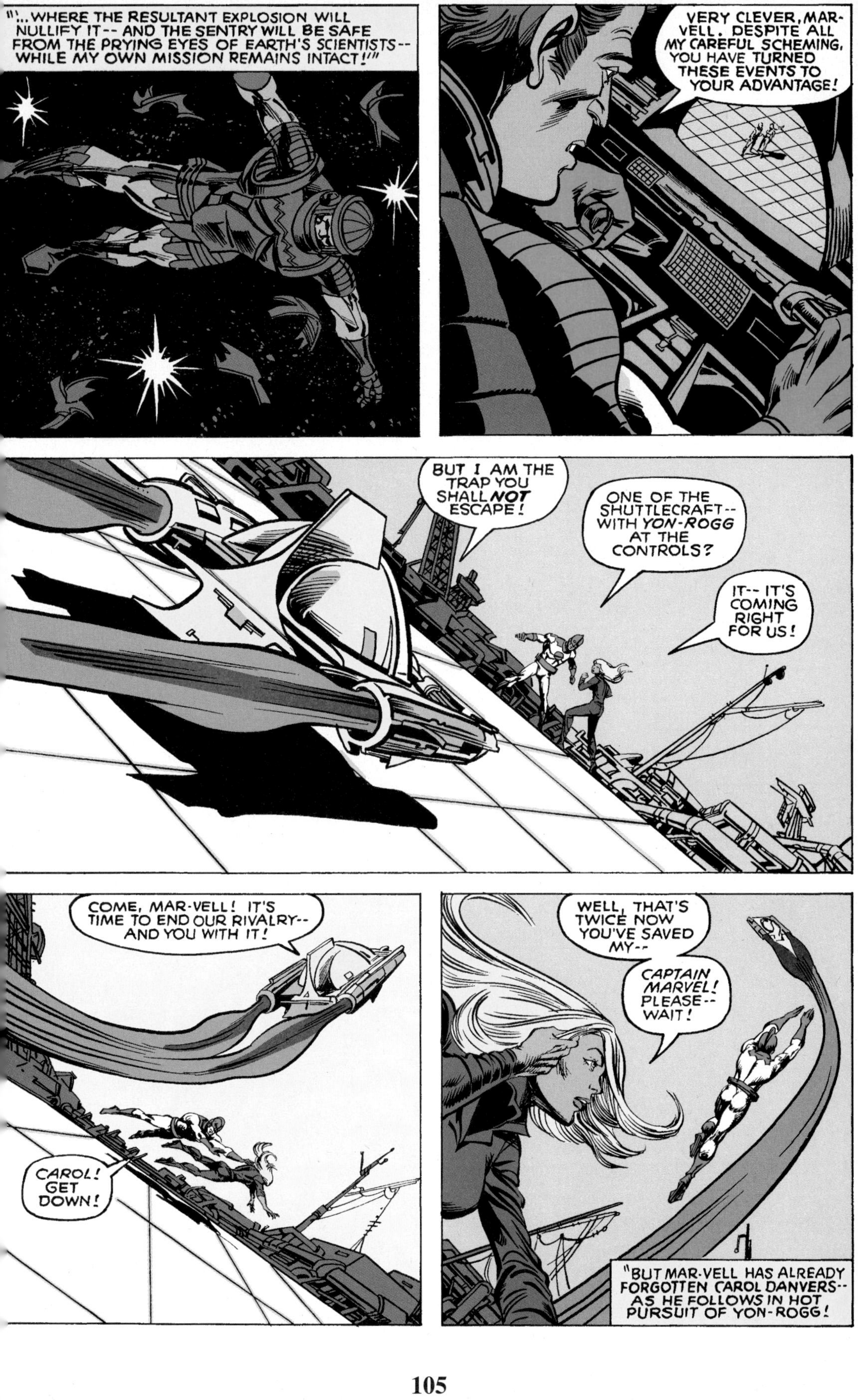
"...WHERE THE RESULTANT EXPLOSION WILL NULLIFY IT -- AND THE SENTRY WILL BE SAFE FROM THE PRYING EYES OF EARTH'S SCIENTISTS -- WHILE MY OWN MISSION REMAINS INTACT!'"
VERY CLEVER, MAR-VELL. DESPITE ALL MY CAREFUL SCHEMING, YOU HAVE TURNED THESE EVENTS TO YOUR ADVANTAGE!
BUT I AM THE TRAP YOU SHALL NOT ESCAPE!
ONE OF THE SHUTTLECRAFT -- WITH YON-ROGG AT THE CONTROLS?
IT-- IT'S COMING RIGHT FOR US!
COME, MAR-VELL! IT'S TIME TO END OUR RIVALRY -- AND YOU WITH IT!
CAROL! GET DOWN!
WELL, THAT'S TWICE NOW YOU'VE SAVED MY--
CAPTAIN MARVEL! PLEASE -- WAIT!
"BUT MAR-VELL HAS ALREADY FORGOTTEN CAROL DANVERS -- AS HE FOLLOWS IN HOT PURSUIT OF YON-ROGG!

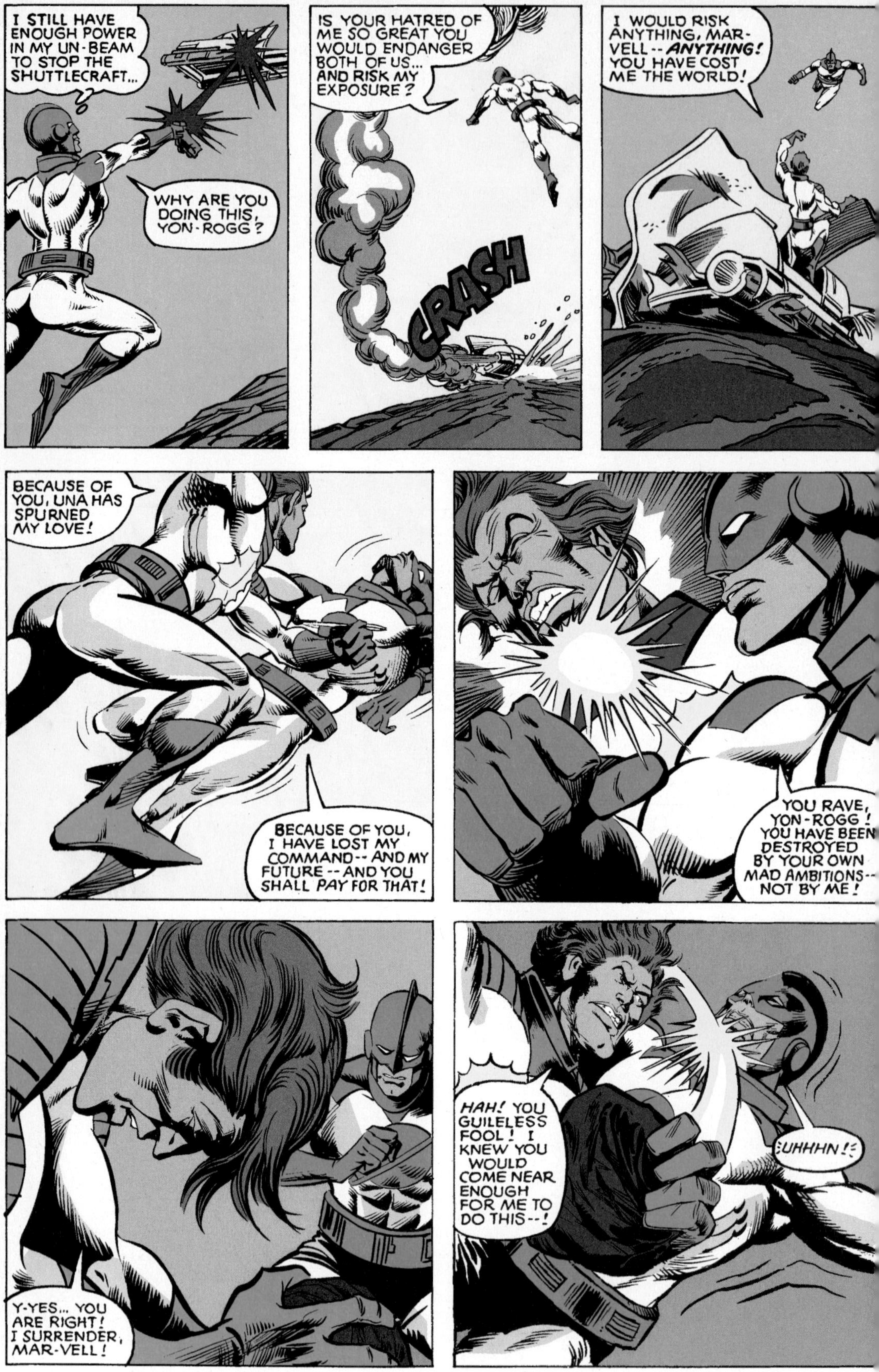
I STILL HAVE ENOUGH POWER IN MY UN-BEAM TO STOP THE SHUTTLECRAFT...
WHY ARE YOU DOING THIS, YON-ROGG?
IS YOUR HATRED OF ME SO GREAT YOU WOULD ENDANGER BOTH OF US... AND RISK MY EXPOSURE?
CRASH
I WOULD RISK ANYTHING, MAR-VELL -- ANYTHING! YOU HAVE COST ME THE WORLD!
BECAUSE OF YOU, UNA HAS SPURNED MY LOVE!
BECAUSE OF YOU, I HAVE LOST MY COMMAND -- AND MY FUTURE -- AND YOU SHALL PAY FOR THAT!
YOU RAVE, YON-ROGG! YOU HAVE BEEN DESTROYED BY YOUR OWN MAD AMBITIONS -- NOT BY ME!
Y-YES... YOU ARE RIGHT! I SURRENDER, MAR-VELL!
HAH! YOU GUILELESS FOOL! I KNEW YOU WOULD COME NEAR ENOUGH FOR ME TO DO THIS --!
UHHHN!

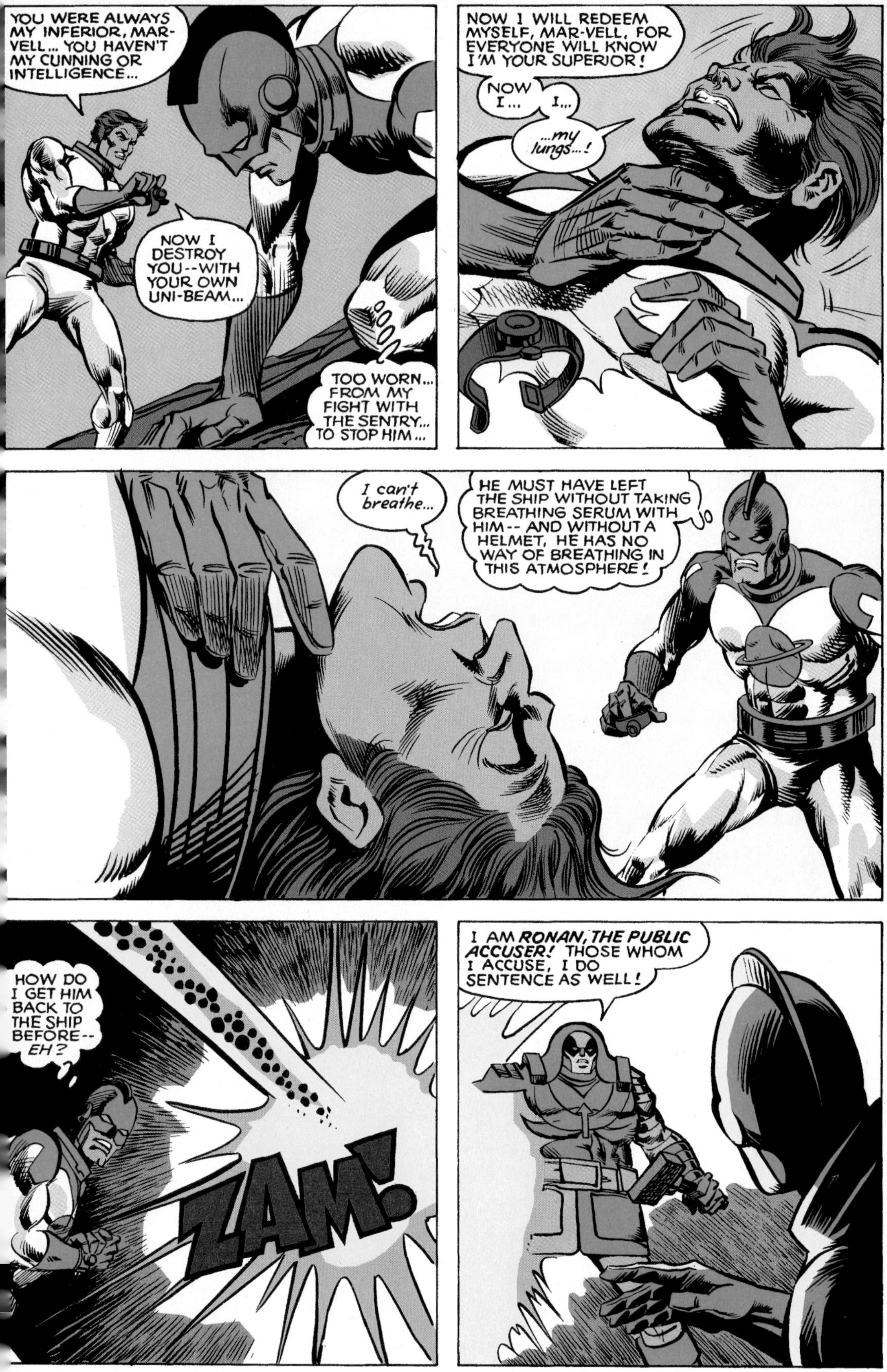

YOU WERE ALWAYS MY INFERIOR, MAR-VELL... YOU HAVEN'T MY CUNNING OR INTELLIGENCE...
NOW I DESTROY YOU--WITH YOUR OWN UNI-BEAM...
TOO WORN... FROM MY FIGHT WITH THE SENTRY... TO STOP HIM...
NOW I WILL REDEEM MYSELF, MAR-VELL, FOR EVERYONE WILL KNOW I'M YOUR SUPERIOR!
NOW I... I...
...my lungs...!
I can't breathe...
HE MUST HAVE LEFT THE SHIP WITHOUT TAKING BREATHING SERUM WITH HIM-- AND WITHOUT A HELMET, HE HAS NO WAY OF BREATHING IN THIS ATMOSPHERE!
HOW DO I GET HIM BACK TO THE SHIP BEFORE-- EH?
ZAM!
I AM RONAN, THE PUBLIC ACCUSER! THOSE WHOM I ACCUSE, I DO SENTENCE AS WELL!

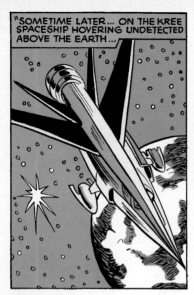

"SOMETIME LATER... ON THE KREE SPACESHIP HOVERING UNDETECTED ABOVE THE EARTH...

HAIL, MAR-VELL-- AND HEAR THE WORDS OF *ZAREK, THE IMPERIAL MINISTER...*

WE HAVE STUDIED THE RECENT EVENTS ON THE PLANET KNOWN AS *THE EARTH*.

IT IS OUR FINDING THAT YOU HAVE HANDLED YOURSELF WITH UTMOST SKILL AND INGENUITY.

AS YOU KNOW, YOUR MISSION IS ONE OF EXTREME SENSITIVITY AND OF THE GREATEST IMPORTANCE TO THE FUTURE OF THE EMPIRE. THE EARTHLINGS ARE A VERY FORBIDDING RACE...

IT IS YOUR MISSION TO STUDY THESE PRIMITIVE BEINGS--SO THAT WE MAY PREDICT WHERE THEIR CIVILIZATION WILL LEAD THEM, AND TAKE STEPS TO NEUTRALIZE THEM SHOULD THEY APPEAR A *THREAT!*

IT IS OUR DECISION THAT YOU ARE MOST QUALIFIED TO HANDLE OUR INTERESTS HERE. IT IS IN YOUR HANDS THAT WE PLACE THIS MISSION--

COLONEL MAR-VELL!

THANK YOU, SIR! I WILL ENDEAVOR TO BE WORTHY OF YOUR TRUST!

I AM PROUD OF YOU, MY DARLING! BUT-- WHAT ARE YOUR FEELINGS FOR THE PLANET EARTH?

--THEN LET THE EARTHLINGS *BEWARE!*

MY LOYALTIES LIE WITH THE EMPIRE, UNA. IF THE EARTHLINGS INDEED PROVE TO BE A MENACE TO THE KREE--

"AND, IN THIS REALITY, A DOOR SILENTLY SHUTS ON THE EARTH..."

end

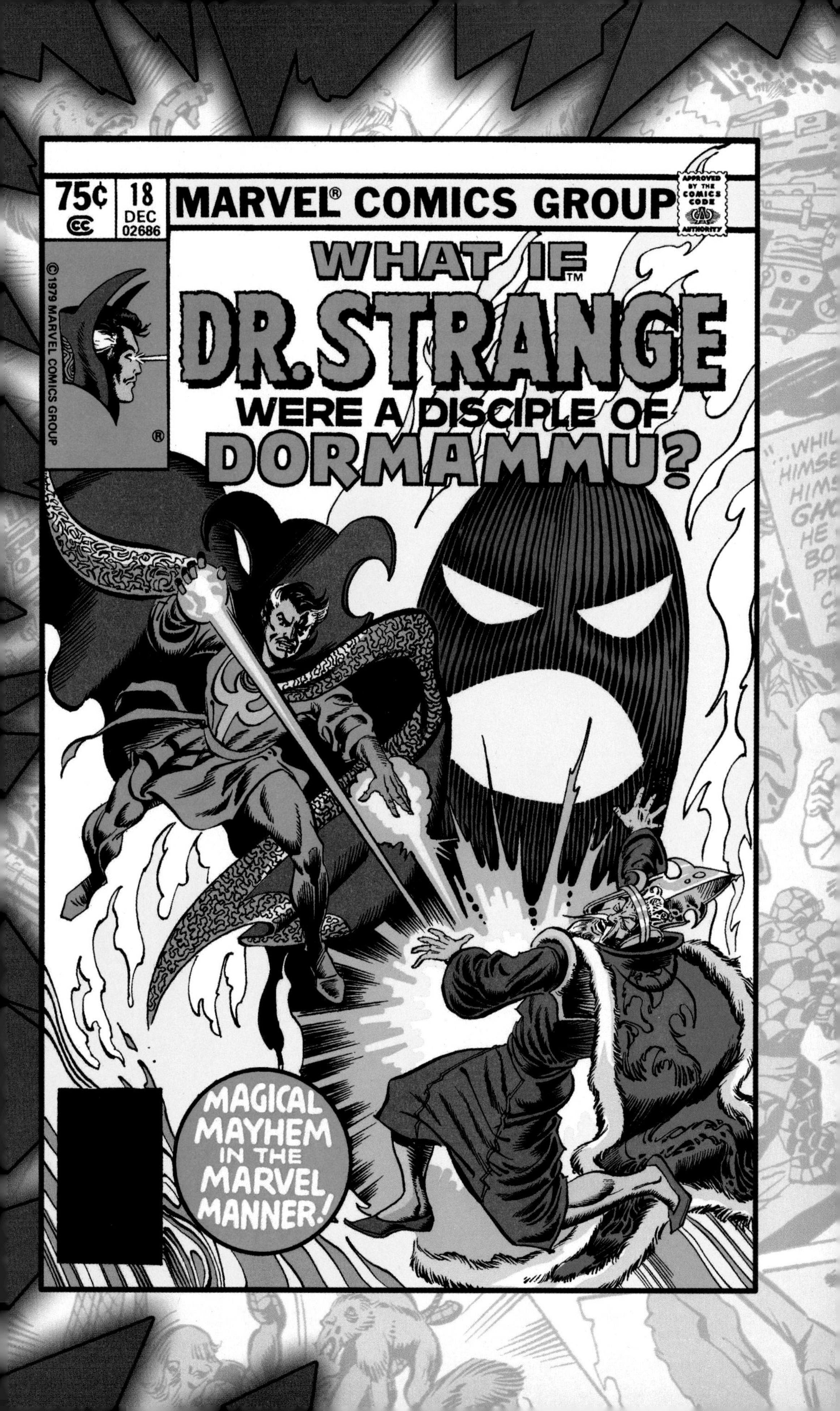
75¢
18
DEC
02686
MARVEL® COMICS GROUP
APPROVED BY THE COMICS CODE AUTHORITY
© 1979 MARVEL COMICS GROUP
WHAT IF™
DR. STRANGE
WERE A DISCIPLE OF
DORMAMMU?
MAGICAL MAYHEM IN THE MARVEL MANNER!

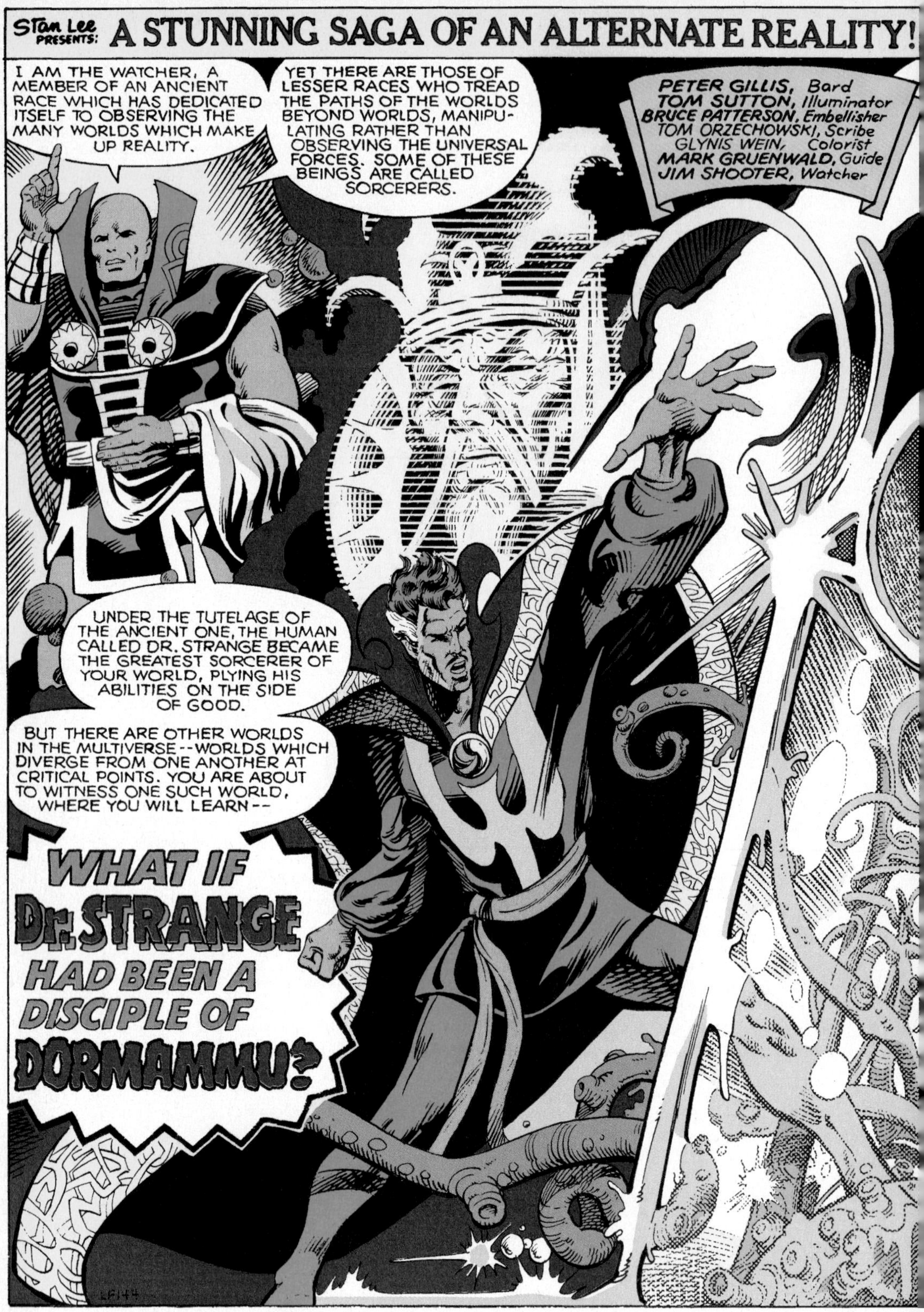
Stan Lee PRESENTS: A STUNNING SAGA OF AN ALTERNATE REALITY!
I AM THE WATCHER, A MEMBER OF AN ANCIENT RACE WHICH HAS DEDICATED ITSELF TO OBSERVING THE MANY WORLDS WHICH MAKE UP REALITY.
YET THERE ARE THOSE OF LESSER RACES WHO TREAD THE PATHS OF THE WORLDS BEYOND WORLDS, MANIPULATING RATHER THAN OBSERVING THE UNIVERSAL FORCES. SOME OF THESE BEINGS ARE CALLED SORCERERS.
PETER GILLIS, Bard
TOM SUTTON, Illuminator
BRUCE PATTERSON, Embellisher
TOM ORZECHOWSKI, Scribe
GLYNIS WEIN, Colorist
MARK GRUENWALD, Guide
JIM SHOOTER, Watcher
UNDER THE TUTELAGE OF THE ANCIENT ONE, THE HUMAN CALLED DR. STRANGE BECAME THE GREATEST SORCERER OF YOUR WORLD, PLYING HIS ABILITIES ON THE SIDE OF GOOD.
BUT THERE ARE OTHER WORLDS IN THE MULTIVERSE--WORLDS WHICH DIVERGE FROM ONE ANOTHER AT CRITICAL POINTS. YOU ARE ABOUT TO WITNESS ONE SUCH WORLD, WHERE YOU WILL LEARN--
WHAT IF Dr. STRANGE HAD BEEN A DISCIPLE OF DORMAMMU?

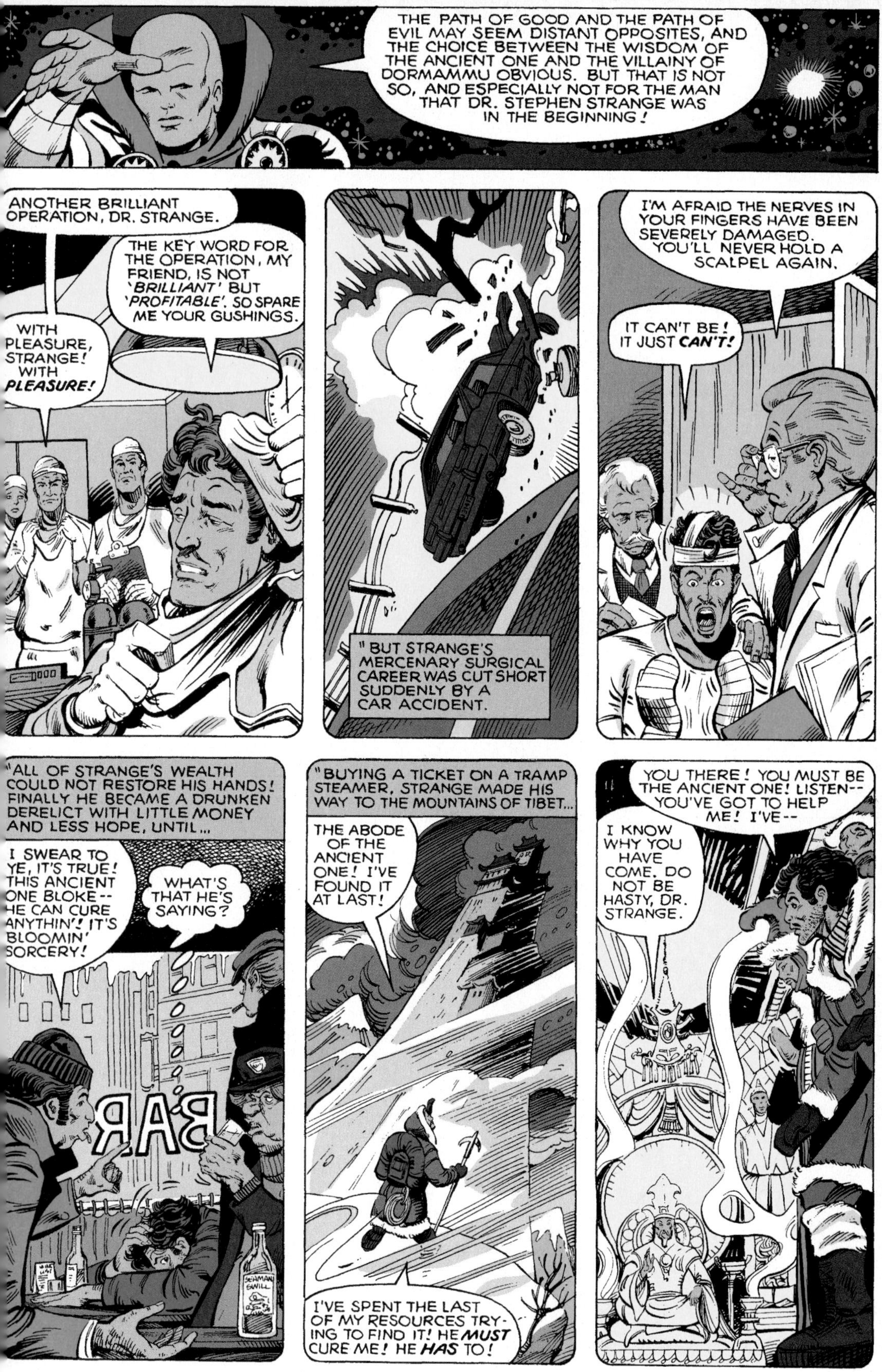
THE PATH OF GOOD AND THE PATH OF EVIL MAY SEEM DISTANT OPPOSITES, AND THE CHOICE BETWEEN THE WISDOM OF THE ANCIENT ONE AND THE VILLAINY OF DORMAMMU OBVIOUS. BUT THAT IS NOT SO, AND ESPECIALLY NOT FOR THE MAN THAT DR. STEPHEN STRANGE WAS IN THE BEGINNING!
ANOTHER BRILLIANT OPERATION, DR. STRANGE.
THE KEY WORD FOR THE OPERATION, MY FRIEND, IS NOT 'BRILLIANT' BUT 'PROFITABLE'. SO SPARE ME YOUR GUSHINGS.
WITH PLEASURE, STRANGE! WITH PLEASURE!
"BUT STRANGE'S MERCENARY SURGICAL CAREER WAS CUT SHORT SUDDENLY BY A CAR ACCIDENT.
I'M AFRAID THE NERVES IN YOUR FINGERS HAVE BEEN SEVERELY DAMAGED. YOU'LL NEVER HOLD A SCALPEL AGAIN.
IT CAN'T BE! IT JUST CAN'T!
"ALL OF STRANGE'S WEALTH COULD NOT RESTORE HIS HANDS! FINALLY HE BECAME A DRUNKEN DERELICT WITH LITTLE MONEY AND LESS HOPE, UNTIL...
I SWEAR TO YE, IT'S TRUE! THIS ANCIENT ONE BLOKE -- HE CAN CURE ANYTHIN'! IT'S BLOOMIN' SORCERY!
WHAT'S THAT HE'S SAYING?
BAR
"BUYING A TICKET ON A TRAMP STEAMER, STRANGE MADE HIS WAY TO THE MOUNTAINS OF TIBET...
THE ABODE OF THE ANCIENT ONE! I'VE FOUND IT AT LAST!
I'VE SPENT THE LAST OF MY RESOURCES TRYING TO FIND IT! HE MUST CURE ME! HE HAS TO!
YOU THERE! YOU MUST BE THE ANCIENT ONE! LISTEN-- YOU'VE GOT TO HELP ME! I'VE--
I KNOW WHY YOU HAVE COME. DO NOT BE HASTY, DR. STRANGE.

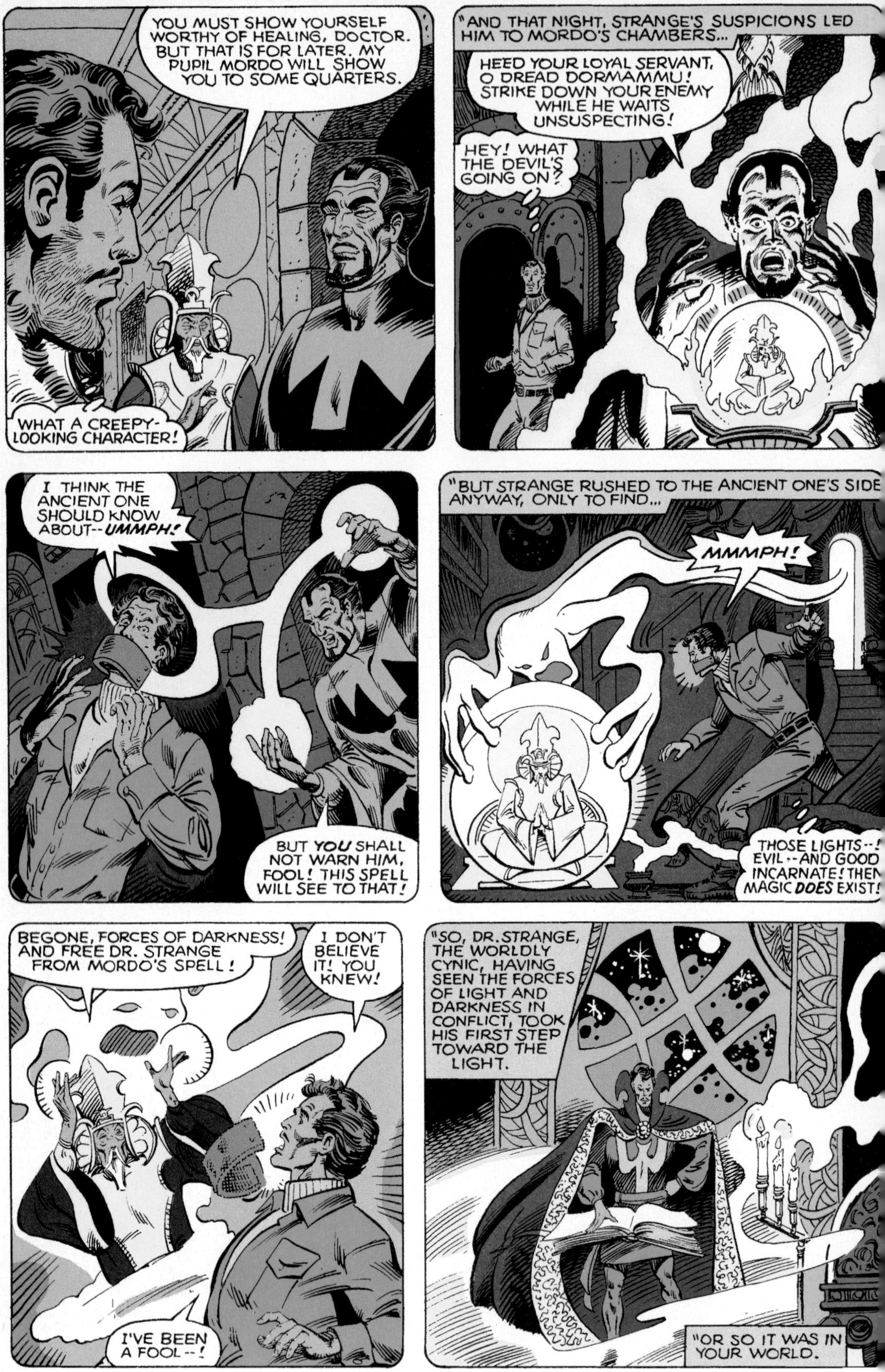
YOU MUST SHOW YOURSELF WORTHY OF HEALING, DOCTOR. BUT THAT IS FOR LATER. MY PUPIL MORDO WILL SHOW YOU TO SOME QUARTERS.
WHAT A CREEPY-LOOKING CHARACTER!
"AND THAT NIGHT, STRANGE'S SUSPICIONS LED HIM TO MORDO'S CHAMBERS...
HEED YOUR LOYAL SERVANT, O DREAD DORMAMMU! STRIKE DOWN YOUR ENEMY WHILE HE WAITS UNSUSPECTING!
HEY! WHAT THE DEVIL'S GOING ON?
I THINK THE ANCIENT ONE SHOULD KNOW ABOUT-- UMMPH!
BUT YOU SHALL NOT WARN HIM, FOOL! THIS SPELL WILL SEE TO THAT!
"BUT STRANGE RUSHED TO THE ANCIENT ONE'S SIDE ANYWAY, ONLY TO FIND...
MMMPH!
THOSE LIGHTS--! EVIL--AND GOOD INCARNATE! THEN MAGIC DOES EXIST!
BEGONE, FORCES OF DARKNESS! AND FREE DR. STRANGE FROM MORDO'S SPELL!
I DON'T BELIEVE IT! YOU KNEW!
I'VE BEEN A FOOL--!
"SO, DR. STRANGE, THE WORLDLY CYNIC, HAVING SEEN THE FORCES OF LIGHT AND DARKNESS IN CONFLICT, TOOK HIS FIRST STEP TOWARD THE LIGHT.
"OR SO IT WAS IN YOUR WORLD.

BUT SO MOMENTOUS AN EVENT AS THE INITIATION OF A SORCERER SUPREME IS FRAUGHT WITH CRITICAL POINTS, WHICH MIGHT HAVE LED TO IRREVOCABLE DIFFERENCES...

--MORDO WILL SHOW YOU TO SOME QUARTERS!

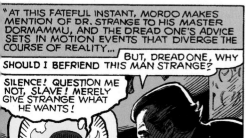

"AT THIS FATEFUL INSTANT, MORDO MAKES MENTION OF DR. STRANGE TO HIS MASTER DORMAMMU, AND THE DREAD ONE'S ADVICE SETS IN MOTION EVENTS THAT DIVERGE THE COURSE OF REALITY...

BUT, DREAD ONE, WHY SHOULD I BEFRIEND THIS MAN STRANGE?

SILENCE! QUESTION ME NOT, SLAVE! MERELY GIVE STRANGE WHAT HE WANTS!

"AND, SO...

YOU WANTED TO SEE ME, MORDO?

MORE THAN THAT, MY FRIEND! I WANT TO HELP YOU!

THE ANCIENT ONE, ALAS, IS SENILE! HE WILL DITHER ABOUT 'BEING WORTHY' AND DO NOTHING! BUT I CAN HEAL YOUR HANDS!

THEN JUST DO IT, MISTER! I DON'T CARE TWO BITS ABOUT MAGIC OR EVIL OR ANY OF THAT! I ONLY CARE ABOUT RESULTS! DO IT, AND I'LL PAY ANY PRICE!

YOU SHALL LEARN THE PRICE LATER, STRANGE!

WAIT! WHAT--?

MY FINGERS-- I CAN FEEL THEM HEALING!

"THE ANCIENT ONE WATCHES WITH GROWING CONCERN-- BUT AS YET HE CAN DO NOTHING.

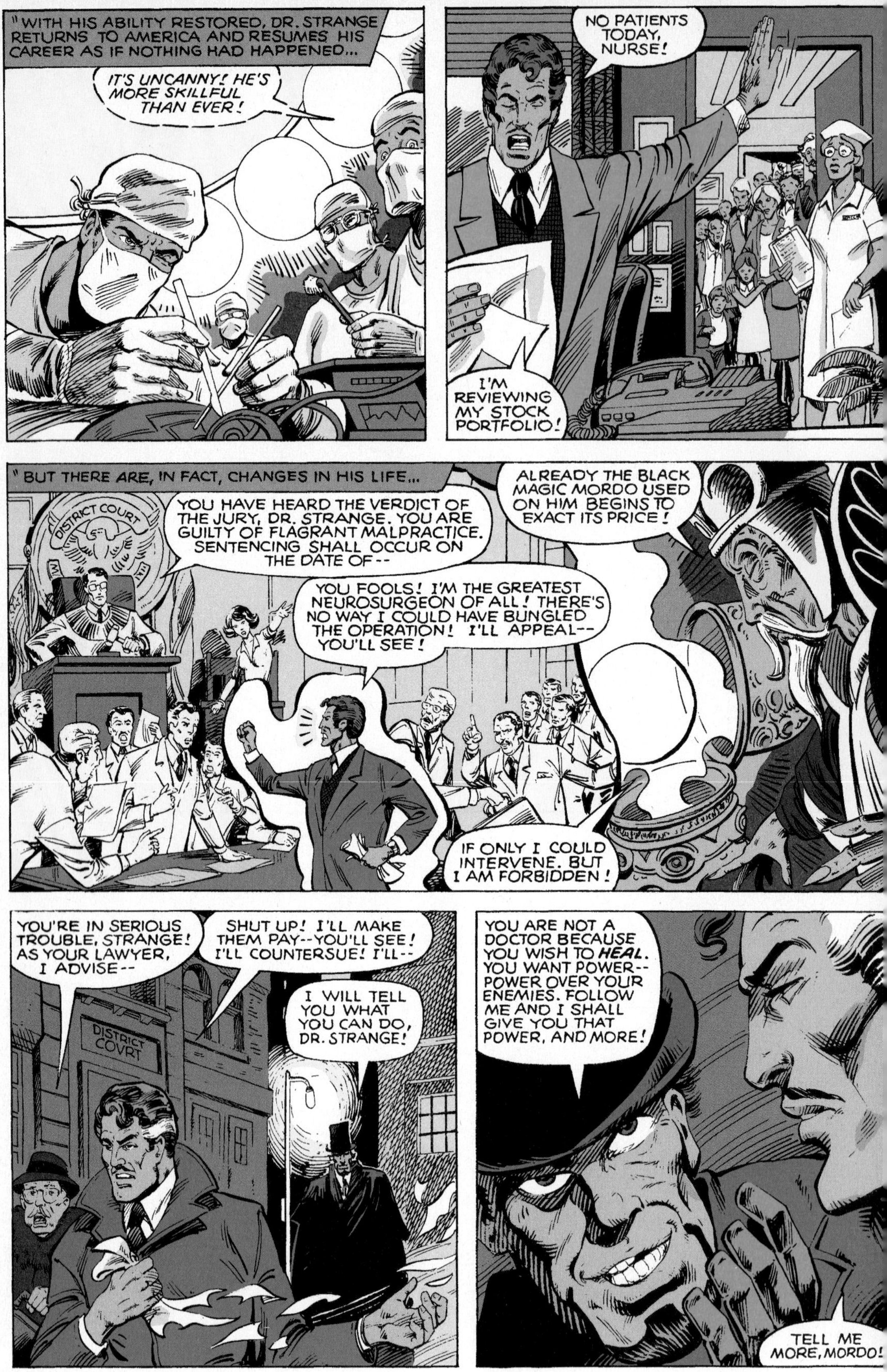

"WITH HIS ABILITY RESTORED, DR. STRANGE RETURNS TO AMERICA AND RESUMES HIS CAREER AS IF NOTHING HAD HAPPENED...
IT'S UNCANNY! HE'S MORE SKILLFUL THAN EVER!
NO PATIENTS TODAY, NURSE!
I'M REVIEWING MY STOCK PORTFOLIO!
"BUT THERE ARE, IN FACT, CHANGES IN HIS LIFE...
DISTRICT COURT
YOU HAVE HEARD THE VERDICT OF THE JURY, DR. STRANGE. YOU ARE GUILTY OF FLAGRANT MALPRACTICE. SENTENCING SHALL OCCUR ON THE DATE OF--
YOU FOOLS! I'M THE GREATEST NEUROSURGEON OF ALL! THERE'S NO WAY I COULD HAVE BUNGLED THE OPERATION! I'LL APPEAL--YOU'LL SEE!
ALREADY THE BLACK MAGIC MORDO USED ON HIM BEGINS TO EXACT ITS PRICE!
IF ONLY I COULD INTERVENE. BUT I AM FORBIDDEN!
YOU'RE IN SERIOUS TROUBLE, STRANGE! AS YOUR LAWYER, I ADVISE--
SHUT UP! I'LL MAKE THEM PAY--YOU'LL SEE! I'LL COUNTERSUE! I'LL--
DISTRICT COVRT
I WILL TELL YOU WHAT YOU CAN DO, DR. STRANGE!
YOU ARE NOT A DOCTOR BECAUSE YOU WISH TO HEAL. YOU WANT POWER--POWER OVER YOUR ENEMIES. FOLLOW ME AND I SHALL GIVE YOU THAT POWER, AND MORE!
TELL ME MORE, MORDO!

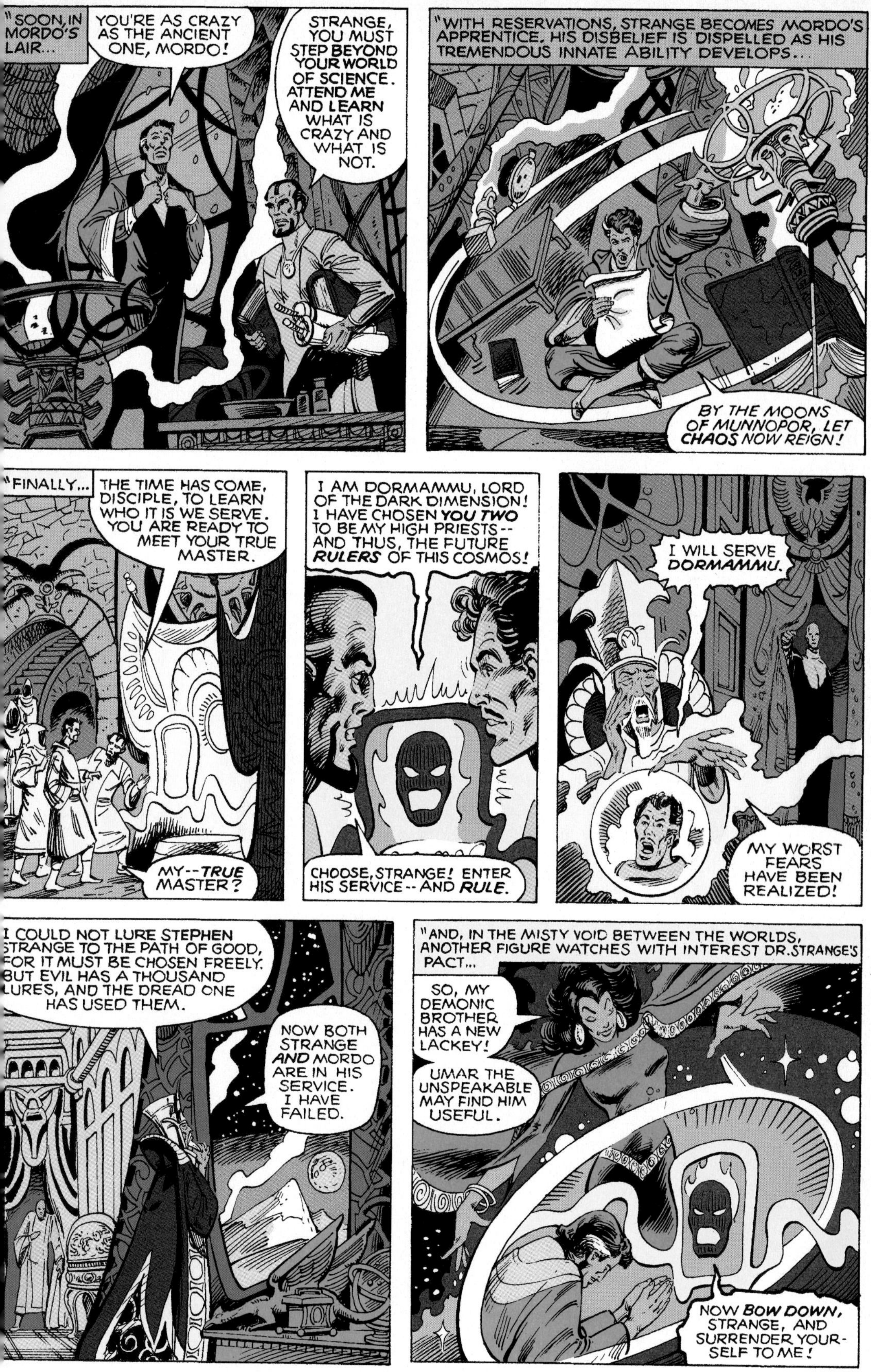
"SOON, IN MORDO'S LAIR...
YOU'RE AS CRAZY AS THE ANCIENT ONE, MORDO!
STRANGE, YOU MUST STEP BEYOND YOUR WORLD OF SCIENCE. ATTEND ME AND LEARN WHAT IS CRAZY AND WHAT IS NOT.
"WITH RESERVATIONS, STRANGE BECOMES MORDO'S APPRENTICE. HIS DISBELIEF IS DISPELLED AS HIS TREMENDOUS INNATE ABILITY DEVELOPS...
BY THE MOONS OF MUNNOPOR, LET CHAOS NOW REIGN!
"FINALLY...
THE TIME HAS COME, DISCIPLE, TO LEARN WHO IT IS WE SERVE. YOU ARE READY TO MEET YOUR TRUE MASTER.
MY--TRUE MASTER?
I AM DORMAMMU, LORD OF THE DARK DIMENSION! I HAVE CHOSEN YOU TWO TO BE MY HIGH PRIESTS-- AND THUS, THE FUTURE RULERS OF THIS COSMOS!
CHOOSE, STRANGE! ENTER HIS SERVICE-- AND RULE.
I WILL SERVE DORMAMMU.
MY WORST FEARS HAVE BEEN REALIZED!
I COULD NOT LURE STEPHEN STRANGE TO THE PATH OF GOOD, FOR IT MUST BE CHOSEN FREELY. BUT EVIL HAS A THOUSAND LURES, AND THE DREAD ONE HAS USED THEM.
NOW BOTH STRANGE AND MORDO ARE IN HIS SERVICE. I HAVE FAILED.
"AND, IN THE MISTY VOID BETWEEN THE WORLDS, ANOTHER FIGURE WATCHES WITH INTEREST DR. STRANGE'S PACT...
SO, MY DEMONIC BROTHER HAS A NEW LACKEY!
UMAR THE UNSPEAKABLE MAY FIND HIM USEFUL.
NOW BOW DOWN, STRANGE, AND SURRENDER YOURSELF TO ME!

"AND, AS DR. STRANGE FREELY SUBMITS TO DORMAMMU'S RULE, HALF A WORLD AWAY, ANOTHER MAN BEARING THE TITLE 'DOCTOR' WILL SOON MAKE AN EQUALLY MOMENTOUS DECISION...

ENOUGH! I CAN TORTURE MYSELF *NO MORE!*

I AM DOCTOR DOOM! I POSSESS VAST POWER, UNTOLD WEALTH, AND UNEQUALLED GENIUS! THEN WHY AM I CURSED BY THIS RAVAGED FACE? WHY CAN I NEVER KNOW THE PEACE OF PERFECTION?

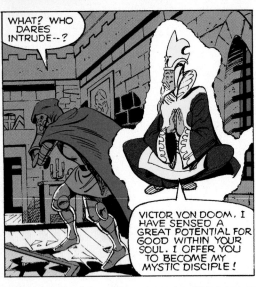

WHAT? WHO DARES INTRUDE--?

VICTOR VON DOOM, I HAVE SENSED A GREAT POTENTIAL FOR GOOD WITHIN YOUR SOUL. I OFFER YOU TO BECOME MY MYSTIC DISCIPLE!

DISCIPLE?? DOCTOR DOOM IS NO MAN'S INFERIOR!

STILL, THERE IS MUCH I CAN TEACH YOU.

AND FOR YOUR AID, I CAN OFFER YOU MUCH IN RETURN!

I CAN FREE YOU FROM THE CURSE OF YOUR FACE, VON DOOM, IF YOU WILL LEARN THE MYSTIC ARTS FROM ME!

NEVER! THE MONARCH OF LATVERIA RELIES ONLY ON HIMSELF! *HIMSELF!*

I-- SEE.

MASTER! HOW DID YOU FARE?

I-- SHOULD HAVE KNOWN BETTER, FAITHFUL HAMIR.

ARE THE OTHERS ASSEMBLED?

THEY ARE.

IN THIS DARK HOUR, EVEN THE GREATEST ASSEMBLAGE OF WHITE MAGICIANS ON EARTH MAY NOT BE ENOUGH!

"THE ANCIENT ONE PASSES INTO HIS INNER SANCTUM, THERE TO SILENTLY GREET THE NINE HE HAS SUMMONED:

"AND, ASSISTING HAMIR THE HERMIT AS ACOLYTES-- VICTORIA BENTLEY AND WONG!

"THE SENILE BUT STILL POWERFUL GENGHIS!

"DR. ANTHONY DRUID!

"TURAN BARIM!

"LORD PHYFFE!

"RAMA KALIPH!

"COUNT CAREZZI!

"AGATHA HARKNESS OF WHISPER HILL!

YOU KNOW WHY YOU'VE BEEN SENT FOR. I SHALL NOT MISLEAD YOU: WE ARE THE WORLD'S LAST HOPE AGAINST DORMAMMU. SHOULD WE FAIL, THERE SHALL BE NONE TO STAND AGAINST HIM.

BUT, WISE ONE --! THE DREAD DORMAMMU IS LIKE UNTO A *GOD!* AND IF THE *TWO MOST POWERFUL ADEPTS* IN THE COSMOS ARE IN HIS CAMP--

--HAVE WE *ANY* HOPE? IS THERE ANY POWER WE CAN CALL ON-- OR ARE WE HERE MERELY TO DIE AMONG FRIENDS?

WE ARE NOT WITHOUT RESOURCES, DR. DRUID--

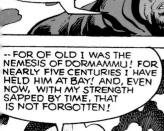

--FOR OF OLD I WAS THE NEMESIS OF DORMAMMU! FOR NEARLY FIVE CENTURIES I HAVE HELD HIM AT BAY! AND, EVEN NOW, WITH MY STRENGTH SAPPED BY TIME, THAT IS NOT FORGOTTEN!

BEHOLD THE TALISMAN WITH WHICH EACH OF DORMAMMU'S ARCH-FOES HAS EVER DEFIED HIM!

BEHOLD THE LIGHT OF TRUTH!

IT IS THE EYE OF AGAMOTTO --

--AND ITS SECRETS MAY PROVE OUR ONLY REMAINING HOPE OF VICTORY!

117

"NO ONE KNOWS THE ORIGIN OF THE ALL-SEEING EYE--

--BUT FOR AGES IT DRIFTED AMONG STRANGE STARS AND SKIES--

"--UNTIL IT WAS DISCOVERED, IT IS SAID, BY THE WIZARD AGAMOTTO, THE FIRST SORCERER SUPREME, IN ONE OF HIS MANY GUISES.

"BUT, THOUGH IT WAS HANDED DOWN THROUGH THE AGES, IT WAS ONLY I WHO DISCOVERED THAT THE AMULET WAS A GATEWAY TO--

"--ETERNITY!! YES, I, AMONG ALL MORTALS, HAVE STEPPED THROUGH THE DOOR OF THE EYE TO SPEAK WITH THAT AWESOME BEING WHO IS EVERYTHING THAT DORMAMMU IS NOT!

BUT I WAS NOT JUDGED WORTHY BY ETERNITY, AND I WAS CAST AWAY.

HE TOLD ME, HOWEVER, TO HOLD THE AMULET IN TRUST FOR MY SUCCESSOR, WHO WOULD STAND BEFORE HIM FREELY!

"EMERGING FROM THE EYE, I LAY NEAR DEATH ON A MOUNTAINSIDE FOR SEVEN DAYS AND SEVEN NIGHTS. I HAVE NEVER TRIED AGAIN, FOR IT WOULD MEAN MY DOOM!"

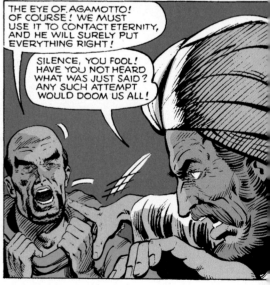

THE EYE OF AGAMOTTO! OF COURSE! WE MUST USE IT TO CONTACT ETERNITY, AND HE WILL SURELY PUT EVERYTHING RIGHT!

SILENCE, YOU FOOL! HAVE YOU NOT HEARD WHAT WAS JUST SAID? ANY SUCH ATTEMPT WOULD DOOM US ALL!

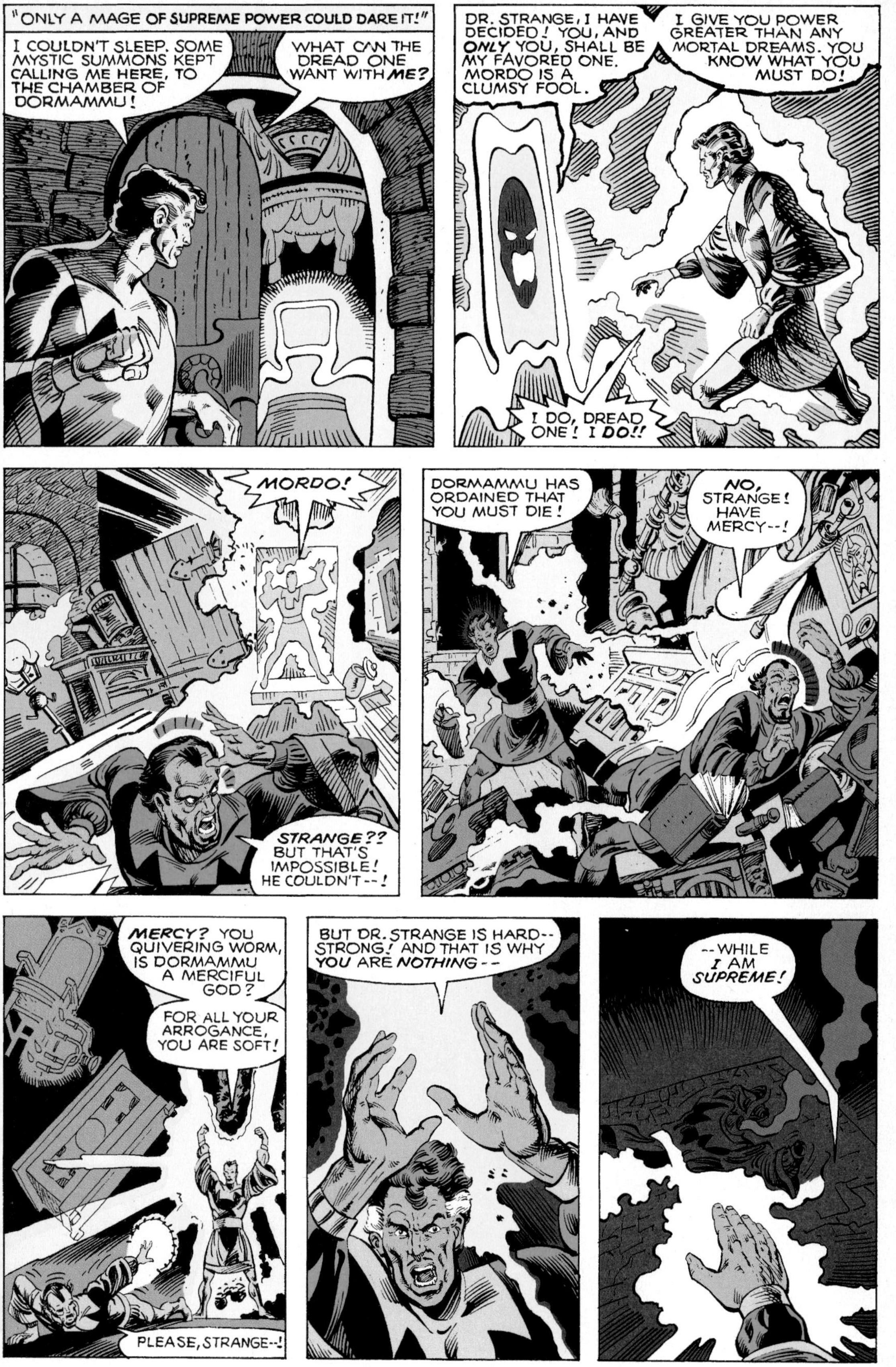
"ONLY A MAGE OF SUPREME POWER COULD DARE IT!"
I COULDN'T SLEEP. SOME MYSTIC SUMMONS KEPT CALLING ME HERE, TO THE CHAMBER OF DORMAMMU!
WHAT CAN THE DREAD ONE WANT WITH ME?
DR. STRANGE, I HAVE DECIDED! YOU, AND ONLY YOU, SHALL BE MY FAVORED ONE. MORDO IS A CLUMSY FOOL.
I GIVE YOU POWER GREATER THAN ANY MORTAL DREAMS. YOU KNOW WHAT YOU MUST DO!
I DO, DREAD ONE! I DO!!
MORDO!
STRANGE?? BUT THAT'S IMPOSSIBLE! HE COULDN'T--!
DORMAMMU HAS ORDAINED THAT YOU MUST DIE!
NO, STRANGE! HAVE MERCY--!
MERCY? YOU QUIVERING WORM, IS DORMAMMU A MERCIFUL GOD?
FOR ALL YOUR ARROGANCE, YOU ARE SOFT!
PLEASE, STRANGE--!
BUT DR. STRANGE IS HARD-- STRONG! AND THAT IS WHY YOU ARE NOTHING--
--WHILE I AM SUPREME!

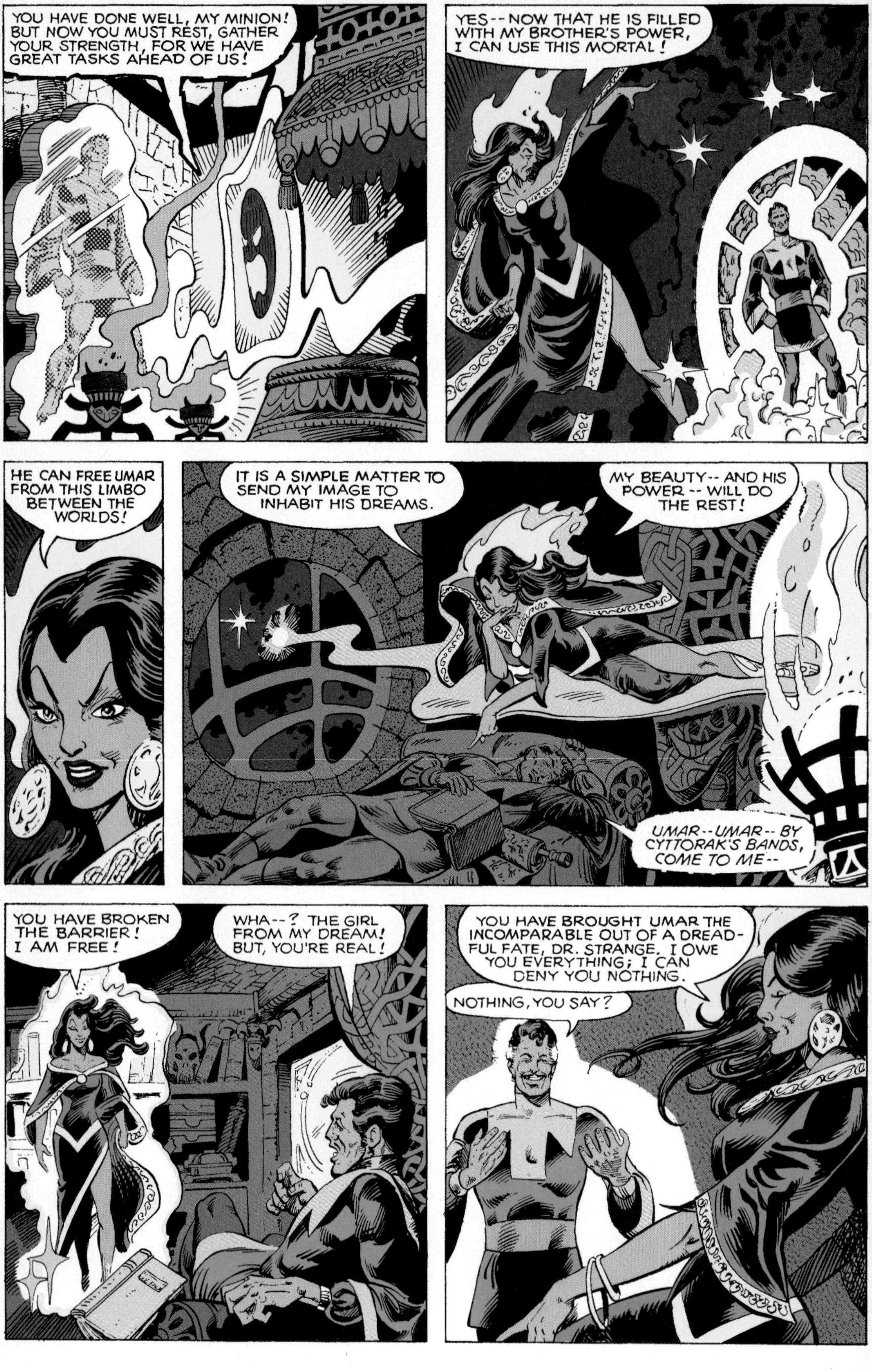
YOU HAVE DONE WELL, MY MINION! BUT NOW YOU MUST REST, GATHER YOUR STRENGTH, FOR WE HAVE GREAT TASKS AHEAD OF US!
YES--NOW THAT HE IS FILLED WITH MY BROTHER'S POWER, I CAN USE THIS MORTAL!
HE CAN FREE UMAR FROM THIS LIMBO BETWEEN THE WORLDS!
IT IS A SIMPLE MATTER TO SEND MY IMAGE TO INHABIT HIS DREAMS.
MY BEAUTY-- AND HIS POWER -- WILL DO THE REST!
UMAR--UMAR-- BY CYTTORAK'S BANDS, COME TO ME--
YOU HAVE BROKEN THE BARRIER! I AM FREE!
WHA--? THE GIRL FROM MY DREAM! BUT, YOU'RE REAL!
YOU HAVE BROUGHT UMAR THE INCOMPARABLE OUT OF A DREADFUL FATE, DR. STRANGE. I OWE YOU EVERYTHING; I CAN DENY YOU NOTHING.
NOTHING, YOU SAY?

"MEANWHILE, IN THE CASTLE OF THE ANCIENT ONE, THE ASSEMBLAGE OF SORCERERS HAS TEMPORARILY ADJOURNED...

I DON'T CARE WHAT THEY SAY! SOMEHOW WE MUST CONTACT ETERNITY!

I HAVE IT! DR. DRUID-- I HAVE IT!

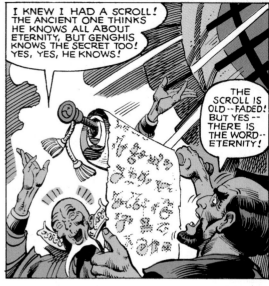

I KNEW I HAD A SCROLL! THE ANCIENT ONE THINKS HE KNOWS ALL ABOUT ETERNITY, BUT GENGHIS KNOWS THE SECRET TOO! YES, YES, HE KNOWS!

THE SCROLL IS OLD--FADED! BUT YES-- THERE IS THE WORD-- ETERNITY!

"LATER, UMAR PAYS A VISIT TO DORMAMMU'S REALM...

OH, STOP FUMING, BROTHER DEAR! I'M FREE AGAIN, AND THAT'S THAT!

CURSE YOU, UMAR! I BANISHED YOU ONCE BECAUSE YOU WERE A THREAT, AND I'LL DO SO AGAIN!

BUT YOU WON'T TRICK ME AS YOU DID LAST TIME, BELOVED!

BESIDES, I HAVE ACQUIRED MORE -- SENSUAL AMBITIONS OF LATE!

IF YOU MEAN STRANGE --

--HE IS THE TOOL WITH WHICH I SHALL BREAK DOWN THE GATES OF ORDER!

ALL THE MYRIAD WORLDS SHALL BECOME DARK DIMENSIONS-- PLACES OF CHAOS! AND ALL UNDER THE RULE OF--DORMAMMU!

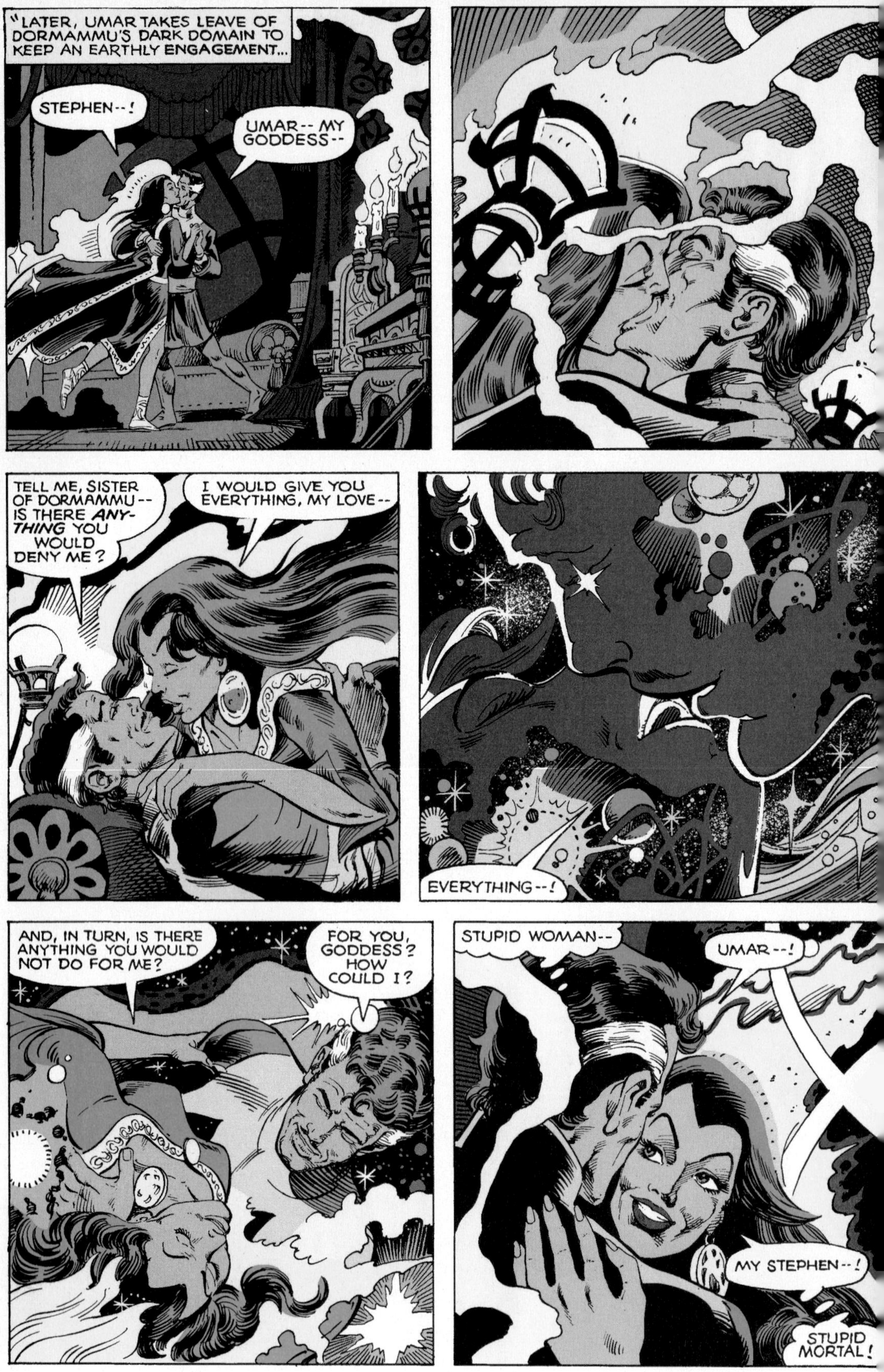
"LATER, UMAR TAKES LEAVE OF DORMAMMU'S DARK DOMAIN TO KEEP AN EARTHLY ENGAGEMENT...
STEPHEN--!
UMAR-- MY GODDESS--
TELL ME, SISTER OF DORMAMMU-- IS THERE *ANYTHING* YOU WOULD DENY ME?
I WOULD GIVE YOU EVERYTHING, MY LOVE--
EVERYTHING--!
AND, IN TURN, IS THERE ANYTHING YOU WOULD NOT DO FOR ME?
FOR YOU, GODDESS? HOW COULD I?
STUPID WOMAN--
UMAR--!
MY STEPHEN--!
STUPID MORTAL!

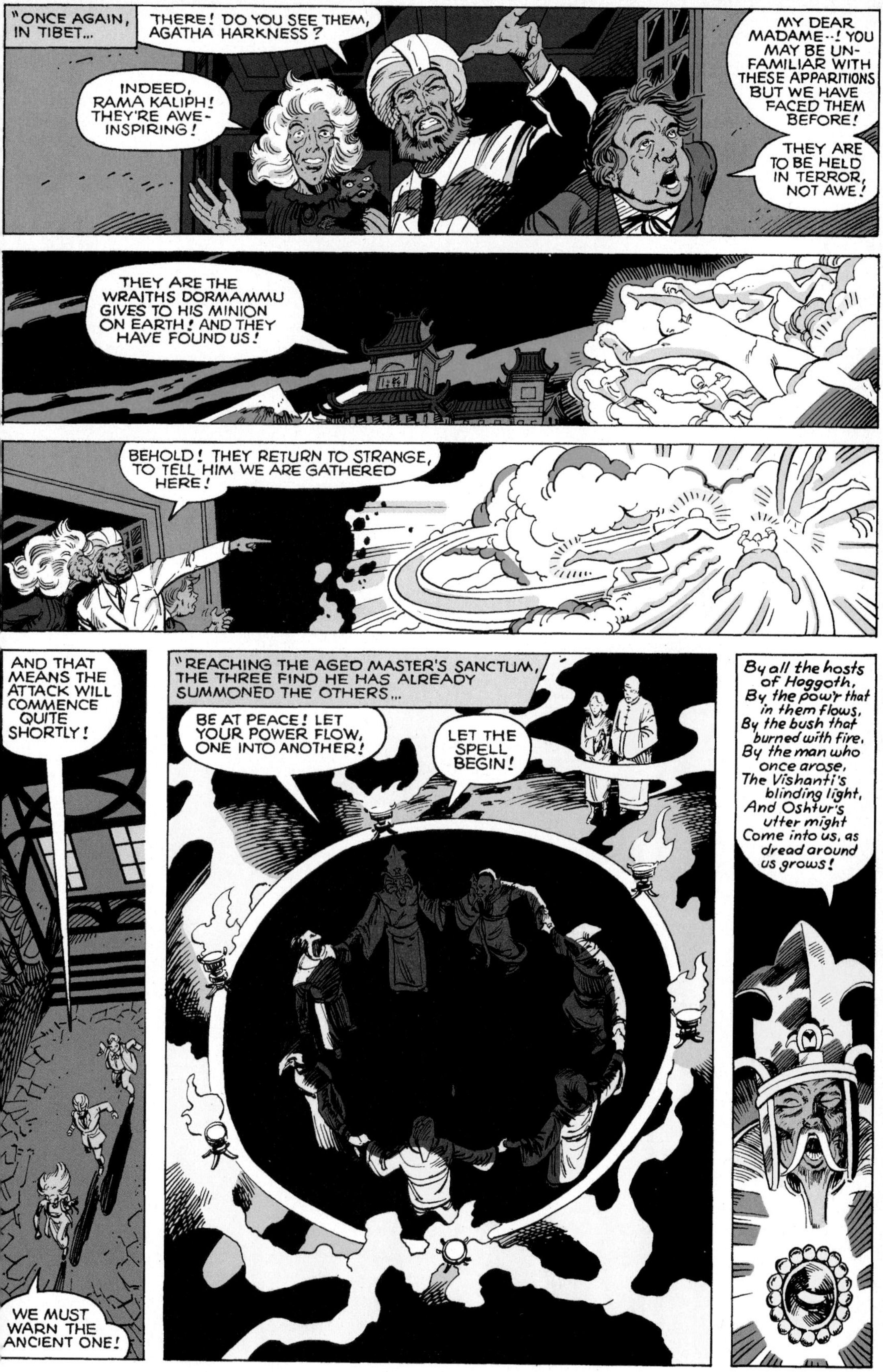
"ONCE AGAIN, IN TIBET...
THERE! DO YOU SEE THEM, AGATHA HARKNESS?
INDEED, RAMA KALIPH! THEY'RE AWE-INSPIRING!
MY DEAR MADAME--! YOU MAY BE UN-FAMILIAR WITH THESE APPARITIONS BUT WE HAVE FACED THEM BEFORE!
THEY ARE TO BE HELD IN TERROR, NOT AWE!
THEY ARE THE WRAITHS DORMAMMU GIVES TO HIS MINION ON EARTH! AND THEY HAVE FOUND US!
BEHOLD! THEY RETURN TO STRANGE, TO TELL HIM WE ARE GATHERED HERE!
AND THAT MEANS THE ATTACK WILL COMMENCE QUITE SHORTLY!
WE MUST WARN THE ANCIENT ONE!
"REACHING THE AGED MASTER'S SANCTUM, THE THREE FIND HE HAS ALREADY SUMMONED THE OTHERS...
BE AT PEACE! LET YOUR POWER FLOW, ONE INTO ANOTHER!
LET THE SPELL BEGIN!
By all the hosts of Hoggoth, By the pow'r that in them flows, By the bush that burned with fire, By the man who once arose, The Vishanti's blinding light, And Oshtur's utter might Come into us, as dread around us grows!

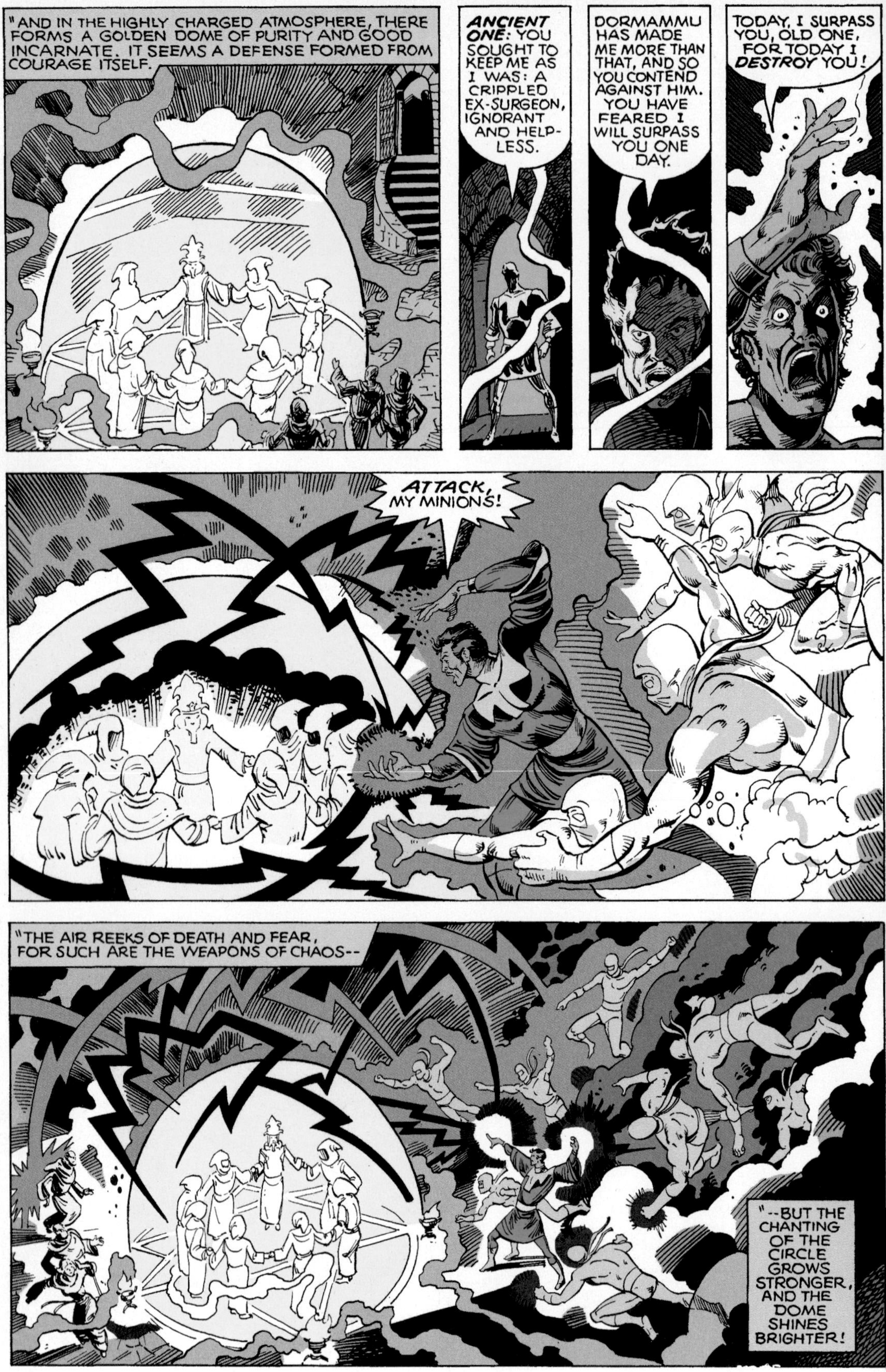
"AND IN THE HIGHLY CHARGED ATMOSPHERE, THERE FORMS A GOLDEN DOME OF PURITY AND GOOD INCARNATE. IT SEEMS A DEFENSE FORMED FROM COURAGE ITSELF.
ANCIENT ONE: YOU SOUGHT TO KEEP ME AS I WAS: A CRIPPLED EX-SURGEON, IGNORANT AND HELPLESS.
DORMAMMU HAS MADE ME MORE THAN THAT, AND SO YOU CONTEND AGAINST HIM. YOU HAVE FEARED I WILL SURPASS YOU ONE DAY.
TODAY, I SURPASS YOU, OLD ONE, FOR TODAY I DESTROY YOU!
ATTACK, MY MINIONS!
"THE AIR REEKS OF DEATH AND FEAR, FOR SUCH ARE THE WEAPONS OF CHAOS--
"--BUT THE CHANTING OF THE CIRCLE GROWS STRONGER, AND THE DOME SHINES BRIGHTER!

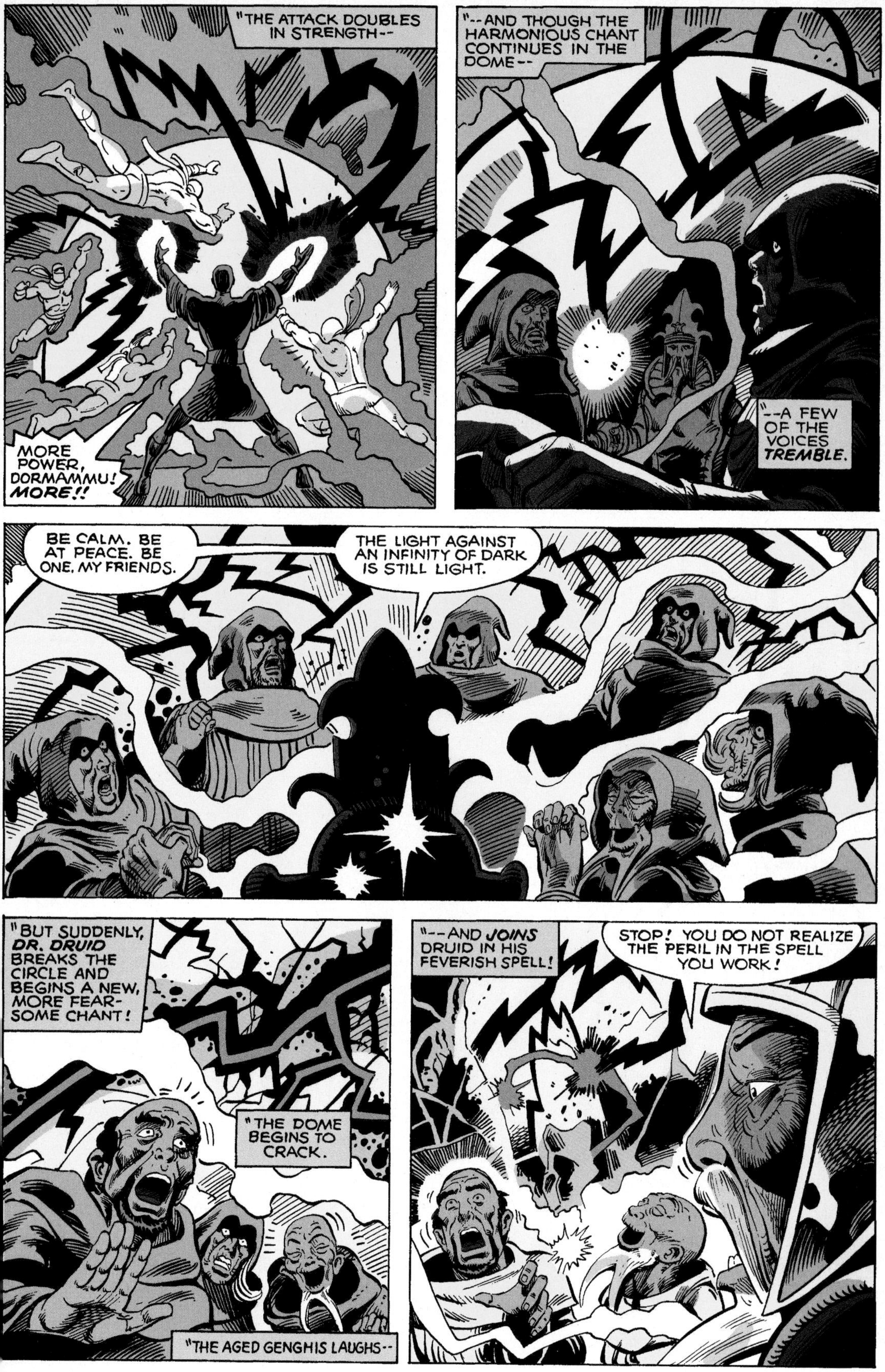
"THE ATTACK DOUBLES IN STRENGTH--
MORE POWER, DORMAMMU! MORE!!
"--AND THOUGH THE HARMONIOUS CHANT CONTINUES IN THE DOME--
"--A FEW OF THE VOICES TREMBLE.
BE CALM. BE AT PEACE. BE ONE, MY FRIENDS.
THE LIGHT AGAINST AN INFINITY OF DARK IS STILL LIGHT.
"BUT SUDDENLY, DR. DRUID BREAKS THE CIRCLE AND BEGINS A NEW, MORE FEAR-SOME CHANT!
"THE DOME BEGINS TO CRACK.
"THE AGED GENGHIS LAUGHS--
"--AND JOINS DRUID IN HIS FEVERISH SPELL!
STOP! YOU DO NOT REALIZE THE PERIL IN THE SPELL YOU WORK!

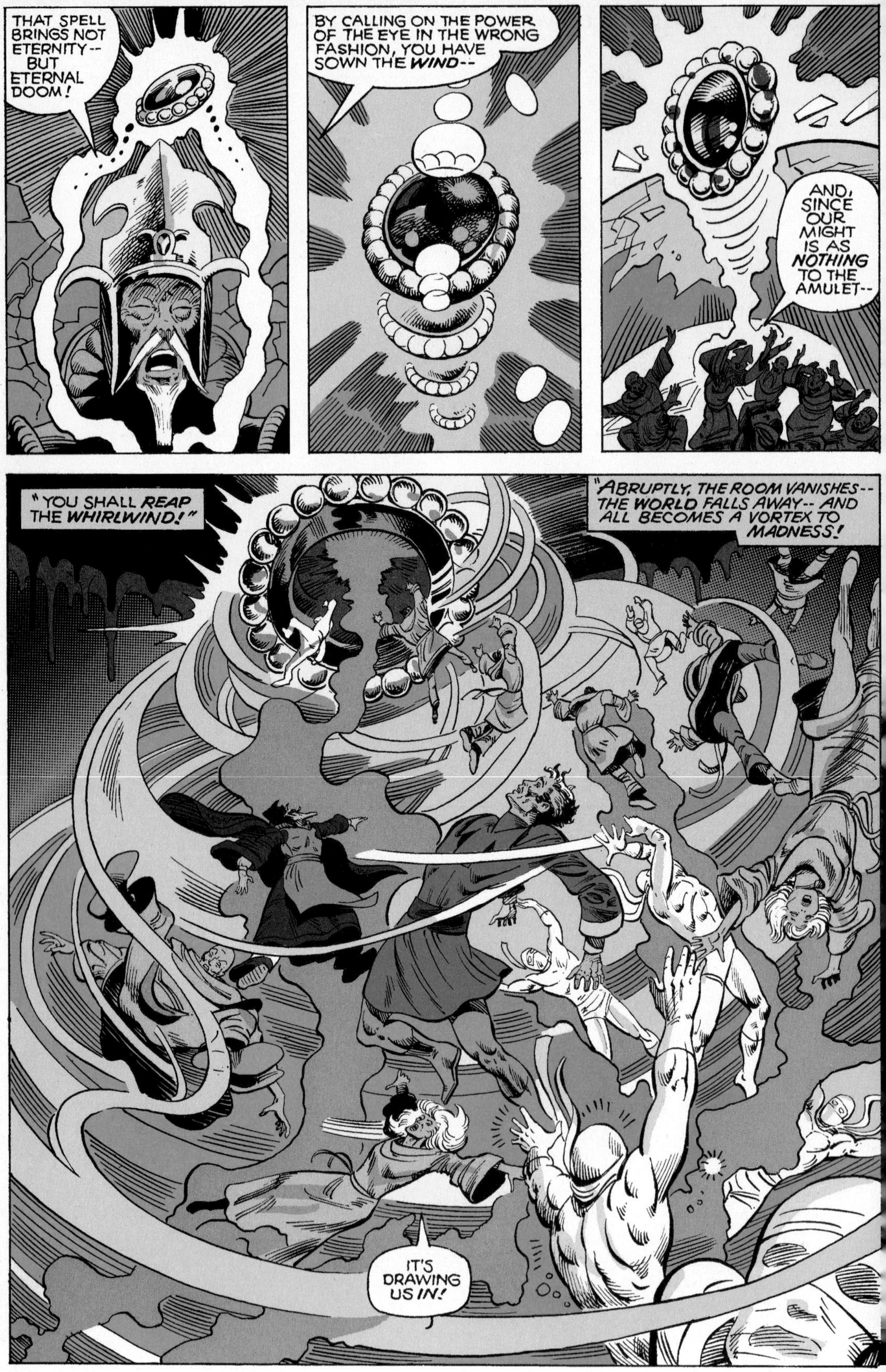
THAT SPELL BRINGS NOT ETERNITY-- BUT ETERNAL DOOM!
BY CALLING ON THE POWER OF THE EYE IN THE WRONG FASHION, YOU HAVE SOWN THE WIND--
AND, SINCE OUR MIGHT IS AS NOTHING TO THE AMULET--
"YOU SHALL REAP THE WHIRLWIND!"
"ABRUPTLY, THE ROOM VANISHES-- THE WORLD FALLS AWAY-- AND ALL BECOMES A VORTEX TO MADNESS!
IT'S DRAWING US IN!

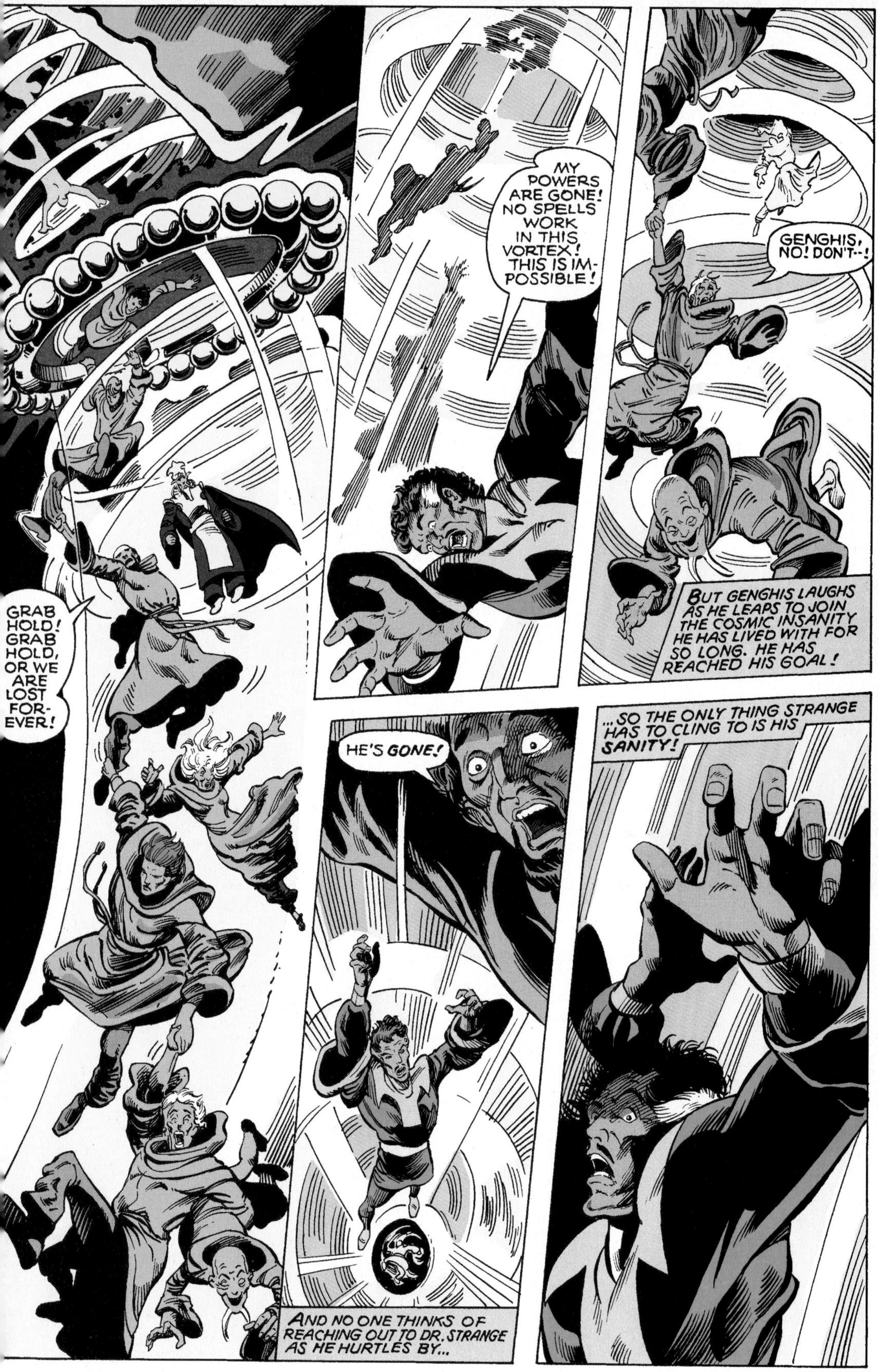
GRAB HOLD! GRAB HOLD, OR WE ARE LOST FOR-EVER!
MY POWERS ARE GONE! NO SPELLS WORK IN THIS VORTEX! THIS IS IM-POSSIBLE!
GENGHIS, NO! DON'T--!
BUT GENGHIS LAUGHS AS HE LEAPS TO JOIN THE COSMIC INSANITY HE HAS LIVED WITH FOR SO LONG. HE HAS REACHED HIS GOAL!
HE'S GONE!
AND NO ONE THINKS OF REACHING OUT TO DR. STRANGE AS HE HURTLES BY...
...SO THE ONLY THING STRANGE HAS TO CLING TO IS HIS SANITY!

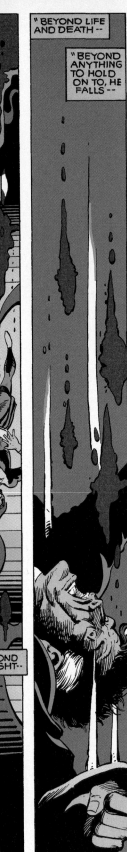

"AS HE FALLS--

"BEYOND DREAMS--

"BEYOND SPACE--

"BEYOND TIME--

"BEYOND THOUGHT--

"BEYOND LIFE AND DEATH--

"BEYOND ANYTHING TO HOLD ON TO, HE FALLS--

"TO LAND--

"WHERE?

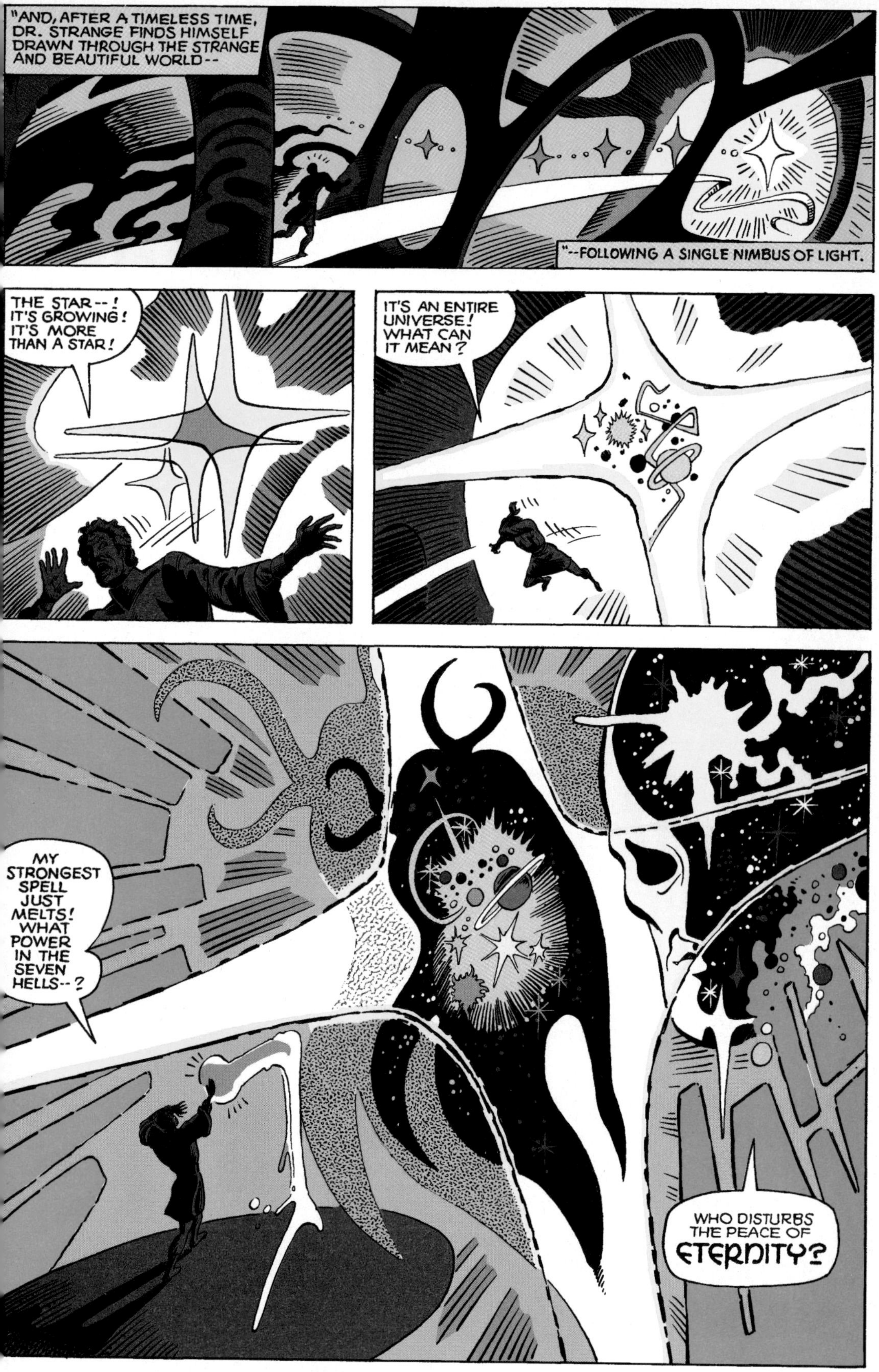
"AND, AFTER A TIMELESS TIME, DR. STRANGE FINDS HIMSELF DRAWN THROUGH THE STRANGE AND BEAUTIFUL WORLD--
"--FOLLOWING A SINGLE NIMBUS OF LIGHT.
THE STAR--! IT'S GROWING! IT'S MORE THAN A STAR!
IT'S AN ENTIRE UNIVERSE! WHAT CAN IT MEAN?
MY STRONGEST SPELL JUST MELTS! WHAT POWER IN THE SEVEN HELLS--?
WHO DISTURBS THE PEACE OF ETERNITY?

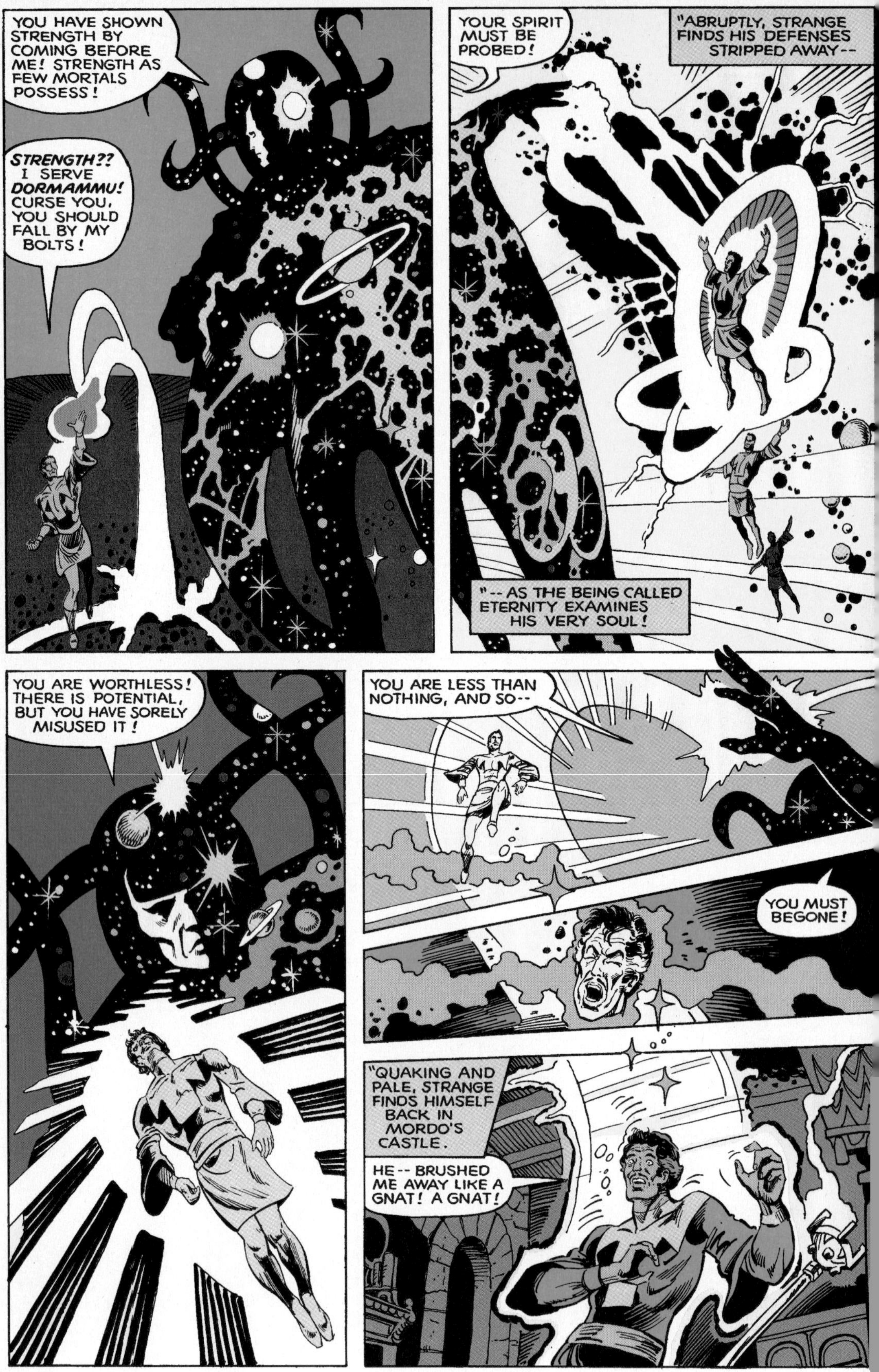
YOU HAVE SHOWN STRENGTH BY COMING BEFORE ME! STRENGTH AS FEW MORTALS POSSESS!
STRENGTH?? I SERVE DORMAMMU! CURSE YOU, YOU SHOULD FALL BY MY BOLTS!
YOUR SPIRIT MUST BE PROBED!
"ABRUPTLY, STRANGE FINDS HIS DEFENSES STRIPPED AWAY--
"--AS THE BEING CALLED ETERNITY EXAMINES HIS VERY SOUL!
YOU ARE WORTHLESS! THERE IS POTENTIAL, BUT YOU HAVE SORELY MISUSED IT!
YOU ARE LESS THAN NOTHING, AND SO--
YOU MUST BEGONE!
"QUAKING AND PALE, STRANGE FINDS HIMSELF BACK IN MORDO'S CASTLE.
HE-- BRUSHED ME AWAY LIKE A GNAT! A GNAT!

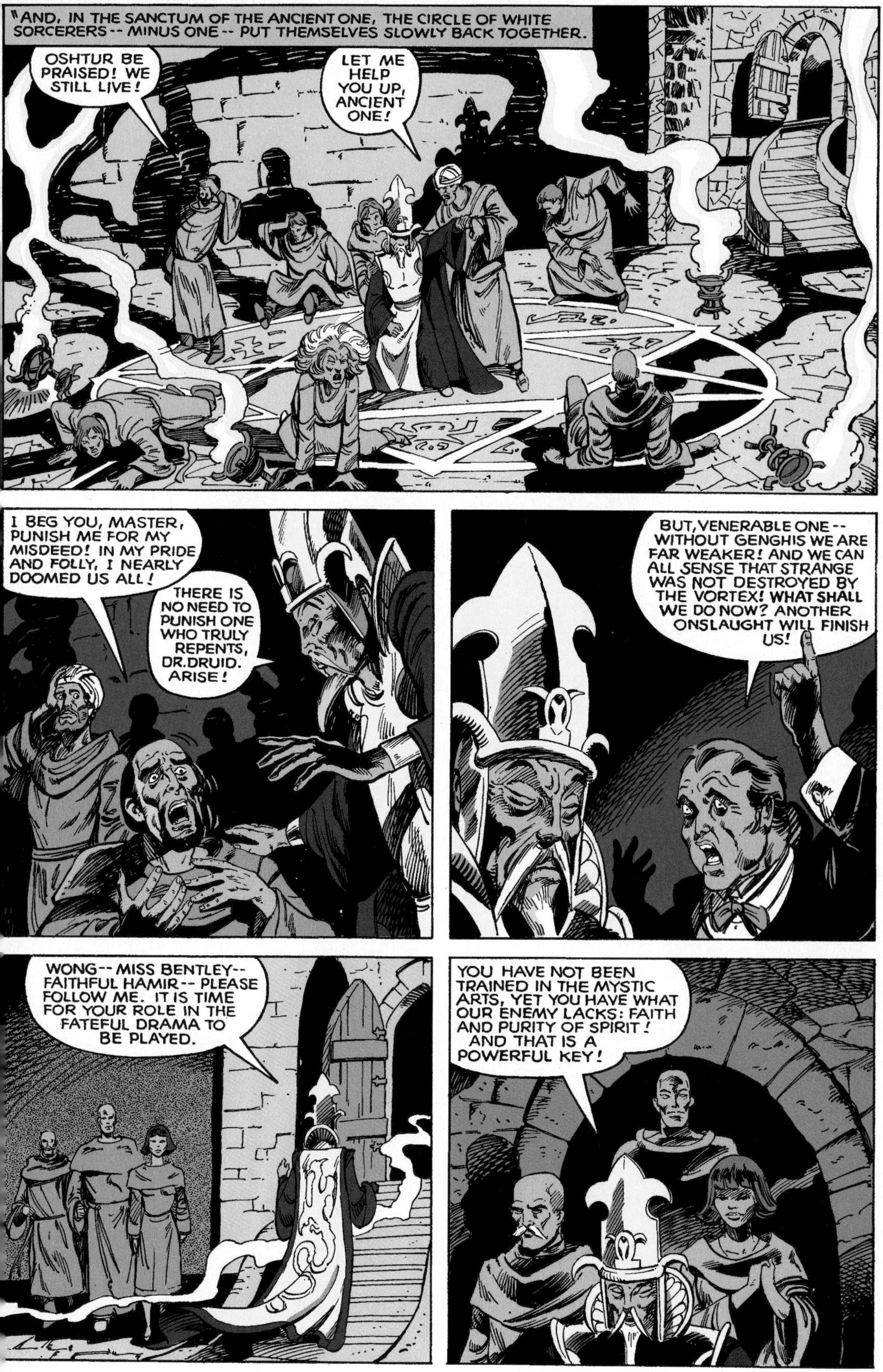
"AND, IN THE SANCTUM OF THE ANCIENT ONE, THE CIRCLE OF WHITE SORCERERS -- MINUS ONE -- PUT THEMSELVES SLOWLY BACK TOGETHER.
OSHTUR BE PRAISED! WE STILL LIVE!
LET ME HELP YOU UP, ANCIENT ONE!
I BEG YOU, MASTER, PUNISH ME FOR MY MISDEED! IN MY PRIDE AND FOLLY, I NEARLY DOOMED US ALL!
THERE IS NO NEED TO PUNISH ONE WHO TRULY REPENTS, DR. DRUID. ARISE!
BUT, VENERABLE ONE -- WITHOUT GENGHIS WE ARE FAR WEAKER! AND WE CAN ALL SENSE THAT STRANGE WAS NOT DESTROYED BY THE VORTEX! WHAT SHALL WE DO NOW? ANOTHER ONSLAUGHT WILL FINISH US!
WONG -- MISS BENTLEY -- FAITHFUL HAMIR -- PLEASE FOLLOW ME. IT IS TIME FOR YOUR ROLE IN THE FATEFUL DRAMA TO BE PLAYED.
YOU HAVE NOT BEEN TRAINED IN THE MYSTIC ARTS, YET YOU HAVE WHAT OUR ENEMY LACKS: FAITH AND PURITY OF SPIRIT! AND THAT IS A POWERFUL KEY!

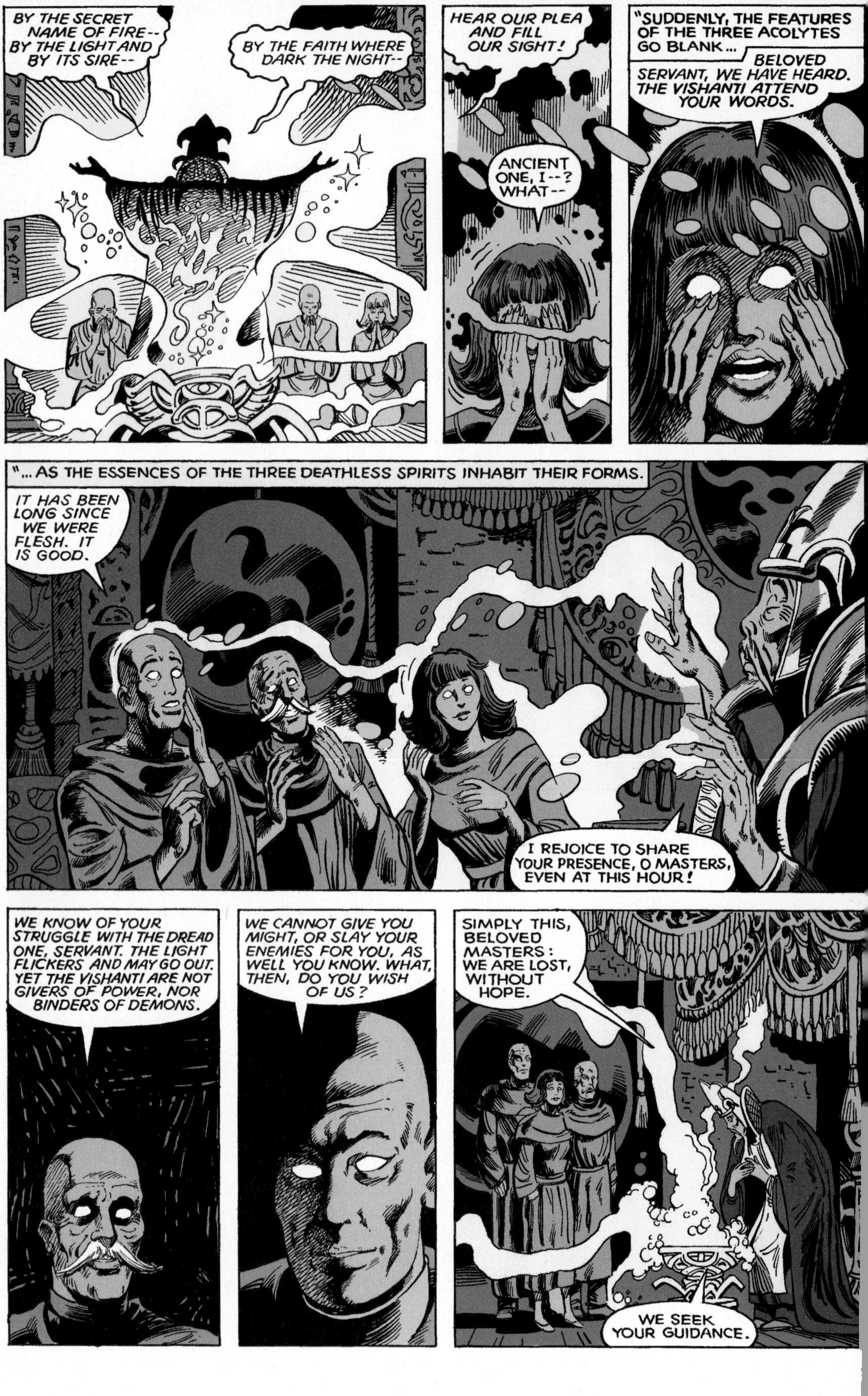
BY THE SECRET NAME OF FIRE-- BY THE LIGHT AND BY ITS SIRE--
BY THE FAITH WHERE DARK THE NIGHT--
HEAR OUR PLEA AND FILL OUR SIGHT!
ANCIENT ONE, I--? WHAT--
"SUDDENLY, THE FEATURES OF THE THREE ACOLYTES GO BLANK...
BELOVED SERVANT, WE HAVE HEARD. THE VISHANTI ATTEND YOUR WORDS.
"... AS THE ESSENCES OF THE THREE DEATHLESS SPIRITS INHABIT THEIR FORMS.
IT HAS BEEN LONG SINCE WE WERE FLESH. IT IS GOOD.
I REJOICE TO SHARE YOUR PRESENCE, O MASTERS, EVEN AT THIS HOUR!
WE KNOW OF YOUR STRUGGLE WITH THE DREAD ONE, SERVANT. THE LIGHT FLICKERS AND MAY GO OUT. YET THE VISHANTI ARE NOT GIVERS OF POWER, NOR BINDERS OF DEMONS.
WE CANNOT GIVE YOU MIGHT, OR SLAY YOUR ENEMIES FOR YOU, AS WELL YOU KNOW. WHAT, THEN, DO YOU WISH OF US?
SIMPLY THIS, BELOVED MASTERS: WE ARE LOST, WITHOUT HOPE.
WE SEEK YOUR GUIDANCE.

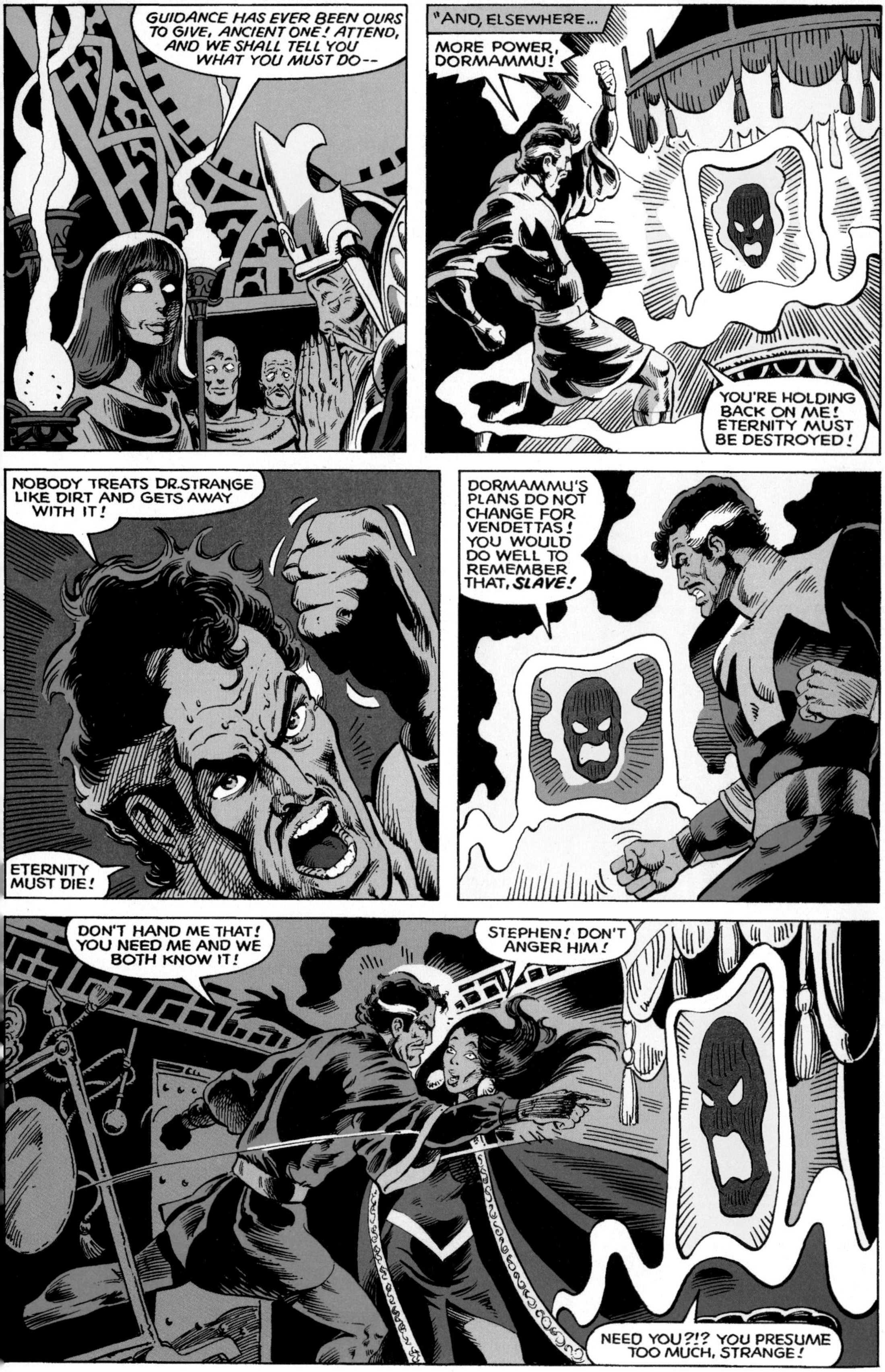
GUIDANCE HAS EVER BEEN OURS TO GIVE, ANCIENT ONE! ATTEND, AND WE SHALL TELL YOU WHAT YOU MUST DO--
"AND, ELSEWHERE...
MORE POWER, DORMAMMU!
YOU'RE HOLDING BACK ON ME! ETERNITY MUST BE DESTROYED!
NOBODY TREATS DR. STRANGE LIKE DIRT AND GETS AWAY WITH IT!
ETERNITY MUST DIE!
DORMAMMU'S PLANS DO NOT CHANGE FOR VENDETTAS! YOU WOULD DO WELL TO REMEMBER THAT, SLAVE!
DON'T HAND ME THAT! YOU NEED ME AND WE BOTH KNOW IT!
STEPHEN! DON'T ANGER HIM!
NEED YOU?!? YOU PRESUME TOO MUCH, STRANGE!

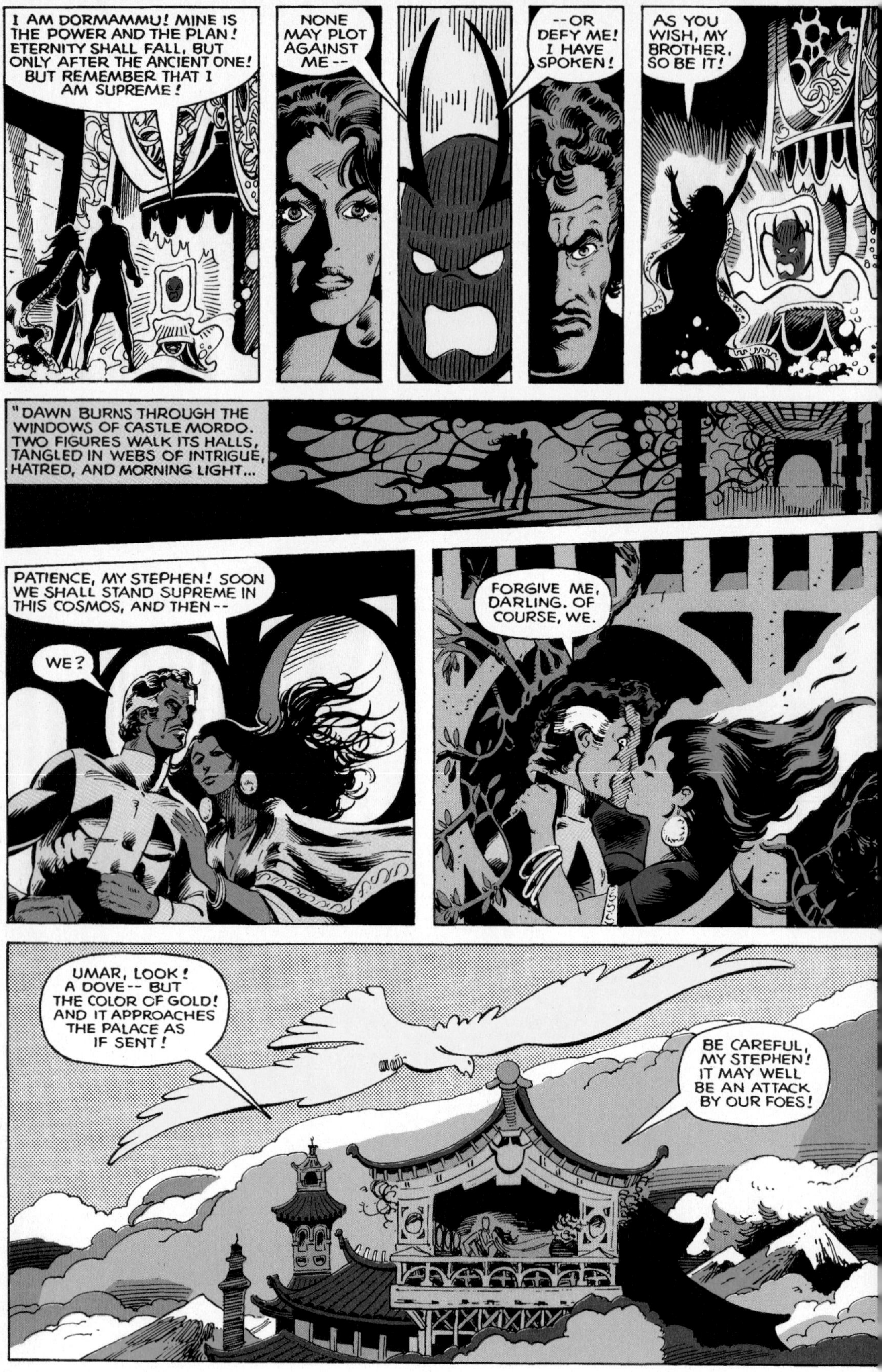
I AM DORMAMMU! MINE IS THE POWER AND THE PLAN! ETERNITY SHALL FALL, BUT ONLY AFTER THE ANCIENT ONE! BUT REMEMBER THAT I AM SUPREME!
NONE MAY PLOT AGAINST ME --
--OR DEFY ME! I HAVE SPOKEN!
AS YOU WISH, MY BROTHER. SO BE IT!
"DAWN BURNS THROUGH THE WINDOWS OF CASTLE MORDO. TWO FIGURES WALK ITS HALLS, TANGLED IN WEBS OF INTRIGUE, HATRED, AND MORNING LIGHT...
PATIENCE, MY STEPHEN! SOON WE SHALL STAND SUPREME IN THIS COSMOS, AND THEN --
WE?
FORGIVE ME, DARLING. OF COURSE, WE.
UMAR, LOOK! A DOVE -- BUT THE COLOR OF GOLD! AND IT APPROACHES THE PALACE AS IF SENT!
BE CAREFUL, MY STEPHEN! IT MAY WELL BE AN ATTACK BY OUR FOES!

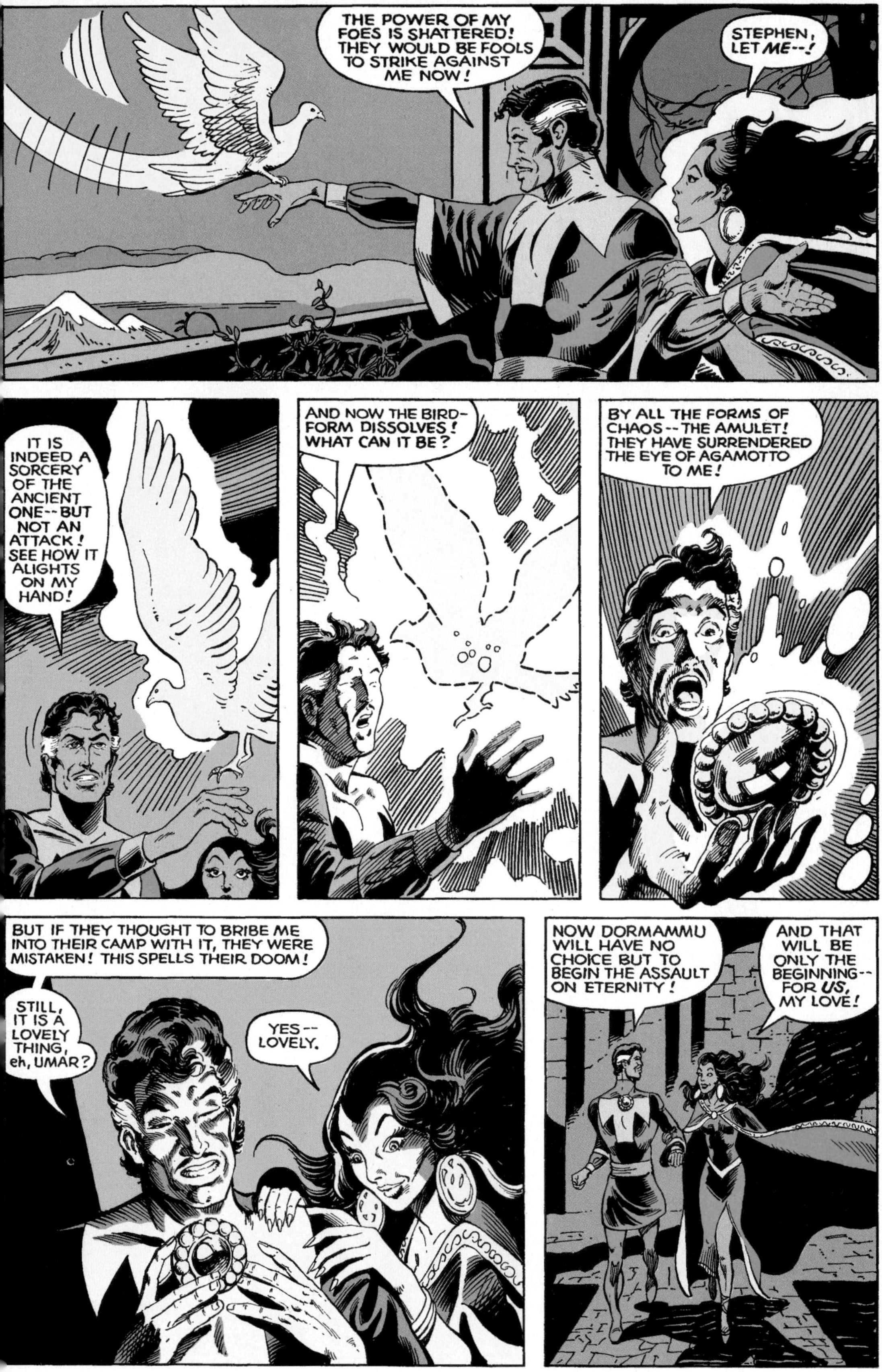
THE POWER OF MY FOES IS SHATTERED! THEY WOULD BE FOOLS TO STRIKE AGAINST ME NOW!
STEPHEN, LET ME--!
IT IS INDEED A SORCERY OF THE ANCIENT ONE-- BUT NOT AN ATTACK! SEE HOW IT ALIGHTS ON MY HAND!
AND NOW THE BIRD-FORM DISSOLVES! WHAT CAN IT BE?
BY ALL THE FORMS OF CHAOS -- THE AMULET! THEY HAVE SURRENDERED THE EYE OF AGAMOTTO TO ME!
BUT IF THEY THOUGHT TO BRIBE ME INTO THEIR CAMP WITH IT, THEY WERE MISTAKEN! THIS SPELLS THEIR DOOM!
STILL, IT IS A LOVELY THING, eh, UMAR?
YES-- LOVELY.
NOW DORMAMMU WILL HAVE NO CHOICE BUT TO BEGIN THE ASSAULT ON ETERNITY!
AND THAT WILL BE ONLY THE BEGINNING-- FOR US, MY LOVE!

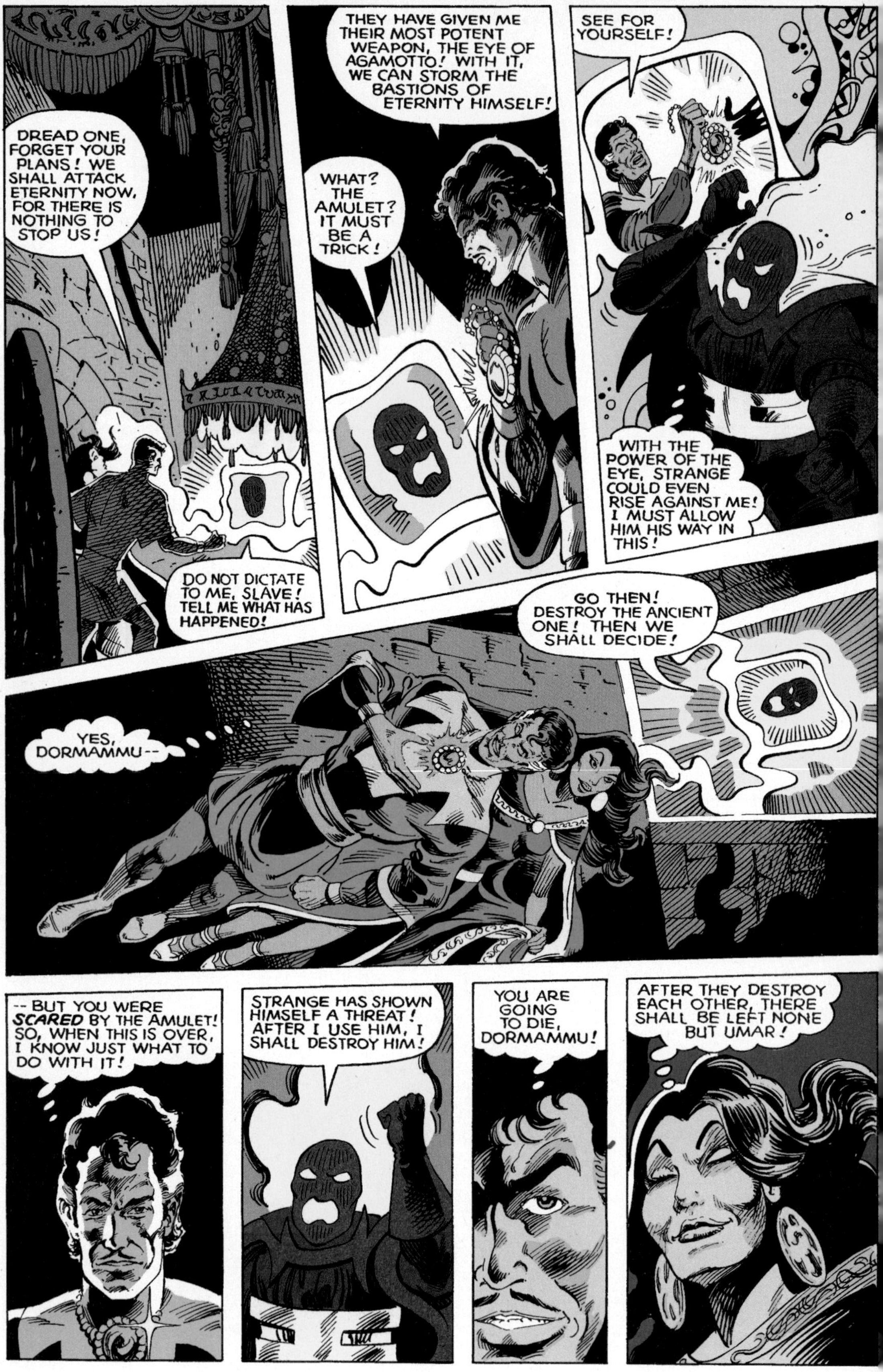
DREAD ONE, FORGET YOUR PLANS! WE SHALL ATTACK ETERNITY NOW, FOR THERE IS NOTHING TO STOP US!
DO NOT DICTATE TO ME, SLAVE! TELL ME WHAT HAS HAPPENED!
THEY HAVE GIVEN ME THEIR MOST POTENT WEAPON, THE EYE OF AGAMOTTO! WITH IT, WE CAN STORM THE BASTIONS OF ETERNITY HIMSELF!
WHAT? THE AMULET? IT MUST BE A TRICK!
SEE FOR YOURSELF!
WITH THE POWER OF THE EYE, STRANGE COULD EVEN RISE AGAINST ME! I MUST ALLOW HIM HIS WAY IN THIS!
GO THEN! DESTROY THE ANCIENT ONE! THEN WE SHALL DECIDE!
YES, DORMAMMU--
-- BUT YOU WERE SCARED BY THE AMULET! SO, WHEN THIS IS OVER, I KNOW JUST WHAT TO DO WITH IT!
STRANGE HAS SHOWN HIMSELF A THREAT! AFTER I USE HIM, I SHALL DESTROY HIM!
YOU ARE GOING TO DIE, DORMAMMU!
AFTER THEY DESTROY EACH OTHER, THERE SHALL BE LEFT NONE BUT UMAR!

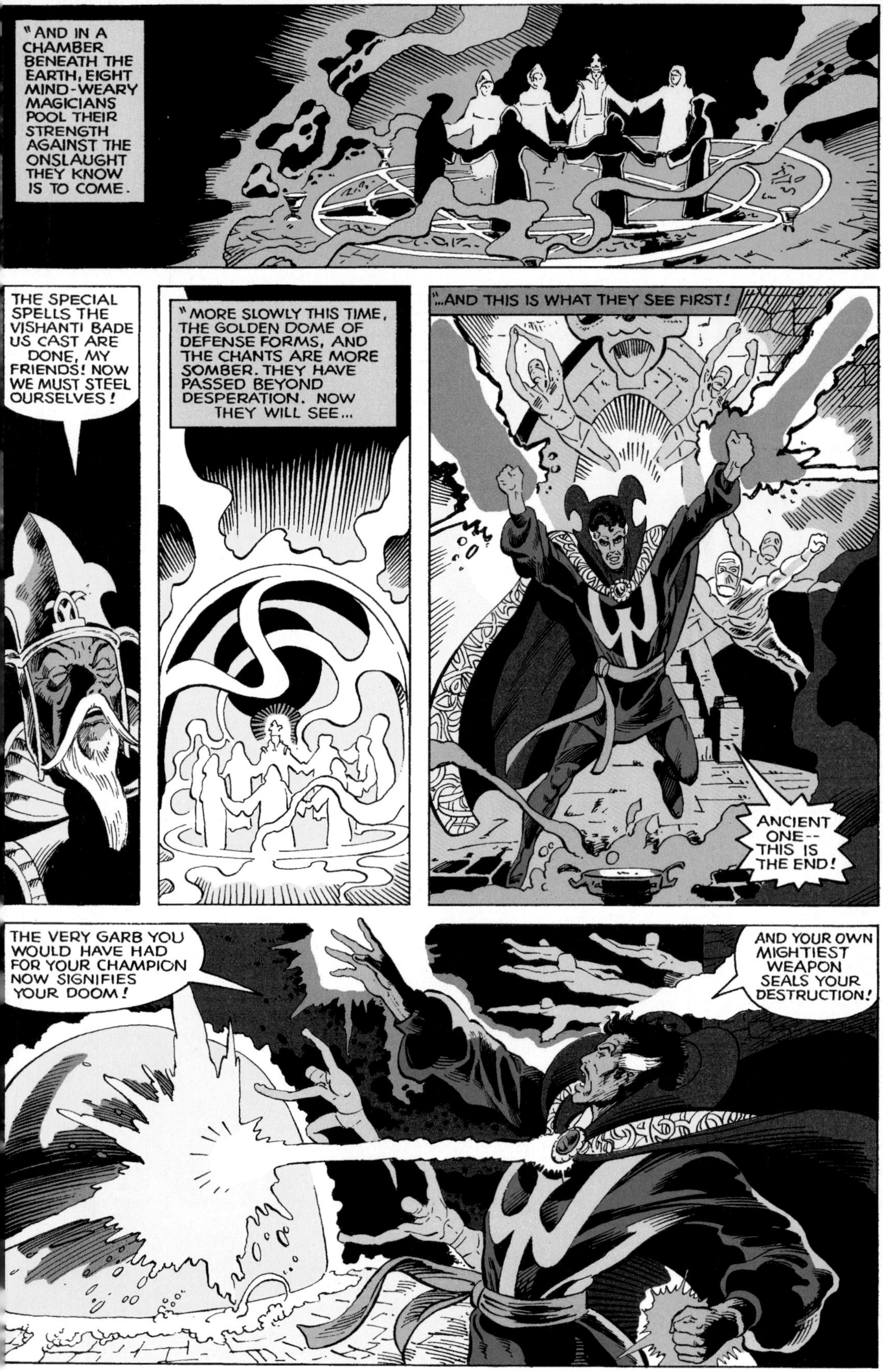
"AND IN A CHAMBER BENEATH THE EARTH, EIGHT MIND-WEARY MAGICIANS POOL THEIR STRENGTH AGAINST THE ONSLAUGHT THEY KNOW IS TO COME.
THE SPECIAL SPELLS THE VISHANTI BADE US CAST ARE DONE, MY FRIENDS! NOW WE MUST STEEL OURSELVES!
"MORE SLOWLY THIS TIME, THE GOLDEN DOME OF DEFENSE FORMS, AND THE CHANTS ARE MORE SOMBER. THEY HAVE PASSED BEYOND DESPERATION. NOW THEY WILL SEE...
"...AND THIS IS WHAT THEY SEE FIRST!
ANCIENT ONE-- THIS IS THE END!
THE VERY GARB YOU WOULD HAVE HAD FOR YOUR CHAMPION NOW SIGNIFIES YOUR DOOM!
AND YOUR OWN MIGHTIEST WEAPON SEALS YOUR DESTRUCTION!

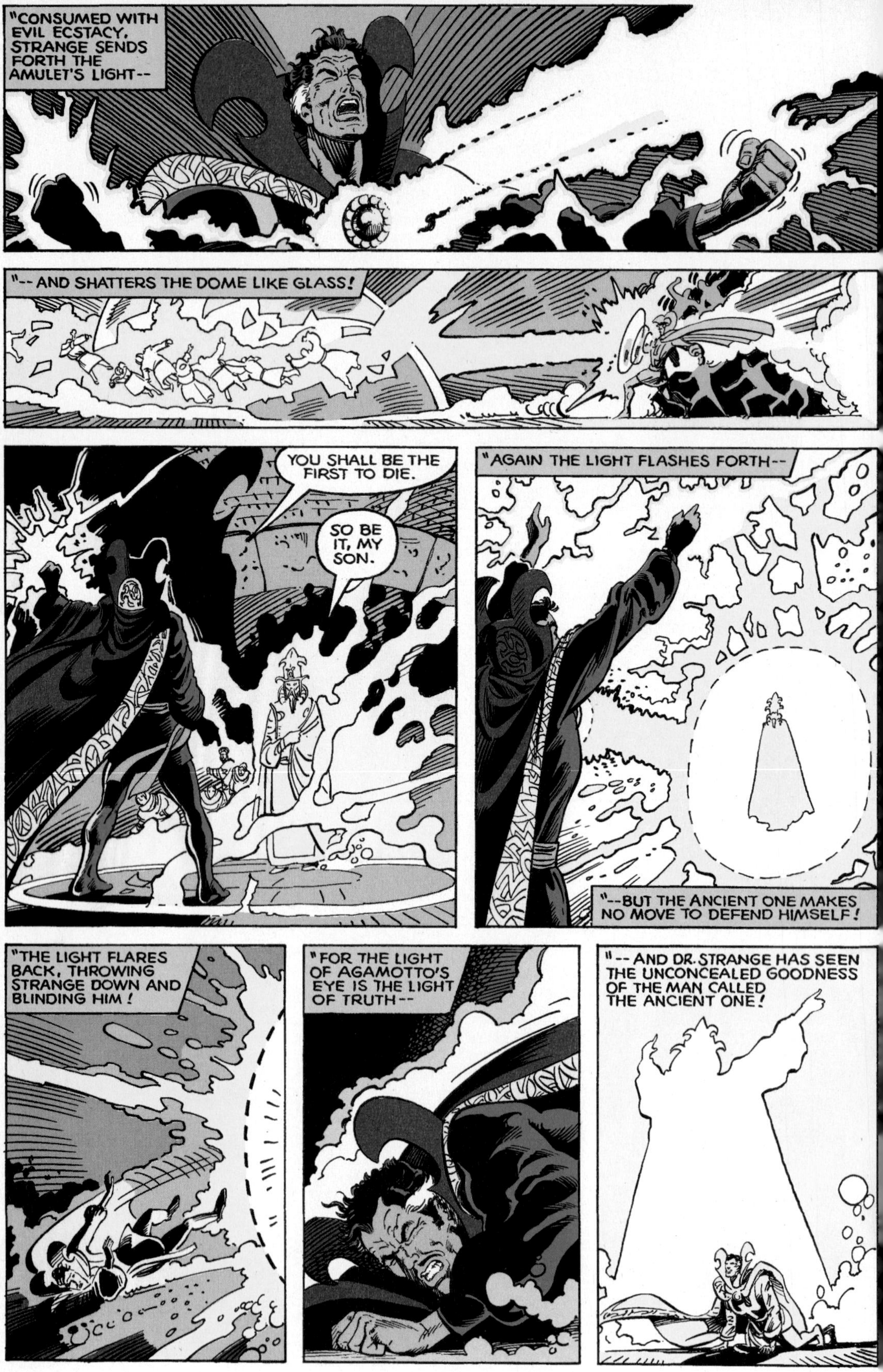
"CONSUMED WITH EVIL ECSTACY, STRANGE SENDS FORTH THE AMULET'S LIGHT--
"--AND SHATTERS THE DOME LIKE GLASS!
YOU SHALL BE THE FIRST TO DIE.
SO BE IT, MY SON.
"AGAIN THE LIGHT FLASHES FORTH--
"--BUT THE ANCIENT ONE MAKES NO MOVE TO DEFEND HIMSELF!
"THE LIGHT FLARES BACK, THROWING STRANGE DOWN AND BLINDING HIM!
"FOR THE LIGHT OF AGAMOTTO'S EYE IS THE LIGHT OF TRUTH--
"--AND DR. STRANGE HAS SEEN THE UNCONCEALED GOODNESS OF THE MAN CALLED THE ANCIENT ONE!

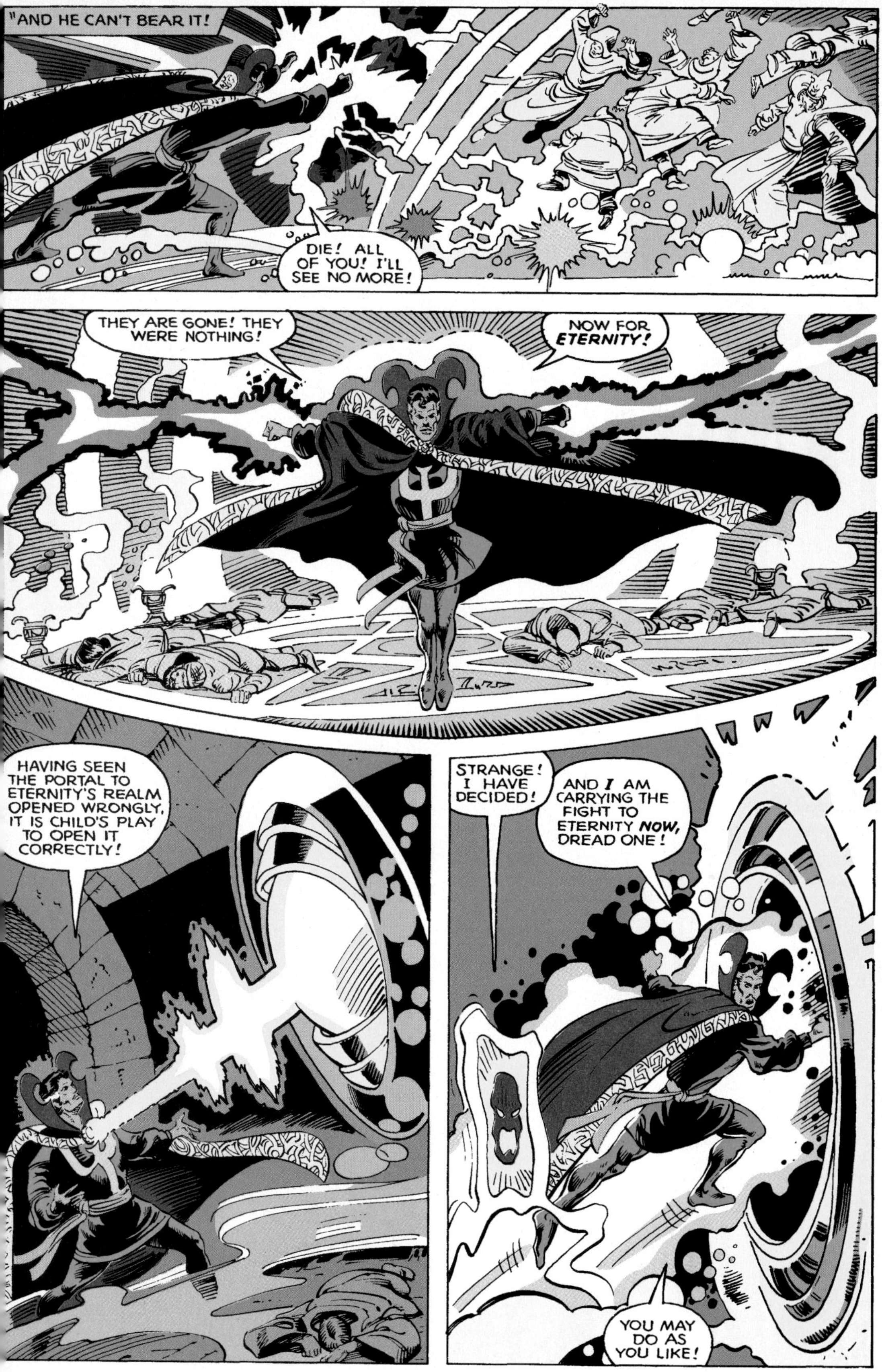
"AND HE CAN'T BEAR IT!
DIE! ALL OF YOU! I'LL SEE NO MORE!
THEY ARE GONE! THEY WERE NOTHING!
NOW FOR ETERNITY!
HAVING SEEN THE PORTAL TO ETERNITY'S REALM OPENED WRONGLY, IT IS CHILD'S PLAY TO OPEN IT CORRECTLY!
STRANGE! I HAVE DECIDED!
AND I AM CARRYING THE FIGHT TO ETERNITY NOW, DREAD ONE!
YOU MAY DO AS YOU LIKE!

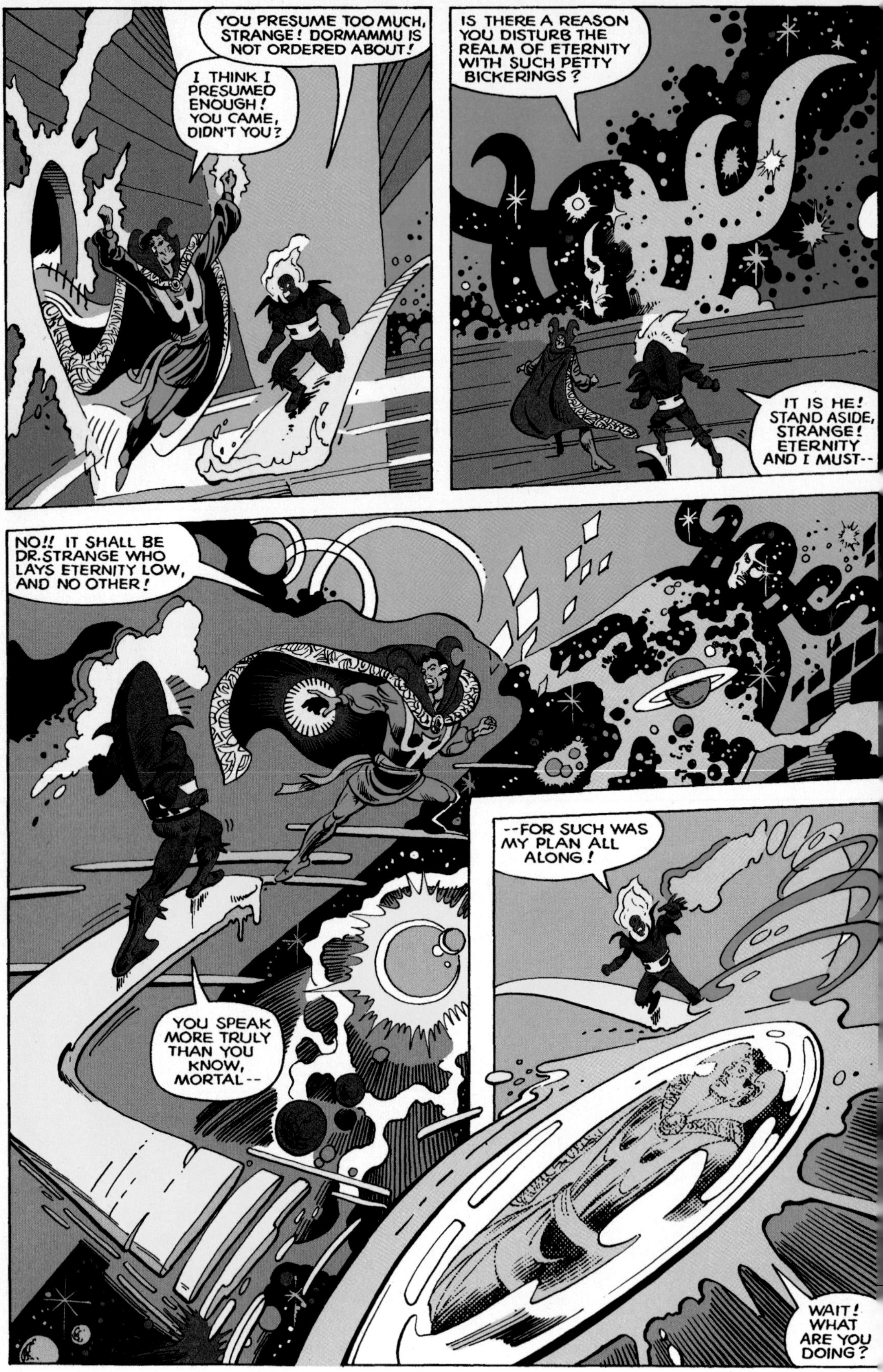

YOU PRESUME TOO MUCH, STRANGE! DORMAMMU IS NOT ORDERED ABOUT!
I THINK I PRESUMED ENOUGH! YOU CAME, DIDN'T YOU?
IS THERE A REASON YOU DISTURB THE REALM OF ETERNITY WITH SUCH PETTY BICKERINGS?
IT IS HE! STAND ASIDE, STRANGE! ETERNITY AND I MUST--
NO!! IT SHALL BE DR. STRANGE WHO LAYS ETERNITY LOW, AND NO OTHER!
YOU SPEAK MORE TRULY THAN YOU KNOW, MORTAL--
--FOR SUCH WAS MY PLAN ALL ALONG!
WAIT! WHAT ARE YOU DOING?

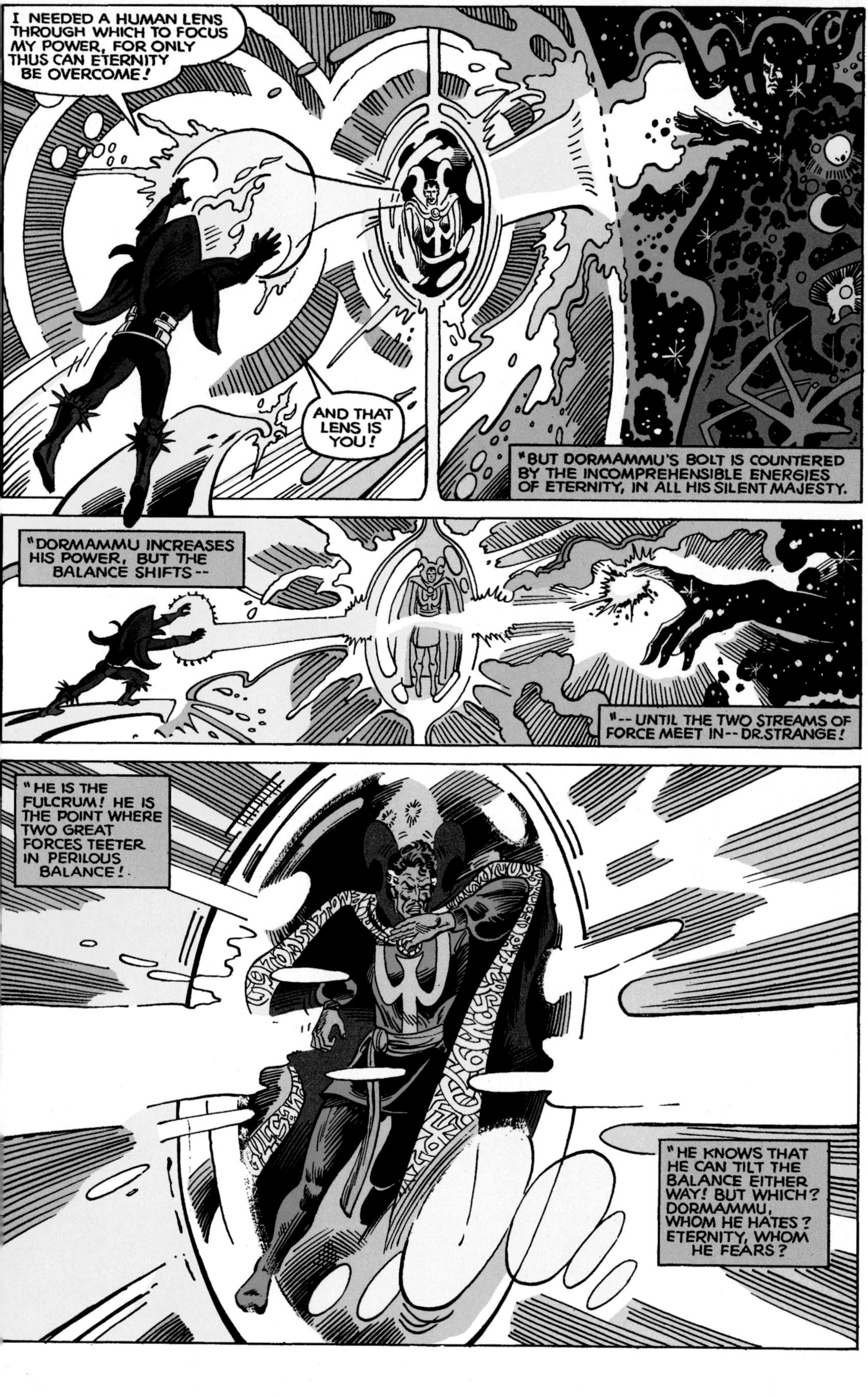
I NEEDED A HUMAN LENS THROUGH WHICH TO FOCUS MY POWER, FOR ONLY THUS CAN ETERNITY BE OVERCOME!
AND THAT LENS IS YOU!
"BUT DORMAMMU'S BOLT IS COUNTERED BY THE INCOMPREHENSIBLE ENERGIES OF ETERNITY, IN ALL HIS SILENT MAJESTY.
"DORMAMMU INCREASES HIS POWER, BUT THE BALANCE SHIFTS--
"--UNTIL THE TWO STREAMS OF FORCE MEET IN--DR. STRANGE!
"HE IS THE FULCRUM! HE IS THE POINT WHERE TWO GREAT FORCES TEETER IN PERILOUS BALANCE!
"HE KNOWS THAT HE CAN TILT THE BALANCE EITHER WAY! BUT WHICH? DORMAMMU, WHOM HE HATES? ETERNITY, WHOM HE FEARS?

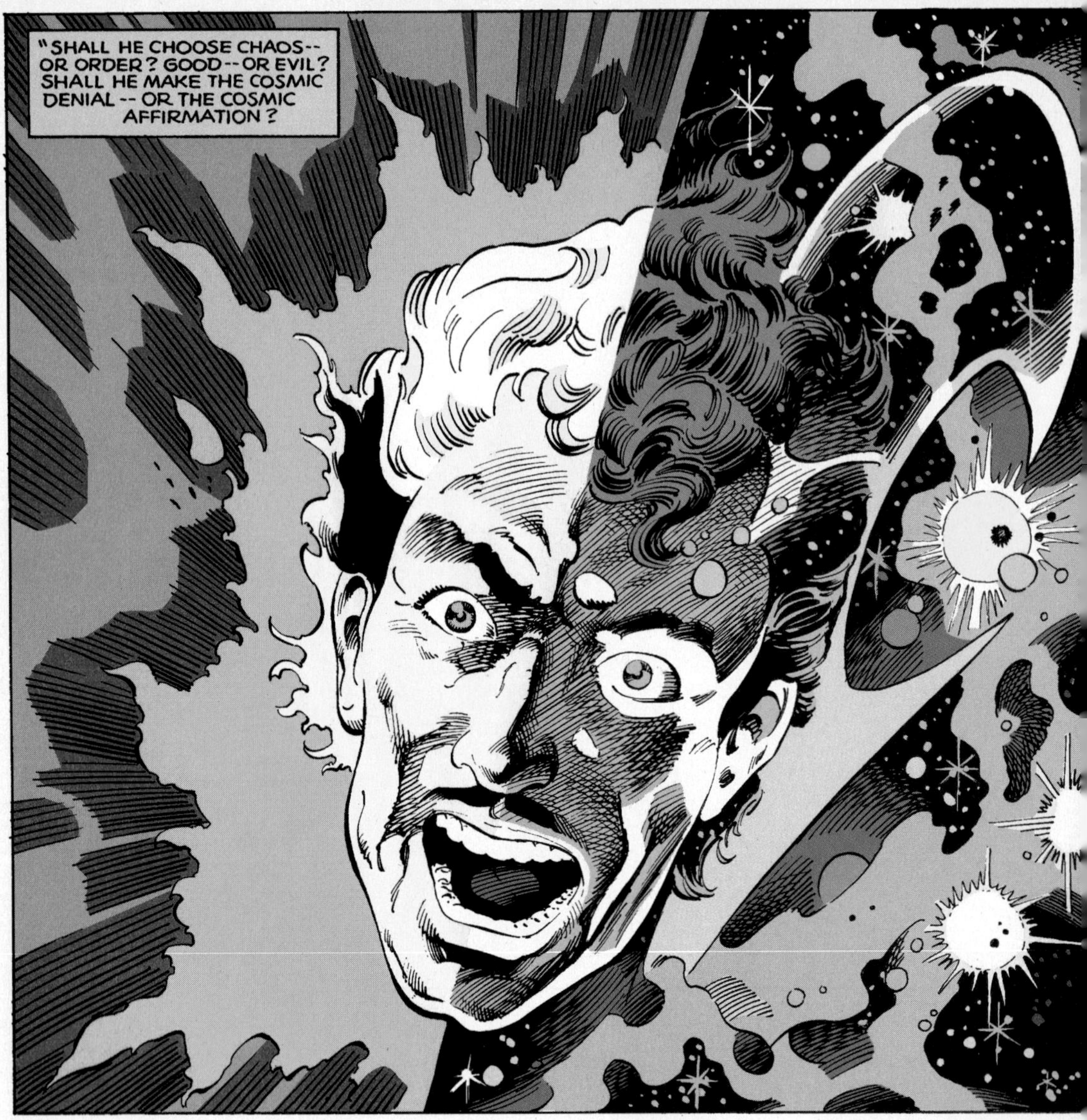
"SHALL HE CHOOSE CHAOS--
OR ORDER? GOOD--OR EVIL?
SHALL HE MAKE THE COSMIC
DENIAL--OR THE COSMIC
AFFIRMATION?

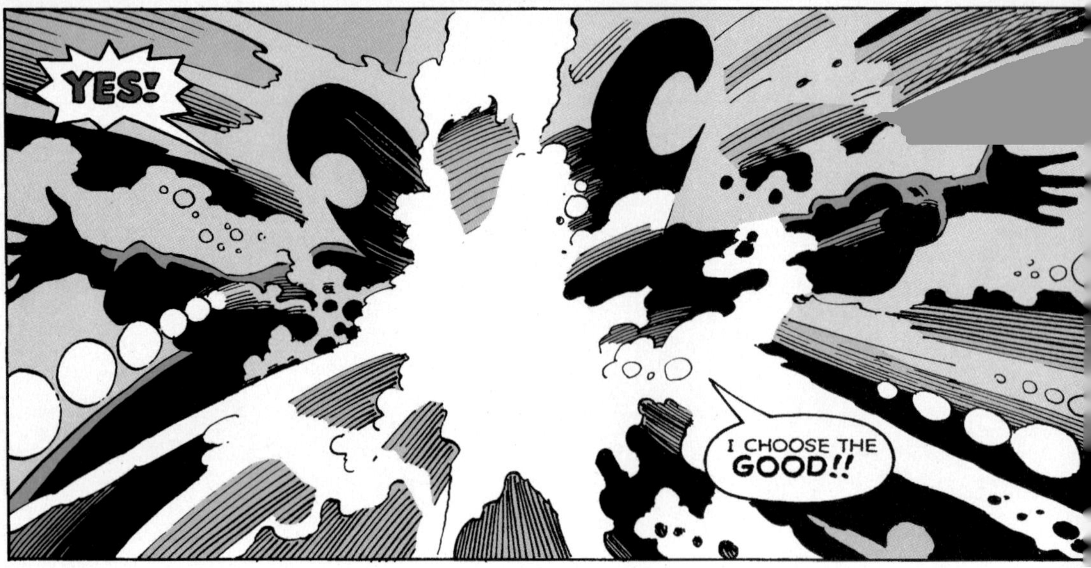
YES!
I CHOOSE THE GOOD!!

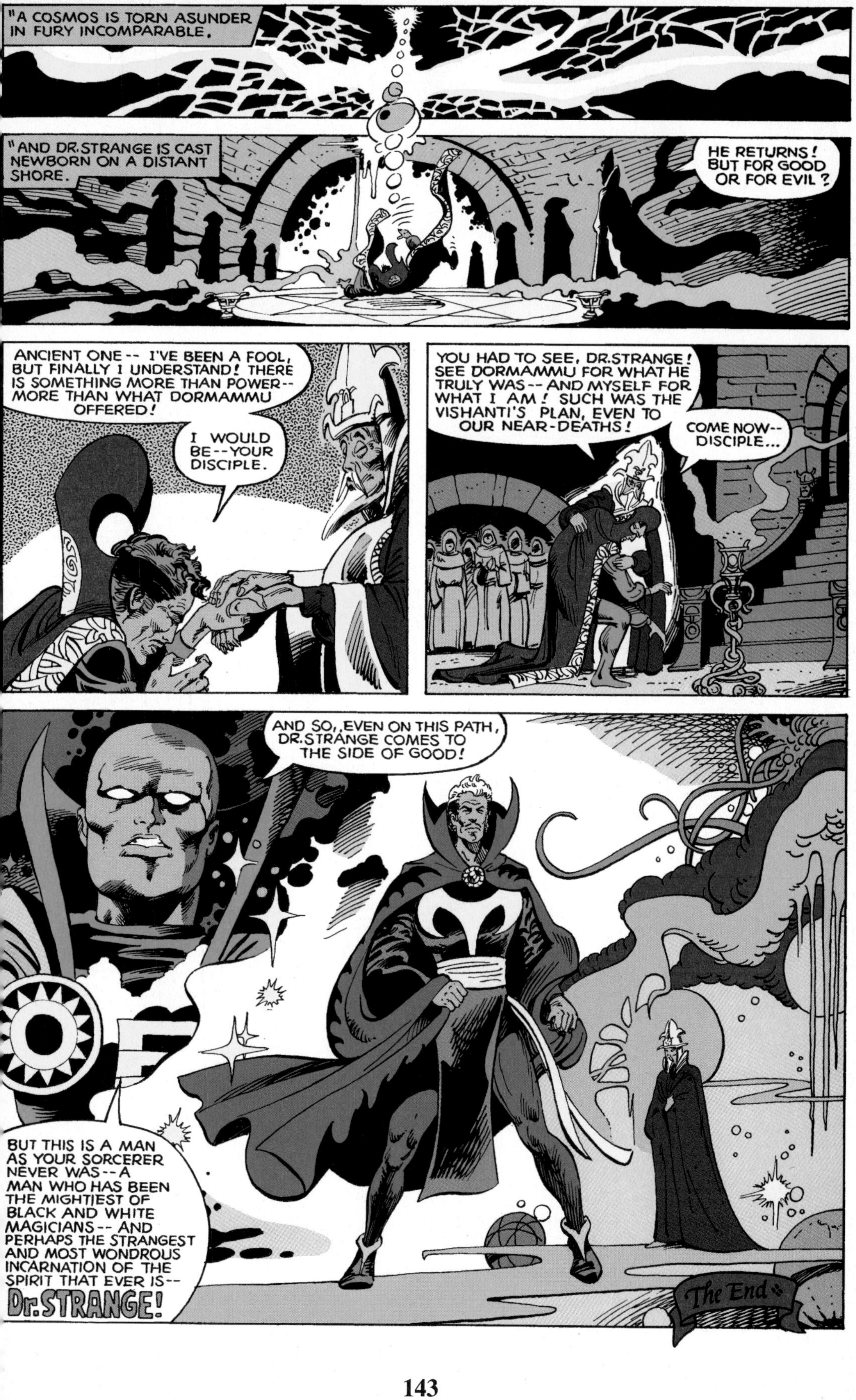
"A COSMOS IS TORN ASUNDER IN FURY INCOMPARABLE.
"AND DR. STRANGE IS CAST NEWBORN ON A DISTANT SHORE.
HE RETURNS! BUT FOR GOOD OR FOR EVIL?
ANCIENT ONE -- I'VE BEEN A FOOL, BUT FINALLY I UNDERSTAND! THERE IS SOMETHING MORE THAN POWER-- MORE THAN WHAT DORMAMMU OFFERED!
I WOULD BE--YOUR DISCIPLE.
YOU HAD TO SEE, DR. STRANGE! SEE DORMAMMU FOR WHAT HE TRULY WAS-- AND MYSELF FOR WHAT I AM! SUCH WAS THE VISHANTI'S PLAN, EVEN TO OUR NEAR-DEATHS!
COME NOW-- DISCIPLE...
AND SO, EVEN ON THIS PATH, DR. STRANGE COMES TO THE SIDE OF GOOD!
BUT THIS IS A MAN AS YOUR SORCERER NEVER WAS--A MAN WHO HAS BEEN THE MIGHTIEST OF BLACK AND WHITE MAGICIANS-- AND PERHAPS THE STRANGEST AND MOST WONDROUS INCARNATION OF THE SPIRIT THAT EVER IS-- Dr. STRANGE!
The End

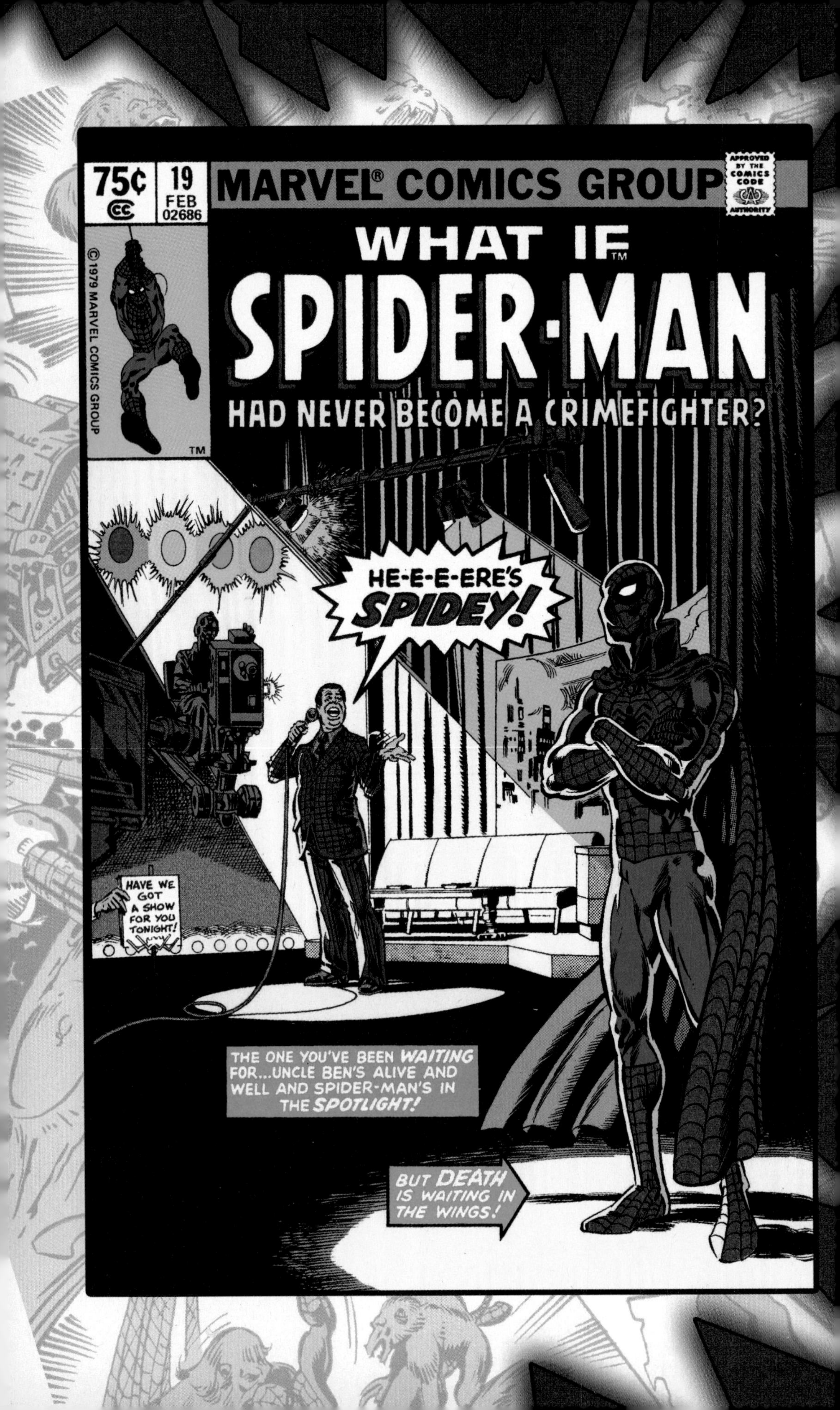
75¢
19
FEB
02686
MARVEL® COMICS GROUP
APPROVED BY THE COMICS CODE AUTHORITY
©1979 MARVEL COMICS GROUP
WHAT IF™
SPIDER-MAN
HAD NEVER BECOME A CRIMEFIGHTER?
HE-E-E-ERE'S SPIDEY!
HAVE WE GOT A SHOW FOR YOU TONIGHT!
THE ONE YOU'VE BEEN WAITING FOR...UNCLE BEN'S ALIVE AND WELL AND SPIDER-MAN'S IN THE SPOTLIGHT!
BUT DEATH IS WAITING IN THE WINGS!

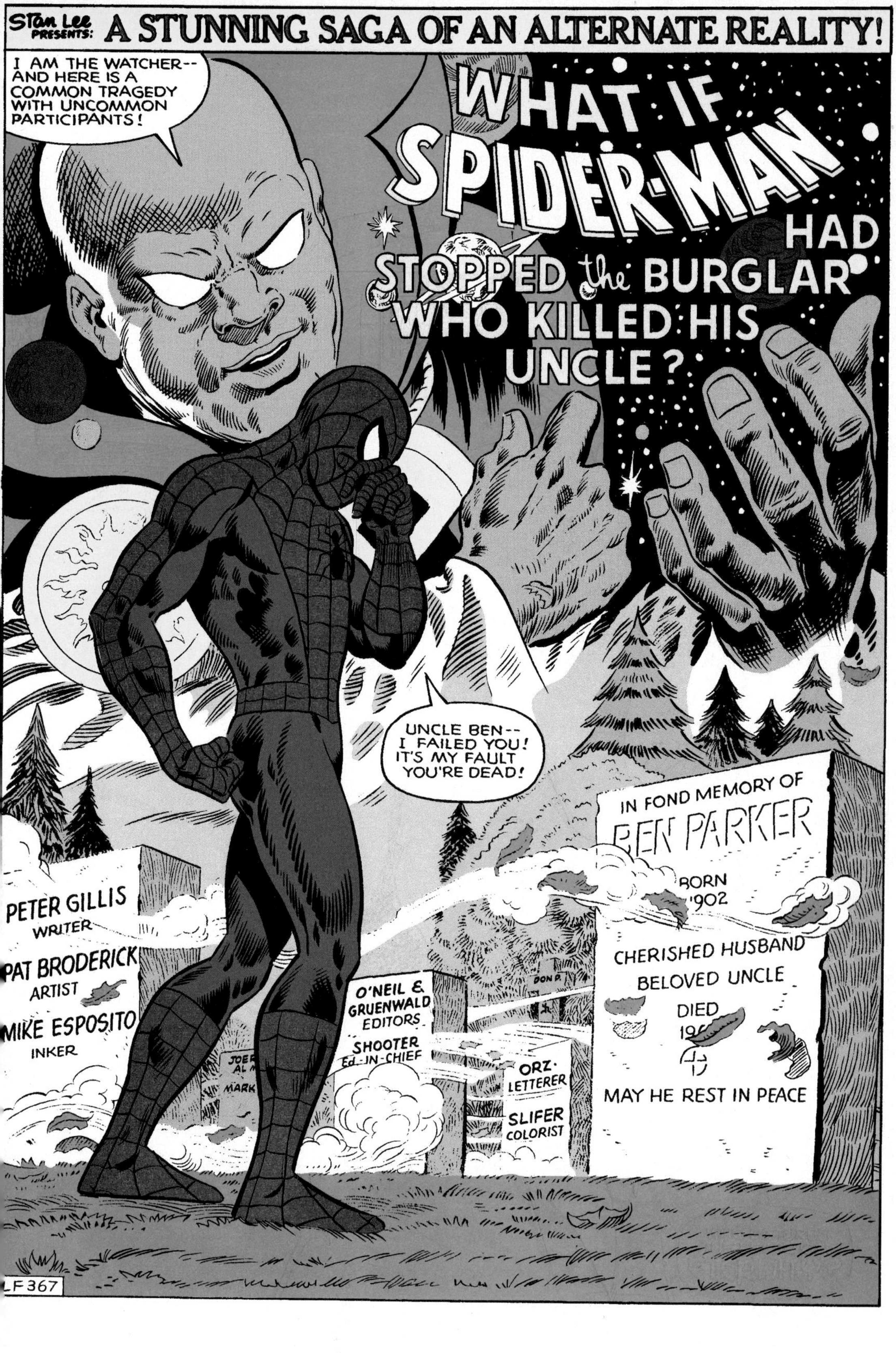
STAN LEE PRESENTS: A STUNNING SAGA OF AN ALTERNATE REALITY!
I AM THE WATCHER-- AND HERE IS A COMMON TRAGEDY WITH UNCOMMON PARTICIPANTS!
WHAT IF SPIDER-MAN HAD STOPPED the BURGLAR WHO KILLED HIS UNCLE?
UNCLE BEN-- I FAILED YOU! IT'S MY FAULT YOU'RE DEAD!
IN FOND MEMORY OF BEN PARKER
BORN 1902
CHERISHED HUSBAND
BELOVED UNCLE
DIED
MAY HE REST IN PEACE
PETER GILLIS WRITER
PAT BRODERICK ARTIST
MIKE ESPOSITO INKER
O'NEIL & GRUENWALD EDITORS
SHOOTER Ed.-IN-CHIEF
ORZ. LETTERER
SLIFER COLORIST
LF367

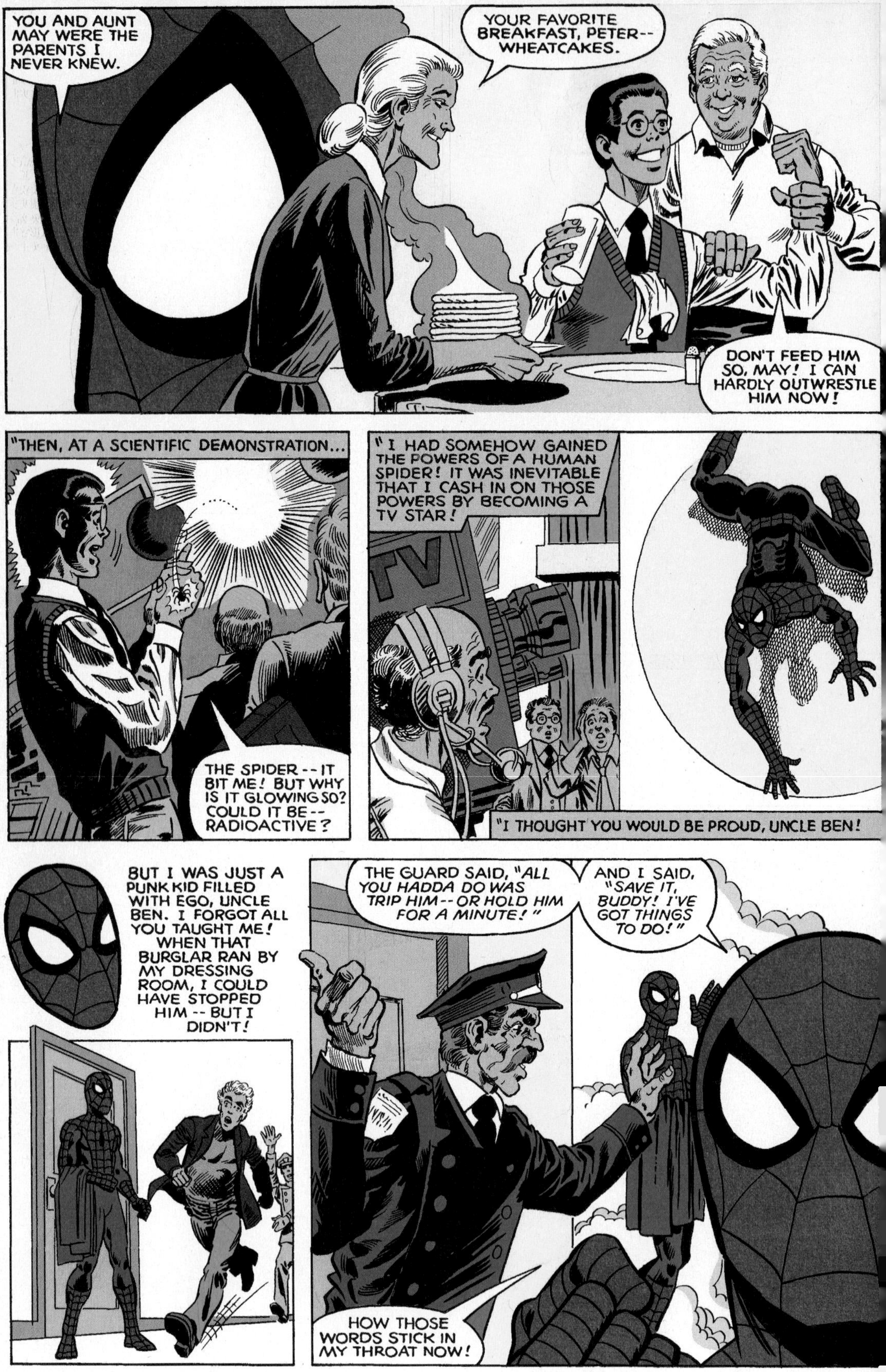
YOU AND AUNT MAY WERE THE PARENTS I NEVER KNEW.
YOUR FAVORITE BREAKFAST, PETER-- WHEATCAKES.
DON'T FEED HIM SO, MAY! I CAN HARDLY OUTWRESTLE HIM NOW!
"THEN, AT A SCIENTIFIC DEMONSTRATION...
THE SPIDER--IT BIT ME! BUT WHY IS IT GLOWING SO? COULD IT BE-- RADIOACTIVE?
"I HAD SOMEHOW GAINED THE POWERS OF A HUMAN SPIDER! IT WAS INEVITABLE THAT I CASH IN ON THOSE POWERS BY BECOMING A TV STAR!
TV
"I THOUGHT YOU WOULD BE PROUD, UNCLE BEN!
BUT I WAS JUST A PUNK KID FILLED WITH EGO, UNCLE BEN. I FORGOT ALL YOU TAUGHT ME! WHEN THAT BURGLAR RAN BY MY DRESSING ROOM, I COULD HAVE STOPPED HIM -- BUT I DIDN'T!
THE GUARD SAID, "ALL YOU HADDA DO WAS TRIP HIM--OR HOLD HIM FOR A MINUTE!"
AND I SAID, "SAVE IT, BUDDY! I'VE GOT THINGS TO DO!"
HOW THOSE WORDS STICK IN MY THROAT NOW!

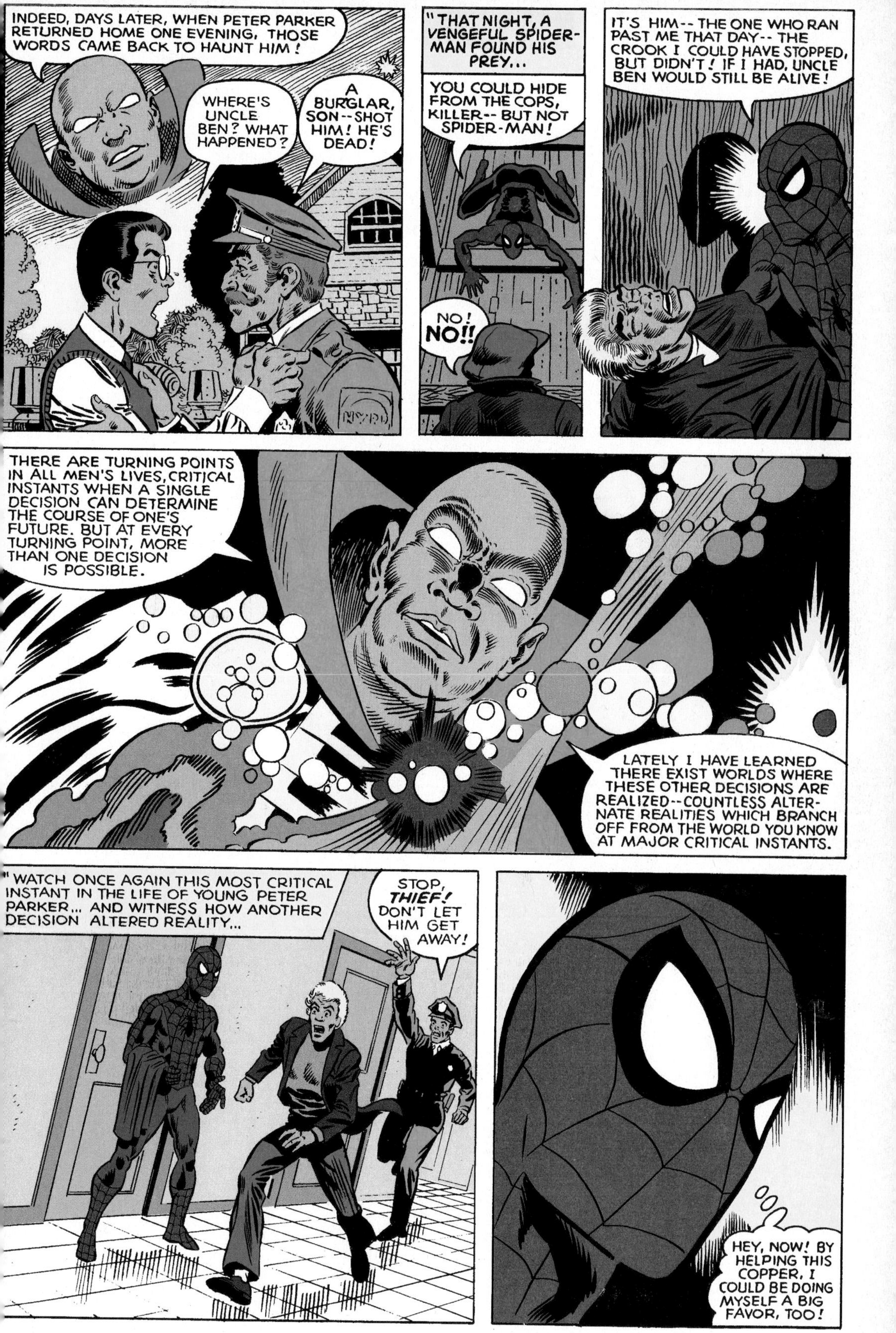
INDEED, DAYS LATER, WHEN PETER PARKER RETURNED HOME ONE EVENING, THOSE WORDS CAME BACK TO HAUNT HIM!
WHERE'S UNCLE BEN? WHAT HAPPENED?
A BURGLAR, SON--SHOT HIM! HE'S DEAD!
NYPD
"THAT NIGHT, A VENGEFUL SPIDER-MAN FOUND HIS PREY...
YOU COULD HIDE FROM THE COPS, KILLER-- BUT NOT SPIDER-MAN!
NO! NO!!
IT'S HIM-- THE ONE WHO RAN PAST ME THAT DAY-- THE CROOK I COULD HAVE STOPPED, BUT DIDN'T! IF I HAD, UNCLE BEN WOULD STILL BE ALIVE!
THERE ARE TURNING POINTS IN ALL MEN'S LIVES, CRITICAL INSTANTS WHEN A SINGLE DECISION CAN DETERMINE THE COURSE OF ONE'S FUTURE. BUT AT EVERY TURNING POINT, MORE THAN ONE DECISION IS POSSIBLE.
LATELY I HAVE LEARNED THERE EXIST WORLDS WHERE THESE OTHER DECISIONS ARE REALIZED--COUNTLESS ALTERNATE REALITIES WHICH BRANCH OFF FROM THE WORLD YOU KNOW AT MAJOR CRITICAL INSTANTS.
"WATCH ONCE AGAIN THIS MOST CRITICAL INSTANT IN THE LIFE OF YOUNG PETER PARKER... AND WITNESS HOW ANOTHER DECISION ALTERED REALITY...
STOP, THIEF! DON'T LET HIM GET AWAY!
HEY, NOW! BY HELPING THIS COPPER, I COULD BE DOING MYSELF A BIG FAVOR, TOO!

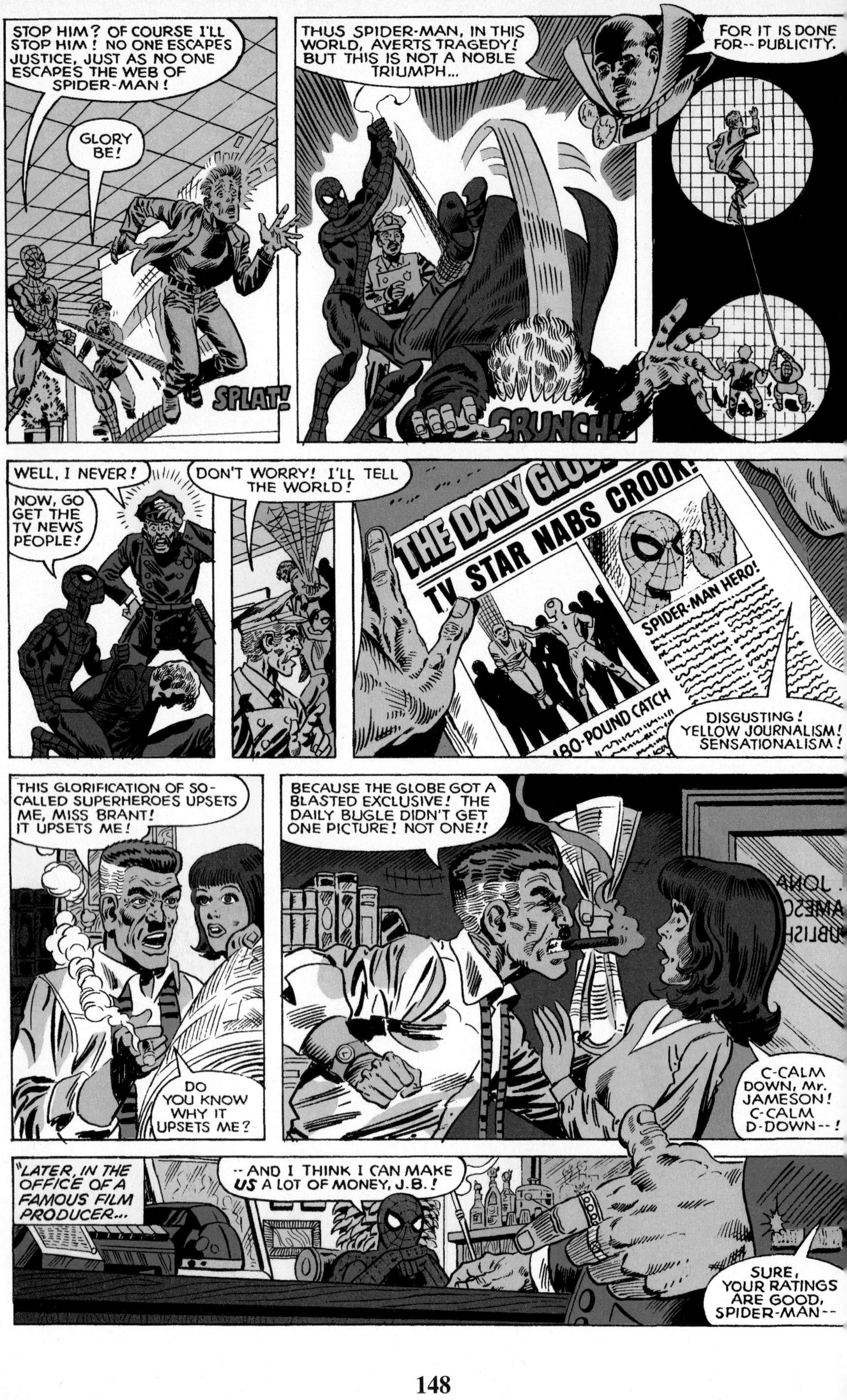

STOP HIM? OF COURSE I'LL STOP HIM! NO ONE ESCAPES JUSTICE, JUST AS NO ONE ESCAPES THE WEB OF SPIDER-MAN!
GLORY BE!
SPLAT!
THUS SPIDER-MAN, IN THIS WORLD, AVERTS TRAGEDY! BUT THIS IS NOT A NOBLE TRIUMPH...
CRUNCH!
FOR IT IS DONE FOR-- PUBLICITY.
WELL, I NEVER!
NOW, GO GET THE TV NEWS PEOPLE!
DON'T WORRY! I'LL TELL THE WORLD!
TV STAR NABS CROOK!
SPIDER-MAN HERO!
DISGUSTING! YELLOW JOURNALISM! SENSATIONALISM!
THIS GLORIFICATION OF SO-CALLED SUPERHEROES UPSETS ME, MISS BRANT! IT UPSETS ME!
DO YOU KNOW WHY IT UPSETS ME?
BECAUSE THE GLOBE GOT A BLASTED EXCLUSIVE! THE DAILY BUGLE DIDN'T GET ONE PICTURE! NOT ONE!!
C-CALM DOWN, Mr. JAMESON! C-CALM D-DOWN--!
LATER, IN THE OFFICE OF A FAMOUS FILM PRODUCER...
--AND I THINK I CAN MAKE US A LOT OF MONEY, J.B.!
SURE, YOUR RATINGS ARE GOOD, SPIDER-MAN--

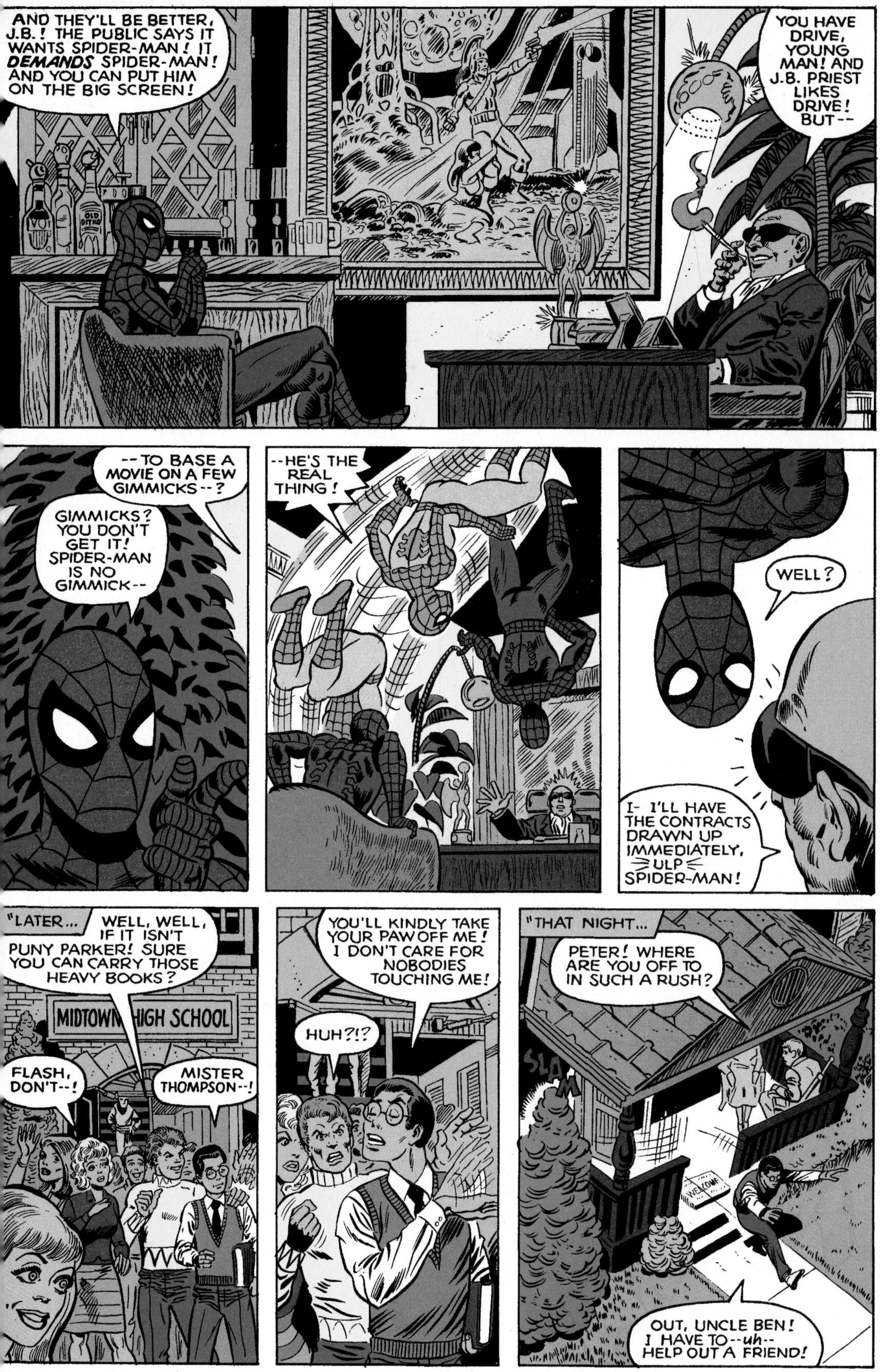
AND THEY'LL BE BETTER, J.B.! THE PUBLIC SAYS IT WANTS SPIDER-MAN! IT *DEMANDS* SPIDER-MAN! AND YOU CAN PUT HIM ON THE BIG SCREEN!
YOU HAVE DRIVE, YOUNG MAN! AND J.B. PRIEST LIKES DRIVE! BUT--
--TO BASE A MOVIE ON A FEW GIMMICKS--?
GIMMICKS? YOU DON'T GET IT! SPIDER-MAN IS NO GIMMICK--
--HE'S THE REAL THING!
WELL?
I- I'LL HAVE THE CONTRACTS DRAWN UP IMMEDIATELY, ULP SPIDER-MAN!
"LATER...
WELL, WELL, IF IT ISN'T PUNY PARKER! SURE YOU CAN CARRY THOSE HEAVY BOOKS?
MIDTOWN HIGH SCHOOL
FLASH, DON'T--!
MISTER THOMPSON--!
YOU'LL KINDLY TAKE YOUR PAW OFF ME! I DON'T CARE FOR NOBODIES TOUCHING ME!
HUH?!?
"THAT NIGHT...
PETER! WHERE ARE YOU OFF TO IN SUCH A RUSH?
SLAM
OUT, UNCLE BEN! I HAVE TO--*uh*--HELP OUT A FRIEND!

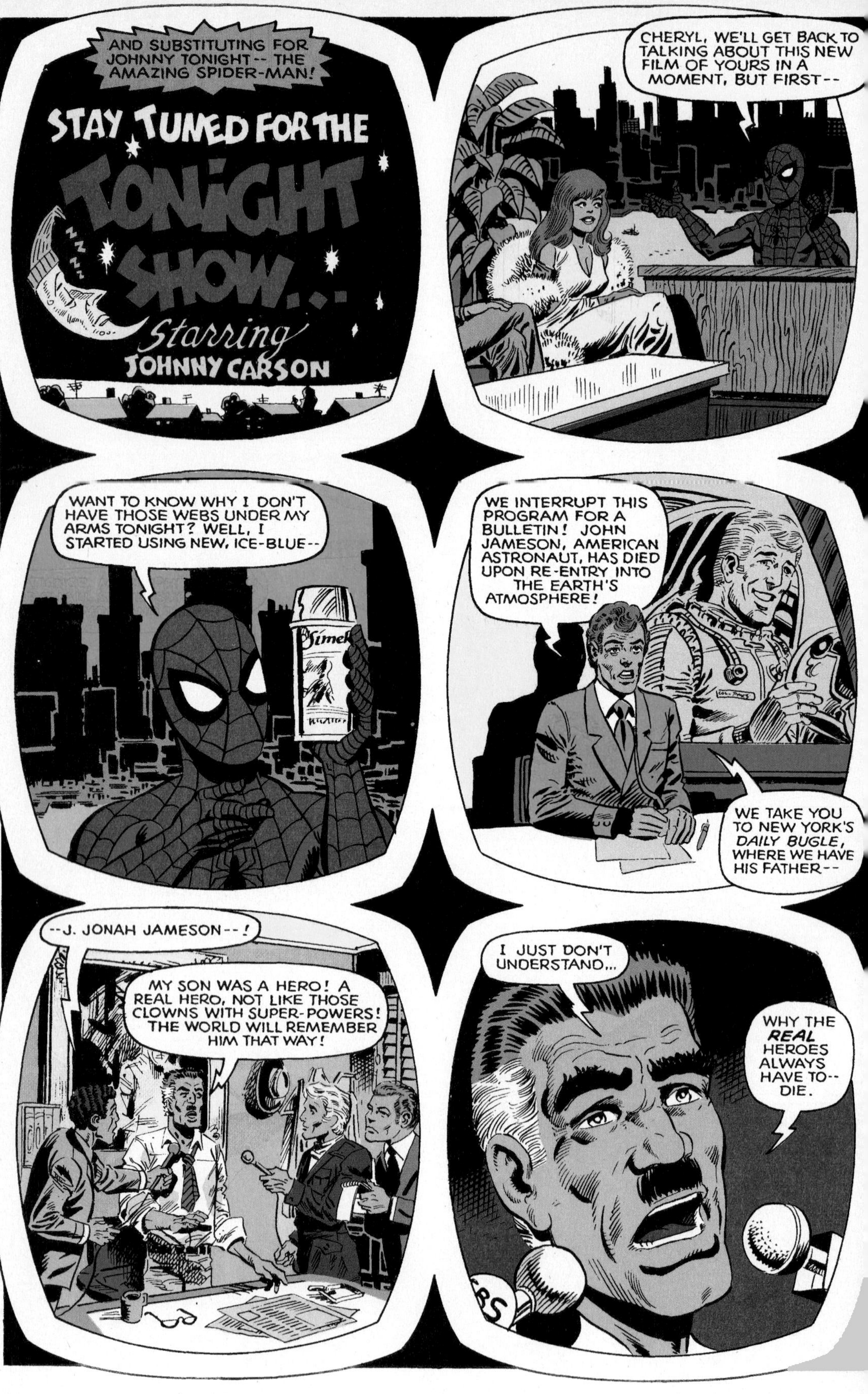
AND SUBSTITUTING FOR JOHNNY TONIGHT-- THE AMAZING SPIDER-MAN!
STAY TUNED FOR THE TONIGHT SHOW... Starring JOHNNY CARSON
CHERYL, WE'LL GET BACK TO TALKING ABOUT THIS NEW FILM OF YOURS IN A MOMENT, BUT FIRST--
WANT TO KNOW WHY I DON'T HAVE THOSE WEBS UNDER MY ARMS TONIGHT? WELL, I STARTED USING NEW, ICE-BLUE--
WE INTERRUPT THIS PROGRAM FOR A BULLETIN! JOHN JAMESON, AMERICAN ASTRONAUT, HAS DIED UPON RE-ENTRY INTO THE EARTH'S ATMOSPHERE!
WE TAKE YOU TO NEW YORK'S *DAILY BUGLE*, WHERE WE HAVE HIS FATHER--
--J. JONAH JAMESON--!
MY SON WAS A HERO! A REAL HERO, NOT LIKE THOSE CLOWNS WITH SUPER-POWERS! THE WORLD WILL REMEMBER HIM THAT WAY!
I JUST DON'T UNDERSTAND...
WHY THE *REAL* HEROES ALWAYS HAVE TO-- DIE.

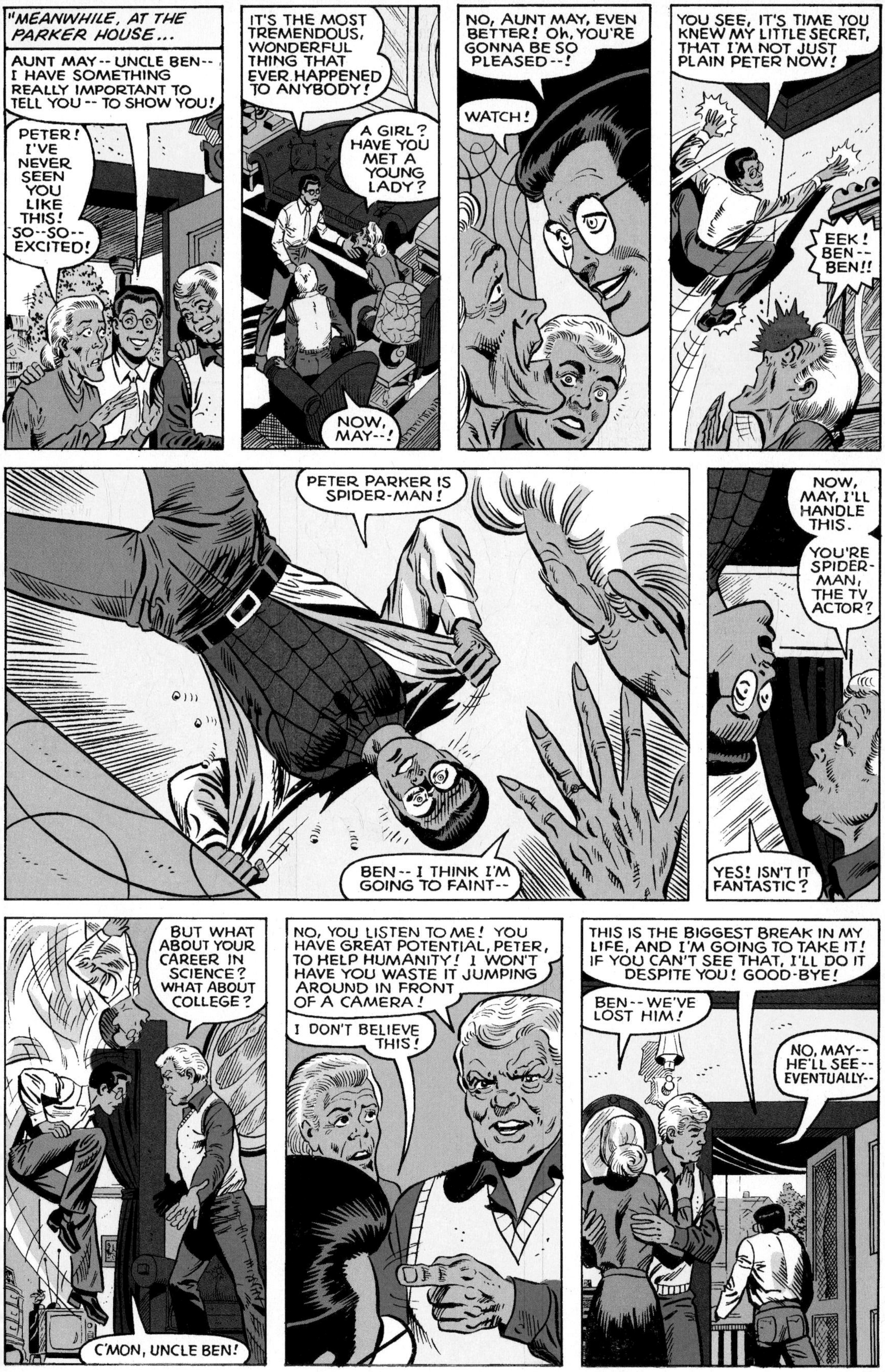
MEANWHILE, AT THE PARKER HOUSE...
AUNT MAY -- UNCLE BEN -- I HAVE SOMETHING REALLY IMPORTANT TO TELL YOU -- TO SHOW YOU!
PETER! I'VE NEVER SEEN YOU LIKE THIS! SO--SO-- EXCITED!
IT'S THE MOST TREMENDOUS, WONDERFUL THING THAT EVER HAPPENED TO ANYBODY!
A GIRL? HAVE YOU MET A YOUNG LADY?
NOW, MAY--!
NO, AUNT MAY, EVEN BETTER! Oh, YOU'RE GONNA BE SO PLEASED--!
WATCH!
YOU SEE, IT'S TIME YOU KNEW MY LITTLE SECRET, THAT I'M NOT JUST PLAIN PETER NOW!
EEK! BEN-- BEN!!
PETER PARKER IS SPIDER-MAN!
BEN-- I THINK I'M GOING TO FAINT--
NOW, MAY, I'LL HANDLE THIS.
YOU'RE SPIDER-MAN, THE TV ACTOR?
YES! ISN'T IT FANTASTIC?
BUT WHAT ABOUT YOUR CAREER IN SCIENCE? WHAT ABOUT COLLEGE?
C'MON, UNCLE BEN!
NO, YOU LISTEN TO ME! YOU HAVE GREAT POTENTIAL, PETER, TO HELP HUMANITY! I WON'T HAVE YOU WASTE IT JUMPING AROUND IN FRONT OF A CAMERA!
I DON'T BELIEVE THIS!
THIS IS THE BIGGEST BREAK IN MY LIFE, AND I'M GOING TO TAKE IT! IF YOU CAN'T SEE THAT, I'LL DO IT DESPITE YOU! GOOD-BYE!
BEN-- WE'VE LOST HIM!
NO, MAY-- HE'LL SEE-- EVENTUALLY--

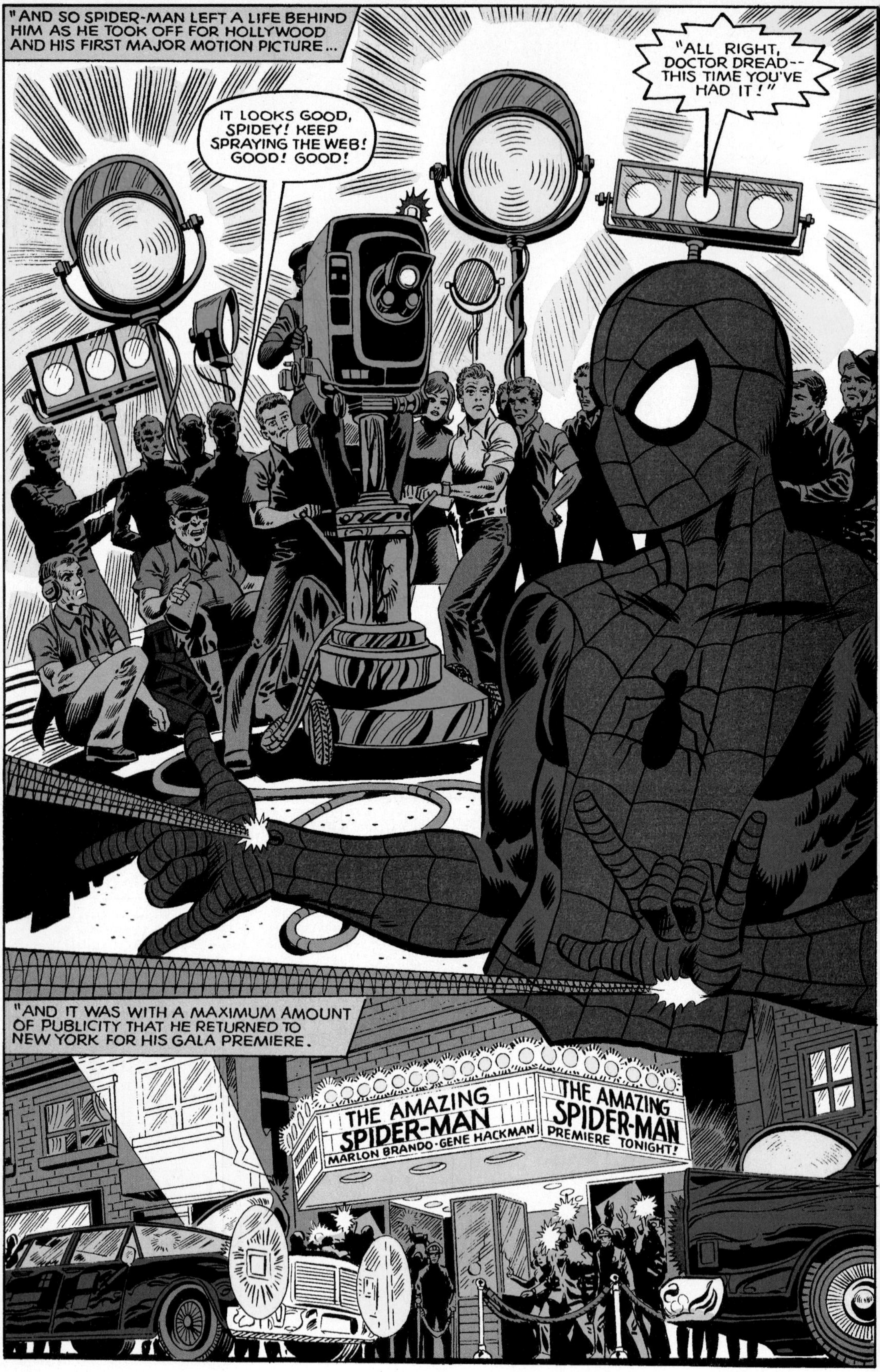
"AND SO SPIDER-MAN LEFT A LIFE BEHIND HIM AS HE TOOK OFF FOR HOLLYWOOD AND HIS FIRST MAJOR MOTION PICTURE...
IT LOOKS GOOD, SPIDEY! KEEP SPRAYING THE WEB! GOOD! GOOD!
"ALL RIGHT, DOCTOR DREAD-- THIS TIME YOU'VE HAD IT!"
"AND IT WAS WITH A MAXIMUM AMOUNT OF PUBLICITY THAT HE RETURNED TO NEW YORK FOR HIS GALA PREMIERE.
THE AMAZING SPIDER-MAN
MARLON BRANDO · GENE HACKMAN
THE AMAZING SPIDER-MAN
PREMIERE TONIGHT!

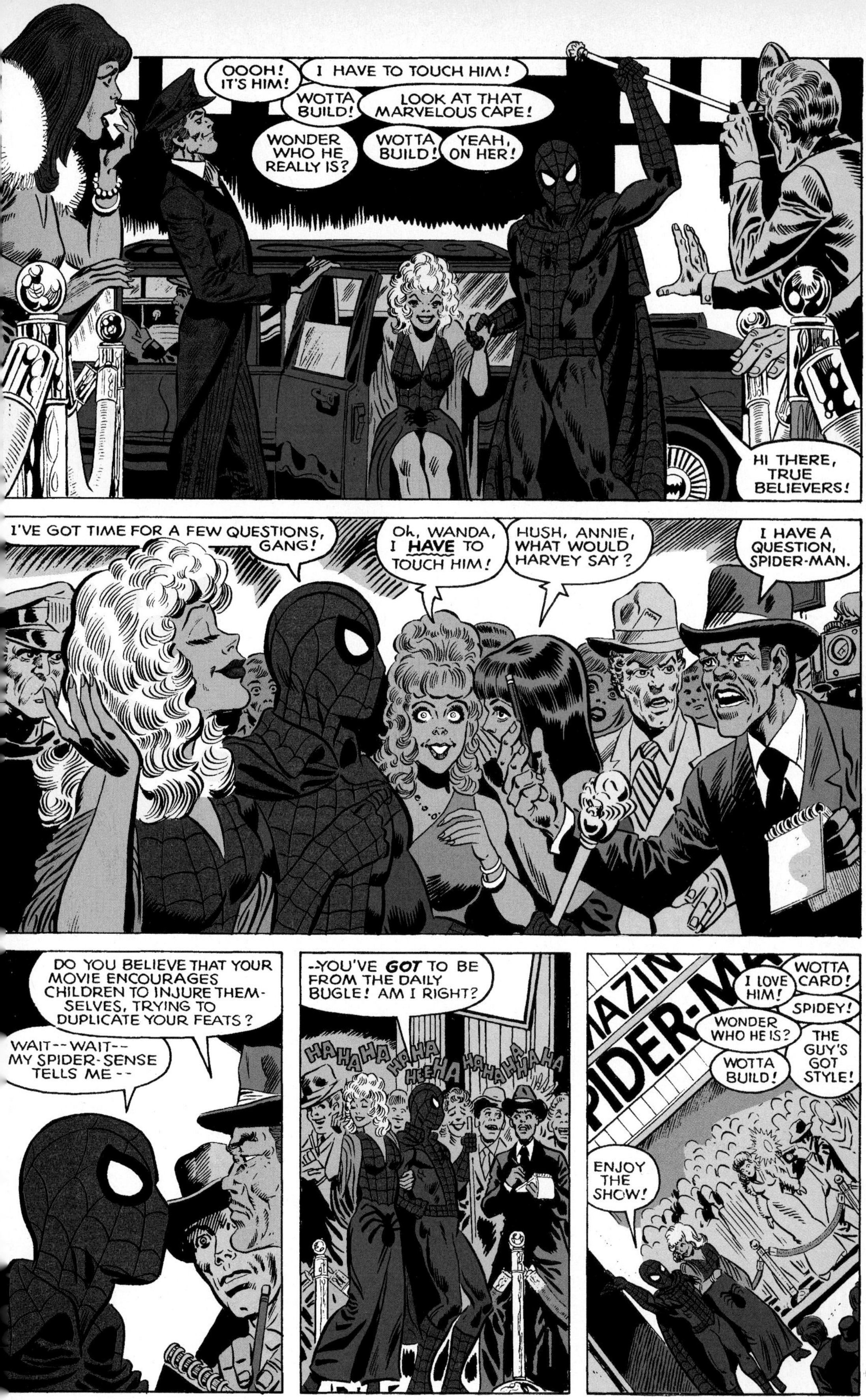
OOOH! IT'S HIM!
I HAVE TO TOUCH HIM!
WOTTA BUILD!
LOOK AT THAT MARVELOUS CAPE!
WONDER WHO HE REALLY IS?
WOTTA BUILD!
YEAH, ON HER!
HI THERE, TRUE BELIEVERS!
I'VE GOT TIME FOR A FEW QUESTIONS, GANG!
Oh, WANDA, I HAVE TO TOUCH HIM!
HUSH, ANNIE, WHAT WOULD HARVEY SAY?
I HAVE A QUESTION, SPIDER-MAN.
DO YOU BELIEVE THAT YOUR MOVIE ENCOURAGES CHILDREN TO INJURE THEMSELVES, TRYING TO DUPLICATE YOUR FEATS?
WAIT--WAIT-- MY SPIDER-SENSE TELLS ME--
--YOU'VE GOT TO BE FROM THE DAILY BUGLE! AM I RIGHT?
HAHAHA HAHA HEHA HAHAHA HAHAHA
MAZIN SPIDER-MA
I LOVE HIM!
WOTTA CARD!
SPIDEY!
WONDER WHO HE IS?
THE GUY'S GOT STYLE!
WOTTA BUILD!
ENJOY THE SHOW!

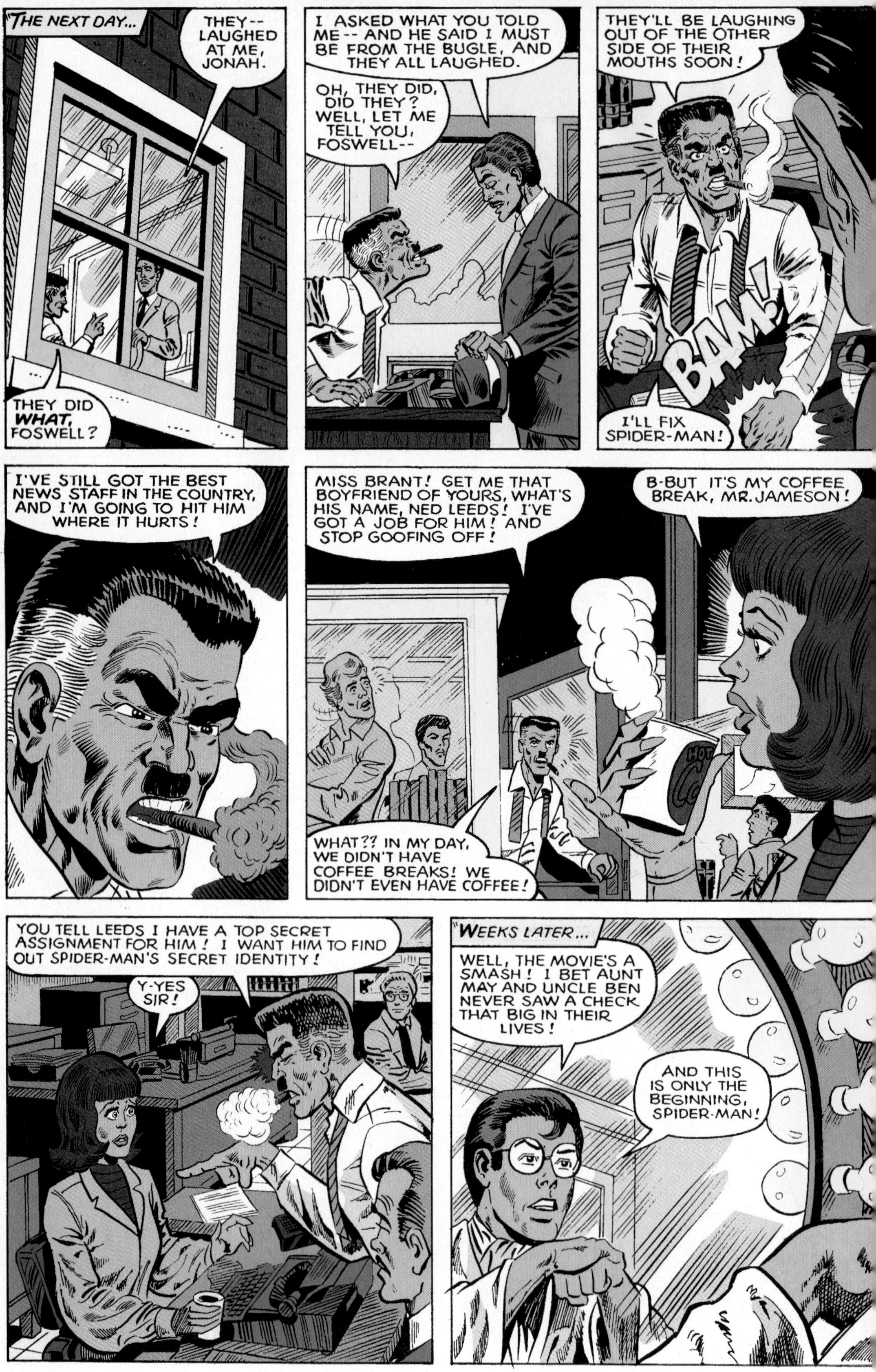

THE NEXT DAY...
THEY-- LAUGHED AT ME, JONAH.
THEY DID WHAT, FOSWELL?
I ASKED WHAT YOU TOLD ME -- AND HE SAID I MUST BE FROM THE BUGLE, AND THEY ALL LAUGHED.
OH, THEY DID, DID THEY? WELL, LET ME TELL YOU, FOSWELL--
THEY'LL BE LAUGHING OUT OF THE OTHER SIDE OF THEIR MOUTHS SOON!
BAM!
I'LL FIX SPIDER-MAN!
I'VE STILL GOT THE BEST NEWS STAFF IN THE COUNTRY, AND I'M GOING TO HIT HIM WHERE IT HURTS!
MISS BRANT! GET ME THAT BOYFRIEND OF YOURS, WHAT'S HIS NAME, NED LEEDS! I'VE GOT A JOB FOR HIM! AND STOP GOOFING OFF!
B-BUT IT'S MY COFFEE BREAK, MR. JAMESON!
WHAT?? IN MY DAY, WE DIDN'T HAVE COFFEE BREAKS! WE DIDN'T EVEN HAVE COFFEE!
YOU TELL LEEDS I HAVE A TOP SECRET ASSIGNMENT FOR HIM! I WANT HIM TO FIND OUT SPIDER-MAN'S SECRET IDENTITY!
Y-YES SIR!
WEEKS LATER...
WELL, THE MOVIE'S A SMASH! I BET AUNT MAY AND UNCLE BEN NEVER SAW A CHECK THAT BIG IN THEIR LIVES!
AND THIS IS ONLY THE BEGINNING, SPIDER-MAN!

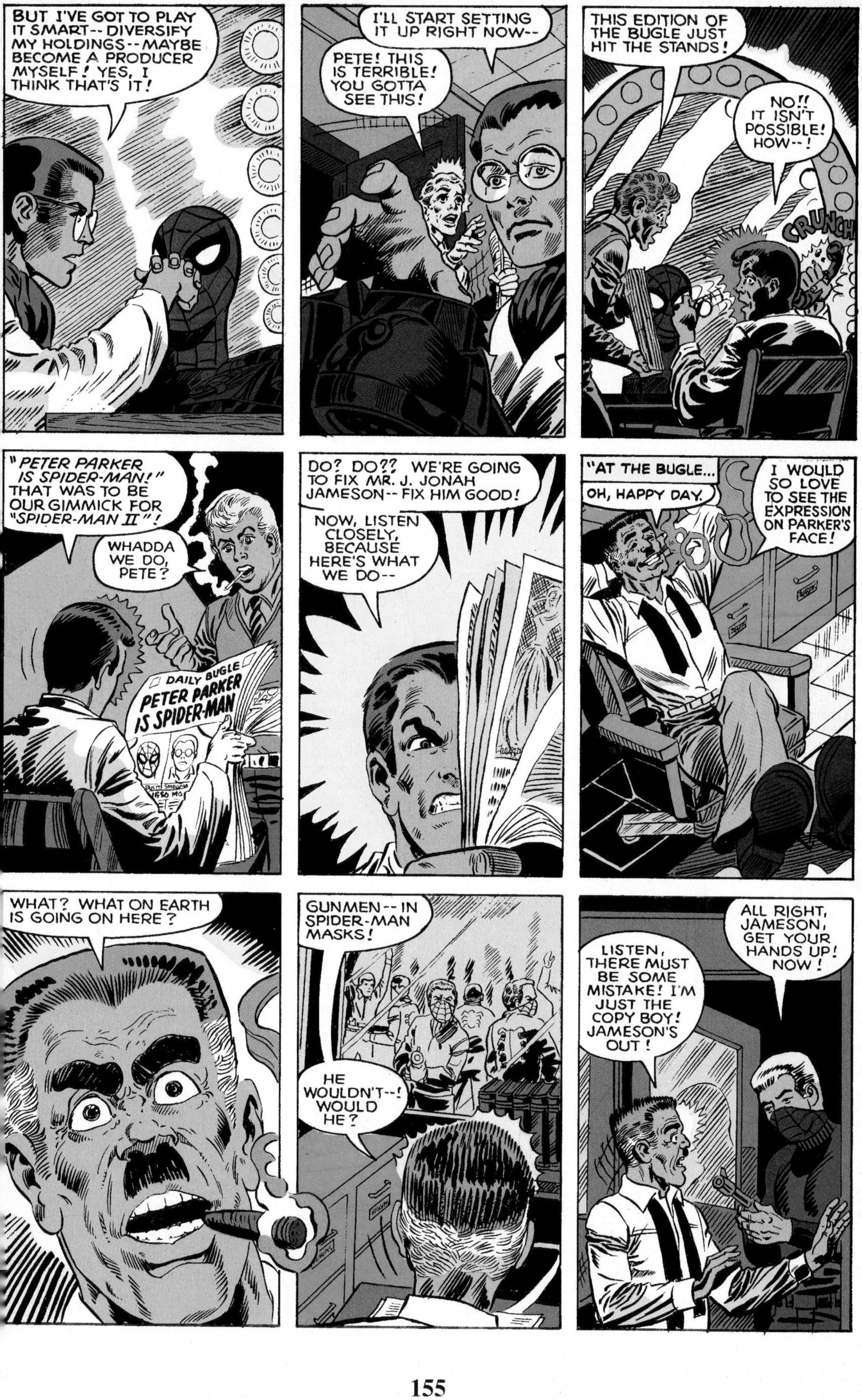
BUT I'VE GOT TO PLAY IT SMART-- DIVERSIFY MY HOLDINGS-- MAYBE BECOME A PRODUCER MYSELF! YES, I THINK THAT'S IT!
I'LL START SETTING IT UP RIGHT NOW--
PETE! THIS IS TERRIBLE! YOU GOTTA SEE THIS!
THIS EDITION OF THE BUGLE JUST HIT THE STANDS!
NO!! IT ISN'T POSSIBLE! HOW--!
CRUNCH
"PETER PARKER IS SPIDER-MAN!" THAT WAS TO BE OUR GIMMICK FOR "SPIDER-MAN II"!
WHADDA WE DO, PETE?
DAILY BUGLE
PETER PARKER IS SPIDER-MAN
DO? DO?? WE'RE GOING TO FIX MR. J. JONAH JAMESON-- FIX HIM GOOD!
NOW, LISTEN CLOSELY, BECAUSE HERE'S WHAT WE DO--
"AT THE BUGLE...
OH, HAPPY DAY.
I WOULD SO LOVE TO SEE THE EXPRESSION ON PARKER'S FACE!
WHAT? WHAT ON EARTH IS GOING ON HERE?
GUNMEN-- IN SPIDER-MAN MASKS!
HE WOULDN'T--! WOULD HE?
ALL RIGHT, JAMESON, GET YOUR HANDS UP! NOW!
LISTEN, THERE MUST BE SOME MISTAKE! I'M JUST THE COPY BOY! JAMESON'S OUT!

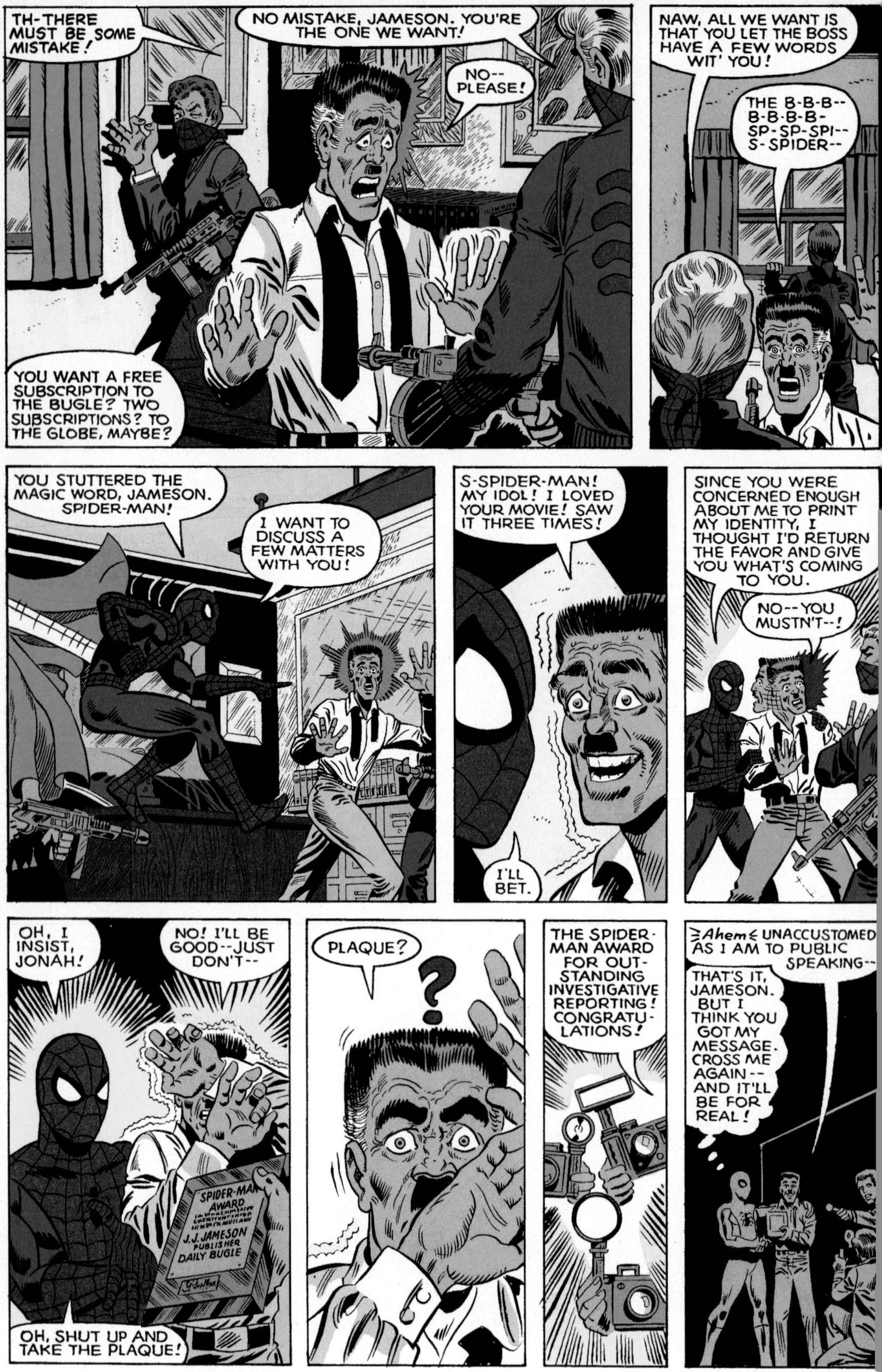
TH-THERE MUST BE SOME MISTAKE!
NO MISTAKE, JAMESON. YOU'RE THE ONE WE WANT!
NO-- PLEASE!
YOU WANT A FREE SUBSCRIPTION TO THE BUGLE? TWO SUBSCRIPTIONS? TO THE GLOBE, MAYBE?
NAW, ALL WE WANT IS THAT YOU LET THE BOSS HAVE A FEW WORDS WIT' YOU!
THE B-B-B-- B-B-B-B- SP-SP-SPI-- S-SPIDER--
YOU STUTTERED THE MAGIC WORD, JAMESON. SPIDER-MAN!
I WANT TO DISCUSS A FEW MATTERS WITH YOU!
S-SPIDER-MAN! MY IDOL! I LOVED YOUR MOVIE! SAW IT THREE TIMES!
I'LL BET.
SINCE YOU WERE CONCERNED ENOUGH ABOUT ME TO PRINT MY IDENTITY, I THOUGHT I'D RETURN THE FAVOR AND GIVE YOU WHAT'S COMING TO YOU.
NO--YOU MUSTN'T--!
OH, I INSIST, JONAH!
NO! I'LL BE GOOD--JUST DON'T--
SPIDER-MAN AWARD
J.J. JAMESON PUBLISHER DAILY BUGLE
OH, SHUT UP AND TAKE THE PLAQUE!
PLAQUE?
THE SPIDER-MAN AWARD FOR OUT-STANDING INVESTIGATIVE REPORTING! CONGRATU-LATIONS!
Ahem UNACCUSTOMED AS I AM TO PUBLIC SPEAKING--
THAT'S IT, JAMESON. BUT I THINK YOU GOT MY MESSAGE. CROSS ME AGAIN--AND IT'LL BE FOR REAL!

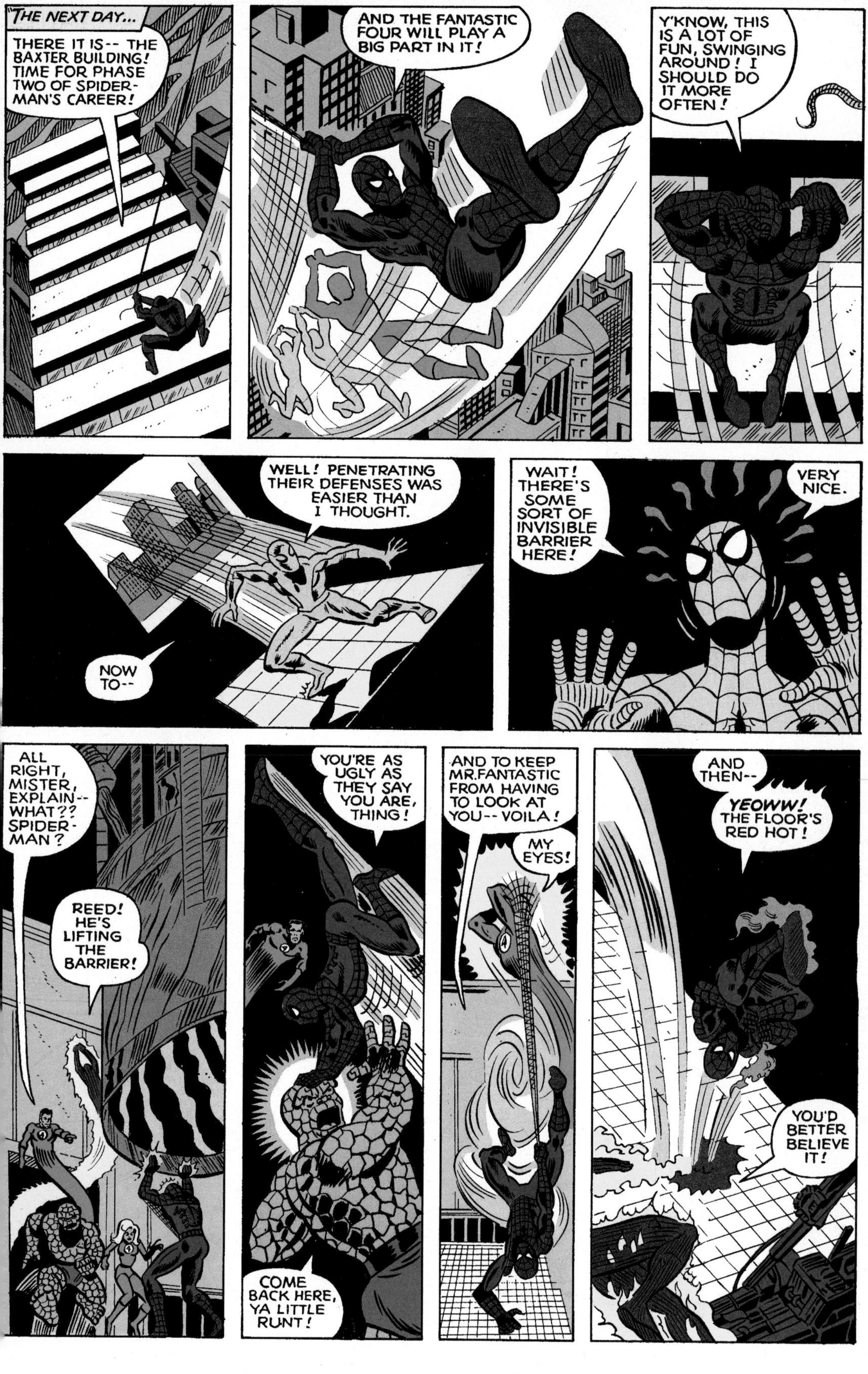
THE NEXT DAY...
THERE IT IS-- THE BAXTER BUILDING! TIME FOR PHASE TWO OF SPIDER-MAN'S CAREER!
AND THE FANTASTIC FOUR WILL PLAY A BIG PART IN IT!
Y'KNOW, THIS IS A LOT OF FUN, SWINGING AROUND! I SHOULD DO IT MORE OFTEN!
WELL! PENETRATING THEIR DEFENSES WAS EASIER THAN I THOUGHT.
NOW TO--
WAIT! THERE'S SOME SORT OF INVISIBLE BARRIER HERE!
VERY NICE.
ALL RIGHT, MISTER, EXPLAIN-- WHAT?? SPIDER-MAN?
REED! HE'S LIFTING THE BARRIER!
YOU'RE AS UGLY AS THEY SAY YOU ARE, THING!
COME BACK HERE, YA LITTLE RUNT!
AND TO KEEP MR. FANTASTIC FROM HAVING TO LOOK AT YOU-- VOILA!
MY EYES!
AND THEN-- YEOWW! THE FLOOR'S RED HOT!
YOU'D BETTER BELIEVE IT!

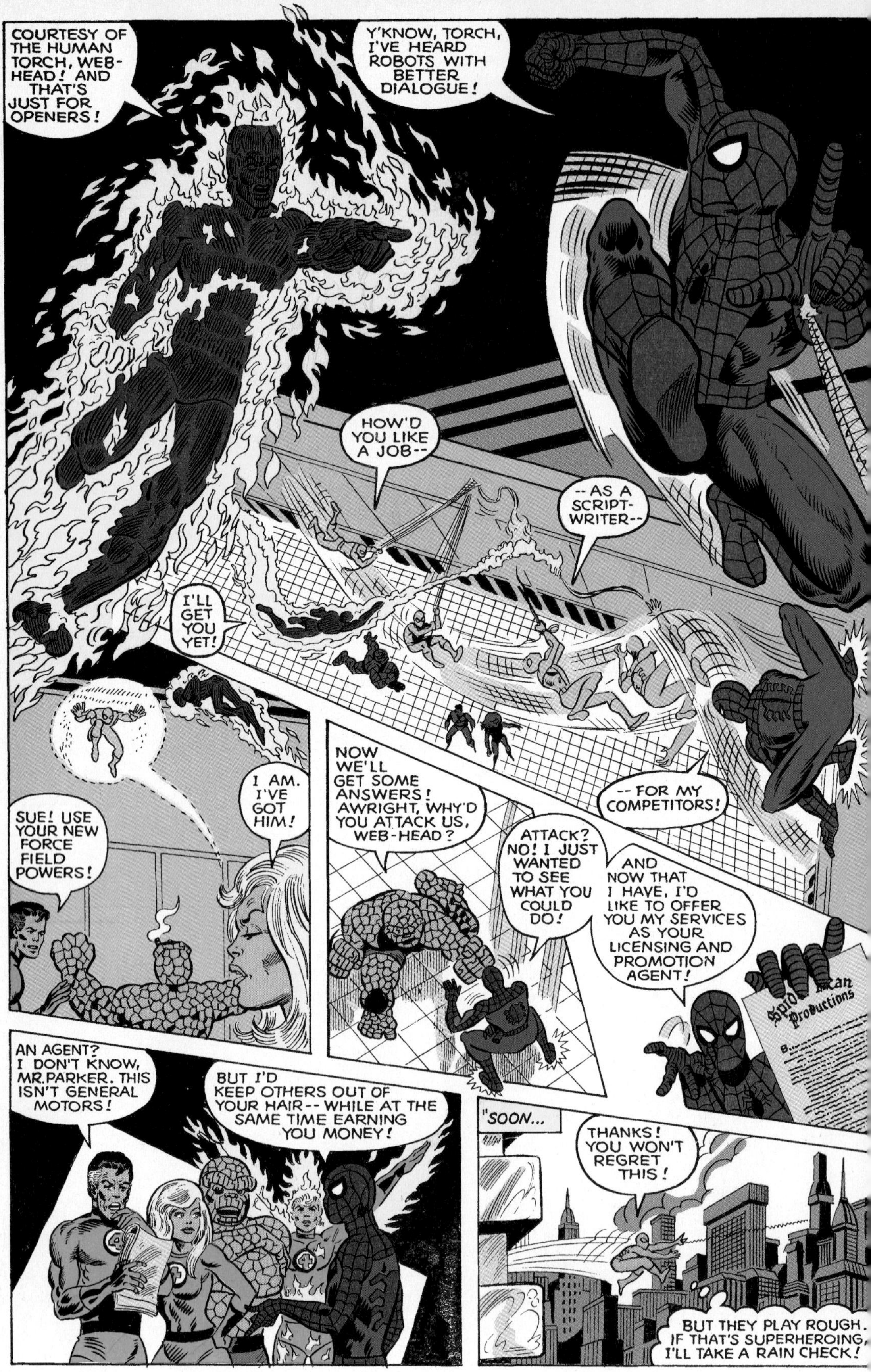
COURTESY OF THE HUMAN TORCH, WEB-HEAD! AND THAT'S JUST FOR OPENERS!
Y'KNOW, TORCH, I'VE HEARD ROBOTS WITH BETTER DIALOGUE!
HOW'D YOU LIKE A JOB--
--AS A SCRIPT-WRITER--
I'LL GET YOU YET!
--FOR MY COMPETITORS!
SUE! USE YOUR NEW FORCE FIELD POWERS!
I AM. I'VE GOT HIM!
NOW WE'LL GET SOME ANSWERS! AWRIGHT, WHY'D YOU ATTACK US, WEB-HEAD?
ATTACK? NO! I JUST WANTED TO SEE WHAT YOU COULD DO!
AND NOW THAT I HAVE, I'D LIKE TO OFFER YOU MY SERVICES AS YOUR LICENSING AND PROMOTION AGENT!
Spider-Man Productions
AN AGENT? I DON'T KNOW, MR. PARKER. THIS ISN'T GENERAL MOTORS!
BUT I'D KEEP OTHERS OUT OF YOUR HAIR-- WHILE AT THE SAME TIME EARNING YOU MONEY!
"SOON...
THANKS! YOU WON'T REGRET THIS!
BUT THEY PLAY ROUGH. IF THAT'S SUPERHEROING, I'LL TAKE A RAIN CHECK!

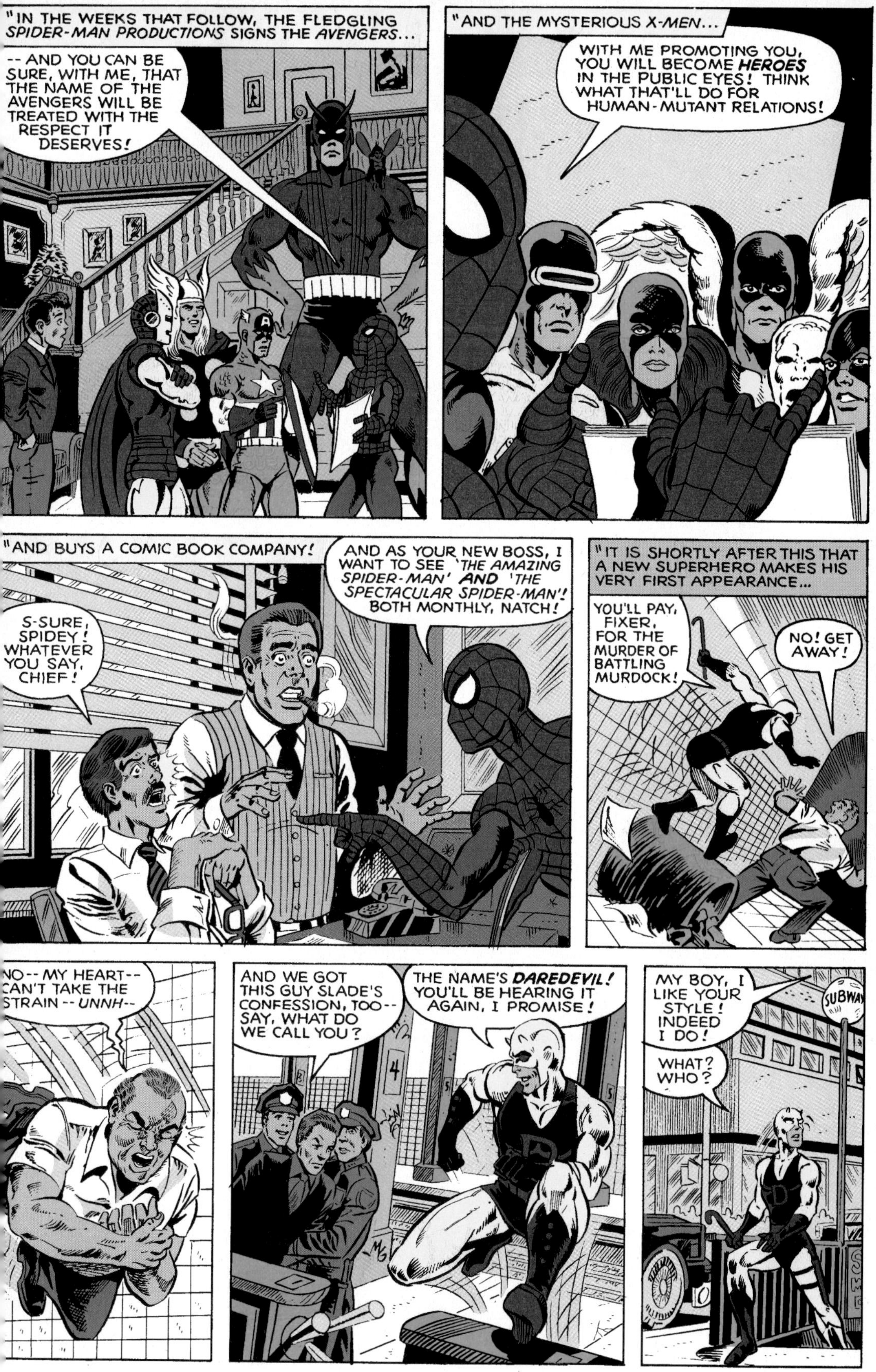
"IN THE WEEKS THAT FOLLOW, THE FLEDGLING SPIDER-MAN PRODUCTIONS SIGNS THE AVENGERS...
-- AND YOU CAN BE SURE, WITH ME, THAT THE NAME OF THE AVENGERS WILL BE TREATED WITH THE RESPECT IT DESERVES!
"AND THE MYSTERIOUS X-MEN...
WITH ME PROMOTING YOU, YOU WILL BECOME HEROES IN THE PUBLIC EYES! THINK WHAT THAT'LL DO FOR HUMAN-MUTANT RELATIONS!
"AND BUYS A COMIC BOOK COMPANY!
AND AS YOUR NEW BOSS, I WANT TO SEE 'THE AMAZING SPIDER-MAN' AND 'THE SPECTACULAR SPIDER-MAN'! BOTH MONTHLY, NATCH!
S-SURE, SPIDEY! WHATEVER YOU SAY, CHIEF!
"IT IS SHORTLY AFTER THIS THAT A NEW SUPERHERO MAKES HIS VERY FIRST APPEARANCE...
YOU'LL PAY, FIXER, FOR THE MURDER OF BATTLING MURDOCK!
NO! GET AWAY!
NO-- MY HEART-- CAN'T TAKE THE STRAIN -- UNNH--
AND WE GOT THIS GUY SLADE'S CONFESSION, TOO-- SAY, WHAT DO WE CALL YOU?
THE NAME'S DAREDEVIL! YOU'LL BE HEARING IT AGAIN, I PROMISE!
MY BOY, I LIKE YOUR STYLE! INDEED I DO!
WHAT? WHO?
SUBWAY

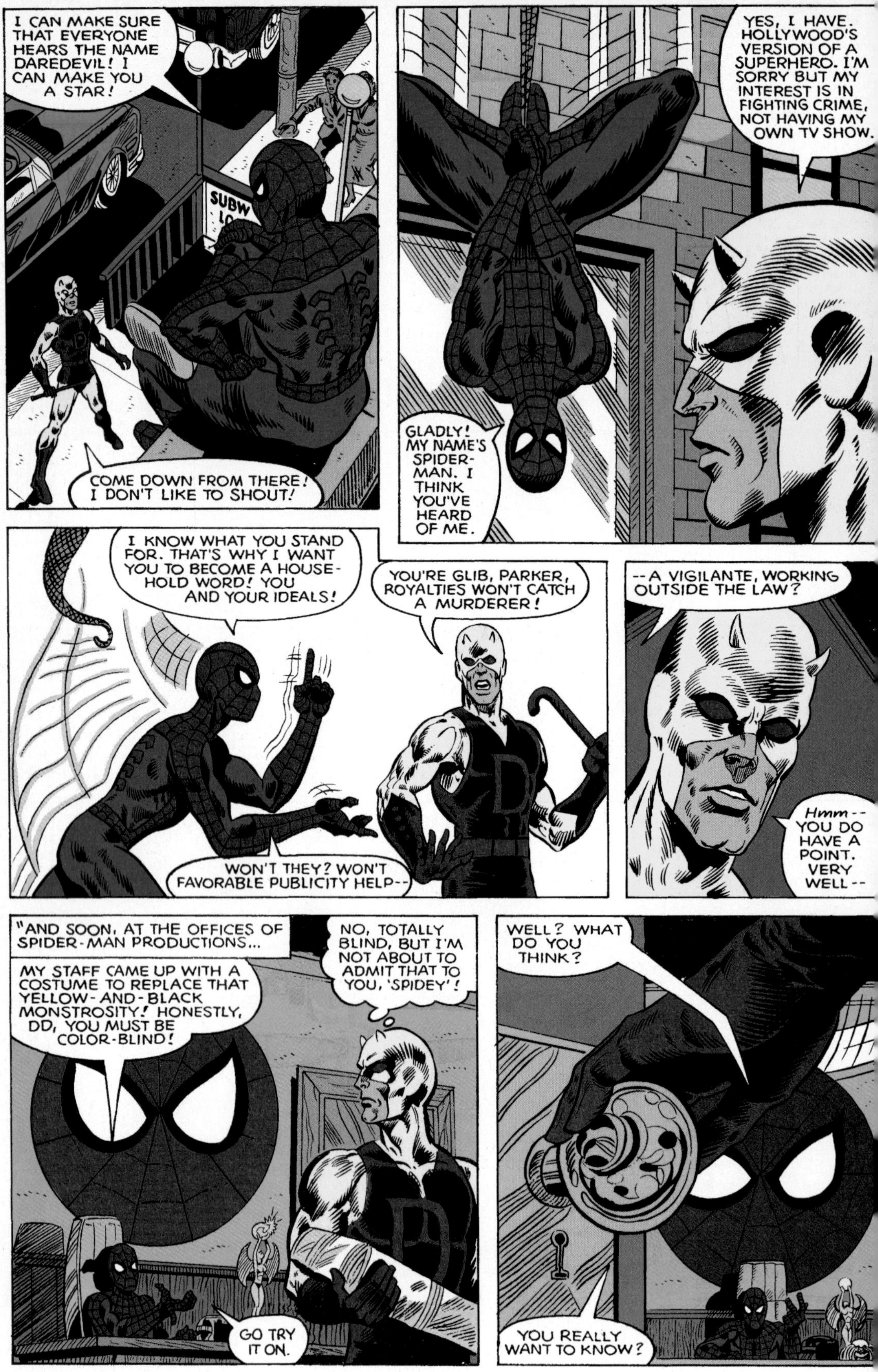
I CAN MAKE SURE THAT EVERYONE HEARS THE NAME DAREDEVIL! I CAN MAKE YOU A STAR!
SUBW
COME DOWN FROM THERE! I DON'T LIKE TO SHOUT!
GLADLY! MY NAME'S SPIDER-MAN. I THINK YOU'VE HEARD OF ME.
YES, I HAVE. HOLLYWOOD'S VERSION OF A SUPERHERO. I'M SORRY BUT MY INTEREST IS IN FIGHTING CRIME, NOT HAVING MY OWN TV SHOW.
I KNOW WHAT YOU STAND FOR. THAT'S WHY I WANT YOU TO BECOME A HOUSE-HOLD WORD! YOU AND YOUR IDEALS!
YOU'RE GLIB, PARKER, ROYALTIES WON'T CATCH A MURDERER!
WON'T THEY? WON'T FAVORABLE PUBLICITY HELP--
--A VIGILANTE, WORKING OUTSIDE THE LAW?
Hmm-- YOU DO HAVE A POINT. VERY WELL--
"AND SOON, AT THE OFFICES OF SPIDER-MAN PRODUCTIONS...
MY STAFF CAME UP WITH A COSTUME TO REPLACE THAT YELLOW-AND-BLACK MONSTROSITY! HONESTLY, DD, YOU MUST BE COLOR-BLIND!
NO, TOTALLY BLIND, BUT I'M NOT ABOUT TO ADMIT THAT TO YOU, 'SPIDEY'!
GO TRY IT ON.
WELL? WHAT DO YOU THINK?
YOU REALLY WANT TO KNOW?

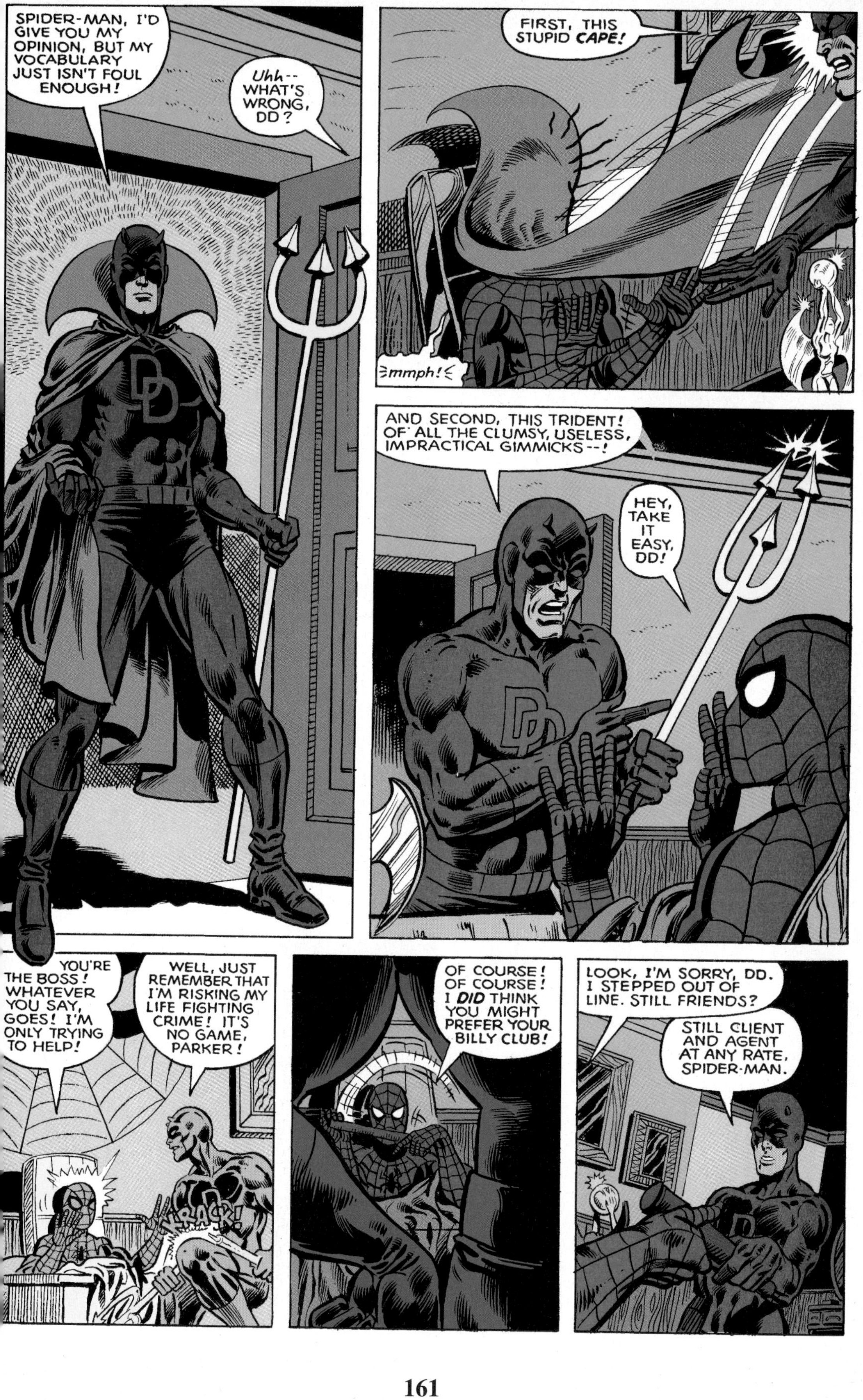
SPIDER-MAN, I'D GIVE YOU MY OPINION, BUT MY VOCABULARY JUST ISN'T FOUL ENOUGH!
Uhh-- WHAT'S WRONG, DD?
FIRST, THIS STUPID CAPE!
mmph!
AND SECOND, THIS TRIDENT! OF ALL THE CLUMSY, USELESS, IMPRACTICAL GIMMICKS--!
HEY, TAKE IT EASY, DD!
YOU'RE THE BOSS! WHATEVER YOU SAY, GOES! I'M ONLY TRYING TO HELP!
WELL, JUST REMEMBER THAT I'M RISKING MY LIFE FIGHTING CRIME! IT'S NO GAME, PARKER!
OF COURSE! OF COURSE! I DID THINK YOU MIGHT PREFER YOUR BILLY CLUB!
LOOK, I'M SORRY, DD. I STEPPED OUT OF LINE. STILL FRIENDS?
STILL CLIENT AND AGENT AT ANY RATE, SPIDER-MAN.

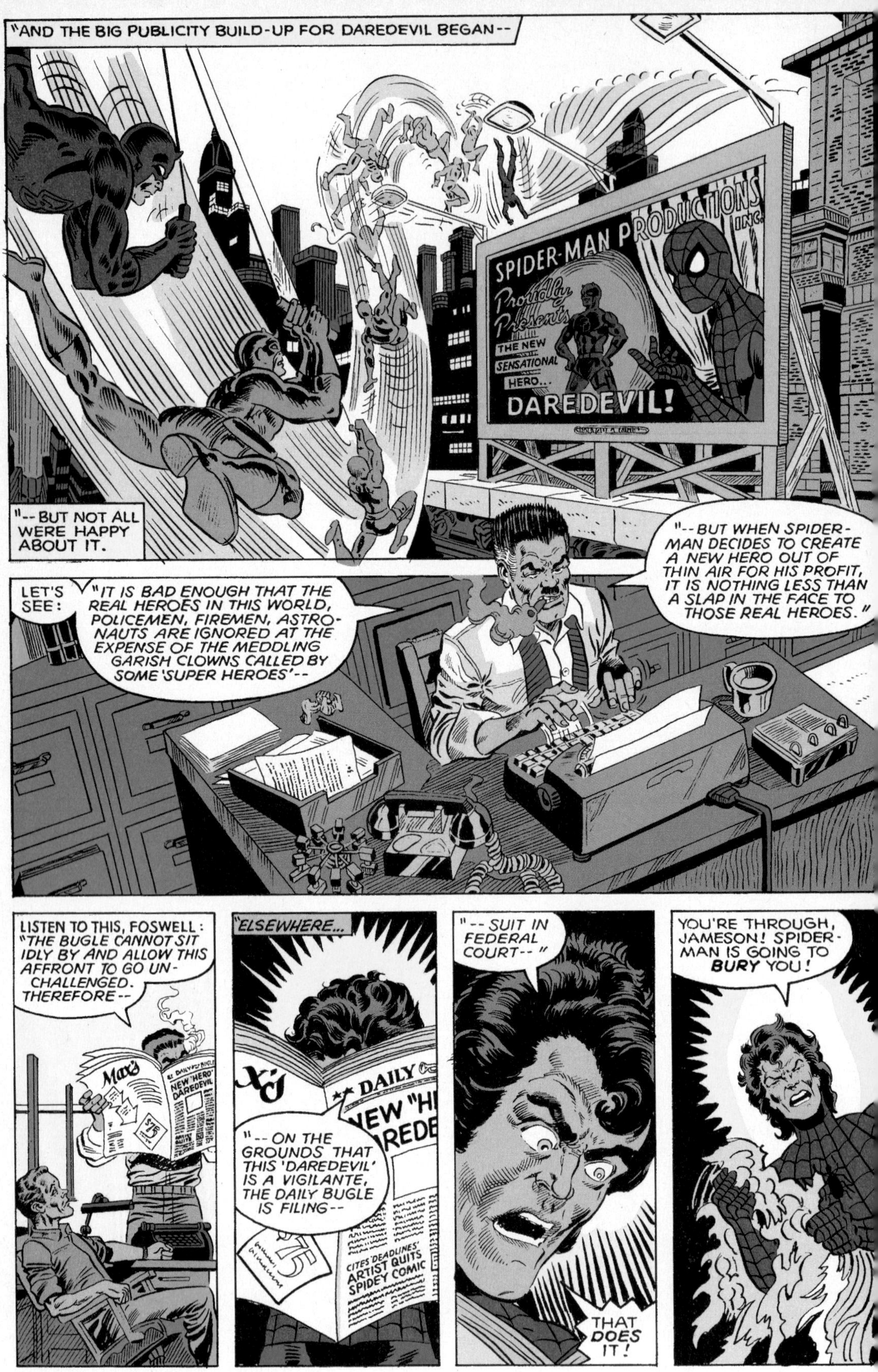
"AND THE BIG PUBLICITY BUILD-UP FOR DAREDEVIL BEGAN--
SPIDER-MAN PRODUCTIONS INC.
Proudly Presents
THE NEW SENSATIONAL HERO...
DAREDEVIL!
"--BUT NOT ALL WERE HAPPY ABOUT IT.
LET'S SEE:
"IT IS BAD ENOUGH THAT THE REAL HEROES IN THIS WORLD, POLICEMEN, FIREMEN, ASTRONAUTS ARE IGNORED AT THE EXPENSE OF THE MEDDLING GARISH CLOWNS CALLED BY SOME 'SUPER HEROES'--
"--BUT WHEN SPIDER-MAN DECIDES TO CREATE A NEW HERO OUT OF THIN AIR FOR HIS PROFIT, IT IS NOTHING LESS THAN A SLAP IN THE FACE TO THOSE REAL HEROES."
LISTEN TO THIS, FOSWELL: "THE BUGLE CANNOT SIT IDLY BY AND ALLOW THIS AFFRONT TO GO UNCHALLENGED. THEREFORE--
Max's
NEW 'HERO' DAREDEVIL
"ELSEWHERE...
DAILY
"--ON THE GROUNDS THAT THIS 'DAREDEVIL' IS A VIGILANTE, THE DAILY BUGLE IS FILING--
CITES 'DEADLINES' ARTIST QUITS SPIDEY COMIC
"--SUIT IN FEDERAL COURT--"
THAT DOES IT!
YOU'RE THROUGH, JAMESON! SPIDER-MAN IS GOING TO BURY YOU!

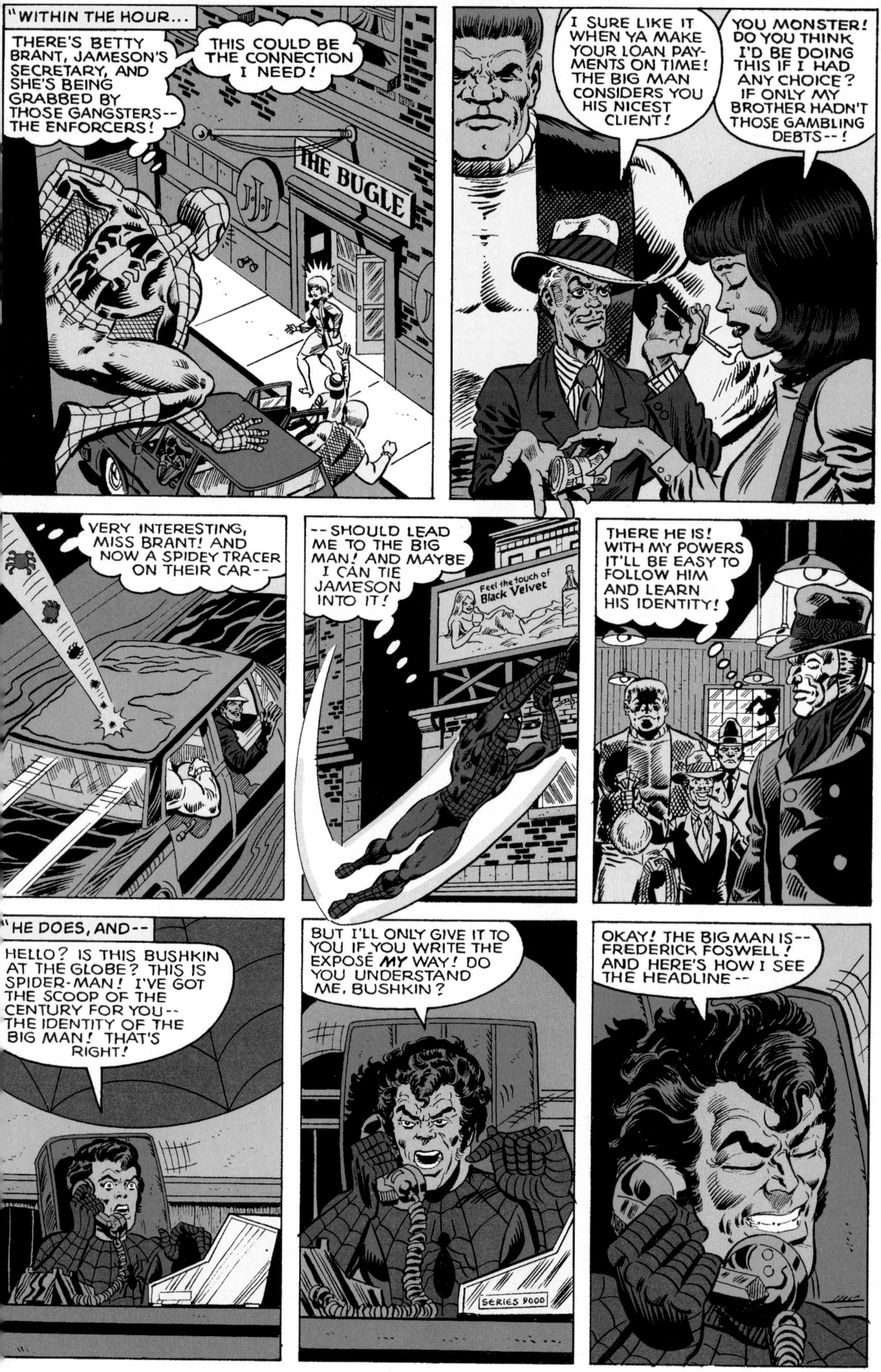
"WITHIN THE HOUR...
THERE'S BETTY BRANT, JAMESON'S SECRETARY, AND SHE'S BEING GRABBED BY THOSE GANGSTERS-- THE ENFORCERS!
THIS COULD BE THE CONNECTION I NEED!
THE BUGLE
I SURE LIKE IT WHEN YA MAKE YOUR LOAN PAY-MENTS ON TIME! THE BIG MAN CONSIDERS YOU HIS NICEST CLIENT!
YOU MONSTER! DO YOU THINK I'D BE DOING THIS IF I HAD ANY CHOICE? IF ONLY MY BROTHER HADN'T THOSE GAMBLING DEBTS--!
VERY INTERESTING, MISS BRANT! AND NOW A SPIDEY TRACER ON THEIR CAR--
--SHOULD LEAD ME TO THE BIG MAN! AND MAYBE I CAN TIE JAMESON INTO IT!
Feel the touch of Black Velvet
THERE HE IS! WITH MY POWERS IT'LL BE EASY TO FOLLOW HIM AND LEARN HIS IDENTITY!
"HE DOES, AND--
HELLO? IS THIS BUSHKIN AT THE GLOBE? THIS IS SPIDER-MAN! I'VE GOT THE SCOOP OF THE CENTURY FOR YOU-- THE IDENTITY OF THE BIG MAN! THAT'S RIGHT!
BUT I'LL ONLY GIVE IT TO YOU IF YOU WRITE THE EXPOSÉ MY WAY! DO YOU UNDERSTAND ME, BUSHKIN?
SERIES 9000
OKAY! THE BIG MAN IS-- FREDERICK FOSWELL! AND HERE'S HOW I SEE THE HEADLINE--

TODAY
Variable cloudiness, mid 60s

TONIGHT
Chance of showers, near 50

TOMORROW
Mostly sunny, low 60s
Details, Page 2

TV listings: P. 32

THE DAILY GLOBE

METRO
TODAY'S RACING

WEDNESDAY, OCTOBER 17, 1973   20 CENTS   © 1973 News Group Publications, Inc.   R   Vol. 178. No. 284

DAILY SALES NOW EXCEED **630,000**

BERNARD BUSHKIN. EDITOR   *   CHARLES FOSTER KANE. FOUNDER

CRIME SYNDICATE RUN FROM BUGLE OFFICES!

Sgt. Edward Via detaining Publisher J. Jonah Jameson for questioning as Foswell arrested.

After long weeks of investigation, reporters for the GLOBE today finally uncovered the identity of the notorious Big Man, boss of most of the New York Rackets. He was found to be Frederick Foswell, right hand man to J. Jonah Jameson, publisher of the Daily Bugle. Jameson seemed to be completely surprised by the revelation, but was taken downtown for questioning nevertheless. Reports linking Jameson directly to the rackets have been current among informed sources, but so far have not been adequately substantiated. Foswell was apprehended by police while in conference with Jameson at the Bugle offices, and surrendered without a struggle. It is thought that the Big Man, using his trio of thugs known as the Enforcers, had taken over nearly three-quarters of the New York rackets, including gambling, prostitution, narcotics, and turning tennis balls into MacRonald Hamburgers. No connection with Donald MacRonald seems to be indicated at this time, however. (Cont. on page 34)

Should Jameson Resign?

AN EDITORIAL BY

BERNARD BUSHKIN

Scandal. It's an ugly word, and an even uglier reality. The fact that it's hit--and seemingly struck down--one of us, in the newspaper business, doesn't make it any nicer.

Should Jameson resign? The signs are all there: corruption among his aides; arrests--shouldn't he resign? One might say yes.

But I've known J. Jonah Jameson for years. Known him as an honest, generous, warm and often funny man. I've known him through triumph and tragedy, the worst tragedy being the loss of his son, John. This is not a man who could be corrupted! And so I say to my good friend Jonah, who is also the friend of those who love the freedom of the American press and way of life, to stay at the helm, and not resign! Unless, of course, he's guilty. Then the scurrilous hyena should be dragged away in disgrace! Fie on him, for defiling the good name Newspaper! He should -- (to page 57)

164

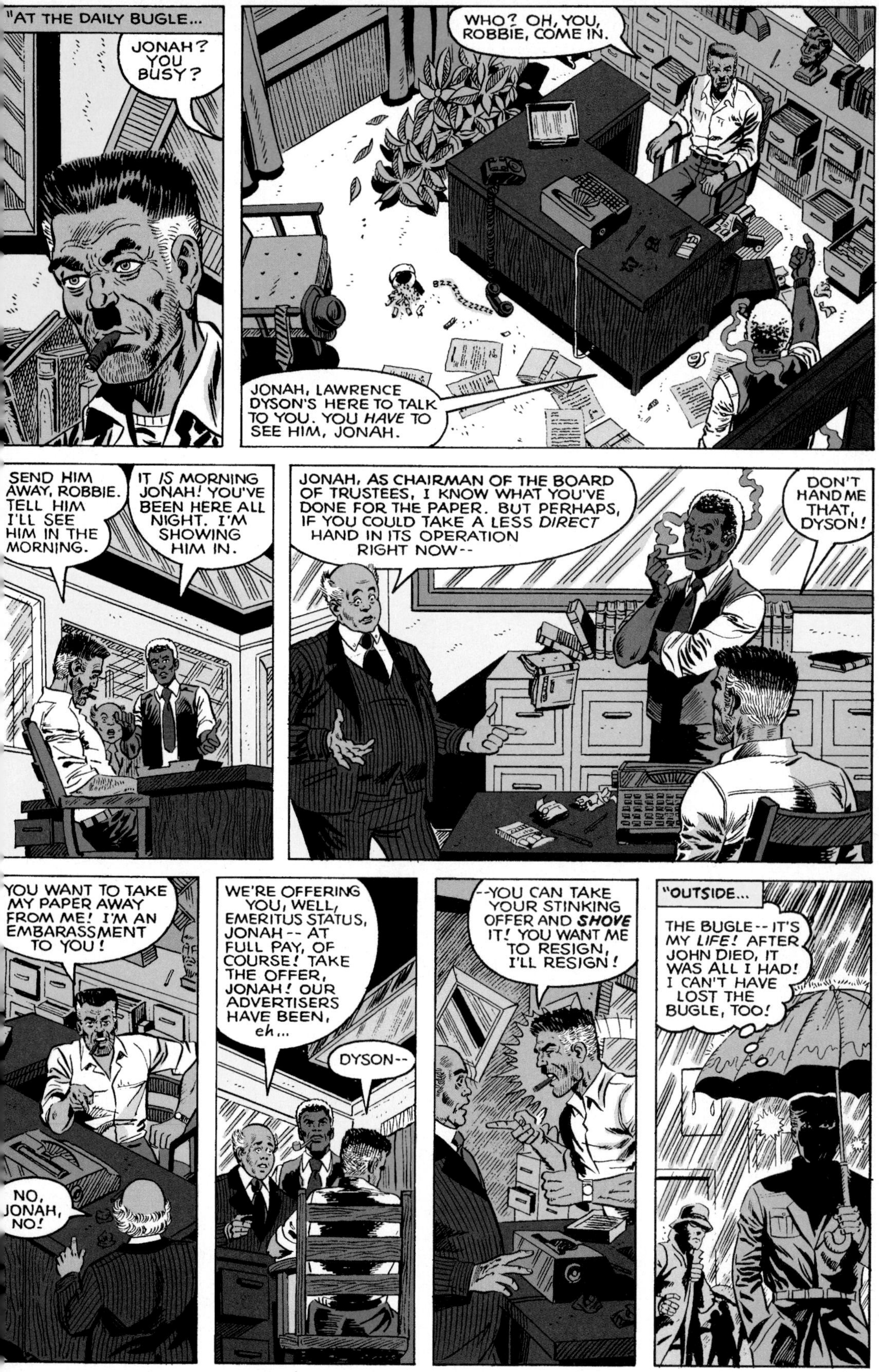
"AT THE DAILY BUGLE...
JONAH? YOU BUSY?
WHO? OH, YOU, ROBBIE, COME IN.
JONAH, LAWRENCE DYSON'S HERE TO TALK TO YOU. YOU HAVE TO SEE HIM, JONAH.
SEND HIM AWAY, ROBBIE. TELL HIM I'LL SEE HIM IN THE MORNING.
IT IS MORNING JONAH! YOU'VE BEEN HERE ALL NIGHT. I'M SHOWING HIM IN.
JONAH, AS CHAIRMAN OF THE BOARD OF TRUSTEES, I KNOW WHAT YOU'VE DONE FOR THE PAPER. BUT PERHAPS, IF YOU COULD TAKE A LESS DIRECT HAND IN ITS OPERATION RIGHT NOW--
DON'T HAND ME THAT, DYSON!
YOU WANT TO TAKE MY PAPER AWAY FROM ME! I'M AN EMBARASSMENT TO YOU!
NO, JONAH, NO!
WE'RE OFFERING YOU, WELL, EMERITUS STATUS, JONAH -- AT FULL PAY, OF COURSE! TAKE THE OFFER, JONAH! OUR ADVERTISERS HAVE BEEN, eh...
DYSON--
--YOU CAN TAKE YOUR STINKING OFFER AND SHOVE IT! YOU WANT ME TO RESIGN, I'LL RESIGN!
"OUTSIDE...
THE BUGLE -- IT'S MY LIFE! AFTER JOHN DIED, IT WAS ALL I HAD! I CAN'T HAVE LOST THE BUGLE, TOO!

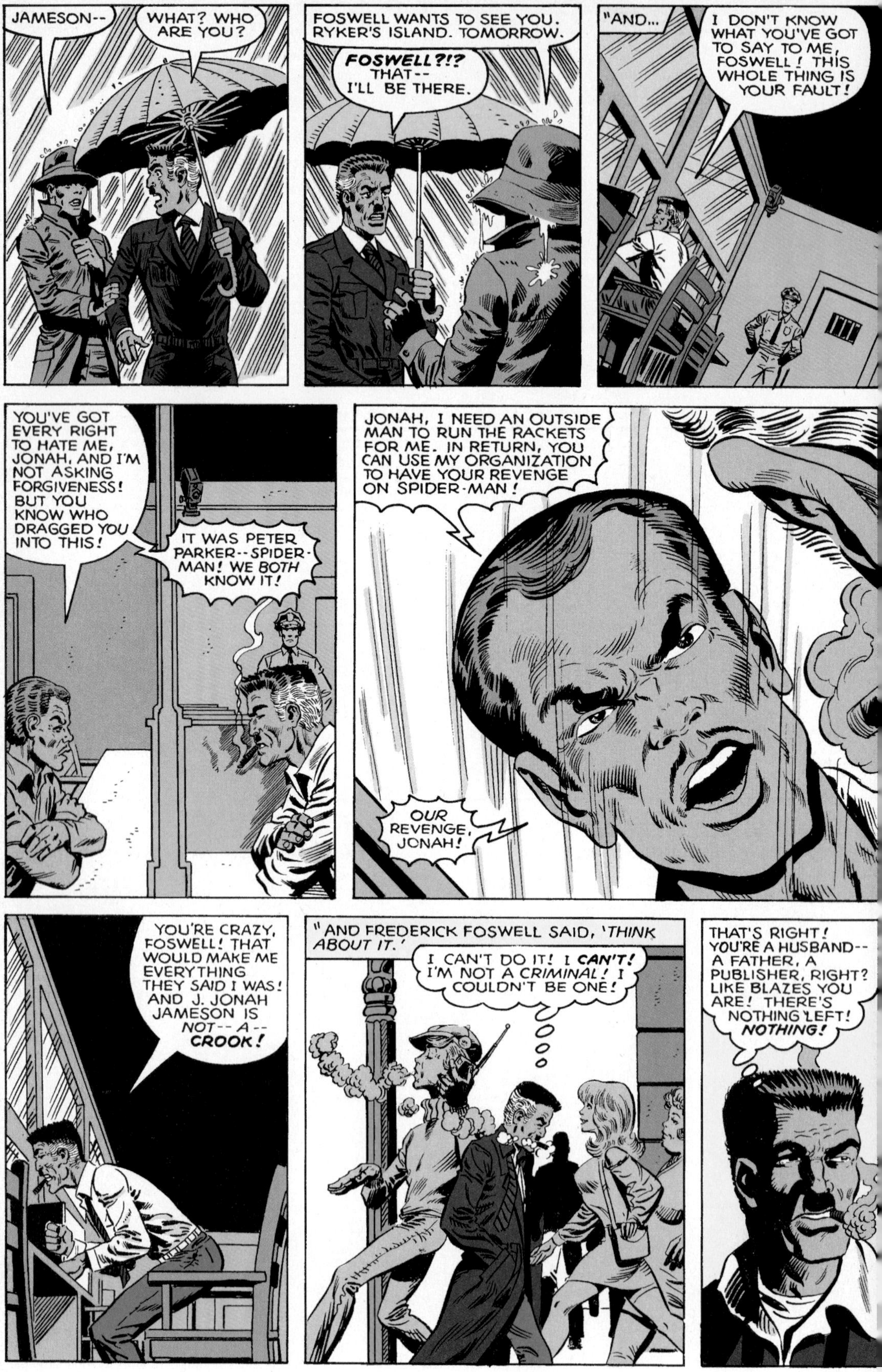
JAMESON--
WHAT? WHO ARE YOU?
FOSWELL WANTS TO SEE YOU. RYKER'S ISLAND. TOMORROW.
FOSWELL?!? THAT-- I'LL BE THERE.
"AND...
I DON'T KNOW WHAT YOU'VE GOT TO SAY TO ME, FOSWELL! THIS WHOLE THING IS YOUR FAULT!
YOU'VE GOT EVERY RIGHT TO HATE ME, JONAH, AND I'M NOT ASKING FORGIVENESS! BUT YOU KNOW WHO DRAGGED YOU INTO THIS!
IT WAS PETER PARKER--SPIDER-MAN! WE BOTH KNOW IT!
JONAH, I NEED AN OUTSIDE MAN TO RUN THE RACKETS FOR ME. IN RETURN, YOU CAN USE MY ORGANIZATION TO HAVE YOUR REVENGE ON SPIDER-MAN!
OUR REVENGE, JONAH!
YOU'RE CRAZY, FOSWELL! THAT WOULD MAKE ME EVERYTHING THEY SAID I WAS! AND J. JONAH JAMESON IS NOT-- A-- CROOK!
"AND FREDERICK FOSWELL SAID, 'THINK ABOUT IT.'
I CAN'T DO IT! I CAN'T! I'M NOT A CRIMINAL! I COULDN'T BE ONE!
THAT'S RIGHT! YOU'RE A HUSBAND-- A FATHER, A PUBLISHER, RIGHT? LIKE BLAZES YOU ARE! THERE'S NOTHING LEFT! NOTHING!

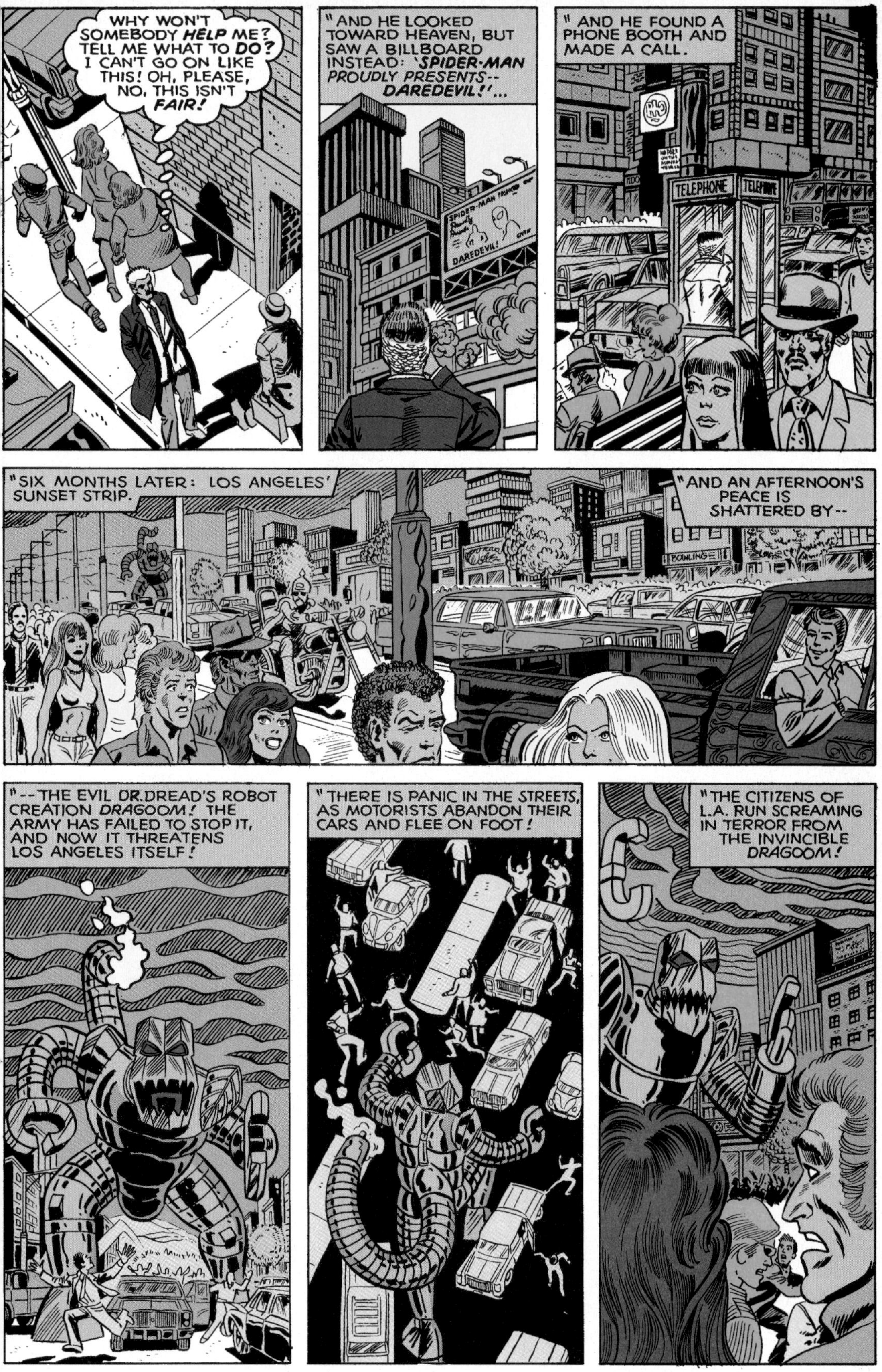
WHY WON'T SOMEBODY HELP ME? TELL ME WHAT TO DO? I CAN'T GO ON LIKE THIS! OH, PLEASE, NO, THIS ISN'T FAIR!
"AND HE LOOKED TOWARD HEAVEN, BUT SAW A BILLBOARD INSTEAD: 'SPIDER-MAN PROUDLY PRESENTS-- DAREDEVIL!'...
DAREDEVIL!
"AND HE FOUND A PHONE BOOTH AND MADE A CALL.
TELEPHONE
"SIX MONTHS LATER: LOS ANGELES' SUNSET STRIP.
"AND AN AFTERNOON'S PEACE IS SHATTERED BY--
BOWLING
"--THE EVIL DR. DREAD'S ROBOT CREATION DRAGOOM! THE ARMY HAS FAILED TO STOP IT, AND NOW IT THREATENS LOS ANGELES ITSELF!
"THERE IS PANIC IN THE STREETS, AS MOTORISTS ABANDON THEIR CARS AND FLEE ON FOOT!
"THE CITIZENS OF L.A. RUN SCREAMING IN TERROR FROM THE INVINCIBLE DRAGOOM!

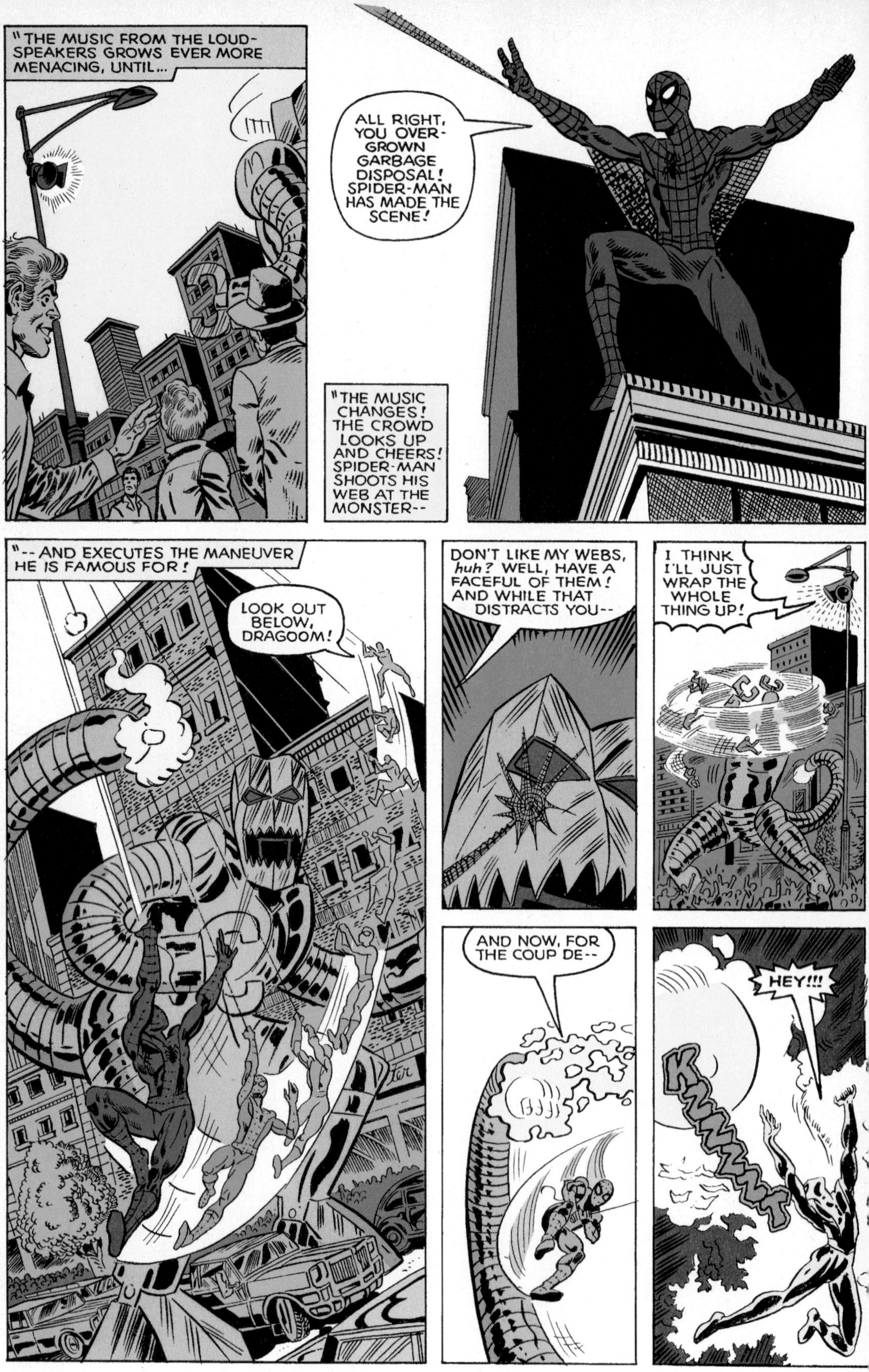
"THE MUSIC FROM THE LOUD-SPEAKERS GROWS EVER MORE MENACING, UNTIL...
ALL RIGHT, YOU OVER-GROWN GARBAGE DISPOSAL! SPIDER-MAN HAS MADE THE SCENE!
"THE MUSIC CHANGES! THE CROWD LOOKS UP AND CHEERS! SPIDER-MAN SHOOTS HIS WEB AT THE MONSTER--
"--AND EXECUTES THE MANEUVER HE IS FAMOUS FOR!
LOOK OUT BELOW, DRAGOOM!
DON'T LIKE MY WEBS, *huh?* WELL, HAVE A FACEFUL OF THEM! AND WHILE THAT DISTRACTS YOU--
I THINK I'LL JUST WRAP THE WHOLE THING UP!
AND NOW, FOR THE COUP DE--
HEY!!!
KWWNNNT

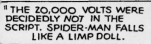

"THE 20,000 VOLTS WERE DECIDEDLY *NOT* IN THE SCRIPT. SPIDER-MAN FALLS LIKE A LIMP DOLL.

YES, FOLKS, BE SURE TO WATCH FOR IT! 'SPIDER-MAN VS. THE MONSTER THAT ATE LOS ANGELES!' AT A THEATRE NEAR YOU!

TH-THANKS, DD! NOW ACT NATURAL!

"THEN, FROM OUT OF NOWHERE...

DON'T WORRY, PARKER! I'VE GOT YOU!

WHA--? DAREDEVIL--?

"LATER, AT PETER PARKER'S MANSION...

THAT COULD HAVE KILLED YOU, PARKER!

PLEASE, DD, IT WAS NOTHING!

I SWEAH, SPIDEY, YOU GOT THE SEXIEST CLIENTS I EVAH SEEN!

I TOLD YOU, PARKER-- THE WORD IS OUT IN NEW YORK THAT YOU'RE TO BE HIT!

WHO? ME? I'M JUST AN ACTOR! WHO'D WANT TO KILL ME?

CLICK

CHUCKIE, BE A DOLL AND *FIRE* WHOEVER PUT THE CHARGE IN DRAGOOM'S TAIL!

YOU BUZZED, SPIDEY?

ROGER WILCO, SPIDEY! ANYTHING ELSE?

YEAH, CHUCKIE! TIME FOR MY WORK-OUT!

IF YOU DON'T MIND, PARKER, I'D LIKE TO... WATCH!

YOU JUST MAY NEED PROTECTING!

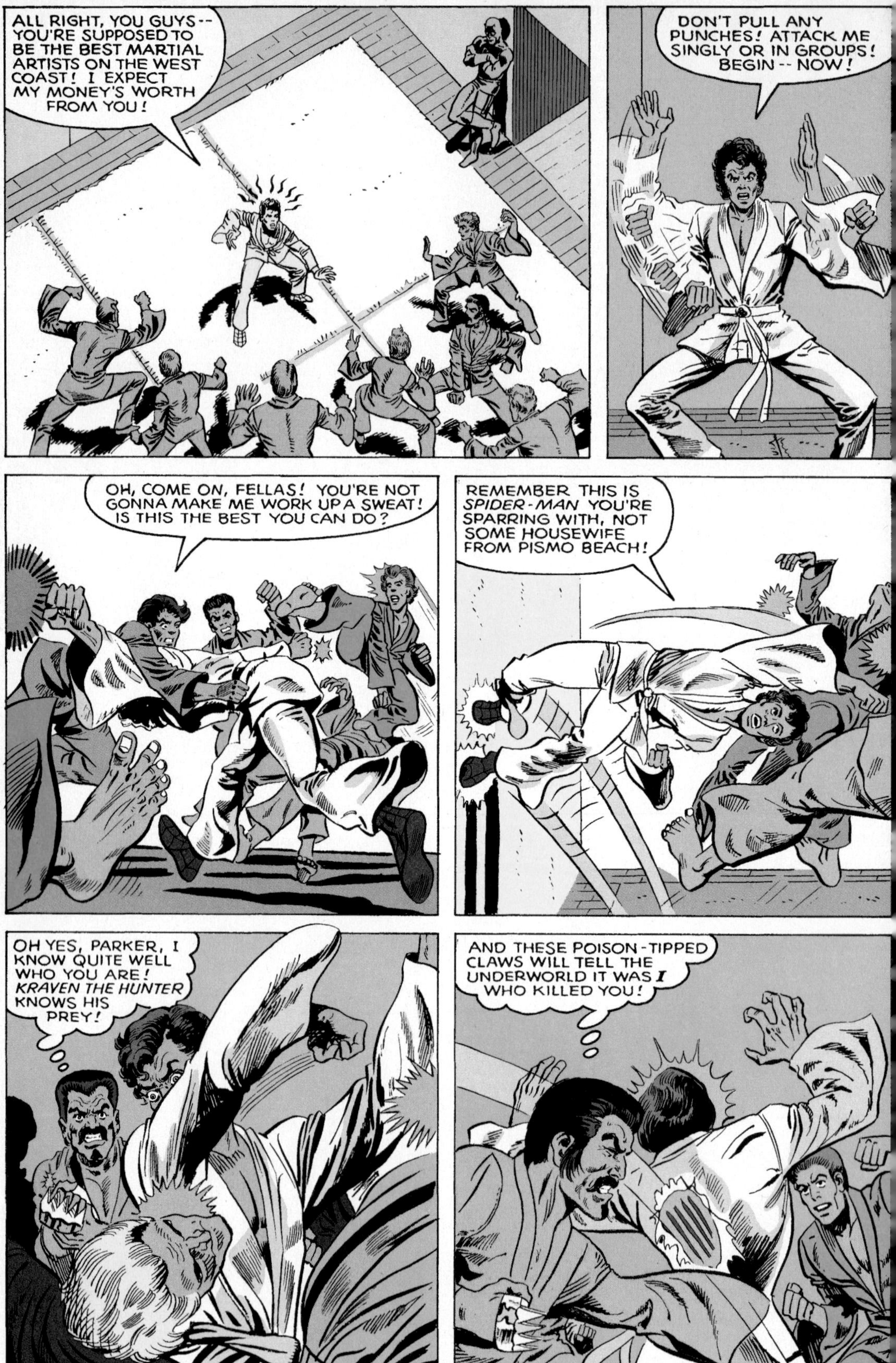
ALL RIGHT, YOU GUYS-- YOU'RE SUPPOSED TO BE THE BEST MARTIAL ARTISTS ON THE WEST COAST! I EXPECT MY MONEY'S WORTH FROM YOU!
DON'T PULL ANY PUNCHES! ATTACK ME SINGLY OR IN GROUPS! BEGIN -- NOW!
OH, COME ON, FELLAS! YOU'RE NOT GONNA MAKE ME WORK UP A SWEAT! IS THIS THE BEST YOU CAN DO?
REMEMBER THIS IS SPIDER-MAN YOU'RE SPARRING WITH, NOT SOME HOUSEWIFE FROM PISMO BEACH!
OH YES, PARKER, I KNOW QUITE WELL WHO YOU ARE! KRAVEN THE HUNTER KNOWS HIS PREY!
AND THESE POISON-TIPPED CLAWS WILL TELL THE UNDERWORLD IT WAS I WHO KILLED YOU!

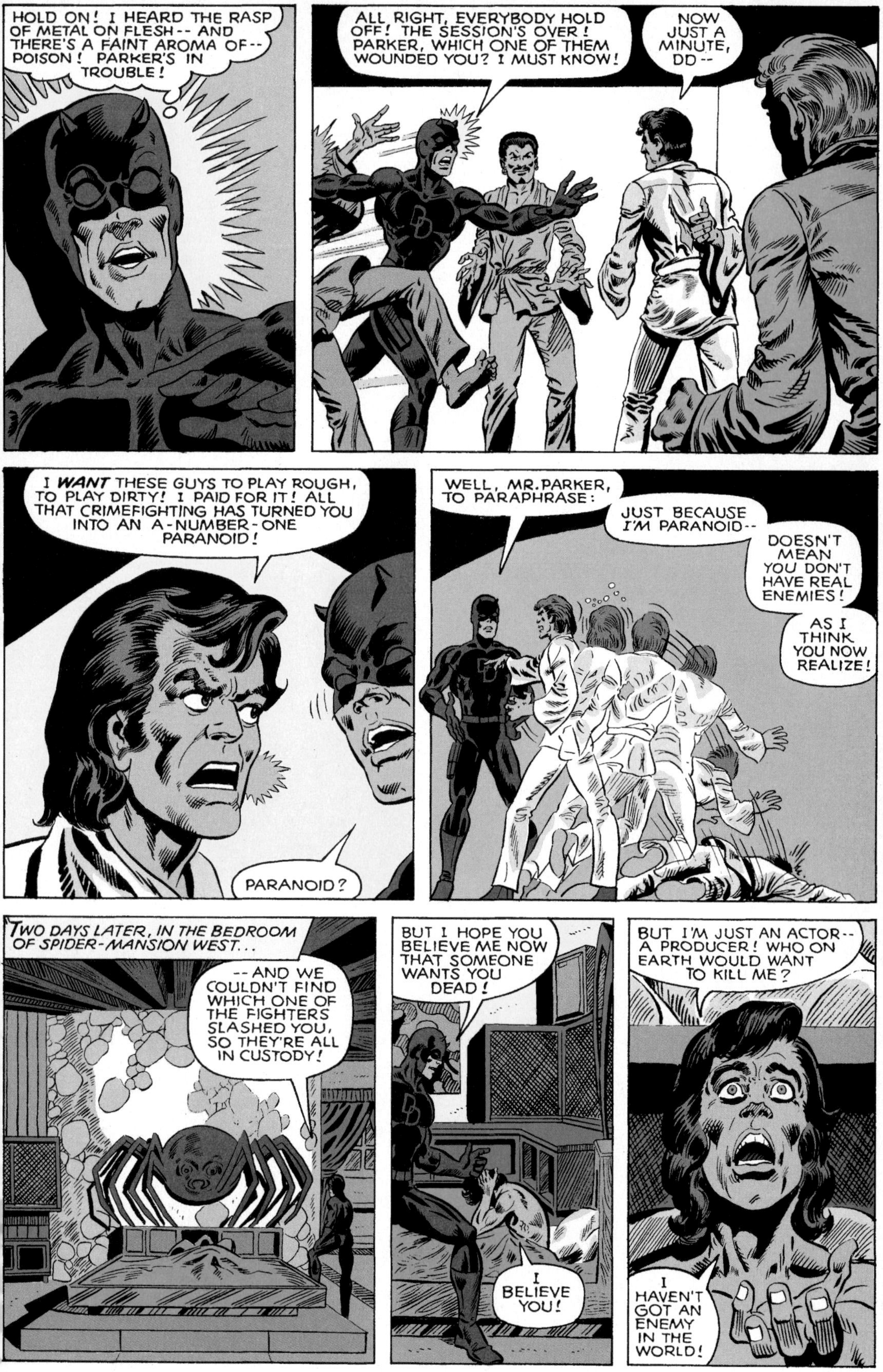
HOLD ON! I HEARD THE RASP OF METAL ON FLESH -- AND THERE'S A FAINT AROMA OF -- POISON! PARKER'S IN TROUBLE!
ALL RIGHT, EVERYBODY HOLD OFF! THE SESSION'S OVER! PARKER, WHICH ONE OF THEM WOUNDED YOU? I MUST KNOW!
NOW JUST A MINUTE, DD --
I WANT THESE GUYS TO PLAY ROUGH, TO PLAY DIRTY! I PAID FOR IT! ALL THAT CRIMEFIGHTING HAS TURNED YOU INTO AN A-NUMBER-ONE PARANOID!
PARANOID?
WELL, MR. PARKER, TO PARAPHRASE:
JUST BECAUSE I'M PARANOID --
DOESN'T MEAN YOU DON'T HAVE REAL ENEMIES!
AS I THINK YOU NOW REALIZE!
TWO DAYS LATER, IN THE BEDROOM OF SPIDER-MANSION WEST...
-- AND WE COULDN'T FIND WHICH ONE OF THE FIGHTERS SLASHED YOU, SO THEY'RE ALL IN CUSTODY!
BUT I HOPE YOU BELIEVE ME NOW THAT SOMEONE WANTS YOU DEAD!
I BELIEVE YOU!
BUT I'M JUST AN ACTOR -- A PRODUCER! WHO ON EARTH WOULD WANT TO KILL ME?
I HAVEN'T GOT AN ENEMY IN THE WORLD!

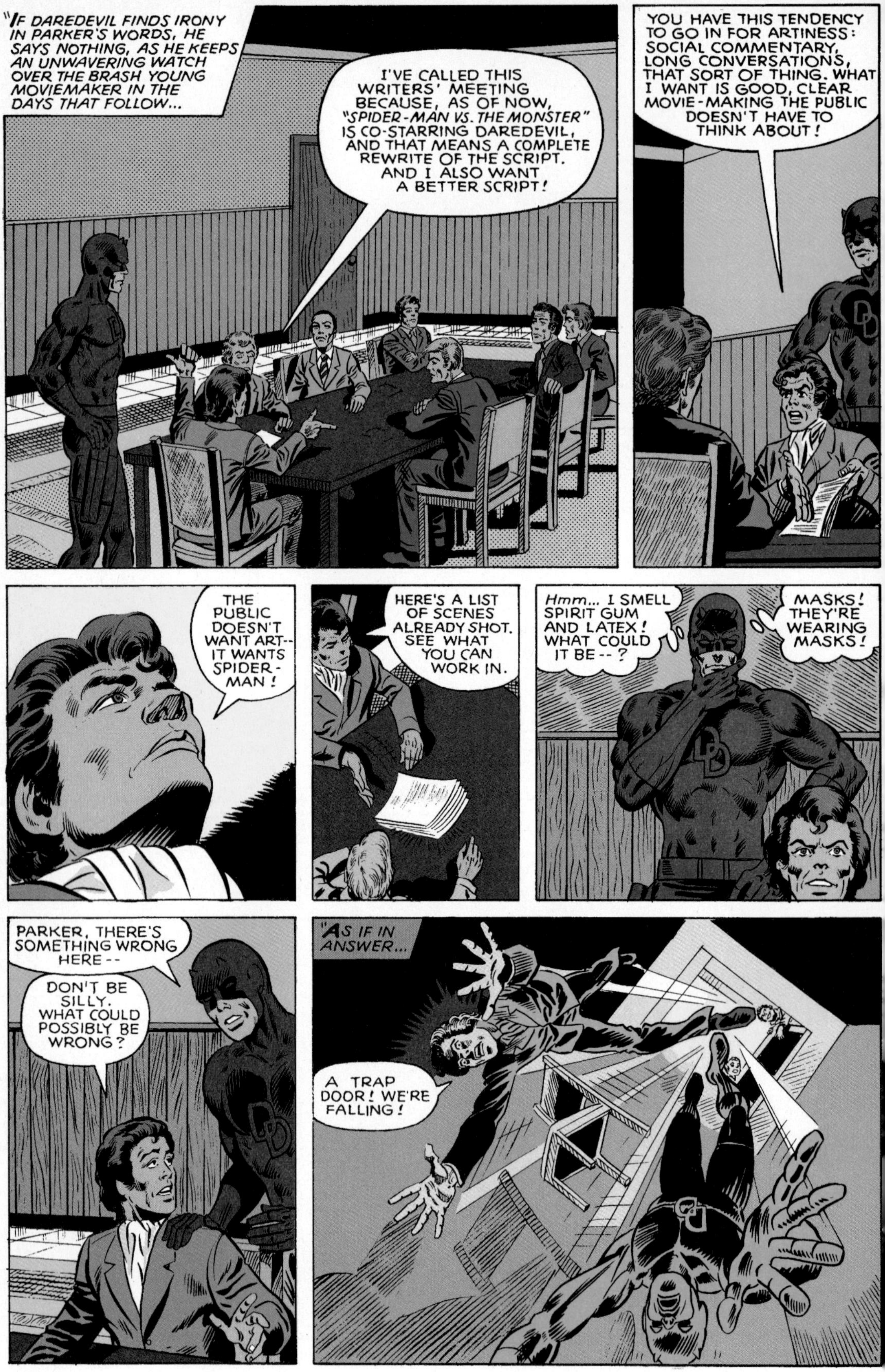
"IF DAREDEVIL FINDS IRONY IN PARKER'S WORDS, HE SAYS NOTHING, AS HE KEEPS AN UNWAVERING WATCH OVER THE BRASH YOUNG MOVIEMAKER IN THE DAYS THAT FOLLOW...
I'VE CALLED THIS WRITERS' MEETING BECAUSE, AS OF NOW, "SPIDER-MAN VS. THE MONSTER" IS CO-STARRING DAREDEVIL, AND THAT MEANS A COMPLETE REWRITE OF THE SCRIPT. AND I ALSO WANT A BETTER SCRIPT!
YOU HAVE THIS TENDENCY TO GO IN FOR ARTINESS: SOCIAL COMMENTARY, LONG CONVERSATIONS, THAT SORT OF THING. WHAT I WANT IS GOOD, CLEAR MOVIE-MAKING THE PUBLIC DOESN'T HAVE TO THINK ABOUT!
THE PUBLIC DOESN'T WANT ART-- IT WANTS SPIDER-MAN!
HERE'S A LIST OF SCENES ALREADY SHOT. SEE WHAT YOU CAN WORK IN.
Hmm... I SMELL SPIRIT GUM AND LATEX! WHAT COULD IT BE -- ?
MASKS! THEY'RE WEARING MASKS!
PARKER, THERE'S SOMETHING WRONG HERE --
DON'T BE SILLY. WHAT COULD POSSIBLY BE WRONG?
"AS IF IN ANSWER...
A TRAP DOOR! WE'RE FALLING!

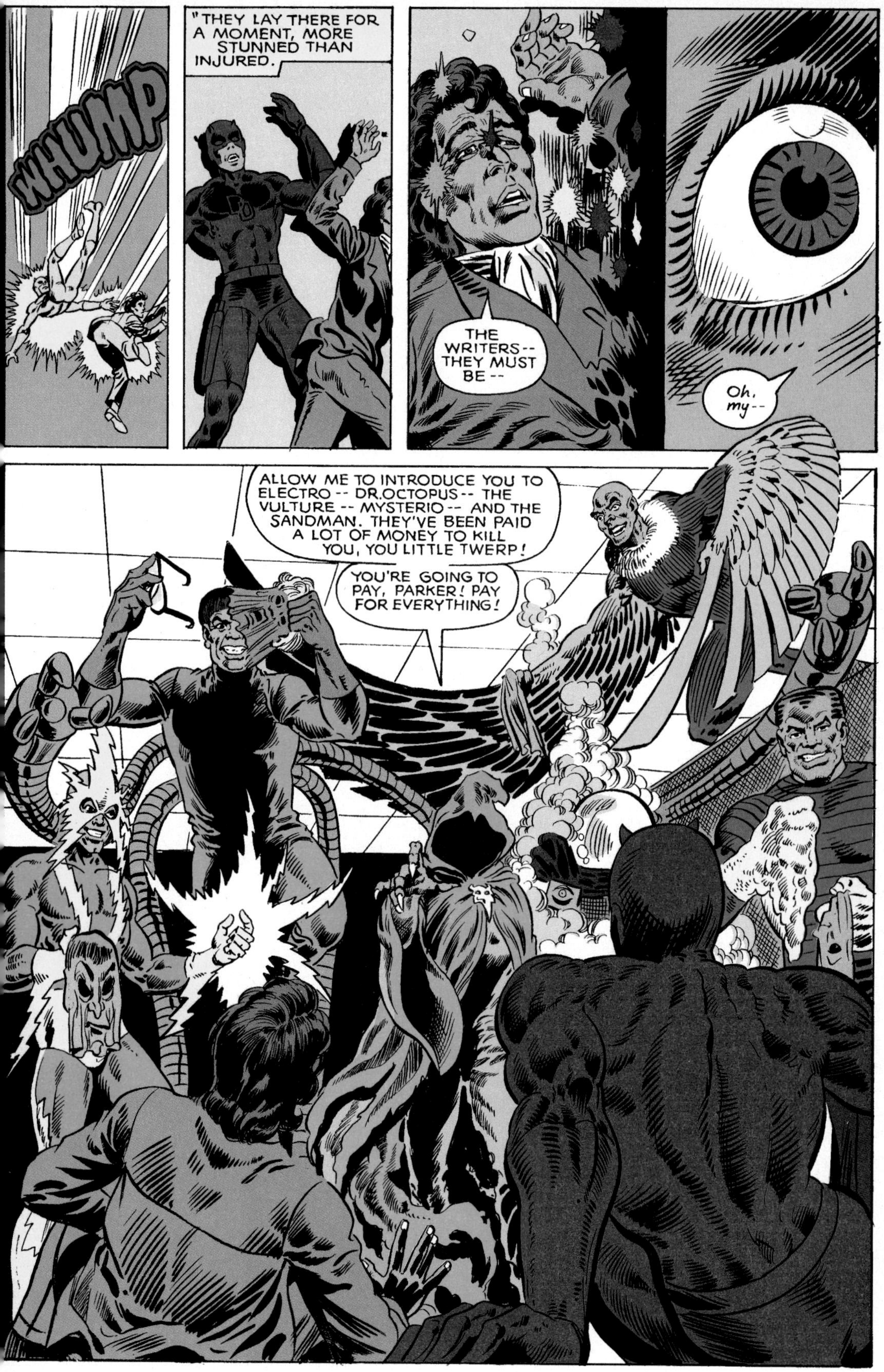
WHUMP
"THEY LAY THERE FOR A MOMENT, MORE STUNNED THAN INJURED.
THE WRITERS -- THEY MUST BE --
Oh, my --
ALLOW ME TO INTRODUCE YOU TO ELECTRO -- DR. OCTOPUS -- THE VULTURE -- MYSTERIO -- AND THE SANDMAN. THEY'VE BEEN PAID A LOT OF MONEY TO KILL YOU, YOU LITTLE TWERP!
YOU'RE GOING TO PAY, PARKER! PAY FOR EVERYTHING!

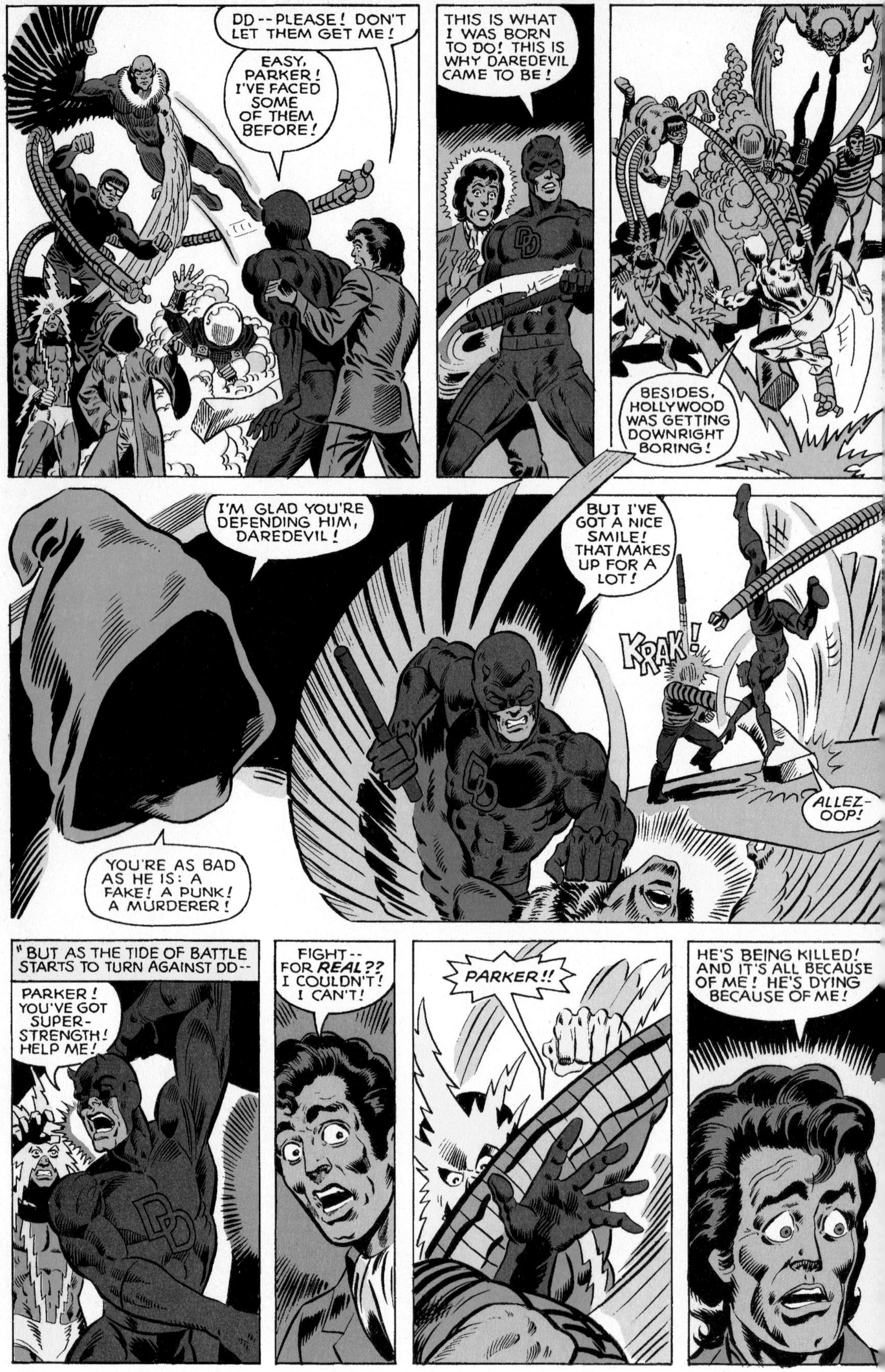
DD--PLEASE! DON'T LET THEM GET ME!
EASY, PARKER! I'VE FACED SOME OF THEM BEFORE!
THIS IS WHAT I WAS BORN TO DO! THIS IS WHY DAREDEVIL CAME TO BE!
BESIDES, HOLLYWOOD WAS GETTING DOWNRIGHT BORING!
I'M GLAD YOU'RE DEFENDING HIM, DAREDEVIL!
YOU'RE AS BAD AS HE IS: A FAKE! A PUNK! A MURDERER!
BUT I'VE GOT A NICE SMILE! THAT MAKES UP FOR A LOT!
KRAK!
ALLEZ-OOP!
"BUT AS THE TIDE OF BATTLE STARTS TO TURN AGAINST DD--
PARKER! YOU'VE GOT SUPER-STRENGTH! HELP ME!
FIGHT-- FOR REAL?? I COULDN'T! I CAN'T!
PARKER!!
HE'S BEING KILLED! AND IT'S ALL BECAUSE OF ME! HE'S DYING BECAUSE OF ME!

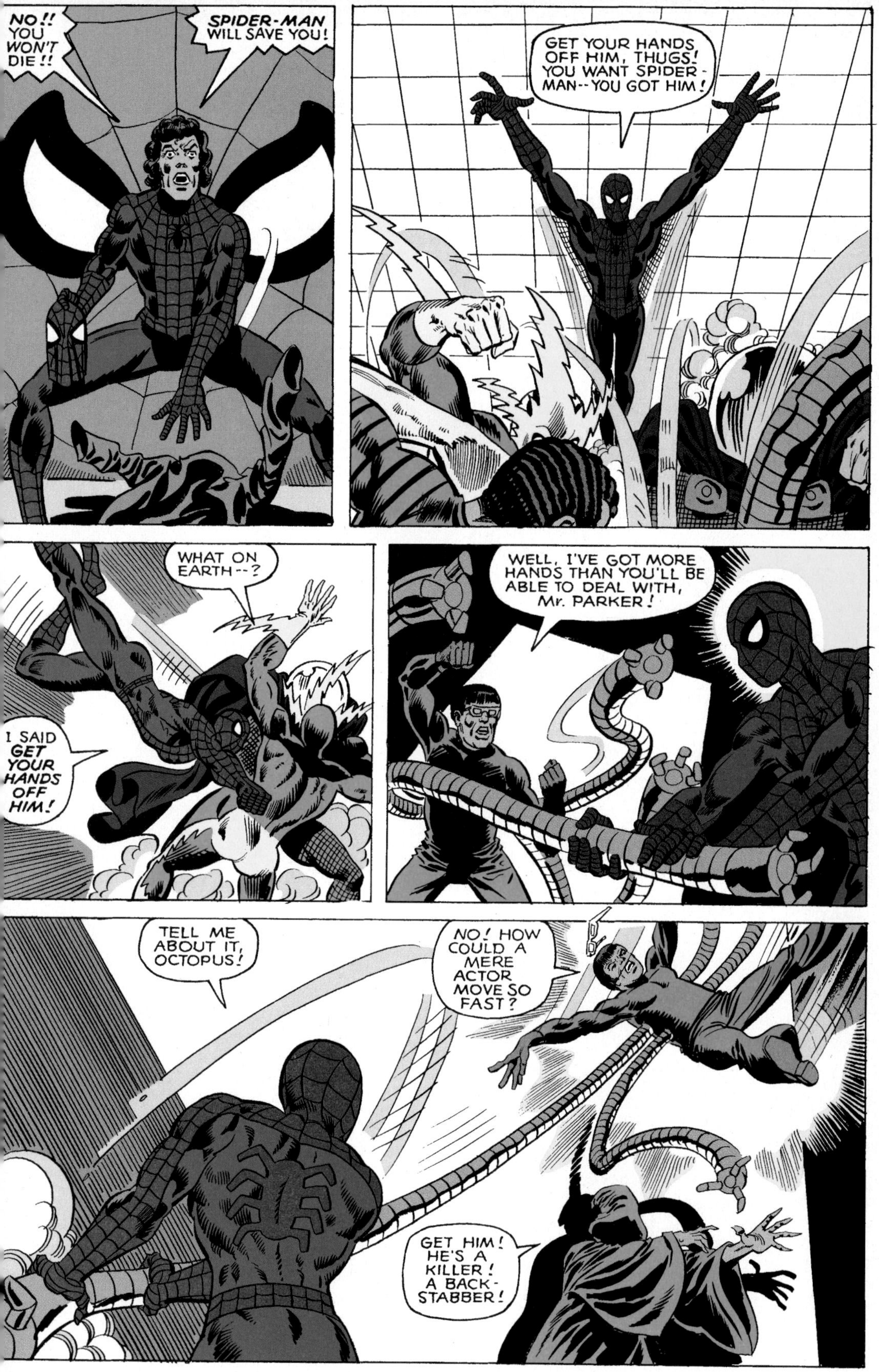
NO!! YOU WON'T DIE!!
SPIDER-MAN WILL SAVE YOU!
GET YOUR HANDS OFF HIM, THUGS! YOU WANT SPIDER-MAN--YOU GOT HIM!
WHAT ON EARTH--?
I SAID GET YOUR HANDS OFF HIM!
WELL, I'VE GOT MORE HANDS THAN YOU'LL BE ABLE TO DEAL WITH, Mr. PARKER!
TELL ME ABOUT IT, OCTOPUS!
NO! HOW COULD A MERE ACTOR MOVE SO FAST?
GET HIM! HE'S A KILLER! A BACK-STABBER!

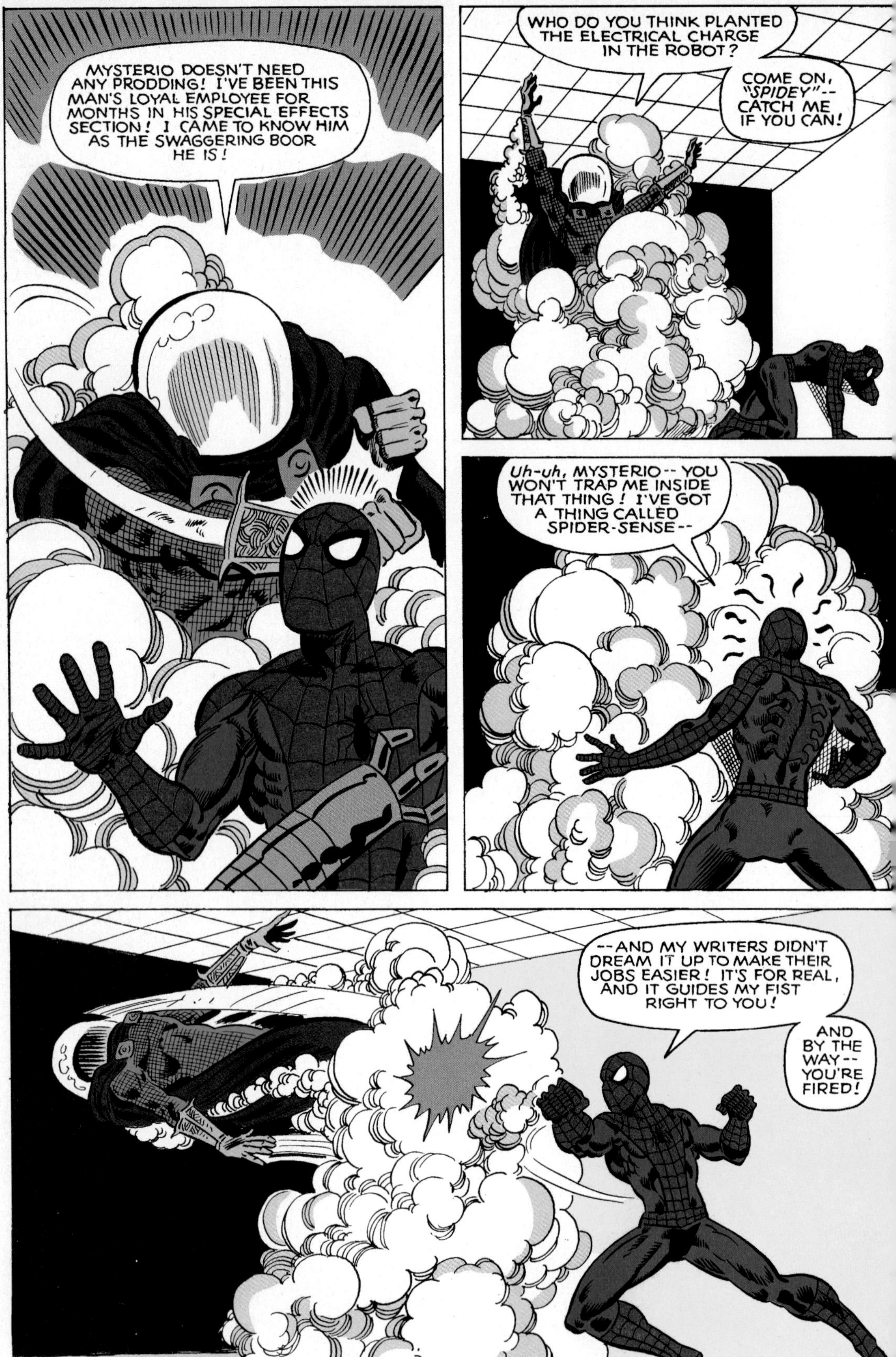
MYSTERIO DOESN'T NEED ANY PRODDING! I'VE BEEN THIS MAN'S LOYAL EMPLOYEE FOR MONTHS IN HIS SPECIAL EFFECTS SECTION! I CAME TO KNOW HIM AS THE SWAGGERING BOOR HE IS!
WHO DO YOU THINK PLANTED THE ELECTRICAL CHARGE IN THE ROBOT?
COME ON, "SPIDEY"-- CATCH ME IF YOU CAN!
Uh-uh, MYSTERIO-- YOU WON'T TRAP ME INSIDE THAT THING! I'VE GOT A THING CALLED SPIDER-SENSE--
--AND MY WRITERS DIDN'T DREAM IT UP TO MAKE THEIR JOBS EASIER! IT'S FOR REAL, AND IT GUIDES MY FIST RIGHT TO YOU!
AND BY THE WAY-- YOU'RE FIRED!

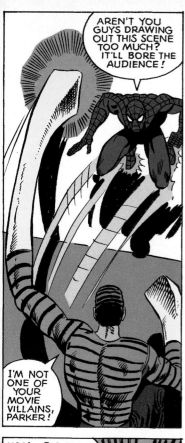

AREN'T YOU GUYS DRAWING OUT THIS SCENE TOO MUCH? IT'LL BORE THE AUDIENCE!

I'M NOT ONE OF YOUR MOVIE VILLAINS, PARKER!

I'M THE SANDMAN, AND I'VE FOUGHT THE FANTASTIC FOUR THEM- SELVES! YOU CAN'T TOUCH ME -- AND YOU CAN'T STOP ME FROM KILLING YOU!

AND IF YOU THINK THAT DOUSING ME WITH LIBRARY PASTE WILL STOP ME, YOU'RE WELCOME TO TRY!

OH, IT'S MORE THAN LIBRARY PASTE! I ALWAYS FIGURED IF MY ACTING CAREER WENT BUST, I'D MARKET MY WEB- FLUID FORMULA! IT'S SUCH A GOOD GLUE THAT IT SHOULD BIND YOUR SAND PARTICLES TOGETHER!

WHA--? I CAN'T MOVE! I CAN'T EVEN CHANGE!

BRIGHT BOY!

"THE FLUSH OF VICTORY VANISHES AS SPIDER- MAN TURNS TO THE FALLEN DAREDEVIL, NOW BARELY BREATHING...

DD! OH LORD, WHY'D YOU SACRIFICE YOURSELF FOR ME? I'M NOT WORTH THE PRICE OF YOUR LIFE!

YOU! YOU GIBBERING LUNATIC, YOU'RE RESPONSIBLE FOR THIS! YOU'LL PAY!

177

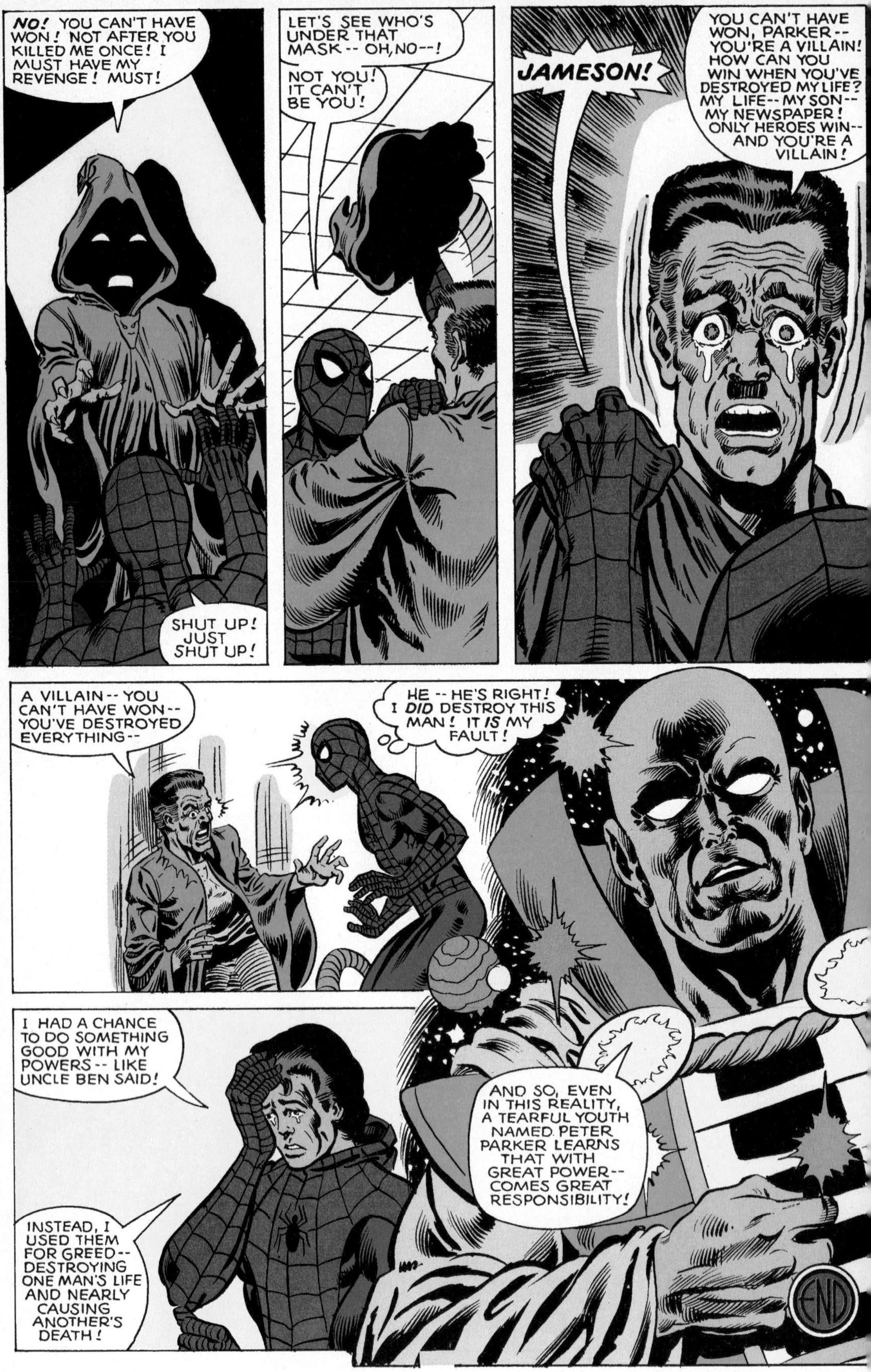
NO! YOU CAN'T HAVE WON! NOT AFTER YOU KILLED ME ONCE! I MUST HAVE MY REVENGE! MUST!
SHUT UP! JUST SHUT UP!
LET'S SEE WHO'S UNDER THAT MASK -- OH, NO--!
NOT YOU! IT CAN'T BE YOU!
JAMESON!
YOU CAN'T HAVE WON, PARKER -- YOU'RE A VILLAIN! HOW CAN YOU WIN WHEN YOU'VE DESTROYED MY LIFE? MY LIFE-- MY SON-- MY NEWSPAPER! ONLY HEROES WIN-- AND YOU'RE A VILLAIN!
A VILLAIN -- YOU CAN'T HAVE WON -- YOU'VE DESTROYED EVERYTHING--
HE -- HE'S RIGHT! I DID DESTROY THIS MAN! IT IS MY FAULT!
I HAD A CHANCE TO DO SOMETHING GOOD WITH MY POWERS -- LIKE UNCLE BEN SAID!
INSTEAD, I USED THEM FOR GREED -- DESTROYING ONE MAN'S LIFE AND NEARLY CAUSING ANOTHER'S DEATH!
AND SO, EVEN IN THIS REALITY, A TEARFUL YOUTH NAMED PETER PARKER LEARNS THAT WITH GREAT POWER -- COMES GREAT RESPONSIBILITY!
END

WHY NOT?

c/o MARVEL COMICS GROUP
575 Madison Avenue
New York, New York 10022

DENNIS O'NEIL
EDITOR
MARK GRUENWALD
ASSISTANT EDITOR

Response to the NOVA issue of WHAT IF has been heavy, people. It seems like more than a few of you out there liked a certain human rocket and were sorry to see his magazine make a rest stop in Comicbook Limbo recently. However, by far the biggest percentage of the mail we received on WHAT IF #15 concerned a different matter: namely, the oxygen-supply in Nova's helmet. See, we've established in a number of stories that the helmet has a built-in breathing system that has seemed to kick on automatically when cut off from air— but, in the first of our four tales of alternate Novas, the helmet did not become activated when the Invisible Girl's forcefield encompassed our female rocketeer. A good number of you Nova-fans caught the slip and respectfully tendered your request for a no-prize. The only problem is: not one of you rapacious readers bothered to offer your agonizing editors a solution to the mess we got ourselves into. Shucks, folks, we'll admit to our mistakes if that's what you want; after all, we're only human and we're bound to make some. But whatever happened to the ol' Marvel fan creativity—when these letters pages were not filled with recitations of our occasional foul-ups, but rather with lively letters to help us solve the continuity conundrums and logic loopholes that we bullpenners sometimes find ourselves in? There was a time when a no-prize was a reward for meritorious service to the Marvel Universe, not a badge for a notorious nit-picker. So if anyone wants to consider themselves no-prized for your goof-up sightings, be our guest. But if anyone wants to be No-Prized, exercise your imagination and see if you can help your hard-working hero-makers out. Send your suggestions to "WHY NOT Put the Know Back in the No-Prize?" in care of this magazine. (You might also tell us what you think of our stories, in spite of our mistakes!)

Now, what say we get onto your letters. . .?

Dear Folks,

I care next to nothing for Nova, even though I had high hopes for him at first, so when I saw "What If Four Other People Had Been Nova?" I said, "Who cares?" However, I did find myself enjoying WHAT IF #15 by ignoring what I thought of Nova and concentrating on Marv Wolfman's theme for the issue: the effects of power. I found the exploration of this topic enthralling. I must admit that using the random-granted Nova-powers was a very useful vehicle in treating this theme.

Sam Hays
Arlington, VA 22209

Dear Roy and Marv,

I found the cover to WHAT IF #15 partially misleading. I don't know about anyone else who bought the issue, but I thought the four Novas would be people already familiar to us scholars of the Marvel Universe, but look what we got— two newcomers (one of which wasn't even in a world of Marvel super heroes), one veteran, and something else I'm not sure of. Nova #1 reminded me of a certain 40-year old hero who admires bats, especially in her dialog and thirst for vengeance. Nova #2 was cute, but stupid. Nuff said. Nova #3 was the best one of the issue, because it was Peter Parker, the neurotic we all know and love. It also gave us a preview of a (hopefully) future issue of WHAT IF?— "What If Aunt May Died?" Nova #4 was very confusing. Exactly who was he? He talks and smokes a cigar like Sgt. Fury, but I doubt it's him. (Incidentally, were any of those faces superimposed on the Sphinx on the last page supposed to resemble anyone in particular? I think one of them looks like Rascally Roy, but I can't be sure.)

Gary Dunaier
Flushing, NY 11365

Good observation, Gary. Yes indeed, there's a whole slew of bullpenners and other famous people represented in that full-pager, courtesy of George Perez and Tom Palmer.

Dear People,

Although the only story I liked of the four in WHAT IF #15 in terms of what happened was the second one, each had a definite message, as the Watcher himself noted. In story one, the message was "Power corrupts." We've seen this idea done before (the majority of comicbook villains are examples), but I've never seen it done quite this way. The poor woman thinks she's a hero. In story two, it was "Self sacrifice." Sound familiar? It should. My only gripe is the choice of villains. Why not use Zorr from NOVA #1? He's just as big a menace as the Skrulls (who, without the FF to stop them might have overrun the Earth a long time ago, anyway). It doesn't make sense that Zorr never showed up here (or in any of the stories) since he seemed so linked with the transition of the Nova-power. But, all in all, this story was my favorite of the lot. Story three: "Power refused." It was not bad, but I fully expected a Spider-powered Peter Parker to be "SKA-BAMM"ed. I think it would have made for a better story, if not thematically better. The Amazing Spider-Nova has a nice ring, no? I didn't like this type-casting of Parker as a total loser. True, that's what makes Spider-Man special, but does he have to lose out in every alternate universe, too? Story four: "Power abused." I could see it a mile away. With four choices, I knew there would be at least one villain. I was glad to see this particular Nova bite the dust. Really. Although it was not the most sensational epic of the month (I thought FF #208 was), WHAT IF #15 has given me something to think about. I wonder if I would be oozing with altruism if I were suddenly handed the powers of a centurion.

Steve Swope
Overland, MO 63114

Dear Marvel,

As in the previous WHAT IF with Sgt. Fury fighting WWII in space, I had difficulties with the Nova Four-in-One in WHAT IF #15. It seems to me that you're letting your writers get away from the WHAT IF premise as established in the very first issue. Namely, a WHAT IF tale is one that diverges from mainstream Marvel history at some point to explore an alternate history. The problem with WHAT IF #14 and #15 (and several others, for that matter) is that they're NOT proceeding from any known point in Marvel history. Sorry, folks, but Leonardo da Vinci building flying machines in the 15th Century is not my idea of a branching off point in Marvel history. Other than its basic absurdity, why should there even be a Nick Fury by 1945 if the last five centuries were so dramatically different? In the Nova issue, two out of the four stories didn't qualify as true WHAT IFfers. In the story of the black Nova getting powers in a world without super heroes, the divergence point was not the fellow getting zapped by the Nova-centurion, it was whatever wiped out all the other heroes before the story opened. (I'm assuming it's a tangent of the Marvel Universe because of the Skrulls.) In the Peter Parker tale, the divergence point was not Parker getting Nova-ed, it was the radioactive spider getting a larger dose of radiation than the Marvel-Earth counterpart did. By slipping in these prior divergences, you're undermining the impact of the set of stories, since it seems as if you're stacking the deck to make a point. (By the way, Marv, I hope you realize that this story in effect establishes that the choosing of Rich Rider as Nova on Marvel-Earth was a totally random occurrence, that anyone might have been the recipient of the Nova-power.) I must admit that I do enjoy these multiple story issues, I just wish you wouldn't play fast and loose with the WHAT IF concept.

Gene Entwender
Racine, WI 53403

You raise some sticky points, Gene, and about all we can say is that we intend to watch out for just the problems you mention.

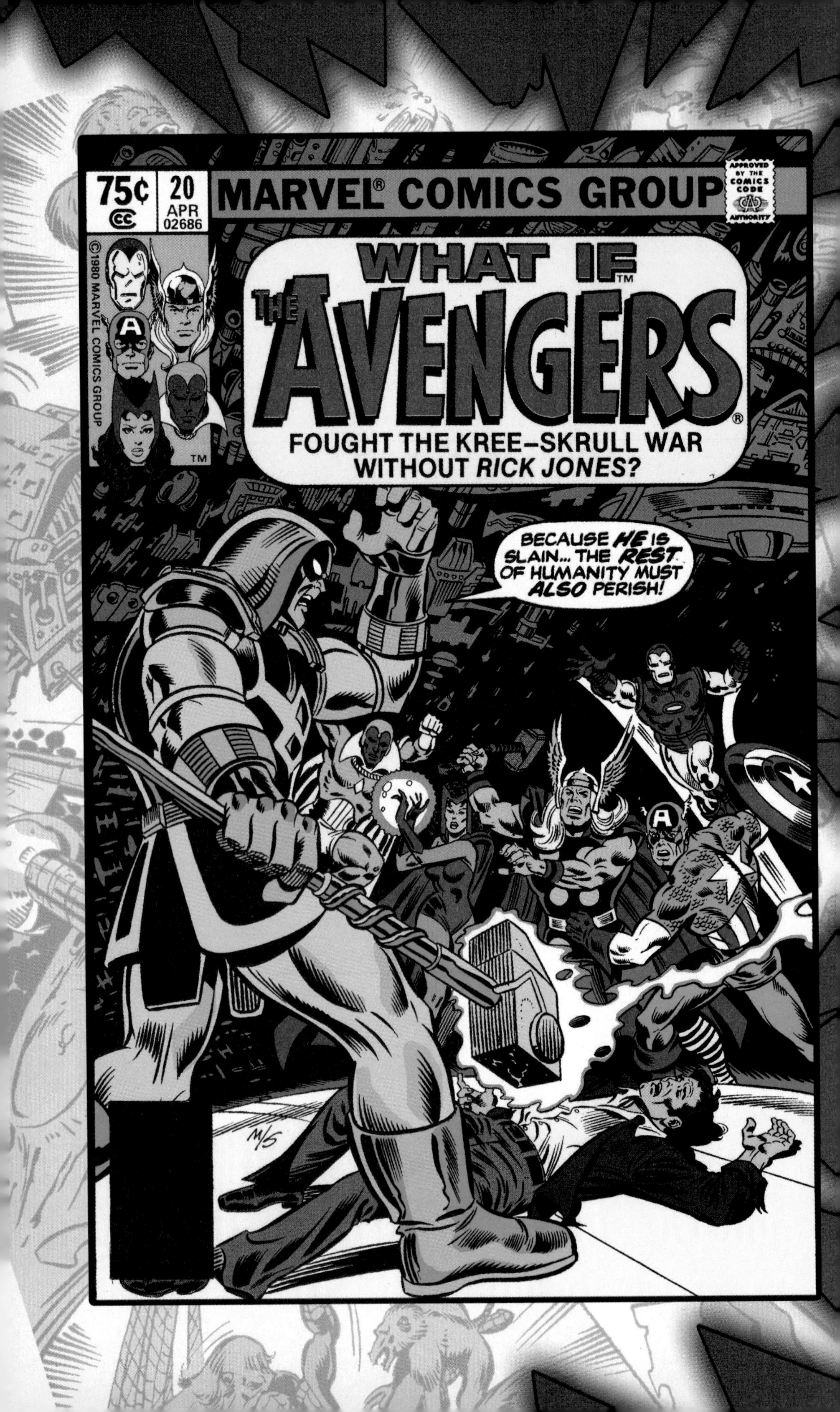
75¢
20
APR
02686
MARVEL® COMICS GROUP
APPROVED BY THE COMICS CODE AUTHORITY
©1980 MARVEL COMICS GROUP
WHAT IF™
THE AVENGERS®
FOUGHT THE KREE–SKRULL WAR
WITHOUT RICK JONES?
BECAUSE HE IS SLAIN... THE REST OF HUMANITY MUST ALSO PERISH!

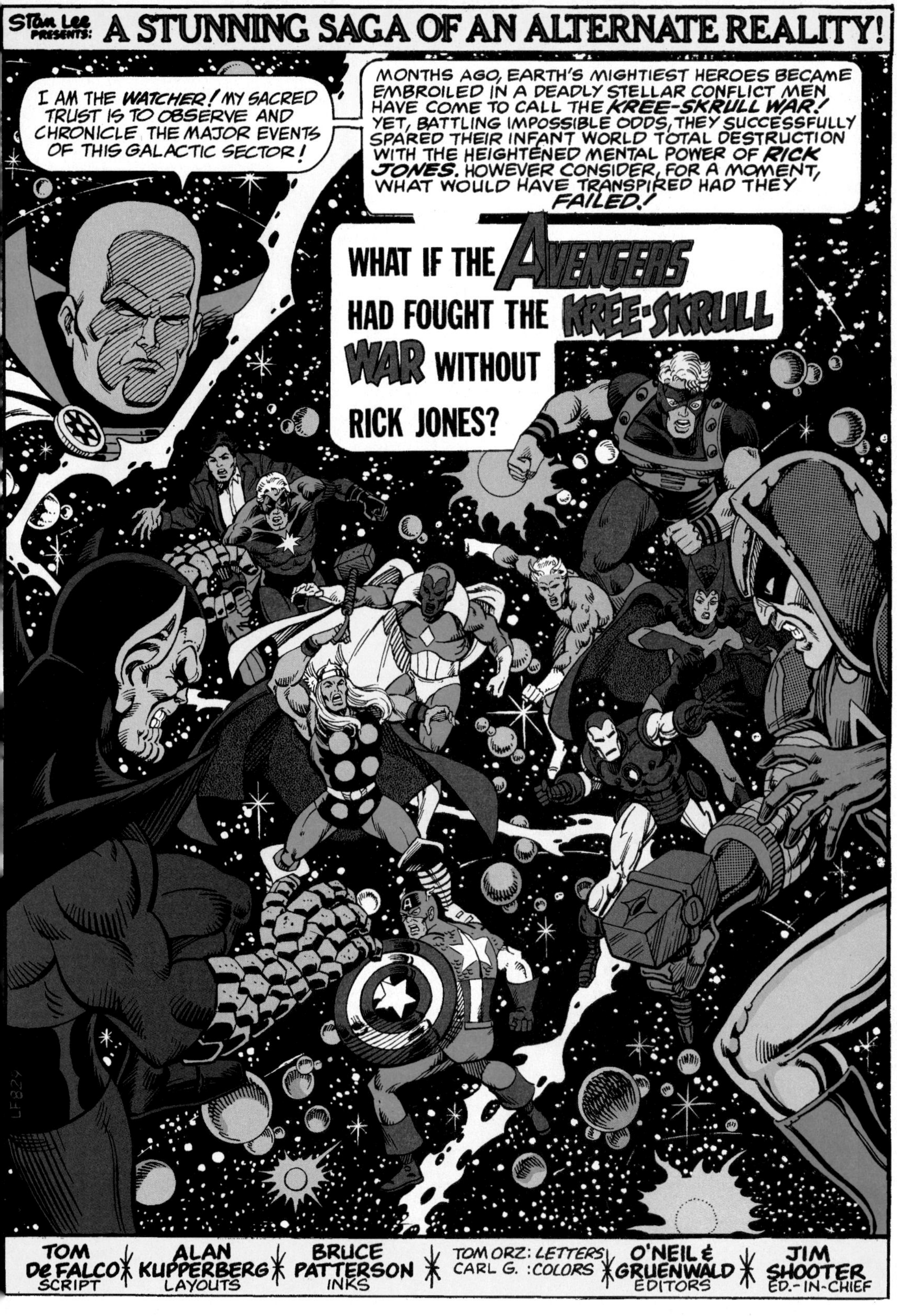

Stan Lee PRESENTS: A STUNNING SAGA OF AN ALTERNATE REALITY!
I AM THE WATCHER! MY SACRED TRUST IS TO OBSERVE AND CHRONICLE THE MAJOR EVENTS OF THIS GALACTIC SECTOR!
MONTHS AGO, EARTH'S MIGHTIEST HEROES BECAME EMBROILED IN A DEADLY STELLAR CONFLICT MEN HAVE COME TO CALL THE KREE-SKRULL WAR! YET, BATTLING IMPOSSIBLE ODDS, THEY SUCCESSFULLY SPARED THEIR INFANT WORLD TOTAL DESTRUCTION WITH THE HEIGHTENED MENTAL POWER OF RICK JONES. HOWEVER CONSIDER, FOR A MOMENT, WHAT WOULD HAVE TRANSPIRED HAD THEY FAILED!
WHAT IF THE AVENGERS HAD FOUGHT THE KREE-SKRULL WAR WITHOUT RICK JONES?
TOM DeFALCO SCRIPT
ALAN KUPPERBERG LAYOUTS
BRUCE PATTERSON INKS
TOM ORZ: LETTERS
CARL G.: COLORS
O'NEIL & GRUENWALD EDITORS
JIM SHOOTER ED.-IN-CHIEF

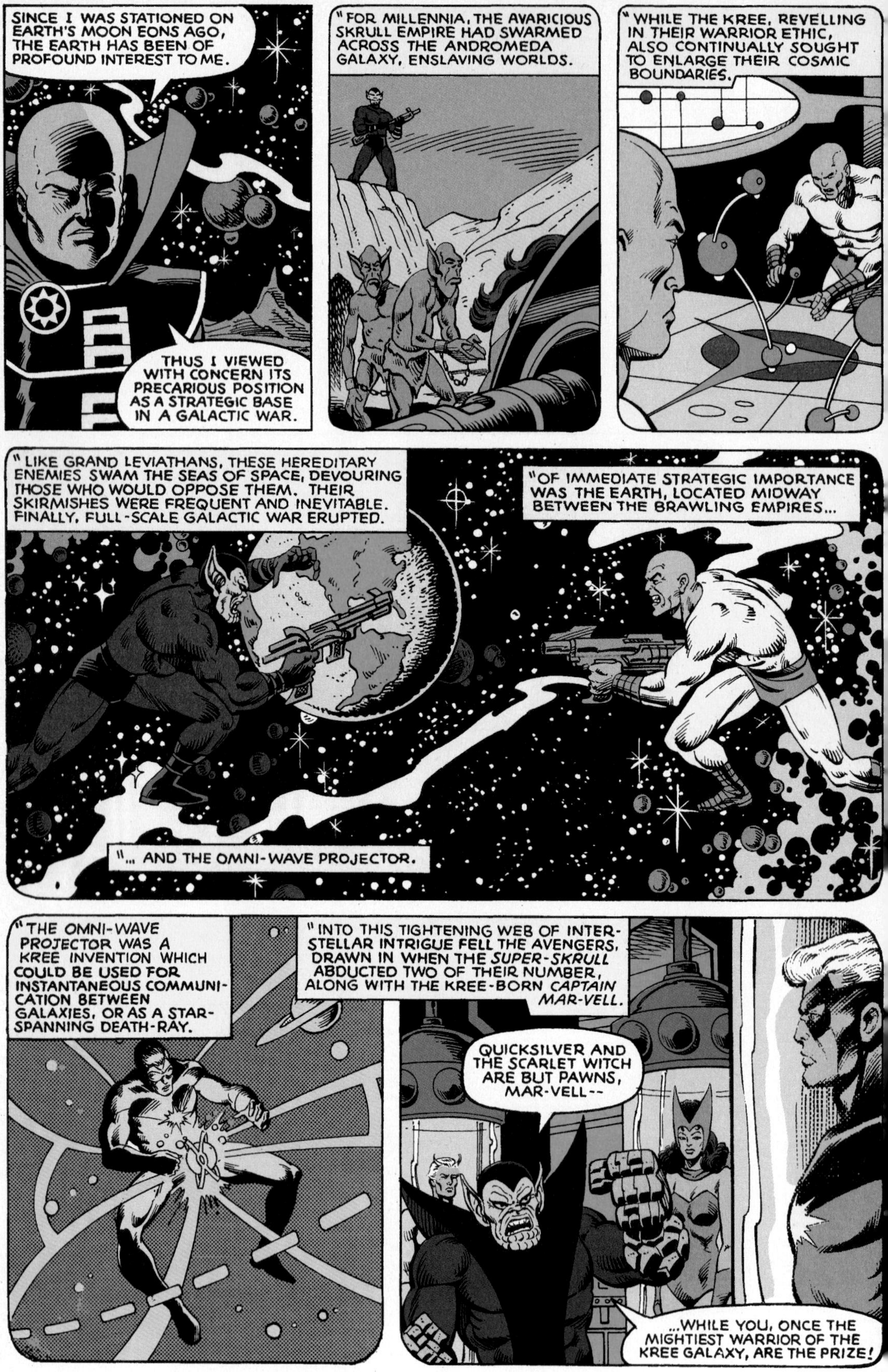
SINCE I WAS STATIONED ON EARTH'S MOON EONS AGO, THE EARTH HAS BEEN OF PROFOUND INTEREST TO ME.
THUS I VIEWED WITH CONCERN ITS PRECARIOUS POSITION AS A STRATEGIC BASE IN A GALACTIC WAR.
"FOR MILLENNIA, THE AVARICIOUS SKRULL EMPIRE HAD SWARMED ACROSS THE ANDROMEDA GALAXY, ENSLAVING WORLDS.
"WHILE THE KREE, REVELLING IN THEIR WARRIOR ETHIC, ALSO CONTINUALLY SOUGHT TO ENLARGE THEIR COSMIC BOUNDARIES.
"LIKE GRAND LEVIATHANS, THESE HEREDITARY ENEMIES SWAM THE SEAS OF SPACE, DEVOURING THOSE WHO WOULD OPPOSE THEM. THEIR SKIRMISHES WERE FREQUENT AND INEVITABLE. FINALLY, FULL-SCALE GALACTIC WAR ERUPTED.
"OF IMMEDIATE STRATEGIC IMPORTANCE WAS THE EARTH, LOCATED MIDWAY BETWEEN THE BRAWLING EMPIRES...
"... AND THE OMNI-WAVE PROJECTOR.
"THE OMNI-WAVE PROJECTOR WAS A KREE INVENTION WHICH COULD BE USED FOR INSTANTANEOUS COMMUNICATION BETWEEN GALAXIES, OR AS A STAR-SPANNING DEATH-RAY.
"INTO THIS TIGHTENING WEB OF INTERSTELLAR INTRIGUE FELL THE AVENGERS, DRAWN IN WHEN THE *SUPER-SKRULL* ABDUCTED TWO OF THEIR NUMBER, ALONG WITH THE KREE-BORN *CAPTAIN MAR-VELL*.
QUICKSILVER AND THE SCARLET WITCH ARE BUT PAWNS, MAR-VELL--
...WHILE YOU, ONCE THE MIGHTIEST WARRIOR OF THE KREE GALAXY, ARE THE PRIZE!

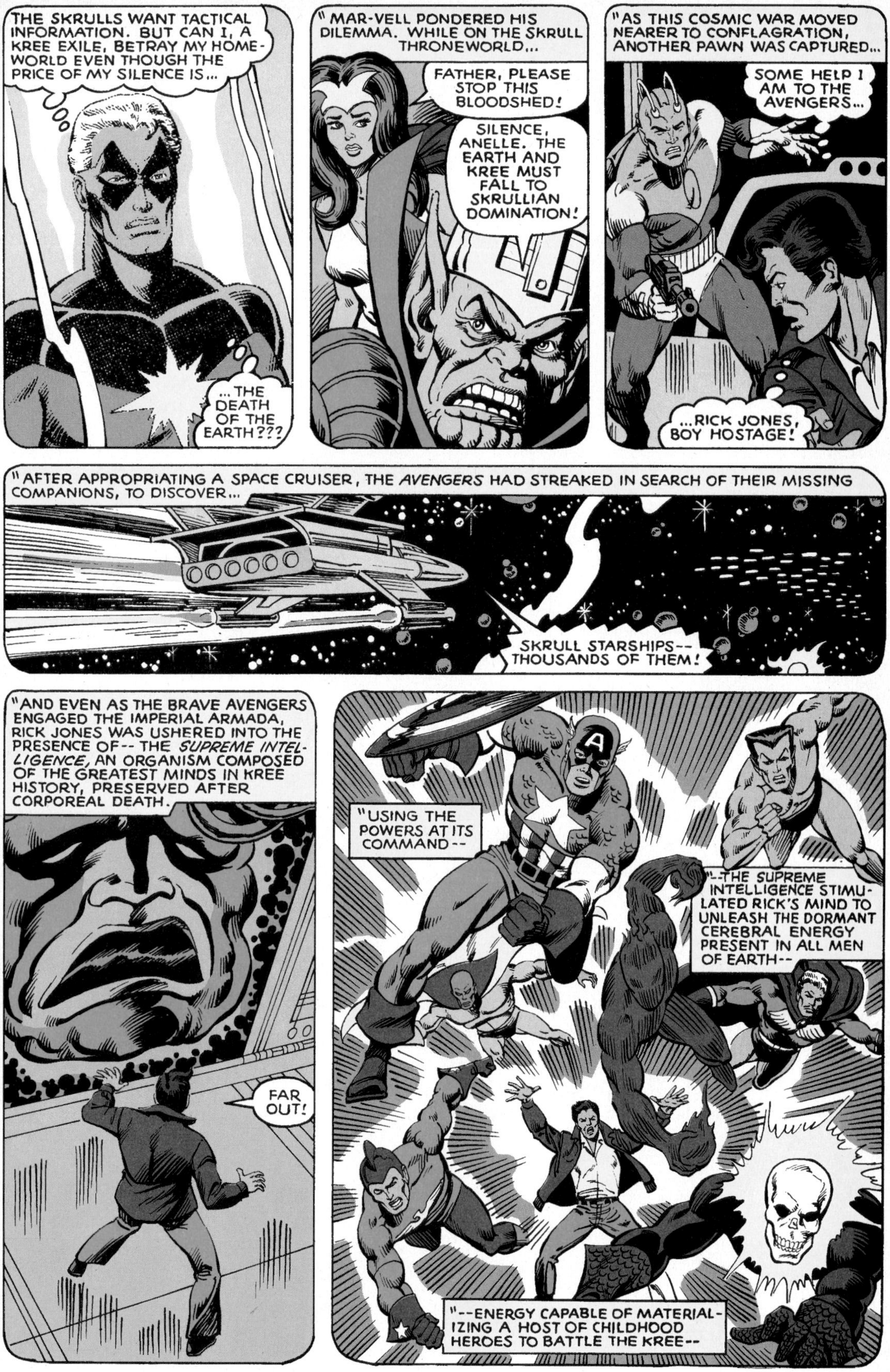
THE SKRULLS WANT TACTICAL INFORMATION. BUT CAN I, A KREE EXILE, BETRAY MY HOME-WORLD EVEN THOUGH THE PRICE OF MY SILENCE IS...
...THE DEATH OF THE EARTH???
"MAR-VELL PONDERED HIS DILEMMA. WHILE ON THE SKRULL THRONEWORLD...
FATHER, PLEASE STOP THIS BLOODSHED!
SILENCE, ANELLE. THE EARTH AND KREE MUST FALL TO SKRULLIAN DOMINATION!
"AS THIS COSMIC WAR MOVED NEARER TO CONFLAGRATION, ANOTHER PAWN WAS CAPTURED...
SOME HELP I AM TO THE AVENGERS...
...RICK JONES, BOY HOSTAGE!
"AFTER APPROPRIATING A SPACE CRUISER, THE *AVENGERS* HAD STREAKED IN SEARCH OF THEIR MISSING COMPANIONS, TO DISCOVER...
SKRULL STARSHIPS--THOUSANDS OF THEM!
"AND EVEN AS THE BRAVE AVENGERS ENGAGED THE IMPERIAL ARMADA, RICK JONES WAS USHERED INTO THE PRESENCE OF-- THE *SUPREME INTELLIGENCE*, AN ORGANISM COMPOSED OF THE GREATEST MINDS IN KREE HISTORY, PRESERVED AFTER CORPOREAL DEATH.
FAR OUT!
"USING THE POWERS AT ITS COMMAND--
"--THE *SUPREME* INTELLIGENCE STIMULATED RICK'S MIND TO UNLEASH THE DORMANT CEREBRAL ENERGY PRESENT IN ALL MEN OF EARTH--
"--ENERGY CAPABLE OF MATERIALIZING A HOST OF CHILDHOOD HEROES TO BATTLE THE KREE--

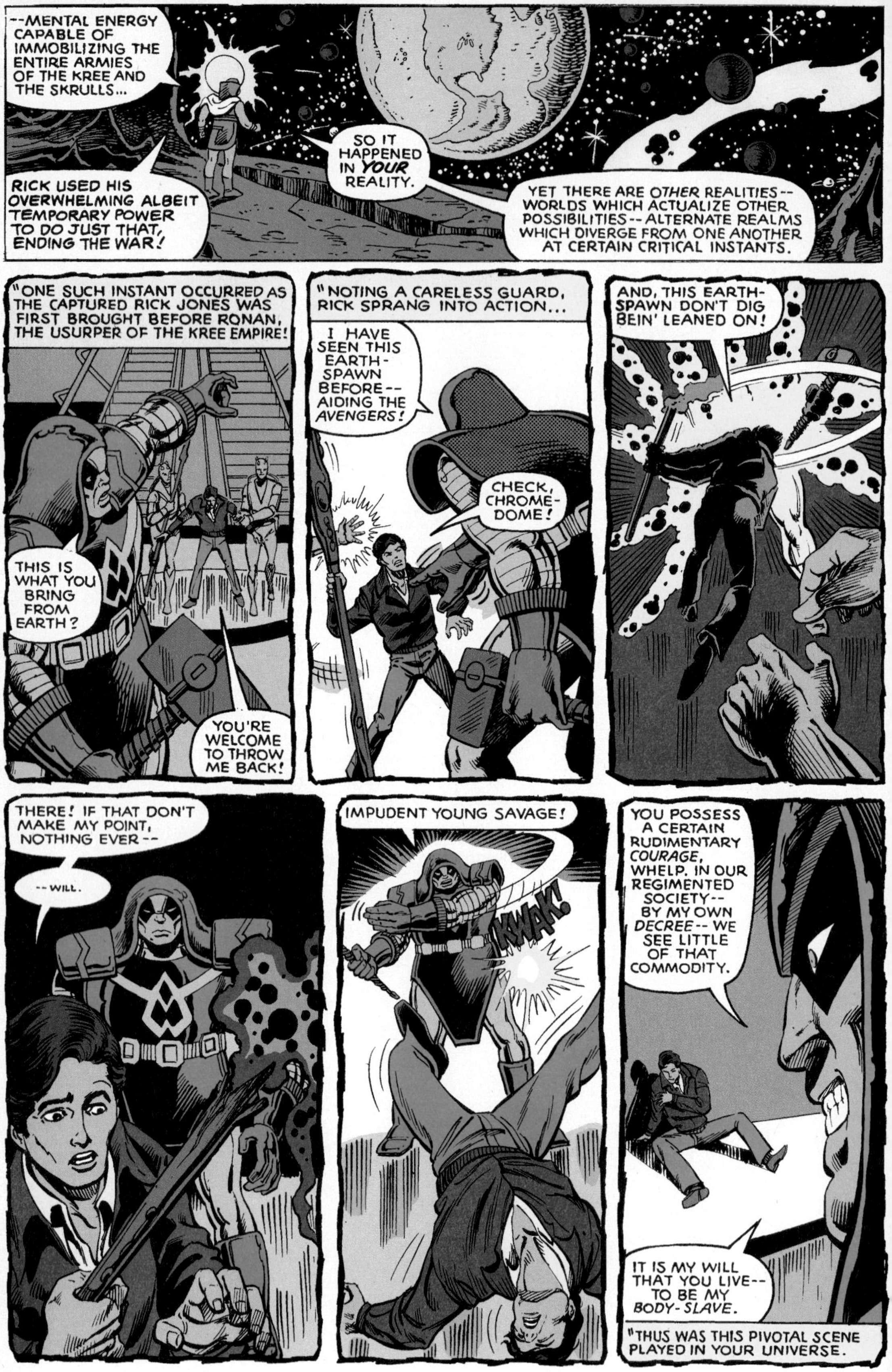

--MENTAL ENERGY CAPABLE OF IMMOBILIZING THE ENTIRE ARMIES OF THE KREE AND THE SKRULLS...
RICK USED HIS OVERWHELMING ALBEIT TEMPORARY POWER TO DO JUST THAT, ENDING THE WAR!
SO IT HAPPENED IN YOUR REALITY.
YET THERE ARE OTHER REALITIES-- WORLDS WHICH ACTUALIZE OTHER POSSIBILITIES-- ALTERNATE REALMS WHICH DIVERGE FROM ONE ANOTHER AT CERTAIN CRITICAL INSTANTS.
"ONE SUCH INSTANT OCCURRED AS THE CAPTURED RICK JONES WAS FIRST BROUGHT BEFORE RONAN, THE USURPER OF THE KREE EMPIRE!
THIS IS WHAT YOU BRING FROM EARTH?
YOU'RE WELCOME TO THROW ME BACK!
"NOTING A CARELESS GUARD, RICK SPRANG INTO ACTION...
I HAVE SEEN THIS EARTH-SPAWN BEFORE-- AIDING THE AVENGERS!
CHECK, CHROME-DOME!
AND, THIS EARTH-SPAWN DON'T DIG BEIN' LEANED ON!
THERE! IF THAT DON'T MAKE MY POINT, NOTHING EVER--
--WILL.
IMPUDENT YOUNG SAVAGE!
KWAK!
YOU POSSESS A CERTAIN RUDIMENTARY COURAGE, WHELP. IN OUR REGIMENTED SOCIETY-- BY MY OWN DECREE-- WE SEE LITTLE OF THAT COMMODITY.
IT IS MY WILL THAT YOU LIVE-- TO BE MY BODY-SLAVE.
"THUS WAS THIS PIVOTAL SCENE PLAYED IN YOUR UNIVERSE.

"HOWEVER, MANY WERE THE EMOTIONS FLASHING THROUGH RONAN'S MIND AS THE YOUNG EARTHLING FUTILELY ATTACKED HIM. ALL IT TAKES IS A SINGLE IMPULSE UNSUPRESSED TO CHANGE THE FUTURE FROM THE ONE YOU MAY HAVE ALREADY SEEN. *

COURAGE-- WE SEE LITTLE OF THAT COMMODITY.

IT IS MY WILL THAT--

*AVENGERS #89-97.--D&M.

-- WE SEE IT NO MORE!

DIE, EARTHSPAWN!

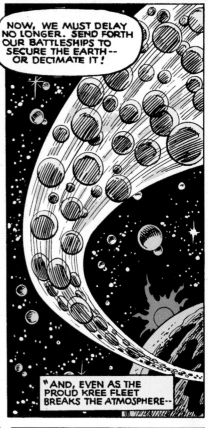

NOW, WE MUST DELAY NO LONGER. SEND FORTH OUR BATTLESHIPS TO SECURE THE EARTH-- OR DECIMATE IT!

"AND, EVEN AS THE PROUD KREE FLEET BREAKS THE ATMOSPHERE--

"-- ACROSS THE COSMOS, THE IMPERIAL SKRULL ARMADA HAS BEEN STORMED BY--

EARTHLINGS! ONE STAR CRUISER--AND THEY DARED BOARD US!

YET, TO WHERE HAVE THE ALIENS VANISHED?

Eh--?

YOU CALLED, GREEN-EYES?

KLANG!

LIST, YE HERALDS OF HATRED AND HOLOCAUST. WE FOUR BE BUT THE MEEKEST HARBINGERS OF THOSE WHO FOLLOW.

TURN BACK THINE ARMADA-- OR FACE THE WRATH OF AN EARTH AROUSED!

KEEP SHOVELLING, THOR! OUR ONLY CHANCE IS TO BLUFF 'EM!

185

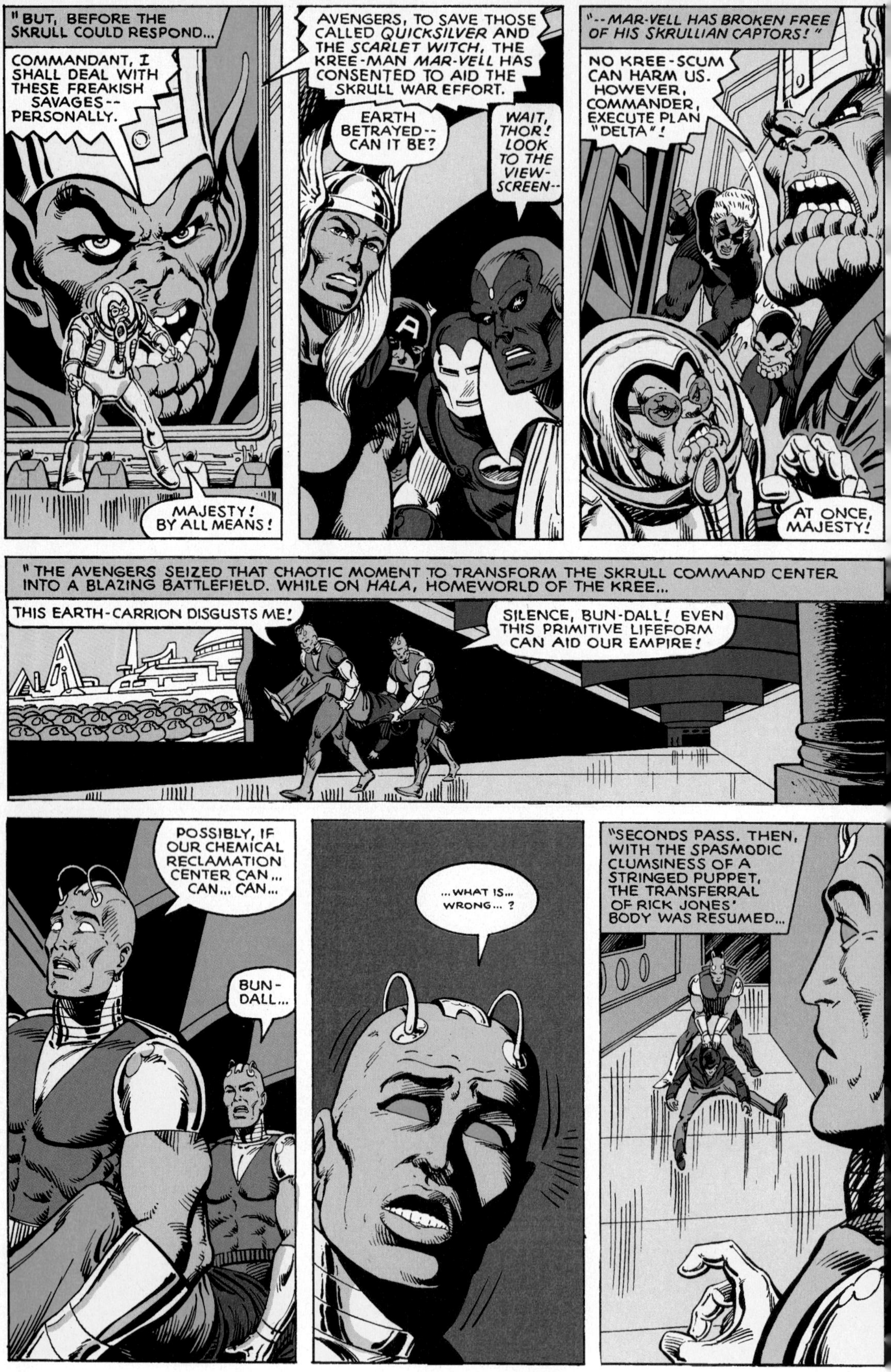
"BUT, BEFORE THE SKRULL COULD RESPOND...
COMMANDANT, I SHALL DEAL WITH THESE FREAKISH SAVAGES-- PERSONALLY.
MAJESTY! BY ALL MEANS!
AVENGERS, TO SAVE THOSE CALLED QUICKSILVER AND THE SCARLET WITCH, THE KREE-MAN MAR-VELL HAS CONSENTED TO AID THE SKRULL WAR EFFORT.
EARTH BETRAYED-- CAN IT BE?
WAIT, THOR! LOOK TO THE VIEW-SCREEN--
"--MAR-VELL HAS BROKEN FREE OF HIS SKRULLIAN CAPTORS!"
NO KREE-SCUM CAN HARM US. HOWEVER, COMMANDER, EXECUTE PLAN "DELTA"!
AT ONCE, MAJESTY!
"THE AVENGERS SEIZED THAT CHAOTIC MOMENT TO TRANSFORM THE SKRULL COMMAND CENTER INTO A BLAZING BATTLEFIELD. WHILE ON HALA, HOMEWORLD OF THE KREE...
THIS EARTH-CARRION DISGUSTS ME!
SILENCE, BUN-DALL! EVEN THIS PRIMITIVE LIFEFORM CAN AID OUR EMPIRE!
POSSIBLY, IF OUR CHEMICAL RECLAMATION CENTER CAN... CAN... CAN...
BUN-DALL...
...WHAT IS... WRONG... ?
"SECONDS PASS. THEN, WITH THE SPASMODIC CLUMSINESS OF A STRINGED PUPPET, THE TRANSFERRAL OF RICK JONES' BODY WAS RESUMED...

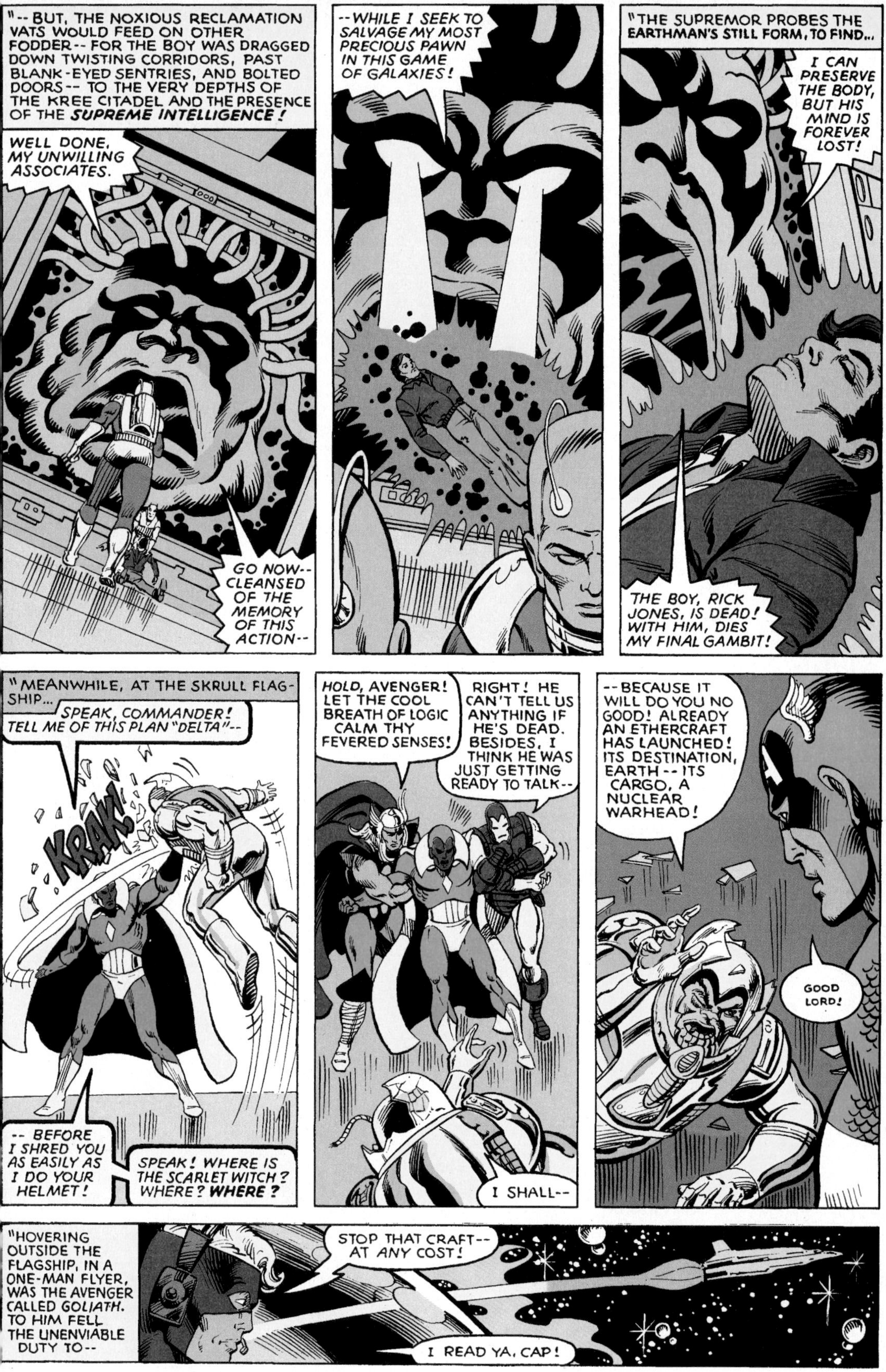
"-- BUT, THE NOXIOUS RECLAMATION VATS WOULD FEED ON OTHER FODDER -- FOR THE BOY WAS DRAGGED DOWN TWISTING CORRIDORS, PAST BLANK-EYED SENTRIES, AND BOLTED DOORS -- TO THE VERY DEPTHS OF THE KREE CITADEL AND THE PRESENCE OF THE SUPREME INTELLIGENCE!
WELL DONE, MY UNWILLING ASSOCIATES.
GO NOW-- CLEANSED OF THE MEMORY OF THIS ACTION--
--WHILE I SEEK TO SALVAGE MY MOST PRECIOUS PAWN IN THIS GAME OF GALAXIES!
"THE SUPREMOR PROBES THE EARTHMAN'S STILL FORM, TO FIND...
I CAN PRESERVE THE BODY, BUT HIS MIND IS FOREVER LOST!
THE BOY, RICK JONES, IS DEAD! WITH HIM, DIES MY FINAL GAMBIT!
"MEANWHILE, AT THE SKRULL FLAGSHIP...
SPEAK, COMMANDER! TELL ME OF THIS PLAN "DELTA"--
KRAK!
-- BEFORE I SHRED YOU AS EASILY AS I DO YOUR HELMET!
SPEAK! WHERE IS THE SCARLET WITCH? WHERE? WHERE?
HOLD, AVENGER! LET THE COOL BREATH OF LOGIC CALM THY FEVERED SENSES!
RIGHT! HE CAN'T TELL US ANYTHING IF HE'S DEAD. BESIDES, I THINK HE WAS JUST GETTING READY TO TALK--
I SHALL--
--BECAUSE IT WILL DO YOU NO GOOD! ALREADY AN ETHERCRAFT HAS LAUNCHED! ITS DESTINATION, EARTH -- ITS CARGO, A NUCLEAR WARHEAD!
GOOD LORD!
"HOVERING OUTSIDE THE FLAGSHIP, IN A ONE-MAN FLYER, WAS THE AVENGER CALLED GOLIATH. TO HIM FELL THE UNENVIABLE DUTY TO--
STOP THAT CRAFT-- AT ANY COST!
I READ YA, CAP!

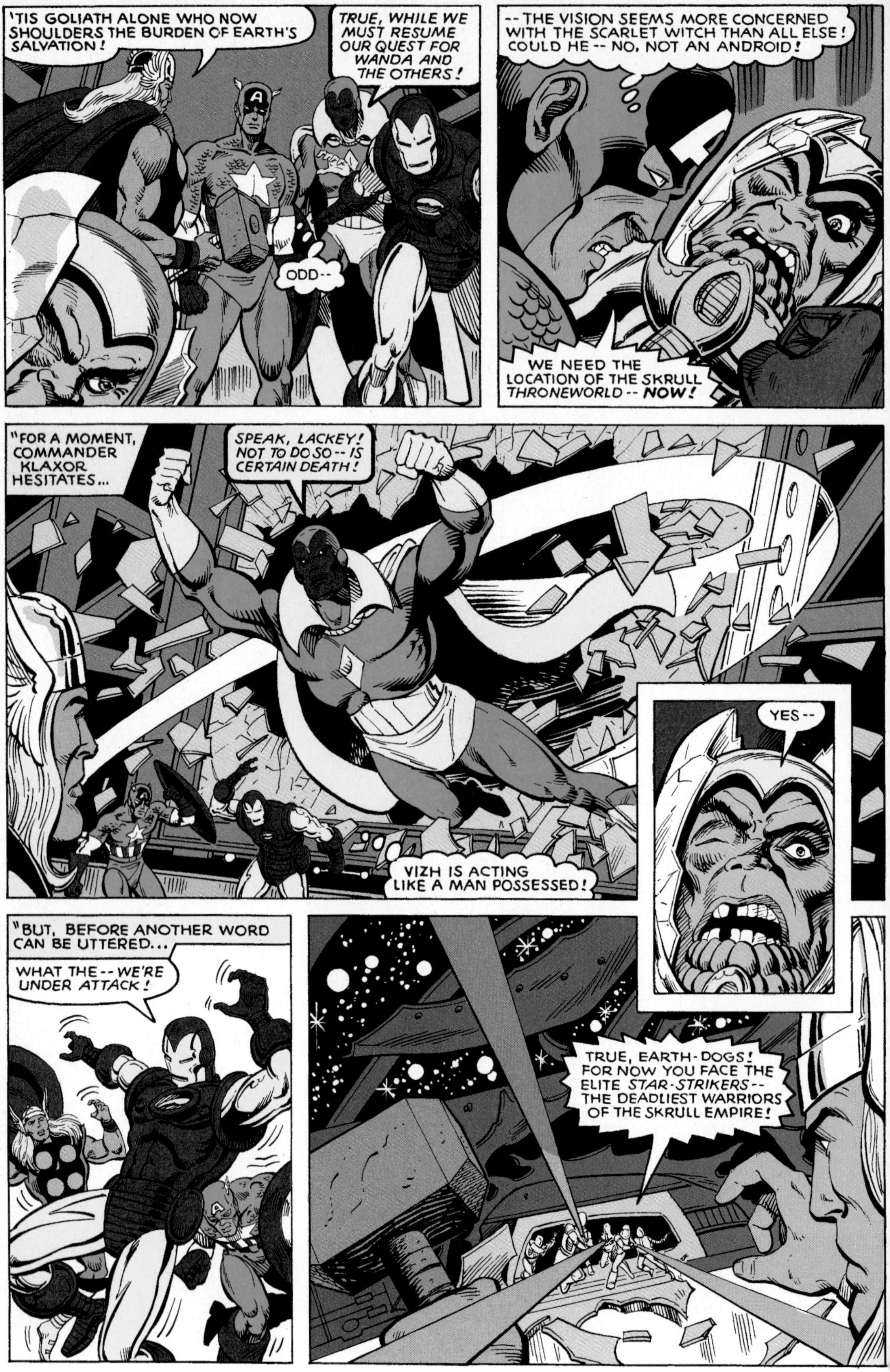
'TIS GOLIATH ALONE WHO NOW SHOULDERS THE BURDEN OF EARTH'S SALVATION!
TRUE, WHILE WE MUST RESUME OUR QUEST FOR WANDA AND THE OTHERS!
ODD--
-- THE VISION SEEMS MORE CONCERNED WITH THE SCARLET WITCH THAN ALL ELSE! COULD HE -- NO, NOT AN ANDROID!
WE NEED THE LOCATION OF THE SKRULL THRONEWORLD -- NOW!
"FOR A MOMENT, COMMANDER KLAXOR HESITATES...
SPEAK, LACKEY! NOT TO DO SO -- IS CERTAIN DEATH!
VIZH IS ACTING LIKE A MAN POSSESSED!
YES --
"BUT, BEFORE ANOTHER WORD CAN BE UTTERED...
WHAT THE -- WE'RE UNDER ATTACK!
TRUE, EARTH-DOGS! FOR NOW YOU FACE THE ELITE STAR-STRIKERS -- THE DEADLIEST WARRIORS OF THE SKRULL EMPIRE!

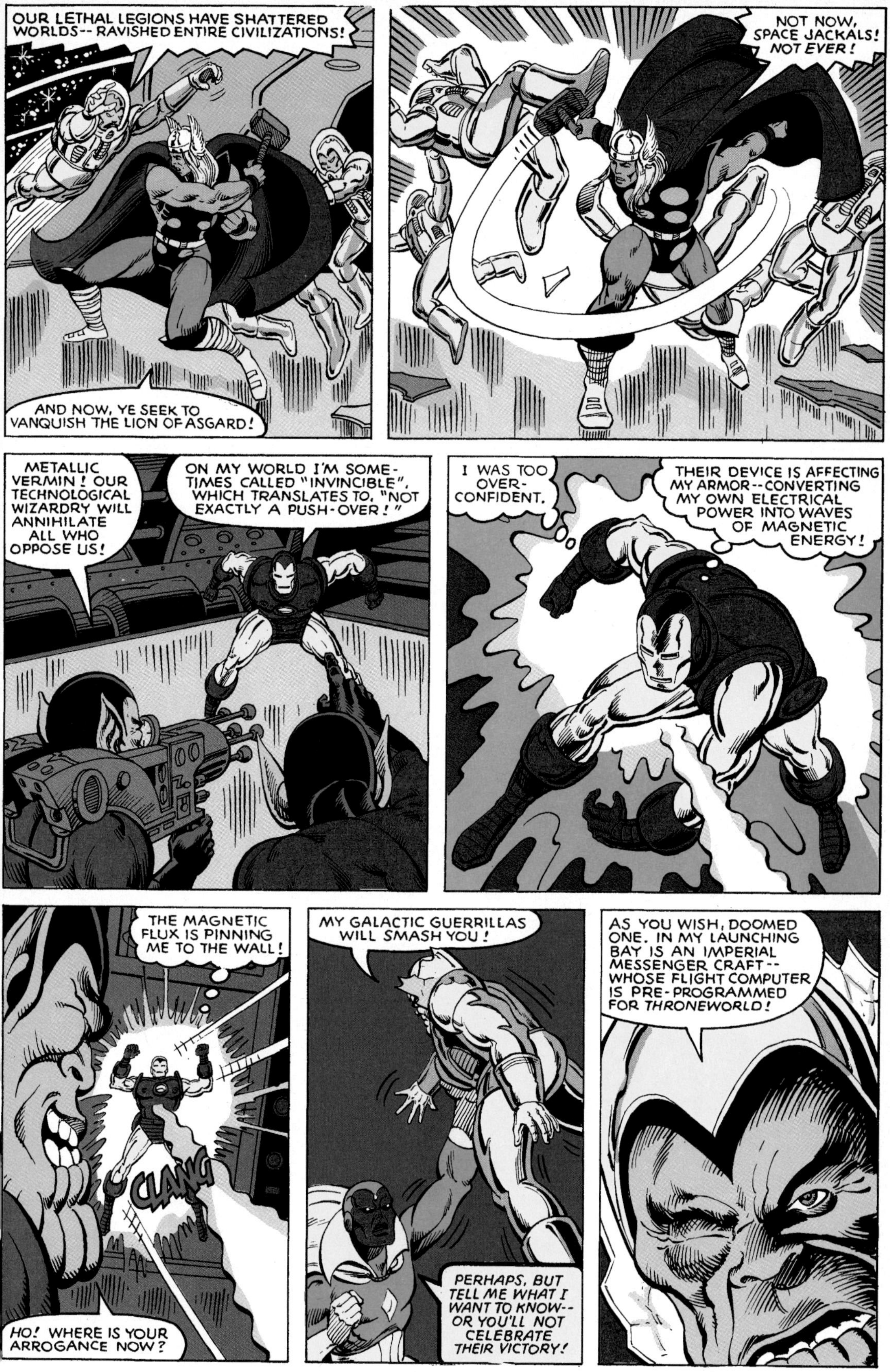
OUR LETHAL LEGIONS HAVE SHATTERED WORLDS-- RAVISHED ENTIRE CIVILIZATIONS!
AND NOW, YE SEEK TO VANQUISH THE LION OF ASGARD!
NOT NOW, SPACE JACKALS! NOT EVER!
METALLIC VERMIN! OUR TECHNOLOGICAL WIZARDRY WILL ANNIHILATE ALL WHO OPPOSE US!
ON MY WORLD I'M SOMETIMES CALLED "INVINCIBLE", WHICH TRANSLATES TO, "NOT EXACTLY A PUSH-OVER!"
I WAS TOO OVER-CONFIDENT.
THEIR DEVICE IS AFFECTING MY ARMOR--CONVERTING MY OWN ELECTRICAL POWER INTO WAVES OF MAGNETIC ENERGY!
THE MAGNETIC FLUX IS PINNING ME TO THE WALL!
CLANG
HO! WHERE IS YOUR ARROGANCE NOW?
MY GALACTIC GUERRILLAS WILL SMASH YOU!
PERHAPS, BUT TELL ME WHAT I WANT TO KNOW-- OR YOU'LL NOT CELEBRATE THEIR VICTORY!
AS YOU WISH, DOOMED ONE. IN MY LAUNCHING BAY IS AN IMPERIAL MESSENGER CRAFT-- WHOSE FLIGHT COMPUTER IS PRE-PROGRAMMED FOR THRONEWORLD!

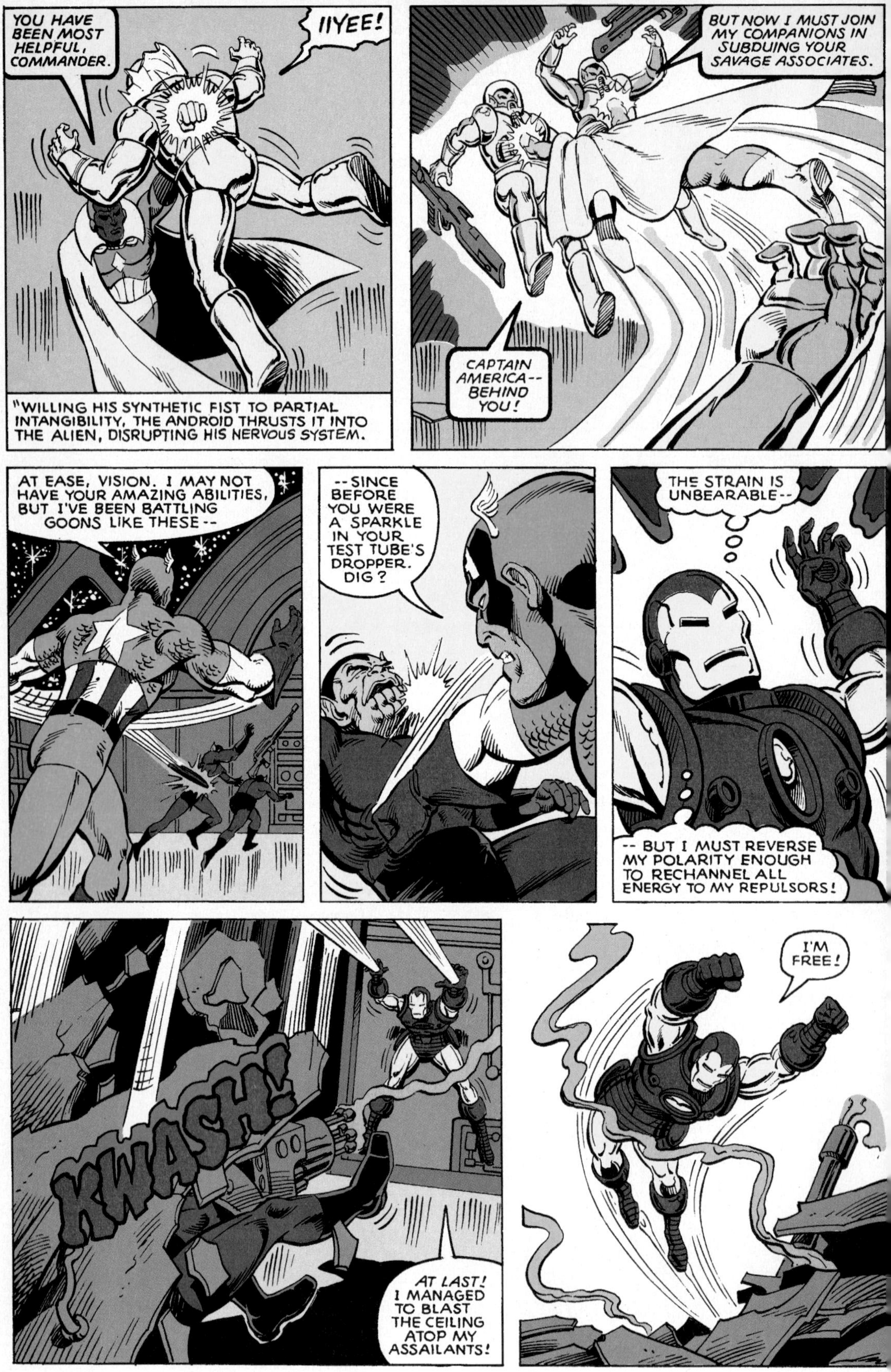
YOU HAVE BEEN MOST HELPFUL, COMMANDER.
IIYEE!
"WILLING HIS SYNTHETIC FIST TO PARTIAL INTANGIBILITY, THE ANDROID THRUSTS IT INTO THE ALIEN, DISRUPTING HIS NERVOUS SYSTEM.
BUT NOW I MUST JOIN MY COMPANIONS IN SUBDUING YOUR SAVAGE ASSOCIATES.
CAPTAIN AMERICA-- BEHIND YOU!
AT EASE, VISION. I MAY NOT HAVE YOUR AMAZING ABILITIES, BUT I'VE BEEN BATTLING GOONS LIKE THESE--
--SINCE BEFORE YOU WERE A SPARKLE IN YOUR TEST TUBE'S DROPPER. DIG?
THE STRAIN IS UNBEARABLE--
-- BUT I MUST REVERSE MY POLARITY ENOUGH TO RECHANNEL ALL ENERGY TO MY REPULSORS!
KWASH!
AT LAST! I MANAGED TO BLAST THE CEILING ATOP MY ASSAILANTS!
I'M FREE!

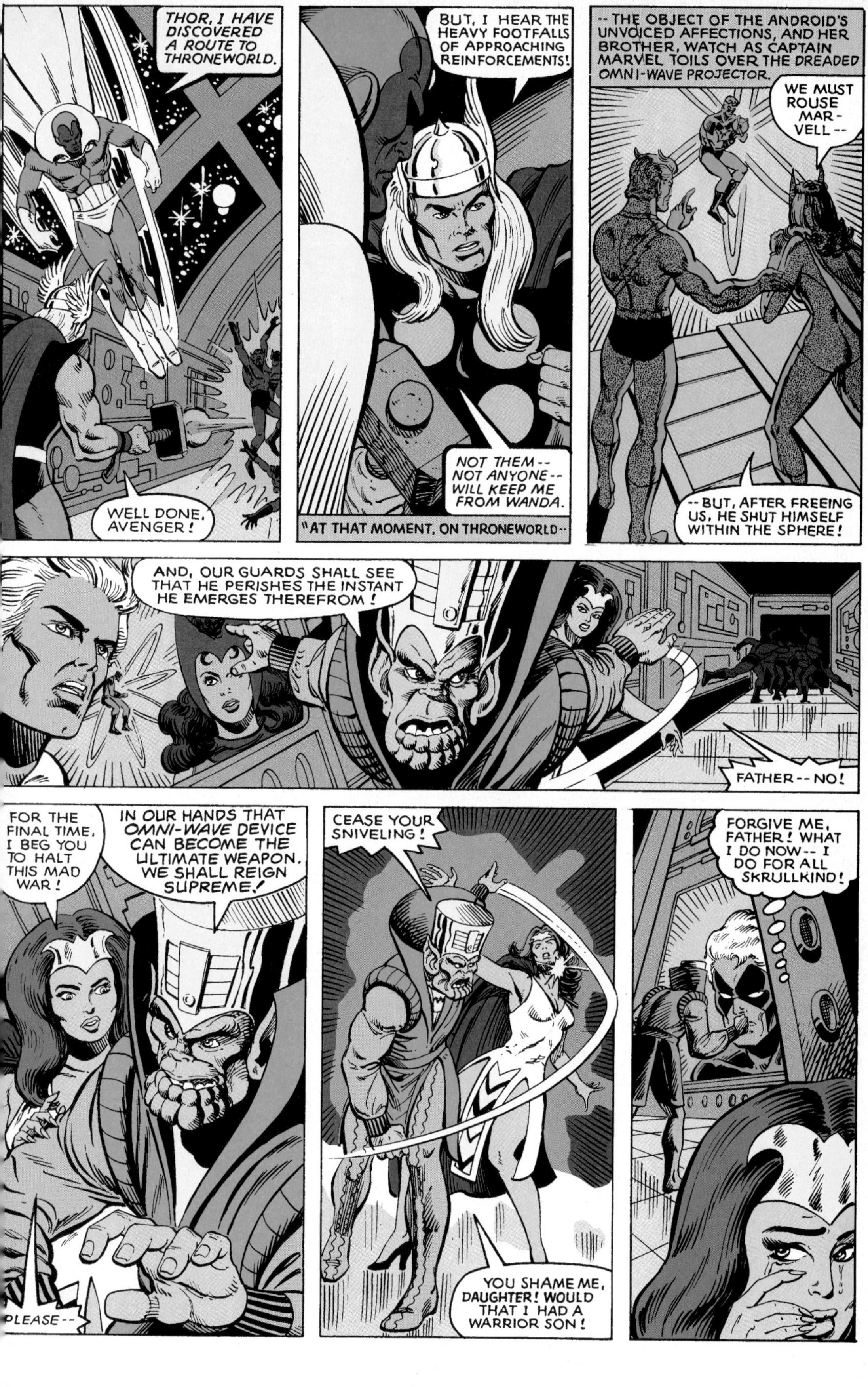
THOR, I HAVE DISCOVERED A ROUTE TO THRONEWORLD.
WELL DONE, AVENGER!
BUT, I HEAR THE HEAVY FOOTFALLS OF APPROACHING REINFORCEMENTS!
NOT THEM -- NOT ANYONE -- WILL KEEP ME FROM WANDA.
"AT THAT MOMENT, ON THRONEWORLD--
-- THE OBJECT OF THE ANDROID'S UNVOICED AFFECTIONS, AND HER BROTHER, WATCH AS CAPTAIN MARVEL TOILS OVER THE DREADED OMNI-WAVE PROJECTOR.
WE MUST ROUSE MAR-VELL --
-- BUT, AFTER FREEING US, HE SHUT HIMSELF WITHIN THE SPHERE!
AND, OUR GUARDS SHALL SEE THAT HE PERISHES THE INSTANT HE EMERGES THEREFROM!
FATHER -- NO!
FOR THE FINAL TIME, I BEG YOU TO HALT THIS MAD WAR!
IN OUR HANDS THAT OMNI-WAVE DEVICE CAN BECOME THE ULTIMATE WEAPON. WE SHALL REIGN SUPREME!
PLEASE --
CEASE YOUR SNIVELING!
YOU SHAME ME, DAUGHTER! WOULD THAT I HAD A WARRIOR SON!
FORGIVE ME, FATHER! WHAT I DO NOW -- I DO FOR ALL SKRULLKIND!

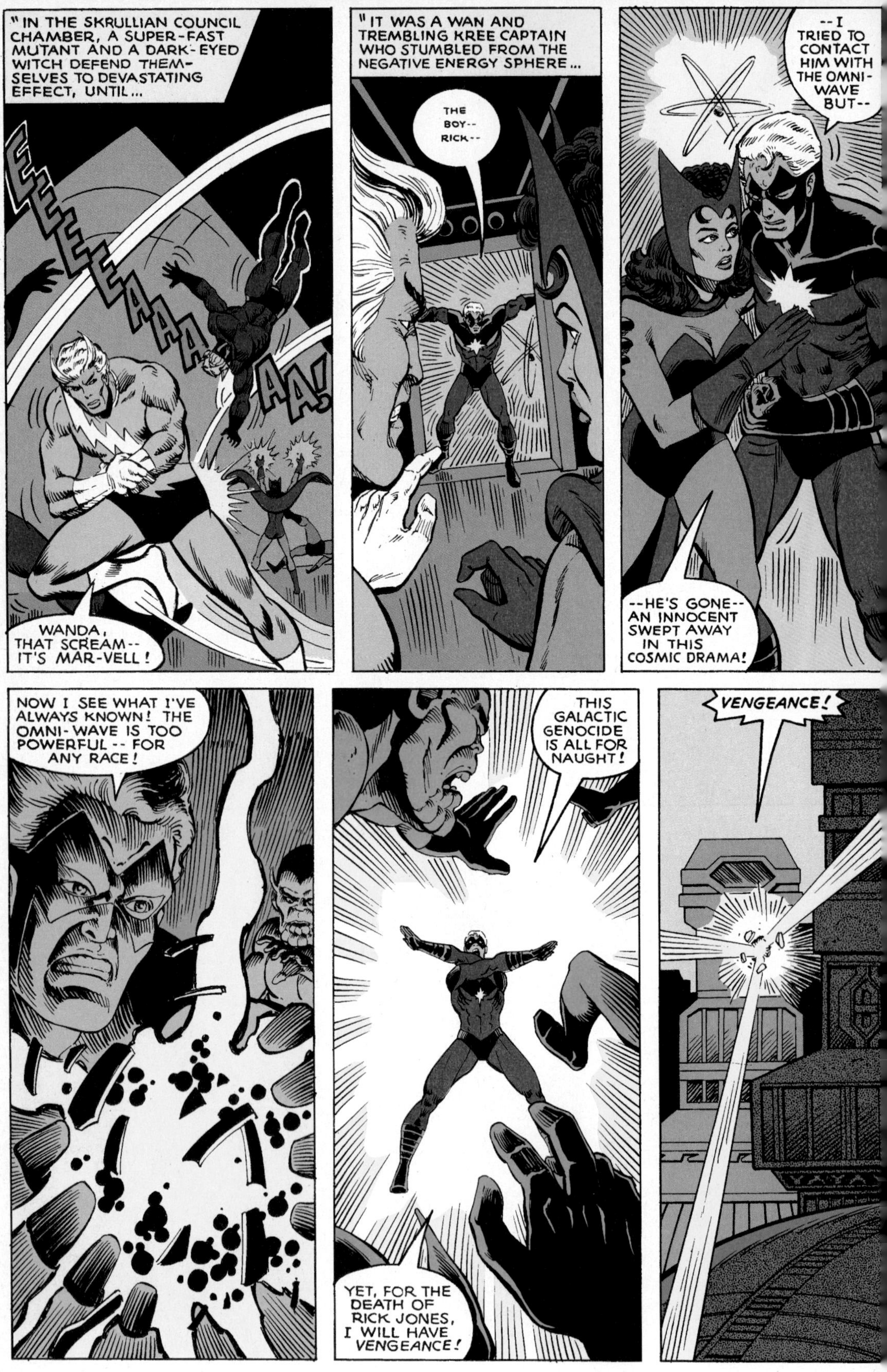
"IN THE SKRULLIAN COUNCIL CHAMBER, A SUPER-FAST MUTANT AND A DARK-EYED WITCH DEFEND THEMSELVES TO DEVASTATING EFFECT, UNTIL...
EEEEEAAAAAAA!
WANDA, THAT SCREAM-- IT'S MAR-VELL!
"IT WAS A WAN AND TREMBLING KREE CAPTAIN WHO STUMBLED FROM THE NEGATIVE ENERGY SPHERE...
THE BOY-- RICK--
--I TRIED TO CONTACT HIM WITH THE OMNI-WAVE BUT--
--HE'S GONE-- AN INNOCENT SWEPT AWAY IN THIS COSMIC DRAMA!
NOW I SEE WHAT I'VE ALWAYS KNOWN! THE OMNI-WAVE IS TOO POWERFUL -- FOR ANY RACE!
THIS GALACTIC GENOCIDE IS ALL FOR NAUGHT!
YET, FOR THE DEATH OF RICK JONES, I WILL HAVE VENGEANCE!
VENGEANCE!

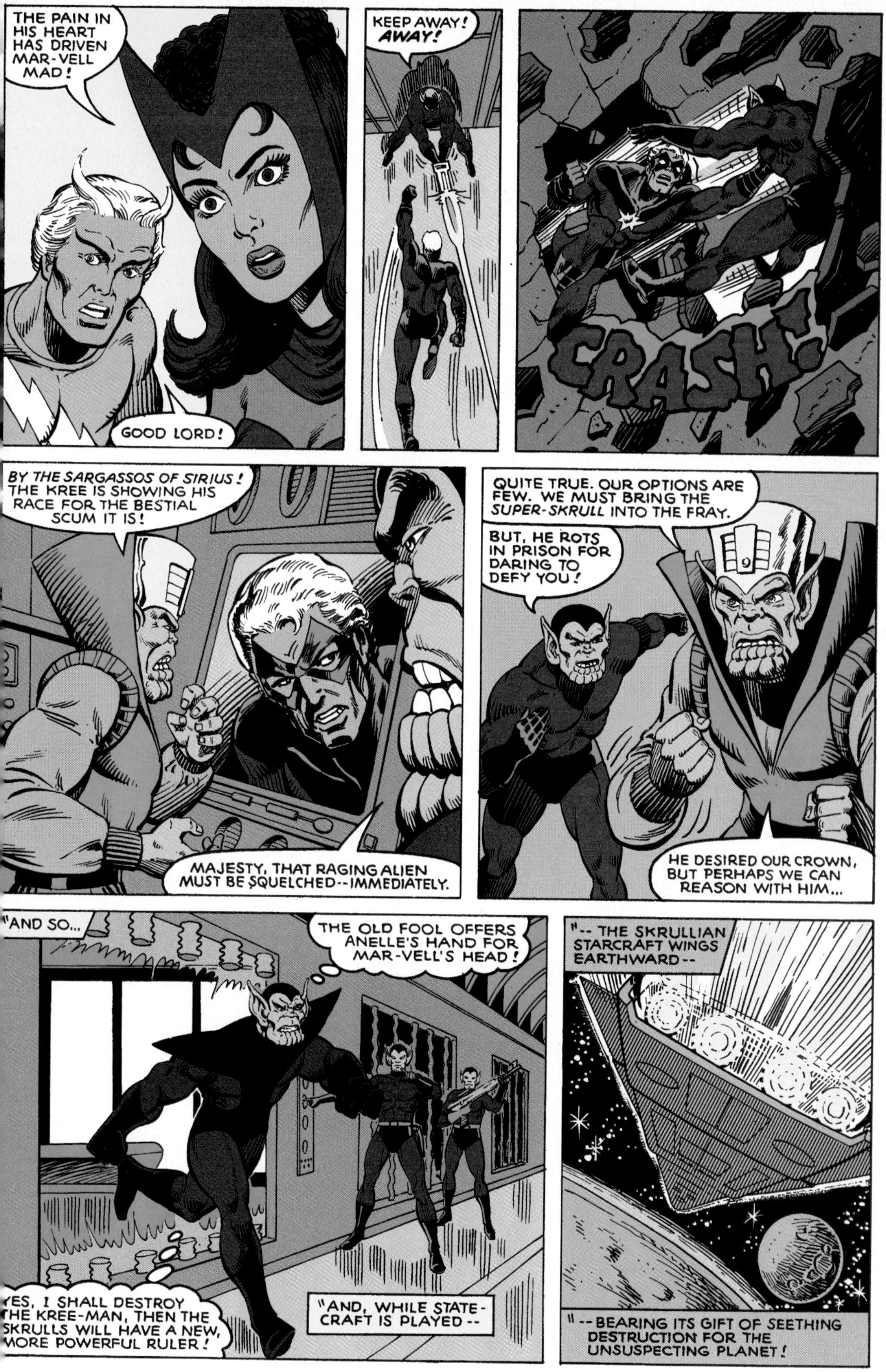
THE PAIN IN HIS HEART HAS DRIVEN MAR-VELL MAD!
GOOD LORD!
KEEP AWAY! AWAY!
CRASH!
BY THE SARGASSOS OF SIRIUS! THE KREE IS SHOWING HIS RACE FOR THE BESTIAL SCUM IT IS!
MAJESTY, THAT RAGING ALIEN MUST BE SQUELCHED--IMMEDIATELY.
QUITE TRUE. OUR OPTIONS ARE FEW. WE MUST BRING THE SUPER-SKRULL INTO THE FRAY.
BUT, HE ROTS IN PRISON FOR DARING TO DEFY YOU!
HE DESIRED OUR CROWN, BUT PERHAPS WE CAN REASON WITH HIM...
"AND SO...
THE OLD FOOL OFFERS ANELLE'S HAND FOR MAR-VELL'S HEAD!
YES, I SHALL DESTROY THE KREE-MAN, THEN THE SKRULLS WILL HAVE A NEW, MORE POWERFUL RULER!
"AND, WHILE STATE-CRAFT IS PLAYED--
"--THE SKRULLIAN STARCRAFT WINGS EARTHWARD--
"--BEARING ITS GIFT OF SEETHING DESTRUCTION FOR THE UNSUSPECTING PLANET!

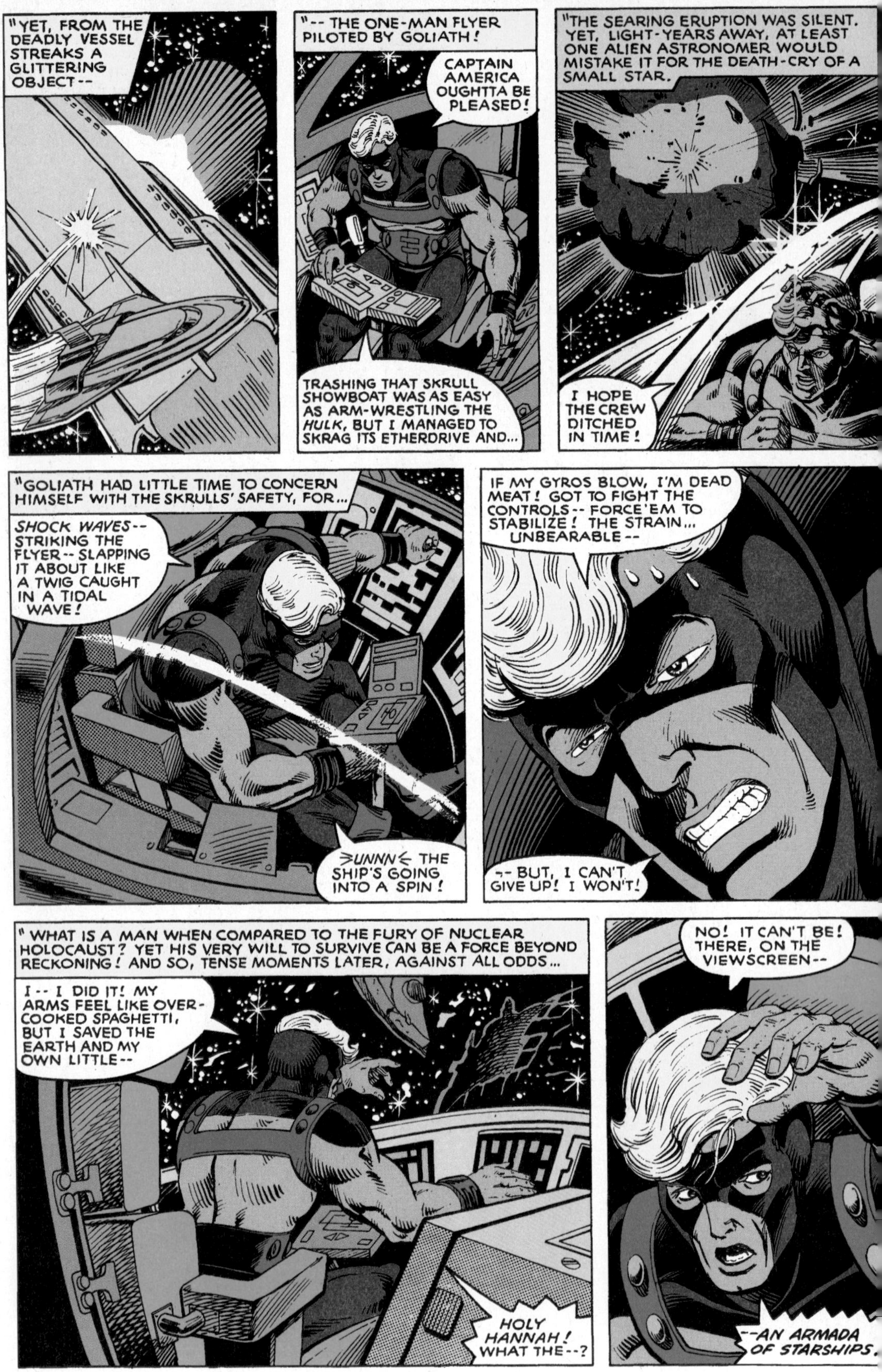
"YET, FROM THE DEADLY VESSEL STREAKS A GLITTERING OBJECT--
"-- THE ONE-MAN FLYER PILOTED BY GOLIATH!
CAPTAIN AMERICA OUGHTTA BE PLEASED!
TRASHING THAT SKRULL SHOWBOAT WAS AS EASY AS ARM-WRESTLING THE HULK, BUT I MANAGED TO SKRAG ITS ETHERDRIVE AND...
"THE SEARING ERUPTION WAS SILENT. YET, LIGHT-YEARS AWAY, AT LEAST ONE ALIEN ASTRONOMER WOULD MISTAKE IT FOR THE DEATH-CRY OF A SMALL STAR.
I HOPE THE CREW DITCHED IN TIME!
"GOLIATH HAD LITTLE TIME TO CONCERN HIMSELF WITH THE SKRULLS' SAFETY, FOR...
SHOCK WAVES-- STRIKING THE FLYER-- SLAPPING IT ABOUT LIKE A TWIG CAUGHT IN A TIDAL WAVE!
UNNN THE SHIP'S GOING INTO A SPIN!
IF MY GYROS BLOW, I'M DEAD MEAT! GOT TO FIGHT THE CONTROLS-- FORCE 'EM TO STABILIZE! THE STRAIN... UNBEARABLE--
-- BUT, I CAN'T GIVE UP! I WON'T!
" WHAT IS A MAN WHEN COMPARED TO THE FURY OF NUCLEAR HOLOCAUST? YET HIS VERY WILL TO SURVIVE CAN BE A FORCE BEYOND RECKONING! AND SO, TENSE MOMENTS LATER, AGAINST ALL ODDS...
I -- I DID IT! MY ARMS FEEL LIKE OVER-COOKED SPAGHETTI, BUT I SAVED THE EARTH AND MY OWN LITTLE--
HOLY HANNAH! WHAT THE--?
NO! IT CAN'T BE! THERE, ON THE VIEWSCREEN--
--AN ARMADA OF STARSHIPS.

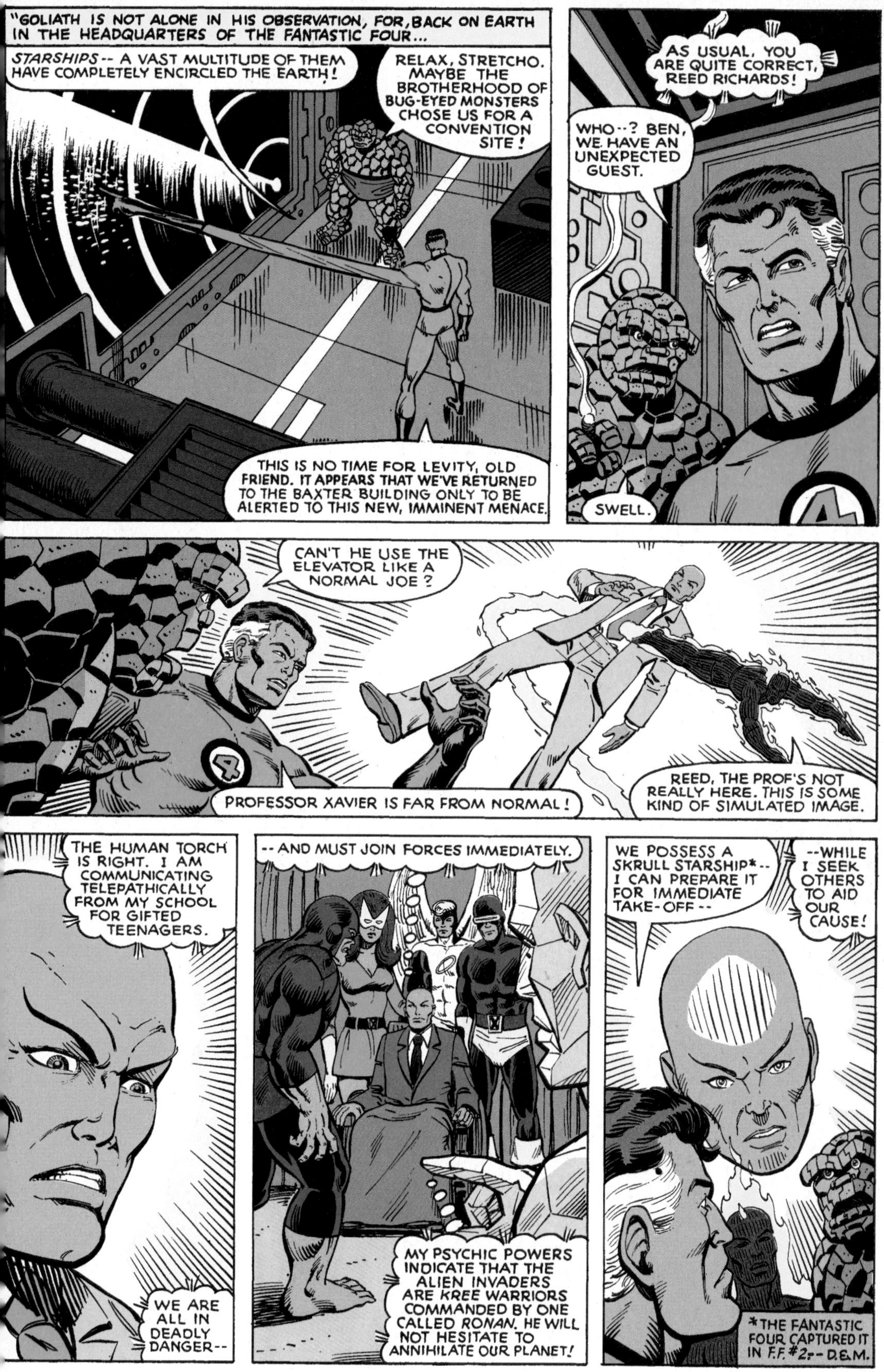
"GOLIATH IS NOT ALONE IN HIS OBSERVATION, FOR, BACK ON EARTH IN THE HEADQUARTERS OF THE FANTASTIC FOUR...
STARSHIPS -- A VAST MULTITUDE OF THEM HAVE COMPLETELY ENCIRCLED THE EARTH!
RELAX, STRETCHO. MAYBE THE BROTHERHOOD OF BUG-EYED MONSTERS CHOSE US FOR A CONVENTION SITE!
THIS IS NO TIME FOR LEVITY, OLD FRIEND. IT APPEARS THAT WE'VE RETURNED TO THE BAXTER BUILDING ONLY TO BE ALERTED TO THIS NEW, IMMINENT MENACE.
AS USUAL, YOU ARE QUITE CORRECT, REED RICHARDS!
WHO--? BEN, WE HAVE AN UNEXPECTED GUEST.
SWELL.
CAN'T HE USE THE ELEVATOR LIKE A NORMAL JOE?
PROFESSOR XAVIER IS FAR FROM NORMAL!
REED, THE PROF'S NOT REALLY HERE. THIS IS SOME KIND OF SIMULATED IMAGE.
THE HUMAN TORCH IS RIGHT. I AM COMMUNICATING TELEPATHICALLY FROM MY SCHOOL FOR GIFTED TEENAGERS.
WE ARE ALL IN DEADLY DANGER--
--AND MUST JOIN FORCES IMMEDIATELY.
MY PSYCHIC POWERS INDICATE THAT THE ALIEN INVADERS ARE KREE WARRIORS COMMANDED BY ONE CALLED RONAN. HE WILL NOT HESITATE TO ANNIHILATE OUR PLANET!
WE POSSESS A SKRULL STARSHIP*-- I CAN PREPARE IT FOR IMMEDIATE TAKE-OFF--
--WHILE I SEEK OTHERS TO AID OUR CAUSE!
*THE FANTASTIC FOUR CAPTURED IT IN F.F. #2.-- D.E.M.

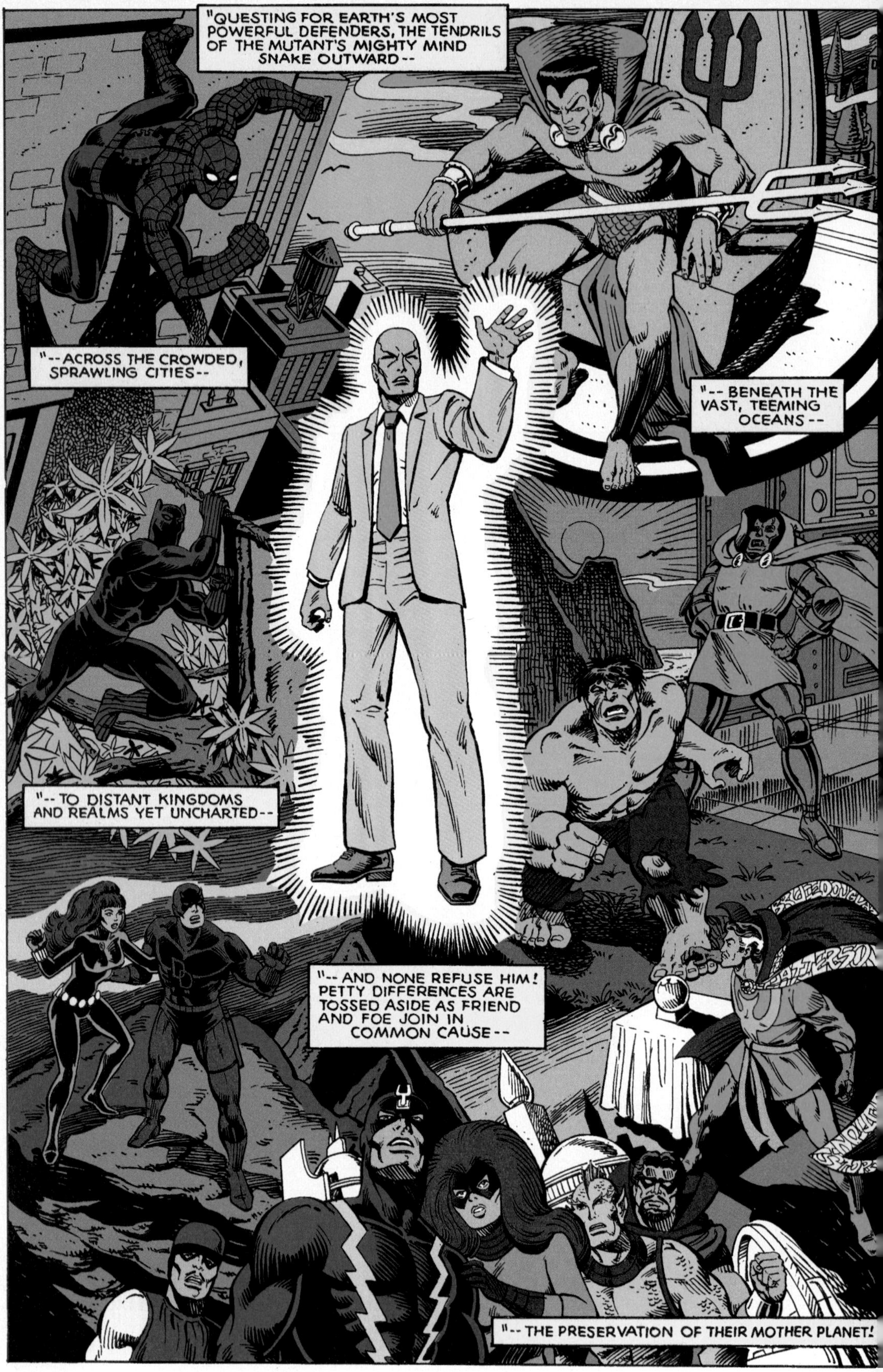
"QUESTING FOR EARTH'S MOST POWERFUL DEFENDERS, THE TENDRILS OF THE MUTANT'S MIGHTY MIND SNAKE OUTWARD--
"--ACROSS THE CROWDED, SPRAWLING CITIES--
"--BENEATH THE VAST, TEEMING OCEANS--
"--TO DISTANT KINGDOMS AND REALMS YET UNCHARTED--
"--AND NONE REFUSE HIM! PETTY DIFFERENCES ARE TOSSED ASIDE AS FRIEND AND FOE JOIN IN COMMON CAUSE--
"--THE PRESERVATION OF THEIR MOTHER PLANET!

"THE MIGHTIEST FORCES ON EARTH GATHERED TOGETHER, WHILE SOME 1,347 MILES ABOVE IT ALL...

GOLIATH TO THE SHIELD HELICARRIER -- REQUESTING PERMISSION TO BOARD! AVENGERS PRIORITY A-1!

IDENTITY CONFIRMED! PERMISSION GRANTED!

"RECEIVING HIS LANDING INSTRUCTIONS, GOLIATH GENTLY GLIDES HIS FLYER TO A REAR HANGAR BAY...

WHEW! I NEVER THOUGHT I'D SUCCESSFULLY RUN THAT KREE BLOCKADE! WE'RE COMPLETELY BOXED IN.

I'VE GOT TO FIND THE COMMAND CENTER AND ADVISE NICK FURY OF THE TOTAL SITUATION!

"THUS, SOON...

AND THE AVENGERS ARE AT THE OTHER END OF THE GALAXY -- HOLDING OFF A FLEET OF SKRULL WAR-SHIPS???

THAT'S ABOUT THE SIZE OF IT!

YER JUST BURSTIN' WITH GOOD NEWS, AIN'T YA?

"JUST THEN...

ATTENTION EARTH-VESSEL: YOU ARE ORBITING IN AIRSPACE RESTRICTED BY THE IMPERIAL KREE COMMAND. SURRENDER YOUR CRAFT OR SUFFER THE CONSEQUENCES!

NUTS!

WE'RE OUTGUNNED AND OUTMANNED, NICK. WHAT ARE YOU GOING TO DO?

WHADDA YA THINK? WE AIN'T GOT A SNOWBALL'S CHANCE, BUT WE DO HAVE A RESPONSIBILITY TO EVERY MAN, WOMAN AND CHILD DOWN BELOW!

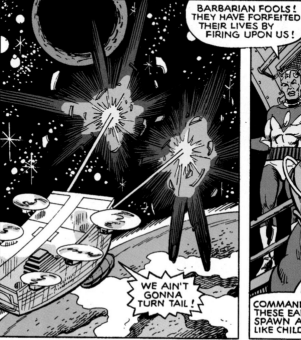

BARBARIAN FOOLS! THEY HAVE FORFEITED THEIR LIVES BY FIRING UPON US!

WE AIN'T GONNA TURN TAIL!

READY THE LASER CANNON!

COMMANDER, THESE EARTH-SPAWN ARE LIKE CHILDREN --

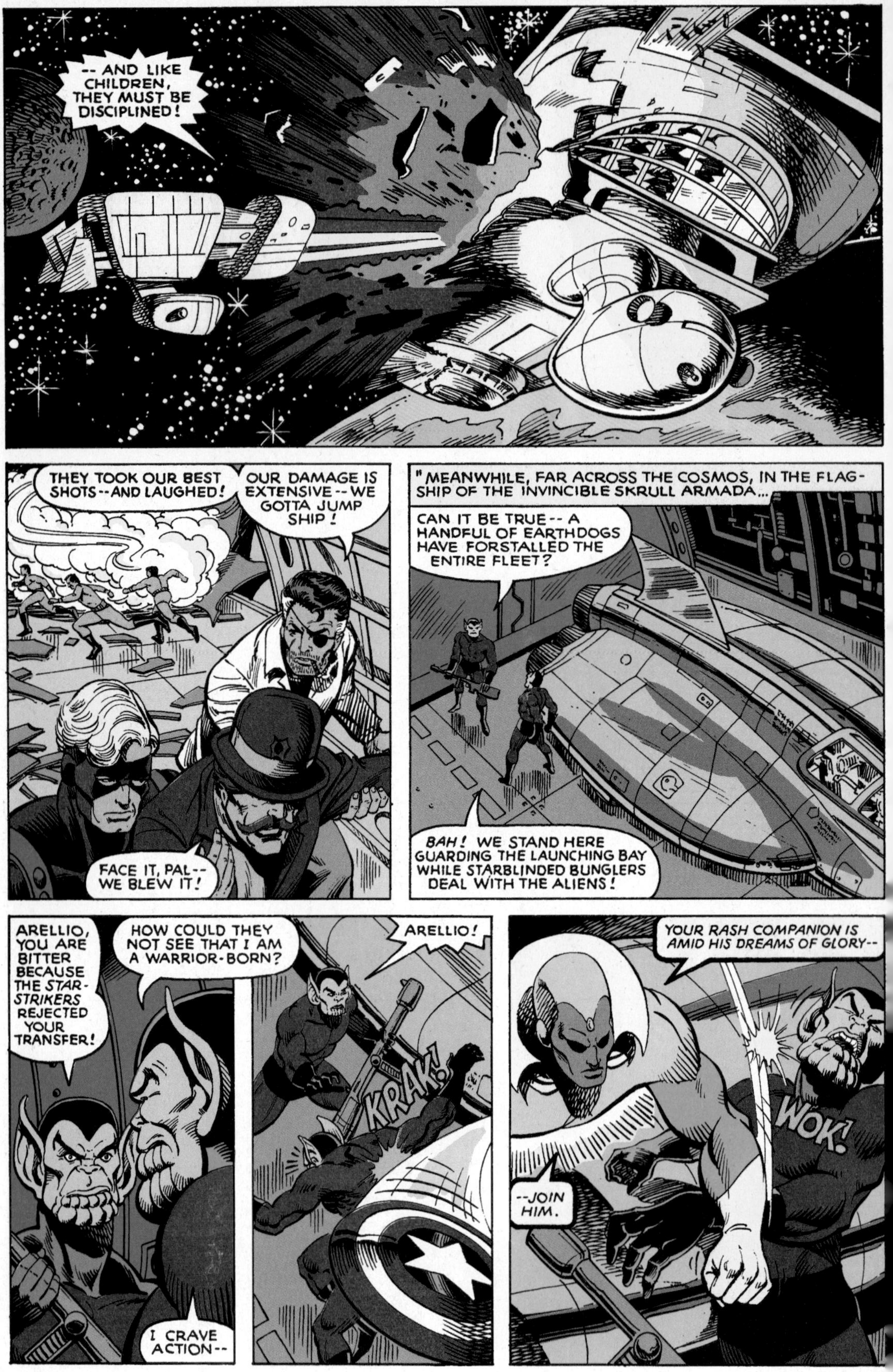
-- AND LIKE CHILDREN, THEY MUST BE DISCIPLINED!
THEY TOOK OUR BEST SHOTS--AND LAUGHED!
OUR DAMAGE IS EXTENSIVE--WE GOTTA JUMP SHIP!
FACE IT, PAL-- WE BLEW IT!
"MEANWHILE, FAR ACROSS THE COSMOS, IN THE FLAG-SHIP OF THE INVINCIBLE SKRULL ARMADA...
CAN IT BE TRUE-- A HANDFUL OF EARTHDOGS HAVE FORSTALLED THE ENTIRE FLEET?
BAH! WE STAND HERE GUARDING THE LAUNCHING BAY WHILE STARBLINDED BUNGLERS DEAL WITH THE ALIENS!
ARELLIO, YOU ARE BITTER BECAUSE THE STAR-STRIKERS REJECTED YOUR TRANSFER!
HOW COULD THEY NOT SEE THAT I AM A WARRIOR-BORN?
I CRAVE ACTION--
ARELLIO!
KRAK!
YOUR RASH COMPANION IS AMID HIS DREAMS OF GLORY--
WOK!
--JOIN HIM.

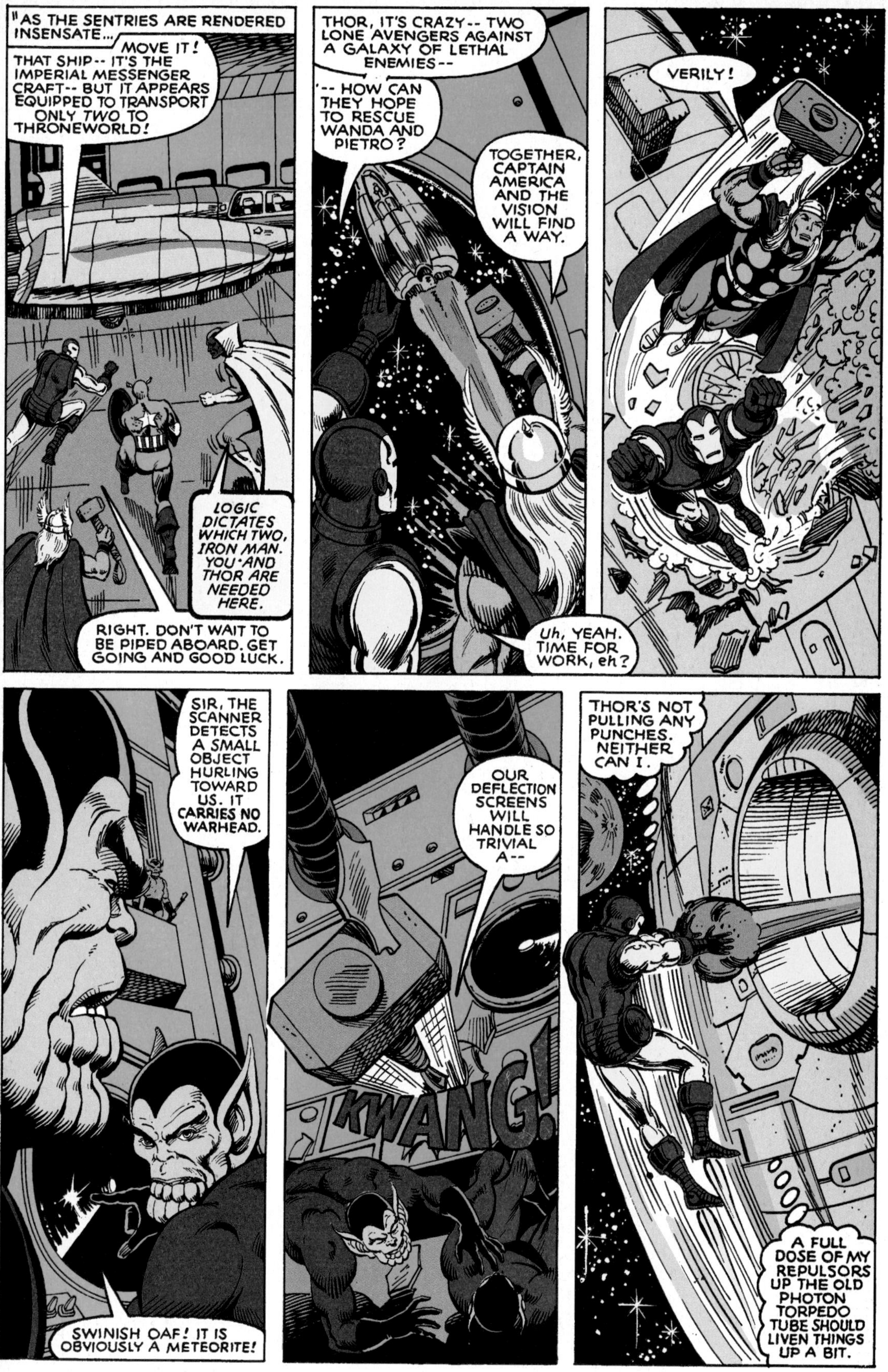

"AS THE SENTRIES ARE RENDERED INSENSATE...
MOVE IT! THAT SHIP-- IT'S THE IMPERIAL MESSENGER CRAFT-- BUT IT APPEARS EQUIPPED TO TRANSPORT ONLY TWO TO THRONEWORLD!
LOGIC DICTATES WHICH TWO, IRON MAN. YOU AND THOR ARE NEEDED HERE.
RIGHT. DON'T WAIT TO BE PIPED ABOARD. GET GOING AND GOOD LUCK.
THOR, IT'S CRAZY-- TWO LONE AVENGERS AGAINST A GALAXY OF LETHAL ENEMIES--
'-- HOW CAN THEY HOPE TO RESCUE WANDA AND PIETRO?
TOGETHER, CAPTAIN AMERICA AND THE VISION WILL FIND A WAY.
Uh, YEAH. TIME FOR WORK, eh?
VERILY!
SIR, THE SCANNER DETECTS A SMALL OBJECT HURLING TOWARD US. IT CARRIES NO WARHEAD.
SWINISH OAF! IT IS OBVIOUSLY A METEORITE!
OUR DEFLECTION SCREENS WILL HANDLE SO TRIVIAL A--
KWANG!
THOR'S NOT PULLING ANY PUNCHES. NEITHER CAN I.
A FULL DOSE OF MY REPULSORS UP THE OLD PHOTON TORPEDO TUBE SHOULD LIVEN THINGS UP A BIT.

UH-OH! I MUST'VE STRUCK A NUCLEAR PROJECTILE READY FOR LAUNCHING. THE CRAFT'S HULL IS TAKING THE BRUNT OF THE BLAST--

-- BUT THE PUNISHMENT IS TOO SEVERE -- MY ARMOR CAN'T--CAN'T-- ≥ Unnnnnnnnnnnn ≤

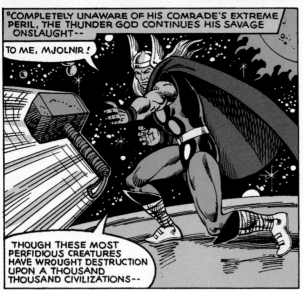

"COMPLETELY UNAWARE OF HIS COMRADE'S EXTREME PERIL, THE THUNDER GOD CONTINUES HIS SAVAGE ONSLAUGHT--

TO ME, MJOLNIR!

THOUGH THESE MOST PERFIDIOUS CREATURES HAVE WROUGHT DESTRUCTION UPON A THOUSAND THOUSAND CIVILIZATIONS--

-- THE HAMMER OF THOR SHALL GIVE THEM PAUSE!

THE EARTH SHALL BE SPARED! SO BE IT!

WUH-WHOOM!

"SUDDENLY, THE ENRAGED IMMORTAL WAS CHILLED WITH HORROR...

IRON MAN! FOULLY STRUCK, HE DRIFTS AIMLESSLY-- LIKE A LOST SOUL OF LIMBO!

FEAR NO MORE, MOST NOBLE ALLY! THIS DAY, THOU SHALT NOT SURRENDER TO THE COLD EMBRACE OF HELA, GODDESS OF DEATH!

THOR SHALL KEEP HER HUNGRY HOUNDS AT BAY!

200

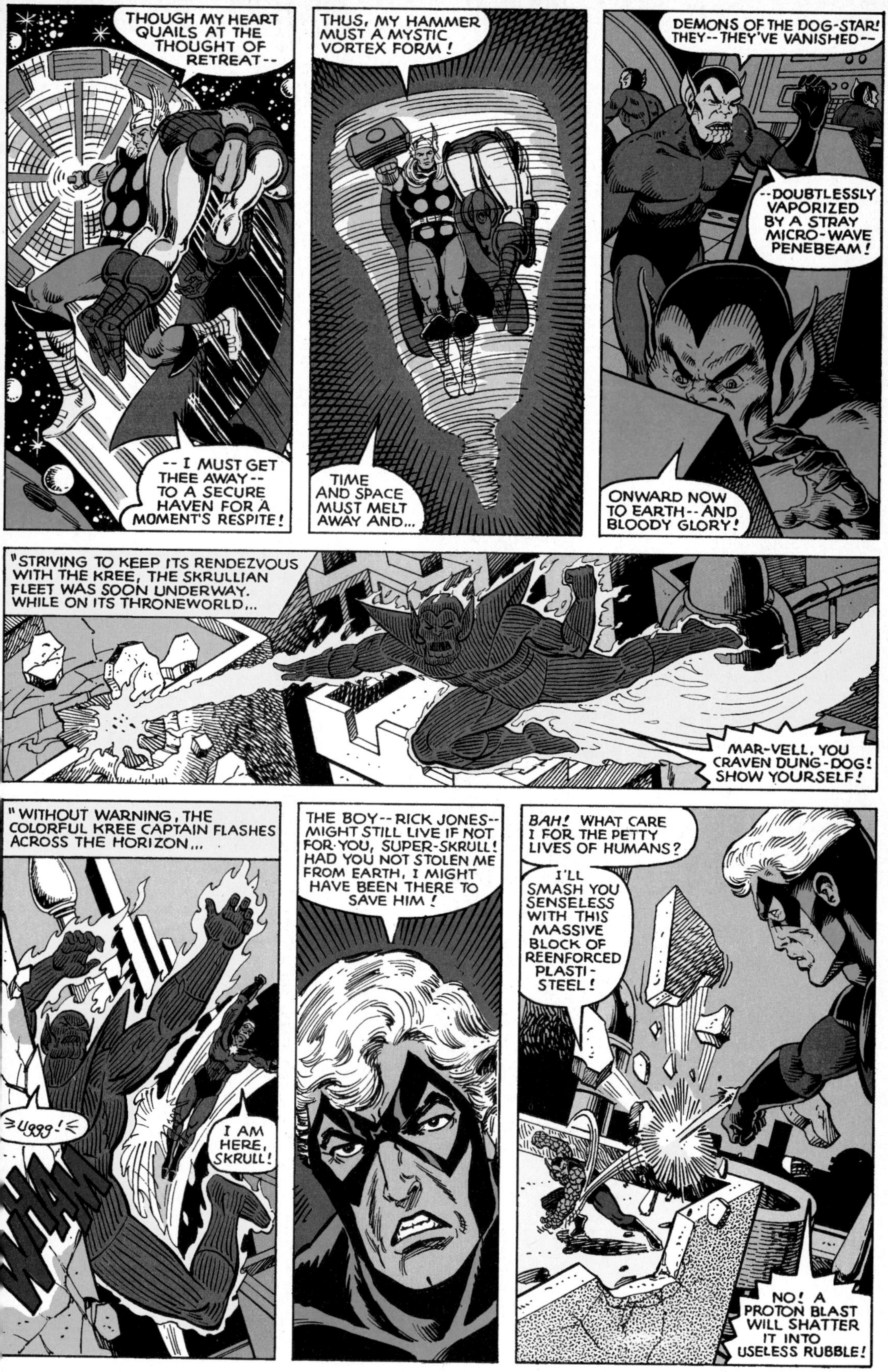
THOUGH MY HEART QUAILS AT THE THOUGHT OF RETREAT--
-- I MUST GET THEE AWAY-- TO A SECURE HAVEN FOR A MOMENT'S RESPITE!
THUS, MY HAMMER MUST A MYSTIC VORTEX FORM!
TIME AND SPACE MUST MELT AWAY AND...
DEMONS OF THE DOG-STAR! THEY-- THEY'VE VANISHED--
--DOUBTLESSLY VAPORIZED BY A STRAY MICRO-WAVE PENEBEAM!
ONWARD NOW TO EARTH-- AND BLOODY GLORY!
"STRIVING TO KEEP ITS RENDEZVOUS WITH THE KREE, THE SKRULLIAN FLEET WAS SOON UNDERWAY. WHILE ON ITS THRONEWORLD...
MAR-VELL, YOU CRAVEN DUNG-DOG! SHOW YOURSELF!
"WITHOUT WARNING, THE COLORFUL KREE CAPTAIN FLASHES ACROSS THE HORIZON...
UGGG!
WHAM
I AM HERE, SKRULL!
THE BOY-- RICK JONES-- MIGHT STILL LIVE IF NOT FOR YOU, SUPER-SKRULL! HAD YOU NOT STOLEN ME FROM EARTH, I MIGHT HAVE BEEN THERE TO SAVE HIM!
BAH! WHAT CARE I FOR THE PETTY LIVES OF HUMANS?
I'LL SMASH YOU SENSELESS WITH THIS MASSIVE BLOCK OF REENFORCED PLASTI-STEEL!
NO! A PROTON BLAST WILL SHATTER IT INTO USELESS RUBBLE!

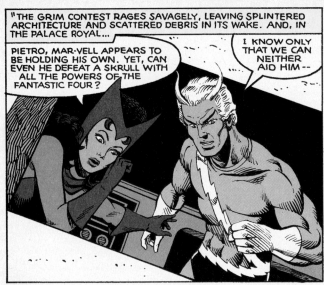

"THE GRIM CONTEST RAGES SAVAGELY, LEAVING SPLINTERED ARCHITECTURE AND SCATTERED DEBRIS IN ITS WAKE. AND, IN THE PALACE ROYAL...

PIETRO, MAR-VELL APPEARS TO BE HOLDING HIS OWN. YET, CAN EVEN HE DEFEAT A SKRULL WITH ALL THE POWERS OF THE FANTASTIC FOUR?

I KNOW ONLY THAT WE CAN NEITHER AID HIM--

--NOR DELAY HERE ANY LONGER!

HO HO! IT'S THE ESCAPED PRIMITIVES--FOR WHOSE SAFE RETURN, OUR GLORIOUS EMPEROR HAS POSTED AN EXTRA SHARE OF PLUNDER!

SKRULL, IF IT'S BLOOD-MONEY YOU CRAVE, YOU'D BEST BE HUNTING OTHER PREY!

EEYII!

QUICKSILVER, THE GUARD'S CRY ALERTED... OTHERS!

AT EASE! ALL SKRULLS ARE CHANGELINGS -- AND THESE SEEK ONLY TO FRIGHTEN US BY ASSUMING MONSTROUS SHAPES!

HUMAN-SCUM, AN ETERNITY OF SUFFERING SHALL BE YOURS!

MY MAGIC CANNOT HOLD THEM BACK! THEY WILL OVERWHELM US BY SHEER NUMBERS!

THEN COME TO ME, WANDA--

--AND FLEE! TOO MUCH DEPENDS UPON OUR ESCAPE TO RISK IT IN MEANINGLESS COMBAT!

BEFORE US IS A PARTIALLY OPENED DOOR. PERHAPS BEHIND IT, WE'LL FIND A MOMENTARY SANCTUARY.

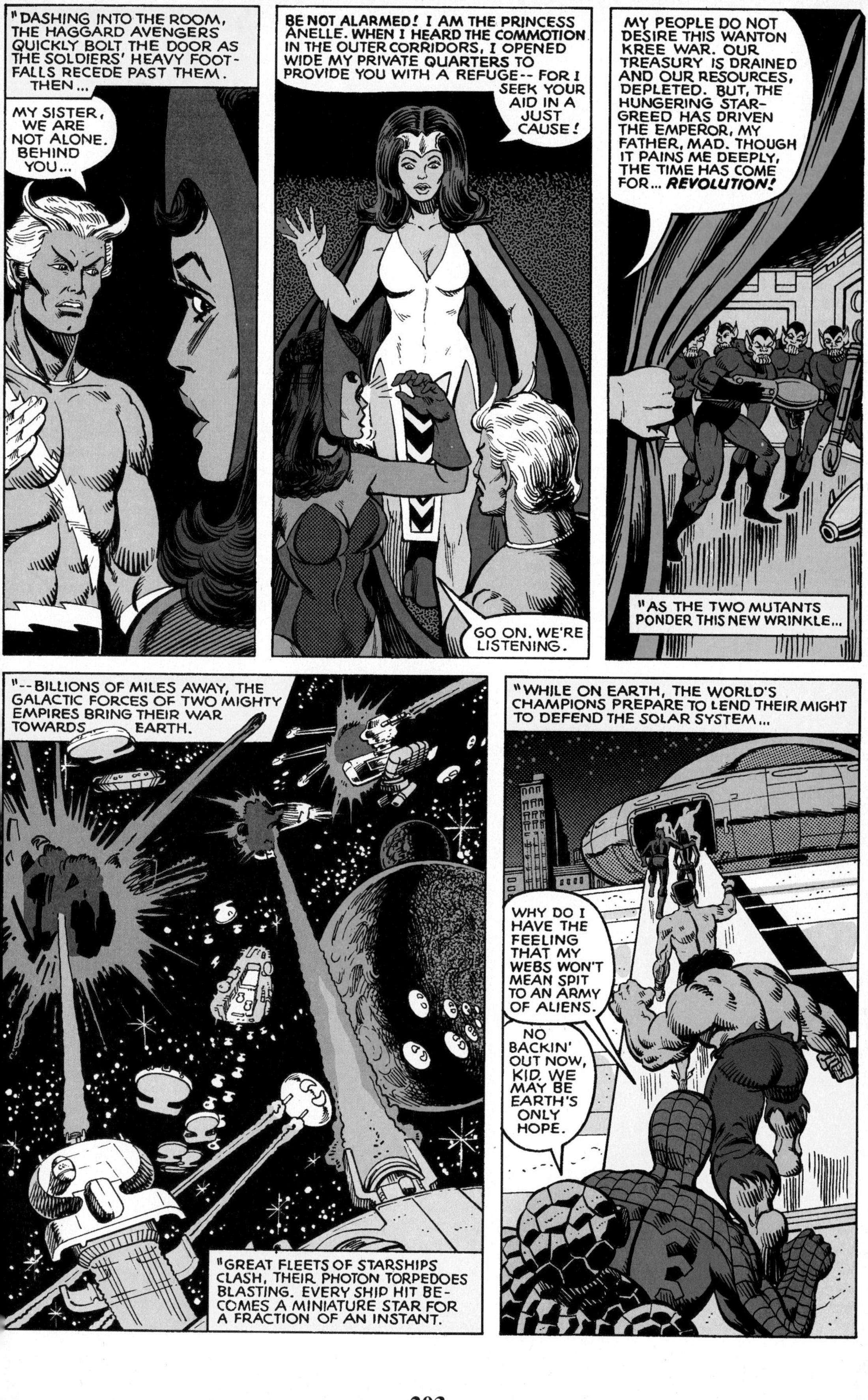
"DASHING INTO THE ROOM, THE HAGGARD AVENGERS QUICKLY BOLT THE DOOR AS THE SOLDIERS' HEAVY FOOT-FALLS RECEDE PAST THEM. THEN...
MY SISTER, WE ARE NOT ALONE. BEHIND YOU...
BE NOT ALARMED! I AM THE PRINCESS ANELLE. WHEN I HEARD THE COMMOTION IN THE OUTER CORRIDORS, I OPENED WIDE MY PRIVATE QUARTERS TO PROVIDE YOU WITH A REFUGE-- FOR I SEEK YOUR AID IN A JUST CAUSE!
GO ON. WE'RE LISTENING.
MY PEOPLE DO NOT DESIRE THIS WANTON KREE WAR. OUR TREASURY IS DRAINED AND OUR RESOURCES, DEPLETED. BUT, THE HUNGERING STAR-GREED HAS DRIVEN THE EMPEROR, MY FATHER, MAD. THOUGH IT PAINS ME DEEPLY, THE TIME HAS COME FOR... REVOLUTION!
"AS THE TWO MUTANTS PONDER THIS NEW WRINKLE...
"--BILLIONS OF MILES AWAY, THE GALACTIC FORCES OF TWO MIGHTY EMPIRES BRING THEIR WAR TOWARDS EARTH.
"GREAT FLEETS OF STARSHIPS CLASH, THEIR PHOTON TORPEDOES BLASTING. EVERY SHIP HIT BE-COMES A MINIATURE STAR FOR A FRACTION OF AN INSTANT.
"WHILE ON EARTH, THE WORLD'S CHAMPIONS PREPARE TO LEND THEIR MIGHT TO DEFEND THE SOLAR SYSTEM...
WHY DO I HAVE THE FEELING THAT MY WEBS WON'T MEAN SPIT TO AN ARMY OF ALIENS.
NO BACKIN' OUT NOW, KID. WE MAY BE EARTH'S ONLY HOPE.

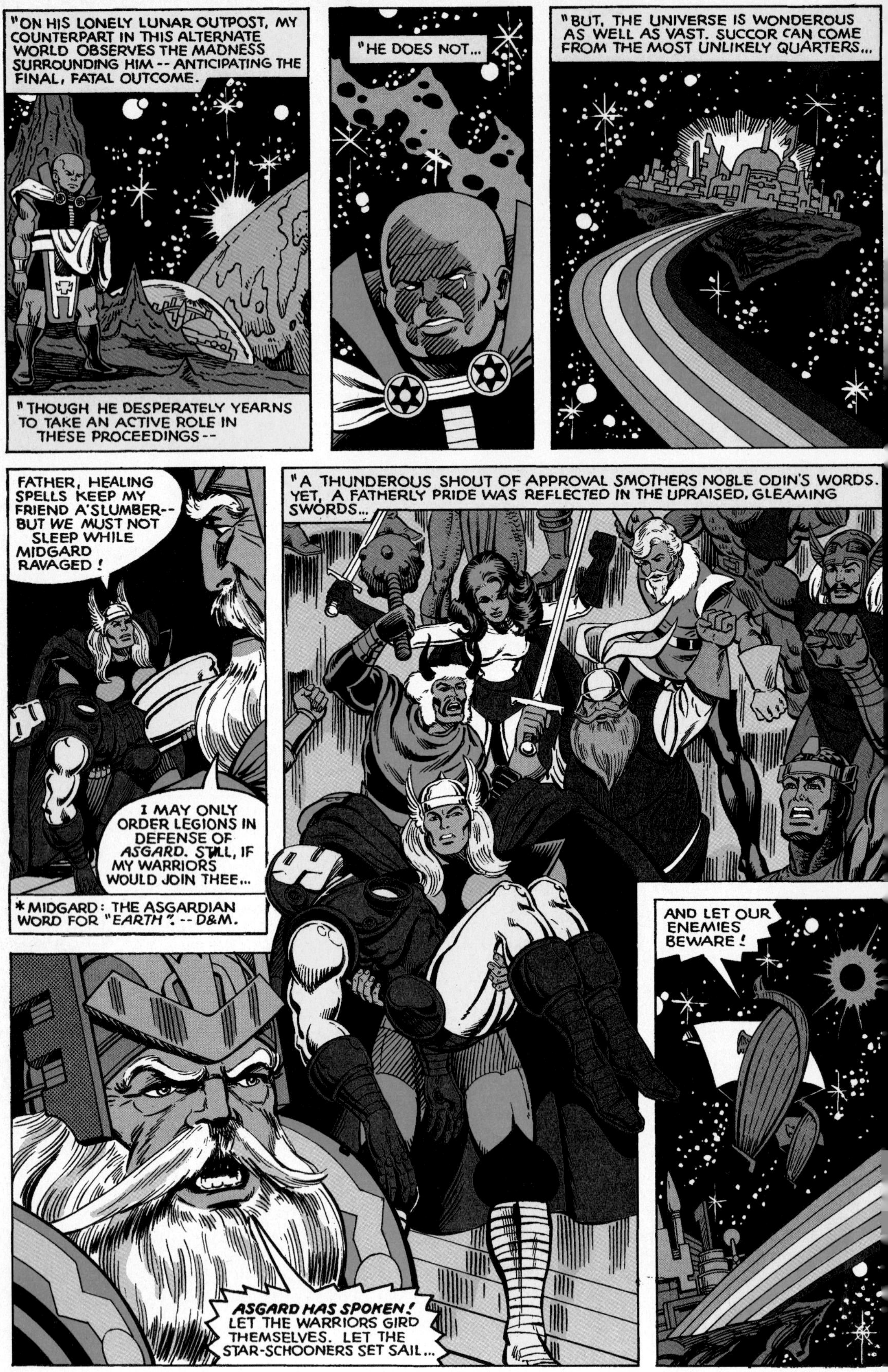
"ON HIS LONELY LUNAR OUTPOST, MY COUNTERPART IN THIS ALTERNATE WORLD OBSERVES THE MADNESS SURROUNDING HIM -- ANTICIPATING THE FINAL, FATAL OUTCOME.
"THOUGH HE DESPERATELY YEARNS TO TAKE AN ACTIVE ROLE IN THESE PROCEEDINGS --
"HE DOES NOT...
"BUT, THE UNIVERSE IS WONDEROUS AS WELL AS VAST. SUCCOR CAN COME FROM THE MOST UNLIKELY QUARTERS...
FATHER, HEALING SPELLS KEEP MY FRIEND A'SLUMBER-- BUT WE MUST NOT SLEEP WHILE MIDGARD RAVAGED!
I MAY ONLY ORDER LEGIONS IN DEFENSE OF ASGARD. STILL, IF MY WARRIORS WOULD JOIN THEE...
*MIDGARD: THE ASGARDIAN WORD FOR "EARTH". -- D&M.
"A THUNDEROUS SHOUT OF APPROVAL SMOTHERS NOBLE ODIN'S WORDS. YET, A FATHERLY PRIDE WAS REFLECTED IN THE UPRAISED, GLEAMING SWORDS...
ASGARD HAS SPOKEN! LET THE WARRIORS GIRD THEMSELVES. LET THE STAR-SCHOONERS SET SAIL...
AND LET OUR ENEMIES BEWARE!

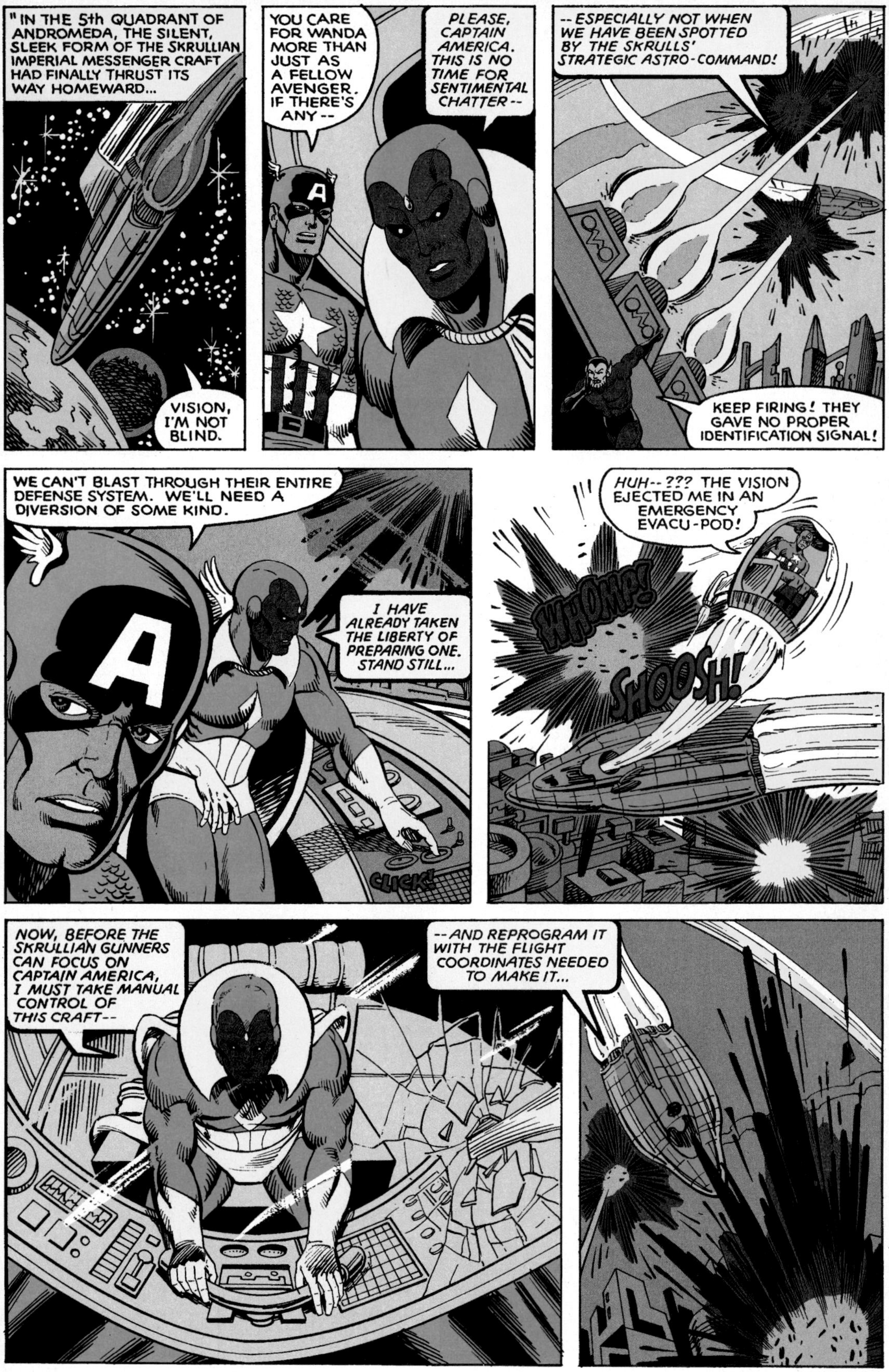

"IN THE 5th QUADRANT OF ANDROMEDA, THE SILENT, SLEEK FORM OF THE SKRULLIAN IMPERIAL MESSENGER CRAFT HAD FINALLY THRUST ITS WAY HOMEWARD...
VISION, I'M NOT BLIND.
YOU CARE FOR WANDA MORE THAN JUST AS A FELLOW AVENGER. IF THERE'S ANY --
PLEASE, CAPTAIN AMERICA. THIS IS NO TIME FOR SENTIMENTAL CHATTER --
-- ESPECIALLY NOT WHEN WE HAVE BEEN SPOTTED BY THE SKRULLS' STRATEGIC ASTRO-COMMAND!
KEEP FIRING! THEY GAVE NO PROPER IDENTIFICATION SIGNAL!
WE CAN'T BLAST THROUGH THEIR ENTIRE DEFENSE SYSTEM. WE'LL NEED A DIVERSION OF SOME KIND.
I HAVE ALREADY TAKEN THE LIBERTY OF PREPARING ONE. STAND STILL...
CLICK!
HUH--??? THE VISION EJECTED ME IN AN EMERGENCY EVACU-POD!
WHOMP!
SHOOSH!
NOW, BEFORE THE SKRULLIAN GUNNERS CAN FOCUS ON CAPTAIN AMERICA, I MUST TAKE MANUAL CONTROL OF THIS CRAFT--
--AND REPROGRAM IT WITH THE FLIGHT COORDINATES NEEDED TO MAKE IT...

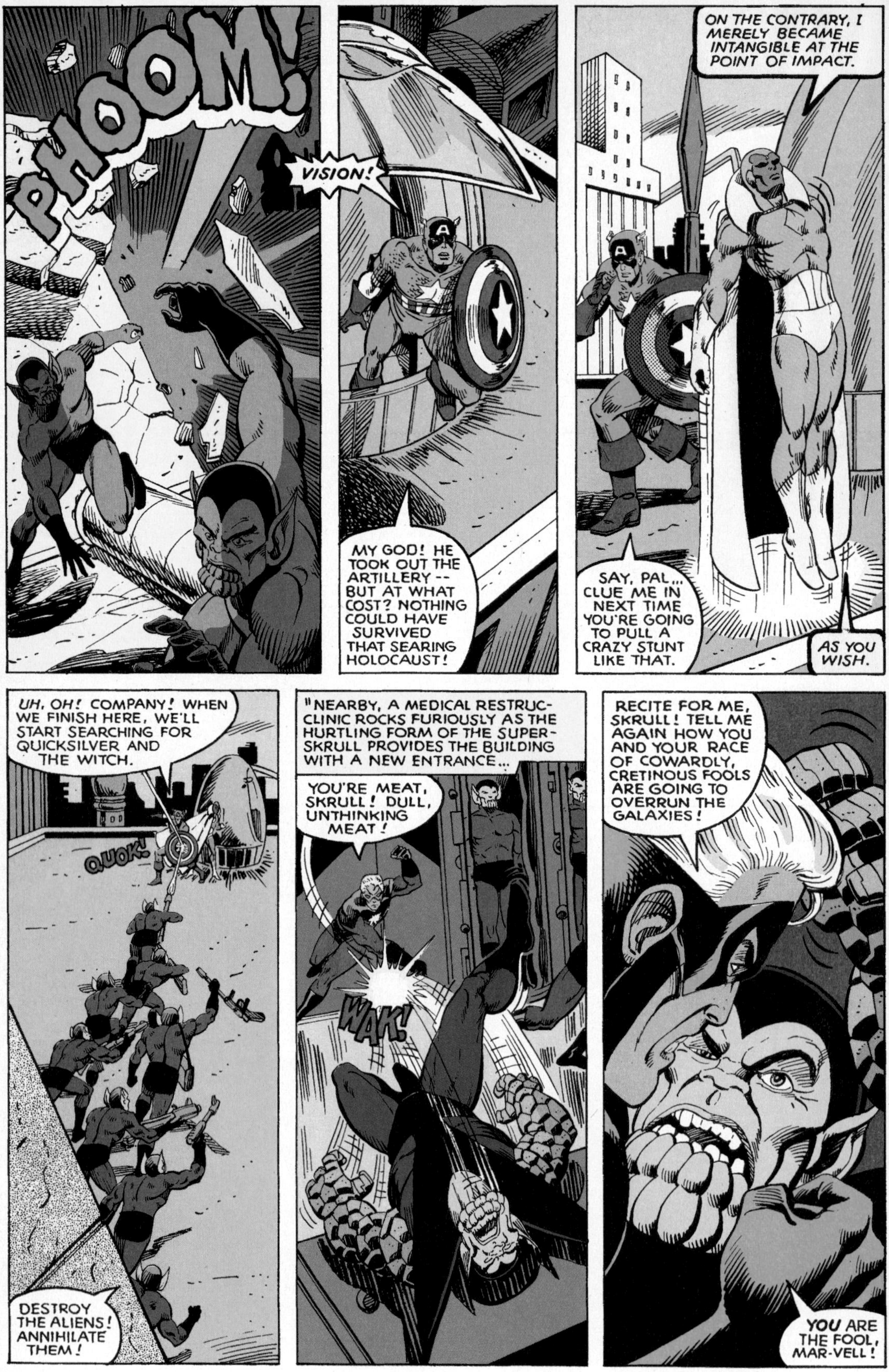
PHOOM!
VISION!
MY GOD! HE TOOK OUT THE ARTILLERY -- BUT AT WHAT COST? NOTHING COULD HAVE SURVIVED THAT SEARING HOLOCAUST!
ON THE CONTRARY, I MERELY BECAME INTANGIBLE AT THE POINT OF IMPACT.
SAY, PAL... CLUE ME IN NEXT TIME YOU'RE GOING TO PULL A CRAZY STUNT LIKE THAT.
AS YOU WISH.
UH, OH! COMPANY! WHEN WE FINISH HERE, WE'LL START SEARCHING FOR QUICKSILVER AND THE WITCH.
QUOK!
DESTROY THE ALIENS! ANNIHILATE THEM!
"NEARBY, A MEDICAL RESTRUC-CLINIC ROCKS FURIOUSLY AS THE HURTLING FORM OF THE SUPER-SKRULL PROVIDES THE BUILDING WITH A NEW ENTRANCE...
YOU'RE MEAT, SKRULL! DULL, UNTHINKING MEAT!
WAK!
RECITE FOR ME, SKRULL! TELL ME AGAIN HOW YOU AND YOUR RACE OF COWARDLY, CRETINOUS FOOLS ARE GOING TO OVERRUN THE GALAXIES!
YOU ARE THE FOOL, MAR-VELL!

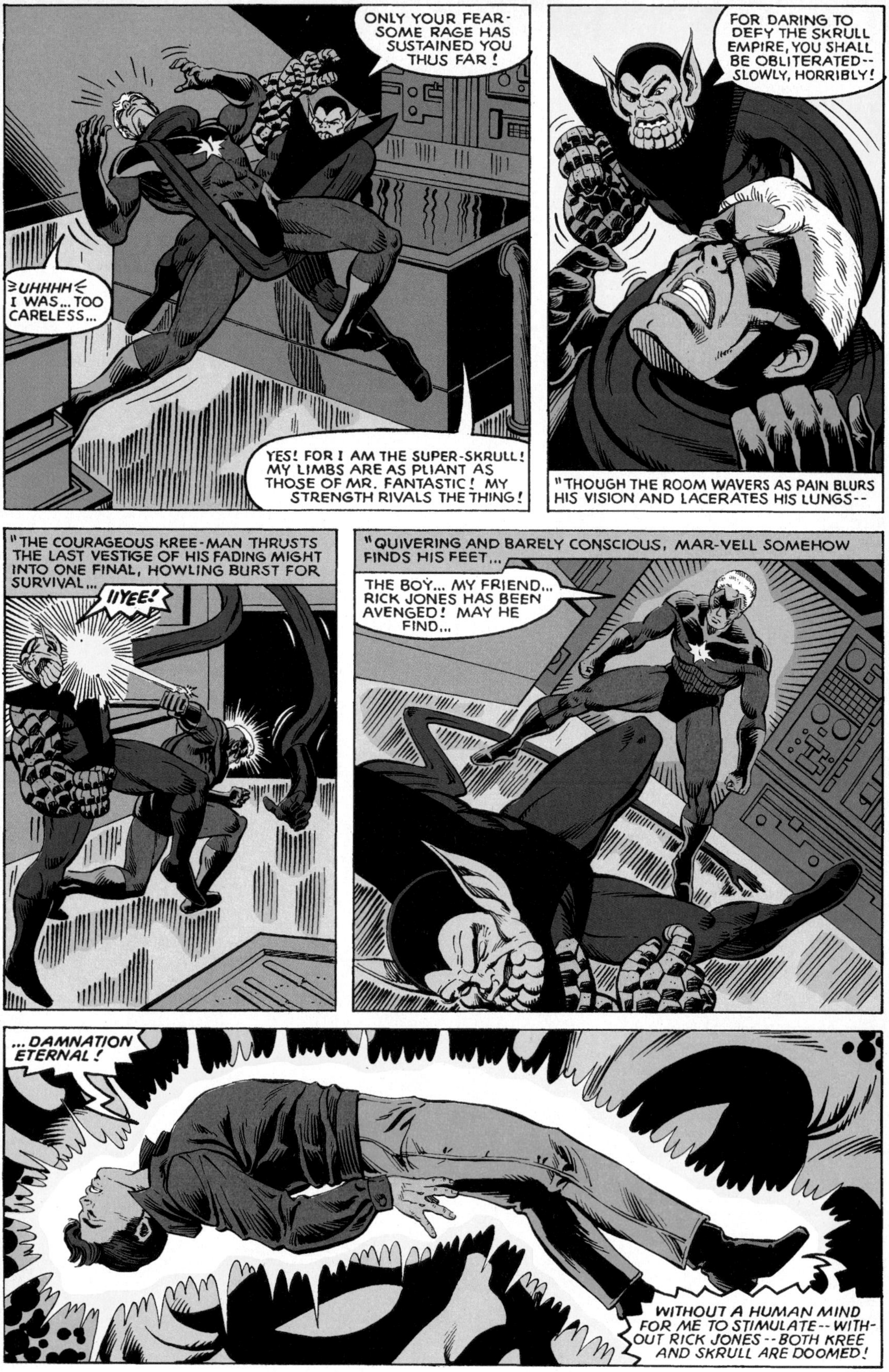

ONLY YOUR FEAR-SOME RAGE HAS SUSTAINED YOU THUS FAR!
≥UHHHH≤ I WAS... TOO CARELESS...
YES! FOR I AM THE SUPER-SKRULL! MY LIMBS ARE AS PLIANT AS THOSE OF MR. FANTASTIC! MY STRENGTH RIVALS THE THING!
FOR DARING TO DEFY THE SKRULL EMPIRE, YOU SHALL BE OBLITERATED-- SLOWLY, HORRIBLY!
"THOUGH THE ROOM WAVERS AS PAIN BLURS HIS VISION AND LACERATES HIS LUNGS--
"THE COURAGEOUS KREE-MAN THRUSTS THE LAST VESTIGE OF HIS FADING MIGHT INTO ONE FINAL, HOWLING BURST FOR SURVIVAL...
IIYEE!
"QUIVERING AND BARELY CONSCIOUS, MAR-VELL SOMEHOW FINDS HIS FEET...
THE BOY... MY FRIEND... RICK JONES HAS BEEN AVENGED! MAY HE FIND...
...DAMNATION ETERNAL!
WITHOUT A HUMAN MIND FOR ME TO STIMULATE--WITH-OUT RICK JONES--BOTH KREE AND SKRULL ARE DOOMED!

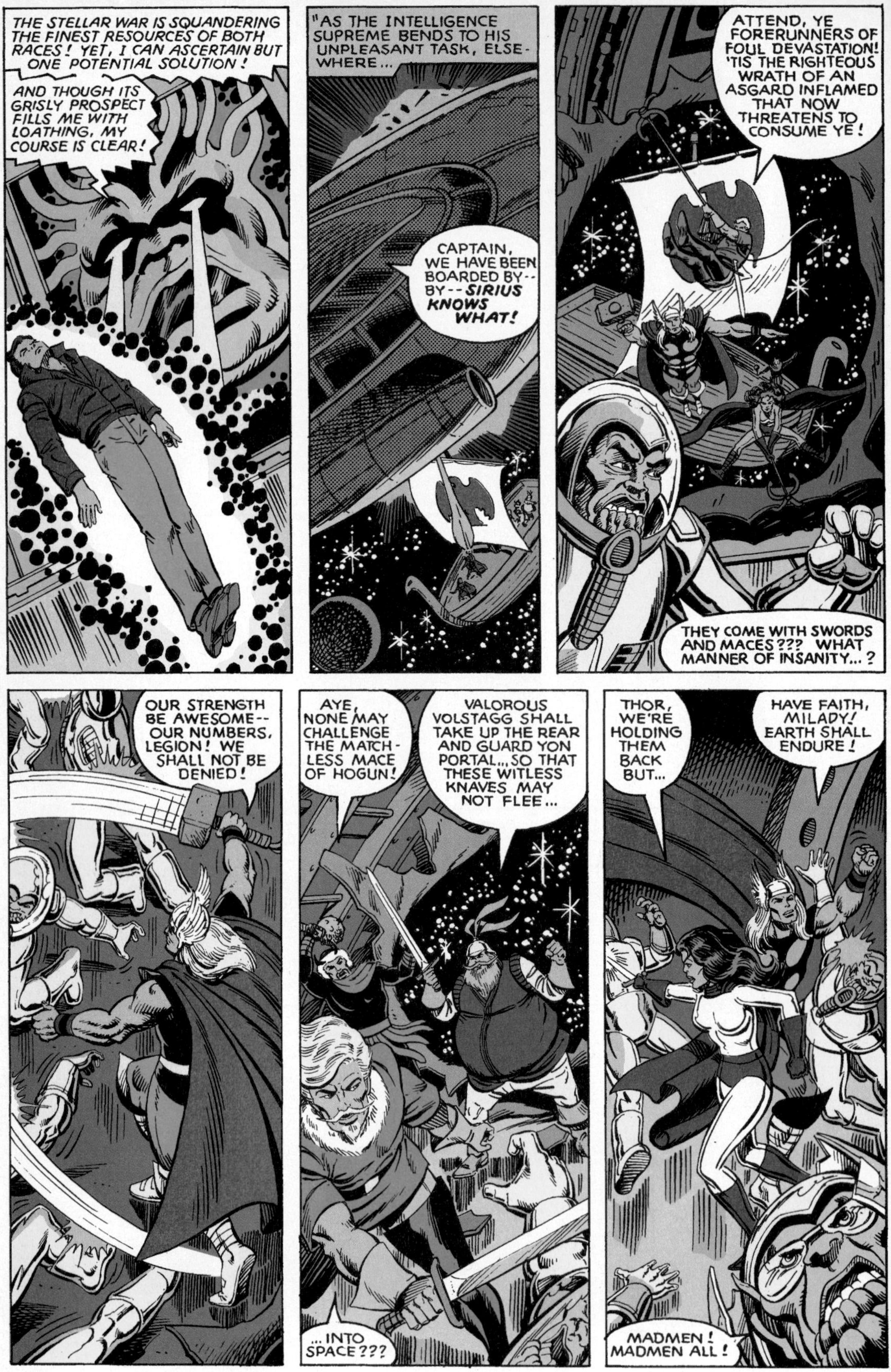
THE STELLAR WAR IS SQUANDERING THE FINEST RESOURCES OF BOTH RACES! YET, I CAN ASCERTAIN BUT ONE POTENTIAL SOLUTION!
AND THOUGH ITS GRISLY PROSPECT FILLS ME WITH LOATHING, MY COURSE IS CLEAR!
"AS THE INTELLIGENCE SUPREME BENDS TO HIS UNPLEASANT TASK, ELSEWHERE...
CAPTAIN, WE HAVE BEEN BOARDED BY-- BY-- SIRIUS KNOWS WHAT!
ATTEND, YE FORERUNNERS OF FOUL DEVASTATION! 'TIS THE RIGHTEOUS WRATH OF AN ASGARD INFLAMED THAT NOW THREATENS TO CONSUME YE!
THEY COME WITH SWORDS AND MACES??? WHAT MANNER OF INSANITY... ?
OUR STRENGTH BE AWESOME-- OUR NUMBERS, LEGION! WE SHALL NOT BE DENIED!
AYE, NONE MAY CHALLENGE THE MATCHLESS MACE OF HOGUN!
VALOROUS VOLSTAGG SHALL TAKE UP THE REAR AND GUARD YON PORTAL... SO THAT THESE WITLESS KNAVES MAY NOT FLEE...
... INTO SPACE???
THOR, WE'RE HOLDING THEM BACK BUT...
HAVE FAITH, MILADY! EARTH SHALL ENDURE!
MADMEN! MADMEN ALL!

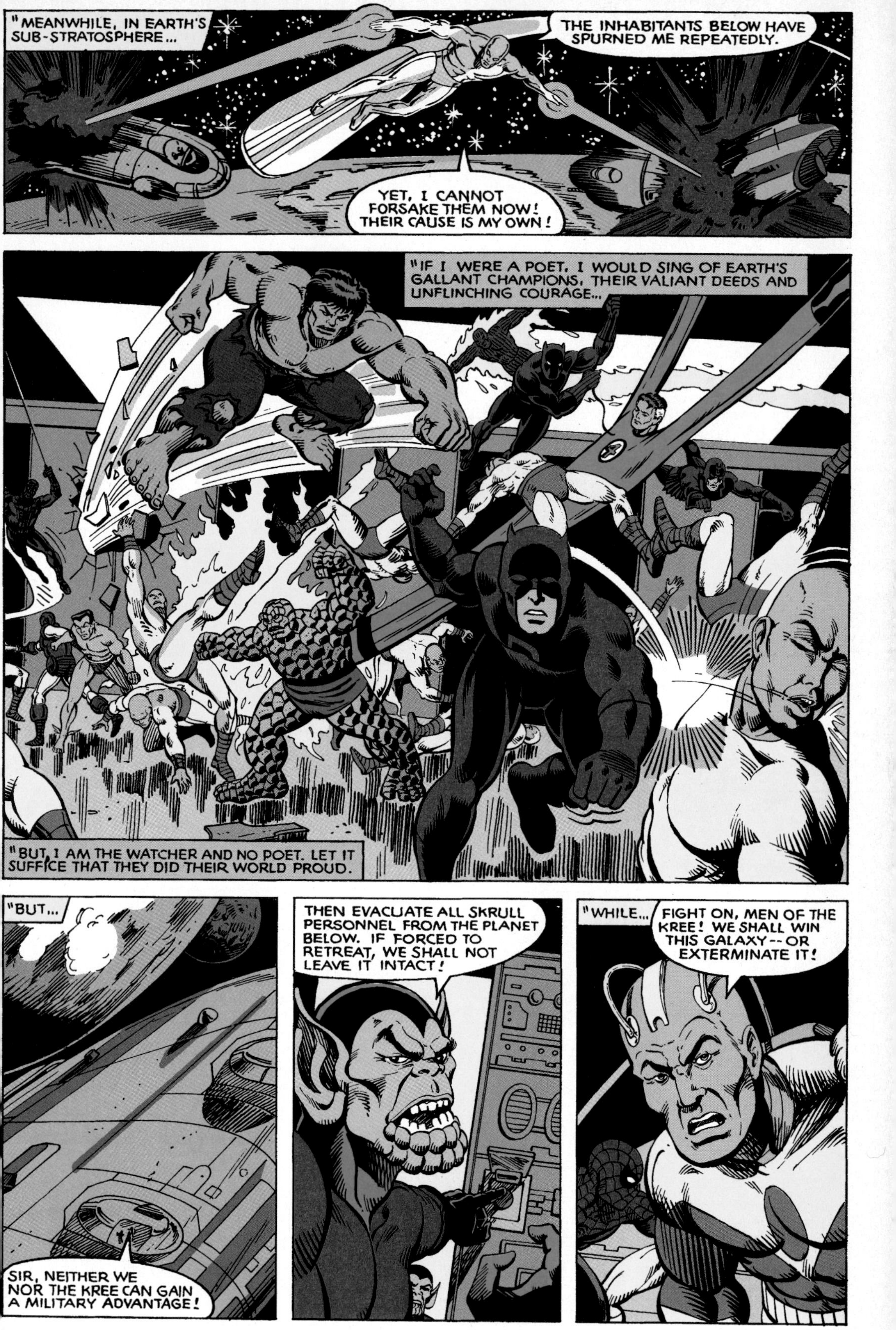
"MEANWHILE, IN EARTH'S SUB-STRATOSPHERE...
THE INHABITANTS BELOW HAVE SPURNED ME REPEATEDLY.
YET, I CANNOT FORSAKE THEM NOW! THEIR CAUSE IS MY OWN!
"IF I WERE A POET, I WOULD SING OF EARTH'S GALLANT CHAMPIONS, THEIR VALIANT DEEDS AND UNFLINCHING COURAGE...
"BUT, I AM THE WATCHER AND NO POET. LET IT SUFFICE THAT THEY DID THEIR WORLD PROUD.
"BUT...
SIR, NEITHER WE NOR THE KREE CAN GAIN A MILITARY ADVANTAGE!
THEN EVACUATE ALL SKRULL PERSONNEL FROM THE PLANET BELOW. IF FORCED TO RETREAT, WE SHALL NOT LEAVE IT INTACT!
"WHILE...
FIGHT ON, MEN OF THE KREE! WE SHALL WIN THIS GALAXY--OR EXTERMINATE IT!

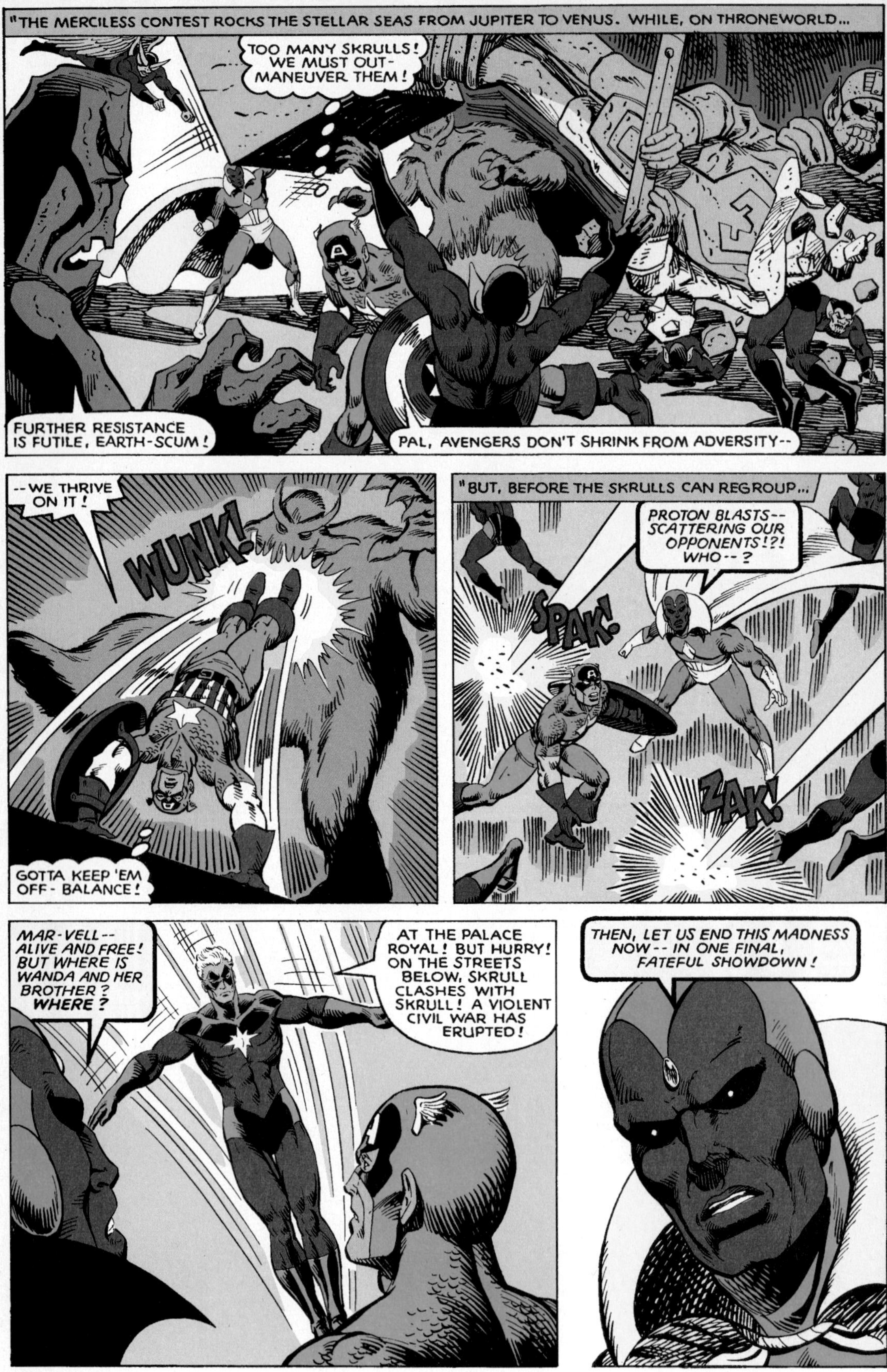
"THE MERCILESS CONTEST ROCKS THE STELLAR SEAS FROM JUPITER TO VENUS. WHILE, ON THRONEWORLD...
TOO MANY SKRULLS! WE MUST OUT-MANEUVER THEM!
FURTHER RESISTANCE IS FUTILE, EARTH-SCUM!
PAL, AVENGERS DON'T SHRINK FROM ADVERSITY--
--WE THRIVE ON IT!
WUNK!
GOTTA KEEP 'EM OFF-BALANCE!
"BUT, BEFORE THE SKRULLS CAN REGROUP...
PROTON BLASTS--SCATTERING OUR OPPONENTS!?! WHO--?
SPAK!
ZAK!
MAR-VELL--ALIVE AND FREE! BUT WHERE IS WANDA AND HER BROTHER? WHERE?
AT THE PALACE ROYAL! BUT HURRY! ON THE STREETS BELOW, SKRULL CLASHES WITH SKRULL! A VIOLENT CIVIL WAR HAS ERUPTED!
THEN, LET US END THIS MADNESS NOW--IN ONE FINAL, FATEFUL SHOWDOWN!

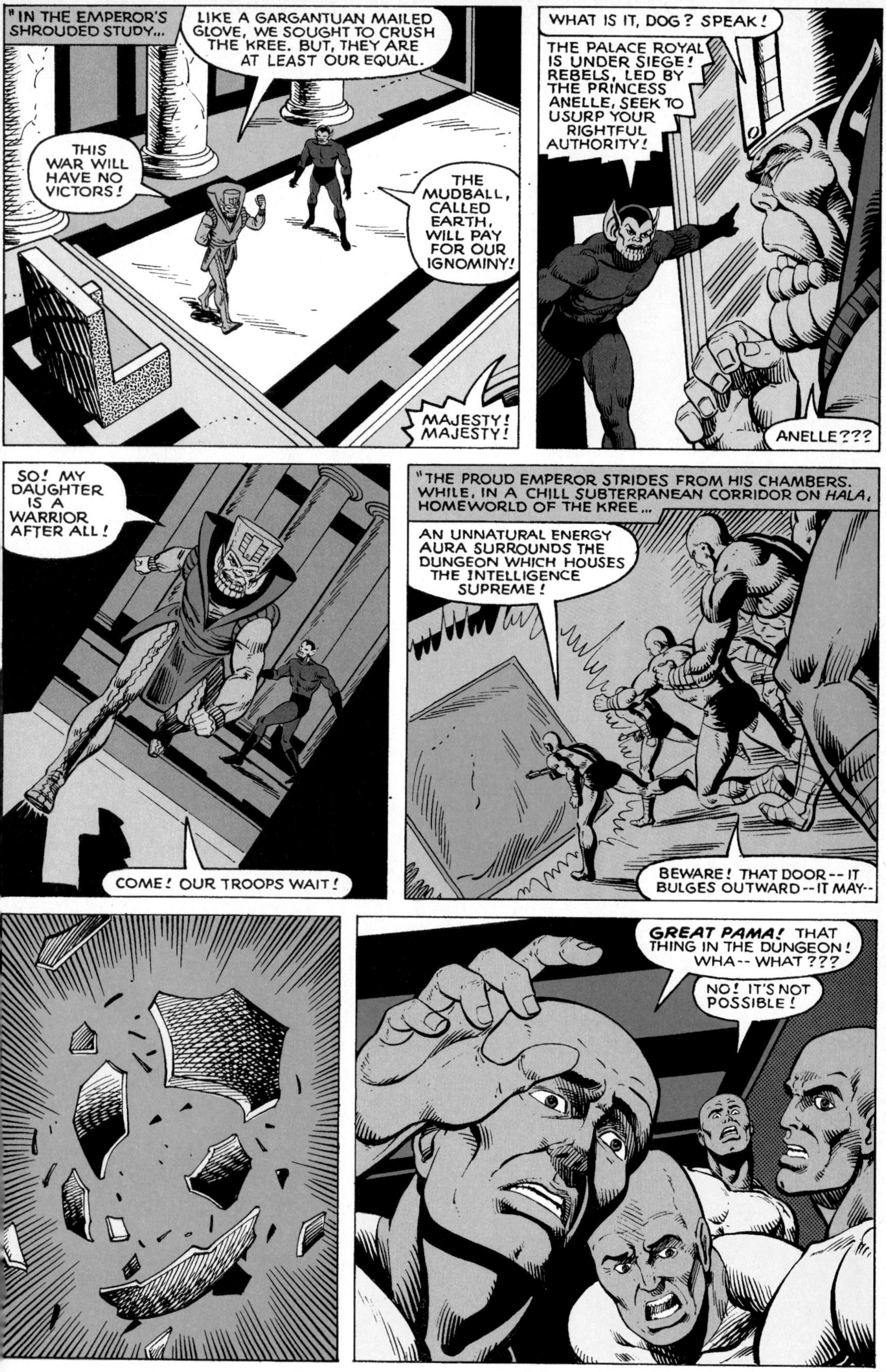
"IN THE EMPEROR'S SHROUDED STUDY...
LIKE A GARGANTUAN MAILED GLOVE, WE SOUGHT TO CRUSH THE KREE. BUT, THEY ARE AT LEAST OUR EQUAL.
THIS WAR WILL HAVE NO VICTORS!
THE MUDBALL, CALLED EARTH, WILL PAY FOR OUR IGNOMINY!
MAJESTY! MAJESTY!
WHAT IS IT, DOG? SPEAK!
THE PALACE ROYAL IS UNDER SIEGE! REBELS, LED BY THE PRINCESS ANELLE, SEEK TO USURP YOUR RIGHTFUL AUTHORITY!
ANELLE???
SO! MY DAUGHTER IS A WARRIOR AFTER ALL!
COME! OUR TROOPS WAIT!
"THE PROUD EMPEROR STRIDES FROM HIS CHAMBERS. WHILE, IN A CHILL SUBTERRANEAN CORRIDOR ON HALA, HOMEWORLD OF THE KREE...
AN UNNATURAL ENERGY AURA SURROUNDS THE DUNGEON WHICH HOUSES THE INTELLIGENCE SUPREME!
BEWARE! THAT DOOR -- IT BULGES OUTWARD -- IT MAY--
GREAT PAMA! THAT THING IN THE DUNGEON! WHA-- WHAT???
NO! IT'S NOT POSSIBLE!

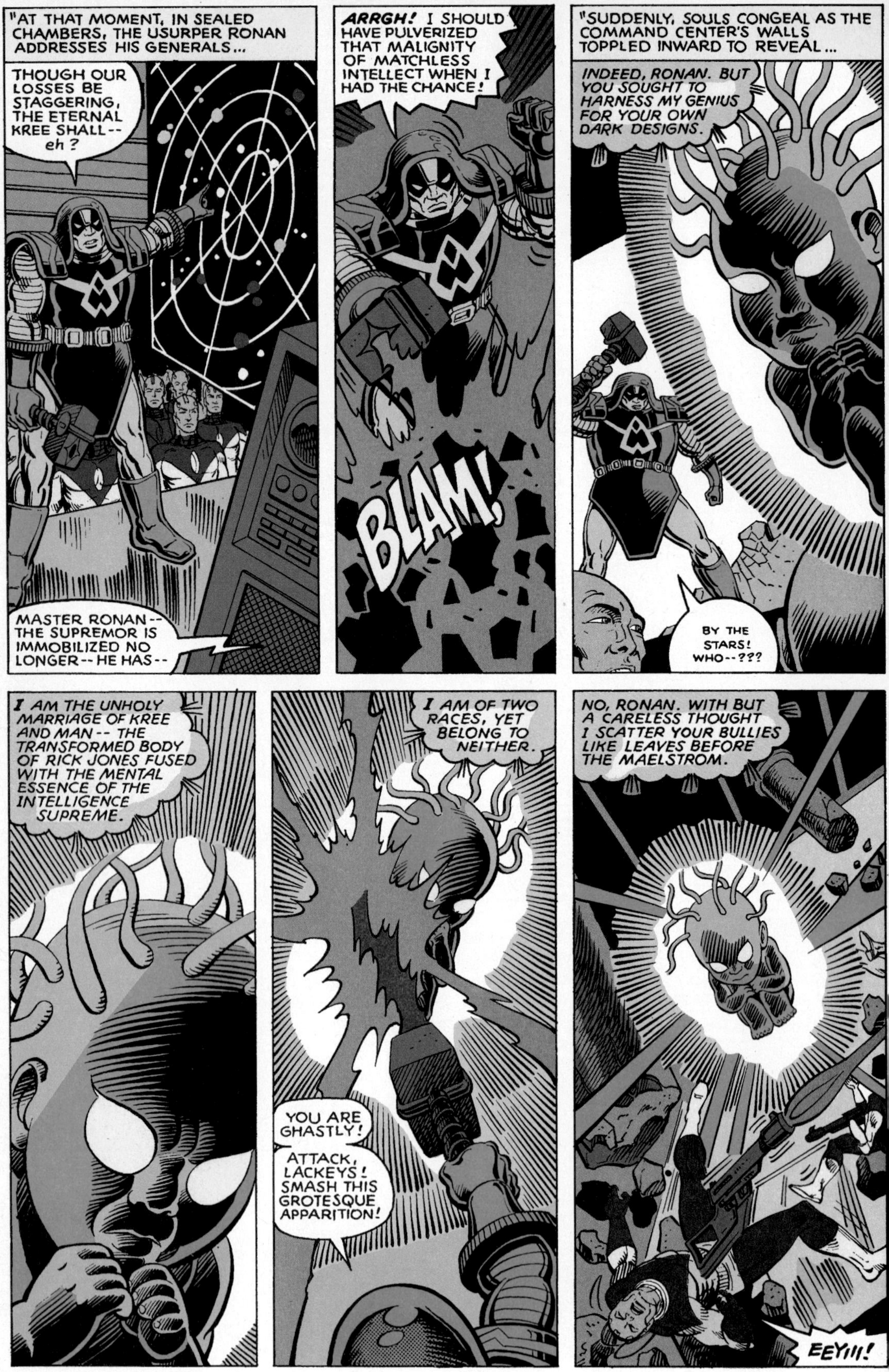
"AT THAT MOMENT, IN SEALED CHAMBERS, THE USURPER RONAN ADDRESSES HIS GENERALS...
THOUGH OUR LOSSES BE STAGGERING, THE ETERNAL KREE SHALL-- eh?
MASTER RONAN-- THE SUPREMOR IS IMMOBILIZED NO LONGER-- HE HAS--
ARRGH! I SHOULD HAVE PULVERIZED THAT MALIGNITY OF MATCHLESS INTELLECT WHEN I HAD THE CHANCE!
BLAM!
"SUDDENLY, SOULS CONGEAL AS THE COMMAND CENTER'S WALLS TOPPLED INWARD TO REVEAL...
INDEED, RONAN. BUT YOU SOUGHT TO HARNESS MY GENIUS FOR YOUR OWN DARK DESIGNS.
BY THE STARS! WHO--???
I AM THE UNHOLY MARRIAGE OF KREE AND MAN-- THE TRANSFORMED BODY OF RICK JONES FUSED WITH THE MENTAL ESSENCE OF THE INTELLIGENCE SUPREME.
I AM OF TWO RACES, YET BELONG TO NEITHER.
YOU ARE GHASTLY!
ATTACK, LACKEYS! SMASH THIS GROTESQUE APPARITION!
NO, RONAN. WITH BUT A CARELESS THOUGHT I SCATTER YOUR BULLIES LIKE LEAVES BEFORE THE MAELSTROM.
EEYIII!

TRAITOR! YOU SACRIFICED YOUR OWN GALACTIC BIRTHRIGHT-- BUT WHY? WHY?

TO SPARE MY FORMER RACE FROM A MADMAN'S DREAMS.

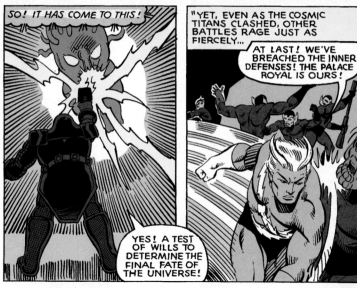

SO! IT HAS COME TO THIS!

YES! A TEST OF WILLS TO DETERMINE THE FINAL FATE OF THE UNIVERSE!

"YET, EVEN AS THE COSMIC TITANS CLASHED, OTHER BATTLES RAGE JUST AS FIERCELY...

AT LAST! WE'VE BREACHED THE INNER DEFENSES! THE PALACE ROYAL IS OURS!

BE CAUTIOUS, PIETRO! THIS BATTLE IS NOT YET ENDED!

FOR ANELLE! FOR LIBERTY!

RAISE HIGH YOUR SONIC-SWORDS AND -- HUMAN!!! BEHIND YOU!

ARRG! MY LEG!

ZAP

"AS THE WOUNDED AVENGER PITCHES FORWARD, THE BATTLE IS JOINED BY UNEXPECTED ARRIVALS...

ALLOW ME TO OFFER MY ASSISTANCE, PRINCESS!

MAR-VELL! THE KREE CAPTAIN!

AT YOUR SERVICE!

"THE TIDE QUICKLY TURNED TOWARD THE REBELS' CAUSE, AND IN THE MIDST OF IT ALL--

WANDA!

VISION!

"--TWO WORDS MADE DO FOR THOUSANDS!

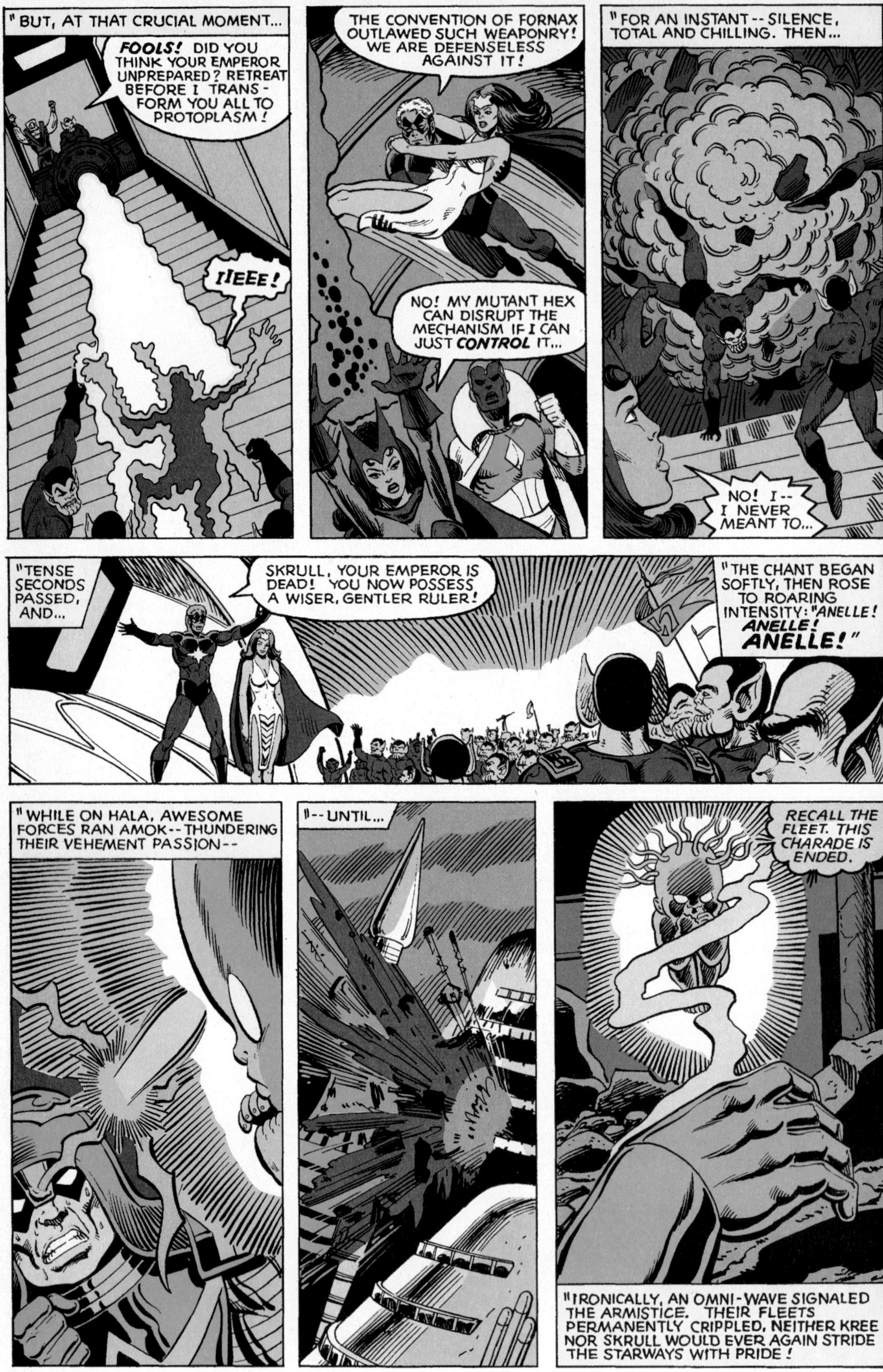
"BUT, AT THAT CRUCIAL MOMENT...
FOOLS! DID YOU THINK YOUR EMPEROR UNPREPARED? RETREAT BEFORE I TRANS-FORM YOU ALL TO PROTOPLASM!
IIEEE!
THE CONVENTION OF FORNAX OUTLAWED SUCH WEAPONRY! WE ARE DEFENSELESS AGAINST IT!
NO! MY MUTANT HEX CAN DISRUPT THE MECHANISM IF I CAN JUST CONTROL IT...
"FOR AN INSTANT -- SILENCE, TOTAL AND CHILLING. THEN...
NO! I -- I NEVER MEANT TO...
"TENSE SECONDS PASSED, AND...
SKRULL, YOUR EMPEROR IS DEAD! YOU NOW POSSESS A WISER, GENTLER RULER!
"THE CHANT BEGAN SOFTLY, THEN ROSE TO ROARING INTENSITY: "ANELLE! ANELLE! ANELLE!"
"WHILE ON HALA, AWESOME FORCES RAN AMOK -- THUNDERING THEIR VEHEMENT PASSION --
"-- UNTIL...
RECALL THE FLEET. THIS CHARADE IS ENDED.
"IRONICALLY, AN OMNI-WAVE SIGNALED THE ARMISTICE. THEIR FLEETS PERMANENTLY CRIPPLED, NEITHER KREE NOR SKRULL WOULD EVER AGAIN STRIDE THE STARWAYS WITH PRIDE!

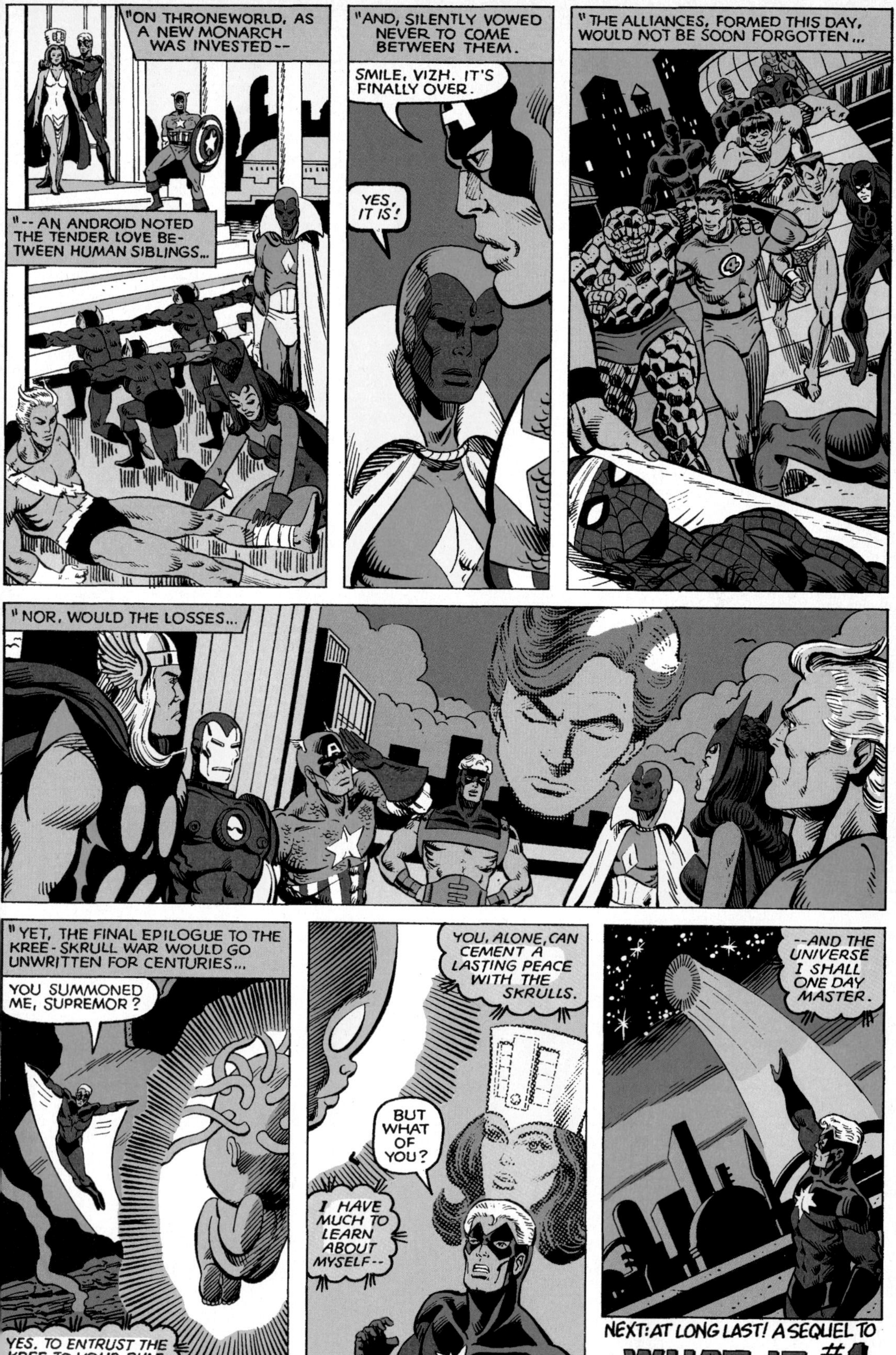
"ON THRONEWORLD, AS A NEW MONARCH WAS INVESTED--
"--AN ANDROID NOTED THE TENDER LOVE BETWEEN HUMAN SIBLINGS...
"AND, SILENTLY VOWED NEVER TO COME BETWEEN THEM.
SMILE, VIZH. IT'S FINALLY OVER.
YES, IT IS!
"THE ALLIANCES, FORMED THIS DAY, WOULD NOT BE SOON FORGOTTEN...
"NOR, WOULD THE LOSSES...
"YET, THE FINAL EPILOGUE TO THE KREE-SKRULL WAR WOULD GO UNWRITTEN FOR CENTURIES...
YOU SUMMONED ME, SUPREMOR?
YES. TO ENTRUST THE KREE TO YOUR RULE.
YOU, ALONE, CAN CEMENT A LASTING PEACE WITH THE SKRULLS.
BUT WHAT OF YOU?
I HAVE MUCH TO LEARN ABOUT MYSELF--
--AND THE UNIVERSE I SHALL ONE DAY MASTER.
NEXT: AT LONG LAST! A SEQUEL TO
WHAT IF #1

WHY NOT?

c/o MARVEL COMICS GROUP
575 Madison Avenue
New York, New York 10022

DENNIS O'NEIL
EDITOR
MARK GRUENWALD
ASSISTANT EDITOR

Due to some extra-long stories squeezing out the letters page for an issue or two, we've got a bit of catching up to do. Here's a grab-bag of responses to WHAT IF #16 and 17...

Dear Roy and Doug,

How alternate are the alternate universes of WHAT IF?

For instance, SPECIAL MARVEL EDITION #15 had Fu Manchu working on animal brain developments (and subsequently the mimosa smuggling in MOKF #18) — *not* a serum of resurrection. I wish you would have made just the one change — Shang-Chi killing Petrie sans interruption — rather than altering *many* paths.

My one irk about the actual writing was that Fu Manchu's speech for killing wasn't any stronger here than in SME #15. Indeed, can a single conversation alter "every spiritual value" in one's life? WHAT IF #16 did not alter Shang-Chi's decision, it only delayed it.

Which brings me to the title(s). In WHAT IF #15: *"Next: What If Shang-Chi Still Served Fu Manchu?"* Great! Shang fighting Smith all these years, perhaps focusing on another turning point in his life. Then, the cover of WHAT IF #16: *"What If Shang-Chi Fought On The Side Of Fu Manchu?"* But he did by killing Petrie! Finally, #16's inside title: *"What If Shang-Chi Had Remained Loyal To Fu Manchu?"* But he didn't remain loyal. He turned away, negating the title. Perhaps a better title would have been, *"What if Shang-Chi Hadn't Realized The Full Evil of Fu Manchu?"*, or, *"What if Shang-Chi Hadn't Devoted His Life To Fighting Fu Manchu?"*

I'm glad Doug handled ther book. His characterizations are as finely honed as ever.

Kevin J. Dooley
756 S. Normandie, #300
Los Angeles, CA 90010

Dear Marvel,

WHAT IF #16 was a real bummer for me. I do not follow the MASTER OF KUNG FU book, and now I know why. Of course, Doug's script wasn't without merit, but he missed my idea of the mark. I had expected something like Shang-Chi becoming a complete believer in his father's empire, but all I got was a mild variation of the regular character. I enjoy WHAT IF issues where a character's situation or actions differ sharply from their Marvel-Earth counterpart. This one left me disappointed.

Roy Valdboom
RR #1
Cedar Grove, WI 53013

Dear Roy, Doug, and Rick,

WHAT IF #16 was one of the best issues in past months. Though I have never read an issue of MASTER OF KUNG FU, I could follow the story, relate to the characters, and enjoy the story. This doesn't happen much with WHAT IF when I am unfamiliar with the lead character. (By the way, when Tarr rips the headstone out of the ground, is the inscription "Sir Hugh Drummond" a joking reference to Bulldog Drummond?)

I hope new editor Mark Gruenwald is able to straighten WHAT IF out, since this issue and the Conan one were the only memorable ones in the last six. I wish you luck.

Michael Samerdyke
14010 Maple Ave.
Maple Heights, OH 44137

Dear Mark, Steven, and Carmine,

WHAT IF #17 was interesting, although the title — "What If _______ became Villains" — was misleading. Not that it was bad, just incorrect. It fit the first story, involving the Ghost Rider. As for Spider-Woman, she thought she was doing what was right. True, she killed Fury, but that was accidental and she only worked with Vermis to find out her origins. She ended up as a fugitive, but I don't think we can consider her to be villainous. As for Captain Marvel, he still proved to be a hero. He defeated the Sentry, correct? Then, after Yon-Rogg is beaten he is promoted to Colonel and only his final statement can be construed as the words of a villain. I feel that, just like on Marvel-Earth, Mar-Vell might well have turned out to be Earth's savior rather than her destroyer.

Just because I disliked the title, that doesn't mean I also disliked the story. Sometimes a blanket title cannot give a clear indication of the contents, and that was the case with WHAT IF #17. I thought the story was very well done, and I like the way you used one long story to tell three shorter tales. I'd like to see that continue.

Roger Schoolcraft
PO Box 281
Follansbee,WV 26037

Dear Speculators,

Having just read WHAT IF #17, I am appalled. Previous issues with more than one story centered on one Marvel character, the reactions of different people to having superpowers, and the conclusions of these people's adventures, and, often, lives.

In #17, you used three separate hero(in)es, leaving two stories unfinished, The artwork was only fair and the actions, if there were any, were uninspired. The entire issue was *dull*. If I wanted any entertainment, I should have bought MARVEL SPOTLIGHT #5 and #32 and MARVEL SUPERHEROES #12-13. It would have cost more, but it would have been infinitely more rewarding.

WHAT IF is not going well. The kind of story I'm looking for is one where something is slightly different from the Marvel Universe, and the results of this difference. Panels recreated from the original stories with slight changes are even better. Stories with totally new situations (#6 and #11) are shoddy and only mildly entertaining. The only time this formula worked was in #16, which was also left unfinished.

Get back to speculation and comparison between worlds, not just action! If you don't, you may as well change the title to *Three 20¢ Stories, Each Worth Every Quarter!*

John Bell
17 Morton St.
Newton, MA 02159

Dear Steven and Carmine,

WHAT IF #17 was one wicked issue. I would place it second only to...uh, *none*. My one complaint is that you had the chance to really do things with Captain Marvel and you let it pass through your fingers. He never really posed a threat to mankind.

Louis Bank
1715 Howard St.
St. Charles, IL 60174

U.S. POSTAL SERVICE
STATEMENT OF OWNERSHIP, MANAGEMENT AND CIRCULATION
(REQUIRED BY 39 U.S.C. 3685)

1. Title of Publication: WHAT IF
2. Date of Filing: October 1, 1979.
3. Frequency of Issue: BI-MONTHLY.
3A. No. of issues published annually: 12
3B. Annual subscription price: $5.00
4. Location of Known Office of Publication: 575 Madison Ave., New York, N.Y. 10022.
5. Location of the Headquarters or General Business Offices of the Publishers: 575 Madison Ave., New York, N.Y. 10022.
6. Names and addresses of the publisher, editor, and managing editor are: Publisher: Stan Lee, 575 Madison Ave., N.Y., N.Y. 10022; Editor: Jim Shooter, 575 Madison Ave., N.Y., N.Y. 10022; Managing Editor: Jim Shooter, 575 Madison Ave., N.Y., N.Y. 10022.
7. Owner (if owned by a corporation, its name and address must be stated and also immediately thereunder the names and addresses of stockholders owning or holding 1 percent or more of total amount of stock. If not owned by a corporation, the names and addresses of the individual owners must be given. If owned by a partnership or other unincorporated firm, its name and address, as well as that of each individual must be given.) Marvel Comics Group, 575 Madison Ave., New York, N.Y. 10022. Cadence Industries Corp., 21 Henderson Drive, West Caldwell, N.J. 07006.
8. Known bondholders, mortgagees, and other security holders owning or holding 1 percent or more of total amount of bonds, mortgages or other securities: None.
9. For completion of nonprofit organizations authorized to mail at special rates (Section 132.122, PSM). The purpose, function, and nonprofit status of this organization and the exempt status for Federal income tax purposes. (Check one.) Have not changed during preceding 12 months. Have changed during preceding 12 months. (If changed, publisher must submit explanation with this statement.)
10. EXTENT AND NATURE OF CIRCULATION.
A. Total No. Copies Printed (net press run): Average no. copies each issue during preceding 12 months: 276,176. Single issue nearest to filing date: 272,602.
B. Paid Circulation: 1) Sales through dealers and carriers, street vendors and counter sales: Average no. copies each issue during preceding 12 months: 133,625. Single issue nearest tc filing date: 145,031. 2) Mail subscriptions: Average no. copies each issue during preceding 12 months: 1,121. Single issue nearest to filing date: 987.
C. Total paid circulation (Sum of 10B1 and 10B2): Average no. copies each issue during preceding 12 months: 134,746. Single issue nearest to filing date: 146,018.
D. Free distribution by mail, carrier or other means, samples, complimentary, and other free copies: Average no. copies each issue during preceding 12 months: 635. Single issue nearest to filing date: 635.
E. Total distribution (Sum of C and D): Average no. copies each issue during preceding 12 months: 135,381. Single issue nearest to filing date: 146,653.
F. Copies not distributed: 1) Office use, left-over, unaccounted, spoiled after printing: Average no. copies each issue during preceding 12 months: 1,1013. Single issue nearest to filing date: 2,150. 2) Returns from News Agents: Average no. copies each issue during preceding 12 months: 141,808. Single issue nearest to filing date: 123,799.
G. Total (Sum of E, F1 and 2 should equal net press run shown in A): Average no. copies each issue during preceding 12 months: 276,176. Single issue nearest to filing date: 272,602.
11. I certify that the statements made by me above are correct and complete.

(signed) Ed Shukin — Business Manager

12. For completion by publishers mailing at the regular rates (Section 132.121, Postal Service Manual) 39 U.S.C. 3626 provides in pertinent part: "No person who would have been entitled to mail matter under former section 4359 of this title shall mail such matter at the rates provided under this subsection unless he files annually with the Postal Service a written request for permission to mail matter at such rates."

In accordance with the provisions of this statute, I hearby request permission to mail the publication named in Item 1 at the reduced postage rates presently authorized by 39 U.S.C. 3626.

(signed) Ed Shukin — Business Manager